Black Book of the Werewolf

Black Book of the Werewolf

A COMET PRESS PRODUCTION

copyright © December 2017
by Comet Press
All rights reserved.

Book Design by Inkubus Design
www.inkubusdesign.com

ISBN 13: 978-1-936964-02-4

First Edition

Visit Comet Press on the web at:
www.cometpress.us
facebook.com/cometpress
twitter.com/cometpress

Table of Contents

The Literary Lair of the Werewolf

This massive collection of 32 gruesome and illuminating werewolf short stories and novellas represent some of the best of the 19th and early 20th century, when the werewolf was at its full height of terror. The werewolf's bestial ferocity, superhuman strength, sadistic cruelty, and ravenous hunger make him (or her) the very epitome of supernatural terror in fur and flesh.

The legends surrounding the werewolf can be traced back to the ancient world. In folklore the werewolf is depicted as the archetype of evil and has dominated above all creatures as the most treacherous, savage, and demonic slaves of Satan.

The werewolf theme in fiction was introduced by Marie de France in her 13th century romance "Lais of the Bisclavret". Though common in folklore, the werewolf doesn't make a major reappearance in fiction until the19th century with the Gothic novel, whose writers drew inspiration from the gruesome legends and folklore of ancient and middle ages, such as "Hugues, the Wer-Wolf" (1839) by Sutherland Menzies, and "The White Wolf of the Hartz Mountains" (1839) by Frederick Marryat, whose villain features a demonic female, with an insatiable appetite for human male flesh.

The late 19th and early 20th century saw an explosion of werewolf short stories and novels, including "The Eyes of the Panther" (1891) by famed occultist Ambrose Bierce and the legendary English occult story writer Algernon Blackwood, who wrote a number of werewolf stories, such as "Running Wolf" (1921). A seductive female who transforms into a werewolf and devours her male victims also make an appearance in Clemence Houseman's acclaimed novella "The Were-wolf" (1896). Rudyard Kipling and Guy de Maupassant are also represented with their respective shapeshifter classics.

Included is "A True Discourse Declaring the Damnable Life and Death of One Stubbe Peeter", written in 1590. Stubbe (died 1589) was a German farmer and alleged serial killer and cannibal, also known as the "Werewolf of Bedburg". He confessed to killing and eating fourteen children, two pregnant women, and their fetuses. One of the children was his own son, whose brain he was reported to have devoured. In addition to this he confessed to having had intercourse with a succubus sent to him by the Devil.

ARREST

memorable de la Cour

de parlement de Dole, donné à l'encontre de Gilles Garnier, Lyonnois, pour auoir en forme de loup garou deuoré plusieurs enfans, & commis autres crimes: enrichy d'aucuns points recueillis de diuers autheurs pour esclarcir la matiere de telle transformation.

Because the stories herein were written in earlier centuries, they read almost as if they were penned as case histories of real-life lycanthropes. And though the style and language may be a bit demanding for readers not accustomed to writings from earlier eras, the payoff comes in the dramatic gravitas of the tales themselves and in the eternal power of exalted storytelling. What you get in return is heightened horror, as evidenced by the following blood-chilling example from "Jean Grenier, A French Were-Wolf" by Sabine Baring-Gould:

"You want to know about the wolf-skin cape?" continued he. "Pierre Labourant gave me that; he wraps it round me, and every Monday, Friday and Sunday, and for about an hour at dusk every other day I am a wolf, a were-wolf. I have killed dogs and drunk their blood; but little girls taste better, their flesh is tender and sweet, their blood rich and warm. I have eaten many a maiden, as I have been on my raids together with my nine companions. I am a were-wolf! Ah, ha! if the sun were to set I would soon fall on one of you and make a meal of you!"

According to the various legends and lore of cultures around the world, there are many ways to become a shapeshifter/werewolf. Being bitten by a wolfman is the most popular, it seems, thanks in large part to Universal Studios. Drinking rainwater from the werewolf's footprint is another, or even drinking downstream from the beast is still another way to get your wolf on. Unless you happen to be born of lycanthropic parentage, you may become a werewolf by doing a shady deal with the Devil, wearing an enchanted belt or wolf skin, eating wolf's brains, being cursed by witchcraft, having sex with a werewolf, or stripping naked in a graveyard, then peeing a circle around your discarded clothes before you go howling off through the tombstones.

We don't recommend you try these or any other bizarre methods. Instead, you can enter the mysterious world of the werewolf and slip inside the skin of the beast through these very pages. You get the same bloody thrills and chills without putting your mortal soul on the line.

The Hour of the Wolf is upon us. Now enter the literary lair of the wolf.

Amongst the tales I tell you once again, I would not forget the Lay of the Were-Wolf. Such beasts as he are known in every land. Bisclavaret he is named in Brittany; whilst the Norman calls him Garwal.

It is a certain thing, and within the knowledge of all, that many a christened man has suffered this change, and ran wild in woods, as a Were-Wolf. The Were-Wolf is a fearsome beast. He lurks within the thick forest, mad and horrible to see. All the evil that he may, he does. He goeth to and fro, about the solitary place, seeking man, in order to devour him. Hearken, now, to the adventure of the Were-Wolf, that I have to tell.

In Brittany there dwelt a baron who was marvellously esteemed of all his fellows. He was a stout knight, and a comely, and a man of office and repute. Right private was he to the mind of his lord, and dear to the counsel of his neighbours. This baron was wedded to a very worthy dame, right fair to see, and sweet of semblance. All his love was set on her, and all her love was given again to him. One only grief had this lady. For three whole days in every week her lord was absent from her side. She knew not where he went, nor on what errand. Neither did any of his house know the business which called him forth.

On a day when this lord was come again to his house, altogether joyous and content, the lady took him to task, right sweetly, in this fashion,

"Husband," said she, "and fair, sweet friend, I have a certain thing to pray of you. Right willingly would I receive this gift, but I fear to anger you in the asking. It is better for me to have an empty hand, than to gain hard words."

When the lord heard this matter, he took the lady in his arms, very tenderly, and kissed her.

"Wife," he answered, "ask what you will. What would you have, for it is yours already?"

"By my faith," said the lady, "soon shall I be whole. Husband, right long and wearisome are the days that you spend away from your home. I rise from my bed in the morning, sick at heart, I know not why. So fearful am I, lest you do aught to your loss, that I may not find any comfort. Very quickly shall I die for reason of my dread. Tell me now, where you go, and on what business! How may the knowledge of one who loves so closely, bring you to harm?"

"Wife," made answer the lord, "nothing but evil can come if I tell you this secret. For the mercy of God do not require it of me. If you but knew, you would withdraw yourself from my love, and I should be lost indeed."

When the lady heard this, she was persuaded that her baron sought to put her by with jesting words. Therefore she prayed and required him the more urgently, with tender looks and speech, till he was overborne, and told her all the story, hiding naught.

"Wife, I become Bisclavaret. I enter in the forest, and live on prey and roots, within the thickest of the wood."

After she had learned his secret, she prayed and entreated the more as to whether he ran in his raiment, or went spoiled of vesture.

"Wife," said he, "I go naked as a beast."

"Tell me, for hope of grace, what you do with your clothing?"

"Fair wife, that will I never. If I should lose my raiment, or even be marked as I quit my vesture, then a Were-Wolf I must go for all the days of my life. Never again should I become man, save in that hour my clothing were given back to me. For this reason never will I show my lair."

"Husband," replied the lady to him, "I love you better than all the world. The less cause have you for doubting my faith, or hiding any tittle from me. What savour is here of friendship? How have I made forfeit of your love; for what sin do you mistrust my honour? Open now your heart, and tell what is good to be known."

So at the end, outwearied and overborne by her importunity, he could no longer refrain, but told her all.

"Wife," said he, "within this wood, a little from the path, there is a hidden way, and at the end thereof an ancient chapel, where oftentimes I have bewailed my lot. Near by is a great hollow stone, concealed by a bush, and there is the secret place where I hide my raiment, till I would return to my own home."

On hearing this marvel the lady became sanguine of visage, because of her exceeding fear. She dared no longer to lie at his side, and turned over in her mind, this way and that, how best she could get her from him. Now there was a certain knight of those parts, who, for a great while, had sought and required this lady for her love. This knight had spent long years in her service, but little enough had he got thereby, not even fair words, or a promise. To him the dame wrote a letter, and meeting, made her purpose plain.

"Fair friend," said she, "be happy. That which you have coveted so long a time, I will grant without delay. Never again will I deny your suit. My heart, and all I have to give, are yours, so take me now as love and dame."

Right sweetly the knight thanked her for her grace, and pledged her faith and fealty. When she had confirmed him by an oath, then she told him all this business of her lord—why he went, and what he became, and of his ravening within the wood. So she showed him of the chapel, and of the hollow stone, and of how to spoil the Were-Wolf of his vesture. Thus, by the kiss of his wife, was Bisclavaret betrayed. Often enough had he ravished his prey in desolate places, but from this journey he never returned. His kinsfolk and acquaintance came together to ask of his tidings, when this absence was noised abroad. Many a man, on many a day, searched the woodland, but none might find him, nor learn where Bisclavaret was gone.

The lady was wedded to the knight who had cherished her for so long a space. More than a year had passed since Bisclavaret disappeared. Then it chanced that the King would hunt in that self-same wood where the Were-Wolf lurked. When the hounds were unleashed they ran this way and that, and swiftly came upon his scent. At the view the huntsman winded on his horn, and the whole pack were at his heels. They followed him from morn to eve, till he was torn and bleeding, and was all adread lest they should pull him down. Now the King was very close to the quarry, and when Bisclavaret looked upon his master, he ran to him for pity and for grace. He took the stirrup within his paws, and fawned upon the prince's foot. The King was very fearful at this sight, but presently he called his courtiers to his aid.

"Lords," cried he, "hasten hither, and see this marvellous thing. Here is a beast who has the sense of man. He abases himself before his foe, and cries for mercy, although he cannot speak. Beat off the hounds, and let no man do him harm. We will hunt no more to-day, but return to our own place, with the wonderful quarry we have taken."

The King turned him about, and rode to his hall, Bisclavaret following at his side. Very near to his master the Were-Wolf went, like any dog, and had no care to seek again the wood. When the King had brought him safely to his own castle, he rejoiced greatly, for the beast was fair and strong, no mightier had any man seen. Much pride had the King in his marvellous beast. He held him so dear, that he bade all those who wished for his love, to cross the Wolf in naught, neither to strike him with a rod, but ever to see that he was richly fed and kennelled warm. This commandment the Court observed willingly. So all the day the Wolf sported with the lords, and at night he lay within the chamber of the King. There was not a man who did not make much of the beast, so frank was he and debonair. None had reason to do him wrong, for ever was he about his master, and for his part did evil to none. Every day were these two companions together, and all perceived that the King loved him as his friend.

Hearken now to that which chanced.

The King held a high Court, and bade his great vassals and barons, and all the lords of his venery to the feast. Never was there a goodlier feast, nor one set forth with sweeter show and pomp. Amongst those who were bidden, came that same knight who had the wife of Bisclavaret for dame. He came to the castle, richly gowned, with a fair company, but little he deemed whom he would find so near. Bisclavaret marked his foe the moment he stood within the hall. He ran towards him, and seized him with his fangs, in the King's very presence, and to the view of all. Doubtless he would have done him much mischief, had not the King called and chidden him, and threatened him with a rod. Once, and twice, again, the Wolf set upon the knight in the very light of day. All men marvelled at his malice, for sweet and serviceable was the beast, and to that hour had shown hatred of none. With one consent the household deemed that this deed was done with full reason, and that the Wolf had suffered at the knight's hand some bitter wrong. Right wary of his foe was the knight until the feast had ended, and all the barons had taken farewell of their lord, and departed, each to his own house. With these, amongst the very first, went that lord whom Bisclavaret so fiercely had assailed. Small was the wonder that he was glad to go.

No long while after this adventure it came to pass that the courteous King would hunt in that forest where Bisclavaret was found. With the prince came his wolf, and a fair company. Now at nightfall the King abode within a certain lodge of that country, and this was known of that dame who before was the wife of Bisclavaret. In the morning the lady clothed her in her most dainty apparel, and hastened to the lodge, since she desired to speak with the King, and to offer him a rich present. When the lady entered in the chamber, neither man nor leash might restrain the fury of the Wolf. He became as a mad dog in his hatred and malice. Breaking from his bonds he sprang at the lady's face, and bit the nose from her visage. From every side men ran to the succour of the dame. They beat off the wolf from his prey, and for a little would have cut him in pieces with their swords. But a certain wise counsellor said to the King,

"Sire, hearken now to me. This beast is always with you, and there is not one of us all who has not known him for long. He goes in and out amongst us, nor has molested any man, neither done wrong or felony to any, save only to this dame, one only time as we have seen. He has done evil to this lady, and to that knight, who is now the husband of the dame. Sire, she was once the wife of that lord who was so close and private to your heart, but who went, and none might find where he had gone. Now, therefore, put the dame in a sure place, and question her straitly, so that she may tell—if perchance she knows thereof—for what reason this Beast holds her in such mortal hate. For many a strange deed has chanced, as well we know, in this marvellous land of Brittany."

The King listened to these words, and deemed the counsel good. He laid hands upon the knight, and put the dame in surety in another place. He caused them to be questioned right straitly, so that their torment was very grievous. At the end, partly because of her distress, and partly by reason of her exceeding fear, the lady's lips were loosed, and she told her tale. She showed them of the betrayal of her lord, and how his raiment was stolen from the hollow stone. Since then she knew not where he went, nor what had befallen him, for he had never come again to his own land. Only, in her heart, well she deemed and was persuaded, that Bisclavaret was he.

Straightway the King demanded the vesture of his baron, whether this were to the wish of the lady, or whether it were against her wish. When the raiment was brought him, he caused it to be spread before Bisclavaret, but the Wolf made as though he had not seen. Then that cunning and crafty counsellor took the King apart, that he might give him a fresh rede.

"Sire," said he, "you do not wisely, nor well, to set this raiment before Bisclavaret, in the sight of all. In shame and much tribulation must he lay aside the beast, and again become man. Carry your wolf within your most secret chamber, and put his vestment therein. Then close the door upon him, and leave him alone for a space. So we shall see presently whether the ravening beast may indeed return to human shape."

The King carried the Wolf to his chamber, and shut the doors upon him fast. He delayed for a brief while, and taking two lords of his fellowship with him, came again to the room. Entering therein, all three, softly together, they found the knight sleeping in the King's bed, like a little child. The King ran swiftly to the bed and taking his friend in his arms, embraced and kissed him fondly, above a hundred times. When man's speech returned once more, he told him of his adventure. Then the King restored to his friend the fief that was stolen from him, and gave such rich gifts, moreover, as I cannot tell. As for the wife who had betrayed Bisclavaret, he bade her avoid his country, and chased her from the realm. So she went forth, she and her second lord together, to seek a more abiding city, and were no more seen.

PEETER STUBBE

A true discourse declaring the damnable life and death of one stubbe peeter

A most wicked sorcerer, who in the likeness of a wolf committed many murders, continuing this devilish practise 25 years, killing and devouring men, women, and children who for the same fact was taken and executed the 31st of october last past in the town of bedbur near the city of collin in germany

Anonymous

1590

In the towns of Cperadt and Bedbur near Collin in high Germany, there was continually brought up and nourished one Stubbe Peeter, who from his youth was greatly inclined to evil and the practising of wicked arts, surfeiting in the damnable desire of magic, necromancy, and sorcery, acquainting himself with many infernal spirits and fiends. The Devil, who hath a ready ear to listen to the lewd motions of cursed men, promised to give him whatsoever his heart desired during his mortal life: whereupon this vile wretch, having a tyrannous heart and a most cruel bloody mind, requested that at his pleasure he might work his malice on men, women, and children, in the shape of some beast, whereby he might live without dread or danger of life, and unknown to be the executor of any bloody enterprise which he meant to commit. The Devil gave him a girdle which, being put around him, he was transformed into the likeness of a greedy, devouring wolf, strong and mighty, with eyes great and large, which in the night sparkled like brands of fire; a mouth great and wide, with most sharp and cruel teeth, a huge body and mighty paws. And no sooner should he put off the same girdle, but presently he should appear in his former shape, according to the proportion of a man, as if he had never been changed.

Stubbe Peeter herewith was exceedingly well pleased, and the shape fitted his fancy and agreed best with his nature, being inclined to blood and cruelty. Therefore, satisfied with this strange and devilish gift (for it was not troublesome but might be hidden in a small room), he proceeded to the execution of heinous and vile murders; for if any person displeased him, he would thirst for revenge, and no sooner should they or any of theirs walk in the fields or the city, but in the shape of a wolf he would presently encounter them, and never rest till he had plucked out their throats and torn their joints asunder. And after he had gotten a taste hereof, he took such pleasure and delight in shedding of blood, that he would night and day walk the fields and work extreme cruelties. And sundry times he would go through the streets of Collin, Bedbur, and Cperadt, in comely habit, and very civilly, as one well known to all the inhabitants thereabout, and oftentimes was he saluted of those whose friends and children he had butchered, though nothing suspected for the same. In these places, I say he would walk up and down, and if he could spy either maid, wife, or child that his eyes liked or his heart lusted after, he would wait their issuing out of the city or town. If he could by any means get them alone, he would in the fields ravish them, and after in his wolvish likeness cruelly murder them. Often it came to pass that as he walked abroad in the fields, if he chanced to spy a company of maidens playing together or else milking their kine, in his wolvish shape he would run among them, and while the rest escaped by flight, he would be sure to lay hold of one, and after his filthy lust fulfilled, he would murder her presently. Besides, if he had liked or known any of them, her he would pursue; such was his swiftness of foot while he continued a wolf that he would outrun the swiftest greyhound in that country; and so much he had practised this wickedness that the whole province was frightened by the cruelty of this bloody and devouring wolf. Thus continuing his devilish and damnable deeds, within the compass of a few years, he had murdered thirteen young children, and two goodly young women bit with child, tearing the children out of their wombs, in most bloody and savage sort, and after ate their hearts panting hot and raw, which he accounted dainty morsels and best agreeing to his appetite.

Moreover, he used many times to kill lambs and kids and such like beasts, feeding on the same most usually raw and bloody, as if he had been a natural wolf indeed.

He had at that time living a fair young daughter, after whom he also lusted most unnaturally, and cruelly committed most wicked incest with her, a most gross and vile sin, far surmounting adultery or fornication, though the least of the three doth drive the soul into hell fire, except hearty repentance, and the great mercy of God. This daughter of his he begot when he was not altogether so wickedly given, who was called by the name of Stubbe Beell, whose beauty and good grace was such as deserved commendations of all those that knew her. And such was his inordinate lust and filthy desire toward her, that he begat a child by her, daily using her as his concubine; but as an insatiate and filthy beast, given over to work evil, with greediness he also lay by his own sister, frequenting her company long time. Moreover being on a time sent for to a Gossip of his there to make merry and good cheer, ere he thence departed he so won the woman by his fair and flattering speech, and so much prevailed, that ere he departed the house, he lay by her, and ever after had her company at his command; this woman had to name Katherine Trompin, a woman of tall and comely stature of exceeding good favour and one that was well esteemed among her neighbours. But his lewd and inordinate lust being not satisfied with the company of many concubines, nor his wicked fancy contented with the beauty of any woman, at length the Devil sent unto him a wicked spirit in the similitude and likeness of a woman, so fair of face and comely of personage, that she resembled rather some heavenly angel than any mortal creature, so far her beauty exceeded the choicest sort of women; and with her, as with his heart's delight, he kept company the space of seven years, though in the end she proved and was found indeed no other than a she-Devil. Notwithstanding, this lewd sin of lechery did not any thing assuage his cruel and bloody mind, but continuing an insatiable bloodsucker, so great was the joy he took therein, that he accounted no day spent in pleasure wherein he had not shed some blood, not respecting so much who he did murder, as how to murder and destroy them, as the matter ensuing doth manifest, which may stand for a special note of a cruel and hard heart. For, having a proper youth to his son, begotten in the flower and strength of his age, the first fruit of his body in whom he took such joy that he did commonly call him his heart's ease, yet so far his delight in murder exceeded the joy he took in his son, that thirsting after his blood, on a time he enticed him into the fields, and from thence into a forest hard by, where, making excuse to stay about the necessaries of nature, while the young man went forward, in the shape and likeness of a wolf he encountered his own son and there most cruelly slew him, which done, he presently ate the brains out of his head as a most savory and dainty delicious means to staunch his greedy appetite: the most monstrous act that ever man heard of, for never was known a wretch from nature so far degenerate.

Long time he continued his vile and villainous life, sometime in the likeness of a wolf, sometime in the habit of a man, sometime in the towns and cities, and sometimes in the woods and thickets to them adjoining, whereas the Dutch copy maketh mention; he on a time met with two men and one woman, whom he greatly desired to murder. In subtle sort he conveyed himself far before them in their way and craftily couched out of their sight; but as soon as they approached near the place where he lay, he called one of them by his name. The party hearing himself called once or twice by his name, supposing it was some familiar friend that in jesting sort stood out of his sight, went from his company toward the place from whence the voice proceeded, of purpose to see who it was; but he was no sooner entered within the danger of this transformed man, but he was murdered in that place; the rest of his company staying for him, expecting still his return, but finding his stay over long, the other man left the woman and went to look for him, by which means the second man was also murdered. The woman then seeing neither of both return again, in heart suspected that some evil had fallen upon them, and therefore, with all the power she had, she sought to save herself by flight, though it nothing prevailed, for, good soul, she was also soon overtaken by this light-footed wolf, whom, when he had first deflowered, he after most cruelly murdered The men were after found mangled in the wood, but the woman's body was never after seen, for she he had most ravenously devoured, whose flesh he esteemed both sweet and dainty in taste.

Thus this damnable Stubbe Peeter lived the term of five and twenty years, unsuspected to be author of so many cruel and unnatural murders, in which time he had destroyed and spoiled an unknown number of men, women, and children, sheep, lambs, and goats, and other cattle; for, when he could not through the wariness of people draw men, women, or children in his danger, then, like a cruel and tyrannous beast, he would work his cruelty on brute beasts in most savage sort, and did act more mischief and cruelty than would be credible, although high Germany hath been forced to taste the truth thereof.

By which means the inhabitants of Collin, Bedbur and Cperadt, seeing themselves so grievously endangered, plagued, and molested by this greedy and cruel wolf, insomuch that few or none durst travel to or from those places without good provision of defence, and all for fear of this devouring and fierce wolf, for oftentimes the inhabitants found the arms and legs of dead men, women, and children scattered up and down the fields, to their great grief and vexation of heart knowing the same to be done by that strange and cruel wolf, whom by no means they could take or overcome, so that if any man or woman missed their child, they were out of hope ever to see it again alive.

And here is to be noted a most strange thing which setteth forth the great power and merciful providence of God to the comfort of each Christian heart. There were not long ago certain small children playing in a meadow together hard by the town, where also some store of kine were feeding, many of them having young calves sucking upon them. And suddenly among these children comes this vile wolf running and caught a pretty fine girl by the collar, with intent to pull out her throat; but such was the will of God, that the wolf could not pierce the collar of the child's coat, being high and very well stiffened and close clasped about her neck; and therewithal the sudden great cry of the rest of the children which escaped so amazed the cattle feeding by, that being fearful to be robbed of their young, they altogether came running against the wolf with such force that he was presently compelled to let go his hold and to run away to escape the danger of their horns; by which means the child was preserved from death, and, God be thanked, remains living at this day.

And that this thing is true, Master Tice Artine, a brewer dwelling at Puddlewharfe in London, being a man of that country born, and one of good reputation and account, is able to justify who is near kinsman to this child, and hath from thence twice received letters concerning the same; and for that the first letter did rather drive him into wondering at the act then yielding credit thereunto, he had shortly after, at request of his writing, another letter sent to him, whereby he was more fully satisfied; and divers other persons of great credit in London hath in like sort received letters from their friends to the like effect.

Likewise in the towns of Germany aforesaid continual prayer was used unto God that it would please Him to deliver them from the danger of this greedy wolf.

And, although they had practised all the means that men could devise to take this ravenous beast, yet until the Lord had determined his fall, they could not in any wise prevail notwithstanding they daily sought to entrap him and for that intent continually maintained great mastiffs and dogs of much strength to hunt and chase the beast. In the end, it pleased God, as they were in readiness and provided to meet with him, that they should espy him in his wolvish likeness at what time they beset him round about, and most circumspectly set their dogs upon him, in such sort that there was no means of escape, at which advantage they never could get him before; but as the Lord delivered Goliath into the hands of David, so was this wolf brought in danger of these men; who, seeing as I said before, no way to escape the imminent danger, being hardly pursued at the heels, presently slipped his girdle from about him, whereby the shape of a wolf clean avoided, and he appeared presently in his true shape and likeness, having in his hand a staff as one walking toward the city; but the hunters, whose eyes were steadfastly bent upon the beast, and seeing him in the same place metamorphosed contrary to their expectation, it wrought a wonderful amazement to their minds; and, had it not been that they knew the man so soon as they saw him, they had surely taken the same to have been some Devil in a mans likeness; but forasmuch as they knew him to be an ancient dweller in the town, they came unto him, and talking with him, they brought him home to his own house, and handing him to be the man indeed, and no delusion or phantastical motion, they had him before the magistrates to be examined.

Thus being apprehended, he was shortly after put to the rack in the town of Bedbur, but fearing the torture, he voluntarily confessed his whole life, and made known the villainies which he had committed for the space of twenty-five years; also he confessed how by sorcery he procured of the Devil a girdle, which being put on, he forthwith became a wolf, which girdle at his apprehension he confessed he cast it off in a certain valley and there left it, which, when the magistrates heard, they sent to the valley for it, but at their coming found nothing at all, for it may be supposed that it was gone to the Devil from whence it came, so that it was not to be found. For the Devil having brought the wretch to all the shame he could, left him to endure the torments which his deeds deserved.

After he had some space been imprisoned, the magistrates found out through due examination of the matter, that his daughter Stubbe Beell and his Gossip Katherine Trompin, were both accessory to divers murders committed, were arraigned, and with Stubbe Peeter condemned, and their several judgements pronounced the 28 of October 1589, in this manner, that is to say Stubbe Peeter as principal malefactor, was judged first to have his body laid on a wheel, and with red hot burning pincers in ten places to have the flesh pulled off from the bones, after that, his legs and arms to be broken with a wooden axe or hatchet, afterward to have his head struck from his body, then to have his carcase burned to ashes.

Also his daughter and his Gossip were judged to be burned quick to ashes, the same time and day with the carcase of the aforesaid Stubbe Peeter. And on the 31st of the same month, they suffered death accordingly in the town of Bedbur in the presence of many peers and princes of Germany.

Thus, Gentle Reader, have I set down the true discourse of this wicked man Stubbe Peeter, which I desire to be a warning to all sorcerers and witches, which unlawfully follow their own devilish imagination to the utter ruin and destruction of their souls eternally, from which wicked and damnable practice, I beseech God keep all good men, and from the cruelty of their wicked hearts. Amen.

After the execution, there was by the advice of the magistrates of the town of Bedbur a high pole set up and strongly framed, which first went through the wheel whereon he was broken, whereunto also it was fastened; after that a little above the wheel the likeness of a wolf was framed in wood, to show unto all men the shape wherein he executed those cruelties. Over that on the top of the stake the sorcerer's head itself was set up, and round about the wheel there hung as it were sixteen pieces of wood about a yard in length which represented the sixteen persons that were perfectly known to be murdered by him. And the same ordained to stand there for a continual monument to all ensuing ages, what murders by Stubbe Peeter were committed, with the order of his judgement, as this picture doth more plainly express.

Witnesses that this is true: Tyse Artyne, William Brewar, Adolf Staedt, George Bores. With divers others that have seen the same.

THE SEVERED ARM

OR, THE WEHR –WOLF OF LIMOUSIN

ANONYMOUS

The adventure that you have heard is no vain fable. Verily and indeed it chanced as I have said. The Lay of the Were-Wolf, truly, was written that it should ever be borne in mind.

The ancient province of Poictou, in France, has long been celebrated in the annals of romance, as one of the most famous haunts of those dreadful animals, whose species is between a phantom and a beast of prey; and which are called by Germans, wehr-wolves, and by the French, Bisclavarets, or Loups Garoux. To the English, these midnight terrors are yet unknown, and almost without a name; but when they are spoken of in this country they are called, by the way of eminence, wild wolves. The common superstition concerning them is, that they are men in compact with the arch enemy, who have the power of assuming the form and nature of wolves at certain periods.

The hilly and woody district of the Upper Limousin, which now forms the southern division of the Upper Vienne, was that particular part of the province which the wehr-wolves were supposed to inhabit: whence, like the animal which gave them their name, they would wander out by midnight, far from their own hills and mountains, and run howling through the silent streets of the nearest towns and villages, to the great terror of all the inhabitants; whose piety however, was somewhat increased by these supernatural visitations.

There once stood in the suburbs of the town of St Yrieux, which is situate in those dangerous parts of ancient Poictou, an old, but handsome *Maison-de-Plaisance*, or, in plain English, a countryhouse, belonging, by ancient descent, to the young Baroness Louise Joliedame; who, out of dread to the terrible Wehr-Wolves, a well-bred horror at the *chambres à l'antique* which it contained, and a greater love for the gallant court of Francis I, let the chateau to strangers; though they occupied but a very small portion of k, whilst the rest was left unrepaired, and was rapidly passing to decay. One of the parties by whom the old mansion was tenanted, was a country chirurgeon, named Antoine du Pilon; who (according to his own account) was not only well acquainted with the science of Galen and Hippocrates, but was also a profound adept in those arts, for the learning of which some men toil their whole lives away, and are none the wiser; such as alchemy, converse with spirits, magic, and so forth. Dr du Pilon had abundant leisure to talk of his knowledge at the cabaret of St Yrieux, which bore the sign of the Chevalier Bayard's arms, where he assembled round him many of the idler members of the town, the chief of whom were Cuirbouilli, the currier; Malbois, the joiner; La Jacquette, the tailor; and Nicole Bonvarlet, his host; together with several other equally arrant gossips, who all swore roundly, at the end of their parleys, that Dr Antoine du Pilon was the best doctor, and the wisest man in the whole world! To remove, however, any wonder that may arise in the reader's mind how a professor of such skill and knowledge should be left to waste his abilities so remote from the patronage of the great, it should be remarked, that in such cases as had already come before him, he had not been quite so successful as could have been expected or desired, since old Genefrede Corbeau, who was frozen almost double with age and ague, he kept cold and fasting to preserve her from fever; and he would have cut off the leg of Pierre Faucile, the reaper, when he wounded his right arm in the harvest time, to prevent his flesh from mortifying downwards!

In a retired apartment of the same deserted mansion where this mirror of chirargeons resided, dwelt a peasant, and his daughter, who had come to St Yrieux from a distant part of Normandy, and of whose history nothing was known, but that they seemed to be in the deepest poverty; although they neither asked relief, nor uttered a single complaint. Indeed, they rather avoided all discourse with their gossiping neighbours, and even with their fellow inmates, excepting so far as the briefest courtesy required; and as they were able, on entering their abode, to place a reasonable security for payment in the hands of old Gervais, the Baroness Joliedame's steward, they were permitted to live in the old chateau with little questioning, and less sympathy. The father appeared in general to be a plain, rude peasant, whom poverty had somewhat tinctured with misanthropy: though there were times when his bluntness towered into a haughtiness not accordant with his present station, but seemed like a relique of a higher sphere, from which he had fallen. He strove, and the very endeavour increased the bitterness of his heart to mankind, to conceal his abject indigence; but that was too apparent to all, since he was rarely to be found at St Yrieux, but led a wild life in the adjacent mountains and forests, occasionally visiting the town to bring to his daughter Adele a portion of the spoil, which as a hunter, he indefatigably sought for the subsistence of both. Adele, on the contrary, though she felt as deeply as her father the sad reverse of fortune to which they were exposed, had more gentleness in her sorrow, and more content in her humiliation. She would, when he returned to the cottage, worn with the fatigue of his forest labours, try, but many times in vain, to bring a smile to his face and consolation to his heart. "My father," she would say, "quit, I beseech you, this wearisome hunting for some safer employment nearer home. You depart, and I watch in vain for your return; days and nights pass away, and you come not!—while my disturbed imagination will ever whisper the danger of a forest midnight, fierce howling wolves, and robbers still more cruel."

"Robbers! girl, sayest thou?" answered her father with a bitter laugh, "and what shall they gain from me, think ye? Is there aught in this worn-out gaberdine to tempt them? Go to, Adele! I am not now Count Gaspar de Marcanville, the friend of the royal Francis, and a knight of the Holy Ghost; but plain Hubert, the Hunter of the Limousin; and wolves, thou trowest, will not prey upon wolves."

"But, my dearest father," said Adele, embracing him, "I would that thou wouldst seek a safer occupation nearer to our dwelling, for I would be by your side."

"What wouldst have me to do, girl?" interrupted Gaspar impatiently; "wouldst have me put this hand to the sickle or the plough, which has so often grasped a sword in the battle, and a banner-lance in the tournament? Or shall a companion of Le Saint Esprit become a fellow-hand-worker with the low artisans of this miserable town? I tell thee, Adele, that but for thy sake I would never again quit the forest, but would remain there in a savage life, till I forgot my language and my species, and become a wehr-wolf or a wild buck!"

Such was commonly the close of their conversation; for if Adele dared to press her entreaties further, Gaspar, half frenzied, would not fail to call to her mind all the unhappy circumstances of his fall, and work himself almost to madness by their repetition. He had, in early life, been introduced by the Count de Saintefleur to the court of Francis I, where he had risen so high in the favour of his sovereign, that he was continually in his society; and in the many wars which so embittered the reign of that excellent monarch, de Marcanville's station was ever by his side. In these conflicts, Gaspar's bosom had often been the shield of Francis even in moments of the most imminent danger; and the grateful king as often showered upon his deliverer those rewards which, to the valiant and high-minded soldier, are far dearer than riches—the glittering jewels of knighthood, and the golden coronal of the peerage. To that friend who had fixed his feet so loftily and securely in the slippery paths of a court, Gaspar felt all the ardour of youthful gratitude; and yet he sometimes imagined, that he could perceive an abatement in the favour of de Saintefleur as that of Francis increased. The truth was, that the gold and rich promises of the king's great enemy, the Emperor Charles V, had induced de Saintefleur to swerve from his allegiance; and he now waited but for a convenient season to put the darkest designs in practice against his sovereign. He also felt no slight degree of envy, even against that very person whom he had been the instrument of raising; and at length an opportunity occurred, when he might gratify both his ambition and his revenge by the same blow. It was in one of those long wars in which the French monarch was engaged, and in which de Saintefleur and de Marcanville were his constant companions, that they were both watching his couch while he slept, when the former, in a low tone of voice, thus began to sound the faith of the latter to his royal master.

"What sayest thou, Gaspar, were not a prince's coronet and a king's revenue in Naples, better than thus ever-toiling in a war that seems unending? Hearest thou, brave de Marcanville? We can close it with the loss of one life only!"

"Queen of Heaven!" ejaculated Gaspar, "what is it thou wouldst say, de Saintefleur?"

"Say! why that there have been other kings in France before this Francis, and will be, when he shall have gone to his place. Thinkest thou that he of the double-headed black eagle, would not amply reward the sword that cut this fading lily from the earth?"

"No more, no more, de Saintefleur," cried Gaspar; "even

from you who placed me where I might flourish beneath the lily's shade, will I not hear this treason. Rest secure that I will not betray thee to the king; my life shall sooner be given for thine; but I will watch thee with more vigilance than the wolf hath when he watcheth the night-fold, and your first step to the heart of Francis shall be over the body of Gaspar de Marcanville."

"Nay, then," said de Saintefleur, aside, "he must be my first victim"; and immediately drawing his sword, he cried aloud, "What, ho! guards! treason!"—whilst Gaspar stood immovable with astonishment and horror. The event is soon related; for Francis was but too easily persuaded that de Marcanville was in reality guilty of the act about to be perpetrated by de Saintefleur; and the magnanimity of Gaspar was such, that not one word which might criminate his former friend could be drawn from him, even to save his own life. The kind-hearted Francis, however, was unable to forget in a moment the favour with which for years he had been accustomed to look upon de Marcanville; and it was only at the earnest solicitation of the courtiers, many of whom were rejoiced at the thought of a powerful rival's removal, that he could be prevailed on to pass upon him even the sentence of degradation and banishment.

Gaspar hastened to his chateau, but the treasures which he was allowed to bear with him into exile, were little more than his wife Rosalie and his daughter Adele; with whom he immured himself in the dark and almost boundless recesses of the Hanoverian Hartz, where his sorrows soon rendered his gaunt and attenuated form altogether unknown. In this savage retirement he drew up a faithful narration of de Saintefleur's treachery; and, in confirmation of its truth, procured a certificate from his confessor, Father Ægidius—one of those holy men, who of old were dwellers in forests and deserts—and directing it "To the King", placed it in the hands of his wife, that if, in any of those hazardous excursions in which he was engaged to procure their daily subsistence, he should perish, it might be delivered to Francis, and his family thus be restored to their rank and estates, when his pledge to de Saintefleur could no longer be claimed. Years passed away, and, in the gloomy recesses of the Hercynian woods, Gaspar acquired considerable skill as a hunter; had it been to preserve his own life only, he had laid him down calmly upon the sod, and resigned that life to famine, or to the hungry wolf; but he had still two objects which bound him to existence, and therefore in the chase the wild buck was too slow to escape his spear, and the bear too weak to resist his attacks.

His fate, notwithstanding, preyed heavily upon him, and he often broke out in fits of vehement passion, and the most bitter lamentations; which at length so wrought upon the grief-worn frame of Rosalie de Marcanville, that about ten years after Gaspar's exile, her death left him a widower, when his daughter Adele was scarcely eighteen years of age. It was then, with a mixture of desperation and distress, that de Marcanville determined to rush forth from his solitude into France; and, careless of the fate which might await him for returning from exile unrecalled, to advance even to the court, and laying his papers at the foot of the throne, to demand the ordeal of combat with de Saintefleur; but when he had arrived at the woody province of Upper Limousin, his purpose failed him, as he saw in the broad daylight, which rarely entered the Hartz Forest, the afflicting changes which ten years of the severest labour, and the most heartfelt sorrow, had made upon his form. He might, indeed, so far as it regarded all recollections of his person, have safely gone even into the court of Francis; but Gaspar also saw, that in the retired forest surrounding St Yrieux, he might still reside unknown to his beloved France; that under the guise of a hunter, he could still provide for the support of his gentle Adele; and that, in the event of his death he should be considerably nearer to the sovereign's abode. It was then, in consequence of these reasons, that de Marcanville employed a part of his small remaining property, in securing a residence in the dilapidated chateau, as it has been already mentioned.

It was some time after their arrival, that the inhabitants of the town of St Yrieux were alarmed by the intelligence that a wehr-wolf, or perhaps a troop of them, certainly inhabited the woods of Limousin. The most terrific howlings were heard in the night, and the wild rush of a chase swept through the deserted streets; yet the townspeople—according to the most approved rules for acting where wehr-wolves are concerned—never once thought of sallying forth in a body, and with weapons and lighted brands, to scare the monsters from their prey; but adding a more secure fastening to every window, which is the wehr-wolf's usual entrance, they deserted such as had already fallen their victims, with one brief expression of pity for them, and many a "Dieu et benit!" for themselves. It was asserted, too, that some of the country people, whose dwellings came more immediately into contact with the Limousin forests, had lost their children; whose lacerated remains, afterwards discovered in the woods, only half devoured, plainly denoted them to have fallen the prey of some abandoned wehr-wolf!

It is not surprising, that in a retired town, where half the people were without employment, and all were thoroughbred gossips, and lovers of wonders, that the inroads of the wehr-wolf formed too important an epoch in their history, to be passed over without a due discussion. Under pretence, therefore, of being a protection to each other, many of the people of St Yrieux, and especially the worthy conclave mentioned at the beginning of this history, were almost eternally convened at the Chevalier Bayard's Arms, talking over their nightly terrors, and filling each other with such affright, by the repetition of many a lying old tale upon the same subject, that, too much alarmed to part, they often agreed to pass the night over Nicole Bonvarlet's wine flask and blazing faggots. Upon a theme so intimately connected with a magical lore as is the history of wehr-wolves, Dr Antoine du Pilon discoursed like a Solomon; citing, to the great edification and wonder of his hearers, such hosts of authors, both sacred and profane, that he who should have hinted, that the wehr-wolves of St Yrieux were simply like other wolves, would have found as little gentleness in his hearers as he would have experienced from the animals themselves.

* * *

"Well, my masters?" began Bonvarlet, one evening when they were met, "I would not, for a tun of malmsey wine now, be in the Limousin forest tonight; for do ye hear how it blusters and pours? By the ship of St Mildred, in a wild night like this, there is no place in the world like your hearthside in a goodly submerge, with a merry host and good liquor; both of which, neighbours, ye have to admiration."

"Ay, Nicole," replied Courbouilli, "it is a foul night, truly, either for man or cattle; and yet I'll warrant ye that the wehr-wolves will be out in it, for their skin is said to be the same as that the fiend himself wears, and that would shut you out water, and storm, and wind, like a castle wall."

"Hark, neighbours, did ye hear that cry? It is a wehr-wolf's bark!" exclaimed Jerome Malbois, starting from his settle.

"Ay, by the bull of St Luke, did I, friend, Jerome," returned Bonvarlet; "surely the great fiend himself can make no worse a howling; I even thought 'twould split the very rafters last night, though I deem they're of good seasoned fir."

"There is the cry again!" exclaimed Malbois, and as the sounds drew nearer, the doctor's audience evinced symptoms of alarm, which were rapidly increasing, when a still louder shriek was heard close to the house.

"What ho, within there!" cried a voice, evidently of one in an agony of terror, "an ye be men, open the door," and the next moment it was burst from its fastenings by the force of a human body falling against it, which dropped without motion upon the floor.

The confusion which this accident created may well be imagined; the doctor, greatly alarmed, retreated into the fireplace, whence he cried out to the equally scared rustics, "It's a wehr-wolf in a human shape; don't touch him, I tell you, but strike him with a fire fork between the eyes, and he'll turn to a wolf and run away."

"Peace, Doctor," said Bonvarlet, the only one of the party who had ventured near the stranger; "he breathes yet, for he's a Christian man like as we are; so come, you prince of all chirurgeons, and bleed him; and when he comes to, why school him yourself."

The doctor advanced from his retreat, with considerable reluctance, to attend upon his patient, who was richly habited in the luxurious fashion of the court of Francis, and appeared to be a middle-aged man, of handsome features, and commanding presence. As the doctor, somewhat reassured, began to remove the short cloak to find out the stranger's arm, he started back with affright, and actually roared with pain at receiving a deep scratch from the huge paw of a wolf, which apparently grew Out from his shoulder. "Avaunt thee, Sathanas!" ejaculated the doctor, "I told thee how it would be, my masters, that this cursed wehr-wolf would bleed us first. By the porker of St Anthony!

Blessed beast! See he hath clawed me from the biceps flexor cubiti, down to the Os Lunare, even as a peasant would plough over a furrow!"

"Ha, ha, ha," laughed Bonvarlet, holding up the dreaded wolf's paw, which was yet bleeding, as if it had been recently separated from the animal. "Here is no wehr-wolf, but a brave hunter, who hath cut off his goodly forepaw in the forest, with his couteau-de-chasse; but soft," he added, throwing it aside, "he recovers!"

"Pierre!—Henri!" said the stranger, recovering, "where are ye? How far is the king behind us? Ha, what place is this? And who are ye?" he continued, looking round.

"This, your good worship, is the Chevalier Bayard's Arms, in the town of St Yrieux, where your honour fell, through loss of blood, as I guess, by this wound. We were fain to keep the door barred for fear of the wehr-wolves; and we half deemed your lordship to be one, at first sight of the great paw you carried, but now I judge you brought it from the forest."

"Ay! yes, thou art in the right on't," said the stranger, recollecting himself. "I was in the forest! I tell thee, host, that I have this night looked upon the arch demon himself!"

"Away, Lucifer!" ejaculated the doctor, devoutly crossing his breast; "and have I received a claw from his forefoot? I feel the enchantment of lycanthropy coming over me; I shall be a wehrwolf myself, shortly; for what saith Hornhoofius, in his Treatise de Diabolus, lib. xiv. cap. xxiii. They who are torn by a wehrwolf—Oh me!—Oh me!—Libera nos Domine. Look to yourselves, neighbours, or I shall raven upon ye all."

"I pray you, Master Doctor," said Bonvarlet, "to let his lordship tell us his story first, and then we'll hear yours.—How was it, fair sir?—but take another cup of wine first."

"My tale is brief," answered the stranger: "The king is passing tonight through the Limousin, and with two of his attendants I rode forward to prepare for his coming; when, in the darkness of the wood, we were separated, and, as I galloped on alone, an enormous wolf, with fiery flashing eyes, leaped out of a brake before me, with the most fearful howlings, and rushed on me with the speed of lightning. As the wolf leaped upon my horse, I drew my couteau-de-chasse, and severed that huge paw which you found upon me: but as the violence of the blow made the weapon fall, I caught up a large forked branch of a tree, and struck the animal upon the forehead: upon which, my horse began to rear and plunge; for, where the wolf stood, I saw by a momentary glimpse of moonlight the form of an ancient enemy, who had long since been banished from France, and whom I believed to have died of famine in the Hartz Forest."

"Look you there now," said du Pilon, "a blow between the eyes with a forked stick—said I not so from Philo-Diamones, lib. xcii? Oh, I'm condemned to be a wehr-wolf of a verity, and I shall eat those of my most intimate acquaintances the first. Masters look to yourselves:—O dies infelix! Oh unhappy man that I am! and with these words he rushed out of the cottage.

"I think the very fiend is in Monsieur the Doctor, to-night," cried the host, "for here he's gone off without dressing his honour's wounds."

"Heed not that, friend, but do thou provide torches and assistance to meet the king; my wound is but small; but when my horse saw the apparition I told you of, he bounded forward like a wild Russian colt, dragged me through all the briers of the forest—for there seemed a troop of a thousand wolves howling behind us—and at the verge of it he dropped lifeless, and left me, still pursued, to gain the town, weak and wounded as I was."

"St Dennis be praised now!" said Bonvarlet, "you showed a good heart, my lord; but we'll at once set out to meet the king; so neighbours take each of ye a good pine faggot off the hearth, and call up more help as you go; and Nicolette and Madeline will prepare for our return."

"But," asked the stranger, "where's the wolf's paw that I brought from the forest?"

"I cast it aside, my lord," answered Bonvarlet, "till you had recovered; but I would fain beg it of you as a gift, for I will hang it over my fireplace, and have its story made into a song by Rowland the minstrel—and, mother of God! What is this?" continued he, putting into his guest's hand a human arm, cut off at the elbow, vested in the worn-out sleeve of a hunter's coat, and bleeding freshly at the part where it was dissevered.

"Holy St Mary!" exclaimed the stranger, regarding the hand attentively, "this is the arm of Gaspar de Marcanville, yet bearing the executioner's brand burnt in his flesh; and he is a wehrwolf!"

"Why," said Bonvarlet, "that's the habit worn by the melancholy hunter, whose daughter lives at the chateau yonder. He rarely comes to St Yrieux, but when he does, he brings more game than any ten of your gentlemen huntsmen ever did. Come, we'll go seek the daughter of this man-wolf, and then on to the forest, for this fellow deserves a stake and a bundle of faggots, as well as ever Jeanne d'Arc did, in my simple thinking."

They then proceeded to Adele, at the dilapidated chateau; and her distress at the foregoing story may better be conceived than described; yet she offered not the slightest resistance to accompanying them to the forest; but when one of the party mentioned their expected meeting with the king, her eyes became suddenly lighted up, and retiring for a moment, she expressed herself in readiness to attend them. At the skirts of the forest they found an elderly man, of a strange, quaint appearance, crouching in the fern like a hare, who called out to them, in a squeaking voice, that was at once familiar to all, "Take care of yourselves, good people, for I am a wehr-wolf, and shall speedily spring upon ye."

"Why, that's our doctor, as I am a sinful man," cried Bonvarlet; "let's try his own cure upon him. Neighbour Malbois, give me a tough forked branch, and I'll disenchant him, I warrant; and you, Courboulli, out with your knife, as though you would skin him"—and then he con-tinued aloud, "Oh, honest friend, you're a wehr-wolf, are you? Why, then, I'll dispossess the devil that's in you. You shall be flayed, and then burnt for a wizard."

With that the rustics of St Yrieux, who enjoyed the jest, fell upon the unhappy doctor, and, by a sound beating, and other rough usage, so convinced him that he was not a wehr-wolf, that he cried Out, "Praised be St Gregory, I am a whole man again. Lo, I am healed, but my bones feel wondrous sore! Who is he that hath cured me?—By the mass, I am grievously bruised!—Thanks to the seraphical Father Francis, the devil hath gone out of me!"

Whilst the peasants were engaged in searching for the king's party and the mutilated wolf, the stranger who was left with Adele de Marcanville, fainted through loss of blood; and, as she bent over him, and stanched his wounds with her scarf, he said, with a faint voice—"Fair one, who is it, thinkest thou, whom thou art so blessedly attending?"

"I wot not," answered she, "but that thou art a man."

"Hear me, then, and throw aside these bandages for my dagger, for I am thy father's ancient enemy, the Count de Saintefleur."

"Heaven forgive you then," returned Adele, "for the time of vengeance belongs to it only."

"And it is come!" cried a loud hoarse voice, as a large wolf, wounded by the loss of a forepaw, leaped upon the count and put an end to his existence. At the same moment, the royal train, which the peasants had discovered, rode up with flambeaux, and a knight, with a large partisan, made a blow at the wolf, whom Adele vainly endeavoured to preserve, since the stroke was of sufficient power to destroy both. The wolf gave one terrific howl, and fell backwards in the form of a tall gaunt man, in a hunting dress; whilst Adele, drawing a packet from her bosom, and offering it to the king, sank lifeless upon the body of her father, Gaspar de Marcanville, the wehr-wolf of Limousin.

HUGUES, THE WER-WOLF
A KENTISH LEGEND OF THE MIDDLE AGES
SUTHERLAND MENZLES

I

"Ye hallowed bells whose voices thro' the
air The awful summons of afflictions bare."

Honoria, or the Day of All Souls.

On the confines of that extensive forest-tract for-merly spreading over so large a portion of the county of Kent, a remnant of which, to this day, is known as the weald[1] of Kent, and where it stretched its almost impervious covert midway between Ashford and Canterbury during the prolonged reign of our second Henry, a family of Norman extraction, by name Hugues (or Wulfric, as they were commonly called by the Saxon inhabitants of that district) had, under protection of the ancient forest laws, furtively erected for themselves a lone and miserable habitation. And amidst those sylvan fast-nesses, ostensibly following the occupation of woodcut-ters, the wretched outcasts, for such, from some cause or other, they evidently were, had for many years maintained a secluded and precarious existence. Whether from the rooted antipathy still actively cherished against all of that usurping nation from which they derived their origin, or from recorded malpractice by their superstitious Anglo-Saxon neighbours, they had long been looked upon as be-longing to the accursed race of wer-wolves, and as such churlishly refused work on the domains of the surrounding franklins or proprietors, so thoroughly was accredited the descent of the original lycanthropic stain transmitted from father to son through several generations. That the Hugues Wulfric reckoned not a single friend among the adjacent homesteads of serf or freedman was not to be wondered at, possessing as they did so unenviable a reputation; for to them was invariably attributed even the misfortunes which chance alone might seem to have given birth. Did midnight fire consume the grange;—did the time-decayed barn, over-stored with an abundant harvest, tumble into ruins;—were the shocks of wheat lain prostrate over the fields by a tempest;—did the smut destroy the grain;—or the cattle perish, decimated by a murrain;—a child sink under some wasting malady;—or a woman give premature birth to her offspring, it was ever the Hugues Wulfric who were openly accused, eyed askaunt with mingled fear and detestation, the finger of young and old pointing them out with bitter execrations—in line, they were almost as nearly classed *feræ natura* as their fabled prototype, and dealt with accordingly.[2]

Terrible, indeed, were the tales told of them round the glowing hearth at eventide, whilst spinning the flax, or plucking the geese; equally affirmed, too, in broad daylight, whilst driving the cows to pasturage, and most circumstantially discussed on Sundays between mass and vespers, by the gossip groups collected within Ashford parvyse, with most seasonable admixture of anathema and devout crossings. Witchcraft, larceny, murder, and sacrilege, formed prominent features in the bloody and mysterious scenes of which the Hugues Wulfric were the alleged actors: sometimes they were ascribed to the father, at others to the mother, and even the sister escaped not her share of vilification; fain would they have attributed an atrocious disposition to the unweaned babe, so great, so universal was the horror in which they held that race of Cain! The churchyard at Ashford, and the stone cross, from whence diverged the several roads to London, Canterbury, and Ashford, situated midway between the two latter places, served, so tradition avouched, as nocturnal theatres for the unhallowed deeds of the Wulfrics, who thither prowled by moonlight, it was said, to batten on the freshly-buried dead, or drain the blood of any living wight who might be rash enough to venture among those solitary spots. True it was that the wolves had, during some of the severe winters, emerged from their forest lairs, and, entering the cemetery by a breach in its walls, goaded by famine, had actually disinterred the dead; true was it, also, that the Wolf's Cross, as the hinds commonly designated it, had been stained with gore on one occasion through the fall of a drunken mendicant, who chanced to fracture his skull against a pointed angle of its basement. But these accidents, as well as a multitude of others, were attributed to the guilty intervention of the Wulfrics, under their fiendish guise of werwolves.

These poor people, moreover, took no pains to justify themselves from a prejudice so monstrous: full well apprised of what calumny they were the victims, but alike conscious of their impotence to contradict it, they tacitly suffered its infliction, and fled all contact with those to whom they knew themselves repulsive. Shunning the highways, and never venturing to pass through the town of Ashford in open day, they pursued such labour as might occupy them within doors, or in unfrequented places. They appeared not at Canterbury market, never numbered themselves amongst the pilgrims at Becket's far-famed shine, or assisted at any sport, merrymaking, hay-cutting, or harvest home: the priest had interdicted them from all communion with the church—the ale-bibbers from the hostelry.

The primitive cabin which they inhabited was built of chalk and clay, with a thatch of straw, in which the high winds had made huge rents, and closed up by a rotten door, exhibiting wide gaps, through which the gusts had free ingress. As this wretched abode was situated at considerable distance from any other, if, perchance, any of the neighbouring serfs strayed within its precincts towards nightfall, their credulous fears made them shun near approach so soon as the vapours of the marsh were seen to blend their ghastly wreaths with the twilight; and as that darkling time drew on which explains the diabolical sense of the old saying, "tween dog and wolf," "'twixt hawk and buzzard," at that hour the will-o'-wisps began to glimmer around the dwelling of the Wulfrics, who patriarchally supped—whenever they had a supper—and forthwith betook themselves to their rest.

Sorrow, misery, and the putrid exhalations of the steeped hemp, from which they manufactured a rude and scanty attire, combined eventually to bring sickness and death into the bosom of this wretched family, who, in their utmost extremity, could neither hope for pity or succour. The father was first attacked, and his corpse was scarce cold ere the mother rendered up her breath. Thus passed that fated couple to their account, unsolaced by the consolation of the confessor, or the medicaments of the leech. Hugues Wulfric, their eldest son, himself dug their grave, laid their bodies within it swathed with hempen shreds for grave cloths, and raised a few clods of earth to mark their last resting-place. A hind, who chanced to see him fulfilling this pious duty in the dusk of evening, crossed himself, and fled as fast as his legs would carry him, fully believing that he had assisted at some hellish incantation. When the real event transpired, the neighbouring gossips congratulated one another upon the double mortality, which they looked upon as the tardy chastisement of heaven: they spoke of ringing the bells, and singing masses of thanks for such an action of grace.

It was All Souls' eve, and the wind howled along the bleak hillside, whistling drearily through the naked branches of the forest trees, whose last leaves it had long since stripped; the sun had disappeared; a dense and chilling fog spread through the air like the mourning veil of the widowed, whose day of love hath early fled. No star shone in the still and murky sky. In that lonely hut, through which death had so lately passed, the orphan survivors held their lonely vigil by the fitful blaze emitted by the reeking logs upon their hearth. Several days had elapsed since their lips had been imprinted for the last time upon the cold hands of their parents; several dreary nights had passed since the sad hour in which their eternal farewell had left them desolate on earth.

Poor lone ones! Both, too, in the flower of their youth—how sad, yet how serene did they appear amid their grief!

But what sudden and mysterious terror is it that seems to overcome them? It is not, alas! the first time since they were left alone upon earth that they have found themselves at this hour of the night by their deserted hearth, enlivened of old by the cheerful tales of their mother. Full often had they wept together over her memory, but never yet had their solitude proved so appalling; and, pallid as very spectres, they tremblingly gazed upon one another as the flickering ray from the wood-fire played over their features.

"Brother! heard you not that loud shriek which every echo of the forest repeated? It sounds to me as if the ground were ringing with the tread of some gigantic phantom, and whose breath seems to have shaken the door of our hut. The breath of the dead they say is icy cold. A mortal shivering has come over me."

"And I, too, sister, thought I heard voices as it were at a distance, murmuring strange words. Tremble not thus—am I not beside you?"

"Oh, brother! let us pray the Holy Virgin, to the end that she may restrain the departed from haunting our dwelling."

"But, perhaps, our mother is amongst them: she comes, unshrived and unshrouded, to visit her forlorn offspring—her well-beloved! For, knowest thou not, sister, 'tis the eve on which the dead forsake their tombs. Let us open the door, that our mother may enter and resume her wonted place by the hearthstone."

"Oh, brother, how gloomy is all without doors, how damp and cold the gust sweeps by. Hearest thou, what groans the dead are uttering round our hut? Oh, close the door, in heaven's name!"

"Take courage, sister, I have thrown upon the fire that holy branch, plucked as it flowered on last Palm Sunday, which thou knowest will drive away all evil spirits, and now our mother can enter alone."

"But how will she look, brother? They say the dead are horrible to gaze upon; that their hair has fallen away; their eyes become hollow; and that, in walking, their bones rattle hideously. Will our mother, then, be thus?"

"No; she will appear with the features we loved to behold; with the affectionate smile that welcomed us home from our perilous labouts; with the voice which, in early youth, sought us when, belated, the closing night surprised us far from our dwelling."

The poor girl busied herself awhile in arranging a few platters of scanty fare upon the tottering board which served them for a table; and this last pious offering of filial love, as she deemed it, appeared accomplished only by the greatest and last effort, so enfeebled had her frame become.

"Let our dearly-loved mother enter then," she exclaimed, sinking exhausted upon the settle. "I have prepared her evening meal, that she may not be angry with me, and all is arranged as she was wont to have it. But what ails thee, my brother, for now thou tremblest as I did awhile agone?"

"See'st thou not, sister, those pale lights which are ris-ing at a distance across the marsh? They are the dead, corning to seat themselves before the repast prepared for them. Hark! list to the funeral tones of the Allhallowtide[3] bells, as they come upon the gale, blended with their hollow voices.—Listen, listen!"

"Brother, this horror grows insupportable. This, I feel, of a verity, will be my last night upon earth! And is there no word of hope to cheer me, mingling with those fearful sounds? Oh, mother! mother!"

"Hush, sister, hush! see'st thou now the ghastly lights which herald the dead, gleaming athwart the horizon? Hearest thou the prolonged tolling of the bell? They come! they come!"

"Eternal repose to their ashes!" exclaimed the bereaved ones, sinking upon their knees, and bowing down their heads in the extremity of terror and lamentation; and as they uttered the words, the door was at the same moment closed with violence, as though it had been slammed to by a vigorous hand. Hugues started to his feet, for the cracking of the timber which supported the roof seemed to announce the fall of the frail tenement; the fire was suddenly extinguished, and a plaintive groan mingled itself with the blast that whistled through the crevices of the door. On raising his sister, Hugues found that she too was no longer to be numbered among the living.

II

Hugues, on becoming the head of his family, composed of two sisters younger than himself, saw them likewise descend into the grave in the short space of a fortnight; and when he had laid the last within her parent earth, he hesitated whether he should not extend himself beside them, and share their peaceful slumber. It was not by tears and sobs that grief so profound as his manifested itself, but in a mute and sullen contemplation over the sepulture of his kindred and his own future happiness. During three consecutive nights he wandered, pale and haggard, from his solitary hut, to prostrate himself and kneel by turns upon the funereal turf. For three days food had not passed his lips.

Winter had interrupted the labours of the woods and fields, and Hugues had presented himself in vain among the neighbouring domains to obtain a few days' employment to thresh grain, cut wood, or drive the plough; no one would employ him from fear of drawing upon himself the fallity attached to all bearing the name of Wulfric. He met with brutal denials at all hands, and not only were these accompanied by taunts and menace, but dogs were let loose upon him to rend his limbs; they deprived him even of the alms accorded to beggars by profession; in short, he found himself overwhelmed with injuries and scorn.

Was he, then, to expire of inanition or deliver himself from the tortures of hunger by suicide? He would have embraced that means, as a last and only consolation, had he not been retained earthward to struggle with his dark fate by a feeling of love. Yes, that abject being, forced in very desperation, against his better self, to abhor the human species in the abstract, and to feel a savage joy in waging war against it; that *paria* who scarce longer felt confidence in that heaven which seemed an apathetic witness of his woes; that man so isolated from those social relations which alone compensate us for the toils and troubles of life, without other stay than that afforded by his conscience, with no other fortune in prospect than the bitter existence and miserable death of his departed kin: worn to the bone by privation and sorrow, swelling with rage and resentment, he yet consented to live—to cling to life; for, strange—he loved! But for that heaven-sent ray gleaming across his thorny path, a pilgrimage so lone and wearisome would he have gladly exchanged for the peaceful slumber of the grave.

Hugues Wulfric would have been the finest youth in all that part of Kent, were it not that the outrages with which he had so unceasingly to contend, and the privations he was forced to undergo, had effaced the colour from his cheeks, and sunk his eyes deep in their orbits: his brows were habitually contracted, and his glance oblique and fierce. Yet, despite that recklessness and anguish which clouded his features, one, incredulous of his atrocities, could not have failed to admire the savage beauty of his head, cast in nature's noblest mould, crowned with a profusion of waving hair, and set upon shoulders whose robust and harmonious proportions were discoverable through the tattered attire investing them. His carriage was firm and majestic; his motions were not without a species of rustic grace, and the tone of his naturally soft voice accorded admirably with the purity in which he spoke his ancestral language—the Norman—French: in short, he differed so widely from people of his imputed condition that one is constrained to believe that jealousy or prejudice must originally have been no stranger to the malicious persecution of which he was the object. The women alone ventured first to pity his forlorn condition, and endeavoured to think of him in a more favourable light.

Branda, niece of Willieblud, the flesher of Ashford, had, among other of the town maidens, noticed Hugues with a not unfavouring eye, as she chanced to pass one day on horseback, through a coppice near the outskirts of the town, into which the latter had been led by the eager chase of a wild hog, and which animal, from the nature of the country was, single-handed, exceedingly difficult of capture. The malignant falsehoods of the ancient crones, continually buzzed in her ears, in nowise diminished the advantageous opinion she had conceived of this ill-treated and good-looking wer-wolf. She sometimes, indeed, went so far as to turn considerably out of her way, in order to meet and exchange his cordial greeting: for Hugues, recognizing the attention of which he had now become the object, had, in his turn, at last summoned up courage to survey more leisurely the pretty Branda; and the result was that he found her as buxom and pretty a lass as, in his hitherto restricted rambles out of the forest, his timorous gaze had ever encountered. His gratitude increased proportion-ally; and at the moment when his domestic losses came one after another to overwhelm him, he was actually on the eve of making Branda, on the first opportunity presenting itself, an avowal of the love he bore her.

It was chill winter—Christmas-tide—the distant roll of the curfew had long ceased, and all the inhabitants of Ashford were safe housed in their tenements for the night. Hugues, solitary, motionless, silent, his forehead grasped between his hands, his gaze dully fixed upon the decaying brands that feebly glimmered upon his hearth: he heeded not the cutting north wind, whose sweeping gusts shook the crazy roof, and whistled through the chinks of the door; he started not at the harsh cries of the herons lighting for prey in the marsh, nor at the dismal croaking of the ravens perched over his smoke-vent. He thought of his departed kindred, and imagined that his hour to join them would soon be at hand; for the intense cold congealed the marrow of his bones, and fell hunger gnawed and twisted his entrails. Yet, at intervals, would a recollection of nascent love, of Branda, suddenly appease his else intolerable anguish, and cause a faint smile to gleam across his wan features.

"Oh, blessed Virgin! grant that my sufferings may speedily cease!" murmured he, despairingly. "Oh, would I might be a wer-wolf, as they call me! I could requite them for all the foul wrong done me. True, I could not nourish myself with their flesh; I would not shed their blood; but I would be able to terrify and torment those who have wrought my parents' and sisters' death—who have persecuted our family even to extermination! Why have I not the power to change my nature into that of a wolf, if, of a verity, my ancestors possessed it, as they avouch? I should at least find carrion to devour,[4] and not die thus horribly. Branda is the sole being in this world who cares for me; and that conviction alone reconciles me to life!"

Hugues gave free current to these gloomy reflections. The smouldering embers now emitted but a feeble and vacillating light, faintly struggling with the surrounding gloom, and Hugues felt the horror of darkness coming strong upon him; frozen with the ague-fit one instant, and troubled the next by the hurried pulsation of his veins, he arose, at last, to seek some fuel, and threw upon the fire a heap of faggot-chips, heath and straw, which soon raised a clear and crackling flame. His stock of wood had become exhausted, and, seeking wherewith to replenish his dying hearth-light, whilst foraging under the rude oven amongst a pile of rubbish placed there by his mother wherewith to bake bread—handles of tools, fractured joint-stools, and cracked platters, he discovered a chest rudely covered with a dressed hide, and which he had never seen before; and seizing upon it as though he had discovered a treasure, broke open the lid, strongly secured by a string.

This chest, which had evidently remained long unopened, contained the complete disguise of a werwolf:—a dyed sheepskin, with gloves in the form of paws, a tail, a mask with an elongated muzzle, and furnished with formidable rows of yellow horse-teeth.

Hugues started backwards, terrified at his discovery—so opportune, that it seemed to him the work of sorcery; then, on recovering from his surprise, he drew forth one by one the several pieces of this strange envelope, which had evidently seen some service, and from long neglect had become somewhat damaged. Then rushed confusedly upon his mind the marvellous recitals made him by his grandfather, as he nursed him upon his knees during earliest childhood; tales, during the narration of which his mother wept silently, as he laughed heartily. In his mind there was a mingled strife of feelings and purposes alike undefinable. He continued his silent examination of this criminal heritage, and by degrees his imagination grew bewildered with vague and extravagant projects.

Hunger and despair conjointly hurried him away: he saw objects no longer save through a bloody prism: he felt his very teeth on edge with an avidity for biting; he experienced an inconceivable desire to run: he set himself to howl as though he had practised werwolfery all his life, and began thoroughly to invest himself with the guise and attributes of his novel vocation. A more startling change could scarcely have been wrought in him, had that so horribly grotesque metamorphosis really been the effect of enchantment; aided, too, as it was, by the fever which generated a temporary insanity in his frenzied brain.

Scarcely did he thus find himself travestied into a werwolf though the influence of his vestment, ere he darted forth from the hut, through the forest and into the open country, white with hoar frost, and across which the bitter north wind swept, howling in a frightful manner and traversing the meadows, fallows, plains, and marshes, like a shadow. But, at that hour, and during such a season, not a single belated wayfarer was there to encounter Hugues, whom the sharpness of the air, and the excitation of his course, had worked up to the highest pitch of extravagance and audacity: he howled the louder proportionally as his hunger increased.

Suddenly the heavy rumbling of an approaching vehicle arrested his attention; at first with indecision, then with a stupid fixity, he struggled with two suggestions, counselling him at one and the same time to fly and to advance. The carriage, or whatever it might be, continued, rolling towards him; the night was not so obscure but that he was enabled to distinguish the tower of Ashford church at a short distance off, and bard by which stood a pile of unhewn stone, destined either for the execution of some repair, or addition to the saintly edifice, in the shade of which he ran to crouch himself down, and so await the arrival of his prey.

It proved to be the covered cart of Willieblud, the Ashford flesher, who was wont twice a week to carry meat to Canterbury, and travelled by night in order that he might be among the first at market-opening. Of this Hugues was fully aware, and the departure of the flesher naturally suggested to him the inference that his niece must be keeping house by herself, for our lusty flesher had been long a widower. For an instant he hesitated whether he should introduce himself there, so favourable an opportunity thus presenting itself, or whether he should attack the uncle and seize upon his viands. Hunger got the better of love this once, and the monotonous whistle with which the driver was accustomed to urge forward his sorry jade warning him to be in readiness, he howled in a plaintive tone, and, rushing forward, seized the horse by the bit.

"Willieblud, flesher," said he, disguising his voice, and speaking to him in the *lingua Franca* of that period, "I hunger; throw me two pounds of meat if thou would'st have me live."

"St. Willifred have mercy on me!" cried the terrified flesher, "is it thou, Hugues Wulfric, of Wealdmarsh, the born wer-wolf?"

"Thou say'st sooth—it is I," replied Hugues, who had sufficient address to avail himself of the credulous superstition of Willieblud; "I would rather have raw meat than eat of thy flesh, plump as thou art. Throw me, therefore, what I crave, and forget not to be ready with the like portion each time thou settest out for Canterbury market; or, failing thereof, I tear thee limb from limb."

Hugues, to display his attributes of a wer-wolf before the gaze of the confounded flesher, had mounted himself upon the spokes of the wheel, and placed his forepaw upon the edge of the cart, which he made semblance of snuffing at with his snout. Willieblud, who believed in wer-wolves as devoutly as he did in his patron saint, had no sooner perceived this monstrous paw, than, uttering a fervent invocation to the latter, he seized upon his daintiest joint of meat, let it fall to the ground, and whilst Hugues sprung eagerly down to pick it up, the butcher at the same instant having bestowed a sudden and violent blow upon the flank of his beast, the latter set off at a round gallop without waiting for any reiterated invitation from the lash.

Hugues was so satisfied with a repast which had cost him far less trouble to procure than any he had long remembered, readily promised himself the renewal of an expedient, the execution of which was at once easy and diverting; for though smitten with the charms of the fair-haired Branda, he not the less found a malicious pleasure in augmenting the terror of her uncle Willieblud. The latter, for a long while, revealed not to the tale of his terrible encounter living being and strange compact, which had varied according to circumstances, and he submitted unmurmuringly to the imposts levied each time the wer-wolf presented himself before him, without being very nice about either the weight or quality of the meat; he no longer even waited to be asked for it, anything to avoid the sight of that fiend-like form clinging to the side of his cart, or being brought into such immediate contact with that hideous mis-shapen paw stretched forth, as it were to strangle him, that paw too, which had once been a human hand. He had become dull and thoughtful of late; he set out to market unwillingly, and seemed to dread the hour of departure as it approached, and no longer beguiled the tedium of his nocturnal journey by whistling to his horse, or trolling snatches of ballads, as was his wont formerly;

he now invariably returned in a melancholy and restless mood.

Branda, at loss to conceive what had given birth to this new and permanent depression which had taken possession of her uncle's mind, after in vain exhausting conjecture, proceeded to interrogate, importune, and supplicate him by turns, until the unhappy flesher, no longer proof against such continued appeals, at last disburthened himself of the load which he had at heart, by recounting the history of his adventure with the wer-wolf.

Branda listened to the whole of the recital without offering interruption or comment; but, at its close—"Hughes is no more a wer-wolf than thou or I," exclaimed she, offended that such unjust suspicion should be cherished against one for whom she had long felt more than an interest; "'tis an idle tale, or some juggling device; I fear me thou must needs dream these sorceries, uncle Willieblud, for Hugues of the Wealdmarsh, or Wulfric, as the silly fools call him, is worth far more, I trow, than his reputation."

"Girl, it boots not saying me nay, in this matter," replied Willieblud, pertinaciously urging the truth of his story; "the family of Hughes, as everybody knows, were wer-wolves born, and, since they are all of late, by the blessing of heaven, defunct, save one, Hughes now inherits the wolf's paw."

"I tell thee, and will avouch it openly, uncle, that Hugues is of too gentle and seemly a nature to serve Satan, and turn himself into a wild beast, and that will I never believe until I have seen the like."

"Mass, and that thou shalt right speedily, if thou wilt but along with me. In very troth 'tis he, besides, he made confession of his name, and did I not recognize his voice, and am I not ever bethinking me of his knavish paw, which he places me on the shaft while he stays the horse. Girl, he is in league with the foul fiend."

Branda had, to a certain degree, imbibed the superstition in the abstract, equally with her uncle, and, excepting so far as it touched the hitherto, as she believed, traduced being on whom her affections, as if in feminine perversity, had so strangely lighted. Her woman's curiosity, in this instance, less determined her resolution to accompany the flesher on his next journey, than the desire to exculpate her lover, fully believing the strange tale of her kinsman's encounter with, and spoliation by the latter, to be the effect of some illusion, and of which to find him guilty, was the sole fear she experienced on mounting the rude vehicle laden with its ensanguined viands.

It was just midnight when they started from Ashford, the hour alike dear to wer-wolves as to spectres of every denomination. Hugues was punctual at the appointed spot; his howlings, as they drew nigh, though horrible enough, had still something human in them, and disconcerted not a little the doubts of Branda. Willieblud, however, trembled even more than she did, and sought for the wolf's portion; the latter raised himself upon his hind legs, and extended one of his forepaws to receive his pittance as soon as the cart stopped at the heap of stones.

"Uncle, I shall swoon with affright," exclaimed Branda, clinging closely to the flesher, and tremblingly pulling the coverchief over her eyes; "loose rein and smite thy beast, or evil will surely betide us."

"Thou are not alone, gossip," cried Hugues, fearful of a snare; "if thou essay'st to play me false, thou art at once undone."

"Harm us not friend Hugues, thou know'st I weigh not my pounds of meat with thee; I shall take care to keep my troth. It is Branda, my niece, who goes with me to-night to buy wares at Canterbury."

"Branda with thee? By the mass 'tis she indeed, more buxom and rosy too, than ever; come pretty one, descend and tarry awhile, that I may have speech with thee."

"I conjure thee, good Hugues, terrify not so cruelly my poor wench, who is wellnigh dead already with fear; suffer us to hold our way, for we have far to go, and the morrow is early market-day."

"Go thy ways then alone, uncle Willieblud, 'tis thy niece I would have speech with, in all courtesy and honour; the which, if thou permittest not readily, and of a good grace, I will rend thee both to death."

All in vain was it that Willieblud exhausted himself in prayers and lamentations in hopes of softening the blood-thirsty wer-wolf, as he believed him to be, refusing as the latter did, every sort of compromise in avoidance of his demand, and at last replying only by horrible threats, which froze the hearts of both. Branda, although especially interested in the debate, neither stirred foot, or opened her mouth, so greatly had terror and surprise overwhelmed her; she kept her eyes fixed upon the wolf, who peered at her likewise through his mask, and felt incapable of offering resistance when she found herself forcibly dragged out of the vehicle, and deposited by an invisible power, as it seemed to her, beside the piles of stones: she swooned without uttering a single scream.

The flesher was no less dumbfounded at the turn which the adventure had taken, and he, too, fell back among his meat as though stricken by a blinding blow; he fancied that the wolf had swept his bushy tail violently across his eyes, and on recovering the use of his senses found himself alone in the cart, which rolled joltingly at a swift pace towards Canterbury. At first he listened, but in vain, for the wind bringing him either the shrieks of his niece, or the howlings of the wolf; but stop his beast he could not, which, panic-stricken, kept trotting as though bewitched, or felt the spur of some fiend pricking her flanks.

Willieblud, however, reached his journey's end in safety, sold his meat, and returned to Ashford, reckoning full sure upon having to say a *De Profundis* for his niece, whose fate he had not ceased to bemoan during the whole night. But how great was his astonishment to find her safe at home, a little pale, from recent fright and want of sleep, but without a scratch; still more was he astonished to hear that the wolf had done her no injury whatsoever, contenting himself, after she had recovered from her swoon, with conducting her back to their dwelling, and acting in every respect like a loyal suitor, rather than a sanguinary wer-wolf Willieblud knew not what to think of it.

This nocturnal gallantry towards his niece had additionally irritated the burly Saxon against the wer-wolf, and although the fear of reprisals kept him from making a direct and public attack upon Hugues, he ruminated not the less upon taking some sure and secret revenge; but previous to putting his design into execution, it struck him that he could not do better than relate his misadventures to the ancient sacristan and parish grave-digger of St. Michael's, a worthy of profound sagacity in those sort of matters, endowed with a clerk-like erudition, and consulted as an oracle by all the old crones and love-loin maidens throughout the township of Ashford and its vicinity.

"Slay a wer-wolf thou canst not," was the repeated rejoinder of the wiseacre to the earnest queries of the tormented flesher; "for his hide is proof against spear or arrow, though vulnerable to the edge of a cutting weapon of steel. I counsel thee to deal him a slight flesh wound, or cut him over the paw, in order to know of a surety whether it really be Hugues or no; thou'lt run no danger, save thou strikest him a blow from which blood flows not therefrom, for, so soon as his skin is severed he taketh flight."

Resolving implicitly to follow the advice of the sacristan, Willieblud that same evening determined to know with what wer-wolf it was with whom he had to do, and with that view hid his cleaver, newly sharpened for the occasion, under the load in his cart, and resolutely prepared to make use of it as a preparatory step towards proving the identity of Hugues with the audacious spoiler of his meat, and eke his peace. The wolf presented himself as usual, and anxiously enquired after Branda, which stimulated the flesher the more firmly to follow out his design.

"Here, Wolf," said Willieblud, stooping down as if to choose a piece of meat; "I give thee double portion tonight; up with thy paw, take toll, and be mindful of my frank alms."

"Sooth, I will remember me, gossip," rejoined our wer-wolf; "but when shall the marriage be solemnized for certain, betwixt the fair Branda and myself?"

Hugues believing he had nothing to fear from the flesher, whose meats he so readily appropriated to himself and of whose fair niece he hoped shortly no less to make lawful possession; both that he really loved, and viewed his union with her as the surest means of placing him within the pale of that sociality from which he had been so unjustly exiled, could he but succeed in making intercession with the holy fathers of the church to remove their interdict. Hugues placed his extended paw upon the edge of the cart; but instead of handing him his joint of beef, or mutton, Willieblud raised his cleaver, and at a single blow lopped off the paw laid there as fittingly for the purpose as though upon a block. The flesher flung down his weapon, and belaboured his beast, the wer-wolf roared aloud with agony, and disappeared amid the dark shades of the forest, in which, aided by the wind, his howling was soon lost.

The next day, on his return, the flesher, chuckling and laughing, deposited a gory cloth upon the table, among the trenchers with which his niece was busied in preparing his noonday meal, and which, on being opened, displayed to her horrified gaze a freshly severed human hand enveloped in wolf-skin. Branda, comprehending what had occurred, shrieked aloud, shed a flood of tears, and then hurriedly throwing her mantle round her, whilst her uncle amused himself by turning and twitching the hand about with a ferocious delight, exclaiming, whilst he staunched the blood which still flowed:

"The sacristan said sooth; the wer-wolf has his need I trow, at last, and now I wot of his nature, I fear no more his witchcraft."

Although the day was fain advanced, Hugues lay writhing in torture upon his couch, his coverings drenched with blood, as well also the floor of his habitation; his countenance of a ghastly pallor, expressed as much moral, as physical pain; tears gushed from beneath his reddened eyelids, and he listened to every noise without, with an increased inquietude, painfully visible upon his distorted features. Footsteps were heard rapidly approaching, the door was hurriedly flung open, and a female threw herself beside his couch, and with mingled sobs and imprecations sought tenderly for his mutilated arm, which, rudely bound round with hempen wrappings, no longer dissembled the absence of its wrist, and from which a crimson stream still trickled. At this piteous spectacle she grew loud in her denunciations against the sanguinary flesher, and sympathetically mingled her lamentations with those of his victim.

These effusions of love and dolour, however, were doomed to sudden interruption; some one knocked at the door. Branda ran to the window that she might recognize who the visitor was that had dared to penetrate the lair of a wer-wolf and on perceiving who it was, she raised her eyes and hands on high, in token of her extremity of despair, whilst the knocking momentarily grew louder.

"'Tis my uncle," faltered she. "Ah! woes me, how shall I escape hence without his seeing me? Whither hide? Oh, here, here, nigh to thee, Hugues, and we will die together," and she crouched herself into an obscure recess behind his couch. "If Willieblud should raise his cleaver to slay thee, he shall first strike through his kinswoman's body."

Branda hastily concealed herself amidst a pile of hemp, whispering Hugues to summon all his courage, who, however, scarce found strength sufficient to raise himself to a sitting posture, whilst his eyes vainly sought around for some weapon of defence.

"A good morrow to thee, Wulfric!" exclaimed Willieblud, as he entered, holding in his hand a napkin tied in a knot, which he proceeded to place upon the coffer beside the sufferer. "I come to offer thee some work, to bind and stack me a faggot-pile, knowing that thou art no laggard at bill-hook and wattle. Wilt do it?"

"I am sick," replied Hugues, repressing the wrath which, despite of pain, sparkled in his wild glance; "I am not in fitting state to work."

"Sick, gossip, sick, art thou indeed? Or is it but a sloth

fit? Come, what ails thee? Where lieth the evil? Your hand, that I may feel thy pulse."

Hugues reddened, and for an instant hesitated whether he should resist a solicitation, the bent of which he too readily comprehended; but in order to avoid exposing Branda to discovery, he thrust forth his left hand from beneath the coverlid, all imbrued in dried gore.

"Not that hand, Hugues, but the other, the right one. Alack, and well-a-day, hast thou lost thy hand, and must I find it for thee?"

Hugues, whose purpling flush of rage changed quickly to a death-like hue, replied not to this taunt, nor testified by the slightest gesture or movement that he was preparing to satisfy a request as cruel in its preconception as the object of it was slenderly cloaked. Willieblud laughed, and ground his teeth in savage glee, maliciously revelling in the tortures he had inflicted upon the sufferer. He seemed already disposed to use violence, rather than allow himself to be baffled in the attainment of the decisive proof he aimed at. Already had he commenced untying the napkin, giving vent all the while to his implacable taunts; one hand alone displaying itself upon the coverlid, and which Hugues, wellnigh senseless with anguish, thought not of withdrawing.

"Why tender me that hand?" continued his unrelenting persecutor, as he imagined himself on the eve of arriving at the conviction he so ardently desired—"That I should lop it off? quick, quick, Master Wulfric, and do my bidding; I demanded to see your right hand."

"Behold it then!" ejaculated a suppressed voice, which belonged to no supernatural being, however it might seem appertaining to such; and Willieblud to his utter confusion and dismay saw a second hand, sound and unmutilated, extend itself towards him as though in silent accusation. He started back; he stammered out a cry for mercy, bent his knees for an instant, and raising himself, palsied with terror, fled from the hut, which he firmly believed under the possession of the foul fiend. He carried not with him the severed hand, which henceforward became a perpetual vision ever present before his eyes, and which all the potent exorcisms of the sacristan, at whose hands be continually sought council and consolation, signally failed to dispel.

"Oh, that hand! To whom then, belongs that accursed hand?" groaned he, continually. "Is it really the fiend's, or that of some wer-wolf? Certain 'tis, that Hugues is innocent, for have I not seen both his hands? But wherefore was one bloody? There's sorcery at bottom of it."

The next morning, early, the first object that struck his sight on entering his stall, was the severed hand that he had left the preceding night upon the coffer in the forest hut; it was stripped of its wolf's-skin covering, and lay among the viands. He dared no longer touch that hand, which now, he verily believed to be enchanted; but in hopes of getting rid of it for ever, he had it flung down a well, and it was with no small increase of despair that he found it shortly afterwards again lying upon his block. He buried it in his garden, but still without being able to rid

himself of it; it returned livid and loathsome to infect his shop, and augment the remorse which was unceasingly revived by the reproaches of his niece.

At last, flattering himself to escape all further persecution from that fatal hand, it struck him that he would have it carried to the cemetery at Canterbury, and try whether exorcism, and sepulture in holy ground would effectually bar its return to the light of day. This was also done; but lo! on the following morning he perceived it nailed to his shutter. Disheartened by these dumb, yet awful reproaches, which wholly robbed him of his peace, and impatient to annihilate all trace of an action with which heaven itself seemed to upbraid him, he quitted Ashford one morning without bidding adieu to his niece, and some days after was found drowned in the river Stour. They drew out his swollen and discoloured body, which was discovered floating on the surface among the sedge, and it was only by piecemeal that they succeeded in tearing away from his death-contracted clutch, the phantom hand, which, in his suicidal convulsions he had retained firmly grasped.

A year after this event, Hugues, although minus a hand, and consequently a confirmed werwolf, married Branda, sole heiress to the stock and chattels of the late unhappy flesher of Ashford.

[1] That woody district, at the period to which our tale belongs, was an immense forest, desolate of inhabitants, and only occupied by wild swine and deer, and though it is now filled with towns and villages and well peopled, the woods that remain sufficiently indicate its former extent. "And being at first," says Hasted, "neither peopled nor cultivated, and only filled with herds of deer and droves of swine, belonged wholly to the king, for there is no mention of it but in royal grants and donations. And it may be presumed that when the weald was first made to belong to certain known owners, as well as the rest of the country, it was not then allotted into tenancies, nor manured like the rest of it; but only as men were contented to inhabit it, and by piecemeal to clear it of the wood, and convert it into tillage."—*Hasted's Kent*, vol. x, p. 134.

[2] King Edgar is said to have been the first who attempted to rid England of these animals; criminals even being pardoned by producing a stated number of these creatures' tongues. Some centuries after they increased to such a degree as to become again the object of royal attention; and Edward I appointed persons to extirpate this obnoxious race. It is one of the principal bearings in armoury. Hugh, surnamed *Lupur*, the first Earl of Kent, bore for his crest a wolf's head.

[3] On this eve formerly the Catholic church performed a most solemn office for the repose of the dead.

[4] Horseflesh was an article of food among our Saxon forefathers in England.

THE WHITE WOLF OF THE HARTZ MOUNTAINS

FREDERICK MARRYAT

I

Before noon Philip and Krantz had embarked, and made sail in the peroqua.

They had no difficulty in steering their course; the islands by day, and the clear stars by night, were their compass. It is true that they did not follow the more direct track, but they followed the more secure, working up the smooth waters, and gaining to the northward more than to the west. Many times they were chased by the Malay proas, which infested the islands, but the swiftness of their little peroqua was their security; indeed, the chase was, generally speaking, abandoned as soon as the smallness of the vessel was made out by the pirates, who expected that little or no booty was to be gained.

One morning, as they were sailing between the isles, with less wind than usual, Philip observed—

"Krantz, you said that there were events in your own life, or connected with it, which would corroborate the mysterious tale I confided to you. Will you now tell me to what you referred?"

"Certainly," replied Krantz; "I have often thought of doing so, but one circumstance or another has hitherto prevented me; this is, however, a fitting opportunity. Prepare therefore to listen to a strange story, quite as strange, perhaps, as your own."

"I take it for granted that you have heard people speak of the Hartz Mountains," observed Krantz.

"I have never heard people speak of them, that I can recollect," replied Philip; "but I have read of them in some book, and of the strange things which have occurred there."

"It is indeed a wild region," rejoined Krantz, "and many strange tales are told of it; but strange as they are. I have good reason for believing them to be true."

"My father was not born, or originally a resident, in the Hartz Mountains; he was a serf of an Hungarian nobleman, of great possessions, in Transylvania; but although a serf, he was not by any means a poor or illiterate man. In fact, he was rich, and his intelligence and respectability were such, that he had been raised by his lord to the stewardship; but whoever may happen to be born a serf, a serf must he remain, even though he become a wealthy man: such was the condition of my father. My father had been married for about five years; and by his marriage had three children—my eldest brother Caesar, myself (Hermann), and a sister named Marcella. You know, Philip, that Latin is still the language spoken in that country; and that will account for our high-sounding names. My mother was a very beautiful woman, unfortunately more beautiful than virtuous; she was seen and admired by the lord of the soil; my father was sent away upon some mission; and during his absence, my mother, flattered by the attentions, and won by the assiduities, of this nobleman, yielded to his wishes. It so happened that my father returned very unexpectedly, and discovered the intrigue. The evidence of my mother's shame was positive: he surprised her in the company of her seducer! Carried away by the impetuosity of his feelings, he watched the opportunity of a meeting taking place between them, and murdered both his wife and her seducer. Conscious that, as a serf, not even the provocation which he had received would be allowed as a justification of his conduct, he hastily collected together what money he could lay his hands upon, and, as we were then in the depth of winter, he put his horses to the sleigh, and taking his children with him, he set off in the middle of the night, and was far away before the tragical circumstance had transpired. Aware that he would be pursued, and that he had no chance of escape if he remained in any portion of his native country (in which the authorities could lay hold of him), he continued his flight without intermission until he had buried himself in the intricacies and seclusions of the Hartz Mountains. Of course, all that I have now told you I learned afterwards. My oldest recollections are knit to a rude, yet comfortable cottage, in which I lived with my father, brother, and sister. It was on the confines of one of those vast forests which cover the northern part of Germany; around it were a few acres of ground, which, during the summer months, my father cultivated, and which, though they yielded a doubtful harvest, were sufficient for our support. In the winter we remained much indoors, for, as my father followed the chase, we were left alone, and the wolves during that season incessantly prowled about. My father had purchased the cottage, and land about it, of one of the rude foresters, who gain their livelihood partly by hunting, and partly by burning charcoal, for the purpose of smelting the ore from the neighbouring mines; it was distant about two miles from any other habitation. I can call to mind the whole landscape now; the tall pines which rose up on the mountain above us, and the wide expanse of the forest beneath, on the topmost boughs and heads of whose trees we looked down from our cottage, as the

mountain below us rapidly descended into the distant valley. In summer time the prospect was beautiful: but during the severe winter a more desolate scene could not well be imagined.

"I said that, in the winter, my father occupied himself with the chase; every day he left us, and often would he lock the door, that we might not leave the cottage. He had no one to assist him, or to take care of us—indeed, it was not easy to find a female servant who would live in such a solitude; but, could he have found one, my father would not have received her, for he had imbibed a horror of the sex, as the difference of his conduct towards us, his two boys, and my poor little sister Marcella evidently proved. You may suppose we were sadly neglected; indeed, we suffered much, for my father, fearful that we might come to some harm, would not allow us fuel when he left the cottage; and we were obliged, therefore, to creep under the heaps of bears' skins, and there to keep ourselves as warm as we could until he returned in the evening, when a blazing fire was our delight. That my father chose this restless sort of life may appear strange, but the fact was, that he could not remain quiet; whether from the remorse for having committed murder, or from the misery consequent on his change of situation, or from both combined, he was never happy unless he was in a state of activity. Children, however, when left so much to themselves, acquire a thoughtfulness not common to their age. So it was with us; and during the short cold days of winter, we would sit silent, longing for the happy hours when the snow would melt and the leaves burst out, and the birds begin their songs, and when we should again be set at liberty.

"Such was our peculiar and savage sort of life until my brother Caesar was nine, myself seven, and my sister five years old, when the circumstances occurred on which is based the extraordinary narrative which I am about to relate.

"One evening my father returned home rather later than usual; he had been unsuccessful, and as the weather was very severe, and many feet of snow were upon the ground, he was not only very cold, but in a very bad humour. He had brought in wood, and we were all three gladly assisting each other in blowing on the embers to create a blaze, when he caught poor little Marcella by the arm and threw her aside; the child fell, struck her mouth, and bled very much. My brother ran to raise her up. Accustomed to ill-usage, and afraid of my father, she did not dare to cry, but looked up in his face very piteously. My father drew his stool nearer to the hearth, muttered something in abuse of women, and busied himself with the fire, which both my brother and I had deserted when our sister was so unkindly treated. A cheerful blaze was soon the result of his exertions; but we did not, as usual, crowd round it. Marcella, still bleeding, retired to a corner, and my brother and I took our seats beside her, while my father hung over the fire gloomily and alone. Such had been our position for about half an hour, when the howl of a wolf, close under the window of the cottage fell on our ears. My father started up, and seized his gun; the howl was repeated; he examined the priming, and then hastily left the cottage, shutting the door after him. We all waited (anxiously listening), for we thought that if he succeeded in shooting the wolf, he would return in a better humour; and, although he was harsh to all of us, and particularly so to our little sister, still we loved our father, and loved to see him cheerful and happy, for what else had we to look up to? And I may here observe, that perhaps there never were three children who were fonder of each other; we did not, like other children, fight and dispute together; and if, by chance. any disagreement did arise, between my elder brother and me, little Marcella would run to us, and kissing us both, seal, through her entreaties, the peace between us. Marcella was a lovely, amiable child; I can recall her beautiful features even now. Alas! poor little Marcella."

"She is dead, then?" observed Philip.

"Dead! yes, dead! but how did she die?—But I must not anticipate. Philip; let me tell my story.

"We waited for some time, but the report of the gun did not reach us, and my elder brother then said, 'Our father has followed the wolf, and will not be back for some time. Marcella, let us wash the blood from your mouth, and then we will leave this corner and go to the fire to warm ourselves.'

"We did so, and remained there until near midnight, every minute wondering, as it grew later, why our father did not return. We had no idea that he was in any danger, but we thought that he must have chased the wolf for a very long time. I will look out and see if father is coming,' said my brother Caesar, going to the door. 'Take care.' said Marcella, 'the wolves must be about now, and we cannot kill them, brother.' My brother opened the door very cautiously, and but a few inches; he peeped out. 'I see nothing.' said he, after a time, and once more he joined us at the fire. 'We have had no supper,' said I, for my father usually cooked the meat as soon as he came home; and during his absence we had nothing but the fragments of the preceding day.

"'And if our father comes home, after his hunt, Caesar,' said Marcella, 'he will be pleased to have some supper; let us cook it for him and for ourselves.' Caesar climbed upon the stool, and reached down some meat—I forget now whether it was venison or bear's meat, but we cut off the usual quantity, and proceeded to dress it, as we used to do under our father's superintendence. We were all busy putting it into the platters before the fire, to await his coming, when we heard the sound of a horn. We listened—there was a noise outside, and a minute afterwards my father entered, ushered in a young female and a large dark man in a hunter's dress.

"Perhaps I had better now relate what was only known to me many years afterwards. When my father had left the cottage, he perceived a large white wolf about thirty yards from him; as soon as the animal saw my father, it retreated slowly, growling and snarling. My father followed; the animal did not run, but always kept at some distance; and my father did not like to fire until he was pretty certain that his ball would take effect; thus they went on for some time, the wolf now leaving my father far behind, and then stopping and snarling defiance at him, and then, again, on his approach, setting off at speed.

"Anxious to shoot the animal (for the white wolf is very rare), my father continued the pursuit for several hours, during which he continually ascended the mountain.

"You must know, Philip, that there are peculiar spots on those mountains which are supposed, and, as my story will prove, truly supposed, to be inhabited by the evil influences: they are well known to the huntsmen, who invariably avoid them. Now, one of these spots, an open space in the pine forest above us, had been pointed out to my father as dangerous on that account. But whether he disbelieved these wild stories, or whether, in his eager pursuit of the case, he disregarded them, I know not; certain, however, it is, that he was decoyed by the white wolf to this open space, when the animal appeared to slacken her speed. My father approached, came close up to her, raised his gun to his shoulder and was about to fire, when the wolf suddenly disappeared. He thought that the snow on the ground must have dazzled his sight, and he let down his gun to look for the beast—but she was gone; how she could have escaped over the clearance, without his seeing her, was beyond his comprehension. Mortified at the ill-success of his chase, he was about to retrace his steps, when he heard the distant sound of a horn. Astonishment at such a sound—at such an hour—in such a wilderness, made him forget for the moment his disappointment, and he remained riveted to the spot. In a minute the horn was blown a second time, and at no great distance; my father stood still, and listened; a third time it was blown. I forget the term used to express it, but it was the signal which, my father well knew, implied that the party was lost in the woods. In a few minutes more my father beheld a man on horseback, with a female seated on the crupper, enter the cleared space, and ride up to him. At first, my father called to mind the strange stories which he had heard of the supernatural beings who were said to frequent these mountains; but the nearer approach of the parties satisfied him that they were mortals like himself. As soon as they came up to him, the man who guided the horse accosted him. 'Friend hunter, you are out late, the better fortune for us; we have ridden far, and are in fear of our lives, which are eagerly sought after. These mountains have enabled us to elude our pursuers; but if we find not shelter and refreshment, that will avail us little, as we must perish from hunger and the inclemency of the night. My daughter, who rides behind me, is now more dead than alive—say, can you assist us in our difficulty?'

"'My cottage is some few miles distant,' replied my father, but I have little to offer you besides a shelter from the weather; to the little I have you are welcome. May I ask whence you come?'

"'Yes, friend, it is no secret now; we have escaped from Transylvania, where my daughter's honour and my life were equally in jeopardy!'

"This information was quite enough to raise an interest in my father's heart. He remembered his own escape: he remembered the loss of his wife's honour, and the tragedy by which it was wound up. He immediately, and warmly, offered all the assistance which he could afford them.

"'There is no time to be lost, then, good sir.' observed the horseman; 'my daughter is chilled with the frost, and cannot hold out much longer against the severity of the weather.'

"'Follow me,' replied my father, leading the way towards his home.

"'I was lured away in pursuit of a large white wolf,' observed my father; 'it came to the very window of my hut, or I should not have been out at this time of night.'

"'The creature passed by us just as we came out of the wood,' said the female, in a silvery tone.

"'I was nearly discharging my piece at it,' observed the hunter; 'but since it did us such good service. I am glad that I allowed it to escape.'

"In about an hour and a half, during which my father walked at a rapid pace, the party arrived at the cottage, and, as I said before, came in.

"'We are in good time, apparently,' observed the dark hunter, catching the smell of the roasted meat, as he walked to the fire and surveyed my brother and sister and myself. 'You have young cooks here, Meinheer.' 'I am glad that we shall not have to wait,' replied my father. 'Come, mistress, seat yourself by the fire; you require warmth after your cold ride.' 'And where can I put up my horse, Meinheer?' observed the huntsman. 'I will take care of him,' replied my father, going out of the cottage door.

"The female must, however, be particularly described. She was young, and apparently twenty years of age. She was dressed in a travelling dress, deeply bordered with white fur, and wore a cap of white ermine on her head. Her features were very beautiful, at least I thought so, and so my father has since declared. Her hair was flaxen, glossy, and shining, and bright as a mirror; and her mouth, although somewhat large when it was open, showed the most brilliant teeth I have ever beheld. But there was something about her eyes, bright as they were, which made us children afraid; they were so restless, so furtive; I could not at that time tell why, but I felt as if there was cruelty in her eye; and when she beckoned us to come to her, we approached her with fear and trembling. Still she was beautiful, very beautiful. She spoke kindly to my brother and myself, patted our heads and caressed us; but Marcella would not come near her; on the contrary, she slunk away, and hid herself in the bed, and would not wait for the supper, which half an hour before she had been so anxious for.

"My father, having put the horse into a close shed, soon returned, and supper was placed on the table. When it was over, my father requested the young lady would take possession of the bed, and he would remain at the fire, and sit up with her father. After some hesitation on her part, this arrangement was agreed to, and I and my brother crept into the other bed with Marcella, for we had as yet always slept together.

"But we could not sleep; there was something so unusual, not only in seeing strange people, but in having those people sleep at the cottage, that we were bewildered. As for poor little Marcella, she was quiet, but I perceived that she trembled during the whole night, and sometimes I thought that she was checking a sob. My father had brought out some spirits, which he rarely used, and he and the strange hunter remained drinking and talking before the fire. Our ears were ready to catch the slightest whisper—so much was our curiosity excited.

"'You said you came from Transylvania?' observed my father. 'Even so, Meinheer,' replied the hunter. 'I was a serf to the noble house of—; my master would insist upon my surrendering up my fair girl to his wishes; it ended in my giving him a few inches of my hunting-knife.'

"'We are countrymen and brothers in misfortune.' replied my father, taking the huntsman's hand and pressing it warmly. "'Indeed! Are you then from that country?' "'Yes; and I too have fled for my life. But mine is a melancholy tale.' "'Your name?' inquired the hunter. "'Krantz.'

"'What! Krantz of—? I have heard your tale; you need not renew your grief by repeating it now. Welcome, most welcome, Meinheer, and, I may say, my worthy kinsman. I am your second cousin, Wilfred of Barnsdorf,' cried the hunter, rising up and embracing my father.

"They filled their horn-mugs to the brim, and drank to one another after the German fashion. The conversation was then carried on in a low tone; all that we could collect from it was that our new relative and his daughter were to take up their abode in our cottage, at least for the present. In about an hour they both fell back in their chairs and appeared to sleep.

"'Marcella, dear, did you hear?' said my brother, in a low tone.

"'Yes,' replied Marcella, in a whisper, 'I heard all. Oh! brother. I cannot bear to look upon that woman—I feel so frightened.'

"My brother made no reply, and shortly afterwards we were all three fast asleep.

"When we awoke the next morning, we found that the hunter's daughter had risen before us. I thought she looked more beautiful than ever. She came up to little Marcella and caressed her; the child burst into tears, and sobbed as if her heart would break. "But not to detain you with too long a story, the huntsman and his daughter were accommodated in the cottage. My father and he went out hunting daily, leaving Christina with us. She performed all the household duties; was very kind to us children and gradually the dislike even of little Marcella wore away. But a great change took place in my father; he appeared to have conquered his aversion to the sex, and was most attentive to Christina. Often, after her father and we were in bed, would he sit up with her, conversing in a low tone by the fire. I ought to have mentioned that my father and the huntsman Wilfred slept in another portion of the cottage, and that the bed which he formerly occupied, and which was in the same room as ours, had been given up to the use of Christina. These visitors had been about three weeks at the cottage, when, one night, after we children had been sent to bed, a consultation was held. My father had asked Christina in marriage, and had obtained both her own consent and that of Wilfred; after this, a conversation took place, which was, as nearly as I can recollect, as follows:—'You may take my child, Meinheer Krantz, and my blessing with her, and I shall then leave you and seek some other habitation—it matters little where.' "'Why not remain here, Wilfred?' "'No, no, I am called elsewhere; let that suffice, and ask no more questions. You have my child.'

"'I thank you for her, and will duly value her; but there is one difficulty.'

"'I know what you would say; there is no priest here in this wild country; true; neither is there any law' to bind. Still must some ceremony pass between you, to satisfy a father. Will you consent to marry her after my fashion? If so. I will marry you directly.'

"'I will,' replied my father.

"'Then take her by the hand. Now, Meinheer, swear.'

"'I swear,' repeated my father.

"'By all the spirits of the Hartz Mountains—'

"'Nay, why not by Heaven?' interrupted my father.

"'Because it is not my humour,' rejoined Wilfred. 'If I prefer that oath, less binding, perhaps, than another, surely you will not thwart me. "'Well, be it so, then; have your humour. Will you make me swear by that in which I do not believe?' "'Yet many do so, who in outward appearance are Christians,' rejoined Wilfred; 'say, will you be married, or shall I take my daughter away with me?' 'Proceed,' replied my father impatiently. "'I swear by all the spirits of the Hartz Mountains, by all their power for good or for evil, that I take Christina for my wedded wife; that I will ever protect her, cherish her, and love her; that my hand shall never be raised against her to harm her.' "My father repeated the words after Wilfred. "'And if I fail in this my vow, may all the vengeance of the spirits fall upon me and upon my children; may they perish by the vulture, by the wolf, or other beasts of the forest; may their flesh be torn from their limbs, and their bones blanch in the wilderness: all this I swear.'

"My father hesitated, as he repeated the last words; little Marcella could not restrain herself, and as my father repeated the last sentence, she burst into tears. This sudden interruption appeared to discompose the party, particularly my father; he spoke harshly to the child, who controlled her sobs, burying her face under the bedclothes.

"Such was the second marriage of my father. The next morning, the hunter Wilfred mounted his horse and rode away.

"My father resumed his bed, which was in the same room as ours; and things went on much as before the marriage, except that our new stepmother did not show any kindness towards us; indeed, during my father's absence, she would often beat us, particularly little Marcella, and her eyes would flash fire, as she looked eagerly upon the fair and lovely child.

"One night my sister awoke me and my brother.

"'What is the matter?' said Caesar.

"'She has gone out,' whispered Marcella.

"'Gone out!'

"'Yes, gone out at the door, in her night-clothes,' replied the child; 'I saw her get out of bed, look at my father to see if he slept, and then she went out at the door.'

"What could induce her to leave her bed, and all undressed to go out, in such bitter wintry weather, with the snow deep on the ground, was to us incomprehensible; we lay awake, and in about an hour we heard the growl of a wolf close under the window.

"'There is a wolf,' said Caesar. 'She will be torn to pieces.

"'Oh, no!' cried Marcella.

"In a few minutes afterwards our stepmother appeared; she was in her night-dress, as Marcella had stated. She let down the latch of the door, so as to make no noise, went to a pail of water, and washed her face and hands, and then slipped into the bed where my father lay.

"We all three trembled—we hardly knew why; but we resolved to watch the next night. We did so; and not only on the ensuing night, but on many others, and always at about the same hour, would our stepmother rise from her bed and leave the cottage; and after she was gone we invariably heard the growl of a wolf under our window, and always saw her on her return wash herself before she retired to bed. We observed also that she seldom sat down to meals, and that when she did she appeared to eat with dislike; but when the meat was taken down to be prepared for dinner, she would often furtively put a raw piece into her mouth.

"My brother Caesar was a courageous boy; he did not like to speak to my father until he knew more. He resolved that he would follow her out, and ascertain what she did. Marcella and I endeavoured to dissuade him from the project; but he would not be controlled; and the very next night he lay down in his clothes, and as soon as our stepmother had left the cottage he jumped up, took down my father's gun, and followed her.

"You may imagine in what a state of suspense Marcella and I remained during his absence. After a few minutes we heard the report of a gun. It did not awaken my father; and we lay trembling with anxiety. In a minute afterwards we saw our stepmother enter the cottage—her dress was bloody. I put my hand to Marcella's mouth to prevent her crying out, although I was myself in great alarm. Our stepmother approached my father's bed, looked to see if he was asleep, and then went to the chimney and blew up the embers into a blaze.

"'Who is there?' said my father, waking up.

"'Lie still, dearest,' replied my stepmother; "it is only me; I have lighted the fire to warm some water; I am not quite well.

"My father turned round, and was soon asleep; but we watched our stepmother. She changed her linen, and threw the garments she had worn into the fire; and we then perceived that her right leg was bleeding profusely, as if from a gun-shot wound. She bandaged it up, and then dressing herself, remained before the fire until the break of day.

"Poor little Marcella, her heart beat quick as she pressed me to her side—so indeed did mine.

"Where was our brother Caesar? How did my stepmother receive the wound unless from his gun? At last my father rose, and then for the first time I spoke, saying, 'Father, where is my brother Caesar?'

"'Your brother?' exclaimed he; 'why, where can he be?'

"'Merciful Heaven! I thought as I lay very restless last night,' observed our stepmother, 'that I heard somebody open the latch of the door; and, dear me, husband, what has become of your gun?'

"My father cast his eyes above the chimney, and perceived that his gun was missing. For a moment he looked perplexed; then, seizing a broad axe, he went out of the cottage without saying another word.

"He did not remain away from us long; in a few minutes he returned, bearing in his arms the mangled body of my poor brother; he laid it down, and covered up his face.

"My stepmother rose up, and looked at the body, while Marcella and I threw ourselves by its side, wailing and sobbing bitterly.

"'Go to bed again, children." said she sharply. 'Husband,' continued she, 'your boy must have taken the gun down to shoot a wolf and the animal has been too powerful for him. Poor boy! he has paid dearly for his rashness.'

"My father made no reply. I wished to speak—to tell all—but Marcella, who perceived my intention, held me by the arm, and looked at me so imploringly, that I desisted.

"My father, therefore, was left in his error; but Marcella and I, although we could not comprehend it, were conscious that our stepmother was in some way connected with my brother's death.

"That day my father went out and dug a grave; and when he laid the body in the earth he piled up stones over it, so that the wolves should not be able to dig it up. The shock of this catastrophe was to my poor father very severe; for several days he never went to the chase, although at times he would utter bitter anathemas and vengeance against the wolves.

"But during this time of mourning on his part, my stepmother's nocturnal wanderings continued with the same regularity as before.

"At last my father took down his gun to repair to the forest; but he soon returned, and appeared much annoyed.

"'Would you believe it, Christina, that the wolves—perdition to the whole race!—have actually contrived to dig up the body of my poor boy, and now there is nothing left of him but his bones.'

"'Indeed!' replied my stepmother. Marcella looked at me, and I saw in her intelligent eye all she would have uttered.

"'A wolf growls under our window every night, father,' said I.

"'Ax', indeed! Why did you not tell me, boy? Wake me the next time you hear it.'

"I saw my stepmother turn away; her eyes flashed fire, and she gnashed her teeth.

"My father went out again, and covered up with a larger pile of stones the little remains of my poor brother which the wolves had spared. Such was the first act of the tragedy.

"The spring now came on; the snow disappeared, and we were permitted to leave the cottage; but never would I quit for one moment my dear little sister, to whom, since the death of my brother, I was more ardently attached than ever; indeed, I was afraid to leave her alone with my stepmother, who appeared to have a particular pleasure in illtreating the child. My father was now employed upon his little farm, and I was able to render him some assistance.

"Marcella used to sit by us while we were at work, leaving my stepmother alone in the cottage.

"I ought to observe that, as the spring advanced, so did my stepmother decrease her nocturnal rambles, and that we never heard the growl of the wolf under the window after I had spoken of it to my father.

"One day, when my father and I were in the field, Marcella being with us, my stepmother came out, saying that she was going into the forest to collect some herbs my father wanted, and that Marcella must go to the cottage and watch the dinner. Marcella went; and my stepmother disappeared in the forest, taking a direction quite contrary to that in which the cottage stood, and leaving my father and me, as it were, between her and Marcella.

"About an hour afterwards we were startled by shrieks from the cottage—evidently the shrieks of little Marcella. 'Marcella has burnt herself, father,' said I, throwing down my spade. My father threw down his, and we both hastened to the cottage. Before we could gain the door, out darted a large white wolf, which fled with the utmost celerity. My father had no weapon; he rushed into the cottage, and there saw poor little Marcella expiring. Her body was dreadfully mangled and the blood pouring from it had formed a large pool on the cottage floor. My father's first intention had been to seize his gun and pursue; but he was checked by this horrid spectacle; he knelt down by his dying child, and burst into tears. Marcella could just look kindly on us for a few seconds, and then her eyes were closed in death.

"My father and I were still hanging over my poor sister's body when my stepmother came in. At the dreadful sight she expressed much concern; but she did not appear to recoil from the sight of blood, as most women do.

"'Poor child!' said she, 'it must have been that great white wolf which passed me just now, and frightened me so. She's quite dead, Krantz.'

"'I know it!—I know it!' cried my father, in agony.

"I thought my father would never recover from the effects of this second tragedy; he mourned bitterly over the body of his sweet child, and for several days would not consign it to its crave, although frequently requested by my stepmother to do so. At last he yielded, and dug a grave for her close by that of my poor brother, and took every precaution that the wolves should not violate her remains.

"I was now really miserable as I lay alone in the bed which I had formerly shared with my brother and sister. I could not help thinking that my stepmother was implicated in both their deaths, although I could not account for the manner; but I no longer felt afraid of her; my little heart was full of hatred and revenge.

"The night after my sister had been buried, as I lay awake, I perceived my stepmother get up and go out of the cottage. I waited some time, then dressed myself, and looked out through the door, which I half opened. The moon shone bright, and I could see the spot where my brother and sister had been buried; and what was my horror when I perceived my stepmother busily removing the stones from Marcella's grave!

"She was in her white night-dress, and the moon shone full upon her. She was digging with her hands, and throwing away the stones behind her with all the ferocity of a wild beast. It was some time before I could collect my senses and decide what I should do. At last I perceived that she had arrived at the body, and raised it up to the side of the grave. I could bear it no longer: I ran to my father and awoke him.

"'Father, father!' cried I, 'dress yourself, and get your gun.'

"'What!' cried my father, 'the wolves are there, are they?'

"He jumped out of bed, threw on his clothes, and in his anxiety did not appear to perceive the absence of his wife. As soon as he was ready I opened the door, he went out, and I followed him.

"Imagine his horror, when (unprepared as he was for such a sight) he beheld, as he advanced towards the grave, not a wolf but his wife, in her night-dress, on her hands and knees, crouching by the body of my sister, and tearing off large pieces of the flesh, and devouring them with all the avidity of a wolf. She was too busy to be aware of our approach. My father dropped his gun; his hair stood on end, so did mine; he breathed heavily, and then his breath for a time stopped. I picked up the gun and put it into his hand. Suddenly he appeared as if concentrated rage had restored him to double vigour; he levelled his piece, fired, and with a loud shriek down fell the wretch whom he had fostered in his bosom.

"'God of heaven!' cried my father, sinking down upon the earth in a swoon, as soon as he had discharged his gun.

"I remained some time by his side before he recovered. 'Where am I?' said he, 'what has happened? Oh!—yes, yes! I recollect now. Heaven forgive me!'

"He rose and we walked up to the grave; what again was our astonishment and horror to find that, instead of the dead body of my stepmother, as we expected, there was lying over the remains of my poor sister a large white she-wolf.

"'The white wolf,' exclaimed my father, 'the white wolf which decoyed me into the forest—I see it all now—I have dealt with the spirits of the Hartz Mountains.'

"For some time my father remained in silence and deep thought. He then carefully lifted up the body of my sister, replaced it in the grave, and covered it over as before, having struck the head of the dead animal with the heel of his boot, and raving like a madman. He walked back to the cottage, shut the door, and threw himself on the bed; I did the same, for I was in a stupor of amazement.

"Early in the morning we were both roused by a loud knocking at the door, and in rushed the hunter Wilfred.

"'My daughter—man—my daughter!—where is my daughter?' cried he in a rage.

"'Where the wretch, the fiend should be, I trust.' replied my father, starting up, and displaying equal choler: 'where she should be—in hell! Leave this cottage, or you may fare worse.'

"'Ha—ha!' replied the hunter, 'would you harm a potent spirit of the Hartz Mountains? Poor mortal, who must needs wed a werewolf.'

"'Out, demon! I defy thee and thy power.'

"'Yet shall you feel it; remember your oath—your solemn oath—never to raise your hand against her to harm her.'

"'I made no compact with evil spirits.'

"'You did, and if you failed in your vow, you were to meet the vengeance of the spirits. Your children were to perish by the vulture, the wolf—' "'Out, out, demon!' "'And their bones blanch in the wilderness. Ha—ha!'

"My father, frantic with rage, seized his axe and raised it over Wilfred's head to strike. "'All this I swear,' continued the huntsman mockingly. "The axe descended; but it passed through the form of the hunter. and my father lost his balance, and fell heavily on the floor.

"'Mortal!' said the hunter, striding over my father's body, 'we have power over those only who have committed murder. You have been guilty of a double murder: you shall pay the penalty attached to your marriage vow. Two of your children are gone, the third is yet to follow—and follow them he will, for your oath is registered. Go—it were kindness to kill thee—your punishment is, that you live!'

"With these words the spirit disappeared. My father rose from the floor, embraced me tenderly, and knelt down in prayer.

"The next morning he quitted the cottage for ever. He took me with him, and bent his steps to Holland, where we safely arrived. He had some little money with him; but he had not been many days in Amsterdam before he was seized with a brain fever, and died raving mad. I was put into the asylum, and afterwards was sent to sea before the mast. You now know all my history. The question is, whether I am to pay the penalty of my father's oath? I am myself perfectly convinced that, in some way or another. I shall."

II

On the twenty-second day the high land of the south of Sumatra was in view: as there were no vessels in sight, they resolved to keep their course through the Straits, and run for Pulo Penang, which they expected, as their vessel lay so close to the wind, to reach in seven or eight days. By constant exposure Philip and Krantz were now so bronzed, that with their long beards and Mussulman dresses, they might easily have passed off for natives. They had steered during the whole of the days exposed to a burning sun; they had lain down and slept in the dew of the night; but their health had not suffered. But for several days, since he had confided the history of his family to Philip, Krantz had become silent and melancholy; his usual flow of spirits had vanished, and Philip had often questioned him as to the cause. As they entered the Straits, Philip talked of what they should do upon their arrival at Goa; when Krantz gravely replied, "For some days, Philip, I have had a presentiment that I shall never see that city."

"You are out of health, Krantz," replied Philip.

"No, I am in sound health, body and mind. I have endeavoured to shake off the presentiment, but in vain; there is a warning voice that continually tells me that I shall not be long with you. Philip, will you oblige me by making me content on one point? I have gold about my person which may be useful to you; oblige me by taking it, and securing it on your own."

"What nonsense, Krantz."

"It is no nonsense, Philip. Have you not had your warnings? Why should I not have mine? You know that I have little fear in my composition, and that I care not about death; but I feel the presentiment which I speak of more strongly every hour. . ."

"These are the imaginings of a disturbed brain, Krantz; why you, young, in full health and vigour, should not pass your days in peace, and live to a good old age, there is no cause for believing. You will be better to-morrow."

"Perhaps so," replied Krantz; "but you still must yield to my whim, and take the gold. If I am wrong, and we do arrive safe, you know, Philip, you can let me have it back," observed Krantz, with a faint smile—"but you forget, our water is nearly out, and we must look out for a rill on the coast to obtain a fresh supply."

"I was thinking of that when you commenced this unwelcome topic. We had better look out for the water before dark, and as soon as we have replenished our jars, we will make sail again."

At the time that this conversation took place, they were on the eastern side of the Strait, about forty miles to the northward. The interior of the coast was rocky and mountainous, but it slowly descended to low land of alternate forest and jungles, which continued to the beach; the country appeared to be uninhabited. Keeping close in to the shore, they discovered, after two hours' run, a fresh stream which burst in a cascade from the mountains, and swept its devious course through the jungle, until it poured its tribute into the waters of the Strait.

They ran close into the mouth of the stream, lowered the sails, and pulled the peroqua against the current, until they had advanced far enough to assure them that the water was quite fresh. The jars were soon filled, and they were a gain thinking of pushing off, when enticed by the beauty of the spot, the coolness of the fresh water, and wearied with their long confinement on board of the peroqua, they proposed to bathe—a luxury hardly to be appreciated by those who have not been in a similar situation. They threw off their Mussulman dresses, and plunged into the stream, where they remained for some time. Krantz was the first to get out; he complained of feeling chilled, and he walked on to the banks where their clothes had been laid. Philip also approached nearer to the beach, intending to follow him.

"And now, Philip," said Krantz. "this will be a good opportunity for me to give you the money. I will open my sash and pour it out, and you can put it into your own before you put it on."

Philip was standing in the water, which was about level with his waist.

"Well, Krantz," said he, "I suppose if it must be so, it must; but it appears to me an idea so ridiculous—however, you shall have your own way."

Philip quitted the run, and sat down by Krantz, who was already busy in shaking the doubloons out of the folds of his sash; at last he said—

"I believe, Philip, you have got them all, now?—I feel satisfied."

"What danger there can be to you, which I am not equally exposed to, I cannot conceive," replied Philip; "however—"

Hardly had he said these words, when there was a tremendous roar—a rush like a mighty wind through the air—a blow which threw him on his back—a loud cry—and a contention. Philip recovered himself, and perceived the naked form of Krantz carried off with the speed of an arrow by an enormous tiger through the jungle. He watched with distended eyeballs; in a few seconds the animal and Krantz had disappeared.

"God of heaven! would that Thou hadst spared me this," cried Philip, throwing himself down in agony on his face. "O Krantz! my friend—my brother—too sure was your presentiment. Merciful God! have pity—but Thy will be done." And Philip burst into a flood of tears.

For more than an hour did he remain fixed upon the spot, careless and indifferent to the danger by which he was surrounded. At last; Somewhat recovered, he rose, dressed himself, and then again sat down—his eves fixed upon the clothes of Krantz, and the gold which still lay on the sand.

"He would give me that gold. He foretold his doom. Yes! yes! it was his destiny, and it has been fulfilled. *His bones will bleach in the wilderness*, and the spirit-hunter and his wolfish daughter are avenged."

JEAN GRENIER, A FRENCH WERE-WOLF

SABINE BARING-GOULD

One fine afternoon in the spring, some village girls were tending their sheep on the sand-dunes which intervene between the vast forests of pine covering the greater portion of the present department of *Landes* in the south of France, and the sea.

The brightness of the sky, the freshness of the air puffing up off the blue twinkling Bay of Biscay, the hum or song of the wind as it made rich music among the pines which stood like a green uplifted wave on the East, the beauty of the sand-hills speckled with golden cistus, or patched with gentian-blue, the charm of the forest-skirts, tinted variously with the foliage of cork-trees, pines, and acacia—all conspired to fill the peasant maidens with joy, and to make their voices rise in song and laughter, which rung merrily over the hills, and through the dark avenues of evergreen trees.

Now a gorgeous butterfly attracted their attention, then a flight of quails skimming the surface.

"Ah!" exclaimed Jacquiline Auzun, "ah, if I had my stilts and bats, I would strike the little birds down, and we should have a fine supper."

"Now, if they would fly ready cooked into one's mouth, as they do in foreign parts!" said another girl.

"Have you got any new clothes for the S. Jean?" asked a third; "my mother has laid by to purchase me a smart cap with gold lace."

"You will turn the head of Etienne altogether, Annette!" said Jeanne Gaboriant. "But what is the matter with the sheep?"

She asked because the sheep which had been quietly browsing before her, on reaching a small depression in the dune, had started away as though frightened at something. At the same time one of the dogs began to growl and show his fangs.

The girls ran to the spot, and saw a little fall in the ground, in which, seated on a log of fir, was a boy of thir-teen. The appearance of the lad was peculiar. His hair was of a tawny red and thickly matted, falling over his shoulders and completely covering his narrow brow. His small pale-grey eyes twinkled with an expression of horrible ferocity and cunning, from deep sunken hollows. The complexion was of a dark olive colour; the teeth were strong and white, and the canine teeth protruded over the lower lip when the mouth was closed. The boy's hands were large and powerful, the nails black and pointed like bird's talons. He was ill clothed, and seemed to be in the most abject poverty. The few garments that he had on him were in tatters, and through the rents the emaciation of his limbs was plainly visible.

The girls stood round him, half frightened and much surprised, but the boy showed no symptoms of astonishment. His face relaxed into a ghastly leer, which showed the whole range of his glittering white fangs.

"Well, my maidens," said he in a harsh voice, "which of you is the prettiest, I should like to know; can you decide among you?"

"What do you want to know for?" asked Jeanne Gaboriant, the eldest of the girls, aged eighteen, who took upon herself to be spokesman for the rest.

"Because I shall marry the prettiest," was the answer.

"Ah!" said Jeanne jokingly; "that is if she will have you, which is not very likely, as we none of us know you, or anything about you."

"I am the son of a priest," replied the boy curtly.

"Is that why you look so dingy and black?"

"No, I am dark-coloured, because I wear a wolf-skin sometimes."

"A wolf-skin!" echoed the girl; "and pray who gave it to you?"

"One called Pierre Labourant."

"There is no man of that name hereabouts. Where does he live?"

A scream of laughter mingled with howls, and breaking into strange gulping bursts of fiendlike merriment from the strange boy.

The girls recoiled, and the youngest took refuge behind Jeanne.

"Do you want to know Pierre Labourant, lass? Hey, he is a man with an iron chain about his neck, which he is ever engaged in gnawing. Do you want to know where he lives, lass? Ha, in a place of gloom and fire, where there are many companions, some seated on iron chairs, burning, burning; others stretched on glowing beds, burning too. Some cast men upon blazing coals, others roast men before fierce flames, others again plunge them into caldrons of liquid fire."

The girls trembled and looked at each other with scared faces, and then again at the hideous being which crouched before them.

"You want to know about the wolf-skin cape?" continued he. "Pierre Labourant gave me that; he wraps it round me, and every Monday, Friday and Sunday, and for about an hour at dusk every other day I am a wolf, a were-wolf. I have killed dogs and drunk their blood; but little girls taste better, their flesh is tender and sweet, their blood rich and warm. I have eaten many a maiden, as I have been on my raids together with my nine companions. I am a were-wolf! Ah, ha! if the sun were to set I would soon fall on one of you and make a meal of you!" Again he burst into one of his frightful paroxysms of laughter, and the girls unable to endure it any longer, fled with precipitation.

Near the village of S. Antoine de Pizon, a little girl of the name of Marguerite Poirier, thirteen years old, was in the habit of tending her sheep, in company with a lad of the same age, whose name was Jean Grenier. The same lad whom Jeanne Gaboriant had questioned.

The little girl often complained to her parents of the conduct of the boy: she said that he frightened her with his horrible stories; but her father and mother thought little of her complaints, till one day she returned home before her usual time so thoroughly alarmed that she had deserted her flock. Her parents now took the matter up and investigated it. Her story was as follows:—

Jean had often told her that he had sold himself to the devil, and that he had acquired the power of ranging the country after dusk, and sometimes in broad day in the form of a wolf. He had assured her that he had killed and devoured many dogs, but that he found their flesh less palatable than the flesh of little girls, which he regarded as a supreme delicacy. He had told her that this had been tasted by him not unfrequently but he had specified only two instances: in one he had eaten as much as he could, and thrown the rest to a wolf, which had come up during the repast. In the other instance he had bitten to death another little girl, had lapped her blood, and, being in a famished condition at the time, had devoured every portion of her, with the exception of the arms and shoulders.

The child told her parents, on the occasion of her return home in a fit of terror, that she had been guiding her sheep as usual, but Grenier had not been present. Hearing a rustle in the bushes she had looked round, and a wild beast had leaped upon her, and torn her clothes on her left side with its sharp fangs. She added that she had defended herself lustily with her shepherd's staff, and had beaten the creature off. It had then retreated a few paces, had seated itself on its hind legs like a dog when it is begging, and had regarded her with such a look of rage, that she had fled in terror. She described the animal as resembling a wolf, but as being shorter and stouter; its hair was red, its tail stumpy, and the head smaller than that of a genuine wolf.

The statement of the child produced general consternation in the parish. It was well known that several little girls had vanished in a most mysterious way of late, and the parents of these little ones were thrown into an agony of terror lest their children had become the prey of the wretched boy accused by Marguerite Poirier. The case was now taken up by the authorities and brought before the parliament of Bordeaux.

The investigation which followed was as complete as could be desired.

Jean Grenier was the son of a poor labourer in the village of S. Antoine de Pizon, and not the son of a priest, as he had asserted. Three months before his seizure he had left home, and had been with several masters doing odd work, or wandering about the country begging. He had been engaged several times to take charge of the flocks belonging to farmers, and had as often been discharged for neglect of his duties. The lad exhibited no reluctance to communicate all he knew about himself, and his statements were tested one by one, and were often proved to be correct.

The story he related of himself before the court was as follows:—

"When I was ten or eleven years old, my neighbour, Duthillaire, introduced me, in the depths of the forest, to a M. de la Forest, a black man, who signed me with his nail, and then gave to me and Duthillaire a salve and a wolf-skin. From that time have I run about the country as a wolf.

"The charge of Marguerite Poirier is correct. My intention was to have killed and devoured her, but she kept me off with a stick. I have only killed one dog, a white one, and I did not drink its blood."

When questioned touching the children, whom he said he had killed and eaten as a wolf, he allowed that he had once entered an empty house on the way between S. Coutras and S. Anlaye, in a small village, the name of which he did not remember, and had found a child asleep in its cradle; and as no one was within to hinder him, he dragged the baby out of its cradle, carried it into the garden, leaped the hedge, and devoured as much of it as satisfied his hunger. What remained he had given to a wolf. In the parish of S. Antoine de Pizon he had attacked a little girl, as she was keeping sheep. She was dressed in a black frock; he did not know her name. He tore her with his nails and teeth, and ate her. Six weeks before his capture he had fallen upon another child, near the stone-bridge, in the same parish. In

Eparon he had assaulted the hound of a certain M. Millon, and would have killed the beast, had not the owner come out with his rapier in his hand.

Jean said that he had the wolf-skin in his possession, and that he went out hunting for children, at the command of his master, the Lord of the Forest. Before transformation he smeared himself with the salve, which he preserved in a small pot, and hid his clothes in the thicket.

He usually ran his courses from one to two hours in the day, when the moon was at the wane, but very often he made his expeditions at night. On one occasion he had accompanied Duthillaire, but they had killed no one.

He accused his father of having assisted him, and of possessing a wolf-skin; he charged him also with having accompanied him on one occasion, when he attacked and ate a girl in the village of Grilland, whom he had found tending a flock of geese. He said that his stepmother was separated from his father. He believed the reason to be, because she had seen him once vomit the paws of a dog and the fingers of a child. He added that the Lord of the Forest had strictly forbidden him to bite the thumb-nail of his left hand, and had warned him never to lose sight of it, as long as he was in his were-wolf disguise.

Duthillaire was apprehended, and the father of Jean Grenier himself claimed to be heard by examination.

The account given by the father and stepmother of Jean coincided in many particulars with the statements made by their son.

The localities where Grenier declared he had fallen on children were identified, the times when he said the deeds had been done accorded with the dates given by the parents of the missing little ones, when their losses had occurred.

The wounds which Jean affirmed that he had made, and the manner in which he had dealt them, coincided with the descriptions given by the children he had assaulted.

He was confronted with Marguerite Poirier, and he singled her out from among five other girls, pointed to the still open gashes in her body, and stated that he had made them with his teeth, when he attacked her in wolf-form, and she had beaten him off with a stick. He described an attack he had made on a little boy whom he would have slain, had not a man come to the rescue, and exclaimed, "I'll have you presently."

The man who saved the child was found, and proved to be the uncle of the rescued lad, and he corroborated the statement of Grenier, that he had used the words mentioned above.

Jean was then confronted with his father. He now began to falter in his story, and to change his statements. The examination had lasted long, and it was seen that the feeble intellect of the boy was wearied out, so the case was adjourned. When next confronted with the elder Grenier, Jean told his story as at first, without changing it in any important particular.

The fact of Jean Grenier having killed and eaten several children, and of his having attacked and wounded others, with intent to take their life, were fully established; but there was no proof whatever of the father having had the least hand in any of the murders, so that he was dismissed from the court without a shadow of guilt upon him.

The only witness who corroborated the assertion of Jean that he changed his shape into that of a wolf was Marguerite Poirier.

Before the court gave judgment, the first president of assize, in an eloquent speech, put on one side all questions of witchcraft and diabolical compact, and bestial transformation, and boldly stated that the court had only to consider the age and the imbecility of the child, who was so dull and idiotic that children of seven or eight years old have usually a larger amount of reason than he. The president went on to say that Lycanthropy and Kuanthropy were mere hallucinations, and that the change of shape existed only in the disorganized brain of the insane, consequently it was not a crime which could be punished. The tender age of the boy must be taken into consideration, and the utter neglect of his education and moral development. The court sentenced Grenier to perpetual imprisonment within the walls of a monastery at Bordeaux, where he might be instructed in his Christian and moral obligations; but any attempt to escape would be punished with death.

No sooner was he admitted into the precincts of the religious house, than he ran frantically about the cloister and gardens upon all fours, and finding a heap of bloody and raw offal, fell upon it and devoured it in an incredibly short space of time.

After seven years in the monastery, he was found to be diminutive in stature, very shy, and unwilling to look any one in the face. His eyes were deep set and restless; his teeth long and protruding; his nails black, and in place worn away; his mind was completely barren; he seemed unable to comprehend the smallest things. He died at the age of twenty.

MONARE

MRS. RICHARD S. GREENOUGH

Night had fallen, covering the broad stretch of the plain with shadow. The little huts which clustered around the massive castle of Ilzerley were hidden from sight; and the presence of the castle itself could be perceived only from a long, pale ray of light which streamed from a narrow window, the window of the chapel where Walter of Ilzerley kept his vigil, watching his armor, for the next day was to see him dubbed a knight.

The castle was filled with lords and ladies from all the country round, come to assist at tomorrow's ceremony. There had been feasting and revelling, dance and song; but now all had retired to rest; and the young man knelt before the altar, companioned by solemn thoughts alone.

The chapel was narrow and high; from niches on either side grim effigies of saints looked down; ranged on either hand stood the suits of armor of the past lords of Ilzerley, each guarding as it were his own tomb. The pavement was worn and uneven. Overhead swung an iron lamp, suspended by a chain. It lighted but faintly the gloom of the chapel; its rays seemed gathered together upon Walter's form as he knelt below it, and were reflected from his snowy vest and curling golden hair.

He knelt and prayed that he might be strengthened worthily to fulfil the vows he was to take on the morrow. He thought of the long line of ancestors from whom he was descended, and his heart burned to emulate their noble deeds. He thought of the woe and wickedness that divided the earth between them; and he longed to grasp his knightly sword to do battle for the oppressed. And as he mused and prayed alternately, the night wore on.

It was at the deepest and the darkest when a low wind swept through the chapel, and waved the banners on the wall. He thought he heard a sad human wail, but the wind died away. He listened. There was no sound. Again he mused and prayed, and again the wind swept through the chapel, louder, stronger than before; and it bore with it the sound of a woman's voice wailing,—

"Who shall deliver me from this captivity?"

Walter of Ilzerley started to his feet. He felt the golden curls rising on his head; but his heart was stout and firm, overflowing the while with tender ruth and compassion.

"Lo, here I stand, Walter of Ilzerley, whom to-morrow will see dubbed a knight; and I will strive, so help me God, to deliver thee from thy captivity."

And as he spoke, a chorus of voices, from the suits of armor of the dead lords standing around, responded:—

"We attest the vow."

And eyes looked steadfastly from the eye-holes of the before empty helmets, and the steel-clad and gauntleted right arms were raised, as if invoking the witness of God's sight, while the banners above waved solemnly, as if conscious of the vow. As the sound of the voices died away, a ruby ring fell at Walter of Ilzerley's feet. As it struck on the pavement before him, the flame of the lamp flickered and went out: but he was not left in darkness; a rosy light flashed from the ring, and filled the chapel with a soft radiance. It gleamed on the iron armor, on the stone saints, on the torn and time-stained banners, and on Walter's awe-struck face. He raised it and placed it on his hand; then, kneeling before the altar, he prayed, with earnestness unknown before, that God would grant him wisdom, valor, and patience to rescue from her captivity the lady who had called him to her aid.

The next day came, and with great pomp and solemnity the gray-headed old Count of Lestuys gave him the knightly accolade, and the two fairest damsels of the assemblage buckled on his golden spurs, and tied his scarf across his breast.

Great preparations had been made for feasting for many days. Minstrels and harpers had flocked to the castle; the pantry and buttery were filled to overflowing with mighty pasties, huge loaves of manchet bread, and great baskets of cakes made with spices and honey. Casks of the oldest and strongest wines were broached, and all was gladness and gayety. But the midnight voice sounded ever in Walter's ear, with its complaint,—

"Who shall deliver me from this captivity?"

He looked at the ruby ring. Its rays seemed hour by hour to pale. He determined to delay no longer, but to set forth that very afternoon. So while all the guests were assembled in the great hall, listening to the minstrels who were singing, turn by turn, the romance of Gui de Provens, he mounted his white horse, took his shield on which he had that day ordered the device of a ring to be painted with the motto, "I seek;" and, without bidding adieu to any one, he crossed the drawbridge, and went on his way.

As his gallant white steed passed across the creaking and groaning bridge, he tossed his head and snorted cheerily; and the ruby ring on Walter of Ilzerley's finger sent forth rays so brilliant that he could scarcely bear to look at it. They lay like a rosy line of light before him; and those whom he met shaded their eyes with their hands, and said,—

"Mort de St. Denis! that young knight's armor shines so bright that one can't look at him."

For they did not know that it was the ruby ring that dazzled them.

He journeyed on all that day. The land was sad and sterile. At intervals rose dark and frowning fortresses, each with a little settlement of huts around it. In the immediate neighborhood of these strongholds he saw cultivated fields, horses and cattle peacefully grazing; but it seemed as if neither peasant nor animal dared venture outside that narrow circuit. The ground between was bare and wild. Ever and anon he would pass an abbey or convent with its towers and its ample domain. There he saw more thrift, wider fields and fairer crops; but there were few of these, not enough to redeem the look of desert solitude of the country.

As night drew on, he found himself on a bleak and sullen sweep. The earth looked as though fire had passed over it, and had left it strewn with ashes. Dismal fogs rose in the distance, and slowly crept forward as if to meet and encircle him. His horse turned his head towards his master and neighed plaintively, as if asking where they were to find shelter. Walter of Ilzerley looked anxiously at his ring as for guidance. As his eye rested on it, it shot forth a long ray that pierced the gathered fog and showed, on a small eminence before him, a low, gray hut. The young man cheered his horse with his voice, and raised him with the bridle; and, avoiding as he best might the pools filled with brackish water which were scattered over the plain, he pressed forward towards the solitary gray hut.

As he approached it, a towering form, clothed in a knight's surcoat, appeared at the door.

"Good knight, I crave your hospitality for the dark hours," said the young man.

"Such as I have to offer is yours," replied the knight in a deep, hoarse voice. And he drew near the steed, as the rider dismounted, stretching out his hand as if to take the bridle. But as he advanced, the horse trembled in every limb, laid his ears close to his head, and started back cowering. The knight turned on his heel without remarking the strange behavior of the steed, and led the way to a sort of cave behind the eminence.

"You will find fodder and water within," he said.

The cave was dark; but the ruby ring lighted its every corner, and showed a clear stream trickling from a rock on one side, and a pile of dried grass.

The knight stood silent at the door while the young man rubbed down and caressed his tired steed. Then, when these kind offices were accomplished, he bade him follow.

He conducted Walter into the hut, which was furnished with a strange mixture of poverty and of luxury. On the rough wooden table lay a cloth broidered with hawks and hounds; on rude shelves stood silver flagons; and on the earthen floor was laid a carpet from Eastern looms. But, peculiar as were these things, Walter of Ilzerley's attention was still more powerfully attracted by a strange odor which pervaded the hut,—a smell as of some wild animal. He glanced around to see whether his host had not some slaughtered creature near. But nothing was to be seen.

The host bade Walter be seated, and gave him bread and wine.

"I have no meat to offer you," he said; and, as he spoke, his eyes grew small and green, he half smiled, and showed white, pointed teeth.

Walter of Ilzerley looked keenly at him; but the knight's eyes were as they had been before, and the points had vanished from his teeth.

"No meat is needed," said Walter; and he crossed himself and gave thanks ere he broke the bread.

The knight breathed hard, and drops stood on his forehead, as he heard the holy words.

When the young man had ended his frugal supper, he arose and requested his host to show him where he was to sleep. The hermit knight drew aside a heavy curtain and revealed a small inner room wherein was a low bed, and bade him sleep, and sleep soundly. His eyes again grew small and green as he spoke; and, as he smiled, he showed again white, pointed teeth.

Walter of Ilzerley knelt before his cross-hilted sword, and, having prayed, took off his armor and lay down upon the low pallet. For some time he could not sleep. The strange odor, as of some wild animal, seemed to taint and poison the air. But at length weariness overcame him, and his eyelids closed.

He was wakened by a vivid flash like lightning across his eyes. He started to his feet, and instinctively grasped the sword which he had laid beside him. The ruby was sending forth fiery darts, and showed, below the heavy curtain of the entrance, the head and shoulders of an enormous wolf, with green eyes, and pointed, glistening teeth. Walter of Ilzerley sprang towards the animal, and smote upon its hairy, bristling neck with his good sword.

A human shriek rent the air; the monster changed before his horror-stricken sight; and there at his feet, the blood pouring from a ghastly wound in his throat, lay the knight who had bidden him welcome,—a were-wolf.

The young man stood for a moment without speech or motion; then he took from the shelf in the next room a tall, long-necked silver flagon, and filled it with the smoking blood; for in those days every one knew that a drop of the blood of a were-wolf, which never curdles, would bring to life his victims, no matter how long they had been dead. This being done, he had no mind to tarry longer in the dead monster's den; and so he saddled and bridled his horse, and rode away over the dark plain.

As the day began to break, he saw, rising from the surface of the plain, large heaps of white stones surmounted by wooden crosses. Most of them seemed to have been there for a long time, but one of them was freshly erected. As he approached, he saw, crouching on the ground beside it, a little boy. The young man's heart melted at the sight of the desolate child crouching on the ground damp with the night dew. He drew near. As the child heard the horse's steps, he looked up and showed a face pale with weeping.

"My child, what brings you here?" said the young knight. "Where is your home, and where are your parents?"

"I have no home. There lies my only parent, killed by the were-wolf, like all the rest," said the child; and he sobbed and wept aloud.

Walter of Ilzerley descended from his horse, and, raising the silver flagon, poured from it one drop upon the stones.

Immediately the heap quaked, and was rent asunder, and forth came a man whole and unharmed, rubbing his eyes like one aroused from slumber.

"Why, Tristam, my son, I wake from an ugly dream. I thought the were-wolf had me.—But what makes you look so pale?" said the man as he patted the head of the child, who was staring at him with widely opened eyes, and cheeks paler than before.

The little boy did not speak, for he was too much frightened; but the young knight told him all that had happened; whereupon the man knelt down and thanked God and Walter of Ilzerley alternately.

The knight gave the man half of the blood, and bade him let fall one drop of it on all the heaps of stones; he charged him also to say himself, and to bid all that the wolf's blood should bring to life to say, three Pater-nosters every morning and every evening for his success in the expedition on which he was bound; then he rode away where the ruby light pointed.

As he reached the border of the plain, he looked back, and saw a kneeling crowd; and, as he strained his ear, the morning wind brought to him the sound of their prayer and praise. And his heart was glad within him, and he journeyed on in the sweet light of the sun, over fields fair with flowers and glittering with dew. Little birds sang on the trees, and the May flies and butterflies sported around him, as he rode on his way, singing an old song of knightly valor and of ladies' grace.

The sun was high overhead when he saw in the distance a castle by the sea. As he came towards it, he saw that it was broad and high, and looked as if it were the residence of some mighty lord; but no knightly banner floated from its walls. A large black pennon drooped sadly against its staff. Walter of Ilzerley rode forward and sounded the horn which hung ready for the use of travellers. A head appeared at the small grated window in the gate, and the porter asked who sounded, and what was his errand.

"Walter of Ilzerley am I called, and my errand is to redress a great wrong," answered the young knight.

"Tarry awhile till I ask what is my lady's will concerning you," said the porter; and he retired from the grate, leaving the traveller much surprised at such an uncourteous reception. He looked around as he sat on his steed waiting. The peasants of the surrounding cottages were busy at their toil in the fields. They were more hale and cheerful than most of their class. They looked well fed and well cared for, but each man wore a black band upon his right arm; and the women and girls, whom he saw busy at their household tasks, all wore black caps and scarfs. Yet they talked and laughed gayly, and seemed to pay no heed to the gloomy tokens they bore.

His marvelling was interrupted by the rattling of the chains that supported the drawbridge, and the groaning of the portcullis as it was raised to admit him. He rode forward. As he entered the court-yard, he perceived that the porter and all the retainers were dressed in black. At the extremity of the court, on the lowest step of a broad flight of stone stairs, stood the seneschal, a venerable, white-bearded man, clothed in black like the rest.

"Welcome, Walter of Ilzerley," he said; "my lady awaits you."

The young knight dismounted, much astonished at all he saw.

He followed the seneschal up the broad stone stairs into a long and lofty room. On either side sat a row of young girls spinning. At the upper end of the room, on a raised dais, sat the lady. She had been beautiful; but sorrow had furrowed her forehead, and quenched the brightness of her eyes. She rose as the young knight approached, and extended her hand.

"Welcome, Walter of Ilzerley," she said; "welcome to a doubly smitten house,—a house reft of its lord and of its child."

"Were your sorrow, lady," answered the young knight, "such as admitted of human aid, then would I bind myself to your service so soon as my present errand be fulfilled; but against such grief as yours the bravest arm lies helpless. I can but grieve with you."

The lady turned to an old priest who sat in the deep embrasure of the window behind her, reading his breviary, and who had not even raised his head at the young man's entrance.

"Father Anselm," she said, "tell this stranger the story of my woe. Perhaps it may be granted to him to succeed in that enterprise wherein those that preceded him have failed."

At these words all the black-robed maidens stopped their spinning, and fastened their eyes sorrowfully on the young knight, and sighed. It was as if a low wind had swept through the hall, and brought back to Walter of Ilzerley's memory the midnight wail in the chapel.

The old priest closed his book, and rose, turning towards the youth.

"My blessing be upon you, my son," he said. "The lady's will shall be obeyed. Follow me to my cell. There will I tell you what grievous woe rests upon this house."

Walter saluted the lady, glanced at the rows of black-robed maidens, who with bowed heads were again busy at their wheels, and retired with the old priest. He followed him through dark, winding passages, cut in the thickness of the stone wall, into his cell; narrow, but lighted by a window which looked out upon the sea. On a little wooden table stood a crucifix and a skull; and the stone floor before it was worn into a hollow where the knees of the good priest had been pressed in his hours of prayer.

"Be seated, my son," said Father Anselm, as he drew forward a wooden stool, and offered it to the youth. He sat down himself upon the low truckle-bed, folded his hands, and heaved a deep sigh. After a pause, during which 'Walter pondered what grief this might be, and what courage and fortune might be necessary to remove it, the old priest thus began:—

"Do not think, my son, that this castle was always the gloomy abode that you now see it. I remember when troops of lords and ladies made it gay with jest and song from morn till midnight. Every day there was hunting and hawking, tilting and jousting; for the count and countess were young, and loved pleasure, like all the young and fortunate. Good were they, and pious also; and on the first day of every month, they and all their guests and all their household, carrying lighted tapers, walked in solemn procession to the shrine of St. Mary of Aspramont, a league away, on the high hill that overhangs the sea.

"It was fourteen years ago,—I shall never forget that glad and sunny morning which was to have so black a close,— fourteen years ago the drawbridge was lowered, and forth walked Count Egbert in his gorgeous dress, leading by her hand his lady all blazing with gold and jewels, both bearing great waxen tapers half an dl high. And all the lords and ladies, magnificently attired and bearing lighted tapers also, and all the household, followed, save two or three old servants who were too infirm to walk so far, and the count and countess' little daughter, their only child, a babe a twelvemonth old, with her nurse. The nurse stood on the lower step of the great stone stairs, and held the child in her arms; and the little thing sprang and laughed for joy as she saw the goodly company and the lighted tapers pass by. Each lord and lady saluted her and bade her good-by as they passed; for she was a sweet and gracious child, and all loved her. Her father and mother looked back and smiled and beckoned with their hand at her as they left the court-yard; but they did not dream that that was to be their last look on their little one.

"The procession passed over the drawbridge and through the pleasant fields, chanting St. Mary's hymn as they went. The sweet voices of the ladies and the deep tones of the knights sounded as though nightingales were singing beside the swelling sea.

"Strange was it that the moment which saw the count and countess bent on such pious intent should have brought to them the misery of their lives. As they rose from their knees before the shrine, one of the knights looked towards the sea and shouted, 'Holy Virgin, the pirates!'

"They all rushed to the edge of the cliff; and there, below them, they saw a great Saracenic galley just entering the bay before the castle. The ladies shrieked and knelt, all save the countess. She snatched the dagger from her husband's belt, and sprang down the steep. The count and all the knights and retainers followed, bounding like deer over the stones, down the broken and rugged way, the countess before them. The way was long,—too long. The castle was hid from their sight by the thick wood. They darted through its shadows, and came out upon the sunny plain. The pirates were already in their boats. Ere the knights could reach the shore, they had gained their vessel; the wind was filling her sails and bearing them away.

"The countess had flown towards the castle. As her husband and his friends, baffled, for they had no vessel wherewith to chase the pirates, crossed the drawbridge which had been left lowered for their return, they saw the murdered bodies of the old servants stretched upon the reddened stones of the court-yard.

" 'My child!' cried the count in a tone of anguish; and he rushed towards his little daughter's room. It was empty of child and nurse. On the floor lay the countess, still and white as though dead. They brought her back to life with much labor and pains; but from that day neither she nor her husband ever smiled again, nor did they ever renew their pilgrimage to St. Mary's shrine, which was a great wrong to the saint. They shut themselves up in their private apartments, and mourned without ceasing. No more mirth or song enlivened the castle, and hospitality was given to strangers for one night only. They brooded over their loss till they fancied themselves aggrieved by Providence;

and they had no thought for the still greater distresses of the poor around them, who that year, for it was a year of famine, saw their children perishing before their eyes for lack of food.

"Another great misery befell on that year. It was the appearance of the were-wolf, which has ever since desolated the country."

At the mention of the were-wolf, the young man bent forward and listened still more attentively.

"The Sieur Nicolas de Maupré was a haughty and lawless lord, whose chief occupation was in waylaying travellers, and his chief pleasure in torturing them until they were fain to ransom themselves at the cost of all they possessed. This wicked lord, as I say, one day disappeared; and no one could imagine what had become of him, until many others disappeared also, and the rumor spread in the country that a were-wolf had taken up its abode near by. Then every one knew that the wicked knight had turned himself into a were-wolf; and all the people since then have lived in terror of their lives, and many have been destroyed in spite of all their precautions; for there lives no beast or being so treacherous, so wily, and so cruel, as the were-wolf. Anathema maranatha!"

And the priest crossed himself.

"But I must go on, and bring my sorrowful history to its close. One afternoon the count wandered forth across the meadows on a solitary walk. Hours passed, the evening meal was ready to be served, but he did not return.

The countess was at prayers in the chapel, and did not perceive her lord's absence; but those of the household began to feel uneasy. They were all watching if they could catch sight of the count returning, when in the dusky twilight they beheld the figure of a boy running towards the castle. As he reached the walls, he shouted,—

" 'The count! the were-wolf!' and sank down upon the stones.

"All the retainers seized torches and weapons and rushed forth in search of their master, taking courage from their numbers; for not one of them, much as they loved their lord, would have dared venture out alone with the chance of meeting the monster.

"Guided by the lad's directions, they sought and found a little brook which ran babbling down from a steep rock into the sea; and on its bank lay all that remained of the count. He had fought manfully against the beast, as the torn and trampled ground proved; but what can one mortal man do against a were-wolf?

"With groans and sobs the retainers took up their lord's remains and bore them to the castle; and not one of them but wept like a child when the countess met them ere they reached the drawbridge. I will not describe her grief. One should have seen it to know what it was.

"The count was buried in the chapel, before the altar; and there three times a day, at morning and noon and night, the countess kneels, and listens to a mass for the dead. And her affliction has borne good fruit. She spends all the rest of her time in caring for the sick, the poor, and the afflicted; deeming her second bereavement a chastisement sent from heaven because of the rebellious manner in which she received the first. And all the country around blesses her, and grieves because of her grief.

"But now, my son, I must leave you, unless, indeed, you will accompany me to the chapel; for noon is at hand, and I must say the mass for the dead."

"One instant, my father," said Walter of Ilzerley; "tarry one instant. Surely by the hand of superhuman wisdom was I brought hither."

And the young knight told the priest how he had slept in the den of the were-wolf, and had slain him, and had brought away his blood. And the old man lifted up his hands and thanked Heaven, while tears of joy ran down his withered cheeks and dropped on his brown robe. Then he led Walter to the chapel, and bade him stand at the foot of the count's tomb.

He had scarcely taken his place there when the countess appeared, followed by all her servants and retainers, and knelt to listen to the mass. But, instead of the service for the dead, the old priest chanted out, in a broken voice, a canticle of thanksgiving. The countess and all her servants were greatly astonished; the more so that they saw the young knight standing with a joyful face, holding a silver flagon upraised in his hand.

When the priest had ended the canticle, he said in a loud voice,—

"Daughter, arise and rejoice. The days of thy mourning are ended."

Thereupon Walter of Ilzerley poured a drop of the were-wolf's blood upon the tomb. And the tomb opened in the middle, and the count arose and came forth, shading his eyes with his hand, as one whom a sudden light wakens. And the chapel was filled with the cries of fright and joy of all the servants and retainers; but the count and countess spake never a word, but stood fast locked in each other's arms.

That night bonfires blazed so broad and high from the walls of the castle, that they reddened the whole sky; and troops of horsemen from all the fortresses for fifteen miles around came hurrying to see what had happened, and to offer their aid. They were all bid right welcome; and oxen were roasted whole, and a great row of wine-casks was brought up from the cellars, and broached and ran without stint or measure. As each successive troop came into the court-yard, and were met by the joyful news, they set up such a shout of joy that it echoed from the castle walls far over the meadows and back to the distant hills. Never was there known such gladness and revelling.

But Walter of Ilzerley, when the evening meal was ended, retired from the great hall, bright with the blaze of a hundred torches, and glad with the voices of the count and countess' fast arriving friends, and took his stand upon the walls and looked towards the dark, scarce seen sea, wondering what errand it might be that he was to undertake at the .countess' behest when his present enterprise should be ended. He was standing, his eyes fixed upon the ruby ring which shone brightly on his hand, but shot forth no guiding ray, when Father Anselm approached him, and begged that he would deign to follow to the presence of the count and countess.

He found them in a small, round room, built in one of the towers. In the middle of the floor stood a child's cradle, the bedclothes tossed here and there in confusion, as if the little creature had been but just snatched up. Around were strewn little playthings; and on a chair lay a child's embroidered dress, but every thing looked old and tarnished.

The countess was standing, her hand clasped in her husband's, her face buried on his shoulder. She raised her head as the young knight entered, and he saw that she had been weeping. The count's face also was sad and sorrowful. The lady spoke.

"Walter of Ilzerley, God knows whether or not I am grateful to you for what you have done this day. Not because I lightly esteem the service already rendered do I sue you for another boon. Father Anselm has told you of our child. Nothing in this room has been touched since she was stolen from it. Each night of these long years have I come hither to mourn for my darling. Two months ago, I was kneeling here at midnight, when I heard a soft low wind come sweeping over the sea, and it bore to my ears my daughter s voice wailing,—

" 'Who shall deliver me from this captivity?' "

When Walter of Ilzerley heard these words, the blood rushed in a mighty column to his heart, and his breath stopped; but he was silent, and the lady went on:—

"Since then two knights have come to this castle, and to each have I told my daughter's prayer. Each has ridden away on the morrow in search of her. From that quest neither has returned. But I feel that to you, perhaps, may be granted what has been denied to the other twain; and I implore you, Walter of Ilzerley, by all that you hold dear in this world and the next, to hear a mother's prayer, and pity a mother's anguish."

And so saying, the countess knelt before the young man's feet, and raised her clasped hands, beseeching him.

Walter of Ilzerley raised the lady, and swore never to return to Christian lands till he had found the maiden, and delivered her from the captivity wherein she was bound.

Then the count grasped him by the hand, and said,—

"Young knight, great as is my debt to you, it is as nought to that which it will be when you restore to me my child. And when she is given back to us, should your eyes love to rest upon her, we will give her to you, as your wife, and she shall have a dowry meet for a king's daughter."

But Walter of Ilzerley still kept silence on the voice that had come to him in the midnight chapel, for he felt as if it would be parting with a precious thing, were any save himself to know of it.

He thought of the maiden all that night, nor had he once closed his eyes to sleep, when the first red streaks of morning shone in the eastern sky. But he felt no fatigue, so bent was his mind upon freeing the count's daughter. He arose, and put on his armor, and, taking leave of the count

and countess, he mounted his white horse, and rode away; while all the retainers bade him adieu, and shouted, "God speed you, brave knight," as he crossed the drawbridge, and came out upon the open plain.

The morning sun shone bright overhead, and the little white clouds floated on the soft blue of the sky, like fairy vessels on a waveless sea. The water danced and sparkled in the light, and the hum of the busy insects, as they flew from flower to flower, filled the air with pleasant sounds. The ruby light lay like a crimson path over the glittering water, and was lost in the distance of the glancing waves.

The knight reined up his horse upon the yellow beach, and looked around for a boat. In a little creek near by he saw a skiff, which two fishermen were dragging into the water.

"Friends, name your price," said the knight, "but I must have your boat."

"It is worth two pieces of gold to us," said the fishermen. The knight gave them four, and, mounting into the little boat with his horse, he pushed off to sea, following the crimson track.

A gentle wind drove forward the skiff, so that the knight had no need to ply the oars. He sat in the stern, his armor flashing back the sunlight; his eyes fixed on the distance where the crimson light pointed; Isis face full of manly courage, yet soft with tender thought.

Three days and three nights did he, with his good steed, float over the sea, borne on by the gentle wind which never varied nor died away; and, on the morning of the fourth day, he saw the minarets and gilded cupolas of a great city on the shore before him. As he floated nearer, he saw the accursed crescent flashing from every high point, and he knew that he had reached the country of the infidels. Suddenly the ruby light vanished, and a shadow seemed to fall upon him. He looked around. The sun was shining brightly as before; but the reflection of his own figure, of his horse, and of the boat, had disappeared, and he saw that he, and all that belonged to him, had become invisible. The boat pressed forward till it reached the shore; and Walter of Ilzerley, leaping from it, knelt on the sands, and thanked Heaven for having brought him so far safely on his way, and implored its assistance in what he had yet to accomplish; then mounting his horse, he turned towards the bronze gates of the city.

As he passed through the portal, a blind beggar, sitting beside the way, held out his hand and begged for alms.

"Fool," said a tall negro who was lounging in the sunshine, "hold your peace. No one comes this way."

The blind man answered,—

"I know by the measured trembling of the ground that a horse and rider are passing by." But the negro could see nothing; and he called to his comrades that the blind man had better eyes than they, for that he could perceive a horse and rider where there was nothing but dust and sunshine. And they all laughed and jeered at the blind man.

The young knight left them behind, and went on through the crowded street that lay before him. It was shaded from the heat of the sun by awnings of crimson silk, which were stretched across from the tops of the houses; and beneath were endless rows of stalls filled with gorgeous silks and jewelry and spices, and merchandise of every sort. Veiled women, preceded by black eunuchs, mingled with the swarthy and turbaned crowd, and shouts and cries and bargaining and chaffering resounded on every side.

Suddenly a blast of trumpets was heard from the upper extremity of the street; and every sound was immediately silenced, and all the people ranged themselves on either side, as a band of slaves dressed in green, with crooked cimeters shining in their hands, came down the way, preceding twelve officers wearing enormous turbans, mounted on black mules, and bearing brazen trumpets. When they reached the centre of the street, they stopped, and the officers sounded their trumpets and made proclamation, saying,—

"O people, listen! Thus saith the sultan, the master of the earth, the ruler of the sea, and the numberer of the stars:—

"Know, O ye people who are so blessed as to live in the city which we honor with our presence, that some child of unfathomable perdition bath stolen from our special treasury, locked with a hundred keys, guarded by a hundred slaves, entered through a labyrinth with a hundred windings, our most precious possession, the ruby ring lost in a wager to our ancestor, the great King Solomon, by the King of the Genii, and handed down ever since that day, in our most glorious and excellent house.

"Out of our great and wonderful clemency, we hereby proclaim that although he who has dared to aspire to the possession of this inestimable gem deserves a thousand deaths; yet, let him return it, and he shall receive free pardon for the offence, and shall furthermore be rewarded with two hundred purses of gold."

Then the brazen trumpets sounded again, and the slaves and the officers moved forward, and the street became more noisy than before; for all the people were wondering and lamenting over the loss from the sultan's treasury, of that wonderful ring.

But Walter of Ilzerley, as he looked around, saw one old woman, dressed as became the slave of a very rich person, who neither wondered nor questioned. She was very pale, and shook all over as she asked the merchant, by whose stall the knight had stopped his horse, whether the blue vest embroidered with gold which her mistress had ordered were finished.

"The vest is finished, and the embroidery is the finest that was ever seen in the city," answered the merchant; "but, know you, that were it not for so illustrious a lady as an inmate of the palace of our exalted master, the sultan, I should have said it had been designed for a dog of a Christian."

"What do you say?" screamed the old woman, in a shrill, quavering voice.

"Look, then," said the merchant, holding up the vest: "is not here on the breast, hidden under the waving lines of the ornaments, the outline of the unclean cross?" And he spat on the ground in sign of abhorrence. "If the lady see it, she will never wear the vest, although she sent the pattern herself."

The old woman said nothing, hut paid the merchant three pieces of gold, and, taking the vest, made her way along the street as fast as she could.

The young knight followed her; but, although he took great pains not to press against any one, the crowd was so great that he constantly pushed those on the right and on the left; and they, not seeing the invisible horse and rider, felt greatly aggrieved, and angrily berated those nearest them, who, knowing themselves innocent of any discourtesy, were not slack in angry retort: and so it happened that the whole street fell into confusion, and threats and blows were exchanged on every side; and so great grew the tumult, that the merchants rose in haste and closed their shops and withdrew the awnings, and the rays of the sun poured down so fiercely that it was like a fiery rain; and so the crowd dispersed to seek shelter elsewhere; while Walter of Ilzerley followed the old woman as she passed through many long and winding streets. At length she halted at a door in a high stone wall. It was the only opening in the face of the wall, which was of great extent.

The old woman knocked three times; and the door was opened by a frightfully ugly slave, whose eyes stood out so far that he looked as if he could see all around him without turning his head. Walter of Ilzerley sprang from his horse, and followed the old woman as she entered; but, although he made all the haste he could, he did not succeed in passing the door ere the frightful slave closed it, and the young knight was caught between the door and the doorpost.

The slave wondered and pushed in vain, for the door could not close, of course, since there was a knight clothed in armor in the way. At last the slave opened widely the door in order to push it to with greater force, and so released the young man, who immediately sprang forward; but the old woman had disappeared through one of the many doors which opened into the circular hall in which he found himself.

He had no clew to guide him in his search, so he opened at random the door nearest him. He saw before him a long, dark, and narrow passage, at the end of which faintly glimmered an uncertain light. He advanced towards the ray, which proceeded from the key-hole of a heavy door, thickly studded with iron nails. A faint odor of gums and spices came to his nostrils; but he could see nothing within save by stooping to look through the key-hole, and to that no knight could condescend. So he drew his sword from its scabbard, and with its hilt knocked loudly at the door. After a short delay it was opened, and the head of an old man clothed, although it was summer, in a furred robe, appeared. His wrinkled forehead was high and broad; his beard was as white as snow; but his eyebrows were black and heavy, and from beneath their shade his small, keen eyes looked piercingly forth. As he cautiously opened the door the young knight passed within.

The old man peered down the passage, then muttering to himself, again closed the door. The room, or rather vault, into which the young knight had penetrated was vast and gloomy. The walls were of stone whereon were deeply graven strange devices and symbols, mixed with Chaldean characters and Coptic signs. In the middle of the vaulted ceiling was a small, round aperture, through which, looking up as through a black tube of great length, the stars could be seen at mid-day. The air was heavy with strange perfumes, which seemed to proceed from a bronze tripod, upon which was burning a fire whose flickering and uncertain flames supplied its only light to the vault.

The old man, still muttering to himself, resumed the occupation which the knight's summons had interrupted. He took some spices and some fine powder of charcoal, and made a paste, which he moulded into the form of a ring, over which he made various signs, turning it constantly, and ever and anon turning it to the four points of the compass. Then he dropped it into the middle of the fire. Immediately a bright flame sprang up, and, detaching itself from the fire below, remained in the shape of a fiery cross, suspended in the air. When the old man saw this, he gnashed his teeth and stamped on the ground.

"What accursed mystery is this?" he exclaimed. "Three times am I foiled. And what shall I say to the sultan when he demands what I have discovered? The ring is without a doubt in Christian hands; but how it came there, it passes my science to discover."

As he said this, the magic flame paled and died away; and, the fire on the tripod likewise sinking, the vault became dark. The old man lighted a tall, green taper at the decaying blaze, and placed it upon a table whereon lay a large, black-covered book, which he began attentively to study. Walter of Ilzerley approached, and looked over the old man's shoulder as he bent over the book, and he saw there written the exact description of the ring, and an explanation of its virtues. There he learnt that the ring had the power, on the approach of danger, of rendering its possessor invisible, and knew why he had become lost to mortal sight from the moment he approached the shore of the infidels. He was reading with avidity the account of all the properties of the ring which had so mysteriously been bestowed upon him, when a loud knock was heard at the iron-studded door. The old man reluctantly arose and opened it; and a slave, richly dressed, entered with a concerned air, and, glancing uneasily around, knelt, and, bending his forehead till it almost touched the ground, said,—

"O most powerful and mighty sage! The sultan, our master, desires your presence forthwith."

The old man, supporting his steps with an ivory cane carved with strange devices, followed the messenger, who seemed in a great hurry to get out of the vault. Walter of Ilzerley accompanied them through numberless passages and halls, until they came to a large room, filled with richly attired officers and slaves, who all drew aside respectfully as the old man passed. At the extremity of the room was a curtain of green brocade, before which stood ten gigantic slaves clothed in yellow, and holding naked cimeters in their hands. They made way as the old man advanced; and the slave who had summoned him drew aside the curtain, and held it up for him to enter. The knight followed close.

As he crossed the threshold, he found himself in a spacious and lofty apartment lighted with many-colored rays. The ceiling was painted to imitate the overhanging branches and green leaves of a forest, and birds of gorgeous plumage swung from it in cages of golden wire. Their songs mixed with the tinkling of a fountain which rose from a crystal tank in the middle of the room, around which grew flowers in rich abundance. Along the walls, which were of cedar inlaid with gold, were divans and cushions of embroidered damask fringed with pearl; and on the marble floor were spread carpets so soft that the footsteps falling on them gave back no sound.

On the divan at the upper end of the room sat a young man magnificently dressed. He was handsome, though very haughty in face and bearing.

The old man knelt and touched his forehead three times to the ground as the curtain fell behind him.

"Approach, O most venerable sage!" said the sultan, "and say how your search has sped. Have you found a clew by which to track the audacious criminal who has dared to violate the sanctity of our private treasury, and to steal from it the ring?"

The sultan knit the black arches of his brows till they met, and his moustaches quivered as he spoke.

"O most glorious and gracious of sultans!" answered the old man; "something truly have I discovered, though less than I had hoped. But that which I have learned makes the loss of the ring more unaccountable than before. I know to a surety that the gem is at this moment in Christian hands."

The sultan started to his feet.

"In the hands of a dog of a Christian!" he exclaimed. "May he and his prophet perish together."

At these impious and insulting words, Walter of Ilzerley lost patience, and, drawing hastily near, he smote the sultan on the face. The blow was well planted, and it tingled sharply on the sultan's olive cheek.

"What demon, miserable old man, have you dared to bring hither with you?" he shouted in a rage, laying his hand on the dagger its his sash. "If you were less useful, your head should within five minutes make acquaintance with the bowstring. Begone I and know that unless, ere three days be over, I see again the ring, I will forget all your past services, and only remember this unheard-of affront."

So saying, the sultan, foaming with rage, clapped his hands together. The curtain was withdrawn, and the old man, half terrified to death, retreated in haste.

The sage had hardly left the room when the curtain was again lifted, and an officer, apparently of high rank, entered and prostrated himself as the old man had done.

"What news do you bring, Mustapha?" said the sultan. "Dare not to say that your quest has been unsuccessful."

"Most illustrious of sovereigns," replied the officer, "this is what I have discovered. On the night before the ring was found to be lost, some fishermen out at sea saw, in the air overhead, a bright stream of rosy light, which flashed from the direction of the city towards the country of the Christians. The night was dark, but so bright was the passing radiance that it streamed like a ruddy pathway over the water, and lighted up all the sea. Further than this, O most merciful of masters! your slave has not been able to trace the ring."

The sultan made no answer, but sat deep in thought for a while, twisting his long, curling moustache and looking on the ground. Then he made a sign to the officer to withdraw.

The sultan clapped his hands together as the officer retired, and a slave entered and prostrated himself.

"Let the great council be summoned," said the sultan; and the slave withdrew.

After a few moments the green curtain was widely withdrawn, and a procession of very old men entered. They all wore green turbans, and their white robes were girded about them by costly shawls. After the due prostrations, at a sign from the sultan they seated themselves cross-legged, folded their arms over their breasts, and waited for him to speak.

"It is known to you," said the sultan, "that our inestimable ruby ring has been audaciously stolen from our especial and private treasury."

Here all the old men bowed their heads.

"I know, from certain information, that it has passed into the unclean hands of a Christian."

Here all the old men spat on the ground, in sign of contempt and abhorrence.

"Furthermore, I have learnt that it is at this moment in the country of the Christians; and I have summoned you, to communicate to you my sovereign will and pleasure that an embassy be immediately despatched to the king of the Christians, demanding the instant return of the ring, and announcing that, should it be refused, I will ravage his country with fire and sword, and will destroy every city and walled town within its borders."

When the great councillors had heard the sultan, they all replied in chorus,—

"O most powerful and illustrious sultan! to hear is to obey."

And they left the room in the same order wherewith they had entered it; and Walter of Ilzerley joined their procession, and passed out with them.

The exterior hall looked out upon a large and shaded garden. Between the trees were seen light kiosks, whose trellised walls were wreathed with roses and jasmine; and from the velvet lawns rose numberless sparkling fountains, cooling the sultry air with their incessant rain.

Unknowing in what direction to turn in order to seek for the old woman who had bought the vest embroidered with the Christian cross, sadly perplexed at the labyrinth of halls and passages which filled the sultan's palace, the young knight passed out through an open door into the garden, and, plunging into one of the thickets of flowering shrubs, threw himself down upon the ground to consider what he was next to do.

He had not yet succeeded in arriving at any definite conclusion, when he heard footsteps coming up the broad walk which led close by him. He raised his head, and saw a hunchbacked old Egyptian female dwarf, whose contorted ugliness seemed insufferably hideous, seen as it was amidst the graceful flowers and silver fountains, and light and glory of the garden. The dwarf advanced till she was close to him; then she stopped, and said,—

"Follow me."

Walter of Ilzerley started to his feet, thinking that the ring had lost its power of concealing him; but, as he stood upright in the sunshine, he saw that his figure cast no shadow upon the ground, and then he perceived that the dwarf must be a sorceress.

He came from the thicket and followed her through the garden, until, turning into a lonely and scarcely trodden path, she stopped at a small, carved minor. She opened it by pressing upon a spring hidden under one of its ornaments, and passed within, followed by the knight. She ascended a narrow and winding staircase, and paused at a door at which she tapped. As the door opened, the dwarf turned her head and beckoned to the invisible knight. The door was opened by the old woman whom he had seen that morning bargaining for the vest. The young man's heart leaped for joy as he saw her; and with eager steps he passed into the room, for he felt assured that he should find there the maiden he sought.

The room was small, but richly decorated and furnished in the Oriental style, with painted arabesques, and the ceiling was carved with curious workmanship; but the knight saw nothing save the figure of a maiden, who was whispering to herself as he entered,—

"Who shall deliver me from this captivity?"

Seated beside an open window, which looked forth upon the sea, and leaning her cheek upon her hand, she was steadfastly gazing upon the glittering expanse of the water. She wore a blue vest embroidered with gold, which half betrayed, half concealed the graceful outlines of her figure; her head was covered on one side by a little embroidered cap, and on the other was placed a bouquet of jewelled flowers; while her long, soft, brown hair, unconfined, fell in heavy waves almost to the ground. On her white arms were clasped golden bracelets; and her little, rosy feet were thrust into crimson slippers embroidered with gold.

The knight had never seen any loveliness to be compared with that of the maiden; and he stood in a trance of wonder and admiration, gazing upon her as though he would never weary.

After a while the maiden turned from looking over the water and spoke in a sorrowful tone to the dwarf.

"Good mother, four days and four nights have I watched the waves; and yet I can see no knight coming to my rescue."

And she sighed, and, turning her head, again fixed her eyes upon the sea.

"I can't help that," 'answered the dwarf, shortly. "Some people see things where there is nothing to be seen, and others see nothing where there is something to be seen. I don't make people's eyes."

And the dwarf sat down on a pile of cushions, and sulked.

The maiden answered nothing, and did not seem to hear the cracked and dissonant tones of the Egyptian; but the old woman who had opened the door rolled up her eyes and groaned, as if to express her disapprobation, though she evidently did not dare to speak.

As if weary of watching, the maiden left the casement, and, crossing the room, seated herself on the pile of cushions beside the dwarf. She took the old Egyptian's brown and wrinkled hand in her soft, white fingers, and said coaxingly,—

"But tell me one thing, good mother: how did you obtain for me the ruby ring? Tell me only that."

"Don't tease me," said the dwarf. "You would be sorry enough if I did tell you. The words I should be obliged to speak would shatter the walls, and bring a host of demons about us."

At these words the old woman whom the young knight had seen in the street, clasped her hands, and implored the maiden not to persist in her entreaties.

"For," said she, "know, my blessed lady, that I can scarcely sleep at nights as it is, knowing as I do that Monarè could have us all strangled by demons ere morning, if she chose. And, if I were once to see a demon, I should die of fright outright, as, indeed, it is a wonder that I did not that day the pirates carried us away. But of that you knew nothing, sweet, unconscious babe that you were."

And the old woman began to weep.

"Don't prate so," said the dwarf, crossly.

"Isn't it bad enough to be stolen by pirates without being told of it all the time? Don't be such a croaking night-owl. I wonder, for my part, why the pirates took you. You never could have had any good looks to boast of."

The old woman, forgetting for the moment her fears, was about to make an angry retort, when the maiden interfered and with gentle words composed the menaced quarrel; then, kissing tenderly the frightful Egyptian dwarf, she said,—

"Good mother, how can I thank you for all that you have done for me? If I obtain my freedom, I will show you what my gratitude is worth."

"Don't talk to me of gratitude," interrupted the dwarf. "I want to know if I haven't cause of gratitude to you. Who was it that saved me from those Mussulman hounds in the bazaar who were going to tear me in pieces for a witch, only because I shortened the leg of one who was going to kick me, so that he couldn't put it down again? Don't talk to me of gratitude! It makes me cross."

But the maiden took no heed of the dwarf's perversity. She kept her seat by her, and caressed her cheek with her white hand.

"Well, good mother," she said, " since you will not tell me how you obtained the ring, tell me at least to whom it was that I sent it with my nightly prayer."

"A good knight and a true," answered the dwarf abruptly.

Walter of Ilzerley, at these words, could have fallen at the dwarf's feet and embraced her knees for very thankfulness, so great was his desire to stand well in the esteem of the beautiful, imprisoned maiden.

"A good knight and a true," repeated the maiden thoughtfully. "But, good mother, tell me something more. Is he young? Is he fair to look upon?"

But the dwarf would not answer a word to the maiden's questions, and only reiterated,—

"A good knight and a true."

Suddenly the maiden sprang to her feet and stood in the attitude of one listening; and the knight perceived the sound of many feet, and the clashing of arms from the garden beneath. He looked from a window that opened over the garden, and saw the old sage advancing at the head of a body of armed slaves. In his hand the old man carried a small, purple snake, which, hissing, stretched out its head in the direction of the little carved door. The old man entered, followed by the slaves, and they heard the noise of many ascending steps. The maiden stood pale and still in the middle of the room, while the old nurse crept trembling into a corner, and the dwarf clenched her teeth and stamped on the floor.

The door was wrenched open from without, and the old man appeared on the threshold. Behind him stood the slaves, filling the entry, and crowding on the stairs. The little purple snake in the sage's hand raised the crest upon its head, and hissed loudly and angrily, turning towards the window where the knight was standing.

As the dwarf caught sight of the snake, her look of rage and perplexity changed into an expression of triumph. She crept behind the maiden, whose flowing robe concealed her from view, and, crossing her hands behind her, she mumbled a few unknown words.

As she spoke them, the little snake writhed violently; then, springing from the old man's hand, it darted to the window, and disappeared.

The old man tore his hair.

"Ten purses of gold to whoever catches the snake!" he shouted. And he and all the armed slaves rushed down the stairs in pursuit of the little purple snake; and the sound of their voices and trampling steps died away.

The old nurse, shaking and trembling, crawled forward and closed the door; while the hideous Egyptian dwarf threw herself on the floor, and rolled her head about in an ecstasy of delight.

"Oh, what a fool, what a world-renowned fool, is that sage! Call him a sage, indeed! Why, if I were to pull out an eyelash, that eyelash would have more knowledge in it than he has in his whole body. I waist to know if he ever lived, like me, in the secret chambers of the great Pyramid, where the books of my ancestors, the Egyptian priests, are stored? What does he know, the bungler! He didn't even know who I was. And to bring that absurd little snake here where I am! Ha, ha, ha!"

And the dwarf rolled about and shrieked with laughter, while the old nurse looked at her aghast, and ever and anon crossed herself; and the maiden stood pressing her hand against her heart, as if to still its frightened beatings; for, at the appearance of the armed slaves, she had anticipated nothing less than instant death.

At length the dwarf's laughter came, as all things will, to an end.

"Do stop crossing yourself," she said peevishly to the old nurse. "Can't any one have a little quiet merriment, but you must put on a long face, and scratch crosses all over yourself?" And she turned her back upon the old woman, and, approaching the trembling maiden, took hold of her hand, and drew her to a divan.

"Sit down, my pearl, my white dove," she said caressingly. "Don't shiver so. Do you think your old Monarè would let any one hurt you? I will make that old fool repent of having frightened my child."

And she began to mutter some strange words. But the maiden laid her hand upon the Egyptian's mouth, and prayed her not to harm the sage.

"You'll make me forget all the curses I ever learned," said the dwarf, sulkily; "but if you don't want him hurt, it's all the same to me."

The maiden rose, and looked out anew upon the waves.

"Good mother, I can see nothing," she said. "When will he come?"

"That's a reasonable question," replied the dwarf, "seeing that he has been in the room for half an hour."

The blood rushed crimson into the maiden's cheeks as she glanced around.

"There's no use in looking for him," said the dwarf. "You can't see him, but I can. Young knight, don't stand there like a stone, with your eyes as wide open as if you were trying to eat her with them. Come here and kiss her hand."

But the young knight did not dare to advance towards the beautiful maiden; and she, on her side, drooped her head, and turned shyly away from that part of the room to which the dwarf directed her eyes.

"I never saw such tiresome people," said the dwarf, in a pet. "There's this young knight, as handsome as he can be, if you could only see him, come over the sea three days and three nights from the country of the Christians, because you called him; and now that he is here, you turn away and won't hold out your hand, and he is afraid to come and take it. I am angry. Hold out your hand; and you, Sir Knight, come forward."

When the maiden heard herself thus rebuked, she held out her hand, blushing all over like the sky at sunrise; and Walter of Ilzerley, advancing, fell on his knees and raised it to his lips. As she felt the invisible lips pressed upon her hand, the maiden uttered a little cry, and drew close to the dwarfs side.

"Don't be frightened," said the dwarf. "You know that you have been looking out of the window four days and four nights, hoping to see him."

At this the maiden blushed more deeply than before, and looked imploringly at the Egyptian.

"Well, well," said the dwarf, "I didn't say any thing, did I? But I must tell now this young knight what he has to do."

So saying, she turned to Walter of Ilzerley. "As soon as it is dark the guards will make their rounds. When they appear you must attack them."

The maiden, hearing this, exclaimed,—

"O good mother I surely you do not wish the knight to fight single-handed against six!"

Walter of Ilzerley would have assured her that he was willing to fight single-handed against sixty, for her sake; but the same charm that rendered him invisible deprived him of the power of speech. He could but clench the handle of his sword and wish for the moment that should prove how little he valued danger in her cause.

He had not long to wait, for the night was fast coming on. It was no sooner dark than heavy steps were heard ascending the stairs; the door was thrown open, and showed the chief of the guard and his armed soldiers, each holding a lighted torch in one hand and a naked cimeter in the other. They gloomily looked around the room to assure themselves of the presence of all its inmates. At that instant Walter of Ilzerley threw from him the ring, and stood in shining armor and with flashing eyes before their astonished sight. They raised their cimeters and rushed upon him, but he sprang to meet them with uplifted sword. The quiet little room was filled with the clashing of weapons and the fierce cries of the guards; but the fray did not last long. One after another fell under the heavy blows of the Christian knight, until all six lay stretched upon the ground.

"That is well done," said the dwarf, who had watched the combat with great delight, clapping her hands and screaming with laughter as each successive guard fell to the ground; while the maiden had thrown herself upon her knees, and, burying her face in her hands, was praying earnestly; and the old nurse had crept under a pile of cushions, where nothing was visible of her save her feet.

"Now," said the dwarf, "take from the sash of the chief of the guard the key which you will find there. It opens every lock in the palace. "With that we can let ourselves out."

The knight took the key from the sash of the chief of the guard, as the dwarf had directed; then taking up the ruby ring, he offered it to the maiden.

"Do as I bid you," said the dwarf, "and put it on your hand again."

The knight would have expostulated, but the Egyptian grew angry, and stretched her hand towards him, making a sign. Immediately the ruby ring slid up his finger, and he again became invisible. He tried to remove it, but it remained fast, and he had nothing to do but to submit.

Led by the dwarf, they descended the stairs, and crept stealthily along the garden. As they came near the guard-room, they heard the soldiers wondering why their chief did not return.

"I always thought harm would happen to some of us," said one of the soldiers, "ever since that Egyptian hag came into the palace. Let us go and look for them; for it grows late, and they should have been back long ago."

And, leaving the guard-room, all the soldiers came in a body into the garden, and spread themselves through it, searching for their comrades. The maiden and her attendants had crouched down in a thick clump of rose-bushes, which grew so high and broad as to quite conceal them. They remained there, until, at a loud shout, which proceeded from that part of the garden on which the little carved door opened, all the soldiers rushed thither, and they heard their cries of rage and astonishment. Then, quickly rising from their hiding-place, the maiden and the women hurried on, accompanied by the invisible knight. They passed into the deserted guard-room, and thence through many passages, until they reached the circular hall into which the knight had come on his first entrance into the palace.

"Stop here," said the Egyptian. "I must go forward and see whether the slave at the door is awake."

She stole cautiously forward, and saw the slave sitting cross-legged on the ground, his great eyes shining in the dark passage like two enormous opals. She came back grinning.

"Now I will show you something amusing," she said; and she began to draw with her 'finger in the air the outline of a gigantic lion. When she had finished, she blew on the air-drawn figure, and it took the form and color of life, and bounded forward with open jaws and fiery eyes in great leaps towards the negro, who, seeing this unexpected sight, yelled, and took to flight, rolling with incredible agility over and over on the floor like a ball.

The Egyptian shrieked with laughter, as the slave, pursued by the phantom of a lion, disappeared. Then leading forward her companions, she unlocked the little door, and they all stood outside the palace, in the street. The knight lifted the maiden upon his invisible horse, and, leading it by the bridle, followed the steps of the dwarf, who conducted them through many dark and silent streets, down to the water's edge.

As they neared the shore, they were startled by a sudden glare; and, looking up, they saw in the distance a great column of fire rising from the watch-tower of the sultan's palace; and the night wind brought to their ears the sound of the clashing of arms, and loud voices.

"We must hurry," said the dwarf; "but, first, I will make sure that we shall not be pursued."

So saying, she stooped and scraped together a handful of sand. Then she bade them enter a boat which lay near by.

The knight lifted the maiden from the horse, and carried her to the boat; for, in truth, she was so terrified that she could not have taken a step. The old nurse hobbled in after them, casting many an affrighted glance over her shoulder at the fast increasing, angry blaze; and the Egyptian took her place, standing in the stern; while the knight dipped the oars into the water, and rowed out to the open sea.

As the boat advanced, the dwarf let the sand fall, grain by grain, from her hand; and, as it fell, the water behind them turned to sand, and all the boats and galleys were buried fast in it, so that they could not be stirred. They saw, as they rowed away, a great crowd, led by the soldiers of the guard-room, come rushing down to the water's edge to pursue them. They heard their angry shouts and cries, and saw their unavailing efforts to raise the half-buried vessels.

The Egyptian turned as the last grain of sand fell from her hand, and, seating herself, composedly said,—

"Now we are safe. Lay down your oars, we do not need them."

A gentle wind sprang up as she spoke, the ruby ring sent forth its rosy light, and the young knight became visible. As he assumed his shape, the maiden raised her eyes timidly to his, intending to thank him; but, perceiving his look riveted upon her, she blushed, and turned away. As the knight looked upon her lovely face, and thought of the delight of her parents when they should receive the maiden from his hands, his eyes filled with tears of joy, and he almost forgot his own promised happiness in the thought of theirs.

Three days and three nights they floated over the sea, borne on by the gentle wind, which never changed nor died away, lighted by the sun by day, and by the rosy radiance of the ring at night. On the fourth night they saw a light far off on the water's edge, at the end, as it were, of the pathway traced by the ruddy rays.

When the dwarf saw the light, she heaved a deep sigh, and said to the knight,—

"Give me now the ring. You have no further need for it."

And the knight drew from his finger the ring, and gave it to her. Then she said to the maiden,—"Child, when you saved me from those who were about to take my life, I vowed one day to repay an equal benefit to you. Look at that light, far in the distance. It shines before your home. There, on. the shore of the sea, stand your father and your mother, with out-stretched arms, waiting to embrace you. I have kept my vow. Kiss me, my child."

The maiden pressed her sweet lips to the old Egyptian's withered cheek, but suddenly she felt upon them nothing but air. The dwarf had vanished utterly, and the rosy light also.

"Monarè! Monarè!" cried the maiden, but no voice replied. Only in the distance, from the bosom of a little white cloud, came a breath that sounded like "Farewell."

The boat sped on, wafted by the wind; and, as it approached, they saw the light higher and broader, and they could distinguish the figures of the count and the countess, surrounded by all their friends and retainers, holding high in the air torches whose waving light flashed out upon the sea, and showed the crowd of eager faces all turned upon the fast advancing boat.

As the keel grated on the shore, Walter of Ilzerley leaped from the boat, bearing the maiden, and delivered her into her parents' arms.

They wept aloud for joy as they kissed and folded to their hearts the beautiful maiden whom they had last seen as a babe in her nurse's arms; and their retainers shouted for gladness in welcome to the daughter of the house; they pressed with joyous acclaim around the knight who had rescued her from the captivity wherein she had been bound, and greeted over and over again the old nurse who had been lost to sight for so many years.

When her parents had kissed and blessed the maiden, Father Anselm advanced, and laid his hand upon her head. Then the maiden and her parents, and Walter of Ilzerley, and all around, knelt upon the shore; and the old priest lifted up his voice, and blessed the maiden, and praised and thanked God.

There was revelling at the count's castle for all that week; and not only the rich and gay, but the poor and lonely rejoiced also, for the count and countess sent out and summoned all the poor of the whole country round, and feasted them in the court-yard, for they wished the sympathy of all in their great joy and happiness. And on the seventh day the maiden was married to the knight by Father Anselm, in the chapel of the castle, before a great crowd of lords and ladies, who had assembled from all the castles far and wide. But there was none among all the ladies who could compare for beauty and gentleness and grace with the maiden, as she stood in her long white robes and snowy veil beside the knight who had delivered her from her captivity.

In the eyes of the villagers of Protogno, Christine Dele-mont was nothing more or less than a witch, a God-forsaken woman, whose life was appointed to be a bane and a terror to all who came in contact with her or with the range of her ill-omened presence. If one yielded credence to all these stories, one would have to believe tales so dark and strange of the doings at her deserted cottage, that one could not but shudder at the very name of so inhuman a woman; and many people were even found to swear that they had been eyewitnesses of Christine's mysterious and cruel doings: how they had seen her child, little Paul, beaten and dashed upon the floor of the cottage and dragged by the hair of his head about the garden. How, also, flames were seen at night-time issuing from the doors and windows of the house, and direful howlings and groanings were heard both by day and night in the woods around. And strange and appalling as were these stories, few voices were raised to deny them, or other tales as extraordinary, which were freely adduced to darken the history of Christine.

But even these wild reports might have found in the few believers, and have perished for want of evidence, had it not been for other and fresh circumstances which fanned into a fiery blaze the smouldering doubts and suspicions of the village folk.

It was late on an autumn afternoon, when the reapers, who had been toiling all day under a blazing sun, were returning from their work into the little town of Protogno. Many had taken off their broad shady hats, so that the little breeze which had sprung up with the decline of the sun might blow through their hair and cool their overheated heads. As if by one accord they filed down the main street of the town, neither halting at house or shop until they reached the marketplace, in front of which stood the Fountain of St Agnes, and whose bright and cool waters had an attraction for their parched lips which only those who, like themselves, had toiled all day long under a meridian sun, could understand. Besides, this fountain was, as it were, the village club. As the hour of six tolled from the high

THE HON. MRS GREENE
BOUND BY A SPELL

bell-tower of the church which crowned the summit of an over-shadowing hill, not only the workmen from the fields, but artisans, shopkeepers, and, above all, the village gossips assembled round the Fountain of St Agnes, which, with its shady row of trees, and comfortable benches set here and there in every nook and corner, made a most inviting resting-place; and here the village politics, the daily doings, the births, deaths, and marriages of the little town were chronicled with more or less solemnity as the importance of the cases required.

This evening the fountain, with its picturesque and quaint carvings, looked particularly tempting, for the sun, which was setting in a crimson flood of light behind the hill, had caught the market-place with its last and most lovely rays, and the fountain, the trees, and the waters tossing high up into the rose-coloured air, looked more like some painted scene in a theatre than the quiet and

every-day resort of the poor and the weary. The benches were speedily filled with those who had already quenched their thirst, their bright sickles lying at their feet on the ground, or hanging from the branches of the trees above their heads. Many were still gathered around the base of the fountain, satisfying their thirst, while a few, who could not find a place by the fountain itself, handed their tin pannikins over the heads of their neighbours into some friendly hands, which returned them again filled with the fresh water their parched throats so much coveted to taste.

But all at once, while the jest and the laugh went round, and Frau Gartmann, the queen-gossip of the town, was quizzing in a covert whisper a handsome couple who stood near the fountain, chatting playfully with each other, there was a sudden hoarse cry of horror and surprise raised amongst the crowd, and, as if to add to the theatrical appearance of the scene, a man suddenly appeared in their midst, whose blood-stained garments, blenched face, and panic-stricken eyes carried a sudden terror into the hearts of all who looked upon him.

It was no other than Silvestro Milano, a reaper like themselves, who had been out all day cutting corn in a distant field near Madeline l'Estrange's Wood. He was a brave and honest-hearted fellow, courageous as a lion, and tender-hearted as a woman, and now he stood among them with his blouse stained with gore, and hanging in ribbons from his bleeding arms; his sickle also had been dipped in blood up to its wooden handle, and he staggered, as he approached the fountain, like a drunken man. He gazed around him at first in a vacant way, and then, pointing towards the fountain, he stretched out his torn and bleeding arm. The neighbours understood his unspoken request, and instantly a score of pannikins running over with clear water were pressed upon his acceptance.

He drank deeply, and then, tottering towards a seat, sank upon it, and remained for some time in a semi-unconscious state, unable to answer the questions of those who pressed around him, and yet looking at them with an anxiety in his eyes which told of a troubled spirit within.

At last he spoke, and so great was the silence that ensued that a grasshopper on a neighbouring tree could be distinctly heard rasping out its evening call.

"I have met the accursed wolf that killed Alexandre Delemont in the forest, and I have slain it. It is now lying cold and dead in the flower-garden where I plunged this sickle into its heart."

At these words a murmur, which had been gradually rising out of the previous hush, now burst into a loud shout or yell of triumph and applause.

"Bravo, bravo, Silvestro! tell us, good friend, how did it all happen?" cried the foremost of the group, as they pressed forwards to catch his gasping efforts at speech.

"Aye, aye; give me time, give me time; for the horror of the thing is still upon me, and I fancy even now I hear the cry of the miserable child."

"What child?"

"Peace, peace! leave me a moment to recall my thoughts. Aye, it was thus that it happened. I had finished my reaping for the day, and I was weary; my back ached and my head was giddy from the long stooping under the most burning sun that ever crossed the sky; so, withdrawing under the shadow of a tree close by the Count's cottage, I sat down to rest, and presently I fell asleep. I do not know how long I slept, but I awoke feeling something soft touching the back of my hand, and then my cheek. I opened my eyes quietly, thinking perhaps a lizard or field mouse had run up my coat-sleeve, when, standing by me, I saw a little child, all dressed in white. I tell ye," cried Silvestro, raising himself up in his excitement, and almost rising to his feet as he spoke, "I tell ye, good folk, I thought it was a vision sent from Heaven. The babe was fair as wax, and beautiful as the child which the Madonna carries in her arms. Its hair, which was of the purest flaxen, hung long over its shoulders, and its eyes gazed into mine as if it sought to gain my love.

"For a moment, awaking as it were from a dream, I thought in my confusion it was our blessed Lord Himself standing once more as a child on the earth beside me—that He had a message, perhaps, to give me; but presently, seeing the boy smile and stretch out his hands to me, I shook off the foolish impression, and I cried out encouragingly, 'Eh, little one, to whom dost thou belong?'

"It smiled again, and with a clear sweet voice it answered me strangely enough, 'A Dieu.'"

Again a low sympathetic murmur rose around Silvestro, but it came chiefly from the women, and there was the sound of a dry sob not far off, followed by the words, "Go on, go on—what next?" and Silvestro, looking up, saw, through a haze of weakness, the lovely face of Marie Fedele gazing earnestly at him.

"Aye, what next?" he repeated, as if questioning himself, for a faintness was stealing over him and his mind was growing clouded and uncertain; "I cannot just now remember what came next, only I know the child, hearing a sound in the garden, turned anxiously and hurried from me, but it cannot have been many minutes, when crossing the field on my way home I heard a piercing cry. May I never hear such a cry on this earth again!" said Silvestro, as he passed his hand languidly across his forehead. "I stopped, and turning towards the cottage, I listened. There was silence for a space, and I was thinking of continuing my way home, whiner I heard the same cry once more, only this the even more bitter in its anguish, and repeated again and yet again.

"I did not hesitate now, but ran as fast as my feet could carry me towards the spot from which the sound came; and as I drew near to the garden hedge, just where a narrow path leads down across the bridge into the forest, I saw a wolf, dark, large, and terrible to look at, hurrying down this very path with something white in its mouth, which all at once I perceived to be nothing else than the child which had stood before me but a few minutes previously, smiling in the security of its innocent trust and love.

"Yes! but the sight was so pitiful, my very limbs seemed to grow weak with horror, and though I strove to ruin, my legs doubled under me like hempstalks. I know not how I ran, nor how often I stumbled in this nightmare chase, until I came on a hock of fair flaxen hair torn from the little one's glossy head and caught on a bramble at my side, and then, as it were, the strength and courage of something more powerful than myself seemed to enter into me. I stumbled no longer, but cutting through the thicket I doubled on the beast, and came, for a moment, face to face with its burning eyes and its bristling mane, while the child still drooped from the creature's mouth, and its white arm trailed along the ground."

"Ah, say no more; is it not dead?" sobbed Marie Fedele, as she laid her head on her husband's shoulder and hid her face from view.

"Have patience for a moment. When I am questioned I lose the thread of my thoughts." Once again Silvestro passed his hand across his eyes as if to hide out some vision of horror, and then he proceeded slowly.

"It turned, the great coward, as I drew my sickle from my belt, and fearing to meet me, it leaped over a low bush, and made back with haste across the wooden bridge towards the house. I saw then what I had to deal with—no common brute such as God Himself places in the forest, but one of those tailless monsters whose existence until now I had never believed in: a wicked were-wolf, with slinking steps, whose every movement filled me with disgust. Full of some strange and ever-increasing strength, I followed after it, gaining each moment on its track, though it hurried forward with ever longer and more sinuous steps. At last, driven as it were almost to bay, it took the direct path towards the cottage, and, slinking through the narrow garden gate, passed in. At ounce I saw my advantage; I closed the gate with a sudden click that sent the hasp straight into the lock, and then, unless it dashed in at the open house-door, it had no mole or possible outlet for escape. Round and round the garden I hunted it, my sharp sickle ever in my outstretched arm, until at last, with a kind of crying snarl, it dropped the child from its blood-stained jaws, and, turning with a sudden fury towards me, it sprang forward to meet me. It was its last hope, its last chance for life, and verily I gave myself up for lost; but seeing the child lie in a white heap on the gravel path, the same infant which had stood before me so lately in its purity and love, I thought of Him who carries the little lambs in His bosom, and though the beast leaped on me, and as it were wrestled with me, and though I felt its jaws snap on my shoulder and its claws tear the flesh from my arm, still the good God guided the weapon in my hand so that I struck it right home to its craven heart, and with a kind of human cry it fell backwards upon the flower-beds behind us, and then rolled over on its side, dead; aye, dead." Silvestro paused: "Aye, dead and stiff, as I shall be myself by-and-by."

It was not a murmur, but a loud yell of stunning overpowering applause which followed on the recital of Silvestro's victory; but he motioned to them to be quiet, and taking up his story from where he had left off, he continued—

"When I saw that the beast was dead, and would no more rise to attack us, I leaped over its carcase, and stepping across a bed of roses and lavender, I came to the spot where the child still lay, to all appearances dead. I stooped to raise it in my arms, but as I did so I heard behind me a loud, sharp cry of pain or anger or surprise, and looking up, I saw Christine Delemont rushing out of the cottage towards the child; she pushed me aside with a frantic gesture, and when I would have stretched out my arm to stay her, she rushed past me and herself lifted up the little one, whose head hung quite loosely to one side, and whose white frock was all stained with blood.

"I know not whether it was a wild despair or a fierce anger or a mad fit which had come over the woman, but Christine screamed and beat herself on her breast and tore her hair from her head, and at length she rushed into the house with the boy in her arms, and the door slammed behind her in my face, in my very face! and though I sought to follow after her, she either did not or would not hear me. I waited in the garden and paced up and down the paths till I grew weak from loss of blood. It was all in vain. At last I turned back and tapped at a window, the curtain of which was drawn. I felt too weak to return without a glass of wine or something wherewith to strengthen myself ere I ventured on the long walk home, but I could obtain no answer; only just as I moved aside, I heard a voice inside the room raised as it were in bitter anguish, and crying aloud, 'Speak, speak, in the name of God, speak, child, speak!' And then, like as it were a sigh or a sound of some far-off voice, I heard the words 'A Dieu,' and I knew it was the babe I had seen in the wood, and I offered up thanks that it still lived."

"Now, Heaven be praised!" cried Marie Fedele; "for if ever there was an angel on earth, it is that child."

"Aye," cried Frau Gartmann, "and if ever there was a foul witch, it is Christine Delemont. From the day she entered that cottage until now, death and destruction have followed in her path."

"Yes," cried a third, "she is a witch, and worse than a witch. It is well known that she keeps that miserable child as a decoy to entice those she hates into her power, and afterwards to wreak her vengeance on them. Ah, the wretch! She ought to be shot through the heart herself; the were-wolf will not cease to haunt the town till her own heart's blood has been spilled."

"How so, Janette?" cried several voices in the crowd; "Did not Silvestro slay it with his sickle?"

"Aye, aye, he slew the shadow, but the real wolf is bound up in the heart of that wicked woman, and, believe me, she will never cease to revenge herself on all who come within her reach until the sickle is plunged into her own bosom. Let those who do not know what a werewolf is, ask me," cried Janette Chaudron; "I can tell them all about it."

"Then how came it to pass that Christine called on God in her anguish? Didst not thou say so, good Silvestro?" said Marie Fedele, her voice tremulous with anger; but if any explanation was given to her question it was lost in the murmur of the crowd, for Silvestro Milano, while speaking, had suddenly fainted away upon the bench, and as his tall son Pierre and others lifted him up tenderly in their arms, it was noticed how, all the time he had been relating his adventure, a pool of blood had been gathering on the ground at his feet.

THE WOLF

GUY DE MAUPASSANT

This is what the old Marquis d'Arville told us after St. Hubert's dinner at the house of the Baron des Ravels.

We had killed a stag that day. The marquis was the only one of the guests who had not taken part in this chase. He never hunted.

During that long repast we had talked about hardly anything but the slaughter of animals. The ladies themselves were interested in bloody and exaggerated tales, and the orators imitated the attacks and the combats of men against beasts, raised their arms, romanced in a thundering voice.

M. d'Arville talked well, in a certain flowery, high-sounding, but effective style. He must have told this story frequently, for he told it fluently, never hesitating for words, choosing them with skill to make his description vivid.

Gentlemen, I have never hunted, neither did my father, nor my grandfather, nor my great-grandfather. This last was the son of a man who hunted more than all of you put together. He died in 1764. I will tell you the story of his death.

His name was Jean. He was married, father of that child who became my great-grandfather, and he lived with his younger brother, Francois d'Arville, in our castle in Lorraine, in the midst of the forest.

Francois d'Arville had remained a bachelor for love of the chase.

They both hunted from one end of the year to the other, without stopping and seemingly without fatigue. They loved only hunting, understood nothing else, talked only of that, lived only for that.

They had at heart that one passion, which was terrible and inexorable. It consumed them, had completely absorbed them, leaving room for no other thought.

They had given orders that they should not be interrupted in the chase for any reason whatever. My great-grandfather was born while his father was following a fox, and Jean d'Arville did not stop the chase, but exclaimed: "The deuce! The rascal might have waited till after the view—halloo!"

His brother Franqois was still more infatuated. On rising he went to see the dogs, then the horses, then he shot little birds about the castle until the time came to hunt some large game.

In the countryside they were called M. le Marquis and M. le Cadet, the nobles then not being at all like the chance nobility of our time, which wishes to establish an hereditary hierarchy in titles; for the son of a marquis is no more a count, nor the son of a viscount a baron, than a son of a general is a colonel by birth. But the contemptible vanity of today finds profit in that arrangement.

My ancestors were unusually tall, bony, hairy, violent and vigorous. The younger, still taller than the older, had a voice so strong that, according to a legend of which he was proud, all the leaves of the forest shook when he shouted.

When they were both mounted to set out hunting, it must have been a superb sight to see those two giants straddling their huge horses.

Now, toward the midwinter of that year, 1764, the frosts were excessive, and the wolves became ferocious.

They even attacked belated peasants, roamed at night outside the houses, howled from sunset to sunrise, and robbed the stables.

And soon a rumor began to circulate. People talked of a colossal wolf with gray fur, almost white, who had eaten two children, gnawed off a woman's arm, strangled all the watch dogs in the district, and even come without fear into the farmyards. The people in the houses affirmed that they had felt his breath, and that it made the flame of the lights flicker. And soon a panic ran through all the province. No one dared go out any more after nightfall. The darkness seemed haunted by the image of the beast.

The brothers d'Arville determined to find and kill him, and several times they brought together all the gentlemen of the country to a great hunt.

They beat the forests and searched the coverts in vain; they never met him. They killed wolves, but not that one. And every night after a battle the beast, as if to avenge himself, attacked some traveller or killed some one's cattle, always far from the place where they had looked for him.

Finally, one night he stole into the pigpen of the Chateau d'Arville and ate the two fattest pigs.

The brothers were roused to anger, considering this attack as a direct insult and a defiance. They took their strong bloodhounds, used to pursue dangerous animals, and they set off to hunt, their hearts filled with rage.

From dawn until the hour when the enpurpled sun descended behind the great naked trees, they beat the woods without finding anything.

At last, furious and disgusted, both were returning, walking their horses along a lane bordered with hedges, and they marvelled that their skill as huntsmen should be baffled by this wolf, and they were suddenly seized with a mysterious fear.

The elder said:

"That beast is not an ordinary one. You would say it had a mind like a man."

The younger answered:

"Perhaps we should have a bullet blessed by our cousin, the bishop, or pray some priest to pronounce the words which are needed."

Then they were silent.

Jean continued:

"Look how red the sun is. The great wolf will do some harm to-night."

He had hardly finished speaking when his horse reared; that of Franqois began to kick. A large thicket covered with dead leaves opened before them, and a mammoth beast, entirely gray, jumped up and ran off through the wood.

Both uttered a kind of grunt of joy, and bending over the necks of their heavy horses, they threw them forward with an impulse from all their body, hurling them on at such a pace, urging them, hurrying them away, exciting them so with voice and with gesture and with spur that the experienced riders seemed to be carrying the heavy beasts between 4 their thighs and to bear them off as if they were flying.

Thus they went, plunging through the thickets, dashing across the beds of streams, climbing the hillsides, descending the gorges, and blowing the horn as loud as they could to attract their people and the dogs.

And now, suddenly, in that mad race, my ancestor struck his forehead against an enormous branch which split his skull; and he fell dead on the ground, while his frightened horse took himself off, disappearing in the gloom which enveloped the woods.

The younger d'Arville stopped quick, leaped to the earth, seized his brother in his arms, and saw that the brains were escaping from the wound with the blood.

Then he sat down beside the body, rested the head, disfigured and red, on his knees, and waited, regarding the immobile face of his elder brother. Little by little a fear possessed him, a strange fear which he had never felt before, the fear of the dark, the fear of loneliness, the fear of the deserted wood, and the fear also of the weird wolf who had just killed his brother to avenge himself upon them both.

The gloom thickened; the acute cold made the trees crack. Francois got up, shivering, unable to remain there longer, feeling himself growing faint. Nothing was to be heard, neither the voice of the dogs nor the sound of the horns-all was silent along the invisible horizon; and this mournful silence of the frozen night had something about it terrific and strange.

He seized in his immense hands the great body of Jean, straightened it, and laid it across the saddle to carry it back to the chateau; then he went on his way softly, his mind troubled as if he were in a stupor, pursued by horrible and fear-giving images.

And all at once, in the growing darkness a great shape crossed his path. It was the beast. A shock of terror shook the hunter; something cold, like a drop of water, seemed to glide down his back, and, like a monk haunted of the devil, he made a great sign of the cross, dismayed at this abrupt return of the horrible prowler. But his eyes fell again on the inert body before him, and passing abruptly from fear to anger, he shook with an indescribable rage.

Then he spurred his horse and rushed after the wolf.

He followed it through the copses, the ravines, and the tall trees, traversing woods which he no longer recognized, his eyes fixed on the white speck which fled before him through the night.

His horse also seemed animated by a force and strength hitherto unknown. It galloped straight ahead with outstretched neck, striking against trees, and rocks, the head and the feet of the dead man thrown across the saddle. The limbs tore out his hair; the brow, beating the huge trunks, spattered them with blood; the spurs tore their ragged coats of bark. Suddenly the beast and the horseman issued from the forest and rushed into a valley, just as the moon appeared above the mountains. The valley here was stony, inclosed by enormous rocks.

Francois then uttered a yell of joy which the echoes repeated like a peal of thunder, and he leaped from his horse, his cutlass in his hand.

The beast, with bristling hair, the back arched, awaited him, its eyes gleaming like two stars. But, before beginning battle, the strong hunter, seizing his brother, seated him on a rock, and, placing stones under his head, which was no more than a mass of blood, he shouted in the ears as if he was talking to a deaf man: "Look, Jean; look at this!"

Then he attacked the monster. He felt himself strong enough to overturn a mountain, to bruise stones in his hands. The beast tried to bite him, aiming for his stomach; but he had seized the fierce animal by the neck, without even using his weapon, and he strangled it gently, listening to the cessation of breathing in its throat and the beatings of its heart. He laughed, wild with joy, pressing closer and closer his formidable embrace, crying in a delirium of joy, "Look, Jean, look!" All resistance ceased; the body of the wolf became limp. He was dead.

Franqois took him up in his arms and carried him to the feet of the elder brother, where he laid him, repeating, in a tender voice: "There, there, there, my little Jean, see him!"

Then he replaced on the saddle the two bodies, one upon the other, and rode away.

He returned to the chateau, laughing and crying, like Gargantua at the birth of Pantagruel, uttering shouts of triumph, and boisterous with joy as he related the death of the beast, and grieving and tearing his beard in telling of that of his brother.

And often, later, when he talked again of that day, he would say, with tears in his eyes: "If only poor Jean could have seen me strangle the beast, he would have died content, that I am sure!"

The widow of my ancestor inspired her orphan son with that horror of the chase which has transmitted itself from father to son as far down as myself.

The Marquis d'Arville was silent. Some one asked:

"That story is a legend, isn't it?"

And the story teller answered:

"I swear to you that it is true from beginning to end."

Then a lady declared, in a little, soft voice

"All the same, it is fine to have passions like that."

THE WHITE WOLF
OF KOSTOPCHIN

SIR GILBERT CAMPBELL

A wide sandy expanse of country, flat and uninteresting in appearance, with a great staring whitewashed house standing in the midst of wide fields of cultivated land; whilst far away were the low sand hills and pine forests to be met with in the district of Lithuania, in Russian Poland. Not far from the great white house was the village in which the serfs dwelt, with the large bakehouse and the public bath which are invariably to be found in all Russian villages, however humble. The fields were negligently cultivated, the hedges broken down and the fences in bad repair, shattered agricultural implements had been carelessly flung aside in remote corners, and the whole estate showed the want of the superintending eye of an energetic master. The great white house was no better looked after, the garden was an utter wilderness, great patches of plaster had fallen from the walls, and many of the Venetian shutters were almost off the hinges. Over all was the dark lowering sky of a Russian autumn, and there were no signs of life to be seen, save a few peasants lounging idly towards the *vodki* ship, and a gaunt halt-starved cat creeping stealthily abroad in quest of a meal.

The estate, which was known by the name of Kostopchin, was the property of Paul Sergevitch, a gentleman of means, and the most discontented man in Russian Poland. Like most wealthy Muscovites , he had traveled much, and had spent the gold which had been amassed by serf labor, like water, in all the dissolute revelries of the capitals of Europe. Paul's figure was as well known in the boudoirs of the *demi mondaines* as his face was familiar at the public gaming tables. He appeared to have no thought for the future, but only to live in the excitement of the mad career of dissipation which he was pursuing. His means, enormous as they were, were all forestalled, and he was continually sending to his intendant for fresh supplies of money. His fortune would not have long held out against the constant inroads that were being made upon it, when an unexpected circumstance took place which stopped his career like a flash of lightning. This was a fatal duel, in which a young man of great promise, the son of the prime minister of the country in which he then resided, fell by his hand. Representatives were made to the Tsar, and Paul Sergevitch was recalled, and, after receiving a severe reprimand was ordered to return to his estates in Lithuania. Horribly discontented, yet not daring to disobey the Imperial mandate, Paul buried himself at Kostopchin, a place he had not visited since his boyhood. At first he endeavored to interest himself in the workings of the vast estate; but agriculture had no charm for him, and the only result was that he quarreled with and dismissed his German intendant, replacing him by an old serf, Michal Vassilitch, who had been his father's valet. Then he took to wandering about the country, gun in hand, and upon his return home would sit moodily drinking brandy and smoking innumerable cigarettes, as he cursed his lord and master, the emperor, for consigning him to such a course of dullness and *ennui*. For a couple of years he led this aimless life, and at last, hardly knowing the reason for so doing, he married the daughter of a neighboring landed proprietor. The marriage was a most unhappy one; the girl had really never cared for Paul, but had married him in obedience to her father's mandates, and the man, whose temper was always brutal and violent, treated her, after a brief interval of contemptuous indifference, with savage cruelty. After three years the unhappy woman expired, leaving behind her two children—a boy, Alexis, and a girl, Katrina. Paul treated his wife's death with the most perfect indifference; but he did not put any one in her place. He was very fond of the little Katrina, but did not take much notice of the boy, and resumed his lonely wanderings about the country with dog and gun. Five years had passed since the death of his wife. Alexis was a fine, healthy boy of seven, whilst Katrina was some eighteen months younger. Paul was lighting one of his eternal cigarettes at the door of his house, when the little girl came running up to him.

"You bad, wicked papa," said she. "How is it that you have never brought me the pretty gray squirrels that you promised I should have the next time you went to the forest?"

"Because I have never yet been able to find any, my treasure," returned her father, taking up his child in his arms and half smothering her with kisses. "Because I have not found them yet, my golden queen; but I am bound to find Ivanovitch, the poacher, smoking about the woods, and if he can't show me where they are, no one can."

"Ah, little father," broke in old Michal, using the term of address with which a Russian of humble position usually accosts his superior; "Ah, little father, take care; you will go to those woods once too often."

"Do you think I am afraid of Ivanovitch?" returned his master, with a coarse laugh. "Why, he and I are the best of friends; at any rate, if he robs me, he does so openly, and keeps other poachers away from my woods."

"It is not of Ivanovitch that I am thinking," answered the old man. "But oh! Gospodin, do not go into these dark solitudes; there are terrible tales told about them, of witches that dance in the moonlight, of strange, shadowy forms that are seen amongst the trunks of the tall pines, and of whispered voices that tempt the listeners to eternal perdition."

Again the rude laugh of the lord of the manor rang out, as Paul observed, "If you go on addling your brain, old man, with these nearly half-forgotten legends, I shall have to look out for a new intendant."

"But I was not thinking of these fearful creatures only," returned Michal, crossing himself piously. "It was against the wolves that I meant to warn you."

"Oh, father, dear, I am frightened now," whimpered little Katrina, hiding her head on her father's shoulder. "Wolves are such cruel, wicked things."

"See there, graybearded dotard," cried Paul, furiously, "you have terrified this sweet angel by your farrago of lies; besides, who ever heard of wolves so early as this? You are dreaming, Michal Vassilitch, or have taken your morning dram of vodki too strong."

"AS I hope for future happiness," answered the old man, solemnly, "as I came through the marsh last night from Kosma the herdsman's cottage—you know, my lord, that he has been bitten by a viper, and is seriously ill—as I came through the marsh, I repeat, I saw something like sparks of fire in the clump of alders on the right-hand side. I was anxious to know what they could be, and cautiously moved a little nearer, recommending my soul to the protection of Saint Vladamir. I had not gone a couple of paces when a wild howl came that chilled the very marrow of my bones, and a pack of some ten or a dozen wolves, gaunt and famished as you see them, my lord, in the winter, rushed out. At their head was a white she-wolf, as big as any of the male ones, with gleaming tusks and a pair of yellow eyes that blazed with lurid fire. I had round my neck a crucifix that had been given me by the priest of Streletza, and the savage beasts knew this and broke away across the marsh, sending up the mud and water in showers in the air; but the white she-wolf, little father, circled round me three times, as though endeavoring to find some place from which to attack me. Three times she did this, and then, with a snap of her teeth and a howl of impotent malice, she galloped away some fifty yards and sat down, watching my every movement with her fiery eyes. I did not delay any longer in so dangerous a spot, as you may well imagine, Gospodin, but walked hurriedly home, crossing myself at every step; but, as I am a living man, that white devil followed me the whole distance, keeping fifty paces in the rear, and every now and then licking her lips with a sound that made my flesh creep. When I got to the last fence before you come to the house I raised up my voice and shouted for the dogs, and soon I heard the deep bay of Troska and Bransköe as they came bounding towards me. The white devil heard it, too, and, giving a high bound into the air, she uttered a loud howl of disappointment, and trotted back leisurely towards the marsh."

"But why did you not set the dogs after her?" asked Paul, interested, in spite of himself, at the old man's narrative. "In the open Troska and Bransköe would run down any wolf that ever set foot to the ground in Lithuania."

"I tried to do so, little father," answered the old man, solemnly; "but directly they got up to the spot where the beast had executed her last devilish gambol, they put their tails between their legs and ran back to the house as fast as their legs could carry them."

"Strange," muttered Paul, thoughtfully, "that is, if it is

truth and not vodki that is speaking."

"My lord," returned the old man, reproachfully, "man and boy, I have served you and my lord your father for fifty years, and no one can say that they ever saw Michal Vassilitch the worse for liquor."

'No one doubts that you are a sly old thief, Michal," returned his master, with his coarse, jarring laugh; "but for all that, your long stories of having been followed by white wolves won't prevent me from going to the forest to-day. A couple of good buckshot cartridges will break any spell, though I don't think that the she-wolf, if she existed anywhere than in your own imagination, has anything to do with magic. Don't be frightened, Katrina, my pet; you shall have a fine white wolf skin to put your feet on, if what this old fool says is right."

"Michal is not a fool," pouted the child, "and it is very wicked of you to call him so. I don't want any nasty wolf skins, I want the gray squirrels."

And you shall have them, my precious," returned her father, setting her down upon the ground. "Be a good girl, and I will not be long away."

"Father," said the little Alexis, suddenly, "let me go with you. I should like to see you kill a wolf, and then I should know how to do so, when I grow older and taller."

"Pshaw," returned his father, irritably. "Boys are always in the way. Take the lad away, Michal; don't you see that he is worrying his sweet little sister?"

"No, no, he does not worry me at all," answered the impetuous little lady, as she flew to her brother and covered him with kisses. "Michal, you shan't take him away, do you hear?"

"There, there, leave the children together," returned Paul, as he shouldered his gun, and kissing the tips of his fingers to Katrina, stepped away rapidly in the direction of the dark pine woods. Paul walked on, humming the fragment of an air that he had heard in a very different place many years ago. A strange feeling of elation crept over him, very different to the false excitement which his solitary drinking bouts were wont to produce. A change seemed to have come over his whole life, the skies looked brighter, the *spiculæ* of the pine trees of a more vivid green, and the landscape seemed to have lost that dull cloud of depression which had for years appeared to hang over it. And beneath all this exaltation of the mind, beneath all this unlooked-for promise of a more happy future, lurked a heavy, inexplicable feeling of a power to come, a something without form or shape, and yet the more terrible because it was shrouded by that thick veil which conceals from the eyes of the soul the strange fantastic designs of the dwellers beyond the line of earthly influences.

There were no signs of the poacher, and wearied with searching for him, Paul made the woods reëcho with his name. The great dog, Troska, which had followed his master, looked up wistfully into his face, and at a second repetition of the name "Ivanovitch," uttered a long plaintive howl, and then, looking round at Paul as though entreating him to follow, moved slowly ahead towards a denser portion of the forest. A little mystified at the hound's unusual proceedings, Paul followed, keeping his gun ready to fire at the least sign of danger. He thought that he knew the forest well, but the dog led the way to a portion which he never remembered to have visited before. He had got away from the pine trees now, and had entered a dense thicket formed of stunted oaks and hollies. The great dog kept only a yard or so ahead; his lips were drawn back, showing the strong white fangs, the hair upon his neck and back was bristling, and his tail firmly pressed between his hind legs. Evidently the animal was in a state of the most extreme terror, and yet it proceeded bravely forward. Struggling through the dense thicket, Paul suddenly found himself in an open space of some ten or twenty yards in diameter. At one end of it was a slimy pool, into the waters of which several strange-looking reptiles glided as the man and dog made their appearance. Almost in the center of the opening was a shattered stone cross, and at its base lay a dark heap, close to which Troska stopped, and again raising his head, uttered a long melancholy howl. For an instant or two, Paul gazed hesitatingly at the shapeless heap that lay beneath the cross, and then, mustering up all his courage, he stepped forwards and bent anxiously over it. Once glance was enough, for he recognized the body of Ivanovitch the poacher, hideously mangled. With a cry of surprise, he turned over the body and shuddered as he gazed upon the terrible injuries that had been inflicted. The unfortunate man had evidently been attacked by some savage beast, for there were marks of teeth upon the throat, and the jugular vein had been almost torn out. The breast of the corpse had been torn open, evidently by long sharp claws, and there was a gaping orifice upon the left side, round which the blood had formed in a thick coagulated patch. The only animals to be found in the forests of Russia capable of inflicting such wounds are the bear or the wolf, and the question as to the class of the assailant was easily settled by a glance at the dank ground, which showed the prints of a wolf so entirely different from the plantegrade traces of the bear.

"Savage brutes," muttered Paul. "So, after all, there may have been some truth in Michal's story, and the old idiot may for once in his life have spoken the truth. Well, it is no concern of mine, and if a fellow chooses to wander about the woods at night to kill my game, instead of remaining in his own hovel, he must take his chance. The strange thing is that the brutes have not eaten him, though they have mauled him so terribly."

He turned away as he spoke, intending to return home and send out some of the serfs to bring in the body of the unhappy man, when his eye was caught by a small white object, hanging from a bramble bush near the pond. He made towards the spot, and taking up the object, examined it curiously. It was a tuft of coarse white hair, evidently belonging to some animal."

"A wolf's hair, or I am much mistaken," muttered Paul, pressing the hair between his fingers, and then applying it to his nose. "And from its color, I should think that it belonged to the white lady who so terribly alarmed old Michal on the occasion of his night walk through the marsh."

Paul found it no easy task to retrace his steps towards those parts of the forest with which he was acquainted, and Troska seemed unable to render him the slightest assistance, but followed moodily behind. Many times Paul found his way blocked by impenetrable thicket or dangerous quagmire, and during his many wanderings he had the ever-present sensation that there was a something close to him, an invisible something, a noiseless something, but for all that a presence which moved as he advanced, and halted as he stopped in vain to listen. The certainty that an impalpable thing of some shape or other was close at hand grew so strong, that as the short autumn day began to close, and darker shadows to fall between the trunks of the lofty trees, it made him hurry on at his utmost speed. At length, when he had grown almost mad with terror, he suddenly came upon a path he knew, and with a feeling of intense relief, he stepped briskly forward in the direction of Kostopchin. As he left the forest and came into the open country, a faint wail seemed to ring through the darkness; but Paul's nerves had been so much shaken that he did not know whether this was an actual fact or only the offspring of his own excited fancy. As he crossed the neglected lawn that lay in front of the house, old Michal came rushing out of the house with terror convulsing every feature.

"Oh, my lord, my lord!" gasped he, "is not this too terrible?"

"Nothing has happened to my Katrina?" cried the father, a sudden sickly feeling of terror passing through his heart.

"No, no, the little lady is quite safe, thanks to the Blessed Virgin and Saint Alexander of Nevskoi," returned Michal; "but oh, my lord, poor Marta, the herd's daughter—"

"Well, what of the slut?" demanded Paul, for now that his momentary fear for the safety of his daughter had passed away, he had but little sympathy to spare for so insignificant a creature as a serf girl.

"I told you that Kosma was dying," answered Michal. "Well, Marta went across the marsh this afternoon to fetch the priest, but alas! she never came back."

"What detained her, then?" asked his master.

"One of the neighbors, going in to see how Kosma was getting on, found the poor old man dead; his face was terribly contorted, and he was half in the bed, and half out, as though he had striven to reach the door. The man ran to the village to give the alarm, and as the men returned to the herdsman's hut, they found the body of Marta in a thicket by the clump of alders on the marsh."

"Her body—she was dead then?" asked Paul.

"Dead, my lord; killed by wolves," answered the old man. "And oh, my lord, it is too horrible, her breast was horribly lacerated, and her heart had been taken out and eaten, for it was nowhere to be found."

Paul started, for the horrible mutilation of the body of Ivanovitch the poacher occurred to his recollection.

"And, my lord," continued the old man, "this is not all;

on a bush close by was this tuft of hair," and, as he spoke, he took it from a piece of paper in which it was wrapped and handed it to his master.

Paul took it and recognized a similar tuft of hair to that which he had seen upon the bramble bush beside the shattered cross.

"Surely, my lord," continued Michal, not heeding his master's look of surprise, "you will have out men and dogs to hunt down this terrible creature, or, better still, send for the priest and holy water, for I have my doubts whether the creature belongs to this earth."

Paul shuddered, and, after a short pause, he told Michal of the ghastly end of Ivanovitch the poacher.

The old man listened with the utmost excitement, crossing himself repeatedly, and muttering invocations to the Blessed Virgin and the saints every instant; but his master would no longer listen to him, and, ordering him to place brandy on the table, sat drinking moodily until daylight.

The next day a fresh horror awaited the inhabitants of Kostopchin. An old man, a confirmed drunkard, had staggered out of the vodki shop with the intention of returning home; three hours later he was found at a turn of the road, horribly scratched and mutilated, with the same gaping orifice in the left side of the breast, from which the heart had been forcibly torn out.

Three several times in the course of the week the same ghastly tragedy occurred—a little child, an able-bodied laborer, and an old woman, were all found with the same terrible marks of mutilation upon them, and in every case the same tuft of white hair was found in the immediate vicinity of the bodies. A frightful panic ensued, and an excited crowd of serfs surrounded the house at Kostopchin, calling upon their master, Paul Sergevitch, to save them from the fiend that had been let loose upon them, and shouting out various remedies, which they insisted upon being carried into effect at once.

Paul felt a strange disinclination to adopt any active measures. A certain feeling which he could not account for urged him to remain quiescent; but the Russian serf when suffering under an access of superstitious terror is a dangerous person to deal with, and, with extreme reluctance, Paul Sergevitch issued instructions for a thorough search through the estate, and a general *battue* of the pine woods.

The army of beaters convened by Michal was ready with the first dawn of sunrise, and formed a strange and almost grotesque-looking assemblage, armed with rusty old firelocks, heavy bludgeons, and scythes fastened on to the end of long poles. Paul, with his double-barreled gun thrown across his shoulder and a keen hunting knife thrust into his belt, marched at the head of the serfs, accompanied by the two great hounds, Troska and Bransköe. Every nook and corner of the hedgerows were examined, and the little outlying clumps were thoroughly searched, but without success; and at last a circle was formed round the larger portion of the forest, and with loud shouts, blowing of horns, and beating of copper cooking utensils, the crowd of eager serfs pushed their way through the brushwood. Frightened birds flew up, whirring through the pine branches; hares and rabbits darted from their hiding places behind tufts and hummocks of grass, and skurried away in the utmost terror. Occasionally a roe deer rushed through the thicket, or a wild boar burst through the thin lines of beaters, but no signs of wolves were to be seen. The circle grew narrower and yet more narrow, when all at once a wild shriek and a confused murmur of voices echoed through the pine trees. All rushed to the spot, and a young lad was discovered weltering in his blood and terribly mutilated, though life still lingered in the mangled frame. A few drops of vodki were poured down the throat, and he managed to gasp out that the white wolf had sprung upon him suddenly, and, throwing him to the ground, had commenced tearing at the flesh over his heart. He would inevitably have been killed, had not the animal quitted him, alarmed by the approach of the other beaters.

"The beast ran into that thicket," gasped the boy, and then once more relapsed into a state on insensibility.

But the words of the wounded boy had been eagerly passed round, and a hundred different propositions were made.

"Set fire to the thicket," exclaimed one.

"Fire a volley into it," suggested another.

"A bold dash in, and trample the beast's life out," shouted a third.

The first proposal was agreed to, and a hundred eager hands collected dried sticks and leaves, and then a light was kindled. Just as the fire was about to be applied, a soft, sweet voice issued from the center of the thicket.

"Do not set fire to the forest, my dear friends; give me time to come out. Is it not enough for me to have been frightened to death by that awful creature?"

All started back in amazement, and Paul felt a strange, sudden thrill pass through his heart as those soft musical accents fell upon his ear.

There was a light rustling in the brushwood, and then a vision suddenly appeared, which filled the souls of the beholders with surprise. As the bushes divided, a fair woman, wrapped in a mantle of soft white fur, with a fantastically shaped traveling cap of green velvet upon her head, stood before them. She was exquisitely fair, and her long Titian red hair hung in disheveled masses over her shoulders.

"My good man," began she, with a certain tinge of aristocratic hauteur in her voice, "is your master here?"

As moved by a spring, Paul stepped forward and mechanically raised his cap.

"I am Paul Sergevitch," said he, "and these woods are on my estate of Kostopchin. A fearful wolf has been committing a series of terrible devastations upon my people, and we have been endeavoring to hunt it down. A boy whom he has just wounded says that he ran into the thicket from which you have just emerged, to the surprise of us all."

"I know," answered the lady, fixing her clear, steel-blue eyes keenly upon Paul's face. "The terrible beast rushed past me, and dived into a large cavity in the earth in the very center of the thicket. It was a huge white wolf, and I greatly feared that it would devour me."

"Ho, my men," cried Paul, "take spade and mattock, and dig out the monster, for she has come to the end of her tether at last. Madam, I do not know what chance has conducted you to this wild solitude, but the hospitality of Kostopchin is at your disposal, and I will, with your permission, conduct you there as soon as this scourge of the countryside has been dispatched."

He offered his hand with some remains of his former courtesy, but started back with an expression of horror on his face.

"Blood," cried he; "why, madam, your hand and fingers are stained with blood."

A faint color rose to the lady's cheek, but it died away in an instant as she answered, with a faint smile:—

"The dreadful creature was all covered with blood, and I suppose I must have stained my hands against the bushes through which it had passed, when I parted them in order to escape from the fiery death with which you threatened me."

There was a ring of suppressed irony in her voice, and Paul felt his eyes drop before the glance of those cold steel-blue eyes. Meanwhile, urged to the utmost exertion by their fears, the serfs plied spade and mattock with the utmost vigor. The cavity was speedily enlarged, but, when a depth of eight feet had been attained, it was found to terminate in a little burrow not large enough to admit a rabbit, much less a creature of the white wolf's size. There were none of the tufts of white hair which had hitherto been always found beside the bodies of the victims, nor did that peculiar rank odor which always indicates the presence of wild animals hang about the spot.

The superstitious Muscovites crossed themselves, and scrambled out of the hole with grotesque alacrity. The mysterious disappearance of the monster which had committed such frightful ravages had cast a chill over the hearts of the ignorant peasants, and, unheeding the shouts of their master, they left the forest, which seemed to be overcast with the gloom of some impending calamity.

"Forgive the ignorance of these boors, madam," said Paul, when he found himself alone with the strange lady, "and permit me to escort you to my poor house, for you must have need of rest and refreshment, and——"

Here Paul checked himself abruptly, and a dark flush of embarrassment passed over his face.

"And," said the lady, with the same faint smile, "and you are dying with curiosity to know how I suddenly made my appearance from a thicket in your forest. You say that you are the lord of Kostopchin; then you are Paul Sergevitch, and should surely know how the ruler of Holy Russia takes upon himself to interfere with the doings of his children?"

"You know me, then?" exclaimed Paul, in some surprise.

"Yes, I have lived in foreign lands, as you have, and have heard your name often. Did you not break the bank at

Blankburg? Did you not carry off Isola Menuti, the dancer, from a host of competitors; and, as a last instance of my knowledge, shall I recall to your memory a certain morning, on a sandy shore, with two men facing each other pistol in hand, the one young, fair, and boyish-looking, hardly twenty-two years of age, the other—"

"Hush!" exclaimed Paul, hoarsely; "you evidently know me, but who in the fiend's name are you?"

"Simply a woman who once moved in society and read the papers, and who is now a hunted fugitive."

"A fugitive!" returned Paul, hotly; "who dare to persecute you?"

The lady moved a little closer to him, and then whispered in his ear:—

"The police!"

"The police!" repeated Paul, stepping back a pace or two. "The police!"

"Yes, Paul Sergevitch, the police," returned the lady, "that body at the mention of which it is said the very Emperor trembles as he sits in his gilded chambers in the Winter Palace. Yes, I have had the imprudence to speak my mind too freely, and—well, you know what women have to dread who fall into the hands of the police in Holy Russia. To avoid such infamous degradations I fled, accompanied by a faithful domestic. I fled in hopes of gaining the frontier, but a few versts from here a body of mounted police rode up. My poor old servant had the imprudence to resist, and was shot dead. Half wild with terror I fled into the forest, and wandered about until I heard the noise your serfs made in the beating of the woods. I thought it was the police, who had organized a search for me, and I crept into the thicket for the purpose of concealment. The rest you know. And now, Paul Sergevitch, tell me whether you dare give shelter to a proscribed fugitive such as I am."

"Madam," returned Paul, gazing into the clear-cut features before him, glowing with the animation of the recital, "Kostopchin is ever open to misfortune—and beauty," added he, with a bow.

"Ah!" cried the lady, with a laugh in which there was something sinister; "I expect that misfortune would knock at your door for a long time, if it was unaccompanied by beauty. However, I thank you, and will accept your hospitality; but if evil come upon you, remember that I am not to be blamed."

"You will be safe enough at Kostopchin," returned Paul. "The police won't trouble their heads about me; they know that since the Emperor drove me to lead this hideous existence, politics have no charm for me, and that the brandy bottle is the only charm of my life."

"Dear me," answered the lady, eyeing him uneasily, "a morbid drunkard, are you? Well, as I am half perished with cold, suppose you take me to Kostopchin; you will be conferring a favor on me, and will get back all the sooner to your favorite brandy."

She placed her hand upon Paul's arm as she spoke, and mechanically he led the way to the great solitary white house. The few servants betrayed no astonishment at the appearance of the lady, for some of the serfs on their way back to the village had spread the report of the sudden appearance of the mysterious stranger; besides, they were not accustomed to question the acts of their somewhat arbitrary master.

Alexis and Katrina had gone to bed, and Paul and his guest sat down to a hastily improvised meal.

"I am no great eater," remarked the lady, as she played with the food before her; and Paul noticed with surprise that scarcely a morsel passed her lips, though she more than once filled and emptied a goblet of the champagne which had been opened in honor of her arrival.

"So it seems," remarked he; "and I do not wonder, for the food in this benighted hole is not what either you or I have been accustomed to."

"Oh, it does well enough," returned the lady, carelessly. "And now, if you have such a thing as a woman in the establishment, you can let her show me to my room, for I am nearly dead for want of sleep."

Paul struck a hand bell that stood on the table beside him, and the stranger rose from her seat, and with a brief "Good night," was moving towards the door, when the old man Michal suddenly made his appearance on the threshold. The aged intendant started backwards as though to avoid a heavy blow, and his fingers at once sought for the crucifix which he wore suspended round his neck, and on whose protection he relied to shield him from the powers of darkness.

"Blessed Virgin!" he exclaimed. "Holy Saint Radislas protect me, where have I seen her before?"

The lady took no notice of the old man's evident terror, but passed away down the echoing corridor.

The old man now timidly approached his master, who, after swallowing a glass of brandy, had drawn his chair up to the stove, and was gazing moodily at its polished surface.

"My lord," said Michal, venturing to touch his master's shoulder, "is that the lady that you found in the forest?"

"Yes," returned Paul, a smile breaking out over his face; "she is very beautiful, is she not?"

"Beautiful!" repeated Michal, crossing himself, "she may have beauty, but it is that of a demon. Where have I seen her before?—where have I seen those shining teeth and those cold eyes? She is not like any one here, and I have never been ten versts from Kostopchin in my life. I am utterly bewildered. Ah, I have it, the dying herdsman—save the mark! Gospodin, have a care. I tell you that the strange lady is the image of the white wolf."

"You old fool," returned his master, savagely, "let me ever hear you repeat such nonsense again, and I will have you skinned alive. The lady is highborn, and of good family; beware how you insult her. Nay, I give you further commands: see that during her sojourn here she is treated with the utmost respect. And communicate this to all the servants. Mind, no more tales about the vision that your addled brain conjured up of wolves in the marsh, and above all do not let me hear that you have been alarming little

Katrina with your senseless babble."

The old man bowed humbly, and, after a short pause, remarked:—

"The lad that was injured at the hunt to-day is dead, my lord."

"Oh, dead is he, poor wretch!" returned Paul, to whom the death of a serf lad was not a matter of overweening importance. "But look here, Michal, remember that if any inquiries are made about the lady, that no one knows anything about her; that, in fact, no one has seen her at all."

"Your lordship shall be obeyed," answered the old man; and then, seeing that his master had relapsed into his former moody reverie, he left the room, crossing himself at every step he took.

Late into the night Paul sat up thinking over the occurrences of the day. He had told Michal that his guest was of noble family, but in reality he knew nothing more of her than she had condescended to tell him."

"Why, I don't even know her name," muttered he; "and yet somehow or other it seems as if a new feature of my life was opening before me. However, I have made one step in advance by getting her here, and if she talks about leaving, why, all that I have to do is threaten her with the police."

After his usual custom he smoked cigarette after cigarette, and poured out copious tumblers of brandy. The attendant serf replenished the stove from a small den which opened into the corridor, and after a time Paul slumbered heavily in his armchair. He was aroused by a light touch upon the shoulder, and, starting up, saw the stranger of the forest standing by his side.

"This is indeed kind of you," said she, with her usual mocking smile. "You felt that I should be strange here, and you got up early to see to the horses, or can it really be, those ends of cigarettes, that empty bottle of brandy? Paul Sergevitch, you have not been to bed at all."

Paul muttered a few indistinct words in reply, and then, ringing the bell furiously, ordered the servant to clear away the *débris* of last night's orgy, and lay the table for breakfast; then, with a hasty apology, he left the room to make a fresh toilet, and in about half an hour returned with his appearance sensibly improved by his ablutions and change of dress.

"I dare say," remarked the lady, as they were seated at the morning meal, for which she manifested the same indifference that she had for the dinner of the previous evening, "that you would like to know my name and who I am. Well, I don't mind telling you my name. It is Ravina, but as to my family and who I am, it will perhaps be best for you to remain in ignorance. A matter of policy, my dear Paul Sergevitch, a mere matter of policy, you see. I leave you to judge from my manners and appearance whether I am of sufficiently good form to be invited to the honor of your table—"

"None more worthy," broke in Paul, whose bemuddled brain was fast succumbing to the charms of his guest; "and surely that is a question upon which I may be deemed a competent judge."

"I do not know about that," returned Ravina, 'for from all accounts the company that you used to keep was not of the most select character."

"No, but hear me," began Paul, seizing her hand and endeavoring to carry it to his lips. But as he did so an unpleasant chill passed over him, for those slender fingers were icy cold.

"Do not be foolish," said Ravina, drawing away her hand, after she had permitted it to rest for an instant in Paul's grasp, "do you not hear someone coming?"

As she spoke the sound of tiny pattering feet was heard in the corridor, then the door was flung violently open, and with a shrill cry of delight, Katrina rushed into the room, followed more slowly by her brother Alexis.

"And are these your children?" asked Ravina, as Paul took up the little girl and placed her fondly upon his knee, whilst the boy stood a few paces from the door gazing with eyes of wonder upon the strange woman, for whose appearance he was utterly unable to account. "Come here, my little man," continued she; "I suppose you are the heir of Kostopchin, though you do not resemble your father much."

"He takes after his mother, I think," returned Paul carelessly; "and how has my darling Katrina been?" he added, addressing his daughter.

"Quite well, papa dear," answered the child; "but where is the fine white wolf skin that you promised me?"

"Your father did not find her," answered Ravina, with a little laugh; "the white wolf was not so easy to catch as he fancied."

Alexis had moved a few steps nearer to the lady, and was listening with grave attention to every word she uttered.

"Are white wolves so difficult to kill, then?" asked he.

"It seems so, my little man," returned the lady, "since your father and all the serfs of Kostopchin were unable to do so."

"I have got a pistol, that good old Michal has taught me to fire, and I am sure I could kill her if ever I got sight of her," observed Alexis, boldly.

"There is a brave boy," returned Ravina, with one of her shrill laughs; "and now, won't you come and sit on my knee, for I am very fond of little boy?"

"No, I don't like you," answered Alexis, after a moment's consideration, "for Michal says—"

"Go to your room, you insolent young brat," broke in the father, in a voice of thunder. "You spend so much of your time with Michal and the serfs that you have learned all their boorish habits."

Two tiny tears rolled down the boy's cheeks as in obedience to his father's orders he turned about and quitted the room, whilst Ravina darted a strange look of dislike after him. As soon, however, as the door had closed, the fair woman addressed Katrina.

"Well, perhaps you will not be so unkind to me as your brother," said she. "Come to me," and as she spoke she held out her arms.

The little girl came to her without hesitation, and began to smooth the silken tresses which were coiled and wreathed around Ravina's head.

"Pretty, pretty," she murmured, "beautiful lady."

"You see, Paul Sergevitch, that your little daughter has taken to me at once," remarked Ravina.

"She takes after her father, who was always noted for his good taste," returned Paul, with a bow; "but take care, madam, or the little puss will have your necklace off."

The child had indeed succeeded in unclasping the glittering ornament, and was now inspecting it in high glee.

"That is a curious ornament," said Paul, stepping up to the child and taking the circlet from her hand.

It was indeed a quaintly fashioned ornament, consisting as it did of a number of what were apparently curved pieces of sharp-pointed horn set in gold, and depending from a snake of the same precious metal.

"Why, these are claws," continued he, as he looked at them more carefully.

"Yes, wolves' claws," answered Ravina, taking the necklet from the child and reclasping it round her neck. "It is a family relic which I have always worn."

Katrina at first seemed inclined to cry at her new plaything being taken from her, but by caresses and endearments Ravina soon contrived to lull her once more into a good temper.

"My daughter has certainly taken to you in a most wonderful manner," remarked Paul, with a pleased smile. "You have quite obtained possession of her heart."

"Not yet, whatever I may do later on," answered the woman, with her strange cold smile, as she pressed the child closer towards her and shot a glance at Paul which made him quiver with an emotion that he had never felt before. Presently, however, the child grew tired of her new acquaintance, and sliding down from her knee, crept from the room in search of her brother Alexis.

Paul and Ravina remained silent for a few instants, and then the woman broke the silence.

"All that remains for me now, Paul Sergevitch, is to trespass on your hospitality, and to ask you to lend me some disguise, and assist me to gain the nearest post town, which, I think, is Vitroski."

"And why should you wish to leave this at all," demanded Paul, a deep flush rising to his cheek. "You are perfectly safe in my house, and if you attempt to pursue your journey there is every chance of your being recognized and captured."

"Why do I wish to leave this house?" answered Ravina, rising to her feet and casting a look of surprise upon her interrogator. "Can you ask me such a question? How is it possible for me to remain here?"

"It is perfectly impossible for you to leave; of that I am quite certain," answered the man, doggedly. "All I know is, that if you leave Kostopchin, you will inevitably fall into the hands of the police."

"And Paul Sergevitch will tell them where they can find me?" questioned Ravina, with an ironical inflection in the tone of her voice.

"I never said so," returned Paul.

"Perhaps not," answered the woman, quickly, "but I am not slow in reading thoughts; they are sometimes plainer to read than words. You are saying to yourself, 'Kostopchin is but a dull hole after all; chance has thrown into my hands a woman whose beauty pleases me; she is utterly friendless, and is in fear of the pursuit of the police; why should I not bend her to my will?' That is what you have been thinking,—is it not so, Paul Sergevitch?"

"I never thought, that is—" stammered the man.

"No, you never thought that I could read you so plainly," pursued the woman, pitilessly; "but it is the truth that I have told you, and sooner than remain an inmate of your house, I would leave it, even if all the police of Russia stood ready to arrest me on its very threshold."

"Stay, Ravina," exclaimed Paul, as the woman made a step towards the door. "I do not say whether your reading of my thoughts is right or wrong, but before you leave, listen to me. I do not speak to you in the usual strain of a pleading lover,—you, who know my past, would laugh at me should I do so; but I tell you plainly that from the first moment that I set eyes upon you, a strange new feeling has risen up in my heart, not the cold thing that society calls love, but a burning resistless flood which flows down like molten lava from the volcano's crater. Stay, Ravina, stay, I implore you, for if you go from here you will take my heart with you."

"You may be speaking more truthfully than you think," returned the fair woman, as, turning back, she came close up to Paul, and placing both her hands upon his shoulders, shot a glance of lurid fire from her eyes. "Still, you have but given me a selfish reason for my staying, only your own self-gratification. Give me one that more nearly affects myself."

Ravina's touch sent a tremor through Paul's whole frame which caused every nerve and sinew to vibrate. Gaze as boldly as he might into those steel-blue eyes, he could not sustain their intensity.

"Be my wife, Ravina," faltered he. "Be my wife. You are safe enough from all pursuit here, and if that does not suit you I can easily convert my estate into a large sum of money, and we can fly to other lands, where you can have nothing to fear from the Russian police."

"And does Paul Sergevitch actually mean to offer his hand to a woman whose name he does not even know, and of whose feelings towards him he is entirely ignorant?" asked the woman, with her customary mocking laugh.

"What do I care for name or birth," returned he, hotly, "I have enough for both, and as for love, my passion would soon kindle some sparks of it in your breast, cold and frozen as it may now be."

"Let me think a little," said Ravina; and throwing herself into an armchair she buried her face in her hands and seemed plunged in deep reflection, whilst Paul paced impatiently up and down the room like a prisoner awaiting the verdict that would restore him to life or doom him to a shameful death.

At length Ravina removed her hands from her face and spoke.

"Listen," said she. "I have thought over your proposal seriously, and upon certain conditions, I will consent to become your wife."

"They are granted in advance," broke in Paul, eagerly.

"Make no bargains blindfold," answered she, "but listen. At the present moment I have no inclination for you, but on the other hand I feel no repugnance for you. I will remain here for a month, and during that time I shall remain in a suite of apartments which you will have prepared for me. Every evening I will visit you here, and upon your making yourself agreeable my ultimate decision will depend."

"And suppose that decision should be an unfavorable one?" asked Paul.

"Then," answered Ravina, with a ringing laugh, "I shall, as you say, leave this and take your heart with me."

"These are hard conditions," remarked Paul. "Why not shorten the time of probation?"

"My conditions are unalterable," answered Ravina, with a little stamp of the foot. "Do you agree to them or not?"

"I have no alternative," answered he, sullenly; "but remember that I am to see you every evening."

"For two hours," said the woman, "so you must try and make yourself as agreeable as you can in that time; and now, if you will give orders regarding my rooms, I will settle myself in them with as little delay as possible."

Paul obeyed her, and in a couple of hours three handsome chambers were got ready for their fair occupant in a distant part of the great rambling house.

The Awakening of the Wolf

The days slipped slowly and wearily away, but Ravina showed no signs of relenting. Every evening, according to her bond, she spent two hours with Paul and made herself most agreeable, listening to his far-fetched compliments and asseverations of love and tenderness either with a cold smile or with one of her mocking laughs. She refused to allow Paul to visit her in her own apartments, and the only intruder she permitted there, save the servants, was little Katrina, who had taken a strange fancy to the fair woman. Alexis, on the contrary, avoided her as much as he possibly could, and the pair hardly ever met. Paul, to while away the time, wandered about the farm and the village, the inhabitants of which had recovered from their panic as the white wolf appeared to have entirely desisted from her murderous attacks upon belated peasants. The shades of evening had closed in as Paul was one day returning from his customary round, rejoiced with the idea that the hour for Ravina's visit was drawing near, when he was startled by a gentle touch upon the shoulder, and turning round, saw the old man Michal standing just behind him. The intendant's face was perfectly livid, his eyes gleamed with the luster of terror, and his fingers kept convulsively clasping and unclasping.

"My lord," exclaimed he, in faltering accents; "oh, my lord, listen to me, for I have terrible news to narrate to you."

"What is the matter?" asked Paul, more impressed than he would have liked to confess by the old man's evident terror.

"The wolf, the white wolf! I have seen it again," whispered Michal.

"You are dreaming," retorted his master, angrily. "You have got the creature on the brain, and have mistaken a white calf or one of the dogs for it."

"I am not mistaken," answered the old man, firmly. "And oh, my lord, do not go into the house, for she is there."

"She—who—what do you mean?" cried Paul.

"The white wolf, my lord. I saw her go in. You know the strange lady's apartments are on the ground floor on the west side of the house. I saw the monster cantering across the lawn, and, as if it knew its way perfectly well, make for the center window of the reception room; it yielded to a touch of the fore paw, and the beast sprang through. Oh, my lord, do not go in; I tell you that it will never harm the strange woman. Ah! let me—"

But Paul cast off the detaining arm with a force that made the old man reel and fall, and then, catching up an ax, dashed into the house, calling upon the servants to follow him to the strange lady's rooms. He tried the handle, but the door was securely fastened, and then, in all the frenzy of terror, he attacked the panels with heavy blows of his ax. For a few seconds no sound was heard save the ring of metal and the shivering of panels, but then the clear tones of Ravina were heard asking the reason for this outrageous disturbance.

"The wolf, the white wolf," shouted half a dozen voices.

"Stand back and I will open the door," answered the fair woman. "You must be mad, for there is no wolf here."

The door flew open and the crowd rushed tumultuously in; every nook and corner were searched, but no signs of the intruder could be discovered, and with many shamefaced glances Paul and his servants were about to return, when the voice of Ravina arrested their steps."

"Paul Sergevitch," sad she, coldly, "explain the meaning of this daring intrusion on my privacy."

She looked very beautiful as she stood before them; her right arm extended and her bosom heaved violently, but this was doubtless caused by her anger at the unlooked-for invasion.

Paul briefly repeated what he had heard from the old serf, and Ravina's scorn was intense.

"And so," cried she, fiercely, "it is to the crotchets of this old dotard that I am indebted for this. Paul, if you ever hope to succeed in winning me, forbid that man ever to enter the house again."

Paul would have sacrificed all his serfs for a whim of the haughty beauty, and Michal was deprived of the office of intendant and exiled to a cabin in the village, with orders never to show his face again near the house. The separation from the children almost broke the old man's heart, but he ventured on no remonstrance and meekly obeyed the mandate which drove him away from all he loved and cherished.

Meanwhile, curious rumors began to be circulated regarding the strange proceedings of the lady who occupied the suite of apartments which had formerly belonged to the wife of the owner of Kostopchin. The servants declared that the food sent up, though hacked about and cut up, was never tasted, but that the raw meat in the larder was frequently missing. Strange sounds were often heard to issue from the rooms as the panic-stricken serfs hurried past the corridor upon which the doors opened, and dwellers in the house were frequently disturbed by the howlings of wolves, the footprints of which were distinctly visible the next morning, and, curiously enough, invariably in the gardens facing the west side of the house in which the lady dwelt. Little Alexis, who found no encouragement to sit with his father, was naturally thrown a great deal amongst the serfs, and heard the subject discussed with many exaggerations. Weird old tales of folklore were often narrated as the servants discussed their evening meal, and the boy's hair would bristle as he listened to the wild and fanciful narratives of wolves, witches, and white ladies with which the superstitious serfs filled his ears. One of his most treasured possessions was an old brass-mounted cavalry pistol, a present from Michal; this he has learned to load, and by using both hands to the cumbrous weapon could contrive to fire it off, as many an ill-starred sparrow could attest. With his mind constantly dwelling upon the terrible tales he had so greedily listened to, this pistol became his daily companion, whether he was wandering about the long echoing corridors of the house or wandering through the neglected shrubberies of the garden. For a fortnight matters went on in this manner, Paul becoming more and more infatuated by the charms of his strange guest, and she every now and then letting drop occasional crumbs of hope which led the unhappy man further and further upon the dangerous course that he was pursuing. A mad, soul-absorbing passion for the fair woman and the deep draughts of brandy with which he consoled himself during her hours of absence were telling upon the brain of the master of Kostopchin, and except during the brief space of Ravina's visit, he would relapse into moods of silent sullenness from which he would occasionally break out into furious bursts of passion for no assignable cause. A shadow seemed to be closing over the house of Kostopchin; it became the abode of grim whispers and undeveloped fears; the men and maid servants went about their work glancing nervously over their shoulders, as though they were apprehensive that some hideous thing was following at their heels.

After three days of exile, poor old Michal could endure the state of suspense regarding the safety of Alexis and Katrina no longer; and, casting aside his superstitious fears, he took to wandering by night about the exterior of the great white house, and peering curiously into such windows as had been left unshuttered. At first he was in continual dread of meeting the terrible white wolf; but his love for the children and his confidence in the crucifix he wore prevailed, and he continued his nocturnal wanderings about Kostopchin and its environs. He kept near the western front of the house, urged on to do so from some vague feeling which he could in no wise account for. One evening as he was making his accustomed tour of inspection, the wail of a child struck upon his ear. He bent down his head and eagerly listened, again he heard the same faint sounds, and in them he fancied he recognized the accents of his dear little Katrina. Hurrying up to one of the ground-floor windows, from which a dim light streamed, he pressed his face against the pane, and looked steadily in. A horrible sight presented itself to his gaze. By the faint light of a shaded lamp, he saw Katrina stretched upon the ground; but her wailing had now ceased, for a shawl had been tied across her little mouth. Over her was bending a hideous shape, which seemed to be clothed in some white and shaggy covering. Katrina lay perfectly motionless, and the hands of the figure were engaged in hastily removing the garments from the child's breast. The task was soon effected; then there was a bright gleam of steel, and the head of the thing bent closely down to the child's bosom.

With a yell of apprehension, the old man dashed in the window frame, and, drawing the cross from his breast, sprang boldly into the room. The creature sprang to its feet, and the white fur cloak falling from its had and shoulders disclosed the pallid features of Ravina, a short, broad knife in her hand, and her lips discolored with blood.

"Vile sorceress!" cried Michal, dashing forward and raising Katrina in his arms. "What hellish work are you about?"

Ravina's eyes gleamed fiercely upon the old man, who had interfered between her and her prey. She raised her dagger, and was about to spring in upon him, when she caught sight of the cross in his extended hand. With a low cry, she dropped the knife, and, staggering back a few paces, wailed out: "I could not help it; I liked the child well enough, but I was so hungry."

Michal paid but little heed to her words, for he was busily engaged in examining the fainting child, whose head was resting helplessly on his shoulder. There was a wound over the left breast, from which the blood was flowing; but the injury appeared slight, and not likely to prove fatal. As soon as he had satisfied himself on this point, he turned to the woman, who was crouching before the cross as a wild beast shrinks before the whip of the tamer.

"I am going to remove the child," said he, slowly. "Dare you to mention a word of what I have done or whither she has gone, and I will arouse the village. Do you know what will happen then? Why, every peasant in the place will hurry here with a lighted brand in his hand to consume this accursed house and the unnatural dwellers in it. Keep silence, and I leave you to your unhallowed work. I will no longer seek to preserve Paul Sergevitch, who has given himself over to the powers of darkness by taking a demon to his bosom."

Ravina listened to him as if she scarcely comprehended him; but, as the old man retreated to the window with his helpless burden, she followed him step by step; and as he turned to cast one last glance at the shattered window, he saw the woman's pale face and bloodstained lips glued against an unbroken pane, with a wild look of unsatiated appetite in her eyes.

Next morning the house of Kostopchin was filled with terror and surprise, for Katrina, the idol of her father's heart, had disappeared, and no signs of her could be discovered. Every effort was made, the woods and fields in the neighborhood were thoroughly searched; but it was at last concluded that robbers had carried off the child for the sake of the ransom that they might be able to extract from the father. This seemed the more likely as one of the windows in the fair stranger's room bore marks of violence, and she declared that, being alarmed by the sound of crashing glass, she had risen and confronted a man who was endeavoring to enter her apartment, but who, on perceiving her, turned and fled away with the utmost precipitation.

Paul Sergevitch did not display as much anxiety as might have been expected from him, considering the devotion which he had ever evinced for the lost Katrina, for his whole soul was wrapped up in one mad, absorbing passion for the fair woman who had so strangely crossed his life. He certainly directed the search, and gave all the necessary orders; but he did so in a listless and half-hearted manner, and hastened back to Kostopchin as speedily as he could as though fearing to be absent for any length of time from the casket in which his new treasure was enshrined. Not so Alexis; he was almost frantic at the loss of his sister, and accompanied the searchers daily until his little legs grew weary, and he had to be carried on the shoulders of a sturdy *moujik*. His treasured brass-mounted pistol was now more than ever his constant companion; and when he met the fair woman who had cast a spell upon his father, his face would flush, and he would grind his teeth in impotent rage.

The day upon which all search had ceased, Ravina glided into the room where she knew that she would find Paul awaiting her. She was fully an hour before her usual time, and the lord of Kostopchin started to his feet in surprise.

"You are surprised to see me," said she; 'but I have only come to pay you a visit for a few minutes. I am convinced that you love me, and could I but relieve a few of the objections that my heart continues to raise, I might be yours."

"Tell me what these scruples are," cried Paul, springing towards her, and seizing her hands in his; "and be sure that I will find means to overcome them."

Even in the midst of all the glow and fervor of anticipated triumph, he could not avoid noticing how icily cold were the fingers that rested in his palm, and how utterly passionless was the pressure with which she slightly returned his enraptured clasp.

"Listen," said she, as she withdrew her hand; "I will take two more hours for consideration. By that time the whole of the house of Kostopchin will be cradled in slumber; then meet me at the old sundial near the yew tree at the bottom of the garden, and I will give you my reply. Nay, not a word," she added, as he seemed about to remonstrate, "for I tell you that I think it will be a favorable one."

"But why not come back here?" urged he; "there is a hard frost to-night, and——"

"Are you so cold a lover," broke in Ravina, with her accustomed laugh, "to dread the changes of the weather? But not another word; I have spoken."

She glided from the room, but uttered a low cry of rage. She had almost fallen over Alexis in the corridor.

"Why is that brat not in his bed? " cried she, angrily; "he gave me quite a turn."

"Go to your room, boy," exclaimed his father, harshly; and with a malignant glance at his enemy, the child slunk away.

Paul Sergevitch paced up and down the room for the two hours that he had to pass before the hour of meeting. His heart was very heavy, and a vague feeling of disquietude began to creep over him. Twenty times he made up his mind not to keep his appointment, and as often the fascination of the fair woman compelled him to rescind his resolution. He remember that he had from childhood disliked that spot by the yew tree, and had always looked upon it as a dreary, uncanny place; and he even now disliked the idea of finding himself here after dark, even with such fair companionship as he had been promised. Counting the minutes, he paced backwards and forwards, as though moved by some concealed machinery. Now and again he glanced at the clock, and at last its deep metallic sound, as it struck the quarter, warned him that he had but little time to lose, if he intended to keep his appointment. Throwing on a heavily furred coat and pulling a traveling cap down over his ears, he opened a side door and sallied out into the grounds. The moon was at its full, and shone coldly down upon the leafless trees, which looked white and ghostlike in its beams. The paths and unkept lawns were now covered with hoar frost, and a keen wind every now and then swept by, which, in spite of his wraps, chilled Paul's blood in his veins. The dark shape of the yew tree soon rose up before him, and in another moment he stood beside its dusky boughs. The old gray sundial stood only a few paces off, and by its side was standing a slender figure, wrapped in a white, fleecy-looking cloak. It was perfectly motionless, and again a terror of undefined dread passed through every nerve and muscle of Paul Sergevitch's body.

"Ravina!" said he, in faltering accents. "Ravina!"

"Did you take me for a ghost?" answered the fair woman, with her shrill laugh; "no, no, I have not come to that yet. Well, Paul Sergevitch, I have come to give you my answer; are you anxious about it?"

"How can you ask me such a question?" returned he; "do you not know that my whole soul has been aglow with anticipations of what your reply might be? Do not keep me any longer in suspense. Is it yes, or no?"

"Paul Sergevitch," answered the young woman, coming

up to him and laying her hands upon his shoulders, and fixing her eyes upon his with that strange weird expression before which he always quailed; "do you really love me, Paul Sergevitch?" asked she.

"Love you!" repeated the lord of Kostopchin; "have I not told you a thousand times how much my whole soul flows out towards you, how I only live and breathe in your presence, and how death at your feet would be more welcome than life without you?"

"People often talk of death, and yet little know how near it is to them," answered the fair lady, a grim smile appearing upon her face; "but say, do you give me your whole heart?"

"All I have is yours, Ravina," returned Paul, "name, wealth, and the devoted love of a lifetime."

"But your heart," persisted she; "it is your heart that I want; tell me, Paul, that it is mine and mine only."

"Yes, my heart is yours, dearest Ravina," answered Paul, endeavoring to embrace the fair form in his impassioned grasp; but she glided from him, and then with a quick bound sprang upon him and glared in his face with a look that was absolutely appalling. Her eyes gleamed with a lurid fire, her lips were drawn back, showing her sharp, white teeth, whilst her breath came in sharp, quick gasps.

"I am hungry," she murmured, "oh, so hungry; but now, Paul Sergevitch, your heart is mine."

Her movement was so sudden and unexpected that he stumbled and fell heavily to the ground, the fair woman clinging to him and falling upon his breast. It was then that the full horror of his position came upon Paul Sergevitch, and he saw his fate clearly before him; but a terrible numbness prevented him from using his hands to free himself from the hideous embrace which was paralyzing all his muscles. The face that was glaring into his seemed to be undergoing some fearful change, and the features to be losing their semblance of humanity. With a sudden, quick movement, she tore open his garments, and in another moment she had perforated his left breast with a ghastly wound, and, plunging in her delicate hands, tore out his heart and bit at it ravenously. Intent upon her hideous banquet she heeded not the convulsive struggles which agitated the dying form of the lord of Kostopchin. She was too much occupied to notice a diminutive form approaching, sheltering itself behind every tree and bush until it had arrived within ten paces of the scene of the terrible tragedy. Then the moonbeams glistened upon the long shining barrel of a pistol, which a boy was leveling with both hands at the murderess. Then quick and sharp rang out the report, and with a wild shriek, in which there was something beastlike, Ravina leaped from the body of the dead man and staggered away to a thick clump of bushes some ten paces distant. The boy Alexis had heard the appointment that had been made, and dogged his father's footsteps to the trysting place. After firing the fatal shot his courage deserted him, and he fled backwards to the house, uttering loud shrieks for help. The startled servants were soon in the presence of their slaughtered master, but

aid was of no avail, for the lord of Kostopchin had passed away. With fear and trembling the superstitious peasants searched the clump of bushes, and started back in horror as they perceived a huge white wolf, lying stark and dead, with a half-devoured human heart clasped between its fore paws.

* * * *

No signs of the fair lady who had occupied the apartments in the western side of the house were ever again seen. She had passed away from Kostopchin like an ugly dream, and as the moujiks of the village sat around their stoves at night they whispered strange stories regarding the fair woman of the forest and the white wolf of Kostopchin. By order of the Tsar a surtee was placed in charge of the estate of Kostopchin, and Alexis was ordered to be sent to a military school until he should be old enough to join the army. The meeting between the boy and his sister, whom the faithful Michal, when all danger was at an end, had produced from his hiding place, was most affecting; but it was not until Katrina had been for some time resident at the house of a distant relative at Vitepak, that she ceased to wake at night and cry out in terror as she again dreamed that she was in the clutches of the white wolf.

The Mark of the Beast

RUDYARD KIPLING

Your Gods and my Gods—do you
or I know which are the stronger?

Native Proverb

East of Suez, some hold, the direct control of Providence ceases; Man being there handed over to the power of the Gods and Devils of Asia, and the Church of England Providence only exercising an occasional and modified supervision in the case of Englishmen.

This theory accounts for some of the more unnecessary horrors of life in India: it may be stretched to explain my story.

My friend Strickland of the Police, who knows as much of natives of India as is good for any man, can bear witness to the facts of the case. Dumoise, our doctor, also saw what Strickland and I saw. The inference which he drew from the

evidence was entirely incorrect. He is dead now; he died, in a rather curious manner, which has been elsewhere described.

When Fleete came to India he owned a little money and some land in the Himalayas, near a place called Dharmsala. Both properties had been left him by an uncle, and he came out to finance them. He was a big, heavy, genial, and inoffensive man. His knowledge of natives was, of course, limited, and he complained of the difficulties of the language.

He rode in from his place in the hills to spend New Year in the station, and he stayed with Strickland. On New Year's Eve there was a big dinner at the club, and the night was excusably wet. When men foregather from the uttermost ends of the Empire, they have a right to be riotous. The Frontier had sent down a contingent o' Catch-'em-Alive-O's who had not seen twenty white faces for a year, and were used to ride fifteen miles to dinner at the next Fort at the risk of a Khyberee bullet where their drinks should lie. They profited by their new security, for they tried to play pool with a curled-up hedgehog found in the garden, and one of them carried the marker round the room in his teeth. Half a dozen planters had come in from the south and were talking "horse' to the Biggest Liar in Asia, who was trying to cap all their stories at once. Everybody was there, and there was a general closing up of ranks and taking stock of our losses in dead or disabled that had fallen during the past year. It was a very wet night, and I remember that we sang "Auld Lang Syne' with our feet in the Polo Championship Cup, and our heads among the stars, and swore that we were all dear friends. Then some of us went away and annexed Burma, and some tried to open up the Soudan and were opened up by Fuzzies in that cruel scrub outside Suakim, and some found stars and medals, and some were married, which was bad, and some did other things which were worse, and the others of us stayed in our chains and strove to make money on insufficient experiences.

Fleete began the night with sherry and bitters, drank champagne steadily up to dessert, then raw, rasping Capri with all the strength of whisky, took Benedictine with his coffee, four or five whiskies and sodas to improve his pool strokes, beer and bones at half-past two, winding up with old brandy. Consequently, when he came out, at half-past three in the morning, into fourteen degrees of frost, he was very angry with his horse for coughing, and tried to leap-frog into the saddle. The horse broke away and went to his stables; so Strickland and I formed a Guard of Dishonour to take Fleete home.

Our road lay through the bazaar, close to a little temple of Hanuman, the Monkey-god, who is a leading divinity worthy of respect. All gods have good points, just as have all priests. Personally, I attach much importance to Hanuman, and am kind to his people—the great gray apes of the hills. One never knows when one may want a friend.

There was a light in the temple, and as we passed, we could hear voices of men chanting hymns. In a native temple, the priests rise at all hours of the night to do honour to their god. Before we could stop him, Fleete dashed up the steps, patted two priests on the back, and was gravely grinding the ashes of his cigar-butt into the forehead of the red stone image of Hanuman. Strickland tried to drag him out, but he sat down and said solemnly:

"Shee that? Mark of the B-beasht! *I* made it. Ishn't it fine?"

In half a minute the temple was alive and noisy, and Strickland, who knew what came of polluting gods, said that things might occur. He, by virtue of his official position, long residence in the country, and weakness for going among the natives, was known to the priests and he felt unhappy. Fleete sat on the ground and refused to move. He said that "good old Hanuman" made a very soft pillow.

Then, without any warning, a Silver Man came out of a recess behind the image of the god. He was perfectly naked in that bitter, bitter cold, and his body shone like frosted silver, for he was what the Bible calls "a leper as white as snow." Also he had no face, because he was a leper of some years' standing and his disease was heavy upon him. We two stooped to haul Fleete up, and the temple was filling and filling with folk who seemed to spring from the earth, when the Silver Man ran in under our arms, making a noise exactly like the mewing of an otter, caught Fleete round the body and dropped his head on Fleete's breast before we could wrench him away. Then he retired to a corner and sat mewing while the crowd blocked all the doors.

The priests were very angry until the Silver Man touched Fleete. That nuzzling seemed to sober them.

At the end of a few minutes' silence one of the priests came to Strickland and said, in perfect English, "Take your friend away. He has done with Hanuman, but Hanuman has not done with him." The crowd gave room and we carried Fleete into the road.

Strickland was very angry. He said that we might all three have been knifed, and that Fleete should thank his stars that he had escaped without injury.

Fleete thanked no one. He said that he wanted to go to bed. He was gorgeously drunk.

We moved on, Strickland silent and wrathful, until Fleete was taken with violent shivering fits and sweating. He said that the smells of the bazaar were overpowering, and he wondered why slaughter-houses were permitted so near English residences. "Can't you smell the blood?" said Fleete.

We put him to bed at last, just as the dawn was breaking, and Strickland invited me to have another whisky and soda. While we were drinking he talked of the trouble in the temple, and admitted that it baffled him completely. Strickland hates being mystified by natives, because his business in life is to overmatch them with their own weapons. He has not yet succeeded in doing this, but in fifteen or twenty years he will have made some small progress.

"They should have mauled us," he said, "instead of mewing at us. I wonder what they meant. I don't like it one little bit."

I said that the Managing Committee of the temple would in all probability bring a criminal action against us for insulting their religion. There was a section of the Indian Penal Code which exactly met Fleete's offence. Strickland said he only hoped and prayed that they would do this. Before I left I looked into Fleete's room, and saw him lying on his right side, scratching his left breast. Then. I went to bed cold, depressed, and unhappy, at seven o'clock in the morning.

At one o'clock I rode over to Strickland's house to inquire after Fleete's head. I imagined that it would be a sore one. Fleete was breakfasting and seemed unwell. His temper was gone, for he was abusing the cook for not supplying him with an underdone chop. A man who can eat raw meat after a wet night is a curiosity. I told Fleete this and he laughed.

"You breed queer mosquitoes in these parts," he said. "I've been bitten to pieces, but only in one place."

"Let's have a look at the bite," said Strickland. "It may have gone down since this morning."

While the chops were being cooked, Fleete opened his shirt and showed us, just over his left breast, a mark, the perfect double of the black rosettes—the five or six irregular blotches arranged in a circle—on a leopard's hide. Strickland looked and said, "It was only pink this morning. It's grown black now."

Fleete ran to a glass.

"By Jove!" he said, "This is nasty. What is it?"

We could not answer. Here the chops came in, all red and juicy, and Fleete bolted three in a most offensive manner. He ate on his right grinders only, and threw his head over his right shoulder as he snapped the meat. When he had finished, it struck him that he had been behaving strangely, for he said apologetically, "I don't think I ever felt so hungry in my life. I've bolted like an ostrich."

After breakfast Strickland said to me, "Don't go. Stay here, and stay for the night."

Seeing that my house was not three miles from Strickland's, this request was absurd. But Strickland insisted, and was going to say something when Fleete interrupted by declaring in a shamefaced way that he felt hungry again. Strickland sent a man to my house to fetch over my bedding and a horse, and we three went down to Strickland's stables to pass the hours until it was time to go out for a ride. The man who has a weakness for horses never wearies of inspecting them; and when two men are killing time in this way they gather knowledge and lies the one from the other.

There were five horses in the stables, and I shall never forget the scene as we tried to look them over. They seemed to have gone mad. They reared and screamed and nearly tore up their pickets; they sweated and shivered and lathered and were distraught with fear. Strickland's horses used to know him as well as his dogs; which made the matter more curious. We left the stable for fear of the brutes throwing themselves in their panic. Then Strickland turned back and called me. The horses were still frightened, but they let us "gentle' and make much of them, and put their heads in our bosoms.

"They aren't afraid of US," said Strickland. "D'you know, I'd give three months' pay if OUTRAGE here could talk."

But Outrage was dumb, and could only cuddle up to his master and blow out his nostrils, as is the custom of horses when they wish to explain things but can't. Fleete came up when we were in the stalls, and as soon as the horses saw him, their fright broke out afresh. It was all that we could do to escape from the place unkicked. Strickland said, "They don't seem to love you, Fleete."

"Nonsense," said Fleete; "my mare will follow me like a dog." He went to her; she was in a loose-box; but as he slipped the bars she plunged, knocked him down, and broke away into the garden. I laughed, but Strickland was not amused. He took his moustache in both fists and pulled at it till it nearly came out. Fleete, instead of going off to chase his property, yawned, saying that he felt sleepy. He went to the house to lie down, which was a foolish way of spending New Year's Day.

Strickland sat with me in the stables and asked if I had noticed anything peculiar in Fleete's manner. I said that he ate his food like a beast; but that this might have been the result of living alone in the hills out of the reach of society as refined and elevating as ours for instance. Strickland was not amused. I do not think that he listened to me, for his next sentence referred to the mark on Fleete's breast, and I said that it might have been caused by blister-flies, or that it was possibly a birth-mark newly born and now visible for the first time. We both agreed that it was unpleasant to look at, and Strickland found occasion to say that I was a fool.

"I can't tell you what I think now," said he, "because you would call me a madman; but you must stay with me for the next few days, if you can. I want you to watch Fleete, but don't tell me what you think till I have made up my mind."

"But I am dining out to-night," I said. "So am I," said Strickland, "and so is Fleete. At least if he doesn't change his mind."

We walked about the garden smoking, but saying nothing—because we were friends, and talking spoils good tobacco—till our pipes were out. Then we went to wake up Fleete. He was wide awake and fidgeting about his room.

"I say, I want some more chops," he said. "Can I get them?"

We laughed and said, "Go and change. The ponies will be round in a minute."

"All right," said Fleete. "I'll go when I get the chops—underdone ones, mind."

He seemed to be quite in earnest. It was four o'clock, and we had had breakfast at one; still, for a long time, he demanded those underdone chops. Then he changed into riding clothes and went out into the verandah. His pony—the mare had not been caught—would not let him come near. All three horses were unmanageable—mad with fear—and finally Fleete said that he would stay at home

and get something to eat. Strickland and I rode out wondering. As we passed the temple of Hanuman, the Silver Man came out and mewed at us.

"He is not one of the regular priests of the temple," said Strickland. "I think I should peculiarly like to lay my hands on him."

There was no spring in our gallop on the racecourse that evening. The horses were stale, and moved as though they had been ridden out.

"The fright after breakfast has been too much for them," said Strickland.

That was the only remark he made through the remainder of the ride. Once or twice I think he swore to himself; but that did not count.

We came back in the dark at seven o'clock, and saw that there were no lights in the bungalow. "Careless ruffians my servants are!" said Strickland.

My horse reared at something on the carriage drive, and Fleete stood up under its nose.

"What are you doing, grovelling about the garden?" said Strickland.

But both horses bolted and nearly threw us. We dismounted by the stables and returned to Fleete, who was on his hands and knees under the orange-bushes.

"What the devil's wrong with you?" said Strickland.

"Nothing, nothing in the world," said Fleete, speaking very quickly and thickly. "I've been gardening-botanising you know. The smell of the earth is delightful. I think I'm going for a walk-a long walk-all night."

Then I saw that there was something excessively out of order somewhere, and I said to Strickland, "I am not dining out."

"Bless you!" said Strickland. "Here, Fleete, get up. You'll catch fever there. Come in to dinner and let's have the lamps lit. We 'll all dine at home."

Fleete stood up unwillingly, and said, "No lamps-no lamps. It's much nicer here. Let's dine outside and have some more chops-lots of 'em and underdone—bloody ones with gristle."

Now a December evening in Northern India is bitterly cold, and Fleete's suggestion was that of a maniac.

"Come in," said Strickland sternly. "Come in at once."

Fleete came, and when the lamps were brought, we saw that he was literally plastered with dirt from head to foot. He must have been rolling in the garden. He shrank from the light and went to his room. His eyes were horrible to look at. There was a green light behind them, not in them, if you understand, and the man's lower lip hung down.

Strickland said, "There is going to be trouble-big trouble-to-night. Don't you change your riding-things."

We waited and waited for Fleete's reappearance, and ordered dinner in the meantime. We could hear him moving about his own room, but there was no light there. Presently from the room came the long-drawn howl of a wolf.

People write and talk lightly of blood running cold and hair standing up and things of that kind. Both sensations are too horrible to be trifled with. My heart stopped as though a knife had been driven through it, and Strickland turned as white as the tablecloth.

The howl was repeated, and was answered by another howl far across the fields.

That set the gilded roof on the horror. Strickland dashed into Fleete's room. I followed, and we saw Fleete getting out of the window. He made beast-noises in the back of his throat. He could not answer us when we shouted at him. He spat.

I don't quite remember what followed, but I think that Strickland must have stunned him with the long boot-jack or else I should never have been able to sit on his chest. Fleete could not speak, he could only snarl, and his snarls were those of a wolf, not of a man. The human spirit must have been giving way all day and have died out with the twilight. We were dealing with a beast that had once been Fleete.

The affair was beyond any human and rational experience. I tried to say "Hydrophobia," but the word wouldn't come, because I knew that I was lying.

We bound this beast with leather thongs of the punkah-rope, and tied its thumbs and big toes together, and gagged it with a shoe-horn, which makes a very efficient gag if you know how to arrange it. Then we carried it into the dining-room, and sent a man to Dumoise, the doctor, telling him to come over at once. After we had despatched the messenger and were drawing breath, Strickland said, "It's no good. This isn't any doctor's work." I, also, knew that he spoke the truth.

The beast's head was free, and it threw it about from side to side. Any one entering the room would have believed that we were curing a wolf's pelt. That was the most loathsome accessory of all.

Strickland sat with his chin in the heel of his fist, watching the beast as it wriggled on the ground, but saying nothing. The shirt had been torn open in the scuffle and showed the black rosette mark on the left breast. It stood out like a blister.

In the silence of the watching we heard something without mewing like a she-otter. We both rose to our feet, and, I answer for myself, not Strickland, felt sick—actually and physically sick. We told each other, as did the men in Pinafore, that it was the cat.

Dumoise arrived, and I never saw a little man so unprofessionally shocked. He said that it was a heart-rending case of hydrophobia, and that nothing could be done. At least any palliative measures would only prolong the agony. The beast was foaming at the mouth. Fleete, as we told Dumoise, had been bitten by dogs once or twice. Any man who keeps half a dozen terriers must expect a nip now and again. Dumoise could offer no help. He could only certify that Fleete was dying of hydrophobia. The beast was then howling, for it had managed to spit out the shoe-horn. Dumoise said that he would be ready to certify to the cause of death, and that the end was certain. He was a good little man, and he offered to remain with us; but Strickland refused the kindness. He did not wish to poison Dumoise's

New Year. He would only ask him not to give the real cause of Fleete's death to the public.

So Dumoise left, deeply agitated; and as soon as the noise of the cart-wheels had died away, Strickland told me, in a whisper, his suspicions. They were so wildly improbable that he dared not say them out aloud; and I, who entertained all Strickland's beliefs, was so ashamed of owning to them that I pretended to disbelieve.

"Even if the Silver Man had bewtiched Fleete for polluting the image of Hanuman, the punishment could not have fallen so quickly."

As I was whispering this the cry outside the house rose again, and the beast fell into a fresh paroxysm of struggling till we were afraid that the thongs that held it would give way.

"Watch!" said Strickland. "If this happens six times I shall take the law into my own hands. I order you to help me."

He went into his room and came out in a few minutes with the barrels of an old shot-gun, a piece of fishing-line, some thick cord, and his heavy wooden bedstead. I reported that the convulsions had followed the cry by two seconds in each case, and the beast seemed perceptibly weaker.

Strickland muttered, "But he can't take away the life! He can't take away the life!"

I said, though I knew that I was arguing against myself, "It may be a cat. It must be a cat. If the Silver Man is responsible, why does he dare to come here?"

Strickland arranged the wood on the hearth, put the gun-barrels into the glow of the fire, spread the twine on the table and broke a walking stick in two. There was one yard of fishing line, gut, lapped with wire, such as is used for mahseer-fishing, and he tied the two ends together in a loop.

Then he said, "How can we catch him? He must be taken alive and unhurt."

I said that we must trust in Providence, and go out softly with polo-sticks into the shrubbery at the front of the house. The man or animal that made the cry was evidently moving round the house as regularly as a night-watchman. We could wait in the bushes till he came by and knock him over.

Strickland accepted this suggestion, and we slipped out from a bath-room window into the front verandah and then across the carriage drive into the bushes.

In the moonlight we could see the leper coming round the corner of the house. He was perfectly naked, and from time to time he mewed and stopped to dance with his shadow. It was an unattractive sight, and thinking of poor Fleete, brought to such degradation by so foul a creature, I put away all my doubts and resolved to help Strickland from the heated gun-barrels to the loop of twine-from the loins to the head and back again—with all tortures that might be needful.

The leper halted in the front porch for a moment and we jumped out on him with the sticks. He was wonderfully strong, and we were afraid that he might escape or be fatally injured before we caught him. We had an idea that lepers were frail creatures, but this proved to be incorrect. Strickland knocked his legs from under him and I put my foot on his neck. He mewed hideously, and even through my riding-boots I could feel that his flesh was not the flesh of a clean man.

He struck at us with his hand and feet-stumps. We looped the lash of a dog-whip round him, under the arm-pits, and dragged him backwards into the hall and so into the dining-room where the beast lay. There we tied him with trunk-straps. He made no attempt to escape, but mewed.

When we confronted him with the beast the scene was beyond description. The beast doubled backwards into a bow as though he had been poisoned with strychnine, and moaned in the most pitiable fashion. Several other things happened also, but they cannot be put down here.

"I think I was right," said Strickland. "Now we will ask him to cure this case."

But the leper only mewed. Strickland wrapped a towel round his hand and took the gun-barrels out of the fire. I put the half of the broken walking stick through the loop of fishing-line and buckled the leper comfortably to Strickland's bedstead. I understood then how men and women and little children can endure to see a witch burnt alive; for the beast was moaning on the floor, and though the Silver Man had no face, you could see horrible feelings passing through the slab that took its place, exactly as waves of heat play across red-hot iron—gun-barrels for instance.

Strickland shaded his eyes with his hands for a moment and we got to work. This part is not to be printed.

The dawn was beginning to break when the leper spoke. His mewings had not been satisfactory up to that point. The beast had fainted from exhaustion and the house was very still. We unstrapped the leper and told him to take away the evil spirit. He crawled to the beast and laid his hand upon the left breast. That was all. Then he fell face down and whined, drawing in his breath as he did so.

We watched the face of the beast, and saw the soul of Fleete coming back into the eyes. Then a sweat broke out on the forehead and the eyes-they were human eyes—closed. We waited for an hour but Fleete still slept. We carried him to his room and bade the leper go, giving him the bedstead, and the sheet on the bedstead to cover his nakedness, the gloves and the towels with which we had touched him, and the whip that had been hooked round his body. He put the sheet about him and went out into the early morning without speaking or mewing.

Strickland wiped his face and sat down. A night-gong, far away in the city, made seven o'clock.

"Exactly four-and-twenty hours!" said Strickland. "And I've done enough to ensure my dismissal from the service, besides permanent quarters in a lunatic asylum. Do you believe that we are awake?"

The red-hot gun-barrel had fallen on the floor and was singeing the carpet. The smell was entirely real.

That morning at eleven we two together went to wake up Fleete. We looked and saw that the black leopard-rosette on his chest had disappeared. He was very drowsy and tired, but as soon as he saw us, he said, "Oh! Confound you fellows. Happy New Year to you. Never mix your liquors. I'm nearly dead."

"Thanks for your kindness, but you're over time," said Strickland. "To-day is the morning of the second. You've slept the clock round with a vengeance."

The door opened, and little Dumoise put his head in. He had come on foot, and fancied that we were laving out Fleete.

"I've brought a nurse," said Dumoise. "I suppose that she can come in for... what is necessary."

"By all means," said Fleete cheerily, sitting up in bed. "Bring on your nurses."

Dumoise was dumb. Strickland led him out and explained that there must have been a mistake in the diagnosis. Dumoise remained dumb and left the house hastily. He considered that his professional reputation had been injured, and was inclined to make a personal matter of the recovery. Strickland went out too. When he came back, he said that he had been to call on the Temple of Hanuman to offer redress for the pollution of the god, and had been solemnly assured that no white man had ever touched the idol and that he was an incarnation of all the virtues labouring under a delusion.

"What do you think?" said Strickland.

I said, "There are more things . . ."

But Strickland hates that quotation. He says that I have worn it threadbare.

One other curious thing happened which frightened me as much as anything in all the night's work. When Fleete was dressed he came into the dining-room and sniffed. He had a quaint trick of moving his nose when he sniffed. "Horrid doggy smell, here," said he. "You should really keep those terriers of yours in better order. Try sulphur, Strick."

But Strickland did not answer. He caught hold of the back of a chair, and, without warning, went into an amazing fit of hysterics. It is terrible to see a strong man overtaken with hysteria. Then it struck me that we had fought for Fleete's soul with the Silver Man in that room, and had disgraced ourselves as Englishmen for ever, and I laughed and gasped and gurgled just as shamefully as Strickland, while Fleete thought that we had both gone mad. We never told him what we had done.

Some years later, when Strickland had married and was a church-going member of society for his wife's sake, we reviewed the incident dispassionately, and Strickland suggested that I should put it before the public.

I cannot myself see that this step is likely to clear up the mystery; because, in the first place, no one will believe a rather unpleasant story, and, in the second, it is well known to every right-minded man that the gods of the heathen are stone and brass, and any attempt to deal with them otherwise is justly condemned.

THE EYES OF THE PANTHER

AMBROSE BIERCE

I

ONE DOES NOT ALWAYS
MARRY WHEN INSANE

A man and a woman—nature had done the grouping—sat on a rustic seat, in the late afternoon. The man was middle-aged, slender, swarthy, with the expression of a poet and the complexion of a pirate—a man at whom one would look again. The woman was young, blonde, graceful, with something in her figure and movements suggesting the word "lithe." She was habited in a gray gown with odd brown markings in the texture. She may have been beautiful; one could not readily say, for her eyes denied attention to all else. They were gray-green, long and narrow, with an expression defying analysis. One could only know that they were disquieting. Cleopatra may have had such eyes.

The man and the woman talked.

"Yes," said the woman, "I love you, God knows! But marry you, no. I cannot, will not."

"Irene, you have said that many times, yet always have denied me a reason. I've a right to know, to understand, to feel and prove my fortitude if I have it. Give me a reason."

"For loving you?"

The woman was smiling through her tears and her pallor. That did not stir any sense of humor in the man.

"No; there is no reason for that. A reason for not marrying me. I've a right to know. I must know. I will know!"

He had risen and was standing before her with clenched hands, on his face a frown—it might have been called a scowl. He looked as if he might attempt to learn by strangling her. She smiled no more—merely sat looking up into his face with a fixed, set regard that was utterly without emotion or sentiment. Yet it had something in it that tamed his resentment and made him shiver.

"You are determined to have my reason?" she asked in a tone that was entirely mechanical—a tone that might have been her look made audible.

"If you please—if I'm not asking too much."

Apparently this lord of creation was yielding some part of his dominion over his co-creature.

"Very well, you shall know: I am insane."

The man started, then looked incredulous and was conscious that he ought to be amused. But, again, the sense of humor failed him in his need and despite his disbelief he was profoundly disturbed by that which he did not believe. Between our convictions and our feelings there is no good understanding.

"That is what the physicians would say," the woman continued—"if they knew. I might myself prefer to call it a case of 'possession.' Sit down and hear what I have to say."

The man silently resumed his seat beside her on the rustic bench by the wayside. Over-against them on the eastern side of the valley the hills were already sunset-flushed and the stillness all about was of that peculiar quality that foretells the twilight. Something of its mysterious and significant solemnity had imparted itself to the man's mood. In the spiritual, as in the material world, are signs and presages of night. Rarely meeting her look, and whenever he did so conscious of the indefinable dread with which, despite their feline beauty, her eyes always affected him, Jenner Brading listened in silence to the story told by Irene Marlowe. In deference to the reader's possible prejudice against the artless method of an unpractised historian the author ventures to substitute his own version for hers.

II

A ROOM MAY BE TOO NARROW FOR THREE,
THOUGH ONE IS OUTSIDE

In a little log house containing a single room sparely and rudely furnished, crouching on the floor against one of the walls, was a woman, clasping to her breast a child. Outside, a dense unbroken forest extended for many miles in every direction. This was at night and the room was black dark: no human eye could have discerned the woman and the child. Yet they were observed, narrowly, vigilantly, with never even a momentary slackening of attention; and that is the pivotal fact upon which this narrative turns.

Charles Marlowe was of the class, now extinct in this country, of woodmen pioneers—men who found their most acceptable surroundings in sylvan solitudes that stretched along the eastern slope of the Mississippi Valley, from the Great Lakes to the Gulf of Mexico. For more than a hundred years these men pushed ever westward, generation after generation, with rifle and ax, reclaiming from Nature and her savage children here and there an isolated acreage for the plow, no sooner reclaimed than surrendered to their less venturesome but more thrifty successors. At last they burst through the edge of the forest into the open country and vanished as if they had fallen over a cliff. The woodman pioneer is no more; the pioneer of the plains—he whose easy task it was to subdue for occupancy two-thirds of the country in a single generation—is another and inferior creation. With Charles Marlowe in the wilderness, sharing the dangers, hardships and privations of that strange, unprofitable life, were his wife and child, to whom, in the manner of his class, in which the domestic virtues were a religion, he was passionately attached. The woman was still young enough to be comely, new enough to the awful isolation of her lot to be cheerful. By withholding the large capacity for happiness which the simple satisfactions of the forest life could not have filled, Heaven had dealt honorably with her. In her light household tasks, her child, her husband and her few foolish books, she found abundant provision for her needs.

One morning in midsummer Marlowe took down his rifle from the wooden hooks on the wall and signified his intention of getting game.

"We've meat enough," said the wife; "please don't go out to-day. I dreamed last night, O, such a dreadful thing! I cannot recollect it, but I'm almost sure that it will come to pass if you go out."

It is painful to confess that Marlowe received this solemn statement with less of gravity than was due to the mysterious nature of the calamity foreshadowed. In truth, he laughed.

"Try to remember," he said. "Maybe you dreamed that Baby had lost the power of speech."

The conjecture was obviously suggested by the fact that Baby, clinging to the fringe of his hunting-coat with all her ten pudgy thumbs was at that moment uttering her sense of the situation in a series of exultant goo-goos inspired by sight of her father's raccoon-skin cap.

The woman yielded: lacking the gift of humor she could not hold out against his kindly badinage. So, with a kiss for the mother and a kiss for the child, he left the house and closed the door upon his happiness forever.

At nightfall he had not returned. The woman prepared supper and waited. Then she put Baby to bed and sang softly to her until she slept. By this time the fire on the hearth, at which she had cooked supper, had burned out and the room was lighted by a single candle. This she afterward placed in the open window as a sign and welcome to the hunter if he should approach from that side. She had thoughtfully closed and barred the door against such wild animals as might prefer it to an open window—of the habits of beasts of prey in entering a house uninvited she was not advised, though with true female prevision she may have considered the possibility of their entrance by way of the chimney. As the night wore on she became not less anxious, but more drowsy, and at last rested her arms upon the bed by the child and her head upon the arms. The candle in the window burned down to the socket, sputtered and flared a moment and went out unobserved; for the woman slept and dreamed.

In her dreams she sat beside the cradle of a second child. The first one was dead. The father was dead. The home in the forest was lost and the dwelling in which she lived was unfamiliar. There were heavy oaken doors, always closed, and outside the windows, fastened into the thick stone walls, were iron bars, obviously (so she thought) a provision against Indians. All this she noted with an infinite self-pity, but without surprise—an emotion unknown in dreams. The child in the cradle was invisible under its coverlet which something impelled her to remove. She did so, disclosing the face of a wild animal! In the shock of this dreadful revelation the dreamer awoke, trembling in the darkness of her cabin in the wood.

As a sense of her actual surroundings came slowly back to her she felt for the child that was not a dream, and assured herself by its breathing that all was well with it; nor could she forbear to pass a hand lightly across its face. Then, moved by some impulse for which she probably could not have accounted, she rose and took the sleeping babe in her arms, holding it close against her breast. The head of the child's cot was against the wall to which the woman now turned her back as she stood. Lifting her eyes she saw two bright objects starring the darkness with a reddish-green glow. She took them to be two coals on the hearth, but with her returning sense of direction came the disquieting consciousness that they were not in that quarter of the room, moreover were too high, being nearly at the level of the eyes—of her own eyes. For these were the eyes of a panther.

The beast was at the open window directly opposite and not five paces away. Nothing but those terrible eyes was visible, but in the dreadful tumult of her feelings as the situation disclosed itself to her understanding she somehow knew that the animal was standing on its hinder feet, supporting itself with its paws on the window-ledge. That signified a malign interest—not the mere gratification of an indolent curiosity. The consciousness of the attitude was an added horror, accentuating the menace of those awful eyes, in whose steadfast fire her strength and courage were alike consumed. Under their silent questioning she shuddered and turned sick. Her knees failed her, and by degrees, instinctively striving to avoid a sudden movement that might bring the beast upon her, she sank to the floor, crouched against the wall and tried to shield the babe with her trembling body without withdrawing her gaze from the luminous orbs that were killing her. No thought of her husband came to her in her agony—no hope nor suggestion of rescue or escape. Her capacity for thought and feeling had narrowed to the dimensions of a single emotion—fear of the animal's spring, of the impact of its body, the buffeting of its great arms, the feel of its teeth in her throat, the mangling of her babe. Motionless now and in absolute silence, she awaited her doom, the moments growing to hours, to years, to ages; and still those devilish eyes maintained their watch.

Returning to his cabin late at night with a deer on his shoulders Charles Marlowe tried the door. It did not yield. He knocked; there was no answer. He laid down his deer and went round to the window. As he turned the angle of the building he fancied he heard a sound as of stealthy footfalls and a rustling in the undergrowth of the forest, but they were too slight for certainty, even to his practised ear. Approaching the window, and to his surprise finding it open, he threw his leg over the sill and entered. All was darkness and silence. He groped his way to the fire-place, struck a match and lit a candle.

Then he looked about. Cowering on the floor against a wall was his wife, clasping his child. As he sprang toward her she rose and broke into laughter, long, loud, and mechanical, devoid of gladness and devoid of sense—the laughter that is not out of keeping with the clanking of a chain. Hardly knowing what he did he extended his arms. She laid the babe in them. It was dead—pressed to death in its mother's embrace.

III
THE THEORY OF THE DEFENSE

That is what occurred during a night in a forest, but not all of it did Irene Marlowe relate to Jenner Brading; not all of it was known to her. When she had concluded the sun was below the horizon and the long summer twilight had begun to deepen in the hollows of the land. For some moments Brading was silent, expecting the narrative to be carried forward to some definite connection with the conversation introducing it; but the narrator was as silent as he, her face averted, her hands clasping and unclasping themselves as they lay in her lap, with a singular suggestion of an activity independent of her will.

"It is a sad, a terrible story," said Brading at last, "but I do not understand. You call Charles Marlowe father; that I know. That he is old before his time, broken by some great sorrow, I have seen, or thought I saw. But, pardon me, you said that you—that you—"

"That I am insane," said the girl, without a movement of head or body.

"But, Irene, you say—please, dear, do not look away from me—you say that the child was dead, not demented."

"Yes, that one—I am the second. I was born three months after that night, my mother being mercifully permitted to lay down her life in giving me mine."

Brading was again silent; he was a trifle dazed and could not at once think of the right thing to say. Her face was still turned away. In his embarrassment he reached impulsively toward the hands that lay closing and unclosing in her lap, but something—he could not have said what—restrained him. He then remembered, vaguely, that he had never altogether cared to take her hand.

"Is it likely," she resumed, "that a person born under such circumstances is like others—is what you call sane?"

Brading did not reply; he was preoccupied with a new thought that was taking shape in his mind—what a scientist would have called an hypothesis; a detective, a theory. It might throw an added light, albeit a lurid one, upon such doubt of her sanity as her own assertion had not dispelled.

The country was still new and, outside the villages, sparsely populated. The professional hunter was still a familiar figure, and among his trophies were heads and pelts of the larger kinds of game. Tales variously credible of nocturnal meetings with savage animals in lonely roads were sometimes current, passed through the customary stages of growth and decay, and were forgotten. A recent addition to these popular apocrypha, originating, apparently, by spontaneous generation in several households, was of a panther which had frightened some of their members by looking in at windows by night. The yarn had caused its little ripple of excitement—had even attained to the distinction of a place in the local newspaper; but Brading had given it no attention. Its likeness to the story to which he had just listened now impressed him as perhaps more than accidental. Was it not possible that the one story had suggested the other—that finding congenial conditions in a morbid mind and a fertile fancy, it had grown to the tragic tale that he had heard?

Brading recalled certain circumstances of the girl's history and disposition, of which, with love's incuriosity, he had hitherto been heedless—such as her solitary life with her father, at whose house no one, apparently, was an acceptable visitor and her strange fear of the night, by which those who knew her best accounted for her never being seen after dark. Surely in such a mind imagination once kindled might burn with a lawless flame, penetrating and enveloping the entire structure. That she was mad, though the conviction gave him the acutest pain, he could no longer doubt; she had only mistaken an effect of her mental disorder for its cause, bringing into imaginary relation with her own personality the vagaries of the local myth-makers. With some vague intention of testing his new "theory," and no very definite notion of how to set about it he said, gravely, but with hesitation:

"Irene, dear, tell me—I beg you will not take offence, but tell me—"

"I have told you," she interrupted, speaking with a passionate earnestness that he had not known her to show—"I have already told you that we cannot marry; is anything else worth saying?"

Before he could stop her she had sprung from her seat and without another word or look was gliding away among the trees toward her father's house. Brading had risen to detain her; he stood watching her in silence until she had vanished in the gloom. Suddenly he started as if he had been shot; his face took on an expression of amazement and alarm: in one of the black shadows into which she had disappeared he had caught a quick, brief glimpse of shining eyes! For an instant he was dazed and irresolute; then he dashed into the wood after her, shouting: "Irene, Irene, look out! The panther! The panther!"

In a moment he had passed through the fringe of forest into open ground and saw the girl's gray skirt vanishing into her father's door. No panther was visible.

IV
AN APPEAL TO THE CONSCIENCE OF GOD

Jenner Brading, attorney-at-law, lived in a cottage at the edge of the town. Directly behind the dwelling was the forest. Being a bachelor, and therefore, by the Draconian moral code of the time and place denied the services of the only species of domestic servant known thereabout, the "hired girl," he boarded at the village hotel, where also was his office. The woodside cottage was merely a lodging maintained—at no great cost, to be sure—as an evidence of prosperity and respectability. It would hardly do for one to whom the local newspaper had pointed with pride as "the foremost jurist of his time" to be "homeless," albeit he may sometimes have suspected that the words "home" and "house" were not strictly synonymous. Indeed, his consciousness of the disparity and his will to harmonize it were matters of logical inference, for it was generally reported that soon after the cottage was built its owner had made a futile venture in the direction of marriage—had, in truth, gone so far as to be rejected by the beautiful but eccentric daughter of Old Man Marlowe, the recluse. This was publicly believed because he had told it himself and she had not—a reversal of the usual order of things which could hardly fail to carry conviction.

Brading's bedroom was at the rear of the house, with a single window facing the forest.

One night he was awakened by a noise at that window; he could hardly have said what it was like. With a little thrill of the nerves he sat up in bed and laid hold of the revolver which, with a forethought most commendable in one addicted to the habit of sleeping on the ground floor with an open window, he had put under his pillow. The room was in absolute darkness, but being unterrified he knew where to direct his eyes, and there he held them, awaiting in silence what further might occur. He could now dimly discern the aperture—a square of lighter black. Presently there appeared at its lower edge two gleaming eyes that burned with a malignant lustre inexpressibly terrible! Brading's heart gave a great jump, then seemed to stand still. A chill passed along his spine and through his hair; he felt the blood forsake his cheeks. He could not have cried out—not to save his life; but being a man of courage he would not, to save his life, have done so if he had been able. Some trepidation his coward body might feel, but his spirit was of sterner stuff. Slowly the shining eyes rose with a steady motion that seemed an approach, and slowly rose Brading's right hand, holding the pistol. He fired!

Blinded by the flash and stunned by the report, Brading nevertheless heard, or fancied that he heard, the wild, high scream of the panther, so human in sound, so devilish in suggestion. Leaping from the bed he hastily clothed himself and, pistol in hand, sprang from the door, meeting two or three men who came running up from the road. A brief explanation was followed by a cautious search of the house. The grass was wet with dew; beneath the window it had been trodden and partly leveled for a wide space, from which a devious trail, visible in the light of a lantern, led away into the bushes. One of the men stumbled and fell upon his hands, which as he rose and rubbed them together were slippery. On examination they were seen to be red with blood.

An encounter, unarmed, with a wounded panther was not agreeable to their taste; all but Brading turned back. He, with lantern and pistol, pushed courageously forward into the wood. Passing through a difficult undergrowth he came into a small opening, and there his courage had its reward, for there he found the body of his victim. But it was no panther. What it was is told, even to this day, upon a weather-worn headstone in the village churchyard, and for many years was attested daily at the graveside by the bent figure and sorrow-seamed face of Old Man Marlowe, to whose soul, and to the soul of his strange, unhappy child, peace. Peace and reparation.

THE OTHER SIDE: A BRETON LEGEND

ERIC STENBOCK

"Not that I like it, but one does feel so much better after it—oh, thank you, Mère Yvonne, yes just a little drop more." So the old crones fell to drinking their hot brandy and water (although of course they only took it medicinally, as a remedy for their rheumatics,) all seated round the big fire and Mère Pinquèle continued her story.

"Oh, yes, then when they get to the top of the hill, there is an altar with six candles quite black and a sort of something in between, that nobody sees quite clearly and the old black ram with the man's face and long horns begins to say Mass in a sort of gibberish nobody understands, and two black strange things like monkeys glide about with the book and the cruets—and there's music too, such music. There are things the top half like black cats, and the bottom part like men only their legs are all covered with close black hair, and they play on the bag-pipes, and when they come to the elevation, then—" Amid the old crones there was lying on the hearth-rug, before the fire, a boy, whose large lovely eyes dilated and whose limbs quivered

in the very ecstasy of terror.

"Is that all true, Mère Pinquèle?" he said.

"Oh, quite true, and not only that, the best part is yet to come; for they take a child and—." Here Mère Pinquèle showed her fang-like teeth.

"Oh! Mère Pinquèle, are you a witch too?"

"Silence, Gabriel," said Mère Yvonne, "how can you say anything so wicked? Why bless me, the boy ought to have been in bed ages ago."

Just then all shuddered, and all made the sign of the cross except Mère Pinquèle, for they heard that most dreadful of dreadful sounds—the howl of a wolf, which begins with three sharp barks and then lifts itself up in a long protracted wail of commingled cruelty and despair, and at last subsides into a whispered growl fraught with eternal malice.

There was a forest and a village and a brook, the village was on one side of the brook, none had dared to cross to the other side. Where the village was, all was green and glad and fertile and fruitful; on the other side the trees never put forth green leaves, and a dark shadow hung over it even at noon-day and in the night-time one could hear the wolves howling—the were-wolves and the wolf-men and the men-wolves; and those very wicked men who for nine days in every year are turned into wolves; but on the green side no wolf was ever seen, and only one little running brook like a silver streak flowed between.

It was spring now and the old crones sat no longer by the fire but before their cottages sunning themselves, and everyone felt so happy that they ceased to tell stories of the "other side." But Gabriel wandered by the brook as he was wont to wander, drawn thither by some strange attraction mingled with intense horror.

His schoolfellows did not like Gabriel; all laughed and jeered at him, because he was less cruel and more gentle of nature than the rest, and even as a rare and beautiful bird escaped from a cage is hacked to death by the common sparrows, so was Gabriel among his fellows. Everyone wondered how Mère Yvonne, that buxom and worthy matron, could have produced a son like this, with strange dreamy eyes, who was as they said "pas comme les autres gamins." His only friends were the Abbé Félicien whose Mass he served each morning, and one little girl called Carmeille, who loved him, no one could make out why.

The sun had already set, Gabriel still wandered by the brook, filled with vague terror and irresistible fascination. The sun set and the moon rose, the full moon; very large and very clear, and the moonlight flooded the forest both this side and "the other side," and just on the "other side" of the brook, hanging over, Gabriel saw a large deep blue flower, whose strange intoxicating perfume reached him and fascinated him even where he stood.

"If I could only make one step across," he thought, "nothing could harm me if I only plucked that one flower, and nobody would know I had been over at all," for the villagers looked with hatred and suspicion on anyone who was said to have crossed to the "other side," so summing up courage he leapt lightly to the other side of the brook. Then the moon breaking from a cloud shone with unusual brilliance, and he saw, stretching before him, long reaches of the same strange blue flowers each one lovelier than the last, till, not being able to make up his mind which one flower to take or whether to take several, he went on and on, and the moon shone very brightly and a strange unseen bird, somewhat like a nightingale, but louder and lovelier, sang, and his heart was filled with longing for he knew not what, and the moon shone and the nightingale sang. But on a sudden a black cloud covered the moon entirely and all was black, utter darkness, and through the darkness he heard wolves howling and shrieking in the hideous ardour of the chase, and there passed before him a horrible procession of wolves (black wolves with red fiery eyes), and with them men that had the heads of wolves and wolves that had the heads of men, and above them flew owls (black owls with red fiery eyes), and bats and long serpentine black things, and last of all seated on an enormous black ram with hideous human face the wolf-keeper

on whose face was eternal shadows but they continued their horrid chase and passed him by and when they had passed the moon shone out more beautiful than ever, and the strange nightingale sang again, and the strange intense blue flowers were in long reaches in front to the right and to the left. But one thing was there which had not been before, among the deep blue flowers walked one with long gleaming golden hair, and she turned once round and her eyes were of the same colour as the strange blue flowers, and she walked on and Gabriel could not choose but follow. But when a cloud passed over the moon he saw no beautiful woman but a wolf, so in utter terror he turned and fled, plucking one of the strange blue flowers on the way and leapt again over the brook and ran home.

When he got home Gabriel could not resist showing his treasure to his mother, though he knew she would not appreciate it; but when she saw the strange blue flower, Mere Yvonne turned pale and said, "Why child, where hast thou been? sure it is the witch flower"; and so saying she snatched it from him and cast it into the corner, and immediately all its beauty and strange fragrance faded from it and it looked charred as though it had been burnt. So Gabriel sat down silently and rather sulkily and having eaten no supper went up to bed, but he did not sleep but waited and waited till all was quiet within the house. Then he crept downstairs in his long white night-shirt and bare feet on the square cold stones and picked hurriedly up the charred and faded flower and put it in his warm bosom next his heart, and immediately the flower bloomed again lovelier than ever, and he fell into a deep sleep, but through his sleep he seemed to hear a soft low voice singing underneath his window in a strange language (in which the subtle sounds melted into one another), but he could distinguish no word except his own name.

When he went forth in the morning to serve Mass, he still kept the flower with him next his heart. Now when the priest began Mass and said "Intriobo ad altare Dei," then said Gabriel "Qui nequiquam laetificavit juventutem meam." And the Abbé Félicien turned round on hearing this strange response, and he saw the boy's face deadly pale, his eyes fixed and his limbs rigid, and as the priest looked on him Gabriel fell fainting to the floor, so the sacristan had to carry him home and seek another acolyte for the Abbé Félicien.

Now when the Abbé Félicien came to see after him, Gabriel felt strangely reluctant to say anything about the blue flower and for the first time he deceived the priest.

In the afternoon as sunset drew nigh he felt better and Carmeille came to see him and begged him to go out with her into the fresh air. So they went out hand in hand, the dark haired, gazelle-eyed boy, and the fair wavy haired girl, and something, he knew not what, led his steps (half knowingly and yet not so, for he could not but walk thither) to the brook, and they sat down together on the bank.

Gabriel thought at least he might tell his secret to Carmeille, so he took out the flower from his bosom and said, "Look here, Carmeille, hast thou seen ever so lovely a flower as this?" but Carmeille turned pale and faint and said, "Oh, Gabriel what is this flower? I but touched it and I felt something strange come over me. No, no, I don't like its perfume, no there's something not quite right about it, oh, dear Gabriel, do let me throw it away," and before he had time to answer, she cast it from her, and again all its beauty and fragrance went from it and it looked charred as though it had been burnt. But suddenly where the flower had been thrown on this side of the brook, there appeared a wolf, which stood and looked at the children.

Carmeille said, "What shall we do," and clung to Gabriel, but the wolf looked at them very steadfastly and Gabriel recognized in the eyes of the wolf the strange deep intense blue eyes of the wolf-woman he had seen on the "other side," so he said, "Stay here, dear Carmeille, see she is looking gently at us and will not hurt us."

"But it is a wolf," said Carmeille, and quivered all over with fear but again Gabriel said languidly, "She will not hurt us." Then Carmeille seized Gabriel's hand in an agony of terror and dragged him along with her till they reached the village, where she gave the alarm and all the lads of the village gathered together. They had never seen a wolf on this side of the brook, so they excited themselves greatly and arranged a grand wolf hunt for the morrow, but Gabriel sat silently apart and said no word..

That night Gabriel could not sleep at all nor could he bring himself to say his prayers; but he sat in his little room by the window with his shirt open at the throat and the strange blue flower at his heart and again this night he heard a voice singing beneath his window in the same soft, subtle, liquid language as before—

> Ma zála liral va jé
> Cwamûlo zhajéla je
> Cárma urádi el java
> Járma, symai,—carmé—
> Zhála javály thra je
> al vú al vlaûde va azré
> Safralje vairálje va já?
> Cárma serâja
> Lâja lâja
> Luzhà!

and as he looked he could see the silvern shadows slide on the limmering light of golden hair, and the strange eyes gleaming dark blue through the night and it seemed to him that he could not but follow, so he walked half clad and bare foot as he was with eyes fixed as in a dream silently down the stairs and out into the night.

And ever and again she turned to look on him with her strange blue eyes full of tenderness and passion and sadness beyond the sadness of things human—and as he foreknew his steps led him to the brink of the brook Then she, taking his hand, familiarly said, "Won't you help me over Gabriel?"

Then it seemed to him as though he had known her all his life—so he went with her to the "other side" but he saw no one by him; and looking again beside him there were *two wolves*. In a frenzy of terror, he (who had never thought to kill any living thing before) seized a log of wood lying by and smote one of the wolves on the head.

Immediately he saw the wolf-woman again at his side with blood streaming from her forehead, staining her wonderful golden hair, and with eyes looking at him with infinite reproach, she said—"Who did this?"

Then she whispered a few words to the other wolf, which leapt over the brook and made its way towards the village, and turning again towards him she said, "Oh Gabriel, how could you strike me, who would have loved you so long and so well." Then it seemed to him again as though he had known her all his life but he felt dazed and said nothing—but she gathered a dark green strangely shaped leaf and holding it to her forehead she said—"Gabriel, kiss the place all will be well again," So he kissed as she had bidden him and he felt the salt taste of blood in his mouth and then he knew no more.

Again he saw the wolf-keeper with his horrible troupe around him, but this time not engaged in the chase but sitting in strange conclave in a circle and the black owls sat in the trees and the black bats hung downwards from the branches. Gabriel stood alone in the middle with a hundred wicked eyes fixed on him. They seemed to deliberate about what should be done with him, speaking in that same strange tongue which he had heard in the songs beneath his window. Suddenly he felt a hand pressing in his and saw the mysterious wolf-woman by his side. Then began what seemed a kind of incantation where human or half human creatures seemed to howl, and beasts to speak with human speech but in the unknown tongue. Then the wolf-keeper whose face was ever veiled in shadow spake some words in a voice that seemed to come from afar off, but all he could distinguish was his own name Gabriel and her name Lilith. Then he felt arms enlacing him.—

Gabriel awoke—in his own room—so it was a dream after all—but what a dreadful dream. Yes, but was it his own room? Of course there was his coat hanging over the chair—yes but—the Crucifix—where was the Crucifix and the benetier and the consecrated palm branch and the antique image of Our Lady perpetuae salutis, with the little ever-burning lamp before it, before which he placed every day the flowers he had gathered, yet had not dared to place the blue flower—

Every morning he lifted his still dream-laden eyes to it and said Ave Maria and made the sign of the cross, which bringeth peace to the soul—but how horrible, how maddening, it was not there, not at all. No surely he could not be awake, at least not quite awake, he would make the benedictive sign and he would be freed from this tearful illusion—yes but the sign, he would make the sign—oh, but what was the sign? Had he forgotten? or was his arm paralyzed? No he could not move. Then he had forgotten—and the prayer—he must remember that A—vae—nunc—mortis—fructus. No surely it did not run thus—but something like it surely—yes, he was awake he could move at any rate—he would reassure himself—he would get up—he would see the grey old church with the exquisitely pointed gables bathed in the light of dawn, and presently the deep solemn bell would toll and he would run down and don his red cassock and lace-worked cotta and light the tall candles on the altar and wait reverently to vest the good and gracious Abbé Félicien, kissing each vestment as he lifted it with reverent hands.

But surely this was not the light of dawn; it was like sunset! He leapt from his small white bed, and a vague terror came over him, he trembled and had to hold on to the chair before he reached the window. No, the solemn spires of the grey church were not to be seen—he was in the depths of the forest, but in a part he had never seen before—but surely he had explored every part, it must be the "other side." To terror succeeded a languor and lassitude not without charm—passivity, acquiescence, indulgence—he felt, as it were, the strong caress of another will flowing over him like water and clothing him with invisible hands in an impalpable garment, so he dressed himself almost mechanically and walked downstairs, the same stairs it seemed to him down which it was his wont to run and spring. The broad square stones seemed singularly beautiful and iridescent with many strange colours—how was it he had never noticed this before—but he was gradually losing the power of wondering—he entered the room below—the wonted coffee and bread-rolls were on the table.

"Why Gabriel, how late you are to-day." The voice was very sweet but the intonation strange—and there sat Lilith, the mysterious wolf-woman, her glittering gold hair tied in a loose knot and an embroidery whereon she was tracing strange serpentine patterns, lay over the lap of her maize coloured garment—and she looked at Gabriel steadfastly with her wonderful dark blue eyes and said, "Why, Gabriel, you are late to-day," and Gabriel answered, "I was tired yesterday, give me some coffee."

A dream within a dream—yes, he had known her all his life, and they dwelt together, had they not always done so? And she would take him through the glades of the forest and gather for him flowers, such as he had never seen before, and tell him stories in her strange, low deep voice, which seemed ever to be accompanied by the faint vibration of strings, looking at him fixedly the while with her marvellous blue eyes.

Little by little the flame of vitality which burned within him seemed to grow fainter and fainter, and his lithe lissom limbs waxed languorous and luxurious—yet was he ever filled with a languid content and a will not his own perpetually overshadowed him.

One day in their wanderings he saw a strange dark blue flower like unto the eyes of Lilith, and a sudden half remembrance flashed through his mind.

"What is this blue flower?" he said, and Lilith shuddered and said nothing; but as they went a little further there was a brook—the brook he thought, and felt his fetters falling off him, and he prepared to spring over the brook; but Lilith seized him by the arm and held him back with all her strength, and trembling all over she said, "Promise me Gabriel that you will not cross over." But he said, "Tell me what is this blue flower, and why you will not tell me?" And she said, "Look Gabriel at the brook." And he looked and saw that though it was just like the brook of separation it was not the same, the waters did not flow.

As Gabriel looked steadfastly into the still waters it seemed to him as though he saw voices—some impression of the Vespers for the Dead. "Hei mihi quia incolatus sum," and again "De profundis clamavi ad te"—oh, that veil, that overshadowing veil! Why could he not hear properly and see, and why did he only remember as one looking through a threefold semitransparent curtain. Yes they were praying for him—but who were they? He heard again the voice of Lilith in whispered anguish, "Come away!"

Then he said, this time in monotone, "What is this blue flower, and what is its use?"

And the low thrilling voice answered, "It is called 'lûli uzhûri,' two drops pressed upon the face of the sleeper and he will *sleep.*"

He was as a child in her hand and suffered himself to be led from thence, nevertheless he plucked listlessly one or the blue flowers, holding it downwards in his hand. What did she mean? Would the sleeper wake? Would the blue flower leave any stain? Could that stain be wiped off?

But as he lay asleep at early dawn he heard voices from afar oft praying for him—the Abbé Félicien, Carmeille, his mother too, then some familiar words struck his ear: "Libera mea porta inferi." Mass was being said for the repose of his soul, he knew this. No, he could not stay, he would leap over the brook, he knew the way—he had forgotten that the brook did not flow. Ah, but Lilith would know—what should he do? The blue flower—there it lay close by his bedside—he understood now, so he crept very silently to where Lilith lay asleep, her long hair glistening gold, shining like a glory round about her. He pressed two drops on her forehead, she sighed once, and a shade of praeternatural anguish passed over her beautiful face. He fled—terror, remorse, and hope tearing his soul and making fleet his feet. He came to the brook—he did not see that the water did not flow—of course it was the brook for separation; one bound, he should be with things human again. He leapt over and—

A change had come over him—what was it? He could not tell—did he walk on all fours? Yes surely. He looked into the brook, whose still waters were fixed as a mirror, and there, horror, he beheld himself; or was it himself? His head and face, yes; but his body transformed to that of a wolf. Even as he looked he heard a sound of hideous mocking laughter behind him. He turned round—there, in a gleam of red lurid light, he saw one whose body was human, but whose head was that of a wolf, with eyes of infinite malice; and, while this hideous being laughed with a loud human laugh, he, essaying to speak, could only utter the prolonged howl of a wolf.

But we will transfer our thoughts from the alien things on the "other side" to the simple human village where Gabriel used to dwell. Mere Yvonne was not much surprised when Gabriel did not turn up to breakfast—he often did not, so absent-minded was he; this time she said, "I suppose he has gone with the others to the wolf hunt." Not that Gabriel was given to hunting, but, as she sagely said, "there was no knowing what he might do next." The boys said, "Of course that muff Gabriel is skulking and hiding himself, he's afraid to join the wolf hunt; why, he wouldn't even kill a cat," for their one notion of excellence was slaughter—so the greater the game the greater the glory. They were chiefly now confined to cats and sparrows, but they all hoped in after time to become generals of armies.

Yet these children had been taught all their life through with the gentle words of Christ—but alas, nearly all the seed falls by the wayside, where it could not bear flower or fruit; how little these know the suffering and bitter anguish or realize the full meaning of the words to those, of whom it is written "Some fell among thorns."

The wolf hunt was so far a success that they did actually see a wolf, but not a success, as they did not kill it before it leapt over the brook to the "other side," where, of course, they were afraid to pursue it. No emotion is more inrooted and intense in the minds of common people than hatred and fear of anything "strange."

Days passed by but Gabriel was nowhere seen—and Mère Yvonne began to see clearly at last how deeply she loved her only son, who was so unlike her that she had thought herself an object of pity to other mothers—the goose and the swan's egg. People searched and pretended to search, they even went to the length of dragging the ponds, which the boys thought very amusing, as it enabled them to kill a great number of water rats, and Carmeille sat in a corner and cried all day long. Mère Pinquèle also sat in a corner and chuckled and said that she had always said Gabriel would come to no good. The Abbé Félicien looked pale and anxious, but said very little, save to God and those that dwelt with God.

At last, as Gabriel was not there, they supposed he must be nowhere—that is *dead*. (Their knowledge of other localities being so limited, that it did not even occur to them to suppose he might be living elsewhere than in the village.) So it was agreed that an empty catafalque should be put up in the church with tall candles round it, and Mere Yvonne said all the prayers that were in her prayer book, beginning at the beginning and ending at the end, regardless of their appropriateness—not even omitting the instructions of the rubrics. And Carmeille sat in the corner of the little side chapel and cried, and cried. And the Abbé Félicien caused the boys to sing the Vespers for the Dead (this did not amuse them so much as dragging the pond), and on the following morning, in the silence of early dawn said the Dirge and the Requiem—and *this Gabriel heard*.

Then the Abbé Félicien received a message to bring the Holy Viaticum to one sick. So they set forth in solemn procession with great torches, and their way lay along the brook of separation.

Essaying to speak he could only utter the prolonged howl of a wolf—the most fearful of all bestial sounds. He howled and howled again—perhaps Lilith would hear him! Perhaps she could rescue him? Then he remembered the blue flower—the beginning and end of all his woe. His cries aroused all the denizens of the forest—the wolves, the wolf-men, and the men-wolves. He fled before them in an agony of terror—behind him, seated on the black ram with human face, was the wolf-keeper, whose face was veiled in eternal shadow. Only once he turned to look behind—for among the shrieks and howls of bestial chase he heard one thrilling voice moan with pain. And there among them he beheld Lilith, her body too was that of a wolf, almost hidden in the masses of her glittering golden hair, on her forehead was a stain of blue, like in colour to her mysterious eyes, now veiled with tears she could not shed.

The way of the Most Holy Viaticum lay along the brook of separation. They heard the fearful howlings afar off, the torch bearers turned pale and trembled—but the Abbé Félicien, holding aloft the Ciborium, said "They cannot harm us."

Suddenly the whole horrid chase came in sight Gabriel sprang over the brook, the Abbé Félicien held the most Blessed Sacrament before him, and his shape was restored to him and he fell down prostrate in adoration. But the Abbé Félicien still held aloft the Sacred Ciborium, and the people fell on their knees in the agony of fear, but the face of the priest seemed to shine with divine effulgence. Then the wolf-keeper held up in his hands the shape of something horrible and inconceivable—a monstrance to the Sacrament of Hell, and three times he raised it, in mockery of the blessed rite of Benediction. And on the third time streams of fire went forth from his fingers, and all the "other side" of the forest took fire, and great darkness was over all.

All who were there and saw and heard it have kept the impress thereof for the rest of their lives—nor till in their death hour was the remembrance thereof absent from their minds. Shrieks, horrible beyond conception, were heard till nightfall—then the rain rained.

The "other side" is harmless now—charred ashes only, but none dares to cross but Gabriel alone—for once a year for nine days a strange madness comes over him.

The great farm hall was ablaze with the fire-light, and noisy with laughter and talk and many-sounding work. None could be idle but the very young and the very old: little Rol, who was hugging a puppy, and old Trella, whose palsied hand fumbled over her knitting. The early evening had closed in, and the farm-servants, come from their outdoor work, had assembled in the ample hall, which gave space for a score or more of workers. Several of the men were engaged in carving, and to these were yielded the best place and light; others made or repaired fishing-tackle and harness, and a great seine net occupied three pairs of hands. Of the women most were sorting and mixing eider feather and chopping straw to add to it. Looms were there, though not in present use, but three wheels whirred emulously, and the finest and swiftest thread of the three ran between the fingers of the house-mistress. Near her were some children, busy too, plaiting wicks for

to find amusement elsewhere.

The baskets of white eider feathers caught his eye far off in a distant corner. He slipped under the table, and crept along on all-fours, the ordinary common-place custom of walking down a room upright not being to his fancy. When close to the women he lay still for a moment watching, with his elbows on the floor and his chin in his palms. One of the women seeing him nodded and smiled, and presently he crept out behind her skirts and passed, hardly noticed, from one to another, till he found opportunity to possess himself of a large handful of feathers. With these he traversed the length of the room, under the table again, and emerged near the spinners. At the feet of the youngest he curled himself round, sheltered by her knees from the observation of the others, and disarmed her of interference by secretly displaying his handful with a confiding smile. A dubious nod satisfied him, and presently he started on the

THE WERE-WOLF

CLEMENCE HOUSMAN

candles and lamps. Each group of workers had a lamp in its centre, and those farthest from the fire had live heat from two braziers filled with glowing wood embers, replenished now and again from the generous hearth. But the flicker of the great fire was manifest to remotest corners, and prevailed beyond the limits of the weaker lights.

Little Rol grew tired of his puppy, dropped it incontinently, and made an onslaught on Tyr, the old wolf-hound, who basked dozing, whimpering and twitching in his hunting dreams. Prone went Rol beside Tyr, his young arms round the shaggy neck, his curls against the black jowl. Tyr gave a perfunctory lick, and stretched with a sleepy sigh. Rol growled and rolled and shoved invitingly, but could only gain from the old dog placid toleration and a half-observant blink. "Take that then!" said Rol, indignant at this ignoring of his advances, and sent the puppy sprawling against the dignity that disdained him as play-mate. The dog took no notice, and the child wandered off

play he had devised. He took a tuft of the white down, and gently shook it free of his fingers close to the whirl of the wheel. The wind of the swift motion took it, spun it round and round in widening circles, till it floated above like a slow white moth. Little Rol's eyes danced, and the row of his small teeth shone in a silent laugh of delight. Another and another of the white tufts was sent whirling round like a winged thing in a spider's web, and floating clear at last. Presently the handful failed.

Rol sprawled forward to survey the room, and contemplate another journey under the table. His shoulder, thrusting forward, checked the wheel for an instant; he shifted hastily. The wheel flew on with a jerk, and the thread snapped. "Naughty Rol!" said the girl. The swiftest wheel stopped also, and the house-mistress, Rol's aunt, leaned forward, and sighting the low curly head, gave a warning against mischief, and sent him off to old Trella's corner.

Rol obeyed, and after a discreet period of obedience,

sidled out again down the length of the room farthest from his aunt's eye. As he slipped in among the men, they looked up to see that their tools might be, as far as possible, out of reach of Rol's hands, and close to their own. Nevertheless, before long he managed to secure a fine chisel and take off its point on the leg of the table. The carver's strong objections to this disconcerted Rol, who for five minutes thereafter effaced himself under the table.

During this seclusion he contemplated the many pairs of legs that surrounded him, and almost shut out the light of the fire. How very odd some of the legs were: some were curved where they should be straight, some were straight where they should be curved, and, as Rol said to himself, "they all seemed screwed on differently." Some were tucked away modestly under the benches, others were thrust far out under the table, encroaching on Rol's own particular domain. He stretched out his own short legs and regarded them critically, and, after comparison, favourably. Why were not all legs made like his, or like *his*?

These legs approved by Rol were a little apart from the rest. He crawled opposite and again made comparison. His face grew quite solemn as he thought of the innumerable days to come before his legs could be as long and strong. He hoped they would be just like those, his models, as straight as to bone, as curved as to muscle.

A few moments later Sweyn of the long legs felt a small hand caressing his foot, and looking down, met the upturned eyes of his little cousin Rol. Lying on his back, still softly patting and stroking the young man's foot, the child was quiet and happy for a good while. He watched the movement of the strong deft hands, and the shifting of the bright tools. Now and then, minute chips of wood, puffed off by Sweyn, fell down upon his face. At last he raised himself, very gently, lest a jog should wake impatience in the carver, and crossing his own legs round Sweyn's ankle, clasping with his arms too, laid his head against the knee. Such act is evidence of a child's most wonderful hero-worship. Quite content was Rol, and more than content when Sweyn paused a minute to joke, and pat his head and pull his curls. Quiet he remained, as long as quiescence is possible to limbs young as his. Sweyn forgot he was near, hardly noticed when his leg was gently released, and never saw the stealthy abstraction of one of his tools.

Ten minutes thereafter was a lamentable wail from low on the floor, rising to the full pitch of Rol's healthy lungs; for his hand was gashed across, and the copious bleeding terrified him. Then was there soothing and comforting, washing and binding, and a modicum of scolding, till the loud outcry sank into occasional sobs, and the child, tear-stained and subdued, was returned to the chimney-corner settle, where Trella nodded.

In the reaction after pain and fright, Rol found that the quiet of that fire-lit corner was to his mind. Tyr, too, disdained him no longer, but, roused by his sobs, showed all the concern and sympathy that a dog can by licking and wistful watching. A little shame weighed also upon his spirits. He wished he had not cried quite so much. He re-

membered how once Sweyn had come home with his arm torn down from the shoulder, and a dead bear; and how he had never winced nor said a word, though his lips turned white with pain. Poor little Rol gave another sighing sob over his own faint-hearted shortcomings.

The light and motion of the great fire began to tell strange stories to the child, and the wind in the chimney roared a corroborative note now and then. The great black mouth of the chimney, impending high over the hearth, received as into a mysterious gulf murky coils of smoke and brightness of aspiring sparks; and beyond, in the high darkness, were muttering and wailing and strange doings, so that sometimes the smoke rushed back in panic, and curled out and up to the roof, and condensed itself to invisibility among the rafters. And then the wind would rage after its lost prey, and rush round the house, rattling and shrieking at window and door.

In a lull, after one such loud gust, Rol lifted his head in surprise and listened. A lull had also come on the babel of talk, and thus could be heard with strange distinctness a sound outside the door—the sound of a child's voice, a child's hands. "Open, open; let me in!" piped the little voice from low down, lower than the handle, and the latch rattled as though a tiptoe child reached up to it, and soft small knocks were struck. One near the door sprang up and opened it. "No one is here," he said. Tyr lifted his head and gave utterance to a howl, loud, prolonged, most dismal.

Sweyn, not able to believe that his ears had deceived him, got up and went to the door. It was a dark night; the clouds were heavy with snow, that had fallen fitfully when the wind lulled. Untrodden snow lay up to the porch; there was no sight nor sound of any human being. Sweyn strained his eyes far and near, only to see dark sky, pure snow, and a line of black fir trees on a hill brow, bowing down before the wind. "It must have been the wind," he said, and closed the door.

Many faces looked scared. The sound of a child's voice had been so distinct—and the words "Open, open; let me in!" The wind might creak the wood, or rattle the latch, but could not speak with a child's voice, nor knock with the soft plain blows that a plump fist gives. And the strange unusual howl of the wolf-hound was an omen to be feared, be the rest what it might. Strange things were said by one and another, till the rebuke of the house-mistress quelled them into far-off whispers. For a time after there was uneasiness, constraint, and silence; then the chill fear thawed by degrees, and the babble of talk flowed on again.

Yet half-an-hour later a very slight noise outside the door sufficed to arrest every hand, every tongue. Every head was raised, every eye fixed in one direction. "It is Christian; he is late," said Sweyn.

No, no; this is a feeble shuffle, not a young man's tread. With the sound of uncertain feet came the hard tap-tap of a stick against the door, and the high-pitched voice of eld, "Open, open; let me in!" Again Tyr flung up his head in a long doleful howl.

Before the echo of the tapping stick and the high voice

had fairly died away, Sweyn had sprung across to the door and flung it wide. "No one again," he said in a steady voice, though his eyes looked startled as he stared out. He saw the lonely expanse of snow, the clouds swagging low, and between the two the line of dark fir-trees bowing in the wind. He closed the door without a word of comment, and re-crossed the room.

A score of blanched faces were turned to him as though he must be solver of the enigma. He could not be unconscious of this mute eye-questioning, and it disturbed his resolute air of composure. He hesitated, glanced towards his mother, the house-mistress, then back at the frightened folk, and gravely, before them all, made the sign of the cross. There was a flutter of hands as the sign was repeated by all, and the dead silence was stirred as by a huge sigh, for the held breath of many was freed as though the sign gave magic relief.

Even the house-mistress was perturbed. She left her wheel and crossed the room to her son, and spoke with him for a moment in a low tone that none could overhear. But a moment later her voice was high-pitched and loud, so that all might benefit by her rebuke of the "heathen chatter" of one of the girls. Perhaps she essayed to silence thus her own misgivings and forebodings.

No other voice dared speak now with its natural fulness. Low tones made intermittent murmurs, and now and then silence drifted over the whole room. The handling of tools was as noiseless as might be, and suspended on the instant if the door rattled in a gust of wind. After a time Sweyn left his work, joined the group nearest the door, and loitered there on the pretence of giving advice and help to the unskilful.

A man's tread was heard outside in the porch. "Christian!" said Sweyn and his mother simultaneously, he confidently, she authoritatively, to set the checked wheels going again. But Tyr flung up his head with an appalling howl.

"Open, open; let me in!"

It was a man's voice, and the door shook and rattled as a man's strength beat against it. Sweyn could feel the planks quivering, as on the instant his hand was upon the door, flinging it open, to face the blank porch, and beyond only snow and sky, and firs aslant in the wind.

He stood for a long minute with the open door in his hand. The bitter wind swept in with its icy chill, but a deadlier chill of fear came swifter, and seemed to freeze the beating of hearts. Sweyn stepped back to snatch up a great bearskin cloak.

"Sweyn, where are you going?"

"No farther than the porch, mother," and he stepped out and closed the door.

He wrapped himself in the heavy fur, and leaning against the most sheltered wall of the porch, steeled his nerves to face the devil and all his works. No sound of voices came from within; the most distinct sound was the crackle and roar of the fire.

It was bitterly cold. His feet grew numb, but he forbore stamping them into warmth lest the sound should strike panic within; nor would he leave the porch, nor print a foot-mark on the untrodden white that declared so absolutely how no human voices and hands could have approached the door since snow fell two hours or more ago. "When the wind drops there will be more snow," thought Sweyn.

For the best part of an hour he kept his watch, and saw no living thing—heard no unwonted sound. "I will freeze here no longer," he muttered, and re-entered.

One woman gave a half-suppressed scream as his hand was laid on the latch, and then a gasp of relief as he came in. No one questioned him, only his mother said, in a tone of forced unconcern, "Could you not see Christian coming?" as though she were made anxious only by the absence of her younger son. Hardly had Sweyn stamped near to the fire than clear knocking was heard at the door. Tyr leapt from the hearth, his eyes red as the fire, his fangs showing white in the black jowl, his neck ridged and bristling; and overleaping Rol, ramped at the door, barking furiously.

Outside the door a clear mellow voice was calling. Tyr's bark made the words undistinguishable. No one offered to stir towards the door before Sweyn.

He stalked down the room resolutely, lifted the latch, and swung back the door.

A white-robed woman glided in.

No wraith! Living—beautiful—young.

Tyr leapt upon her.

Lithely she baulked the sharp fangs with folds of her long fur robe, and snatching from her girdle a small two-edged axe, whirled it up for a blow of defence.

Sweyn caught the dog by the collar, and dragged him off yelling and struggling.

The stranger stood in the doorway motionless, one foot set forward, one arm flung up, till the house-mistress hurried down the room; and Sweyn, relinquishing to others the furious Tyr, turned again to close the door, and offer excuse for so fierce a greeting. Then she lowered her arm, slung the axe in its place at her waist, loosened the furs about her face, and shook over her shoulders the long white robe—all as it were with the sway of one movement.

She was a maiden, tall and very fair. The fashion of her dress was strange, half masculine, yet not unwomanly. A fine fur tunic, reaching but little below the knee, was all the skirt she wore; below were the cross-bound shoes and leggings that a hunter wears. A white fur cap was set low upon the brows, and from its edge strips of fur fell lappet-wise about her shoulders; two of these at her entrance had been drawn forward and crossed about her throat, but now, loosened and thrust back, left unhidden long plaits of fair hair that lay forward on shoulder and breast, down to the ivory-studded girdle where the axe gleamed.

Sweyn and his mother led the stranger to the hearth without question or sign of curiosity, till she voluntarily told her tale of a long journey to distant kindred, a promised guide unmet, and signals and landmarks mistaken.

"Alone!" exclaimed Sweyn in astonishment. "Have you journeyed thus far, a hundred leagues, alone?"

She answered "Yes" with a little smile.

"Over the hills and the wastes! Why, the folk there are savage and wild as beasts."

She dropped her hand upon her axe with a laugh of some scorn.

"I fear neither man nor beast; some few fear me." And then she told strange tales of fierce attack and defence, and of the bold free huntress life she had led.

Her words came a little slowly and deliberately, as though she spoke in a scarce familiar tongue; now and then she hesitated, and stopped in a phrase, as though for lack of some word.

She became the centre of a group of listeners. The interest she excited dissipated, in some degree, the dread inspired by the mysterious voices. There was nothing ominous about this young, bright, fair reality, though her aspect was strange.

Little Rol crept near, staring at the stranger with all his might. Unnoticed, he softly stroked and patted a corner of her soft white robe that reached to the floor in ample folds. He laid his cheek against it caressingly, and then edged up close to her knees.

"What is your name?" he asked.

The stranger's smile and ready answer, as she looked down, saved Rol from the rebuke merited by his unmannerly question.

"My real name," she said, "would be uncouth to your ears and tongue. The folk of this country have given me another name, and from this" (she laid her hand on the fur robe) "they call me 'White Fell.'"

Little Rol repeated it to himself, stroking and patting as before. "White Fell, White Fell."

The fair face, and soft, beautiful dress pleased Rol. He knelt up, with his eyes on her face and an air of uncertain determination, like a robin's on a doorstep, and plumped his elbows into her lap with a little gasp at his own audacity.

"Rol!" exclaimed his aunt; but, "Oh, let him!" said White Fell, smiling and stroking his head; and Rol stayed.

He advanced farther, and panting at his own adventurousness in the face of his aunt's authority, climbed up on to her knees. Her welcoming arms hindered any protest. He nestled happily, fingering the axe head, the ivory studs in her girdle, the ivory clasp at her throat, the plaits of fair hair; rubbing his head against the softness of her fur-clad shoulder, with a child's full confidence in the kindness of beauty.

White Fell had not uncovered her head, only knotted the pendant fur loosely behind her neck. Rol reached up his hand towards it, whispering her name to himself, "White Fell, White Fell," then slid his arms round her neck, and kissed her—once—twice. She laughed delightedly, and kissed him again.

"The child plagues you?" said Sweyn.

"No, indeed," she answered, with an earnestness so intense as to seem disproportionate to the occasion.

Rol settled himself again on her lap, and began to un-

wind the bandage bound round his hand. He paused a little when he saw where the blood had soaked through; then went on till his hand was bare and the cut displayed, gaping and long, though only skin deep. He held it up towards White Fell, desirous of her pity and sympathy.

At sight of it, and the blood-stained linen, she drew in her breath suddenly, clasped Rol to her—hard, hard—till he began to struggle. Her face was hidden behind the boy, so that none could see its expression. It had lighted up with a most awful glee.

Afar, beyond the fir-grove, beyond the low hill behind, the absent Christian was hastening his return. From daybreak he had been afoot, carrying notice of a bear hunt to all the best hunters of the farms and hamlets that lay within a radius of twelve miles. Nevertheless, having been detained till a late hour, he now broke into a run, going with a long smooth stride of apparent ease that fast made the miles diminish.

He entered the midnight blackness of the fir-grove with scarcely slackened pace, though the path was invisible; and passing through into the open again, sighted the farm lying a furlong off down the slope. Then he sprang out freely, and almost on the instant gave one great sideways leap, and stood still. There in the snow was the track of a great wolf.

His hand went to his knife, his only weapon. He stooped, knelt down, to bring his eyes to the level of a beast, and peered about; his teeth set, his heart beat a little harder than the pace of his running insisted on. A solitary wolf, nearly always savage and of large size, is a formidable beast that will not hesitate to attack a single man. This wolf-track was the largest Christian had ever seen, and, so far as he could judge, recently made. It led from under the fir-trees down the slope. Well for him, he thought, was the delay that had so vexed him before: well for him that he had not passed through the dark fir-grove when that danger of jaws lurked there. Going warily, he followed the track.

It led down the slope, across a broad ice-bound stream, along the level beyond, making towards the farm. A less precise knowledge had doubted, and guessed that here might have come straying big Tyr or his like; but Christian was sure, knowing better than to mistake between footmark of dog and wolf.

Straight on—straight on towards the farm.

Surprised and anxious grew Christian, that a prowling wolf should dare so near. He drew his knife and pressed on, more hastily, more keen-eyed. Oh that Tyr were with him!

Straight on, straight on, even to the very door, where the snow failed. His heart seemed to give a great leap and then stop. There the track *ended*.

Nothing lurked in the porch, and there was no sign of return. The firs stood straight against the sky, the clouds lay low; for the wind had fallen and a few snowflakes came drifting down. In a horror of surprise, Christian stood dazed a moment: then he lifted the latch and went in. His glance took in all the old familiar forms and faces, and with them that of the stranger, fur-clad and beautiful. The awful truth flashed upon him: he knew what she was.

Only a few were startled by the rattle of the latch as he entered. The room was filled with bustle and movement, for it was the supper hour, when all tools were laid aside, and trestles and tables shifted. Christian had no knowledge of what he said and did; he moved and spoke mechanically, half thinking that soon he must wake from this horrible dream. Sweyn and his mother supposed him to be cold and dead-tired, and spared all unnecessary questions. And he found himself seated beside the hearth, opposite that dreadful Thing that looked like a beautiful girl; watching her every movement, curdling with horror to see her fondle the child Rol.

Sweyn stood near them both, intent upon White Fell also; but how differently! She seemed unconscious of the gaze of both—neither aware of the chill dread in the eyes of Christian, nor of Sweyn's warm admiration.

These two brothers, who were twins, contrasted greatly, despite their striking likeness. They were alike in regular profile, fair brown hair, and deep blue eyes; but Sweyn's features were perfect as a young god's, while Christian's showed faulty details. Thus, the line of his mouth was set too straight, the eyes shelved too deeply back, and the contour of the face flowed in less generous curves than Sweyn's. Their height was the same, but Christian was too slender for perfect proportion, while Sweyn's well-knit frame, broad shoulders, and muscular arms, made him pre-eminent for manly beauty as well as for strength. As a hunter Sweyn was without rival; as a fisher without rival. All the countryside acknowledged him to be the best wrestler, rider, dancer, singer. Only in speed could he be surpassed, and in that only by his younger brother. All others Sweyn could distance fairly; but Christian could outrun him easily. Ay, he could keep pace with Sweyn's most breathless burst, and laugh and talk the while. Christian took little pride in his fleetness of foot, counting a man's legs to be the least worthy of his members. He had no envy of his brother's athletic superiority, though to several feats he had made a moderate second. He loved as only a twin can love—proud of all that Sweyn did, content with all that Sweyn was; humbly content also that his own great love should not be so exceedingly returned, since he knew himself to be so far less love-worthy.

Christian dared not, in the midst of women and children, launch the horror that he knew into words. He waited to consult his brother; but Sweyn did not, or would not, notice the signal he made, and kept his face always turned towards White Fell. Christian drew away from the hearth, unable to remain passive with that dread upon him.

"Where is Tyr?" he said suddenly. Then, catching sight of the dog in a distant corner, "Why is he chained there?"

"He flew at the stranger," one answered.

Christian's eyes glowed. "Yes?" he said, interrogatively.

"He was within an ace of having his brain knocked out."

"Tyr?"

"Yes; she was nimbly up with that little axe she has at her waist. It was well for old Tyr that his master throttled him off."

Christian went without a word to the corner where Tyr was chained. The dog rose up to meet him, as piteous and indignant as a dumb beast can be. He stroked the black head. "Good Tyr! brave dog!"

They knew, they only; and the man and the dumb dog had comfort of each other.

Christian's eyes turned again towards White Fell: Tyr's also, and he strained against the length of the chain. Christian's hand lay on the dog's neck, and he felt it ridge and bristle with the quivering of impotent fury. Then he began to quiver in like manner, with a fury born of reason, not instinct; as impotent morally as was Tyr physically. Oh! the woman's form that he dare not touch! Anything but that, and he with Tyr would be free to kill or be killed.

Then he returned to ask fresh questions.

"How long has the stranger been here?"

"She came about half-an-hour before you."

"Who opened the door to her?"

"Sweyn: no one else dared."

The tone of the answer was mysterious.

"Why?" queried Christian. "Has anything strange happened? Tell me."

For answer he was told in a low undertone of the summons at the door thrice repeated without human agency; and of Tyr's ominous howls; and of Sweyn's fruitless watch outside.

Christian turned towards his brother in a torment of impatience for a word apart. The board was spread, and Sweyn was leading White Fell to the guest's place. This was more awful: she would break bread with them under the roof-tree!

He started forward, and touching Sweyn's arm, whispered an urgent entreaty. Sweyn stared, and shook his head in angry impatience.

Thereupon Christian would take no morsel of food.

His opportunity came at last. White Fell questioned of the landmarks of the country, and of one Cairn Hill, which was an appointed meeting-place at which she was due that night. The house-mistress and Sweyn both exclaimed.

"It is three long miles away," said Sweyn; "with no place for shelter but a wretched hut. Stay with us this night, and I will show you the way to-morrow."

White Fell seemed to hesitate. "Three miles," she said; "then I should be able to see or hear a signal."

"I will look out," said Sweyn; "then, if there be no signal, you must not leave us."

He went to the door. Christian rose silently, and followed him out.

"Sweyn, do you know what she is?"

Sweyn, surprised at the vehement grasp, and low hoarse voice, made answer:

"She? Who? White Fell?"

"Yes."

"She is the most beautiful girl I have ever seen."

"She is a Were-Wolf."

Sweyn burst out laughing. "Are you mad?" he asked.

"No; here, see for yourself."

Christian drew him out of the porch, pointing to the snow where the footmarks had been. Had been, for now they were not. Snow was falling fast, and every dint was blotted out.

"Well?" asked Sweyn.

"Had you come when I signed to you, you would have seen for yourself."

"Seen what?"

"The footprints of a wolf leading up to the door; none leading away."

It was impossible not to be startled by the tone alone, though it was hardly above a whisper. Sweyn eyed his brother anxiously, but in the darkness could make nothing of his face. Then he laid his hands kindly and re-assuringly on Christian's shoulders and felt how he was quivering with excitement and horror.

"One sees strange things," he said, "when the cold has got into the brain behind the eyes; you came in cold and worn out."

"No," interrupted Christian. "I saw the track first on the brow of the slope, and followed it down right here to the door. This is no delusion."

Sweyn in his heart felt positive that it was. Christian was given to day-dreams and strange fancies, though never had he been possessed with so mad a notion before.

"Don't you believe me?" said Christian desperately. "You must. I swear it is sane truth. Are you blind? Why, even Tyr knows."

"You will be clearer headed to-morrow after a night's rest. Then come too, if you will, with White Fell, to the Hill Cairn; and if you have doubts still, watch and follow, and see what footprints she leaves."

Galled by Sweyn's evident contempt Christian turned abruptly to the door. Sweyn caught him back.

"What now, Christian? What are you going to do?"

"You do not believe me; my mother shall."

Sweyn's grasp tightened. "You shall not tell her," he said authoritatively.

Customarily Christian was so docile to his brother's mastery that it was now a surprising thing when he wrenched himself free vigorously, and said as determinedly as Sweyn, "She shall know!" but Sweyn was nearer the door and would not let him pass.

"There has been scare enough for one night already. If this notion of yours will keep, broach it to-morrow." Christian would not yield.

"Women are so easily scared," pursued Sweyn, "and are ready to believe any folly without shadow of proof. Be a man, Christian, and fight this notion of a Were-Wolf by yourself."

"If you would believe me," began Christian.

"I believe you to be a fool," said Sweyn, losing patience. "Another, who was not your brother, might believe you to be a knave, and guess that you had transformed White Fell into a Were-Wolf because she smiled more readily on me

than on you."

The jest was not without foundation, for the grace of White Fell's bright looks had been bestowed on him, on Christian never a whit. Sweyn's coxcombery was always frank, and most forgiveable, and not without fair colour.

"If you want an ally," continued Sweyn, "confide in old Trella. Out of her stores of wisdom, if her memory holds good, she can instruct you in the orthodox manner of tackling a Were-Wolf. If I remember aright, you should watch the suspected person till midnight, when the beast's form must be resumed, and retained ever after if a human eye sees the change; or, better still, sprinkle hands and feet with holy water, which is certain death. Oh! never fear, but old Trella will be equal to the occasion."

Sweyn's contempt was no longer good-humoured; some touch of irritation or resentment rose at this monstrous doubt of White Fell. But Christian was too deeply distressed to take offence.

"You speak of them as old wives' tales; but if you had seen the proof I have seen, you would be ready at least to wish them true, if not also to put them to the test."

"Well," said Sweyn, with a laugh that had a little sneer in it, "put them to the test! I will not object to that, if you will only keep your notions to yourself. Now, Christian, give me your word for silence, and we will freeze here no longer."

Christian remained silent.

Sweyn put his hands on his shoulders again and vainly tried to see his face in the darkness.

"We have never quarrelled yet, Christian?"

"I have never quarrelled," returned the other, aware for the first time that his dictatorial brother had sometimes offered occasion for quarrel, had he been ready to take it.

"Well," said Sweyn emphatically, "if you speak against White Fell to any other, as to-night you have spoken to me—we shall."

He delivered the words like an ultimatum, turned sharp round, and re-entered the house. Christian, more fearful and wretched than before, followed.

"Snow is falling fast: not a single light is to be seen."

White Fell's eyes passed over Christian without apparent notice, and turned bright and shining upon Sweyn.

"Nor any signal to be heard?" she queried. "Did you not hear the sound of a sea-horn?"

"I saw nothing, and heard nothing; and signal or no signal, the heavy snow would keep you here perforce."

She smiled her thanks beautifully. And Christian's heart sank like lead with a deadly foreboding, as he noted what a light was kindled in Sweyn's eyes by her smile.

That night, when all others slept, Christian, the weariest of all, watched outside the guest-chamber till midnight was past. No sound, not the faintest, could be heard. Could the old tale be true of the midnight change? What was on the other side of the door, a woman or a beast? he would have given his right hand to know. Instinctively he laid his hand on the latch, and drew it softly, though believing that bolts fastened the inner side. The door yielded to his hand;

he stood on the threshold; a keen gust of air cut at him; the window stood open; the room was empty.

So Christian could sleep with a somewhat lightened heart.

In the morning there was surprise and conjecture when White Fell's absence was discovered. Christian held his peace. Not even to his brother did he say how he knew that she had fled before midnight; and Sweyn, though evidently greatly chagrined, seemed to disdain reference to the subject of Christian's fears.

The elder brother alone joined the bear hunt; Christian found pretext to stay behind. Sweyn, being out of humour, manifested his contempt by uttering not a single expostulation.

All that day, and for many a day after, Christian would never go out of sight of his home. Sweyn alone noticed how he manœuvred for this, and was clearly annoyed by it. White Fell's name was never mentioned between them, though not seldom was it heard in general talk. Hardly a day passed but little Rol asked when White Fell would come again: pretty White Fell, who kissed like a snowflake. And if Sweyn answered, Christian would be quite sure that the light in his eyes, kindled by White Fell's smile, had not yet died out.

Little Rol! Naughty, merry, fairhaired little Rol. A day came when his feet raced over the threshold never to return; when his chatter and laugh were heard no more; when tears of anguish were wept by eyes that never would see his bright head again: never again, living or dead.

He was seen at dusk for the last time, escaping from the house with his puppy, in freakish rebellion against old Trella. Later, when his absence had begun to cause anxiety, his puppy crept back to the farm, cowed, whimpering and yelping, a pitiful, dumb lump of terror, without intelligence or courage to guide the frightened search.

Rol was never found, nor any trace of him. Where he had perished was never known; how he had perished was known only by an awful guess—a wild beast had devoured him.

Christian heard the conjecture "a wolf"; and a horrible certainty flashed upon him that he knew what wolf it was. He tried to declare what he knew, but Sweyn saw him start at the words with white face and struggling lips; and, guessing his purpose, pulled him back, and kept him silent, hardly, by his imperious grip and wrathful eyes, and one low whisper.

That Christian should retain his most irrational suspicion against beautiful White Fell was, to Sweyn, evidence of a weak obstinacy of mind that would but thrive upon expostulation and argument. But this evident intention to direct the passions of grief and anguish to a hatred and fear of the fair stranger, such as his own, was intolerable, and Sweyn set his will against it. Again Christian yielded to his brother's stronger words and will, and against his own judgment consented to silence.

Repentance came before the new moon, the first of the year, was old. White Fell came again, smiling as she entered, as though assured of a glad and kindly welcome; and, in truth, there was only one who saw again her fair face and strange white garb without pleasure. Sweyn's face glowed with delight, while Christian's grew pale and rigid as death. He had given his word to keep silence; but he had not thought that she would dare to come again. Silence was impossible, face to face with that Thing, impossible. Irrepressibly he cried out:

"Where is Rol?"

Not a quiver disturbed White Fell's face. She heard, yet remained bright and tranquil. Sweyn's eyes flashed round at his brother dangerously. Among the women some tears fell at the poor child's name; but none caught alarm from its sudden utterance, for the thought of Rol rose naturally. Where was little Rol, who had nestled in the stranger's arms, kissing her; and watched for her since; and prattled of her daily?

Christian went out silently. One only thing there was that he could do, and he must not delay. His horror overmastered any curiosity to hear White Fell's smooth excuses and smiling apologies for her strange and uncourteous departure; or her easy tale of the circumstances of her return; or to watch her bearing as she heard the sad tale of little Rol.

The swiftest runner of the country-side had started on his hardest race: little less than three leagues and back, which he reckoned to accomplish in two hours, though the night was moonless and the way rugged. He rushed against the still cold air till it felt like a wind upon his face. The dim homestead sank below the ridges at his back, and fresh ridges of snowlands rose out of the obscure horizon-level to drive past him as the stirless air drove, and sink away behind into obscure level again. He took no conscious heed of landmarks, not even when all sign of a path was gone under depths of snow. His will was set to reach his goal with unexampled speed; and thither by instinct his physical forces bore him, without one definite thought to guide.

And the idle brain lay passive, inert, receiving into its vacancy restless siftings of past sights and sounds: Rol, weeping, laughing, playing, coiled in the arms of that dreadful Thing: Tyr—O Tyr!—white fangs in the black jowl: the women who wept on The foolish puppy, precious for the child's last touch: footprints from pine wood to door: the smiling face among furs, of such womanly beauty—smiling—smiling: and Sweyn's face.

"Sweyn, Sweyn, O Sweyn, my brother!"

Sweyn's angry laugh possessed his ear within the sound of the wind of his speed; Sweyn's scorn assailed more quick and keen than the biting cold at his throat. And yet he was unimpressed by any thought of how Sweyn's anger and scorn would rise, if this errand were known.

Sweyn was a sceptic. His utter disbelief in Christian's testimony regarding the footprints was based upon positive scepticism. His reason refused to bend in accepting the possibility of the supernatural materialised. That a living beast could ever be other than palpably bestial—pawed, toothed, shagged, and eared as such, was to him incredible;

far more that a human presence could be transformed from its god-like aspect, upright, free-handed, with brows, and speech, and laughter. The wild and fearful legends that he had known from childhood and then believed, he regarded now as built upon facts distorted, overlaid by imagination, and quickened by superstition. Even the strange summons at the threshold, that he himself had vainly answered, was, after the first shock of surprise, rationally explained by him as malicious foolery on the part of some clever trickster, who withheld the key to the enigma.

To the younger brother all life was a spiritual mystery, veiled from his clear knowledge by the density of flesh. Since he knew his own body to be linked to the complex and antagonistic forces that constitute one soul, it seemed to him not impossibly strange that one spiritual force should possess divers forms for widely various manifestation. Nor, to him, was it great effort to believe that as pure water washes away all natural foulness, so water, holy by consecration, must needs cleanse God's world from that supernatural evil Thing. Therefore, faster than ever man's foot had covered those leagues, he sped under the dark, still night, over the waste, trackless snow-ridges to the far-away church, where salvation lay in the holy-water stoup at the door. His faith was as firm as any that wrought miracles in days past, simple as a child's wish, strong as a man's will.

He was hardly missed during these hours, every second of which was by him fulfilled to its utmost extent by extremest effort that sinews and nerves could attain. Within the homestead the while, the easy moments went bright with words and looks of unwonted animation, for the kindly, hospitable instincts of the inmates were roused into cordial expression of welcome and interest by the grace and beauty of the returned stranger.

But Sweyn was eager and earnest, with more than a host's courteous warmth. The impression that at her first coming had charmed him, that had lived since through memory, deepened now in her actual presence. Sweyn, the matchless among men, acknowledged in this fair White Fell a spirit high and bold as his own, and a frame so firm and capable that only bulk was lacking for equal strength. Yet the white skin was moulded most smoothly, without such muscular swelling as made his might evident. Such love as his frank self-love could concede was called forth by an ardent admiration for this supreme stranger. More admiration than love was in his passion, and therefore he was free from a lover's hesitancy and delicate reserve and doubts. Frankly and boldly he courted her favour by looks and tones, and an address that came of natural ease, needless of skill by practice.

Nor was she a woman to be wooed otherwise. Tender whispers and sighs would never gain her ear; but her eyes would brighten and shine if she heard of a brave feat, and her prompt hand in sympathy fall swiftly on the axe-haft and clasp it hard. That movement ever fired Sweyn's admiration anew; he watched for it, strove to elicit it, and glowed when it came. Wonderful and beautiful was that wrist, slender and steel-strong; also the smooth shapely hand, that curved so fast and firm, ready to deal instant death.

Desiring to feel the pressure of these hands, this bold lover schemed with palpable directness, proposing that she should hear how their hunting songs were sung, with a chorus that signalled hands to be clasped. So his splendid voice gave the verses, and, as the chorus was taken up, he claimed her hands, and, even through the easy grip, felt, as he desired, the strength that was latent, and the vigour that quickened the very fingertips, as the song fired her, and her voice was caught out of her by the rhythmic swell, and rang clear on the top of the closing surge.

Afterwards she sang alone. For contrast, or in the pride of swaying moods by her voice, she chose a mournful song that drifted along in a minor chant, sad as a wind that dirges:

"Oh, let me go!
Around spin wreaths of snow;
The dark earth sleeps below.

"Far up the plain
Moans on a voice of pain:
'Where shall my babe be lain?'

"In my white breast
Lay the sweet life to rest!
Lay, where it can lie best!

"'Hush! hush its cries!
Dense night is on the skies:
Two stars are in thine eyes.'

"Come, babe, away!
But lie thou till dawn be grey,
Who must be dead by day.

"This cannot last;
But, ere the sickening blast,
All sorrow shall be past;

"And kings shall be
Low bending at thy knee,
Worshipping life from thee.

"For men long sore
To hope of what's before,—
To leave the things of yore.

"Mine, and not thine,
How deep their jewels shine!
Peace laps thy head, not mine."

Old Trella came tottering from her corner, shaken to additional palsy by an aroused memory. She strained her dim eyes towards the singer, and then bent her head, that the one ear yet sensible to sound might avail of every note. At the close, groping forward, she murmured with the high-pitched quaver of old age:

"So she sang, my Thora; my last and brightest. What is she like, she whose voice is like my dead Thora's? Are her eyes blue?"

"Blue as the sky."

"So were my Thora's! Is her hair fair, and in plaits to the waist?" "Even so," answered White Fell herself, and met the advancing hands with her own, and guided them to corroborate her words by touch.

"Like my dead Thora's," repeated the old woman; and then her trembling hands rested on the fur-clad shoulders, and she bent forward and kissed the smooth fair face that White Fell upturned, nothing loth, to receive and return the caress.

So Christian saw them as he entered.

He stood a moment. After the starless darkness and the icy night air, and the fierce silent two hours' race, his senses reeled on sudden entrance into warmth, and light, and the cheery hum of voices. A sudden unforeseen anguish assailed him, as now first he entertained the possibility of being overmatched by her wiles and her daring, if at the approach of pure death she should start up at bay transformed to a terrible beast, and achieve a savage glut at the last. He looked with horror and pity on the harmless, helpless folk, so unwitting of outrage to their comfort and security. The dreadful Thing in their midst, that was veiled from their knowledge by womanly beauty, was a centre of pleasant interest. There, before him, signally impressive, was poor old Trella, weakest and feeblest of all, in fond nearness. And a moment might bring about the revelation of a monstrous horror—a ghastly, deadly danger, set loose and at bay, in a circle of girls and women and careless defenceless men: so hideous and terrible a thing as might crack the brain, or curdle the heart stone dead.

And he alone of the throng prepared!

For one breathing space he faltered, no longer than that, while over him swept the agony of compunction that yet could not make him surrender his purpose.

He alone? Nay, but Tyr also; and he crossed to the dumb sole sharer of his knowledge.

So timeless is thought that a few seconds only lay between his lifting of the latch and his loosening of Tyr's collar; but in those few seconds succeeding his first glance, as lightning-swift had been the impulses of others, their motion as quick and sure. Sweyn's vigilant eye had darted upon him, and instantly his every fibre was alert with hostile instinct; and, half divining, half incredulous, of Christian's object in stooping to Tyr, he came hastily, wary, wrathful, resolute to oppose the malice of his wild-eyed brother.

But beyond Sweyn rose White Fell, blanching white as her furs, and with eyes grown fierce and wild. She leapt down the room to the door, whirling her long robe closely to her. "Hark!" she panted. "The signal horn! Hark, I must go!" as she snatched at the latch to be out and away.

For one precious moment Christian had hesitated on the half-loosened collar; for, except the womanly form were exchanged for the bestial, Tyr's jaws would gnash to rags his honour of manhood. Then he heard her voice, and turned—too late.

As she tugged at the door, he sprang across grasping his flask, but Sweyn dashed between, and caught him back irresistibly, so that a most frantic effort only availed to wrench one arm free. With that, on the impulse of sheer despair, he cast at her with all his force. The door swung behind her, and the flask flew into fragments against it. Then, as Sweyn's grasp slackened, and he met the questioning astonishment of surrounding faces, with a hoarse inarticulate cry: "God help us all!" he said. "She is a Were-Wolf."

Sweyn turned upon him, "Liar, coward!" and his hands gripped his brother's throat with deadly force, as though the spoken word could be killed so; and as Christian struggled, lifted him clear off his feet and flung him crashing backward. So furious was he, that, as his brother lay motionless, he stirred him roughly with his foot, till their mother came between, crying shame; and yet then he stood by, his teeth set, his brows knit, his hands clenched, ready to enforce silence again violently, as Christian rose staggering and bewildered.

But utter silence and submission were more than he expected, and turned his anger into contempt for one so easily cowed and held in subjection by mere force. "He is mad!" he said, turning on his heel as he spoke, so that he lost his mother's look of pained reproach at this sudden free utterance of what was a lurking dread within her.

Christian was too spent for the effort of speech. His hard-drawn breath laboured in great sobs; his limbs were powerless and unstrung in utter relax after hard service. Failure in his endeavour induced a stupor of misery and despair. In addition was the wretched humiliation of open violence and strife with his brother, and the distress of hearing misjudging contempt expressed without reserve; for he was aware that Sweyn had turned to allay the scared excitement half by imperious mastery, half by explanation and argument, that showed painful disregard of brotherly consideration. All this unkindness of his twin he charged upon the fell Thing who had wrought this their first dissension, and, ah! most terrible thought, interposed between them so effectually, that Sweyn was wilfully blind and deaf on her account, resentful of interference, arbitrary beyond reason.

Dread and perplexity unfathomable darkened upon him; unshared, the burden was overwhelming: a foreboding of unspeakable calamity, based upon his ghastly discovery, bore down upon him, crushing out hope of power to withstand impending fate.

Sweyn the while was observant of his brother, despite the continual check of finding, turn and glance when he would, Christian's eyes always upon him, with a strange look of helpless distress, discomposing enough to the angry aggressor. "Like a beaten dog!" he said to himself, rallying contempt to withstand compunction. Observation set him wondering on Christian's exhausted condition. The heavy labouring breath and the slack inert fall of the limbs told surely of unusual and prolonged exertion. And then why had close upon two hours' absence been followed by open hostility against White Fell?

Suddenly, the fragments of the flask giving a clue, he guessed all, and faced about to stare at his brother in amaze. He forgot that the motive scheme was against White Fell, demanding derision and resentment from him; that was swept out of remembrance by astonishment and admiration for the feat of speed and endurance. In eagerness to question he inclined to attempt a generous part and frankly offer to heal the breach; but Christian's depression and sad following gaze provoked him to self-justification by recalling the offence of that outrageous utterance against White Fell; and the impulse passed. Then other considerations counselled silence; and afterwards a humour possessed him to wait and see how Christian would find opportunity to proclaim his performance and establish the fact, without exciting ridicule on account of the absurdity of the errand.

This expectation remained unfulfilled. Christian never attempted the proud avowal that would have placed his feat on record to be told to the next generation.

That night Sweyn and his mother talked long and late together, shaping into certainty the suspicion that Christian's mind had lost its balance, and discussing the evident cause. For Sweyn, declaring his own love for White Fell, suggested that his unfortunate brother, with a like passion, they being twins in loves as in birth, had through jealousy and despair turned from love to hate, until reason failed at the strain, and a craze developed, which the malice and treachery of madness made a serious and dangerous force.

So Sweyn theorised, convincing himself as he spoke; convincing afterwards others who advanced doubts against White Fell; fettering his judgment by his advocacy, and by his staunch defence of her hurried flight silencing his own inner consciousness of the unaccountability of her action.

But a little time and Sweyn lost his vantage in the shock of a fresh horror at the homestead. Trella was no more, and her end a mystery. The poor old woman crawled out in a bright gleam to visit a bed-ridden gossip living beyond the fir-grove. Under the trees she was last seen, halting for her companion, sent back for a forgotten present. Quick alarm sprang, calling every man to the search. Her stick was found among the brushwood only a few paces from the path, but no track or stain, for a gusty wind was sifting the snow from the branches, and hid all sign of how she came by her death.

So panic-stricken were the farm folk that none dared go singly on the search. Known danger could be braced, but not this stealthy Death that walked by day invisible, that cut off alike the child in his play and the aged woman so near to her quiet grave.

"Rol she kissed; Trella she kissed!" So rang Christian's frantic cry again and again, till Sweyn dragged him away and strove to keep him apart, albeit in his agony of grief and remorse he accused himself wildly as answerable for the tragedy, and gave clear proof that the charge of madness was well founded, if strange looks and desperate, incoherent words were evidence enough.

But thenceforward all Sweyn's reasoning and mastery could not uphold White Fell above suspicion. He was not called upon to defend her from accusation when Christian had been brought to silence again; but he well knew the significance of this fact, that her name, formerly uttered freely and often, he never heard now: it was huddled away into whispers that he could not catch.

The passing of time did not sweep away the superstitious fears that Sweyn despised. He was angry and anxious; eager that White Fell should return, and, merely by her bright gracious presence, reinstate herself in favour; but doubtful if all his authority and example could keep from her notice an altered aspect of welcome; and he foresaw clearly that Christian would prove unmanageable, and might be capable of some dangerous outbreak.

For a time the twins' variance was marked, on Sweyn's part by an air of rigid indifference, on Christian's by heavy downcast silence, and a nervous apprehensive observation of his brother. Superadded to his remorse and foreboding, Sweyn's displeasure weighed upon him intolerably, and the remembrance of their violent rupture was a ceaseless misery. The elder brother, self-sufficient and insensitive, could little know how deeply his unkindness stabbed. A depth and force of affection such as Christian's was unknown to him. The loyal subservience that he could not appreciate had encouraged him to domineer; this strenuous opposition to his reason and will was accounted as furious malice, if not sheer insanity.

Christian's surveillance galled him incessantly, and embarrassment and danger he foresaw as the outcome. Therefore, that suspicion might be lulled, he judged it wise to make overtures for peace. Most easily done. A little kindliness, a few evidences of consideration, a slight return of the old brotherly imperiousness, and Christian replied by a gratefulness and relief that might have touched him had he understood all, but instead, increased his secret contempt.

So successful was this finesse, that when, late on a day, a message summoning Christian to a distance was transmitted by Sweyn, no doubt of its genuineness occurred. When, his errand proved useless, he set out to return, mistake or misapprehension was all that he surmised. Not till he sighted the homestead, lying low between the night-grey snow ridges, did vivid recollection of the time when he had tracked that horror to the door rouse an intense dread, and with it a hardly-defined suspicion.

His grasp tightened on the bear-spear that he carried as a staff; every sense was alert, every muscle strung; excitement urged him on, caution checked him, and the two governed his long stride, swiftly, noiselessly, to the climax he felt was at hand.

As he drew near to the outer gates, a light shadow stirred and went, as though the grey of the snow had taken detached motion. A darker shadow stayed and faced Christian, striking his life-blood chill with utmost despair.

Sweyn stood before him, and surely, the shadow that went was White Fell.

They had been together—close. Had she not been in his arms, near enough for lips to meet?

There was no moon, but the stars gave light enough to show that Sweyn's face was flushed and elate. The flush remained, though the expression changed quickly at sight of his brother. How, if Christian had seen all, should one of his frenzied outbursts be met and managed: by resolution? by indifference? He halted between the two, and as a result, he swaggered.

"White Fell?" questioned Christian, hoarse and breathless.

"Yes?"

Sweyn's answer was a query, with an intonation that implied he was clearing the ground for action.

From Christian came: "Have you kissed her?" like a bolt direct, staggering Sweyn by its sheer prompt temerity.

He flushed yet darker, and yet half-smiled over this earnest of success he had won. Had there been really between himself and Christian the rivalry that he imagined, his face had enough of the insolence of triumph to exasperate jealous rage.

"You dare ask this!"

"Sweyn, O Sweyn, I must know! You have!"

The ring of despair and anguish in his tone angered Sweyn, misconstruing it. Jealousy urging to such presumption was intolerable.

"Mad fool!" he said, constraining himself no longer. "Win for yourself a woman to kiss. Leave mine without question. Such an one as I should desire to kiss is such an one as shall never allow a kiss to you."

Then Christian fully understood his supposition.

"I—I!" he cried. "White Fell—that deadly Thing! Sweyn, are you blind, mad? I would save you from her: a Were-Wolf!"

Sweyn maddened again at the accusation—a dastardly way of revenge, as he conceived; and instantly, for the second time, the brothers were at strife violently.

But Christian was now too desperate to be scrupulous; for a dim glimpse had shot a possibility into his mind, and to be free to follow it the striking of his brother was a necessity. Thank God! he was armed, and so Sweyn's equal.

Facing his assailant with the bear-spear, he struck up his arms, and with the butt end hit hard so that he fell. The matchless runner leapt away on the instant, to follow a forlorn hope. Sweyn, on regaining his feet, was as amazed as angry at this unaccountable flight. He knew in his heart that his brother was no coward, and that it was unlike him to shrink from an encounter because defeat was certain, and cruel humiliation from a vindictive victor probable. Of the uselessness of pursuit he was well aware: he must abide his chagrin, content to know that his time for advantage would come. Since White Fell had parted to the right, Christian to the left, the event of a sequent encounter did not occur to him. And now Christian, acting on the dim glimpse he had had, just as Sweyn turned upon him, of something that moved against the sky along the ridge behind the homestead, was staking his only hope on a chance, and his own superlative speed. If what he saw was really White Fell, he guessed she was bending her steps towards the open wastes; and there was just a possibility that, by a straight dash, and a desperate perilous leap over a sheer bluff, he might yet meet her or head her. And then: he had no further thought.

It was past, the quick, fierce race, and the chance of death at the leap; and he halted in a hollow to fetch his breath and to look: did she come? had she gone?

She came.

She came with a smooth, gliding, noiseless speed, that was neither walking nor running; her arms were folded in her furs that were drawn tight about her body; the white lappets from her head were wrapped and knotted closely beneath her face; her eyes were set on a far distance. So she went till the even sway of her going was startled to a pause by Christian.

"Fell!"

She drew a quick, sharp breath at the sound of her name thus mutilated, and faced Sweyn's brother. Her eyes glittered; her upper lip was lifted, and shewed the teeth. The half of her name, impressed with an ominous sense as uttered by him, warned her of the aspect of a deadly foe. Yet she cast loose her robes till they trailed ample, and spoke as a mild woman.

"What would you?"

Then Christian answered with his solemn dreadful accusation:

"You kissed Rol—and Rol is dead! You kissed Trella: she is dead! You have kissed Sweyn, my brother; but he shall not die!"

He added: "You may live till midnight."

The edge of the teeth and the glitter of the eyes stayed a moment, and her right hand also slid down to the axe haft. Then, without a word, she swerved from him, and sprang out and away swiftly over the snow.

And Christian sprang out and away, and followed her swiftly over the snow, keeping behind, but half-a-stride's length from her side.

So they went running together, silent, towards the vast wastes of snow, where no living thing but they two moved under the stars of night.

Never before had Christian so rejoiced in his powers. The gift of speed, and the training of use and endurance were priceless to him now. Though midnight was hours away, he was confident that, go where that Fell Thing would, hasten as she would, she could not outstrip him nor escape from him. Then, when came the time for transformation, when the woman's form made no longer a shield against a man's hand, he could slay or be slain to save Sweyn. He had struck his dear brother in dire extremity, but he could not, though reason urged, strike a woman.

For one mile, for two miles they ran: White Fell ever foremost, Christian ever at equal distance from her side, so near that, now and again, her out-flying furs touched him. She spoke no word; nor he. She never turned her head to look at him, nor swerved to evade him; but, with set face looking forward, sped straight on, over rough, over smooth, aware of his nearness by the regular beat of his feet, and the sound of his breath behind.

In a while she quickened her pace. From the first, Christian had judged of her speed as admirable, yet with exulting security in his own excelling and enduring whatever her efforts. But, when the pace increased, he found himself put to the test as never had he been before in any race. Her feet, indeed, flew faster than his; it was only by his length of stride that he kept his place at her side. But his heart was high and resolute, and he did not fear failure yet.

So the desperate race flew on. Their feet struck up the powdery snow, their breath smoked into the sharp clear air, and they were gone before the air was cleared of snow and vapour. Now and then Christian glanced up to judge, by the rising of the stars, of the coming of midnight. So long—so long!

White Fell held on without slack. She, it was evident, with confidence in her speed proving matchless, as resolute to outrun her pursuer as he to endure till midnight and fulfil his purpose. And Christian held on, still self-assured. He could not fail; he would not fail. To avenge Rol and Trella was motive enough for him to do what man could do; but for Sweyn more. She had kissed Sweyn, but he should not die too: with Sweyn to save he could not fail.

Never before was such a race as this; no, not when in old Greece man and maid raced together with two fates at stake; for the hard running was sustained unabated, while star after star rose and went wheeling up towards midnight, for one hour, for two hours.

Then Christian saw and heard what shot him through with fear. Where a fringe of trees hung round a slope he saw something dark moving, and heard a yelp, followed by a full horrid cry, and the dark spread out upon the snow, a pack of wolves in pursuit.

Of the beasts alone he had little cause for fear; at the pace he held he could distance them, four-footed though they were. But of White Fell's wiles he had infinite apprehension, for how might she not avail herself of the savage jaws of these wolves, akin as they were to half her nature. She vouchsafed to them nor look nor sign; but Christian, on an impulse to assure himself that she should not escape him, caught and held the back-flung edge of her furs, running still.

She turned like a flash with a beastly snarl, teeth and eyes gleaming again. Her axe shone, on the upstroke, on the downstroke, as she hacked at his hand. She had lopped it off at the wrist, but that he parried with the bear-spear. Even then, she shore through the shaft and shattered the bones of the hand at the same blow, so that he loosed perforce.

Then again they raced on as before, Christian not losing a pace, though his left hand swung useless, bleeding and broken.

The snarl, indubitable, though modified from a wom-an's organs, the vicious fury revealed in teeth and eyes, the sharp arrogant pain of her maiming blow, caught away Christian's heed of the beasts behind, by striking into him close vivid realisation of the infinitely greater danger that ran before him in that deadly Thing.

When he bethought him to look behind, lo! the pack had but reached their tracks, and instantly slunk aside, cowed; the yell of pursuit changing to yelps and whines. So abhorrent was that fell creature to beast as to man.

She had drawn her furs more closely to her, disposing them so that, instead of flying loose to her heels, no drapery hung lower than her knees, and this without a check to her wonderful speed, nor embarrassment by the cumbering of the folds. She held her head as before; her lips were firmly set, only the tense nostrils gave her breath; not a sign of distress witnessed to the long sustaining of that terrible speed.

But on Christian by now the strain was telling palpably. His head weighed heavy, and his breath came labouring in great sobs; the bear spear would have been a burden now. His heart was beating like a hammer, but such a dulness oppressed his brain, that it was only by degrees he could realise his helpless state; wounded and weaponless, chasing that terrible Thing, that was a fierce, desperate, axe-armed woman, except she should assume the beast with fangs yet more formidable.

And still the far slow stars went lingering nearly an hour from midnight.

So far was his brain astray that an impression took him that she was fleeing from the midnight stars, whose gain was by such slow degrees that a time equalling days and days had gone in the race round the northern circle of the world, and days and days as long might last before the end—except she slackened, or except he failed.

But he would not fail yet.

How long had he been praying so? He had started with a self-confidence and reliance that had felt no need for that aid; and now it seemed the only means by which to restrain his heart from swelling beyond the compass of his body, by which to cherish his brain from dwindling and shrivelling quite away. Some sharp-toothed creature kept tearing and dragging on his maimed left hand; he never could see it, he could not shake it off; but he prayed it off at times.

The clear stars before him took to shuddering, and he knew why: they shuddered at sight of what was behind him. He had never divined before that strange things hid themselves from men under pretence of being snow-clad mounds or swaying trees; but now they came slipping out from their harmless covers to follow him, and mock at his impotence to make a kindred Thing resolve to truer form. He knew the air behind him was thronged; he heard the hum of innumerable murmurings together; but his eyes could never catch them, they were too swift and nimble. Yet he knew they were there, because, on a backward glance, he saw the snow mounds surge as they grovelled flatlings out of sight; he saw the trees reel as they screwed themselves rigid past recognition among the boughs.

And after such glance the stars for awhile returned to steadfastness, and an infinite stretch of silence froze upon the chill grey world, only deranged by the swift even beat of the flying feet, and his own—slower from the longer stride, and the sound of his breath. And for some clear moments he knew that his only concern was, to sustain his speed regardless of pain and distress, to deny with every nerve he had her power to outstrip him or to widen the space between them, till the stars crept up to midnight. Then out again would come that crowd invisible, humming and hustling behind, dense and dark enough, he knew, to blot out the stars at his back, yet ever skipping and jerking from his sight.

A hideous check came to the race. White Fell swirled about and leapt to the right, and Christian, unprepared for so prompt a lurch, found close at his feet a deep pit yawning, and his own impetus past control. But he snatched at her as he bore past, clasping her right arm with his one whole hand, and the two swung together upon the brink.

And her straining away in self preservation was vigorous enough to counter-balance his headlong impulse, and brought them reeling together to safety.

Then, before he was verily sure that they were not to perish so, crashing down, he saw her gnashing in wild pale fury as she wrenched to be free; and since her right hand was in his grasp, used her axe left-handed, striking back at him.

The blow was effectual enough even so; his right arm dropped powerless, gashed, and with the lesser bone broken, that jarred with horrid pain when he let it swing as he leaped out again, and ran to recover the few feet she had gained from his pause at the shock.

The near escape and this new quick pain made again every faculty alive and intense. He knew that what he followed was most surely Death animate: wounded and helpless, he was utterly at her mercy if so she should realise and take action. Hopeless to avenge, hopeless to save, his very despair for Sweyn swept him on to follow, and follow, and precede the kiss-doomed to death. Could he yet fail to hunt that Thing past midnight, out of the womanly form alluring and treacherous, into lasting restraint of the bestial, which was the last shred of hope left from the confident purpose of the outset?

"Sweyn, Sweyn, O Sweyn!" He thought he was praying, though his heart wrung out nothing but this: "Sweyn, Sweyn, O Sweyn!"

The last hour from midnight had lost half its quarters, and the stars went lifting up the great minutes; and again his greatening heart, and his shrinking brain, and the sickening agony that swung at either side, conspired to appal the will that had only seeming empire over his feet.

Now White Fell's body was so closely enveloped that not a lap nor an edge flew free. She stretched forward strangely aslant, leaning from the upright poise of a runner. She cleared the ground at times by long bounds, gaining an increase of speed that Christian agonised to equal.

Because the stars pointed that the end was nearing, the black brood came behind again, and followed, noising. Ah! if they could but be kept quiet and still, nor slip their usual harmless masks to encourage with their interest the last speed of their most deadly congener. What shape had they? Should he ever know? If it were not that he was bound to compel the fell Thing that ran before him into her truer form, he might face about and follow them. No—no—not so; if he might do anything but what he did—race, race, and racing bear this agony, he would just stand still and die, to be quit of the pain of breathing.

He grew bewildered, uncertain of his own identity, doubting of his own true form. He could not be really a man, no more than that running Thing was really a woman; his real form was only hidden under embodiment of a man, but what it was he did not know. And Sweyn's real form he did not know. Sweyn lay fallen at his feet, where he had struck him down—his own brother—he: he stumbled over him, and had to overleap him and race harder because she who had kissed Sweyn leapt so fast. "Sweyn, Sweyn, O Sweyn!"

Why did the stars stop to shudder? Midnight else had surely come!

The leaning, leaping Thing looked back at him with a wild, fierce look, and laughed in savage scorn and triumph. He saw in a flash why, for within a time measurable by seconds she would have escaped him utterly. As the land lay, a slope of ice sunk on the one hand; on the other hand a steep rose, shouldering forwards; between the two was space for a foot to be planted, but none for a body to stand; yet a juniper bough, thrusting out, gave a handhold secure enough for one with a resolute grasp to swing past the perilous place, and pass on safe.

Though the first seconds of the last moment were going, she dared to flash back a wicked look, and laugh at the pursuer who was impotent to grasp.

The crisis struck convulsive life into his last supreme effort; his will surged up indomitable, his speed proved matchless yet. He leapt with a rush, passed her before her laugh had time to go out, and turned short, barring the way, and braced to withstand her.

She came hurling desperate, with a feint to the right hand, and then launched herself upon him with a spring like a wild beast when it leaps to kill. And he, with one strong arm and a hand that could not hold, with one strong hand and an arm that could not guide and sustain, he caught and held her even so. And they fell together. And because he felt his whole arm slipping, and his whole hand loosing, to slack the dreadful agony of the wrenched bone above, he caught and held with his teeth the tunic at her knee, as she struggled up and wrung off his hands to overleap him victorious.

Like lightning she snatched her axe, and struck him on the neck, deep—once, twice—his life-blood gushed out, staining her feet.

The stars touched midnight.

The death scream he heard was not his, for his set teeth

had hardly yet relaxed when it rang out; and the dreadful cry began with a woman's shriek, and changed and ended as the yell of a beast. And before the final blank overtook his dying eyes, he saw that She gave place to It; he saw more, that Life gave place to Death—causelessly, incomprehensibly.

For he did not presume that no holy water could be more holy, more potent to destroy an evil thing than the life-blood of a pure heart poured out for another in free willing devotion.

His own true hidden reality that he had desired to know grew palpable, recognisable. It seemed to him just this: a great glad abounding hope that he had saved his brother; too expansive to be contained by the limited form of a sole man, it yearned for a new embodiment infinite as the stars.

What did it matter to that true reality that the man's brain shrank, shrank, till it was nothing; that the man's body could not retain the huge pain of his heart, and heaved it out through the red exit riven at the neck; that the black noise came again hurtling from behind, reinforced by that dissolved shape, and blotted out for ever the man's sight, hearing, sense.

* * * *

In the early grey of day Sweyn chanced upon the footprints of a man—of a runner, as he saw by the shifted snow; and the direction they had taken aroused curiosity, since a little farther their line must be crossed by the edge of a sheer height. He turned to trace them. And so doing, the length of the stride struck his attention—a stride long as his own if he ran. He knew he was following Christian.

In his anger he had hardened himself to be indifferent to the night-long absence of his brother; but now, seeing where the footsteps went, he was seized with compunction and dread. He had failed to give thought and care to his poor frantic twin, who might—was it possible?—have rushed to a frantic death.

His heart stood still when he came to the place where the leap had been taken. A piled edge of snow had fallen too, and nothing but snow lay below when he peered. Along the upper edge he ran for a furlong, till he came to a dip where he could slip and climb down, and then back again on the lower level to the pile of fallen snow. There he saw that the vigorous running had started afresh.

He stood pondering; vexed that any man should have taken that leap where he had not ventured to follow; vexed that he had been beguiled to such painful emotions; guessing vainly at Christian's object in this mad freak. He began sauntering along, half unconsciously following his brother's track; and so in a while he came to the place where the footprints were doubled.

Small prints were these others, small as a woman's, though the pace from one to another was longer than that which the skirts of women allow.

Did not White Fell tread so?

A dreadful guess appalled him, so dreadful that he recoiled from belief. Yet his face grew ashy white, and he gasped to fetch back motion to his checked heart. Unbe-

lievable? Closer attention showed how the smaller footfall had altered for greater speed, striking into the snow with a deeper onset and a lighter pressure on the heels. Unbelievable? Could any woman but White Fell run so? Could any man but Christian run so? The guess became a certainty. He was following where alone in the dark night White Fell had fled from Christian pursuing.

Such villainy set heart and brain on fire with rage and indignation: such villainy in his own brother, till lately love-worthy, praiseworthy, though a fool for meekness. He would kill Christian; had he lives many as the footprints he had trodden, vengeance should demand them all. In a tempest of murderous hate he followed on in haste, for the track was plain enough, starting with such a burst of speed as could not be maintained, but brought him back soon to a plod for the spent, sobbing breath to be regulated. He cursed Christian aloud and called White Fell's name on high in a frenzied expense of passion. His grief itself was a rage, being such an intolerable anguish of pity and shame at the thought of his love, White Fell, who had parted from his kiss free and radiant, to be hounded straightway by his brother mad with jealousy, fleeing for more than life while her lover was housed at his ease. If he had but known, he raved, in impotent rebellion at the cruelty of events, if he had but known that his strength and love might have availed in her defence; now the only service to her that he could render was to kill Christian.

As a woman he knew she was matchless in speed, matchless in strength; but Christian was matchless in speed among men, nor easily to be matched in strength. Brave and swift and strong though she were, what chance had she against a man of his strength and inches, frantic, too, and intent on horrid revenge against his brother, his successful rival?

Mile after mile he followed with a bursting heart; more piteous, more tragic, seemed the case at this evidence of White Fell's splendid supremacy, holding her own so long against Christian's famous speed. So long, so long that his love and admiration grew more and more boundless, and his grief and indignation therewith also. Whenever the track lay clear he ran, with such reckless prodigality of strength, that it soon was spent, and he dragged on heavily, till, sometimes on the ice of a mere, sometimes on a wind-swept place, all signs were lost; but, so undeviating had been their line that a course straight on, and then short questing to either hand, recovered them again.

Hour after hour had gone by through more than half that winter day, before ever he came to the place where the trampled snow showed that a scurry of feet had come—and gone! Wolves' feet—and gone most amazingly! Only a little beyond he came to the lopped point of Christian's bear-spear; farther on he would see where the remnant of the useless shaft had been dropped. The snow here was dashed with blood, and the footsteps of the two had fallen closer together. Some hoarse sound of exultation came from him that might have been a laugh had breath sufficed. "O White Fell, my poor, brave love! Well struck!" he groaned, torn by his pity and great admiration, as he guessed surely how she had turned and dealt a blow.

The sight of the blood inflamed him as it might a beast that ravens. He grew mad with a desire to have Christian by the throat once again, not to loose this time till he had crushed out his life, or beat out his life, or stabbed out his life; or all these, and torn him piecemeal likewise: and ah! then, not till then, bleed his heart with weeping, like a child, like a girl, over the piteous fate of his poor lost love.

On—on—on—through the aching time, toiling and straining in the track of those two superb runners, aware of the marvel of their endurance, but unaware of the marvel of their speed, that, in the three hours before midnight had overpassed all that vast distance that he could only traverse from twilight to twilight. For clear daylight was passing when he came to the edge of an old marl-pit, and saw how the two who had gone before had stamped and trampled together in desperate peril on the verge. And here fresh blood stains spoke to him of a valiant defence against his infamous brother; and he followed where the blood had dripped till the cold had staunched its flow, taking a savage gratification from this evidence that Christian had been gashed deeply, maddening afresh with desire to do likewise more excellently, and so slake his murderous hate. And he began to know that through all his despair he had entertained a germ of hope, that grew apace, rained upon by his brother's blood.

He strove on as best he might, wrung now by an access of hope, now of despair, in agony to reach the end, however terrible, sick with the aching of the toiled miles that deferred it.

And the light went lingering out of the sky, giving place to uncertain stars.

He came to the finish.

Two bodies lay in a narrow place. Christian's was one, but the other beyond not White Fell's. There where the footsteps ended lay a great white wolf.

At the sight Sweyn's strength was blasted; body and soul he was struck down grovelling.

The stars had grown sure and intense before he stirred from where he had dropped prone. Very feebly he crawled to his dead brother, and laid his hands upon him, and crouched so, afraid to look or stir farther.

Cold, stiff, hours dead. Yet the dead body was his only shelter and stay in that most dreadful hour. His soul, stripped bare of all sceptic comfort, cowered, shivering, naked, abject; and the living clung to the dead out of piteous need for grace from the soul that had passed away.

He rose to his knees, lifting the body. Christian had fallen face forward in the snow, with his arms flung up and wide, and so had the frost made him rigid: strange, ghastly, unyielding to Sweyn's lifting, so that he laid him down again and crouched above, with his arms fast round him, and a low heart-wrung groan.

When at last he found force to raise his brother's body and gather it in his arms, tight clasped to his breast, he tried to face the Thing that lay beyond. The sight set his limbs in a palsy with horror and dread. His senses had failed and fainted in utter cowardice, but for the strength that came from holding dead Christian in his arms, enabling him to compel his eyes to endure the sight, and take into the brain the complete aspect of the Thing. No wound, only blood stains on the feet. The great grim jaws had a savage grin, though dead-stiff. And his kiss: he could bear it no longer, and turned away, nor ever looked again.

And the dead man in his arms, knowing the full horror, had followed and faced it for his sake; had suffered agony and death for his sake; in the neck was the deep death gash, one arm and both hands were dark with frozen blood, for his sake! Dead he knew him, as in life he had not known him, to give the right meed of love and worship. Because the outward man lacked perfection and strength equal to his, he had taken the love and worship of that great pure heart as his due; he, so unworthy in the inner reality, so mean, so despicable, callous, and contemptuous towards the brother who had laid down his life to save him. He longed for utter annihilation, that so he might lose the agony of knowing himself so unworthy such perfect love. The frozen calm of death on the face appalled him. He dared not touch it with lips that had cursed so lately, with lips fouled by kiss of the horror that had been death.

He struggled to his feet, still clasping Christian. The dead man stood upright within his arm, frozen rigid. The eyes were not quite closed; the head had stiffened, bowed slightly to one side; the arms stayed straight and wide. It was the figure of one crucified, the blood-stained hands also conforming.

So living and dead went back along the track that one had passed in the deepest passion of love, and one in the deepest passion of hate. All that night Sweyn toiled through the snow, bearing the weight of dead Christian, treading back along the steps he before had trodden, when he was wronging with vilest thoughts, and cursing with murderous hatred, the brother who all the while lay dead for his sake.

Cold, silence, darkness encompassed the strong man bowed with the dolorous burden; and yet he knew surely that that night he entered hell, and trod hell-fire along the homeward road, and endured through it only because Christian was with him. And he knew surely that to him Christian had been as Christ, and had suffered and died to save him from his sins.

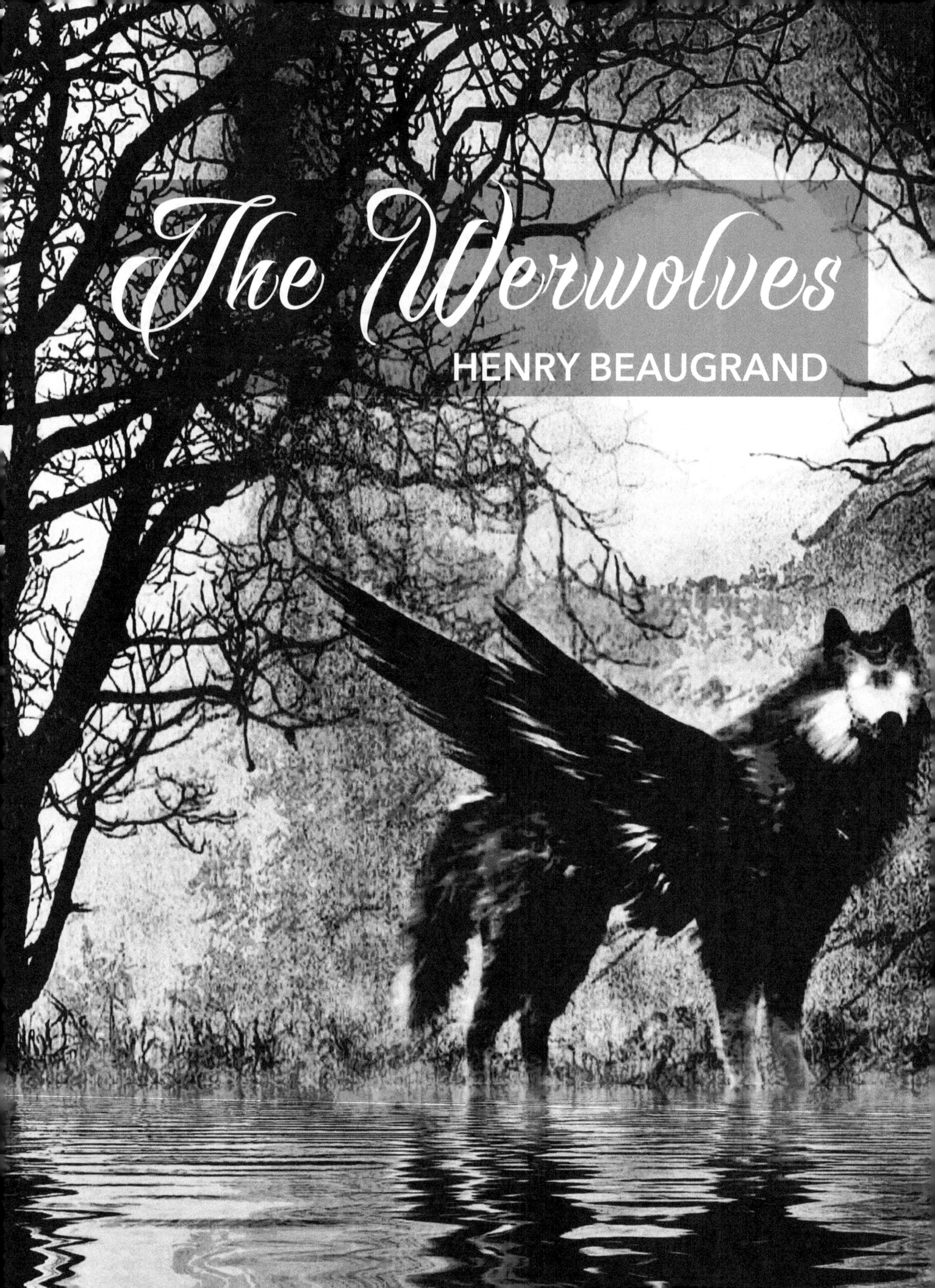

motley and picturesque-looking crowd had gathered within the walls of Fort Richelieu to attend the annual distribution of powder and lead, to take part in the winter drills and target practice, and to join in the Christmas festivities, that would last until the fast-approaching New Year.

Coureurs des bois from the Western country, scouts, hunters, trappers, militiamen, and habitants from the surrounding settlements, Indian warriors from the neighbouring tribe of friendly Abenakis, were all placed under the military instruction of the company of regular marine infantry that garrisoned the fort constructed in 1665, by M. de Saurel, at the mouth of the Richelieu River, where it flows into the waters of the St. Lawrence, forty-five miles below Montreal.

It was on Christmas eve of the year 1706, and the dreaded Iroquois were committing depredations in the surrounding country, burning farm-houses, stealing cattle and horses, and killing every man, woman, and child whom they could not carry away to their own villages to torture at the stake.

The Richelieu River was the natural highway to the Iroquois country during the open season, but now that its waters were icebound, it was hard to tell whence the attacks from those terrible savages could be expected.

The distribution of arms and ammunition having been made, under the joint supervision of the notary royal and the commandant of the fort, the men had retired to the barracks, where they were drinking, singing, and telling stories.

Tales of the most extraordinary adventures were being unfolded by some of the hunters, who were vying with one another in their attempts at relating some unheard-of and fantastic incidents that would create a sensation among their superstitious and wonder-loving comrades.

A sharp lookout was kept outside on the bastions, where four sentries were pacing up and down, repeating every half-hour the familiar watch-cry:

"Sentinelles! Prenez garde . . . vous!"

Old Sergeant Bellehumeur of the regulars, who had seen forty years of service in Canada, and who had come over with the regiment of Carignan-Salieres, was quietly sitting in a corner of the guard-room, smoking his Indian calumet, and watching over and keeping order among the men who were inclined to become boisterous over the oft-repeated libations.

One of the men, who had accompanied La Salle in his first expedition in search of the mouths of the Mississippi, was in the act of reciting his adventures with the hostile tribes that they had met in that far-off country, when the crack of a musket was heard from the outside, through the battlements. A second report immediately followed the first one, and the cry, "Aux armes!" was soon heard, with two more shots following close on each other.

The four sentries had evidently fired their muskets at some enemy or enemies, and the guard tumbled out in a hurry, followed by all the men, who had seized their arms, ready for an emergency.

The officer on duty was already on the spot when Sergeant Bellehumeur arrived to inquire into the cause of all this turmoil.

The sentry who had fired the first shot declared excitedly that all at once, on turning round on his beat, he had seen a party of red devils dancing around a bush fire, a couple of hundred yards away, right across the river from the fort, on the point covered with tall pine-trees. He had fired his musket in their direction, more with the intention of giving alarm than in the hope of hitting any of them at that distance.

The second, third, and fourth shots had been successively fired by the other sentries, who had not seen anything of the Indians, but who had joined in the firing with the idea of calling the guard to the spot, and scaring away the enemy who might be prowling around.

"But where are the Indians now?" inquired the officer, who had climbed on the parapet, "and where is the fire of which you speak?"

"They seem to have disappeared as by enchantment, sir," answered the soldier, in astonishment; "but they were there a few moments ago, when I fired my musket at them."

"Well, we will see," and, turning to Bellehumeur, "Sergeant, take ten men with you, and proceed over there cautiously, to see whether you can discover any signs of the presence of Indians on the point. Meanwhile, see to it that the guard is kept under arms until your return, to prevent any surprise."

Bellehumeur did as he was ordered, picking ten of his best men to accompany him. The gate of the fort was opened, and the drawbridge was lowered to give passage to the party, who proceeded to cross the river, over the ice, marching at first in Indian file. When nearing the opposite shore, near the edge of the wood, the men were seen to scatter, and to advance carefully, taking advantage of every tree to protect themselves against a possible ambush.

The night was a bright one, and any dark object could be plainly seen on the white snow, in the clearing that surrounded the fort.

The men disappeared for a short time, but were soon seen again, coming back in the same order and by the same route.

"Nothing, sir," said the sergeant, in saluting the officer. "Not a sign of fire of any kind, and not a single Indian track, in the snow, over the point."

"Well, that is curious, I declare! Had the sentry been drinking, sergeant, before going on post?"

"No more than the rest of the men, sir; and I could see no sign of liquor on him when the relief was sent out, an hour ago."

"Well, the man must be a fool or a poltroon to raise such an alarm without any cause whatever. See that he is immediately relieved from his post, sergeant, and have him confined in the guard-house until he appears before the commandant in the morning."

The sentry was duly relieved, and calm was restored among the garrison. The men went back to their quarters, and the conversation naturally fell on the peculiar circumstances that had just taken place.

An old weather-beaten trapper who had just returned from the Great Lakes volunteered the remark that, for his part, he was not so very sure that the sentry had not acted in perfect good faith, and had not been deceived by a band of loups-garous—werwolves—who came and went, appeared and disappeared, just as they pleased, under the protection of old Nick himself.

"I have seen them more than once in my travels," continued the trapper; "and only last year I had occasion to fire at just such a band of miscreants, up on the Ottawa River, above the portage of the Grandes-Chaudieres."

"Tell us about it!" chimed in the crowd of superstitious adventurers, whose credulous curiosity was instantly awakened by the promise of a story that would appeal to their love of the supernatural.

And everyone gathered about the old trapper, who was evidently proud to have the occasion to recite his exploits before as distinguished an assemblage of dare-devils as one could find anywhere, from Quebec to Michilimackinac.

"We had left Lachine, twenty-four of us, in three war-canoes, bound for the Illinois country, by way of the Ottawa River and the Upper Lakes; and in four days we had reached the portage of the Grandes-Chaudieres, where we rested for one day to renew our stock of meat, which was getting exhausted. Along with one of my companions, I had followed some deer-tracks, which led us several miles up the river, and we soon succeeded in killing a splendid animal. We divided the meat so as to make it easier for us to carry, and it was getting on toward nightfall when we began to retrace our steps in the direction of the camp. Darkness overtook us on the way, and as we were heavily burdened, we had stopped to rest and to smoke a pipe in a clump of maple trees on the edge of the river. All at once, and without warning of any kind, we saw a bright fire of balsam boughs burning on a small island in the middle of the river. Ten or twelve renegades, half human and half beasts, with heads and tails like wolves, arms, legs, and bodies like men, and eyes glaring like burning coals, were dancing around the fire and barking a sort of outlandish chant that was now and then changed to peals of infernal laughter. We could also vaguely perceive, lying on the ground, the body of a human being that two of the imps were engaged in cutting up, probably getting it ready for the horrible meal that the miscreants would make when the dance would be over. Although we were sitting in the shadow of the trees, partly concealed by the underbrush, we were at once discovered by the dancers, who beckoned to us to go and join them in their disgusting feast. That is the way they entrap unwary hunters for their bloody sacrifices. Our first impulse was to fly toward the woods; but we soon realised that we had to deal with loups-garous; and as we had both been to confession and taken holy communion before embarking at Lachine, we knew we had nothing to fear from them. White loups-garous are bad enough at any time, and you all know that only those who have remained seven years without performing their Easter duties are liable to be changed into wolves, condemned to prowl about at night until they are delivered by some Christian drawing blood from them by inflicting a wound on their forehead in the form of a cross. But we had to deal with Indian renegades, who had accepted the sacraments only in mockery, and we had never since performed any of the duties commanded by the Church. They are the worst loups-garous that one can meet, because they are constantly intent on capturing some misguided Christian, to drink his blood and to eat his flesh in their horrible fricots. Had we been in possession of holy water to sprinkle at them, or of a four-leaved clover to make wadding for our muskets, we might have exterminated the whole crowd, after having cut crosses on the lead of our bullets. But we were powerless to interfere with them, knowing full well that ordinary ammunition was useless, and that bullets would flatten out on their tough and impenetrable hides. Wolves at night, those devils would assume again, during the day, the appearance of ordinary Indians; but their hide is only turned inside out, with the hair growing inward. We were about to proceed on our way to the camp, leaving the loups-garous to continue their witchcraft unmolested, when a thought struck me that we might at least try to give them a couple of parting shots. We both withdrew the bullets from our muskets, cut crosses on them with our hunting-knives, placed them back in the barrels, along with two dizaines [a score] of beads from the blessed rosary which I carried in my pocket. That would surely make the renegades sick, if it did not kill them outright.

"We took good aim, and fired together. Such unearthly howling and yelling I have never heard before or since. Whether we killed any of them I could not say; but the fire instantly disappeared, and the island was left in darkness, while the howls grew fainter and fainter as the loups-garous seemed to be scampering in the distance. We returned to camp, where our companions were beginning to be anxious about our safety.

We found that one man, a hard character who bragged of his misdeeds, had disappeared during the day, and when we left on the following morning he had not yet returned to camp, neither did we ever hear of him afterward. In paddling up the river in our canoes, we passed close to the island where we had seen the loups-garous the night before. We landed, and searched around for some time; but we could find no traces of fire, or any signs of the passage of werewolves or of any other animals. I knew that it would turn out just so, because it is a well-known fact that those accursed brutes never leave any tracks behind them. My opinion was then, and has never changed to this day, that the man who strayed from our camp, and never returned, was captured by the loups-garous, and was being eaten up by them when we disturbed their horrible feast."

"Well, is that all?" inquired Sergeant Bellehumeur, with an ill-concealed contempt.

"Yes, that is all; but is it not enough to make one think that the sentry who has just been confined in the guard-house by the lieutenant for causing a false alarm has been deceived by a band of loups-garous who were picnicking on the point, and who disappeared in a twinkle when they found out that they were discovered?"

THE GRAY CAT

BARRY PAIN

I heard this story from Archdeacon M—. I should imagine that it would not be very difficult, by trimming it a little and altering the facts here and there, to make it capable of some simple explanation; but I have preferred to tell it as it was told to me.

After all, there is some explanation possible, even if there is not one definite and simple explanation clearly indicated. It must rest with the reader whether he will prefer to believe that some of the so-called uncivilized races may possess occult powers transcending anything of which the so-called civilized are capable, or whether he will consider that a series of coincidences is sufficient to account for the extraordinary incidents which, in a plain brief way, I am about to relate. It does not seem to me essential to state which view I hold myself, or if I hold neither, and have reasons for not stating a third possible explanation.

I must add a word or two with regard to Archdeacon M—. At the time of this story he was in his fiftieth year. He was a fine scholar, a man of considerable learning. His religious views were remarkably broad; his enemies said remarkably thin. In his younger days he had been something of an athlete, but owing to age, sedentary habits, and some amount of self-indulgence, he had grown stout, and no longer took exercise in any form. He had no nervous trouble of any kind. His death, from heart disease, took place about three years ago. He told me the story twice, at my request there was an interval of about six weeks between the two narrations; some of the details were elicited by questions of my own. With this preliminary note, we may proceed to the story.

* * *

In January, 1881, Archdeacon M—, who was a great admirer of Tennyson's poetry, came up to London for a few days, chiefly in order to witness the performance of 'The Cup,' at the Lyceum. He was not present on the first night (Monday, January 3), but on a later night in the same week. At that time, of course, the poet had not received his peerage, nor the actor his knighthood.

On leaving the theatre, less satisfied with the play than with the magnificence of the setting, the Archdeacon found some slight difficulty in getting a cab. He walked a little way down the Strand to find one, when he encountered unexpectedly his old friend, Guy Breddon.

Breddon (that was not his real name) was a man of considerable fortune, a member of the learned societies, and devoted to Central African exploration. He was two or three years younger than the Archdeacon, and a man of tremendous physique.

Breddon was surprised to find the Archdeacon in London, and the Archdeacon was equally surprised to find Breddon in England at all. Breddon carried off the Archdeacon with him to his rooms, and sent a servant in a cab to the Langham to pay the Archdeacon's bill and fetch luggage. The Archdeacon protested, but faintly, and Breddon would not hear of his hospitality being refused.

Breddon's rooms were and expensive suite immediately over a ruinous upholsterer's in a street off Berkeley Square. There was a private street-door, and from it a private staircase to the first and second floors.

The suite of rooms on the first floor, occupied by Breddon, was entirely shut off from the staircase by a door. The second floor suite, tenanted by an Irish M. P., was similarly shut off and at that time was unoccupied.

Breddon and the Archdeacon passed through the street-door and up the stairs to the first landing, from whence, by the staircase-door, they entered the flat. Breddon had only recently taken the flat, and the Archdeacon had never been there before. It consisted of a broad L-shaped passage within rooms opening into it. There were many trophies on the walls. Horned heads glared at them; stealthy but stuffed beasts watched them furtively from under tables. There was a perfect arsenal of murderous weapons gleaming brightly under the shaded gaslights.

Breddon's servant prepared supper for them before leaving for the Langham, and soon the two men were discussing Mr. Tennyson, Mr. Irving, and a parody of the 'Queen of the May' which had recently appeared in *Punch*, and doing justice to some oysters, a cold pheasant with an excellent salad, and a bottle of '74 Pommery. It was characteristic of the Archdeacon that he remembered exactly the items of the supper, and that Breddon rather neglected the wine. After supper they passed into the library, where a bright fire was burning. The Archdeacon walked towards the fire, rubbing his plump hands together. As he did so, a portion of the great rug of gray fur on which he was standing seemed to rise up. It was a gray cat of enormous size,

larger than any that the Archdeacon had ever seen before, and of the same colour as the rug on which it had been sleeping. It rubbed itself affectionately against the Archdeacon's leg, and purred as he bent down to stroke it.

'What an extraordinary animal!' said the Archdeacon. 'I had no idea cats could grow to this size. Its head's queer, too—so much too small for the body.'

'Yes,' said Breddon, 'and his feet are just as much too big.'

The gray cat stretched himself voluptuously under the Archdeacon's caressing hand, and the feet could be seen plainly. They were very broad, and the claws, which shot out, seemed unusually powerful and well developed. The beast's coat was short, thick, and wiry.

'Most extraordinary!' the Archdeacon repeated.

He lowered himself into a comfortable chair by the fire. He was still bending over the cat and playing with it when a slight chink made him look up. Breddon was putting something down on the table behind the liquor decanters.

'Any particular breed?' the Archdeacon asked.

'Not that I know of. Freakish, I should say. We found him on board the boat when I left for home—may have come there after mice. He'd have been thrown overboard but for me. I got rather interested in him. Smoke?'

'Oh, thank you.'

Outside a cold north wind screamed in quick gusts. Within came the sharp scratch of the match on the ribbed glass as the Archdeacon lit his cigar, the bubble of the rose-water in Breddon's hookah, the soft step of Breddon's man carrying the Archdeacon's luggage into the bedroom at the end of the L-shaped passage, and the constant purring of the big gray cat.

'And what's the cat's name?' the Archdeacon asked.

Breddon laughed.

'Well, if you must have the plain truth, he's called Gray Devil—or, more frequently, Devil *tout court.*'

Really, now, really, you can't expect an Archdeacon to use such abominable language. I shall call him Gray—or perhaps Mr. Gray would be more respectful, seeing the shortness of our acquaintance. Do you object to the smell of smoke, Mr. Gray? The intelligent beast does not object. Probably you've accustomed him to it.'

'Well, seeing what his name is, he could hardly object to smoke, could he?'

Breddon's servant entered. As the door opened and shut, one heard for a moment the crackle of the newly-hit fire in the room that awaited the Archdeacon. The servant swept up the hearth, and, under Archidiaconal direction, mixed a lengthy brandy-and-soda. He retired with the information that he would not be wanted again that night.

'Did you notice,' asked the Archdeacon, 'the way Mr. Gray followed your man about? I never saw a more affectionate cat.'

'Think so?' said Breddon. 'Watch this time.'

For the first the he approached the gray cat, and stretched out his hand as if to pet him. In an instant the cat seemed to have gone mad. Its claws shot out, its back hooped, its coat bristled, its tail stood erect; it cursed and spat, and its small green eyes glared. But a close observer would have noticed that all the time it watched not only Breddon, but also that object which had chinked as Breddon had put it down behind the decanters.

The Archdeacon lay back in his chair and laughed heartily.

'What funny creatures they are, and never so funny as when they lose their tempers! Really, Mr. Gray, out of respect to my cloth, you might have refrained from swearing like that. Poor Mr. Gray! Poor puss!'

Breddon resumed his seat with a grim smile. The gray cat slowly subsided, and then thrust its head, as though demanding sympathy, into the fat palm of the Archdeacon's dependent hand.

Suddenly the Archdeacon's eye lighted on the object which the cat had been watching, visible now that the servant had displaced the decanters.

'Goodness me!' he exclaimed, 'you've got a revolver there.'

'That is so,' said Breddon. Not loaded, I trust?'

'Oh yes, fully loaded.'

'But isn't that very dangerous?'

'Well, no; I'm used to these things, and I'm not careless with them. I should have thought it more dangerous to have introduced Gray Devil to you without it. Hes much more powerful than an ordinary eat, and I fancy there's something beside cat in his pedigree. When I bring a stranger to see him I keep the cat covered with the revolver until I see how the land lies. To do the brute justice, he has always been most friendly with everybody except myself. I'm his only antipathy. He'd have gone for me just now but that he's smart enough to be afraid of this.'

He tapped the revolver.

'I see,' said the Archdeacon seriously, 'and can guess how it happened. You scared him one day by firing the revolver for joke; the report frightened him, and he's never forgiven you or forgotten the revolver. Wonderful memory some of these animals have!'

'Yes,' said Breddon, 'but that guess won't do. I have never, intentionally or by chance, given the "Devil" any reason for his enmity. So far as I know he has never heard a firearm, and certainly he has never heard one since I made his acquaintance. Somebody may have scared him before, and I'm inclined to think that somebody did, for there can be no doubt that the brute knows all that a cat need know about a revolver, and that he's scared of it.

'The first time we met was almost in darkness. I'd got some cases that I was particular about, and the captain had said I could go down to look after them. Well, this beast suddenly came out of a lump of black and flew at me. I didn't even recognise that it was a cat, because he's so mighty big. I fetched him a clip on the side of the head that knocked him off, and whipped out my iron. He was away in a streak. He knew. And I've had plenty of proof since that he knows. He'd bite me now if he had the chance, but he understands that he hasn't got the chance. I'm often

half inclined to take him on plain—shooting barred—and to feel my own hands breaking his damned neck

'Really, old man, really!' said the Archdeacon in perfunctory protest, as he rose and mixed himself another drink.

'Sorry to use strong language, but I don't love that cat, you know.'

The Archdeacon expressed his surprise that in that case Breddon did not get rid of the brute.

'You come across him on board ship and he flies at you. You save his life, give him board and lodging, and he still hates you so much that he won't let you touch him, and you are no fonder of him than he is of you. Why don't you part company?'

'As for his board, I've rarely known him to eat anything except his own kill. He goes out hunting every night. I keep him simply and solely because I'm afraid of him. As long as I can keep him I know my nerves are all right. If I let my funk of him make any diference—well, I shouldn't be much good in a Central African forest. At first I had some idea of taming him—and, besides, there was a queer coincidence. He rose and opened the window, and Gray Devil slowly slunk up to it. He paused a few moments on the window-sill and then suddenly sprang and vanished.

'What was the coincidence?'

'What do you think of that?'

Breddon handed the Archdeacon a figure of a cat which he had taken from the mantelpiece. It was a little thing about three inches high. In colour, in the small head, enormous feet, and curiously human eyes, it seemed an exact reproduction of Gray Devil.

'A perfect likeness. How did you get it made?'

'I got the likeness before I got the original. A little Jew dealer sold it me the night before I left for England. He thought it was Egyptian, and described it as an idol. Anyhow, it was a niceish piece of jade.'

'I always thought Jade was bright green.

It may be—or white—or brown. It varies. I don't think there can be any doubt that this little figure is old, though I doubt if it's Egyptian.'

Breddon put it back in its place.

By the way, that same nighttime little Jew came to try and buy it back again, he offered me twice what I had given for it. I said he must have found somebody who was pretty keen on it. I asked if it was a collector. The Jew thought not; said it was a coloured gentleman. Well, that finished it. I wasn't going to do anything to oblige a nigger. The Jew pleaded that it was a particularly fine buck-nigger, with mountains of money, who'd been tracking the thing for years, and hinted at all manner of mumbo-jumbo business—to scare me, I suppose. However, I wouldn't listen, and kicked him out. Then came the coincidence. Having bought the likeness, next day I found the living original. Rum, wasn't it?'

At this moment the clock struck, and the Archdeacon recognised with horror that it was very, very much past the time when respectable Archdeacons should be in bed and asleep. He rose and said good night, observing that he'd like to hear more about it on the morrow.

This was extremely unfortunate, for it will be seen it is just at this part of the story that one wants full details, and on the morrow it became impossible to elicit them.

Before leaving the library Breddon closed the window, and the Archdeacon asked how 'Mr. Gray,' as he called him, would get back.

'Very likely he's back already. He's got a special window in the kitchen, made on purpose, just big enough to let him get in and out as he likes.'

'But don't other cats get in, too?'

'No,' said Breddon. 'Other cats avoid Gray Devil.'

The Archdeacon found himself unaccountably nervous when he got to his room. He owned to me that he had to satisfy himself that there was no one concealed under the bed or in the wardrobe. However, he got into bed, and after a little while fell into a deep sleep; his fire was burning brightly, and the room was quite light.

Shortly after four, he was awakened by a loud scream. Still sleepy, he did not for the moment locate the sound, thinking that it must have come from the street outside. But almost immediately afterwards he heard the report of a revolver fired twice in quick succession, and then, after a short pause, a third time. The Archdeacon was terribly frightened, He did not know what had happened, and thought of armed burglars. For a time—he did not think it could have been more than a minute—fear held him motionless. Then with an effort he rose, lit the gas, and hurried on his clothes. As he was dressing, he heard a step down the passage and a knock at his door.

He opened it, and found Breddon's servant. The man had put on a blue overcoat over his night-things, and wore slippers. He was shivering with cold and terror.

'Oh, my God, sir!' he exclaimed, 'Mr. Breddon's shot himself. Would you come, sir?'

The Archdeacon followed the man to Breddon's bedroom. The smoke still hung thickly in the room. A mirror had been smashed, and lay in fragments on the floor. On the bed, with his back to the Archdeacon, lay Breddon, dead.

His right hand still grasped the revolver, and there was a blackened wound behind the right ear.

When the Archdeacon came round to look at the face he turned faint, and the servant took him out into the library and gave him brandy, the glasses and decanters still standing there. Breddon's face certainly had looked very ghastly; it had been scratched, torn and bitten; one eye was gone, and the whole face was covered with blood.

'Do you think it was that brute did it?'

'Sure of it, sir; sprang on his face while he was asleep. I knew it would happen one of these nights. He knew it too; always slept with the revolver by his side. He fired twice at the brute, but couldn't see for the blood. Then he killed himself.'

It seemed likely enough, with his eyesight gone, horribly mauled, in an agony of pain, possibly believing that he was saving himself from a death still more horrible, Breddon might very well have turned the weapon on himself.

'What do we do now?' the man asked.

'We must get a doctor and fetch the police at once. Come on.'

As they turned the corner of the passage, they saw that the door communicating with the staircase was open.

'Did you open that door?' asked the Archdeacon.

'No,' said the man, aghast.

'Then who did?'

'Don't know, sir. Looks as if we weren't at the end of this yet.'

They passed down the stairs together, and found the street-door. also ajar. On the pavement outside lay a Policeman slowly recovering consciousness. Breddon's man took the policeman's whistle and blew it. A passing hansom, going back to the mews, slowed up; the cab was sent to fetch a doctor, and communication with the police-station rapidly followed.

The injured policeman told a curious story. He was passing the house when he heard shots fired. Almost immediately afterwards he heard the bolts of the front-door being drawn, and stepped back into the neighbouring doorway. The front-door opened, and a negro emerged clad in a gray tweed suit with a gray overcoat. The policeman jumped out, and without a second's hesitation the black man felled him. 'It was all done before you could think,' was the policeman's phrase.

'What kind of negro?' asked the Archdeacon.

'A big man—stood over six foot, and black as coal. He never waited to be challenged; the moment he knew that he was seen he hit out.'

The policeman was not a very intelligent fellow, and there was little more to be got out of him. He had heard the shots, seen the street-door open and the man in gray appear, and had been felled by a lightning blow before he had time to do anything.

The doctor, a plain, matter-of-fact little man, had no hesitation in saying that Breddon was dead, and must have died almost immediately.

After the injuries received, respiration and heart-action must have ceased at once. He was explaining something which oozed from the dead man's ear, when the Archdeacon could stand it no longer, and staggered out into the library. There he found Breddon's servant, still in the blue overcoat, explaining to a policeman with a notebook that as far as he knew nothing was fusing except a jade image or idol of cat which formerly stood on the mantelpiece.

The cat known as 'Gray Devil' as also missing, and, although a description of it was circulated in the public press, nothing was ever heard of it again. But gray fur was found in the clenched left hand of the dead man.

The inquest resulted in the customary verdict, and brought to light no new facts. But it may be as well to give what the police theory of the ease was. According to the police the suicide took place much as Breddon's servant had supposed. Mad with pain and unable to bear the thought of his awful mutilation, Breddon had shot himself.

The story of the jade image, as far as it was known, was told at the inquest. The police held that this image was an idol, that some uncivilized tribe was much perturbed by the theft of it, and was ready to pay an enormously high price for its recovery. The negro was assumed to be aware of this, and to have determined to obtain possession of the idol by fair means or foul. Fair means failing, it was suggested that the negro followed Breddon to England, tracked him out, and on the night in question found some means to conceal himself in Breddon's flat. There it was assumed that he fell asleep, was awakened by the screams and the sound of the firing, and, being scared, caught up the jade image and made off. Realizing that the shots would have been heard outside, and that his departure at that moment would be considered extremely suspicious, he was ready as he opened the street-door to fell the first man that he saw. the temporary unconsciousness of the policeman gave him time to get away.

The theory sounds at first sight like the only possible theory. When the Archdeacon first told me the story I tried to find out indirectly whether he accepted it. Finding him rather disposed to fence with my hints and suggestions, I put the question to him plainly and bluntly:

'Do you believe in the police theory?'

He hesitated, and then answered with complete frankness:

'No most emphatically not.'

Why?' I asked; and he went over the evidence with me.

'In the first place, I do not believe that Breddon, in the ordinary sense, committed suicide. No amount of physical pain would have made him even think of it. He had un-ending pluck. He would have taken the facial disfigurement and loss of sight as the chances of war, and would have done the best that could be done by a man with such awful disabilities. One must admit that he fired the fatal shot—the medical evidence on that point is too strong to be gainsaid—but he fired it under circumstances of supernatural horror of which we, thank God! know nothing.'

'I'm naturally slow to admit supernatural explanation.

'Well, let's go on. What's this mysterious tribe the police talk about? I want to know where it lives and what its name is. It's wealthy enough to offer a huge reward; it must be of some importance. The negro managed to get in and secrete himself. How? Where? I know the flat, and that theory won't do. We don't even know that it was the negro who took that little image, though I believe it was. Anyhow, how did the negro get away at that hour of the morning absolutely unobserved? Negroes are not so common in London that they can walk about without being noticed; yet not one trace of him was ever found, and equally mysterious is the disappearance of the Gray Cat. It was such an extraordinary brute, and the description of it was so widely circulated that it would have seemed almost certain we should hear of it again. Well, we've not heard.'

We discussed the Police theory for some little time, and something which he happened to say led me to exclaim:

'Really! do you mean to say that the Gray Cat actually was the negro?'

'No,' he replied, 'not exactly that, but something near it. Cats are strange animals, anyhow. needn't remind you of their connection with certain old religions or with that witchcraft in which even in England to-day some still believe, and not so long ago almost all believed I have never, by way, seen a good explanation of the fact that there are people who cannot bear to be in a room with a cat and are aware of its presence as by some mysterious extra sense. Let me remind you of the belief which undoubtedly exists both in China and Japan, that evil spirits may enter into certain of the lower animals, the fox and badger especially. Every student of demonology knows about these things.

'But that idea of evil spirits taking possession of cats or foxes is surely a heathen superstition which you can't hold.'

'Well, I have read of the evil spirits that entered into the swine. Think it over, and keep an open mind.'

WHERE THERE IS NOTHING, THERE IS GOD

W. B. YEATS

The little wicker houses at Tullagh, where the Brothers were accustomed to pray, or bend over many handicrafts, when twilight had driven them from the fields, were empty, for the hardness of the winter had brought the brotherhood together in the little wooden house under the shadow of the wooden chapel; and Abbot Malathgeneus, Brother Dove, Brother Bald Fox, Brother Peter, Brother Patrick, Brother Bittern, Brother Fair-Brows, and many too young to have won names in the great battle, sat about the fire with ruddy faces, one mending lines to lay in the river for eels, one fashioning a snare for birds, one mending the broken handle of a spade, one writing in a large book, and one shaping a jewelled box to hold the book; and among the rushes at their feet lay the scholars, who would one day be Brothers, and whose school-house it was, and for the succour of whose tender years the great fire was supposed to leap and flicker. One of these, a child of eight or nine years, called Olioll, lay upon his back looking up through the hole in the roof, through which the smoke went, and watching the stars appearing and disappearing in the smoke with mild eyes, like the eyes of a beast of the field. He turned presently to the Brother who wrote in the big book, and whose duty was to teach the children, and said, 'Brother Dove, to what are the stars fastened?' The Brother, rejoicing to see so much curiosity in the stupidest of his scholars, laid down the pen and said, 'There are nine crystalline spheres, and on the first the Moon is fastened, on the second the planet Mercury, on the third the planet Venus, on the fourth the Sun, on the fifth the planet Mars, on the sixth the planet Jupiter, on the seventh the planet Saturn; these are the wandering stars; and on the eighth are fastened the fixed stars; but the ninth sphere is a sphere of the substance on which the breath of God moved in the beginning.'

'What is beyond that?' said the child. 'There is nothing beyond that; there is God.'

And then the child's eyes strayed to the jewelled box, where one great ruby was gleaming in the light of the fire, and he said, 'Why has Brother Peter put a great ruby on the side of the box?'

'The ruby is a symbol of the love of God.'

'Why is the ruby a symbol of the love of God?'

'Because it is red, like fire, and fire burns up everything, and where there is nothing, there is God.'

The child sank into silence, but presently sat up and said, 'There is somebody outside.'

'No,' replied the Brother. 'It is only the wolves; I have heard them moving about in the snow for some time. They are growing very wild, now that the winter drives them from the mountains. They broke into a fold last night and carried off many sheep, and if we are not careful they will devour everything.'

'No, it is the footstep of a man, for it is heavy; but I can hear the footsteps of the wolves also.'

He had no sooner done speaking than somebody rapped three times, but with no great loudness.

'I will go and open, for he must be very cold.'

'Do not open, for it may be a man-wolf, and he may devour us all.'

But the boy had already drawn back the heavy wooden bolt, and all the faces, most of them a little pale, turned towards the slowly-opening door.

'He has beads and a cross, he cannot be a man-wolf,' said the child, as a man with the snow heavy on his long, ragged beard, and on the matted hair, that fell over his shoulders and nearly to his waist, and dropping from the tattered cloak that but half-covered his withered brown body, came in and looked from face to face with mild, ecstatic eyes. Standing some way from the fire, and with eyes that had rested at last upon the Abbot Malathgeneus, he cried out, 'O blessed abbot, let me come to the fire and warm myself and dry the snow from my beard and my hair and my cloak; that I may not die of the cold of the mountains, and anger the Lord with a wilful martyrdom.'

'Come to the fire,' said the abbot, 'and warm yourself, and eat the food the boy Olioll will bring you. It is sad indeed that any for whom Christ has died should be as poor as you.'

The man sat over the fire, and Olioll took away his now dripping cloak and laid meat and bread and wine before him; but he would eat only of the bread, and he put away the wine, asking for water. When his beard and hair had begun to dry a little and his limbs had ceased to shiver with the cold, he spoke again.

'O blessed abbot, have pity on the poor, have pity on a beggar who has trodden the bare world this many a year, and give me some labour to do, the hardest there is, for I am the poorest of God's poor.'

Then the Brothers discussed together what work they could put him to, and at first to little purpose, for there was no labour that had not found its labourer in that busy community; but at last one remembered that Brother Bald Fox, whose business it was to turn the great quern in the quern-house, for he was too stupid for anything else, was getting old for so heavy a labour; and so the beggar was put to the quern from the morrow.

The cold passed away, and the spring grew to summer, and the quern was never idle, nor was it turned with grudging labour, for when any passed the beggar was heard singing as he drove the handle round. The last gloom, too, had passed from that happy community, for Olioll, who had always been stupid and unteachable, grew clever, and this was the more miraculous because it had come of a sudden. One day he had been even duller than usual, and was beaten and told to know his lesson better on the morrow or be sent into a lower class among little boys who would make a joke of him. He had gone out in tears, and when he came the next day, although his stupidity, born of a mind that would listen to every wandering sound and brood upon every wandering light, had so long been the byword of the school, he knew his lesson so well that he passed to the head of the class, and from that day was the best of scholars. At first Brother Dove thought this was an answer to his own prayers to the Virgin, and took it for a great proof of the love she bore him; but when many far more fervid prayers had failed to add a single wheatsheaf to the harvest, he began to think that the child was trafficking with bards, or druids, or witches, and resolved to follow and watch. He had told his thought to the abbot, who bid him come to him the moment he hit the truth; and the next day, which was a Sunday, he stood in the path when the abbot and the Brothers were coming from vespers, with their white habits upon them, and took the abbot by the habit and said, 'The beggar is of the greatest of saints and of the workers of miracle. I followed Olioll but now, and by his slow steps and his bent head I saw that the weariness of his stupidity was over him, and when he came to the little wood by the quern-house I knew by the path broken in the under-wood and by the footmarks in the muddy places that he had gone that way many times. I hid behind a bush where the path doubled upon itself at a sloping place, and understood by the tears in his eyes that his stupidity was too old and his wisdom too new to save him from terror of the rod. When he was in the quern-house I went to the window and looked in, and the birds came down and perched upon my head and my shoulders, for they are not timid in that holy place; and a wolf passed by, his right side shaking my habit, his left the leaves of a bush. Olioll opened his book and turned to the page I had told him to learn, and began to cry, and the beggar sat beside him and comforted him until he fell asleep. When his sleep was of the deepest the beggar knelt down and prayed aloud, and said, "O Thou Who dwellest beyond the stars, show forth Thy power as at the beginning, and let knowledge sent from Thee awaken in his mind, wherein is nothing from the world, that the nine orders of angels may glorify Thy name"; and then a light broke out of the air and wrapped Aodh, and I smelt the breath of roses. I stirred a little in my wonder, and the beggar turned and saw me, and, bending low, said, "O Brother Dove, if I have done wrong, forgive me, and I will do penance. It was my pity moved me"; but I was afraid and I ran away, and did not stop running until I came here.' Then all the Brothers began talking together, one saying it was such and such a saint, and one that it was not he but another; and one that it was none of these, for they were still in their brotherhoods, but that it was such and such a one; and the talk was as near to quarreling as might be in that gentle community, for each would claim so great a saint for his native province. At last the abbot said, 'He is none that you have named, for at Easter I had greeting from all, and each was in his brotherhood; but he is Aengus the Lover of God, and the first of those who have gone to live in the wild places and among the wild beasts. Ten years ago he felt the burden of many labours in a brotherhood under the Hill of Patrick and went into the forest that he might labour only with song to the Lord; but the fame of his holiness brought many thousands to his cell, so that a little pride clung to a soul from which all

else had been driven. Nine years ago he dressed himself in rags, and from that day none has seen him, unless, indeed, it be true that he has been seen living among the wolves on the mountains and eating the grass of the fields. Let us go to him and bow down before him; for at last, after long seeking, he has found the nothing that is God; and bid him lead us in the pathway he has trodden.'

They passed in their white habits along the beaten path in the wood, the acolytes swinging their censers before them, and the abbot, with his crozier studded with precious stones, in the midst of the incense; and came before the quern-house and knelt down and began to pray, awaiting the moment when the child would wake, and the Saint cease from his watch and come to look at the sun going down into the unknown darkness, as his way was.

AMINA

EDWARD LUCAS WHITE

Waldo, brought face to face with the actuality of the unbelievable—as he himself would have worded it—was completely dazed. In silence he suffered the consul to lead him from the tepid gloom of the interior, through the ruinous doorway, out into the hot, stunning brilliance of the desert landscape. Hassan followed, with never a look behind him. Without any word he had taken Waldo's gun from his nerveless hand and carried it, with his own and the consul's.

The consul strode across the gravelly sand, some fifty paces from the southwest corner of the tomb, to a bit of not wholly ruined wall from which there was a clear view of the doorway side of the tomb and of the side with the larger crevice.

"Hassan," he commanded, "watch here."

Hassan said something in Persian.

"How many cubs were there?" the consul asked Waldo. Waldo stared mute.

"How many young ones did you see?" the consul asked again.

"Twenty or more," Waldo made answer.

"That's impossible," snapped the consul.

"There seemed to be sixteen or eighteen," Waldo asserted. Hassan smiled and grunted. The consul took from him two guns, handed Waldo his, and they walked around the tomb to a point about equally distant from the opposite corner. There was another bit of ruin, and in front of it, on the side toward the tomb, was a block of stone mostly in the shadow of the wall.

"Convenient," said the consul. "Sit on that stone and lean against the wall, make yourself comfortable. You are a bit shaken, but you will be all right in a moment. You should have something to eat, but we have nothing. Anyhow, take a good swallow of this."

He stood by him as Waldo gasped over the raw brandy.

"Hassan will bring you his water-bottle before he goes," the consul went on; "drink plenty, for you must stay here for some time. And now, pay attention to me. We must extirpate these vermin. The male, I judge, is absent. If he had been anywhere about, you would not now be alive. The young cannot be as many as you say, but, I take it, we have to deal with ten, a full litter. We must smoke them out. Hassan will go back to camp after fuel and the guard. Meanwhile, you and I must see that none escape."

He took Waldo's gun, opened the breech, shut it, examined the magazine and handed it back to him.

"Now watch me closely," he said. He paced off, looking to his left past the tomb. Presently he stopped and gathered several stones together.

"You see these?" he called.

Waldo shouted an affirmation.

The consul came back, passed on in the same line, looking to his right past the tomb, and presently, at a similar distance, put up another tiny cairn, shouted again and was again answered. Again he returned.

"Now you are sure you cannot mistake those two marks

I have made?"

"Very sure indeed," said Waldo.

"It is important, warned the consul. "I am going back to where I left Hassan, to watch there while he is gone. You will watch here. You may pace as often as you like to either of those stone heaps. From either you can see me on my beat. Do not diverge from the line from one to the other. For as soon as Hassan is out of sight I shall shoot any moving thing I see nearer. Sit here till you see me set up similar limits for my sentry—go on the farther side, then shoot any moving thing not on my line of patrol. Keep a lookout all around you. There is one chance in a million that the male might return in daylight—mostly, they are nocturnal, but this lair is evidently exceptional. Keep a bright lookout.

"And now listen to me. You must not feel any foolish sentimentalism about any fancied resemblance of these vermin to human beings. Shoot, and shoot to kill. Not only is it our duty, in general, to abolish them, but it will be very dangerous for us if we do not. There is little or no solidarity in Mohammedan communities, but on the comparatively few points upon which public opinion exists it acts with amazing promptitude and vigor. One matter as to which there is no disagreement is that it is incumbent upon every man to assist in eradicating these creatures. The good old Biblical custom of stoning to death is the mode of lynching indigenous hereabouts. These modern Asiatics are quite capable of applying it to anyone believed derelict against any of these inimical monsters. If we let one escape and the rumor of it gets about, we may precipitate an outburst of racial prejudice difficult to cope with. Shoot, I say, without hesitation or mercy."

"I understand," said Waldo.

"I 'don't care whether you understand or not," said the consul, "I want you to act. Shoot if needful, and shoot straight." And he tramped off.

Hassan presently appeared, and Waldo drank from his water-bottle as nearly all of its contents as Has-

san would permit. After his departure Waldo's first alertness soon gave place to mere endurance of the monotony of watching and the intensity of the heat. His discomfort became suffering, and what with the fury of the dry glare, the pangs of thirst and his bewilderment of mind, Waldo was moving in a waking dream by the time Hassan returned with two donkeys and a mule laden with brushwood. Behind the beasts straggled the guard.

Waldo's trance became a nightmare when the smoke took effect and the battle began. He was, however, not only not required to join in the killing, but was enjoined to keep back. He did keep very much in the background, seeing only so much of the slaughter as his curiosity would not let him refrain from viewing. Yet he felt all a murderer as he gazed at the ten small carcasses laid out arow, and the memory of his vigil and its end, indeed of the whole day, though it was the day of his most marvelous adventure, remains to him as the broken recollections of a phantasmagoria.

On the morning of his memorable peril Waldo had waked early. The experiences of his sea-voyage, the sights at Gibraltar, at Port Said, in the canal, at Suez, at Aden, at Muscat, and at Basrah had formed an altogether inadequate transition from the decorous regularity of house and school life in New England to the breathless wonder of the desert immensities.

Everything seemed unreal, and yet the reality of its strangeness so besieged him that he could not feel at home in it, he could not sleep heavily in a tent. After composing himself to sleep, he lay long conscious and awakened early, as on this morning, just at the beginning of the false dawn.

The consul was fast asleep, snoring loudly. Waldo dressed quietly and went out; mechanically, without any purpose or forethought, taking his gun. Outside he found Hassan, seated, his gun across his knees, his head sunk forward, as fast asleep as the consul. Ali and Ibrahim had left the camp the day before for supplies. Waldo was the only waking creature

about; for the guards, camped some little distance off, were but logs about the ashes of their fire. Meaning merely to enjoy, under the white glow of the false dawn, the magical reappearance of the constellations and the short last glory of the star-laden firmament, that brief coolness which compensated a trifle for the hot morning, the fiery day and the warmish night, he seated himself on a rock, some paces from the tent and twice as far from the guards. Turning his gun in his hands he felt an irresistible temptation to wander off by himself, to stroll alone through the fascinating emptiness of the arid landscape.

When he had begun camp life he had expected to find the consul, that combination of sportsman, explorer and archaeologist, a particularly easygoing guardian. He had looked forward to absolutely untrameled liberty in the spacious expanse of the limitless wastes. The reality he had found exactly the reverse of his preconceptions. The consul's first injunction was:

"Never let yourself get out of sight of me or of Hassan unless he or I send you off with Au or Ibrahim. Let nothing tempt you to roam about alone. Even a ramble is dangerous. You might lose sight of the camp before you knew it."

At first Waldo acquiesced, later he protested. "I have a good pocket compass. I know how to use it. I never lost my way in the Maine woods."

"No Kourds in the Maine woods," said the consul.

Yet before long Waldo noticed that the few Kourds they encountered seemed simple-hearted, peaceful folk. No semblance of danger or even of adventure had appeared. Their armed guard of a dozen greasy tatterdemalions had passed their time in uneasy loafing.

Likewise Waldo noticed that the consul seemed indifferent to the ruins they passed by or encamped among, that his feeling for sites and topography was cooler than lukewarm, that he showed no ardor in the pursuit of the scanty and uninteresting game. He had picked up enough of several dialects to hear repeated conversations about "them." "Have you heard of any about here?" "Has one been killed?" "Any traces of them in this district?" And such queries he could make out in the various talks with the natives they met, as to what "they" were he received no enlightenment.

Then he had questioned Hassan as to why he was so restricted in his movements. Hassan spoke some English and regaled him with tales of Afrits, ghouls, specters and other uncanny legendary presences; of the jinn of the waste, appearing in human shape, talking all languages, ever on the alert to ensnare infidels; of the woman whose feet turned the wrong way at the ankles, luring the unwary to a pool and there drowning her victims; of the malignant ghosts of dead brigands, more terrible than their living fellows; of the spirit in the shape of a wild ass, or of a gazelle, enticing its pursuers to the brink of a precipice and itself seeming to run ahead upon an expanse of sand, a mere mirage, dissolving as the victim passed the brink and fell to death; of the sprite in the semblance of a hare feigning a limp, or of a ground bird feigning a broken wing, drawing its pursuer after it till he met death in an unseen pit or well shaft.

Ali and Ibrahim spoke no English. As far as Waldo could understand their long harangues, they told similar stories or hinted at dangers equally vague and imaginary. These childish bogy-tales merely whetted Waldo's craving for independence.

Now, as he sat on a rock, longing to enjoy the perfect sky, the clear, early air, the wide, lonely landscape, along with the sense of having it to himself, it seemed to him that the consul was merely innately cautious, overcautious. There was no danger. He would have a fine leisurely stroll, kill something perhaps, and certainly be back in camp before the sun grew hot. He stood up.

Some hours later he was seated on a fallen coping stone in the shadow of a ruined tomb. All the country they had been traversing is full of tombs and remains of tombs, prehistoric, Bactrian, old Persian, Parthian, Sassanian, or Mohammedan, scattered everywhere in groups or solitary.

Vanished utterly are the faintest traces of the cities, towns, and villages, ephemeral houses or temporary huts, in which had lived the countless generations of mourners who had reared these tombs.

The tombs, built more durably than mere dwellings of the living, remained. Complete or ruinous, or reduced to mere fragments, they were everywhere. In that district they were all of one type. Each was domed and below was square, its one door facing eastward and opening into a large empty room, behind which were the mortuary chambers.

In the shadow of such a tomb Waldo sat. He had shot nothing, had lost his way, had no idea of the direction of the camp, was tired, warm, and thirsty. He had forgotten his water-bottle.

He swept his gaze over the vast, desolate prospect, the unvaried turquoise of the sky arched above the rolling desert. Far reddish hills along the skyline hooped in the less distant brown hillocks which, without diversifying it, hum-

mocked the yellow landscape. Sand and rocks with a lean, starved bush or two made up the nearer view, broken here and there by dazzling white or streaked, grayish, crumbling ruins. The sun had not been long above the horizon, yet the whole surface of the desert was quivering with heat.

As Waldo sat viewing the outlook a woman came round the corner of the tomb. All the village women Waldo had seen had worn yashmaks or some other form of face covering or veil. This woman was bareheaded and unveiled. She wore some sort of yellowish-brown garment which enveloped her from neck to ankles, showing no waist line. Her feet, in defiance of the blistering sands, were bare.

At sight of Waldo she stopped and stared at him as he at her. He remarked the un-European posture of her feet, not at all turned out, but with the inner lines parallel. She wore no anklets, he observed, no bracelets, no necklace or earrings. Her bare arms he thought the most muscular he had ever seen on a human being. Her nails were pointed and long, both on her hands and feet. Her hair was black, short, and tousled, yet she did not look wild or uncomely. Her eyes smiled and her lips had the effect of smiling, though they did not part ever so little, not showing at all the teeth behind them.

"What a pity," said Waldo aloud, "that she does not speak English."

"I do speak English," said the woman, and Waldo noticed that as she spoke, her lips did not perceptibly open. "What does the gentleman want?"

"You speak English!" Waldo exclaimed, jumping to his feet. "What luck! Where did you learn it?"

"At the mission school," she replied, an amused smile playing about the corners of her rather wide, unopening mouth. "What can be done for you?" She spoke with scarcely any foreign accent, but very slowly and with a sort of growl running along from syllable to syllable.

"I am thirsty," said Waldo, "and I have lost my way."

"Is the gentleman living in a brown tent, shaped like half a melon?" she inquired, the queer, rumbling note drawling from one word to the next, her lips barely separated.

"Yes, that is our camp," said Waldo.

"I could guide the gentleman that way," she droned; "but it is far, and there is no water on that side."

"I want water first," said Waldo, "or milk."

"If you mean cow's milk, we have none. But we have goat's milk. There is to drink where I dwell," she said, sing-songing the words. "It is not far. It is the other way."

"Show me," said he.

She began to walk, Waldo, his gun under his arm, beside her. She trod noiselessly and fast. Waldo could scarcely keep up with her. As they walked he often fell behind and noted how her swathing garments clung to a lithe, shapely back, neat waist, and firm hips. Each time he hurried and caught up with her, he scanned her with intermittent glances, puzzled that her waist, so well-marked at the spine, showed no particular definition in front; that the outline of her from neck to knees, perfectly shapeless under her wrappings, was without any waistline or suggestion of firmness or undulation. Likewise he remarked the amused flicker in her eyes and the compressed line of her red, her too-red lips.

"How long were you in the mission school?" he inquired.

"Four years," she replied.

"Are you a Christian?" he asked.

"The Free-folk do not submit to baptism," she stated simply, but with rather more of the droning growl between her words.

He felt a queer shiver as he watched the scarcely moved lips through which the syllables edged their way.

"But you are not veiled," he could not resist saying.

"The Free-folk," she rejoined, "are never veiled."

"Then you are not a Mohammedan?" he ventured.

"The Free-folk are not Moslems."

"Who are the Free-folk?" he blurted out incautiously.

She shot one baleful glance at him. Waldo remembered that he had to do with an Asiatic. He recalled the three permitted questions.

"What is your name?" he inquired.

"Amina," she told him.

That is a name from the 'Arabian Nights'," he hazarded.

"From the foolish tales of the believers," she sneered. "The Free-folk know nothing of such follies." The unvarying shutness of her speaking lips, the drawly burr between the syllables, struck him all the more as her lips curled but did not open.

"You utter your words in a strange way," he said.

"Your language is not mine," she replied.

"How is it that you learned my language at the mission school and are not a Christian?"

"They teach all at the mission school," she said, "and the maidens of the Free-folk are like the other maidens they teach, though the Free-folk when grown are not as town-dwellers are. Therefore they taught me as any town-bred girl, not knowing me for what I am."

"They taught you well," he commented.

"I have the gift of tongues," she uttered enigmatically, with an odd note of triumph burring the words through her unmoving lips.

Waldo felt a horrid shudder all over him, not only at her uncanny words, but also from mere faintness.

"Is it far to your home?" he breathed.

"It is there," she said, pointing to the doorway of a large tomb just before them.

The wholly open arch admitted them into a fairly spacious interior, cool with the abiding temperature of thick masonry. There was no rubbish on the floor. Waldo, relieved to escape the blistering glare outside, seated himself on a block of stone midway between the door and the inner partition wall, resting his gun butt on the floor. For the moment he was blinded by the change from the insistent brilliance of the desert morning to the blurred gray light of the interior.

When his sight cleared he looked about and remarked, opposite the door, the ragged hole which laid open the desecrated mausoleum. As his eyes grew accustomed to the dimness he was so startled that he stood up. It seemed to him that from its four corners the room swarmed with naked children. To his inexperienced conjecture they seemed about two years old, but they moved with the assurance of boys of eight or ten.

"Whose are these children?" he exclaimed.

"Mine," she said.

"All yours?" he protested.

"All mine," she replied, a curious suppressed boisterousness in her demeanor.

"But there are twenty of them," he cried.

"You count badly in the dark," she told him. "There are fewer."

"There certainly are a dozen," he maintained, spinning round as they danced and scampered about.

"The Free-people have large families," she said.

"But they are all of one age," Waldo exclaimed, his tongue dry against the roof of his mouth.

She laughed, an unpleasant, mocking laugh, clapping her hands. She was between him and the doorway, and as most of the light came from it he could not see her lips.

"Is not that like a man! No woman would have made that mistake."

Waldo was confuted and sat down again. The children circulated around him, chattering, laughing, giggling, snickering, making noises indicative of glee.

"Please get me something cool to drink," said Waldo, and his tongue was not only dry but big in his mouth.

"We shall have to drink shortly," she said, "but it will be warm."

Waldo began to feel uneasy. The children pranced around him, jabbering strange, guttural noises, licking their lips, pointing at him, their eyes fixed on him, with now and then a glance at their mother.

"Where is the water?"

The woman stood silent, her arms hanging at her sides, and it seemed to Waldo she was shorter than she had been.

"Where is the water?" he repeated.

"Patience, patience," she growled, and came a step near to him.

The sunlight struck upon her back and made a sort of halo about her hips. She seemed still shorter than before. There was a something furtive in her bearing, and the little ones sniggered evilly.

At that instant two rifle shots rang out almost as one. The woman fell face downward on the floor. The babies shrieked in a shrill chorus. Then she leapt up from all fours with an explosive suddenness, staggered in a hurled, lurching rush toward the hole in the wall, and, with a frightful yell, threw up her arms and whirled backward to the ground, doubled and contorted like a dying fish, stiffened, shuddered and was still. Waldo, his horrified eyes fixed on her face, even in his amazement noted that her lips did not open.

The children, squealing faint cries of dismay, scrambled

through the hole in the inner wall, vanishing into the inky void beyond. The last had hardly gone when the consul appeared in the doorway, his smoking gun in his hand.

"Not a second too soon, my boy," he ejaculated. "She was just going to spring."

He cocked his gun and prodded the body with the muzzle.

"Good and dead," he commented. "What luck! Generally it takes three or four bullets to finish one. I've known one with two bullets through her lungs to kill a man."

"Did you murder this woman?" Waldo demanded fiercely.

"Murder?" the consul snorted. "Murder! Look at that."

He knelt down and pulled open the full, close lips, disclosing not human teeth, but small incisors, cusped grinders, wide-spaced; and long, keen, overlapping canines, like those of a greyhound: a fierce, deadly, carnivorous dentition, menacing and combative.

Waldo felt a qualm, yet the face and form still swayed his horrified sympathy for their humanness.

"Do you shoot women because they have long teeth?" Waldo insisted, revolted at the horrid death he had watched.

"You are hard to convince," said the consul sternly. "Do you call that a woman?"

He stripped the clothing from the carcass.

Waldo sickened all over. What he saw was not the front of a woman, but more like the underside of an old fox-terrier with puppies, or of a white sow, with her second litter; from collarbone to groin ten lolloping udders, two rows, mauled, stringy, and flaccid.

"What kind of a creature is it?" he asked faintly.

"A Ghoul, my boy," the consul answered solemnly, almost in a whisper.

"I thought they did not exist," Waldo babbled. "I thought they were mythical; I thought there were none.

"I can very well believe that there are none in Rhode Island," the consul said gravely. "This is in Persia, and Persia is in Asia."

THE CAMP OF THE DOG

ALGERNON BLACKWOOD

I

Islands of all shapes and sizes troop northward from Stockholm by the hundred, and the little steamer that threads their intricate mazes in summer leaves the traveller in a somewhat bewildered state as regards the points of the compass when it reaches the end of its journey at Waxholm. But it is only after Waxholm that the true islands begin, so to speak, to run wild, and start up the coast on their tangled course of a hundred miles of deserted loveliness, and it was in the very heart of this delightful confusion that we pitched our tents for a summer holiday. A veritable wilderness of islands lay about us: from the mere round button of a rock that bore a single fir, to the mountainous stretch of a square mile, densely wooded, and bounded by precipitous cliffs; so close together often that a strip of water ran between no wider than a country lane, or, again, so far that an expanse stretched like the open sea for miles.

Although the larger islands boasted farms and fishing stations, the majority were uninhabited. Carpeted with moss and heather, their coast-lines showed a series of ravines and clefts and little sandy bays, with a growth of splendid pine-woods that came down to the water's edge and led the eye through unknown depths of shadow and mystery into the very heart of primitive forest.

The particular islands to which we had camping rights by virtue of paying a nominal sum to a Stockholm merchant lay together in a picturesque group far beyond the reach of the steamer, one being a mere reef with a fringe of fairy-like birches, and two others, cliff-bound monsters rising with wooded heads out of the sea. The fourth, which we selected because it enclosed a little lagoon suitable for anchorage, bathing, night-lines, and what-not, shall have what description is necessary as the story proceeds; but, so far as paying rent was concerned, we might equally well have pitched our tents on any one of a hundred others that clustered about us as thickly as a swarm of bees.

It was in the blaze of an evening in July, the air clear as crystal, the sea a cobalt blue, when we left the steamer on the borders of civilisation and sailed away with maps, compasses, and provisions for the little group of dots in the Skägård that were to be our home for the next two months. The dinghy and my Canadian canoe trailed behind us, with tents and dunnage carefully piled aboard, and when the point of cliff intervened to hide the steamer and the Waxholm hotel we realised for the first time that the horror of trains and houses was far behind us, the fever of men and cities, the weariness of streets and confined spaces. The wilderness opened up on all sides into endless blue reaches, and the map and compasses were so frequently called into requisition that we went astray more often than not and progress was enchantingly slow. It took us, for instance, two whole days to find our crescent-shaped home, and the camps we made on the way were so fascinating that we left them with difficulty and regret, for each island seemed more desirable than the one before it, and over all lay the spell of haunting peace, remoteness from the turmoil of the world, and the freedom of open and desolate spaces.

And so many of these spots of world-beauty have I sought out and dwelt in, that in my mind remains only a composite memory of their faces, a true map of heaven, as it were, from which this particular one stands forth with unusual sharpness because of the strange things that happened there, and also, I think, because anything in which John Silence played a part has a habit of fixing itself in the mind with a living and lasting quality of vividness.

For the moment, however, Dr. Silence was not of the party. Some private case in the interior of Hungary claimed his attention, and it was not till later—the 15th of August, to be exact—that I had arranged to meet him in Berlin and then return to London together for our harvest of winter work. All the members of our party, however, were known to him more or less well, and on this third day as we sailed through the narrow opening into the lagoon and saw the circular ridge of trees in a gold and crimson sunset before us, his last words to me when we parted in London for some unaccountable reason came back very sharply to my memory, and recalled the curious impression of prophecy with which I had first heard them:

"Enjoy your holiday and store up all the force you can," he had said as the train slipped out of Victoria; "and we will meet in Berlin on the 15th—unless you should send for me sooner."

And now suddenly the words returned to me so clearly that it seemed I almost heard his voice in my ear: "Unless you should send for me sooner"; and returned, moreover, with a significance I was wholly at a loss to understand that touched somewhere in the depths of my mind a vague sense of apprehension that they had all along been intended in the nature of a prophecy.

In the lagoon, then, the wind failed us this July evening, as was only natural behind the shelter of the belt of woods, and we took to the oars, all breathless with the beauty of this first sight of our island home, yet all talking in somewhat hushed voices of the best place to land, the depth of water, the safest place to anchor, to put up the tents in, the most sheltered spot for the camp-fires, and a dozen things of importance that crop up when a home in the wilderness has actually to be made.

And during this busy sunset hour of unloading before the dark, the souls of my companions adopted the trick of presenting themselves very vividly anew before my mind, and introducing themselves afresh.

In reality, I suppose, our party was in no sense singular. In the conventional life at home they certainly seemed ordinary enough, but suddenly, as we passed through these gates of the wilderness, I saw them more sharply than before, with characters stripped of the atmosphere of men and cities. A complete change of setting often furnishes a startlingly new view of people hitherto held for well-known; they present another facet of their personalities. I seemed to see my own party almost as new people—people I had not known properly hitherto, people who would drop all disguises and henceforth reveal themselves as they really were. And each one seemed to say: "Now you will see me as I am. You will see me here in this primitive life of the wilderness without clothes. All my masks and veils I have left behind in the abodes of men. So, look out for surprises!"

The Reverend Timothy Maloney helped me to put up the tents, long practice making the process easy, and while he drove in pegs and tightened ropes, his coat off, his flannel collar flying open without a tie, it was impossible to avoid the conclusion that he was cut out for the life of a pioneer rather than the church. He was fifty years of age, muscular, blue-eyed and hearty, and he took his share of the work, and more, without shirking. The way he handled the axe in cutting down saplings for the tent-poles was a delight to see, and his eye in judging the level was unfailing.

Bullied as a young man into a lucrative family living, he had in turn bullied his mind into some semblance of orthodox beliefs, doing the honours of the little country church with an energy that made one think of a coal-heaver tending china; and it was only in the past few years that he had resigned the living and taken instead to cramming young men for their examinations. This suited him better. It enabled him, too, to indulge his passion for spells of "wild life," and to spend the summer months of most years under canvas in one part of the world or another where he could take his young men with him and combine "reading" with open air.

His wife usually accompanied him, and there was no doubt she enjoyed the trips, for she possessed, though in less degree, the same joy of the wilderness that was his own distinguishing characteristic. The only difference was that while he regarded it as the real life, she regarded it as an interlude. While he camped out with his heart and mind, she played at camping out with her clothes and body. None the less, she made a splendid companion, and to watch her busy cooking dinner over the fire we had built among the stones was to understand that her heart was in the business for the moment and that she was happy even with the detail.

Mrs. Maloney at home, knitting in the sun and believing that the world was made in six days, was one woman; but Mrs. Maloney, standing with bare arms over the smoke of a wood fire under the pine trees, was another; and Peter Sangree, the Canadian pupil, with his pale skin, and his loose, though not ungainly figure, stood beside her in very unfavourable contrast as he scraped potatoes and sliced bacon with slender white fingers that seemed better suited to hold a pen than a knife. She ordered him about like a slave, and he obeyed, too, with willing pleasure, for in spite of his general appearance of debility he was as happy to be in camp as any of them.

But more than any other member of the party, Joan Maloney, the daughter, was the one who seemed a natural and genuine part of the landscape, who belonged to it all just in the same way that the trees and the moss and the grey rocks running out into the water belonged to it. For she was obviously in her right and natural setting, a creature of the wilds, a gipsy in her own home.

To any one with a discerning eye this would have been more or less apparent, but to me, who had known her during all the twenty-two years of her life and was familiar with the ins and outs of her primitive, utterly un-modern type, it was strikingly clear. To see her there made it impossible to imagine her again in civilisation. I lost all recollection of how she looked in a town. The memory somehow evaporated. This slim creature before me, flitting to and fro with the grace of the woodland life, swift, supple, adroit, on her knees blowing the fire, or stirring the frying-pan through a veil of smoke, suddenly seemed the only way I had ever really seen her. Here she was at home; in London she became some one concealed by clothes, an artificial doll overdressed and moving by clockwork, only a portion of her alive. Here she was alive all over.

I forget altogether how she was dressed, just as I forget how any particular tree was dressed, or how the markings ran on any one of the boulders that lay about the Camp. She looked just as wild and natural and untamed as everything else that went to make up the scene, and more than that I cannot say.

Pretty, she was decidedly not. She was thin, skinny, dark-haired, and possessed of great physical strength in the form of endurance. She had, too, something of the force and vigorous purpose of a man, tempestuous sometimes and wild to passionate, frightening her mother, and puzzling her easy-going father with her storms of waywardness, while at the same time she stirred his admiration by her violence. A pagan of the pagans she was besides, and with some haunting suggestion of old-world pagan beauty about her dark face and eyes. Altogether an odd and difficult character, but with a generosity and high courage that made her very lovable.

In town life she always seemed to me to feel cramped, bored, a devil in a cage, in her eyes a hunted expression as though any moment she dreaded to be caught. But up in these spacious solitudes all this disappeared. Away from the limitations that plagued and stung her, she would show at her best, and as I watched her moving about the Camp I repeatedly found myself thinking of a wild creature that had just obtained its freedom and was trying its muscles.

Peter Sangree, of course, at once went down before her. But she was so obviously beyond his reach, and besides so well able to take care of herself, that I think her parents gave the matter but little thought, and he himself worshipped at a respectful distance, keeping admirable control of his passion in all respects save one; for at his age the eyes are difficult to master, and the yearning, almost the devouring, expression often visible in them was probably there unknown even to himself. He, better than any one else, understood that he had fallen in love with something most hard of attainment, something that drew him to the very edge of life, and almost beyond it. It, no doubt, was a secret and terrible joy to him, this passionate worship from afar; only I think he suffered more than any one guessed, and that his want of vitality was due in large measure to the constant stream of unsatisfied yearning that poured for ever from his soul and body. Moreover, it seemed to me, who now saw them for the first time together, that there was an unnamable something—an elusive quality of some kind—that marked them as belonging to the same world, and that although the girl ignored him she was secretly, and perhaps unknown to herself, drawn by some attribute very deep in her own nature to some quality equally deep in his.

This, then, was the party when we first settled down into our two months' camp on the island in the Baltic Sea. Other figures flitted from time to time across the scene, and sometimes one reading man, sometimes another, came to join us and spend his four hours a day in the clergyman's tent, but they came for short periods only, and they went without leaving much trace in my memory, and certainly they played no important part in what subsequently happened.

The weather favoured us that night, so that by sunset the tents were up, the boats unloaded, a store of wood collected and chopped into lengths, and the candle-lanterns hung round ready for lighting on the trees. Sangree, too, had picked deep mattresses of balsam boughs for the women's beds, and had cleared little paths of brushwood from their tents to the central fireplace. All was prepared for bad weather. It was a cosy supper and a well-cooked one that we sat down to and ate under the stars, and, according to the clergyman, the only meal fit to eat we had seen since we left London a week before.

The deep stillness, after that roar of steamers, trains, and tourists, held something that thrilled, for as we lay round the fire there was no sound but the faint sighing of the pines and the soft lapping of the waves along the shore and against the sides of the boat in the lagoon. The ghostly outline of her white sails was just visible through the trees, idly rocking to and fro in her calm anchorage, her sheets flapping gently against the mast. Beyond lay the dim blue shapes of other islands floating in the night, and from all the great spaces about us came the murmur of the sea and the soft breathing of great woods. The odours of the wilderness—smells of wind and earth, of trees and water, clean, vigorous, and mighty—were the true odours of a virgin world unspoilt by men, more penetrating and more subtly intoxicating than any other perfume in the whole world. Oh!—and dangerously strong, too, no doubt, for some natures!

"Ahhh!" breathed out the clergyman after supper, with an indescribable gesture of satisfaction and relief. "Here there is freedom, and room for body and mind to turn in. Here one can work and rest and play. Here one can be alive and absorb something of the earth-forces that never get within touching distance in the cities. By George, I shall make a permanent camp here and come when it is time to die!"

The good man was merely giving vent to his delight at being under canvas. He said the same thing every year, and he said it often. But it more or less expressed the superficial feelings of us all. And when, a little later, he turned to compliment his wife on the fried potatoes, and discovered that she was snoring, with her back against a tree, he grunted with content at the sight and put a ground-sheet over her feet, as if it were the most natural thing in the world for her to fall asleep after dinner, and then moved back to his own corner, smoking his pipe with great satisfaction.

And I, smoking mine too, lay and fought against the most delicious sleep imaginable, while my eyes wandered from the fire to the stars peeping through the branches, and then back again to the group about me. The Rev. Timothy soon let his pipe go out, and succumbed as his wife had done, for he had worked hard and eaten well. Sangree, also smoking, leaned against a tree with his gaze fixed on the girl, a depth of yearning in his face that he could not hide, and that really distressed me for him. And Joan herself, with wide staring eyes, alert, full of the new forces of the place, evidently keyed up by the magic of finding herself among all the things her soul recognised as "home," sat rigid by the fire, her thoughts roaming through the spaces, the blood stirring about her heart. She was as unconscious of the Canadian's gaze as she was that her parents both slept. She looked to me more like a tree, or something that had grown out of the island, than a living girl of the century; and when I spoke across to her in a whisper and suggested a tour of investigation, she started and looked up at me as though she heard a voice in her dreams.

Sangree leaped up and joined us, and without waking the others we three went over the ridge of the island and made our way down to the shore behind. The water lay like a lake before us still coloured by the sunset. The air was keen and scented, wafting the smell of the wooded islands that hung about us in the darkening air. Very small waves tumbled softly on the sand. The sea was sown with stars, and everywhere breathed and pulsed the beauty of the northern summer night. I confess I speedily lost consciousness of the human presences beside me, and I have little doubt Joan did too. Only Sangree felt otherwise, I suppose, for presently we heard him sighing; and I can well imagine that he absorbed the whole wonder and passion of the scene into his aching heart, to swell the pain there that was more searching even than the pain at the sight of such matchless and incomprehensible beauty.

The splash of a fish jumping broke the spell.

"I wish we had the canoe now," remarked Joan; "we could paddle out to the other islands."

"Of course," I said; "wait here and I'll go across for it," and was turning to feel my way back through the darkness when she stopped me in a voice that meant what it said.

"No; Mr. Sangree will get it. We will wait here and cooee to guide him."

The Canadian was off in a moment, for she had only to hint of her wishes and he obeyed.

"Keep out from shore in case of rocks," I cried out as he went, "and turn to the right out of the lagoon. That's the shortest way round by the map."

My voice travelled across the still waters and woke

echoes in the distant islands that came back to us like people calling out of space. It was only thirty or forty yards over the ridge and down the other side to the lagoon where the boats lay, but it was a good mile to coast round the shore in the dark to where we stood and waited. We heard him stumbling away among the boulders, and then the sounds suddenly ceased as he topped the ridge and went down past the fire on the other side.

"I didn't want to be left alone with him," the girl said presently in a low voice. "I'm always afraid he's going to say or do something—" She hesitated a moment, looking quickly over her shoulder towards the ridge where he had just disappeared—"something that might lead to unpleasantness."

She stopped abruptly.

"*You* frightened, Joan!" I exclaimed, with genuine surprise. "This is a new light on your wicked character. I thought the human being who could frighten you did not exist." Then I suddenly realised she was talking seriously—looking to me for help of some kind—and at once I dropped the teasing attitude.

"He's very far gone, I think, Joan," I added gravely. "You must be kind to him, whatever else you may feel. He's exceedingly fond of you."

"I know, but I can't help it," she whispered, lest her voice should carry in the stillness; "there's something about him that—that makes me feel creepy and half afraid."

"But, poor man, it's not his fault if he is delicate and sometimes looks like death," I laughed gently, by way of defending what I felt to be a very innocent member of my sex.

"Oh, but it's not that I mean," she answered quickly; "it's something I feel about him, something in his soul, something he hardly knows himself, but that may come out if we are much together. It draws me, I feel, tremendously. It stirs what is wild in me—deep down—oh, very deep down,—yet at the same time makes me feel afraid."

"I suppose his thoughts are always playing about you," I said, "but he's nice-minded and—"

"Yes, yes," she interrupted impatiently, "I can trust myself absolutely with him. He's gentle and singularly pure-minded. But there's something else that—" She stopped again sharply to listen. Then she came up close beside me in the darkness, whispering—

"You know, Mr. Hubbard, sometimes my intuitions warn me a little too strongly to be ignored. Oh, yes, you needn't tell me again that it's difficult to distinguish between fancy and intuition. I know all that. But I also know that there's something deep down in that man's soul that calls to something deep down in mine. And at present it frightens me. Because I cannot make out what it is; and I know, I *know*, he'll do something some day that—that will shake my life to the very bottom." She laughed a little at the strangeness of her own description.

I turned to look at her more closely, but the darkness was too great to show her face. There was an intensity, almost of suppressed passion, in her voice that took me completely by surprise.

"Nonsense, Joan," I said, a little severely; "you know him well. He's been with your father for months now."

"But that was in London; and up here it's different—I mean, I feel that it may be different. Life in a place like this blows away the restraints of the artificial life at home. I know, oh, I know what I'm saying. I feel all untied in a place like this; the rigidity of one's nature begins to melt and flow. Surely *you* must understand what I mean!"

"Of course I understand," I replied, yet not wishing to encourage her in her present line of thought, "and it's a grand experience—for a short time. But you're overtired to-night, Joan, like the rest of us. A few days in this air will set you above all fears of the kind you mention."

Then, after a moment's silence, I added, feeling I should estrange her confidence altogether if I blundered any more and treated her like a child—

"I think, perhaps, the true explanation is that you pity him for loving you, and at the same time you feel the repulsion of the healthy, vigorous animal for what is weak and timid. If he came up boldly and took you by the throat and shouted that he would force you to love him—well, then you would feel no fear at all. You would know exactly how to deal with him. Isn't it, perhaps, something of that kind?"

The girl made no reply, and when I took her hand I felt that it trembled a little and was cold.

"It's not his love that I'm afraid of," she said hurriedly, for at this moment we heard the dip of a paddle in the water, "it's something in his very soul that terrifies me in a way I have never been terrified before,—yet fascinates me. In town I was hardly conscious of his presence. But the moment we got away from civilisation, it began to come. He seems so—so *real* up here. I dread being alone with him. It makes me feel that something must burst and tear its way out—that he would do something—or I should do something—I don't know exactly what I mean, probably,—but that I should let myself go and scream—"

"Joan!"

"Don't be alarmed," she laughed shortly; "I shan't do anything silly, but I wanted to tell you my feelings in case I needed your help. When I have intuitions as strong as this they are never wrong, only I don't know yet what it means exactly."

"You must hold out for the month, at any rate," I said in as matter-of-fact a voice as I could manage, for her manner had somehow changed my surprise to a subtle sense of alarm. "Sangree only stays the month, you know. And, anyhow, you are such an odd creature yourself that you should feel generously towards other odd creatures," I ended lamely, with a forced laugh.

She gave my hand a sudden pressure. "I'm glad I've told you at any rate," she said quickly under her breath, for the canoe was now gliding up silently like a ghost to our feet, "and I'm glad you're here, too," she added as we moved down towards the water to meet it.

I made Sangree change into the bows and got into the

steering seat myself, putting the girl between us so that I could watch them both by keeping their outlines against the sea and stars. For the intuitions of certain folk—women and children usually, I confess—I have always felt a great respect that has more often than not been justified by experience; and now the curious emotion stirred in me by the girl's words remained somewhat vividly in my consciousness. I explained it in some measure by the fact that the girl, tired out by the fatigue of many days' travel, had suffered a vigorous reaction of some kind from the strong, desolate scenery, and further, perhaps, that she had been treated to my own experience of seeing the members of the party in a new light—the Canadian, being partly a stranger, more vividly than the rest of us. But, at the same time, I felt it was quite possible that she had sensed some subtle link between his personality and her own, some quality that she had hitherto ignored and that the routine of town life had kept buried out of sight. The only thing that seemed difficult to explain was the fear she had spoken of, and this I hoped the wholesome effects of camp-life and exercise would sweep away naturally in the course of time.

We made the tour of the island without speaking. It was all too beautiful for speech. The trees crowded down to the shore to hear us pass. We saw their fine dark heads, bowed low with splendid dignity to watch us, forgetting for a moment that the stars were caught in the needled network of their hair. Against the sky in the west, where still lingered the sunset gold, we saw the wild toss of the horizon, shaggy with forest and cliff, gripping the heart like the motive in a symphony, and sending the sense of beauty all a-shiver through the mind—all these surrounding islands standing above the water like low clouds, and like them seeming to post along silently into the engulfing night. We heard the musical drip-drip of the paddle, and the little wash of our waves on the shore, and then suddenly we found ourselves at the opening of the lagoon again, having made the complete circuit of our home.

The Reverend Timothy had awakened from sleep and was singing to himself; and the sound of his voice as we glided down the fifty yards of enclosed water was pleasant to hear and undeniably wholesome. We saw the glow of the fire up among the trees on the ridge, and his shadow moving about as he threw on more wood.

"There you are!" he called aloud. "Good again! Been setting the night-lines, eh? Capital! And your mother's still fast asleep, Joan."

His cheery laugh floated across the water; he had not been in the least disturbed by our absence, for old campers are not easily alarmed.

"Now, remember," he went on, after we had told our little tale of travel by the fire, and Mrs. Maloney had asked for the fourth time exactly where her tent was and whether the door faced east or south, "every one takes their turn at cooking breakfast, and one of the men is always out at sunrise to catch it first. Hubbard, I'll toss you which you do in the morning and which I do!" He lost the toss. "Then I'll catch it," I said, laughing at his discomfiture, for I knew he

loathed stirring porridge. "And mind you don't burn it as you did every blessed time last year on the Volga," I added by way of reminder.

Mrs. Maloney's fifth interruption about the door of her tent, and her further pointed observation that it was past nine o'clock, set us lighting lanterns and putting the fire out for safety.

But before we separated for the night the clergyman had a time-honoured little ritual of his own to go through that no one had the heart to deny him. He always did this. It was a relic of his pulpit habits. He glanced briefly from one to the other of us, his face grave and earnest, his hands lifted to the stars and his eyes all closed and puckered up beneath a momentary frown. Then he offered up a short, almost inaudible prayer, thanking Heaven for our safe arrival, begging for good weather, no illness or accidents, plenty of fish, and strong sailing winds.

And then, unexpectedly—no one knew why exactly—he ended up with an abrupt request that nothing from the kingdom of darkness should be allowed to afflict our peace, and no evil thing come near to disturb us in the night-time.

And while he uttered these last surprising words, so strangely unlike his usual ending, it chanced that I looked up and let my eyes wander round the group assembled about the dying fire. And it certainly seemed to me that Sangree's face underwent a sudden and visible alteration. He was staring at Joan, and as he stared the change ran over it like a shadow and was gone. I started in spite of myself, for something oddly concentrated, potent, collected, had come into the expression usually so scattered and feeble. But it was all swift as a passing meteor, and when I looked a second time his face was normal and he was looking among the trees.

And Joan, luckily, had not observed him, her head being bowed and her eyes tightly closed while her father prayed.

"The girl has a vivid imagination indeed," I thought, half laughing, as I lit the lanterns, "if her thoughts can put a glamour upon mine in this way"; and yet somehow, when we said good-night, I took occasion to give her a few vigorous words of encouragement, and went to her tent to make sure I could find it quickly in the night in case anything happened. In her quick way the girl understood and thanked me, and the last thing I heard as I moved off to the men's quarters was Mrs. Maloney crying that there were beetles in her tent, and Joan's laughter as she went to help her turn them out.

Half an hour later the island was silent as the grave, but for the mournful voices of the wind as it sighed up from the sea. Like white sentries stood the three tents of the men on one side of the ridge, and on the other side, half hidden by some birches, whose leaves just shivered as the breeze caught them, the women's tents, patches of ghostly grey, gathered more closely together for mutual shelter and protection. Something like fifty yards of broken ground, grey rock, moss and lichen, lay between, and over all lay the curtain of the night and the great whispering winds from the forests of Scandinavia.

And the very last thing, just before floating away on that mighty wave that carries one so softly off into the deeps of forgetfulness, I again heard the voice of John Silence as the train moved out of Victoria Station; and by some subtle connection that met me on the very threshold of consciousness there rose in my mind simultaneously the memory of the girl's half-given confidence, and of her distress. As by some wizardry of approaching dreams they seemed in that instant to be related; but before I could analyse the why and the wherefore, both sank away out of sight again, and I was off beyond recall.

"Unless you should send for me sooner."

II

Whether Mrs. Maloney's tent door opened south or east I think she never discovered, for it is quite certain she always slept with the flap tightly fastened; I only know that my own little "five by seven, all silk" faced due east, because next morning the sun, pouring in as only the wilderness sun knows how to pour, woke me early, and a moment later, with a short run over soft moss and a flying dive from the granite ledge, I was swimming in the most sparkling water imaginable.

It was barely four o'clock, and the sun came down a long vista of blue islands that led out to the open sea and Finland. Nearer by rose the wooded domes of our own property, still capped and wreathed with smoky trails of fast-melting mist, and looking as fresh as though it was the morning of Mrs. Maloney's Sixth Day and they had just issued, clean and brilliant, from the hands of the great Architect.

In the open spaces the ground was drenched with dew, and from the sea a cool salt wind stole in among the trees and set the branches trembling in an atmosphere of shimmering silver. The tents shone white where the sun caught them in patches. Below lay the lagoon, still dreaming of the summer night; in the open the fish were jumping busily, sending musical ripples towards the shore; and in the air hung the magic of dawn—silent, incommunicable.

I lit the fire, so that an hour later the clergyman should find good ashes to stir his porridge over, and then set forth upon an examination of the island, but hardly had I gone a dozen yards when I saw a figure standing a little in front of me where the sunlight fell in a pool among the trees.

It was Joan. She had already been up an hour, she told me, and had bathed before the last stars had left the sky. I saw at once that the new spirit of this solitary region had entered into her, banishing the fears of the night, for her face was like the face of a happy denizen of the wilderness, and her eyes stainless and shining. Her feet were bare, and drops of dew she had shaken from the branches hung in her loose-flying hair. Obviously she had come into her own.

"I've been all over the island," she announced laughingly, "and there are two things wanting."

"You're a good judge, Joan. What are they?"

"There's no animal life, and there's no—water."

"They go together," I said. "Animals don't bother with a rock like this unless there's a spring on it."

And as she led me from place to place, happy and excited, leaping adroitly from rock to rock, I was glad to note that my first impressions were correct. She made no reference to our conversation of the night before. The new spirit had driven out the old. There was no room in her heart for fear or anxiety, and Nature had everything her own way.

The island, we found, was some three-quarters of a mile from point to point, built in a circle, or wide horseshoe, with an opening of twenty feet at the mouth of the lagoon. Pine-trees grew thickly all over, but here and there were patches of silver birch, scrub oak, and considerable colonies of wild raspberry and gooseberry bushes. The two ends of the horseshoe formed bare slabs of smooth granite running into the sea and forming dangerous reefs just below the surface, but the rest of the island rose in a forty-foot ridge and sloped down steeply to the sea on either side, being nowhere more than a hundred yards wide.

The outer shore-line was much indented with numberless coves and bays and sandy beaches, with here and there caves and precipitous little cliffs against which the sea broke in spray and thunder. But the inner shore, the shore of the lagoon, was low and regular, and so well protected by the wall of trees along the ridge that no storm could ever send more than a passing ripple along its sandy marges. Eternal shelter reigned there.

On one of the other islands, a few hundred yards away—for the rest of the party slept late this first morning, and we took to the canoe—we discovered a spring of fresh water untainted by the brackish flavour of the Baltic, and having thus solved the most important problem of the Camp, we next proceeded to deal with the second—fish. And in half an hour we reeled in and turned homewards, for we had no means of storage, and to clean more fish than may be stored or eaten in a day is no wise occupation for experienced campers.

And as we landed towards six o'clock we heard the clergyman singing as usual and saw his wife and Sangree shaking out their blankets in the sun, and dressed in a fashion that finally dispelled all memories of streets and civilisation.

"The Little People lit the fire for me," cried Maloney, looking natural and at home in his ancient flannel suit and breaking off in the middle of his singing, "so I've got the porridge going—and this time it's *not* burnt."

We reported the discovery of water and held up the fish.

"Good! Good again!" he cried. "We'll have the first decent breakfast we've had this year. Sangree'll clean 'em in no time, and the Bo'sun's Mate—"

"Will fry them to a turn," laughed the voice of Mrs. Maloney, appearing on the scene in a tight blue jersey and sandals, and catching up the frying-pan. Her husband always called her the Bo'sun's Mate in Camp, because it was her duty, among others, to pipe all hands to meals.

"And as for you, Joan," went on the happy man, "you look like the spirit of the island, with moss in your hair and wind in your eyes, and sun and stars mixed in your face." He looked at her with delighted admiration. "Here, Sangree, take these twelve, there's a good fellow, they're the biggest; and we'll have 'em in butter in less time than you can say Baltic island!"

I watched the Canadian as he slowly moved off to the cleaning pail. His eyes were drinking in the girl's beauty, and a wave of passionate, almost feverish, joy passed over his face, expressive of the ecstasy of true worship more than anything else. Perhaps he was thinking that he still had three weeks to come with that vision always before his eyes; perhaps he was thinking of his dreams in the night. I cannot say. But I noticed the curious mingling of yearning and happiness in his eyes, and the strength of the impression touched my curiosity. Something in his face held my gaze for a second, something to do with its intensity. That so timid, so gentle a personality should conceal so virile a passion almost seemed to require explanation.

But the impression was momentary, for that first breakfast in Camp permitted no divided attentions, and I dare swear that the porridge, the tea, the Swedish "flatbread," and the fried fish flavoured with points of frizzled bacon, were better than any meal eaten elsewhere that day in the whole world.

The first clear day in a new camp is always a furiously busy one, and we soon dropped into the routine upon which in large measure the real comfort of every one depends. About the cooking-fire, greatly improved with stones from the shore, we built a high stockade consisting of upright poles thickly twined with branches, the roof lined with moss and lichen and weighted with rocks, and round the interior we made low wooden seats so that we could lie round the fire even in rain and eat our meals in peace. Paths, too, outlined themselves from tent to tent, from the bathing places and the landing stage, and a fair division of the island was decided upon between the quarters of the men and the women. Wood was stacked, awkward trees and boulders removed, hammocks slung, and tents strengthened. In a word, Camp was established, and duties were assigned and accepted as though we expected to live on this Baltic island for years to come and the smallest detail of the Community life was important.

Moreover, as the Camp came into being, this sense of a community developed, proving that we were a definite whole, and not merely separate human beings living for a while in tents upon a desert island. Each fell willingly into the routine. Sangree, as by natural selection, took upon himself the cleaning of the fish and the cutting of the wood into lengths sufficient for a day's use. And he did it well. The pan of water was never without a fish, cleaned and scaled, ready to fry for whoever was hungry; the nightly fire never died down for lack of material to throw on without going farther afield to search.

And Timothy, once reverend, caught the fish and chopped down the trees. He also assumed responsibility for the condition of the boat, and did it so thoroughly that nothing in the little cutter was ever found wanting. And when, for any reason, his presence was in demand, the first place to look for him was—in the boat, and there, too, he was usually found, tinkering away with sheets, sails, or rudder and singing as he tinkered.

'Nor was the "reading" neglected; for most mornings there came a sound of droning voices form the white tent by the raspberry bushes, which signified that Sangree, the tutor, and whatever other man chanced to be in the party at the time, were hard at it with history or the classics.

And while Mrs. Maloney, also by natural selection, took charge of the larder and the kitchen, the mending and general supervision of the rough comforts, she also made herself peculiarly mistress of the megaphone which summoned to meals and carried her voice easily from one end of the island to the other; and in her hours of leisure she daubed the surrounding scenery on to a sketching block with all the honesty and devotion of her determined but unreceptive soul.

Joan, meanwhile, Joan, elusive creature of the wilds, became I know not exactly what. She did plenty of work in the Camp, yet seemed to have no very precise duties. She was everywhere and anywhere. Sometimes she slept in her tent, sometimes under the stars with a blanket. She knew every inch of the island and kept turning up in places where she was least expected—for ever wandering about, reading her books in sheltered corners, making little fires on sunless days to "worship by to the gods," as she put it, ever finding new pools to dive and bathe in, and swimming day and night in the warm and waveless lagoon like a fish in a huge tank. She went bare-legged and bare-footed, with her hair down and her skirts caught up to the knees, and if ever a human being turned into a jolly savage within the compass of a single week, Joan Maloney was certainly that human being. She ran wild.

So completely, too, was she possessed by the strong spirit of the place that the little human fear she had yielded to so strangely on our arrival seemed to have been utterly dispossessed. As I hoped and expected, she made no reference to our conversation of the first evening. Sangree bothered her with no special attentions, and after all they were very little together. His behaviour was perfect in that respect, and I, for my part, hardly gave the matter another thought. Joan was ever a prey to vivid fancies of one kind or another, and this was one of them. Mercifully for the happiness of all concerned, it had melted away before the spirit of busy, active life and deep content that reigned over the island. Every one was intensely alive, and peace was upon all.

* * *

Meanwhile the effect of the camp-life began to tell. Always a searching test of character, its results, sooner or later, are infallible, for it acts upon the soul as swiftly and surely as the hypo bath upon the negative of a photograph. A readjustment of the personal forces takes place quickly;

some parts of the personality go to sleep, others wake up: but the first sweeping change that the primitive life brings about is that the artificial portions of the character shed themselves one after another like dead skins. Attitudes and poses that seemed genuine in the city drop away. The mind, like the body, grows quickly hard, simple, uncomplex. And in a camp as primitive and close to nature as ours was, these effects became speedily visible.

Some folk, of course, who talk glibly about the simple life when it is safely out of reach, betray themselves in camp by for ever peering about for the artificial excitements of civilisation which they miss. Some get bored at once; some grow slovenly; some reveal the animal in most unexpected fashion; and some, the select few, find themselves in very short order and are happy.

And, in our little party, we could flatter ourselves that we all belonged to the last category, so far as the general effect was concerned. Only there were certain other changes as well, varying with each individual, and all interesting to note.

It was only after the first week or two that these changes became marked, although this is the proper place, I think, to speak of them. For, having myself no other duty than to enjoy a well-earned holiday, I used to load my canoe with blankets and provisions and journey forth on exploration trips among the islands of several days together; and it was on my return from the first of these—when I rediscovered the party, so to speak—that these changes first presented themselves vividly to me, and in one particular instance produced a rather curious impression.

In a word, then, while every one had grown wilder, naturally wilder, Sangree, it seemed to me, had grown much wilder, and what I can only call unnaturally wilder. He made me think of a savage.

To begin with, he had changed immensely in mere physical appearance, and the full brown cheeks, the brighter eyes of absolute health, and the general air of vigour and robustness that had come to replace his customary lassitude and timidity, had worked such an improvement that I hardly knew him for the same man. His voice, too, was deeper and his manner bespoke for the first time a greater measure of confidence in himself. He now had some claims to be called nice-looking, or at least to a certain air of virility that would not lessen his value in the eyes of the opposite sex.

All this, of course, was natural enough, and most welcome. But, altogether apart from this physical change, which no doubt had also been going forward in the rest of us, there was a subtle note in his personality that came to me with a degree of surprise that almost amounted to shock.

And two things—as he came down to welcome me and pull up the canoe—leaped up in my mind unbidden, as though connected in some way I could not at the moment divine—first, the curious judgment formed of him by Joan; and secondly, that fugitive expression I had caught in his face while Maloney was offering up his strange prayer for special protection from Heaven.

The delicacy of manner and feature—to call it by no milder term—which had always been a distinguishing characteristic of the man, had been replaced by something far more vigorous and decided, that yet utterly eluded analysis. The change which impressed me so oddly was not easy to name. The others—singing Maloney, the bustling Bo'sun's Mate, and Joan, that fascinating half-breed of undine and salamander—all showed the effects of a life so close to nature; but in their case the change was perfectly natural and what was to be expected, whereas with Peter Sangree, the Canadian, it was something unusual and unexpected.

It is impossible to explain how he managed gradually to convey to my mind the impression that something in him had turned savage, yet this, more or less, is the impression that he did convey. It was not that he seemed really less civilised, or that his character had undergone any definite alteration, but rather that something in him, hitherto dormant, had awakened to life. Some quality, latent till now—so far, at least, as we were concerned, who, after all, knew him but slightly—had stirred into activity and risen to the surface of his being.

And while, for the moment, this seemed as far as I could get, it was but natural that my mind should continue the intuitive process and acknowledge that John Silence, owing to his peculiar faculties, and the girl, owing to her singularly receptive temperament, might each in a different way have divined this latent quality in his soul, and feared its manifestation later.

On looking back to this painful adventure, too, it now seems equally natural that the same process, carried to its logical conclusion, should have wakened some deep instinct in me that, wholly without direction from my will, set itself sharply and persistently upon the watch from that very moment. Thenceforward the personality of Sangree was never far from my thoughts, and I was for ever analysing and searching for the explanation that took so long in coming.

"I declare, Hubbard, you're tanned like an aboriginal, and you look like one, too," laughed Maloney.

"And I can return the compliment," was my reply, as we all gathered round a brew of tea to exchange news and compare notes.

And later, at supper, it amused me to observe that the distinguished tutor, once clergyman, did not eat his food quite as "nicely" as he did at home—he devoured it; that Mrs. Maloney ate more, and, to say the least, with less delay, than was her custom in the select atmosphere of her English dining-room; and that while Joan attacked her tin plateful with genuine avidity, Sangree, the Canadian, bit and gnawed at his, laughing and talking and complimenting the cook all the while, and making me think with secret amusement of a starved animal at its first meal. While, from their remarks about myself, I judged that I had changed and grown wild as much as the rest of them.

In this and in a hundred other little ways the change

showed, ways difficult to define in detail, but all proving—not the coarsening effect of leading the primitive life, but, let us say, the more direct and unvarnished methods that became prevalent. For all day long we were in the bath of the elements—wind, water, sun—and just as the body became insensible to cold and shed unnecessary clothing, the mind grew straightforward and shed many of the disguises required by the conventions of civilisation.

And in each, according to temperament and character, there stirred the life-instincts that were natural, untamed, and, in a sense—savage.

III

So it came about that I stayed with our island party, putting off my second exploring trip from day to day, and I think that this far-fetched instinct to watch Sangree was really the cause of my postponement.

For another ten days the life of the Camp pursued its even and delightful way, blessed by perfect summer weather, a good harvest of fish, fine winds for sailing, and calm, starry nights. Maloney's selfish prayer had been favourably received. Nothing came to disturb or perplex. There was not even the prowling of night animals to vex the rest of Mrs. Maloney; for in previous camps it had often been her peculiar affliction that she heard the porcupines scratching against the canvas, or the squirrels dropping fir-cones in the early morning with a sound of miniature thunder upon the roof of her tent. But on this island there was not even a squirrel or a mouse. I think two toads and a small and harmless snake were the only living creatures that had been discovered during the whole of the first fortnight. And these two toads in all probability were not two toads, but one toad.

Then, suddenly, came the terror that changed the whole aspect of the place—the devastating terror.

It came, at first, gently, but from the very start it made me realise the unpleasant loneliness of our situation, our remote isolation in this wilderness of sea and rock, and how the islands in this tideless Baltic ocean lay about us like the advance guard of a vast besieging army. Its entry, as I say, was gentle, hardly noticeable, in fact, to most of us: singularly undramatic it certainly was. But, then, in actual life this is often the way the dreadful climaxes move upon us, leaving the heart undisturbed almost to the last minute, and then overwhelming it with a sudden rush of horror. For it was the custom at breakfast to listen patiently while each in turn related the trivial adventures of the night—how they slept, whether the wind shook their tent, whether the spider on the ridge pole had moved, whether they had heard the toad, and so forth—and on this particular morning Joan, in the middle of a little pause, made a truly novel announcement:

"In the night I heard the howling of a dog," she said, and then flushed up to the roots of her hair when we burst out laughing. For the idea of there being a dog on this forsaken island that was only able to support a snake and two toads was distinctly ludicrous, and I remember Ma-

loney, half-way through his burnt porridge, capping the announcement by declaring that he had heard a "Baltic turtle" in the lagoon, and his wife's expression of frantic alarm before the laughter undeceived her.

But the next morning Joan repeated the story with additional and convincing detail.

"Sounds of whining and growling woke me," she said, "and I distinctly heard sniffing under my tent, and the scratching of paws."

"Oh, Timothy! Can it be a porcupine?" exclaimed the Bo'sun's Mate with distress, forgetting that Sweden was not Canada.

But the girl's voice had sounded to me in quite another key, and looking up I saw that her father and Sangree were staring at her hard. They, too, understood that she was in earnest, and had been struck by the serious note in her voice.

"Rubbish, Joan! You are always dreaming something or other wild," her father said a little impatiently.

"There's not an animal of any size on the whole island," added Sangree with a puzzled expression. He never took his eyes from her face.

"But there's nothing to prevent one swimming over," I put in briskly, for somehow a sense of uneasiness that was not pleasant had woven itself into the talk and pauses. "A deer, for instance, might easily land in the night and take a look round—"

"Or a bear!" gasped the Bo'sun's Mate, with a look so portentous that we all welcomed the laugh.

But Joan did not laugh. Instead, she sprang up and called to us to follow.

"There," she said, pointing to the ground by her tent on the side farthest from her mother's; "there are the marks close to my head. You can see for yourselves."

We saw plainly. The moss and lichen—for earth there was hardly any—had been scratched up by paws. An animal about the size of a large dog it must have been, to judge by the marks. We stood and stared in a row.

"Close to my head," repeated the girl, looking round at us. Her face, I noticed, was very pale, and her lip seemed to quiver for an instant. Then she gave a sudden gulp—and burst into a flood of tears.

The whole thing had come about in the brief space of a few minutes, and with a curious sense of inevitableness, moreover, as though it had all been carefully planned from all time and nothing could have stopped it. It had all been rehearsed before—had actually happened before, as the strange feeling sometimes has it; it seemed like the opening movement in some ominous drama, and that I knew exactly what would happen next. Something of great moment was impending.

For this sinister sensation of coming disaster made itself felt from the very beginning, and an atmosphere of gloom and dismay pervaded the entire Camp from that moment forward.

I drew Sangree to one side and moved away, while Maloney took the distressed girl into her tent, and his wife followed them, energetic and greatly flustered.

For thus, in undramatic fashion, it was that the terror I have spoken of first attempted the invasion of our Camp, and, trivial and unimportant though it seemed, every little detail of this opening scene is photographed upon my mind with merciless accuracy and precision. It happened exactly as described. This was exactly the language used. I see it written before me in black and white. I see, too, the faces of all concerned with the sudden ugly signature of alarm where before had been peace. The terror had stretched out, so to speak, a first tentative feeler toward us and had touched the hearts of each with a horrid directness. And from this moment the Camp changed.

Sangree in particular was visibly upset. He could not bear to see the girl distressed, and to hear her actually cry was almost more than he could stand. The feeling that he had no right to protect her hurt him keenly, and I could see that he was itching to do something to help, and liked him for it. His expression said plainly that he would tear in a thousand pieces anything that dared to injure a hair of her head.

We lit our pipes and strolled over in silence to the men's quarters, and it was his odd Canadian expression "Gee whiz!" that drew my attention to a further discovery.

"The brute's been scratching round my tent too," he cried, as he pointed to similar marks by the door and I stooped down to examine them. We both stared in amazement for several minutes without speaking.

"Only I sleep like the dead," he added, straightening up again, "and so heard nothing, I suppose."

We traced the paw-marks from the mouth of his tent in a direct line across to the girl's, but nowhere else about the Camp was there a sign of the strange visitor. The deer, dog, or whatever it was that had twice favoured us with a visit in the night, had confined its attentions to these two tents. And, after all, there was really nothing out of the way about these visits of an unknown animal, for although our own island was destitute of life, we were in the heart of a wilderness, and the mainland and larger islands must be swarming with all kinds of four-footed creatures, and no very prolonged swimming was necessary to reach us. In any other country it would not have caused a moment's interest—interest of the kind we felt, that is. In our Canadian camps the bears were for ever grunting about among the provision bags at night, porcupines scratching unceasingly, and chipmunks scuttling over everything.

"My daughter is overtired, and that's the truth of it," explained Maloney presently when he rejoined us and had examined in turn the other paw-marks. "She's been overdoing it lately, and camp-life, you know, always means a great excitement to her. It's natural enough, if we take no notice she'll be all right." He paused to borrow my tobacco pouch and fill his pipe, and the blundering way he filled it and spilled the precious weed on the ground visibly belied the calm of his easy language. "You might take her out for a bit of fishing, Hubbard, like a good chap; she's hardly up to the long day in the cutter. Show her some of the other islands in your canoe, perhaps. Eh?"

And by lunch-time the cloud had passed away as suddenly, and as suspiciously, as it had come.

But in the canoe, on our way home, having till then purposely ignored the subject uppermost in our minds, she suddenly spoke to me in a way that again touched the note of sinister alarm—the note that kept on sounding and sounding until finally John Silence came with his great vibrating presence and relieved it; yes, and even after he came, too, for a while.

"I'm ashamed to ask it," she said abruptly, as she steered me home, her sleeves rolled up, her hair blowing in the wind, "and ashamed of my silly tears too, because I really can't make out what caused them; but, Mr. Hubbard, I want you to promise me not to go off for your long expeditions—just yet. I beg it of you." She was so in earnest that she forgot the canoe, and the wind caught it sideways and made us roll dangerously. "I have tried hard not to ask this," she added, bringing the canoe round again, "but I simply can't help myself."

It was a good deal to ask, and I suppose my hesitation was plain; for she went on before I could reply, and her beseeching expression and intensity of manner impressed me very forcibly.

"For another two weeks only—"

"Mr. Sangree leaves in a fortnight," I said, seeing at once what she was driving at, but wondering if it was best to encourage her or not.

"If I knew you were to be on the island till then," she said, her face alternately pale and blushing, and her voice trembling a little, "I should feel so much happier."

I looked at her steadily, waiting for her to finish.

"And safer," she added almost in a whisper; "especially—at night, I mean."

"Safer, Joan?" I repeated, thinking I had never seen her eyes so soft and tender. She nodded her head, keeping her gaze fixed on my face.

It was really difficult to refuse, whatever my thoughts and judgment may have been, and somehow I understood that she spoke with good reason, though for the life of me I could not have put it into words.

"Happier—and safer," she said gravely, the canoe giving a dangerous lurch as she leaned forward in her seat to catch my answer. Perhaps, after all, the wisest way was to grant her request and make light of it, easing her anxiety without too much encouraging its cause.

"All right, Joan, you queer creature; I promise," and the instant look of relief in her face, and the smile that came back like sunlight to her eyes, made me feel that, unknown to myself and the world, I was capable of considerable sacrifice after all.

"But, you know, there's nothing to be afraid of," I added sharply; and she looked up in my face with the smile women use when they know we are talking idly, yet do not wish to tell us so.

"*You* don't feel afraid, I know," she observed quietly.

"Of course not; why should I?"

"So, if you will just humour me this once I—I will never ask anything foolish of you again as long as I live," she said gratefully.

"You have my promise," was all I could find to say.

She headed the nose of the canoe for the lagoon lying a quarter of a mile ahead, and paddled swiftly; but a minute or two later she paused again and stared hard at me with the dripping paddle across the thwarts.

"You've not heard anything at night yourself, have you?" she asked.

"I never hear anything at night," I replied shortly, "from the moment I lie down till the moment I get up."

"That dismal howling, for instance," she went on, determined to get it out, "far away at first and then getting closer, and stopping just outside the Camp?"

"Certainly not."

"Because, sometimes I think I almost dreamed it."

"Most likely you did," was my unsympathetic response.

"And you don't think father has heard it either, then?"

"No. He would have told me if he had."

This seemed to relieve her mind a little. "I know mother hasn't," she added, as if speaking to herself, "for she hears nothing—ever.

* * *

It was two nights after this conversation that I woke out of deep sleep and heard sounds of screaming. The voice was really horrible, breaking the peace and silence with its shrill clamour. In less than ten seconds I was half dressed and out of my tent. The screaming had stopped abruptly, but I knew the general direction, and ran as fast as the darkness would allow over to the women's quarters, and on getting close I heard sounds of suppressed weeping. It was Joan's voice. And just as I came up I saw Mrs. Maloney, marvellously attired, fumbling with a lantern. Other voices became audible in the same moment behind me, and Timothy Maloney arrived, breathless, less than half dressed, and carrying another lantern that had gone out on the way from being banged against a tree. Dawn was just breaking, and a chill wind blew in from the sea. Heavy black clouds drove low overhead.

The scene of confusion may be better imagined than described. Questions in frightened voices filled the air against this background of suppressed weeping. Briefly—Joan's silk tent had been torn, and the girl was in a state bordering upon hysterics. Somewhat reassured by our noisy presence, however,—for she was plucky at heart,—she pulled herself together and tried to explain what had happened; and her broken words, told there on the edge of night and morning upon this wild island ridge, were oddly thrilling and distressingly convincing.

"Something touched me and I woke," she said simply, but in a voice still hushed and broken with the terror of it, "something pushing against the tent; I felt it through the canvas. There was the same sniffing and scratching as before, and I felt the tent give a little as when wind shakes it. I heard breathing—very loud, very heavy breathing—and then came a sudden great tearing blow, and the canvas ripped open close to my face."

She had instantly dashed out through the open flap and screamed at the top of her voice, thinking the creature had actually got into the tent. But nothing was visible, she declared, and she heard not the faintest sound of an animal making off under cover of the darkness. The brief account seemed to exercise a paralysing effect upon us all as we listened to it. I can see the dishevelled group to this day, the wind blowing the women's hair, and Maloney craning his head forward to listen, and his wife, open-mouthed and gasping, leaning against a pine tree.

"Come over to the stockade and we'll get the fire going," I said; "that's the first thing," for we were all shaking with the cold in our scanty garments. And at that moment Sangree arrived wrapped in a blanket and carrying his gun; he was still drunken with sleep.

"The dog again," Maloney explained briefly, forestalling his questions; "been at Joan's tent. Torn it, by Gad! this time. It's time we did something." He went on mumbling confusedly to himself.

Sangree gripped his gun and looked about swiftly in the darkness. I saw his eyes aflame in the glare of the flickering lanterns. He made a movement as though to start out and hunt—and kill. Then his glance fell on the girl crouching on the ground, her face hidden in her hands, and there leaped into his features an expression of savage anger that transformed them. He could have faced a dozen lions with a walking stick at that moment, and again I liked him for the strength of his anger, his self-control, and his hopeless devotion.

But I stopped him going off on a blind and useless chase.

"Come and help me start the fire, Sangree," I said, anxious also to relieve the girl of our presence; and a few minutes later the ashes, still growing from the night's fire, had kindled the fresh wood, and there was a blaze that warmed us well while it also lit up the surrounding trees within a radius of twenty yards.

"I heard nothing," he whispered; "what in the world do you think it is? It surely can't be only a dog!"

"We'll find that out later," I said, as the others came up to the grateful warmth; "the first thing is to make as big a fire as we can."

Joan was calmer now, and her mother had put on some warmer, and less miraculous, garments. And while they stood talking in low voices Maloney and I slipped off to examine the tent. There was little enough to see, but that little was unmistakable. Some animal had scratched up the ground at the head of the tent, and with a great blow of a powerful paw—a paw clearly provided with good claws—had struck the silk and torn it open. There was a hole large enough to pass a fist and arm through.

"It can't be far away," Maloney said excitedly. "We'll organise a hunt at once; this very minute."

We hurried back to the fire, Maloney talking boisterously about his proposed hunt. "There's nothing like prompt action to dispel alarm," he whispered in my ear; and then turned to the rest of us.

"We'll hunt the island from end to end at once," he said, with excitement; "that's what we'll do. The beast can't be far away. And the Bo'sun's Mate and Joan must come too, because they can't be left alone. Hubbard, you take the right shore, and you, Sangree, the left, and I'll go in the middle with the women. In this way we can stretch clean across the ridge, and nothing bigger than a rabbit can possibly escape us." He was extraordinarily excited, I thought. Anything affecting Joan, of course, stirred him prodigiously. "Get your guns and we'll start the drive at once," he cried. He lit another lantern and handed one each to his wife and Joan, and while I ran to fetch my gun I heard him singing to himself with the excitement of it all.

Meanwhile the dawn had come on quickly. It made the flickering lanterns look pale. The wind, too, was rising, and I heard the trees moaning overhead and the waves breaking with increasing clamour on the shore. In the lagoon the boat dipped and splashed, and the sparks from the fire were carried aloft in a stream and scattered far and wide.

We made our way to the extreme end of the island, measured our distances carefully, and then began to advance. None of us spoke. Sangree and I, with cocked guns, watched the shore lines, and all within easy touch and speaking distance. It was a slow and blundering drive, and there were many false alarms, but after the best part of half an hour we stood on the farther end, having made the complete tour, and without putting up so much as a squirrel. Certainly there was no living creature on that island but ourselves.

"I know what it is!" cried Maloney, looking out over the dim expanse of grey sea, and speaking with the air of a man making a discovery; "it's a dog from one of the farms on the larger islands"—he pointed seawards where the archipelago thickened—"and it's escaped and turned wild. Our fires and voices attracted it, and it's probably half starved as well as savage, poor brute!"

No one said anything in reply, and he began to sing again very low to himself.

The point where we stood—a huddled, shivering group—faced the wider channels that led to the open sea and Finland. The grey dawn had broken in earnest at last, and we could see the racing waves with their angry crests of white. The surrounding islands showed up as dark masses in the distance, and in the east, almost as Maloney spoke, the sun came up with a rush in a stormy and magnificent sky of red and gold. Against this splashed and gorgeous background black clouds, shaped like fantastic and legendary animals, filed past swiftly in a tearing stream, and to this day I have only to close my eyes to see again that vivid and hurrying procession in the air. All about us the pines made black splashes against the sky. It was an angry sunrise. Rain, indeed, had already begun to fall in big drops.

We turned, as by a common instinct, and, without speech, made our way back slowly to the stockade, Maloney humming snatches of his songs, Sangree in front with his gun, prepared to shoot at a moment's notice, and the women floundering in the rear with myself and the extinguished lanterns.

Yet it was only a dog!

Really, it was most singular when one came to reflect soberly upon it all. Events, say the occultists, have souls, or at least that agglomerate life due to the emotions and thoughts of all concerned in them, so that cities, and even whole countries, have great astral shapes which may become visible to the eye of vision; and certainly here, the soul of this drive—this vain, blundering, futile drive—stood somewhere between ourselves and—laughed.

All of us heard that laugh, and all of us tried hard to smother the sound, or at least to ignore it. Every one talked at once, loudly, and with exaggerated decision, obviously trying to say something plausible against heavy odds, striving to explain naturally that an animal might so easily conceal itself from us, or swim away before we had time to light upon its trail. For we all spoke of that "trail" as though it really existed, and we had more to go upon than the mere marks of paws about the tents of Joan and the Canadian. Indeed, but for these, and the torn tent, I think it would, of course, have been possible to ignore the existence of this beast intruder altogether.

And it was here, under this angry dawn, as we stood in the shelter of the stockade from the pouring rain, weary yet so strangely excited—it was here, out of this confusion of voices and explanations, that—very stealthily—the ghost of something horrible slipped in and stood among us. It made all our explanations seem childish and untrue; the false relation was instantly exposed. Eyes exchanged quick, anxious glances, questioning, expressive of dismay. There was a sense of wonder, of poignant distress, and of trepidation. Alarm stood waiting at our elbows. We shivered.

Then, suddenly, as we looked into each other's faces, came the long, unwelcome pause in which this new arrival established itself in our hearts.

And, without further speech, or attempt at explanation, Maloney moved off abruptly to mix the porridge for an early breakfast; Sangree to clean the fish; myself to chop wood and tend the fire; Joan and her mother to change their wet garments; and, most significant of all, to prepare her mother's tent for its future complement of two.

Each went to his duty, but hurriedly, awkwardly, silently; and this new arrival, this shape of terror and distress stalked, viewless, by the side of each.

"If only I could have traced that dog," I think was the thought in the minds of all.

But in Camp, where every one realises how important the individual contribution is to the comfort and well-being of all, the mind speedily recovers tone and pulls itself together.

During the day, a day of heavy and ceaseless rain, we kept more or less to our tents, and though there were signs of mysterious conferences between the three members of the Maloney family, I think that most of us slept a good deal and stayed alone with his thoughts. Certainly, I did, because when Maloney came to say that his wife invited us all to a special "tea" in her tent, he had to shake me awake before I realised that he was there at all.

And by supper-time we were more or less even-minded again, and almost jolly. I only noticed that there was an undercurrent of what is best described as "jumpiness," and that the merest snapping of a twig, or plop of a fish in the lagoon, was sufficient to make us start and look over our shoulders. Pauses were rare in our talk, and the fire was never for one instant allowed to get low. The wind and rain had ceased, but the dripping of the branches still kept up an excellent imitation of a downpour. In particular, Maloney was vigilant and alert, telling us a series of tales in which the wholesome humorous element was especially strong. He lingered, too, behind with me after Sangree had gone to bed, and while I mixed myself a glass of hot Swedish punch, he did a thing I had never known him do before—he mixed one for himself, and then asked me to light him over to his tent. We said nothing on the way, but I felt that he was glad of my companionship.

I returned alone to the stockade, and for a long time after that kept the fire blazing, and sat up smoking and thinking. I hardly knew why; but sleep was far from me for one thing, and for another, an idea was taking form in my mind that required the comfort of tobacco and a bright fire for its growth. I lay against a corner of the stockade seat, listening to the wind whispering and to the ceaseless drip-drip of the trees. The night, otherwise, was very still, and the sea quiet as a lake. I remember that I was conscious, peculiarly conscious, of this host of desolate islands crowding about us in the darkness, and that we were the one little spot of humanity in a rather wonderful kind of wilderness.

But this, I think, was the only symptom that came to warn me of highly strung nerves, and it certainly was not sufficiently alarming to destroy my peace of mind. One thing, however, did come to disturb my peace, for just as I finally made ready to go, and had kicked the embers of the fire into a last effort, I fancied I saw, peering at me round the farther end of the stockade wall, a dark and shadowy mass that might have been—that strongly resembled, in fact—the body of a large animal. Two glowing eyes shone for an instant in the middle of it. But the next second I saw that it was merely a projecting mass of moss and lichen in the wall of our stockade, and the eyes were a couple of wandering sparks from the dying ashes I had kicked. It was easy enough, too, to imagine I saw an animal moving here and there between the trees, as I picked my way stealthily to my tent. Of course, the shadows tricked me.

And though it was after one o'clock, Maloney's light was still burning, for I saw his tent shining white among the pines.

It was, however, in the short space between consciousness and sleep—that time when the body is low and the voices of the submerged region tell sometimes true—that the idea which had been all this while maturing reached the point of an actual decision, and I suddenly realised that I had resolved to send word to Dr. Silence. For, with a sudden wonder that I had hitherto been so blind, the

unwelcome conviction dawned upon me all at once that some dreadful thing was lurking about us on this island, and that the safety of at least one of us was threatened by something monstrous and unclean that was too horrible to contemplate. And, again remembering those last words of his as the train moved out of the platform, I understood that Dr. Silence would hold himself in readiness to come.

"Unless you should send for me sooner," he had said.

* * *

I found myself suddenly wide awake. It is impossible to say what woke me, but it was no gradual process, seeing that I jumped from deep sleep to absolute alertness in a single instant. I had evidently slept for an hour and more, for the night had cleared, stars crowded the sky, and a pallid half-moon just sinking into the sea threw a spectral light between the trees.

I went outside to sniff the air, and stood upright. A curious impression that something was astir in the Camp came over me, and when I glanced across at Sangree's tent, some twenty feet away, I saw that it was moving. He too, then, was awake and restless, for I saw the canvas sides bulge this way and that as he moved within.

The flap pushed forward. He was coming out, like myself, to sniff the air; and I was not surprised, for its sweetness after the rain was intoxicating. And he came on all fours, just as I had done. I saw a head thrust round the edge of the tent.

And then I saw that it was not Sangree at all. It was an animal. And the same instant I realised something else too—it was *the* animal; and its whole presentment for some unaccountable reason was unutterably malefic.

A cry I was quite unable to suppress escaped me, and the creature turned on the instant and stared at me with baleful eyes. I could have dropped on the spot, for the strength all ran out of my body with a rush. Something about it touched in me the living terror that grips and paralyses. If the mind requires but the tenth of a second to form an impression, I must have stood there stockstill for several seconds while I seized the ropes for support and stared. Many and vivid impressions flashed through my mind, but not one of them resulted in action, because I was in instant dread that the beast any moment would leap in my direction and be upon me. Instead, however, after what seemed a vast period, it slowly turned its eyes from my face, uttered a low whining sound, and came out altogether into the open.

Then, for the first time, I saw it in its entirety and noted two things: it was about the size of a large dog, but at the same time it was utterly unlike any animal that I had ever seen. Also, that the quality that had impressed me first as being malefic was really only its singular and original strangeness. Foolish as it may sound, and impossible as it is for me to adduce proof, I can only say that the animal seemed to me then to be—not real.

But all this passed through my mind in a flash, almost subconsciously, and before I had time to check my impressions, or even properly verify them, I made an involuntary movement, catching the tight rope in my hand so that it twanged like a banjo string, and in that instant the creature turned the corner of Sangree's tent and was gone into the darkness.

Then, of course, my senses in some measure returned to me, and I realised only one thing: it had been inside his tent!

I dashed out, reached the door in half a dozen strides, and looked in. The Canadian, thank God! lay upon his bed of branches. His arm was stretched outside, across the blankets, the fist tightly clenched, and the body had an appearance of unusual rigidity that was alarming. On his face there was an expression of effort, almost of painful effort, so far as the uncertain light permitted me to see, and his sleep seemed to be very profound. He looked, I thought, so stiff, so unnaturally stiff, and in some indefinable way, too, he looked smaller—shrunken.

I called to him to wake, but called many times in vain. Then I decided to shake him, and had already moved forward to do so vigorously when there came a sound of footsteps padding softly behind me, and I felt a stream of hot breath burn my neck as I stooped. I turned sharply. The tent door was darkened and something silently swept in. I felt a rough and shaggy body push past me, and knew that the animal had returned. It seemed to leap forward between me and Sangree—in fact, to leap upon Sangree, for its dark body hid him momentarily from view, and in that moment my soul turned sick and coward with a horror that rose from the very dregs and depths of life, and gripped my existence at its central source.

The creature seemed somehow to melt away into him, almost as though it belonged to him and were a part of himself, but in the same instant—that instant of extraordinary confusion and terror in my mind—it seemed to pass over and behind him, and, in some utterly unaccountable fashion, it was gone. And the Canadian woke and sat up with a start.

"Quick! You fool!" I cried, in my excitement, "the beast has been in your tent, here at your very throat while you sleep like the dead. Up, man! Get your gun! Only this second it disappeared over there behind your head. Quick! or Joan—!"

And somehow the fact that he was there, wide-awake now, to corroborate me, brought the additional conviction to my own mind that this was no animal, but some perplexing and dreadful form of life that drew upon my deeper knowledge, that much reading had perhaps assented to, but that had never yet come within actual range of my senses.

He was up in a flash, and out. He was trembling, and very white. We searched hurriedly, feverishly, but found only the traces of paw-marks passing from the door of his own tent across the moss to the women's. And the sight of the tracks about Mrs. Maloney's tent, where Joan now slept, set him in a perfect fury.

"Do you know what it is, Hubbard, this beast?" he hissed under his breath at me; "it's a damned wolf, that's

what it is—a wolf lost among the islands, and starving to death—desperate. So help me God, I believe it's that!"

He talked a lot of rubbish in his excitement. He declared he would sleep by day and sit up every night until he killed it. Again his rage touched my admiration; but I got him away before he made enough noise to wake the whole Camp.

"I have a better plan than that," I said, watching his face closely. "I don't think this is anything we can deal with. I'm going to send for the only man I know who can help. We'll go to Waxholm this very morning and get a telegram through."

Sangree stared at me with a curious expression as the fury died out of his face and a new look of alarm took its place.

"John Silence," I said, "will know—"

"You think it's something—of that sort?" he stammered.

"I am sure of it."

There was a moment's pause. "That's worse, far worse than anything material," he said, turning visibly paler. He looked from my face to the sky, and then added with sudden resolution, "Come; the wind's rising. Let's get off at once. From there you can telephone to Stockholm and get a telegram sent without delay."

I sent him down to get the boat ready, and seized the opportunity myself to run and wake Maloney. He was sleeping very lightly, and sprang up the moment I put my head inside his tent. I told him briefly what I had seen, and he showed so little surprise that I caught myself wondering for the first time whether he himself had seen more going on than he had deemed wise to communicate to the rest of us.

He agreed to my plan without a moment's hesitation, and my last words to him were to let his wife and daughter think that the great psychic doctor was coming merely as a chance visitor, and not with any professional interest.

So, with frying-pan, provisions, and blankets aboard, Sangree and I sailed out of the lagoon fifteen minutes later, and headed with a good breeze for the direction of Waxholm and the borders of civilisation.

IV

Although nothing John Silence did ever took me, properly speaking, by surprise, it was certainly unexpected to find a letter from Stockholm waiting for me. "I have finished my Hungary business," he wrote, "and am here for ten days. Do not hesitate to send if you need me. If you telephone any morning from Waxholm I can catch the afternoon steamer."

My years of intercourse with him were full of "coincidences" of this description, and although he never sought to explain them by claiming any magical system of communication with my mind, I have never doubted that there actually existed some secret telepathic method by which he knew my circumstances and gauged the degree of my need. And that this power was independent of time in the sense that it saw into the future, always seemed to me equally apparent.

Sangree was as much relieved as I was, and within an hour of sunset that very evening we met him on the arrival of the little coasting steamer, and carried him off in the dinghy to the camp we had prepared on a neighbouring island, meaning to start for home early next morning.

"Now," he said, when supper was over and we were smoking round the fire, "let me hear your story." He glanced from one to the other, smiling.

"You tell it, Mr. Hubbard," Sangree interrupted abruptly, and went off a little way to wash the dishes, yet not so far as to be out of earshot. And while he splashed with the hot water, and scraped the tin plates with sand and moss, my voice, unbroken by a single question from Dr. Silence, ran on for the next half-hour with the best account I could give of what had happened.

My listener lay on the other side of the fire, his face half hidden by a big sombrero; sometimes he glanced up questioningly when a point needed elaboration, but he uttered no single word till I had reached the end, and his manner all through the recital was grave and attentive. Overhead, the wash of the wind in the pine branches filled in the pauses; the darkness settled down over the sea, and the stars came out in thousands, and by the time I finished the moon had risen to flood the scene with silver. Yet, by his face and eyes, I knew quite well that the doctor was listening to something he had expected to hear, even if he had not actually anticipated all the details.

"You did well to send for me," he said very low, with a significant glance at me when I finished; "very well,"—and for one swift second his eye took in Sangree,—"for what we have to deal with here is nothing more than a werewolf—rare enough, I am glad to say, but often very sad, and sometimes very terrible."

I jumped as though I had been shot, but the next second was heartily ashamed of my want of control; for this brief remark, confirming as it did my own worst suspicions, did more to convince me of the gravity of the adventure than any number of questions or explanations. It seemed to draw close the circle about us, shutting a door somewhere that locked us in with the animal and the horror, and turning the key. Whatever it was had now to be faced and dealt with.

"No one has been actually injured so far?" he asked aloud, but in a matter-of-fact tone that lent reality to grim possibilities.

"Good heavens, no!" cried the Canadian, throwing down his dishcloths and coming forward into the circle of firelight. "Surely there can be no question of this poor starved beast injuring anybody, can there?"

His hair straggled untidily over his forehead, and there was a gleam in his eyes that was not all reflection from the fire. His words made me turn sharply. We all laughed a little short, forced laugh.

"I trust not, indeed," Dr. Silence said quietly. "But what makes you think the creature is starved?" He asked the question with his eyes straight on the other's face. The prompt question explained to me why I had started, and I waited with just a tremor of excitement for the reply.

Sangree hesitated a moment, as though the question took him by surprise. But he met the doctor's gaze unflinchingly across the fire, and with complete honesty.

"Really," he faltered, with a little shrug of the shoulders, "I can hardly tell you. The phrase seemed to come out of its own accord. I have felt from the beginning that it was in pain and—starved, though why I felt this never occurred to me till you asked."

"You really know very little about it, then?" said the other, with a sudden gentleness in his voice.

"No more than that," Sangree replied, looking at him with a puzzled expression that was unmistakably genuine. "In fact, nothing at all, really," he added, by way of further explanation.

"I am glad of that," I heard the doctor murmur under his breath, but so low that I only just caught the words, and Sangree missed them altogether, as evidently he was meant to do.

"And now," he cried, getting on his feet and shaking himself with a characteristic gesture, as though to shake out the horror and the mystery, "let us leave the problem till to-morrow and enjoy this wind and sea and stars. I've been living lately in the atmosphere of many people, and feel that I want to wash and be clean. I propose a swim and then bed. Who'll second me?" And two minutes later we were all diving from the boat into cool, deep water, that reflected a thousand moons as the waves broke away from us in countless ripples.

We slept in blankets under the open sky, Sangree and I taking the outside places, and were up before sunrise to catch the dawn wind. Helped by this early start we were half-way home by noon, and then the wind shifted to a few points behind us so that we fairly ran. In and out among a thousand islands, down narrow channels where we lost the wind, out into open spaces where we had to take in a reef, racing along under a hot and cloudless sky, we flew through the very heart of the bewildering and lonely scenery.

"A real wilderness," cried Dr. Silence from his seat in the bows where he held the jib sheet. His hat was off, his hair tumbled in the wind, and his lean brown face gave him the touch of an Oriental. Presently he changed places with Sangree, and came down to talk with me by the tiller.

"A wonderful region, all this world of islands," he said, waving his hand to the scenery rushing past us, "but doesn't it strike you there's something lacking?"

"It's—hard," I answered, after a moment's reflection. "It has a superficial, glittering prettiness, without—" I hesitated to find the word I wanted.

John Silence nodded his head with approval.

"Exactly," he said. "The picturesqueness of stage scenery that is not real, not alive. It's like a landscape by a clever painter, yet without true imagination. Soulless—that's the word you wanted."

"Something like that," I answered, watching the gusts of wind on the sails. "Not dead so much, as without soul. That's it."

"Of course," he went on, in a voice calculated, it seemed to me, not to reach our companion in the bows, "to live long in a place like this—long and alone—might bring about a strange result in some men."

I suddenly realised he was talking with a purpose and pricked up my ears.

"There's no life here. These islands are mere dead rocks pushed up from below the sea—not living land; and there's nothing really alive on them. Even the sea, this tideless, brackish sea, neither salt water nor fresh, is dead. It's all a pretty image of life without the real heart and soul of life. To a man with too strong desires who came here and lived close to nature, strange things might happen."

"Let her out a bit," I shouted to Sangree, who was coming aft. "The wind's gusty and we've got hardly any ballast."

He went back to the bows, and Dr. Silence continued—

"Here, I mean, a long sojourn would lead to deterioration, to degeneration. The place is utterly unsoftened by human influences, by any humanising associations of history, good or bad. This landscape has never awakened into life; it's still dreaming in its primitive sleep."

"In time," I put in, "you mean a man living here might become brutal?"

"The passions would run wild, selfishness become supreme, the instincts coarsen and turn savage probably."

"But—"

"In other places just as wild, parts of Italy for instance, where there are other moderating influences, it could not happen. The character might grow wild, savage too in a sense, but with a human wildness one could understand and deal with. But here, in a hard place like this, it might be otherwise." He spoke slowly, weighing his words carefully.

I looked at him with many questions in my eyes, and a precautionary cry to Sangree to stay in the fore part of the boat, out of earshot.

"First of all there would come callousness to pain, and indifference to the rights of others. Then the soul would turn savage, not from passionate human causes, or with enthusiasm, but by deadening down into a kind of cold, primitive, emotionless savagery—by turning, like the landscape, soulless."

"And a man with strong desires, you say, might change?"

"Without being aware of it, yes; he might turn savage, his instincts and desires turn animal. And if"—he lowered his voice and turned for a moment towards the bows, and then continued in his most weighty manner—"owing to delicate health or other predisposing causes, his Double—you know what I mean, of course—his etheric Body of Desire, or astral body, as some term it—that part in which the emotions, passions and desires reside—if this, I say, were for some constitutional reason loosely joined to his physi-

cal organism, there might well take place an occasional projection—"

Sangree came aft with a sudden rush, his face aflame, but whether with wind or sun, or with what he had heard, I cannot say. In my surprise I let the tiller slip and the cutter gave a great plunge as she came sharply into the wind and flung us all together in a heap on the bottom. Sangree said nothing, but while he scrambled up and made the jib sheet fast my companion found a moment to add to his unfinished sentence the words, too low for any ear but mine—

"Entirely unknown to himself, however."

We righted the boat and laughed, and then Sangree produced the map and explained exactly where we were. Far away on the horizon, across an open stretch of water, lay a blue cluster of islands with our crescent-shaped home among them and the safe anchorage of the lagoon. An hour with this wind would get us there comfortably, and while Dr. Silence and Sangree fell into conversation, I sat and pondered over the strange suggestions that had just been put into my mind concerning the "Double," and the possible form it might assume when dissociated temporarily from the physical body.

The whole way home these two chatted, and John Silence was as gentle and sympathetic as a woman. I did not hear much of their talk, for the wind grew occasionally to the force of a hurricane and the sails and tiller absorbed my attention; but I could see that Sangree was pleased and happy, and was pouring out intimate revelations to his companion in the way that most people did—when John Silence wished them to do so.

But it was quite suddenly, while I sat all intent upon wind and sails, that the true meaning of Sangree's remark about the animal flared up in me with its full import. For his admission that he knew it was in pain and starved was in reality nothing more or less than a revelation of his deeper self. It was in the nature of a confession. He was speaking of something that he knew positively, something that was beyond question or argument, something that had to do directly with himself. "Poor starved beast" he had called it in words that had "come out of their own accord," and there had not been the slightest evidence of any desire to conceal or explain away. He had spoken instinctively—from his heart, and as though about his own self.

And half an hour before sunset we raced through the narrow opening of the lagoon and saw the smoke of the dinner-fire blowing here and there among the trees, and the figures of Joan and the Bo'sun's Mate running down to meet us at the landing-stage.

V

Everything changed from the moment John Silence set foot on that island; it was like the effect produced by calling in some big doctor, some great arbiter of life and death, for consultation. The sense of gravity increased a hundredfold. Even inanimate objects took upon themselves a subtle alteration, for the setting of the adventure—this deserted bit of sea with its hundreds of uninhabited islands—somehow turned sombre. An element that was mysterious, and in a sense disheartening, crept unbidden into the severity of grey rock and dark pine forest and took the sparkle from the sunshine and the sea.

I, at least, was keenly aware of the change, for my whole being shifted, as it were, a degree higher, becoming keyed up and alert. The figures from the background of the stage moved forward a little into the light—nearer to the inevitable action. In a word this man's arrival intensified the whole affair.

And, looking back down the years to the time when all this happened, it is clear to me that he had a pretty sharp idea of the meaning of it from the very beginning. How much he knew beforehand by his strange divining powers, it is impossible to say, but from the moment he came upon the scene and caught within himself the note of what was going on amongst us, he undoubtedly held the true solution of the puzzle and had no need to ask questions. And this certitude it was that set him in such an atmosphere of power and made us all look to him instinctively; for he took no tentative steps, made no false moves, and while the rest of us floundered he moved straight to the climax. He was indeed a true diviner of souls.

I can now read into his behaviour a good deal that puzzled me at the time, for though I had dimly guessed the solution, I had no idea how he would deal with it. And the conversations I can reproduce almost verbatim, for, according to my invariable habit, I kept full notes of all he said.

To Mrs. Maloney, foolish and dazed; to Joan, alarmed, yet plucky; and to the clergyman, moved by his daughter's distress below his usual shallow emotions, he gave the best possible treatment in the best possible way, yet all so easily and simply as to make it appear naturally spontaneous. For he dominated the Bo'sun's Mate, taking the measure of her ignorance with infinite patience; he keyed up Joan, stirring her courage and interest to the highest point for her own safety; and the Reverend Timothy he soothed and comforted, while obtaining his implicit obedience, by taking him into his confidence, and leading him gradually to a comprehension of the issue that was bound to follow.

And Sangree—here his wisdom was most wisely calculated—he neglected outwardly because inwardly he was the object of his unceasing and most concentrated attention. Under the guise of apparent indifference his mind kept the Canadian under constant observation.

There was a restless feeling in the Camp that evening and none of us lingered round the fire after supper as usual. Sangree and I busied ourselves with patching up the torn tent for our guest and with finding heavy stones to hold the ropes, for Dr. Silence insisted on having it pitched on the highest point of the island ridge, just where it was most rocky and there was no earth for pegs. The place, moreover, was midway between the men's and women's tents, and, of course, commanded the most comprehensive view of the Camp.

"So that if your dog comes," he said simply, "I may be able to catch him as he passes across."

The wind had gone down with the sun and an unusual warmth lay over the island that made sleep heavy, and in the morning we assembled at a late breakfast, rubbing our eyes and yawning. The cool north wind had given way to the warm southern air that sometimes came up with haze and moisture across the Baltic, bringing with it the relaxing sensations that produced enervation and listlessness.

And this may have been the reason why at first I failed to notice that anything unusual was about, and why I was less alert than normally; for it was not till after breakfast that the silence of our little party struck me and I discovered that Joan had not yet put in an appearance. And then, in a flash, the last heaviness of sleep vanished and I saw that Maloney was white and troubled and his wife could not hold a plate without trembling.

A desire to ask questions was stopped in me by a swift glance from Dr. Silence, and I suddenly understood in some vague way that they were waiting till Sangree should have gone. How this idea came to me I cannot determine, but the soundness of the intuition was soon proved, for the moment he moved off to his tent, Maloney looked up at me and began to speak in a low voice.

"You slept through it all," he half whispered.

"Through what?" I asked, suddenly thrilled with the knowledge that something dreadful had happened.

"We didn't wake you for fear of getting the whole Camp up," he went on, meaning, by the Camp, I supposed, Sangree. "It was just before dawn when the screams woke me."

"The dog again?" I asked, with a curious sinking of the heart.

"Got right into the tent," he went on, speaking passionately but very low, "and woke my wife by scrambling all over her. Then she realised that Joan was struggling beside her. And, by God! the beast had torn her arm; scratched all down the arm she was, and bleeding."

"Joan injured?" I gasped.

"Merely scratched—this time," put in John Silence, speaking for the first time; "suffering more from shock and fright than actual wounds."

"Isn't it a mercy the doctor was here?" said Mrs. Maloney, looking as if she would never know calmness again. "I think we should both have been killed."

"It has been a most merciful escape," Maloney said, his pulpit voice struggling with his emotion. "But, of course, we cannot risk another—we must strike Camp and get away at once—"

"Only poor Mr. Sangree must not know what has happened. He is so attached to Joan and would be so terribly upset," added the Bo'sun's Mate distractedly, looking all about in her terror.

"It is perhaps advisable that Mr. Sangree should not know what has occurred," Dr. Silence said with quiet authority, "but I think, for the safety of all concerned, it will be better not to leave the island just now." He spoke with great decision and Maloney looked up and followed his words closely.

"If you will agree to stay here a few days longer, I have no doubt we can put an end to the attentions of your strange visitor, and incidentally have the opportunity of observing a most singular and interesting phenomenon—"

"What!" gasped Mrs. Maloney, "a phenomenon?—you mean that you know what it is?"

"I am quite certain I know what it is," he replied very low, for we heard the footsteps of Sangree approaching, "though I am not so certain yet as to the best means of dealing with it. But in any case it is not wise to leave precipitately—"

"Oh, Timothy, does he think it's a devil—?" cried the Bo'sun's Mate in a voice that even the Canadian must have heard.

"In my opinion," continued John Silence, looking across at me and the clergyman, "it is a case of modern lycanthropy with other complications that may—" He left the sentence unfinished, for Mrs. Maloney got up with a jump and fled to her tent fearful she might hear a worse thing, and at that moment Sangree turned the corner of the stockade and came into view.

"There are footmarks all round the mouth of my tent," he said with excitement. "The animal has been here again in the night. Dr. Silence, you really must come and see them for yourself. They're as plain on the moss as tracks in snow."

But later in the day, while Sangree went off in the canoe to fish the pools near the larger islands, and Joan still lay, bandaged and resting, in her tent, Dr. Silence called me and the tutor and proposed a walk to the granite slabs at the far end. Mrs. Maloney sat on a stump near her daughter, and busied herself energetically with alternate nursing and painting.

"We'll leave you in charge," the doctor said with a smile that was meant to be encouraging, "and when you want us for lunch, or anything, the megaphone will always bring us back in time."

For, though the very air was charged with strange emotions, every one talked quietly and naturally as with a definite desire to counteract unnecessary excitement.

"I'll keep watch," said the plucky Bo'sun's Mate, "and meanwhile I find comfort in my work." She was busy with the sketch she had begun on the day after our arrival. "For even a tree," she added proudly, pointing to her little easel, "is a symbol of the divine, and the thought makes me feel safer." We glanced for a moment at a daub which was more like the symptom of a disease than a symbol of the divine—and then took the path round the lagoon.

At the far end we made a little fire and lay round it in the shadow of a big boulder. Maloney stopped his humming suddenly and turned to his companion.

"And what do you make of it all?" he asked abruptly.

"In the first place," replied John Silence, making himself comfortable against the rock, "it is of human origin, this animal; it is undoubted lycanthropy."

His words had the effect precisely of a bombshell. Maloney listened as though he had been struck.

"You puzzle me utterly," he said, sitting up closer and staring at him.

"Perhaps," replied the other, "but if you'll listen to me for a few moments you may be less puzzled at the end—or more. It depends how much you know. Let me go further and say that you have underestimated, or miscalculated, the effect of this primitive wild life upon all of you."

"In what way?" asked the clergyman, bristling a trifle.

"It is strong medicine for any town-dweller, and for some of you it has been too strong. One of you has gone wild." He uttered these last words with great emphasis.

"Gone savage," he added, looking from one to the other.

Neither of us found anything to reply.

"To say that the brute has awakened in a man is not a mere metaphor always," he went on presently.

"Of course not!"

"But, in the sense I mean, may have a very literal and terrible significance," pursued Dr. Silence. "Ancient instincts that no one dreamed of, least of all their possessor, may leap forth—"

"Atavism can hardly explain a roaming animal with teeth and claws and sanguinary instincts," interrupted Maloney with impatience.

"The term is of your own choice," continued the doctor equably, "not mine, and it is a good example of a word that indicates a result while it conceals the process; but the explanation of this beast that haunts your island and attacks your daughter is of far deeper significance than mere atavistic tendencies, or throwing back to animal origin, which I suppose is the thought in your mind."

"You spoke just now of lycanthropy," said Maloney, looking bewildered and anxious to keep to plain facts evidently; "I think I have come across the word, but really—really—it can have no actual significance to-day, can it? These superstitions of mediaeval times can hardly—"

He looked round at me with his jolly red face, and the expression of astonishment and dismay on it would have made me shout with laughter at any other time. Laughter, however, was never farther from my mind than at this moment when I listened to Dr. Silence as he carefully suggested to the clergyman the very explanation that had gradually been forcing itself upon my own mind.

"However mediaeval ideas may have exaggerated the idea is not of much importance to us now," he said quietly, "when we are face to face with a modern example of what, I take it, has always been a profound fact. For the moment let us leave the name of any one in particular out of the matter and consider certain possibilities."

We all agreed with that at any rate. There was no need to speak of Sangree, or of any one else, until we knew a little more.

"The fundamental fact in this most curious case," he went on, "is that the 'Double' of a man—"

"You mean the astral body? I've heard of that, of course," broke in Maloney with a snort of triumph.

"No doubt," said the other, smiling, "no doubt you

have;—that this Double, or fluidic body of a man, as I was saying, has the power under certain conditions of projecting itself and becoming visible to others. Certain training will accomplish this, and certain drugs likewise; illnesses, too, that ravage the body may produce temporarily the result that death produces permanently, and let loose this counterpart of a human being and render it visible to the sight of others.

"Every one, of course, knows this more or less to-day; but it is not so generally known, and probably believed by none who have not witnessed it, that this fluidic body can, under certain conditions, assume other forms than human, and that such other forms may be determined by the dominating thought and wish of the owner. For this Double, or astral body as you call it, is really the seat of the passions, emotions and desires in the psychical economy. It is the Passion Body; and, in projecting itself, it can often assume a form that gives expression to the overmastering desire that moulds it; for it is composed of such tenuous matter that it lends itself readily to the moulding by thought and wish."

"I follow you perfectly," said Maloney, looking as if he would much rather be chopping firewood elsewhere and singing.

"And there are some persons so constituted," the doctor went on with increasing seriousness, "that the fluid body in them is but loosely associated with the physical, persons of poor health as a rule, yet often of strong desires and passions; and in these persons it is easy for the Double to dissociate itself during deep sleep from their system, and, driven forth by some consuming desire, to assume an animal form and seek the fulfilment of that desire."

There, in broad daylight, I saw Maloney deliberately creep closer to the fire and heap the wood on. We gathered in to the heat, and to each other, and listened to Dr. Silence's voice as it mingled with the swish and whirr of the wind about us, and the falling of the little waves.

"For instance, to take a concrete example," he resumed; "suppose some young man, with the delicate constitution I have spoken of, forms an overpowering attachment to a young woman, yet perceives that it is not welcomed, and is man enough to repress its outward manifestations. In such a case, supposing his Double be easily projected, the very repression of his love in the daytime would add to the intense force of his desire when released in deep sleep from the control of his will, and his fluidic body might issue forth in monstrous or animal shape and become actually visible to others. And, if his devotion were dog-like in its fidelity, yet concealing the fires of a fierce passion beneath, it might well assume the form of a creature that seemed to be half dog, half wolf—"

"A werewolf, you mean?" cried Maloney, pale to the lips as he listened.

John Silence held up a restraining hand. "A werewolf," he said, "is a true psychical fact of profound significance, however absurdly it may have been exaggerated by the imaginations of a superstitious peasantry in the days of unenlightenment, for a werewolf is nothing but the savage, and possibly sanguinary, instincts of a passionate man scouring the world in his fluidic body, his passion body, his body of desire. As in the case at hand, he may not know it—"

"It is not necessarily deliberate, then?" Maloney put in quickly, with relief.

"—It is hardly ever deliberate. It is the desires released in sleep from the control of the will finding a vent. In all savage races it has been recognised and dreaded, this phenomenon styled 'Wehr Wolf,' but to-day it is rare. And it is becoming rarer still, for the world grows tame and civilised, emotions have become refined, desires lukewarm, and few men have savagery enough left in them to generate impulses of such intense force, and certainly not to project them in animal form."

"By Gad!" exclaimed the clergyman breathlessly, and with increasing excitement, "then I feel I must tell you—what has been given to me in confidence—that Sangree has in him an admixture of savage blood—of Red Indian ancestry—"

"Let us stick to our supposition of a man as described," the doctor stopped him calmly, "and let us imagine that he has in him this admixture of savage blood; and further, that he is wholly unaware of his dreadful physical and psychical infirmity; and that he suddenly finds himself leading the primitive life together with the object of his desires; with the result that the strain of the untamed wild-man in his blood—"

"Red Indian, for instance," from Maloney.

"Red Indian, perfectly," agreed the doctor; "the result, I say, that this savage strain in him is awakened and leaps into passionate life. What then?"

He looked hard at Timothy Maloney, and the clergyman looked hard at him.

"The wild life such as you lead here on this island, for instance, might quickly awaken his savage instincts—his buried instincts—and with profoundly disquieting results."

"You mean his Subtle Body, as you call it, might issue forth automatically in deep sleep and seek the object of its desire?" I said, coming to Maloney's aid, who was finding it more and more difficult to get words.

"Precisely;—yet the desire of the man remaining utterly unmalefic—pure and wholesome in every sense—"

"Ah!" I heard the clergyman gasp.

"The lover's desire for union run wild, run savage, tearing its way out in primitive, untamed fashion, I mean," continued the doctor, striving to make himself clear to a mind bounded by conventional thought and knowledge; "for the desire to possess, remember, may easily become importunate, and, embodied in this animal form of the Subtle Body which acts as its vehicle, may go forth to tear in pieces all that obstructs, to reach to the very heart of the loved object and seize it. *Au fond*, it is nothing more than the aspiration for union, as I said—the splendid and perfectly clean desire to absorb utterly into itself—"

He paused a moment and looked into Maloney's eyes.

"To bathe in the very heart's blood of the one desired," he added with grave emphasis.

The fire spurted and crackled and made me start, but Maloney found relief in a genuine shudder, and I saw him turn his head and look about him from the sea to the trees. The wind dropped just at that moment and the doctor's words rang sharply through the stillness.

"Then it might even kill?" stammered the clergyman presently in a hushed voice, and with a little forced laugh by way of protest that sounded quite ghastly.

"In the last resort it might kill," repeated Dr. Silence. Then, after another pause, during which he was clearly debating how much or how little it was wise to give to his audience, he continued: "And if the Double does not succeed in getting back to its physical body, that physical body would wake an imbecile—an idiot—or perhaps never wake at all."

Maloney sat up and found his tongue.

"You mean that if this fluid animal thing, or whatever it is, should be prevented getting back, the man might never wake again?" he asked, with shaking voice.

"He might be dead," replied the other calmly. The tremor of a positive sensation shivered in the air about us.

"Then isn't that the best way to cure the fool—the brute—?" thundered the clergyman, half rising to his feet.

"Certainly it would be an easy and undiscoverable form of murder," was the stern reply, spoken as calmly as though it were a remark about the weather.

Maloney collapsed visibly, and I gathered the wood over the fire and coaxed up a blaze.

"The greater part of the man's life—of his vital forces—goes out with this Double," Dr. Silence resumed, after a moment's consideration, "and a considerable portion of the actual material of his physical body. So the physical body that remains behind is depleted, not only of force, but of matter. You would see it small, shrunken, dropped together, just like the body of a materialising medium at a seance. Moreover, any mark or injury inflicted upon this Double will be found exactly reproduced by the phenomenon of repercussion upon the shrunken physical body lying in its trance—"

"An injury inflicted upon the one you say would be reproduced also on the other?" repeated Maloney, his excitement growing again.

"Undoubtedly," replied the other quietly; "for there exists all the time a continuous connection between the physical body and the Double—a connection of matter, though of exceedingly attenuated, possibly of etheric, matter. The wound *travels*, so to speak, from one to the other, and if this connection were broken the result would be death."

"Death," repeated Maloney to himself, "death!" He looked anxiously at our faces, his thoughts evidently beginning to clear.

"And this solidity?" he asked presently, after a general pause; "this tearing of tents and flesh; this howling, and the marks of paws? You mean that the Double—?"

"Has sufficient material drawn from the depleted body to produce physical results? Certainly!" the doctor took him up. "Although to explain at this moment such problems as the passage of matter through matter would be as difficult as to explain how the thought of a mother can actually break the bones of the child unborn."

Dr. Silence pointed out to sea, and Maloney, looking wildly about him, turned with a violent start. I saw a canoe, with Sangree in the stern-seat, slowly coming into view round the farther point. His hat was off, and his tanned face for the first time appeared to me—to us all, I think—as though it were the face of some one else. He looked like a wild man. Then he stood up in the canoe to make a cast with the rod, and he looked for all the world like an Indian. I recalled the expression of his face as I had seen it once or twice, notably on that occasion of the evening prayer, and an involuntary shudder ran down my spine.

At that very instant he turned and saw us where we lay, and his face broke into a smile, so that his teeth showed white in the sun. He looked in his element, and exceedingly attractive. He called out something about his fish, and soon after passed out of sight into the lagoon.

For a time none of us said a word.

"And the cure?" ventured Maloney at length.

"Is not to quench this savage force," replied Dr. Silence, "but to steer it better, and to provide other outlets. This is the solution of all these problems of accumulated force, for this force is the raw material of usefulness, and should be increased and cherished, not by separating it from the body by death, but by raising it to higher channels. The best and quickest cure of all," he went on, speaking very gently and with a hand upon the clergyman's arm, "is to lead it towards its object, provided that object is not unalterably hostile—to let it find rest where—"

He stopped abruptly, and the eyes of the two men met in a single glance of comprehension.

"Joan?" Maloney exclaimed, under his breath.

"Joan!" replied John Silence.

* * *

We all went to bed early. The day had been unusually warm, and after sunset a curious hush descended on the island. Nothing was audible but that faint, ghostly singing which is inseparable from a pinewood even on the stillest day—a low, searching sound, as though the wind had hair and trailed it o'er the world.

With the sudden cooling of the atmosphere a sea fog began to form. It appeared in isolated patches over the water, and then these patches slid together and a white wall advanced upon us. Not a breath of air stirred; the firs stood like flat metal outlines; the sea became as oil. The whole scene lay as though held motionless by some huge weight in the air; and the flames from our fire—the largest we had ever made—rose upwards, straight as a church steeple.

As I followed the rest of our party tent-wards, having kicked the embers of the fire into safety, the advance guard of the fog was creeping slowly among the trees, like white arms feeling their way. Mingled with the smoke was the odour of moss and soil and bark, and the peculiar flavour of the Baltic, half salt, half brackish, like the smell of an estuary at low water.

It is difficult to say why it seemed to me that this deep stillness masked an intense activity; perhaps in every mood lies the suggestion of its opposite, so that I became aware of the contrast of furious energy, for it was like moving through the deep pause before a thunderstorm, and I trod gently lest by breaking a twig or moving a stone I might set the whole scene into some sort of tumultuous movement. Actually, no doubt, it was nothing more than a result of overstrung nerves.

There was no more question of undressing and going to bed than there was of undressing and going to bathe. Some sense in me was alert and expectant. I sat in my tent and waited. And at the end of half an hour or so my waiting was justified, for the canvas suddenly shivered, and some one tripped over the ropes that held it to the earth. John Silence came in.

The effect of his quiet entry was singular and prophetic: it was just as though the energy lying behind all this stillness had pressed forward to the edge of action. This, no doubt, was merely the quickening of my own mind, and had no other justification; for the presence of John Silence always suggested the near possibility of vigorous action, and as a matter of fact, he came in with nothing more than a nod and a significant gesture.

He sat down on a corner of my ground-sheet, and I pushed the blanket over so that he could cover his legs. He drew the flap of the tent after him and settled down, but hardly had he done so when the canvas shook a second time, and in blundered Maloney.

"Sitting in the dark?" he said self-consciously, pushing his head inside, and hanging up his lantern on the ridge-pole nail. "I just looked in for a smoke. I suppose—"

He glanced round, caught the eye of Dr. Silence, and stopped. He put his pipe back into his pocket and began to hum softly—that underbreath humming of a nondescript melody I knew so well and had come to hate.

Dr. Silence leaned forward, opened the lantern and blew the light out. "Speak low," he said, "and don't strike matches. Listen for sounds and movements about the Camp, and be ready to follow me at a moment's notice." There was light enough to distinguish our faces easily, and I saw Maloney glance again hurriedly at both of us.

"Is the Camp asleep?" the doctor asked presently, whispering.

"Sangree is," replied the clergyman, in a voice equally low. "I can't answer for the women; I think they're sitting up."

"That's for the best." And then he added: "I wish the fog would thin a bit and let the moon through; later—we may want it."

"It is lifting now, I think," Maloney whispered back. "It's over the tops of the trees already."

I cannot say what it was in this commonplace exchange of remarks that thrilled. Probably Maloney's swift acqui-escence in the doctor's mood had something to do with it; for his quick obedience certainly impressed me a good deal. But, even without that slight evidence, it was clear that each recognised the gravity of the occasion, and understood that sleep was impossible and sentry duty was the order of the night.

"Report to me," repeated John Silence once again, "the least sound, and do nothing precipitately."

He shifted across to the mouth of the tent and raised the flap, fastening it against the pole so that he could see out. Maloney stopped humming and began to force the breath through his teeth with a kind of faint hissing, treating us to a medley of church hymns and popular songs of the day.

Then the tent trembled as though some one had touched it.

"That's the wind rising," whispered the clergyman, and pulled the flap open as far as it would go. A waft of cold damp air entered and made us shiver, and with it came a sound of the sea as the first wave washed its way softly along the shores.

"It's got round to the north," he added, and follow-ing his voice came a long-drawn whisper that rose from the whole island as the trees sent forth a sighing response. "The fog'll move a bit now. I can make out a lane across the sea already."

"Hush!" said Dr. Silence, for Maloney's voice had risen above a whisper, and we settled down again to another long period of watching and waiting, broken only by the occasional rubbing of shoulders against the canvas as we shifted our positions, and the increasing noise of waves on the outer coast-line of the island. And over all whirred the murmur of wind sweeping the tops of the trees like a great harp, and the faint tapping on the tent as drops fell from the branches with a sharp pinging sound.

We had sat for something over an hour in this way, and Maloney and I were finding it increasingly hard to keep awake, when suddenly Dr. Silence rose to his feet and peered out. The next minute he was gone.

Relieved of the dominating presence, the clergyman thrust his face close into mine. "I don't much care for this waiting game," he whispered, "but Silence wouldn't hear of my sitting up with the others; he said it would prevent anything happening if I did."

"He knows," I answered shortly.

"No doubt in the world about that," he whispered back; "it's this 'Double' business, as he calls it, or else it's ob-session as the Bible describes it. But it's bad, whichever it is, and I've got my Winchester outside ready cocked, and I brought this too." He shoved a pocket Bible under my nose. At one time in his life it had been his inseparable companion.

"One's useless and the other's dangerous," I replied un-der my breath, conscious of a keen desire to laugh, and leaving him to choose. "Safety lies in following our lead-er—"

"I'm not thinking of myself," he interrupted sharply;

"only, if anything happens to Joan to-night I'm going to shoot first—and pray afterwards!"

Maloney put the book back into his hip-pocket, and peered out of the doorway. "What is he up to now, in the devil's name, I wonder!" he added; "going round Sangree's tent and making gestures. How weird he looks disappearing in and out of the fog."

"Just trust him and wait," I said quickly, for the doctor was already on his way back. "Remember, he has the knowledge, and knows what he's about. I've been with him through worse cases than this."

Maloney moved back as Dr. Silence darkened the doorway and stooped to enter.

"His sleep is very deep," he whispered, seating himself by the door again. "He's in a cataleptic condition, and the Double may be released any minute now. But I've taken steps to imprison it in the tent, and it can't get out till I permit it. Be on the watch for signs of movement." Then he looked hard at Maloney. "But no violence, or shooting, remember, Mr. Maloney, unless you want a murder on your hands. Anything done to the Double acts by repercussion upon the physical body. You had better take out the cartridges at once."

His voice was stern. The clergyman went out, and I heard him emptying the magazine of his rifle. When he returned he sat nearer the door than before, and from that moment until we left the tent he never once took his eyes from the figure of Dr. Silence, silhouetted there against sky and canvas.

And, meanwhile, the wind came steadily over the sea and opened the mist into lanes and clearings, driving it about like a living thing.

It must have been well after midnight when a low booming sound drew my attention; but at first the sense of hearing was so strained that it was impossible exactly to locate it, and I imagined it was the thunder of big guns far out at sea carried to us by the rising wind. Then Maloney, catching hold of my arm and leaning forward, somehow brought the true relation, and I realised the next second that it was only a few feet away.

"Sangree's tent," he exclaimed in a loud and startled whisper.

I craned my head round the corner, but at first the effect of the fog was so confusing that every patch of white driving about before the wind looked like a moving tent and it was some seconds before I discovered the one patch that held steady. Then I saw that it was shaking all over, and the sides, flapping as much as the tightness of the ropes allowed, were the cause of the booming sound we had heard. Something alive was tearing frantically about inside, banging against the stretched canvas in a way that made me think of a great moth dashing against the walls and ceiling of a room. The tent bulged and rocked.

"It's trying to get out, by Jupiter!" muttered the clergyman, rising to his feet and turning to the side where the unloaded rifle lay. I sprang up too, hardly knowing what purpose was in my mind, but anxious to be prepared for anything. John Silence, however, was before us both, and his figure slipped past and blocked the doorway of the tent. And there was some quality in his voice next minute when he began to speak that brought our minds instantly to a state of calm obedience.

"First—the women's tent," he said low, looking sharply at Maloney, "and if I need your help, I'll call."

The clergyman needed no second bidding. He dived past me and was out in a moment. He was labouring evidently under intense excitement. I watched him picking his way silently over the slippery ground, giving the moving tent a wide berth, and presently disappearing among the floating shapes of fog.

Dr. Silence turned to me. "You heard those footsteps about half an hour ago?" he asked significantly.

"I heard nothing."

"They were extraordinarily soft—almost the soundless tread of a wild creature. But now, follow me closely," he added, "for we must waste no time if I am to save this poor man from his affliction and lead his werewolf Double to its rest. And, unless I am much mistaken"—he peered at me through the darkness, whispering with the utmost distinctness—"Joan and Sangree are absolutely made for one another. And I think she knows it too—just as well as he does."

My head swam a little as I listened, but at the same time something cleared in my brain and I saw that he was right. Yet it was all so weird and incredible, so remote from the commonplace facts of life as commonplace people know them; and more than once it flashed upon me that the whole scene—people, words, tents, and all the rest of it—were delusions created by the intense excitement of my own mind somehow, and that suddenly the sea-fog would clear off and the world become normal again.

The cold air from the sea stung our cheeks sharply as we left the close atmosphere of the little crowded tent. The sighing of the trees, the waves breaking below on the rocks, and the lines and patches of mist driving about us seemed to create the momentary illusion that the whole island had broken loose and was floating out to sea like a mighty raft.

The doctor moved just ahead of me, quickly and silently; he was making straight for the Canadian's tent where the sides still boomed and shook as the creature of sinister life raced and tore about impatiently within. A little distance from the door he paused and held up a hand to stop me. We were, perhaps, a dozen feet away.

"Before I release it, you shall see for yourself," he said, "that the reality of the werewolf is beyond all question. The matter of which it is composed is, of course, exceedingly attenuated, but you are partially clairvoyant—and even if it is not dense enough for normal sight you will see something."

He added a little more I could not catch. The fact was that the curiously strong vibrating atmosphere surrounding his person somewhat confused my senses. It was the result, of course, of his intense concentration of mind and forces, and pervaded the entire Camp and all the persons in it. And as I watched the canvas shake and heard it boom and flap I heartily welcomed it. For it was also protective.

At the back of Sangree's tent stood a thin group of pine trees, but in front and at the sides the ground was comparatively clear. The flap was wide open and any ordinary animal would have been out and away without the least trouble. Dr. Silence led me up to within a few feet, evidently careful not to advance beyond a certain limit, and then stooped down and signalled to me to do the same. And looking over his shoulder I saw the interior lit faintly by the spectral light reflected from the fog, and the dim blot upon the balsam boughs and blankets signifying Sangree; while over him, and round him, and up and down him, flew the dark mass of "something" on four legs, with pointed muzzle and sharp ears plainly visible against the tent sides, and the occasional gleam of fiery eyes and white fangs.

I held my breath and kept utterly still, inwardly and outwardly, for fear, I suppose, that the creature would become conscious of my presence; but the distress I felt went far deeper than the mere sense of personal safety, or the fact of watching something so incredibly active and real. I became keenly aware of the dreadful psychic calamity it involved. The realisation that Sangree lay confined in that narrow space with this species of monstrous projection of himself—that he was wrapped there in the cataleptic sleep, all unconscious that this thing was masquerading with his own life and energies—added a distressing touch of horror to the scene. In all the cases of John Silence—and they were many and often terrible—no other psychic affliction has ever, before or since, impressed me so convincingly with the pathetic impermanence of the human personality, with its fluid nature, and with the alarming possibilities of its transformations.

"Come," he whispered, after we had watched for some minutes the frantic efforts to escape from the circle of thought and will that held it prisoner, "come a little farther away while I release it."

We moved back a dozen yards or so. It was like a scene in some impossible play, or in some ghastly and oppressive nightmare from which I should presently awake to find the blankets all heaped up upon my chest.

By some method undoubtedly mental, but which, in my confusion and excitement, I failed to understand, the doctor accomplished his purpose, and the next minute I heard him say sharply under his breath, "It's out! Now watch!"

At this very moment a sudden gust from the sea blew aside the mist, so that a lane opened to the sky, and the moon, ghastly and unnatural as the effect of stage lime-light, dropped down in a momentary gleam upon the door of Sangree's tent, and I perceived that something had moved forward from the interior darkness and stood clearly defined upon the threshold. And, at the same moment, the tent ceased its shuddering and held still.

There, in the doorway, stood an animal, with neck and muzzle thrust forward, its head poking into the night, its whole body poised in that attitude of intense rigidity that precedes the spring into freedom, the running leap of attack. It seemed to be about the size of a calf, leaner than a mastiff, yet more squat than a wolf, and I can swear that I saw the fur ridged sharply upon its back. Then its upper lip slowly lifted, and I saw the whiteness of its teeth.

Surely no human being ever stared as hard as I did in those next few minutes. Yet, the harder I stared the clearer appeared the amazing and monstrous apparition. For, after all, it was Sangree—and yet it was not Sangree. It was the head and face of an animal, and yet it was the face of Sangree: the face of a wild dog, a wolf, and yet his face. The eyes were sharper, narrower, more fiery, yet they were his eyes—his eyes run wild; the teeth were longer, whiter, more pointed—yet they were his teeth, his teeth grown cruel; the expression was flaming, terrible, exultant—yet it was his expression carried to the border of savagery—his expression as I had already surprised it more than once, only dominant now, fully released from human constraint, with the mad yearning of a hungry and importunate soul. It was the soul of Sangree, the long suppressed, deeply loving Sangree, expressed in its single and intense desire—pure utterly and utterly wonderful.

Yet, at the same time, came the feeling that it was all an illusion. I suddenly remembered the extraordinary changes the human face can undergo in circular insanity, when it changes from melancholia to elation; and I recalled the effect of hascheesh, which shows the human countenance in the form of the bird or animal to which in character it most approximates; and for a moment I attributed this mingling of Sangree's face with a wolf to some kind of similar delusion of the senses. I was mad, deluded, dreaming! The excitement of the day, and this dim light of stars and bewildering mist combined to trick me. I had been amazingly imposed upon by some false wizardry of the senses. It was all absurd and fantastic; it would pass.

And then, sounding across this sea of mental confusion like a bell through a fog, came the voice of John Silence bringing me back to a consciousness of the reality of it all—

"Sangree—in his Double!"

And when I looked again more calmly, I plainly saw that it was indeed the face of the Canadian, but his face turned animal, yet mingled with the brute expression a curiously pathetic look like the soul seen sometimes in the yearning eyes of a dog,—the face of an animal shot with vivid streaks of the human.

The doctor called to him softly under his breath—

"Sangree! Sangree, you poor afflicted creature! Do you know me? Can you understand what it is you're doing in your 'Body of Desire'?"

For the first time since its appearance the creature moved. Its ears twitched and it shifted the weight of its body on to the hind legs. Then, lifting its head and muzzle to the sky, it opened its long jaws and gave vent to a dismal and prolonged howling.

But, when I heard that howling rise to heaven, the breath caught and strangled in my throat and it seemed that my heart missed a beat; for, though the sound was entirely animal, it was at the same time entirely human. But, more than that, it was the cry I had so often heard in the Western States of America where the Indians still fight and hunt and struggle—it was the cry of the Redskin!

"The Indian blood!" whispered John Silence, when I caught his arm for support; "the ancestral cry."

And that poignant, beseeching cry, that broken human voice, mingling with the savage howl of the brute beast, pierced straight to my very heart and touched there something that no music, no voice, passionate or tender, of man, woman or child has ever stirred before or since for one second into life. It echoed away among the fog and the trees and lost itself somewhere out over the hidden sea. And some part of myself—something that was far more than the mere act of intense listening—went out with it, and for several minutes I lost consciousness of my surroundings and felt utterly absorbed in the pain of another stricken fellow-creature.

Again the voice of John Silence recalled me to myself.

"Hark!" he said aloud. "Hark!"

His tone galvanised me afresh. We stood listening side by side.

Far across the island, faintly sounding through the trees and brushwood, came a similar, answering cry. Shrill, yet wonderfully musical, shaking the heart with a singular wild sweetness that defies description, we heard it rise and fall upon the night air.

"It's across the lagoon," Dr. Silence cried, but this time in full tones that paid no tribute to caution. "It's Joan! She's answering him!"

Again the wonderful cry rose and fell, and that same instant the animal lowered its head, and, muzzle to earth, set off on a swift easy canter that took it off into the mist and out of our sight like a thing of wind and vision.

The doctor made a quick dash to the door of Sangree's tent, and, following close at his heels, I peered in and caught a momentary glimpse of the small, shrunken body lying upon the branches but half covered by the blankets—the cage from which most of the life, and not a little of the actual corporeal substance, had escaped into that other form of life and energy, the body of passion and desire.

By another of those swift, incalculable processes which at this stage of my apprenticeship I failed often to grasp, Dr. Silence reclosed the circle about the tent and body.

"Now it cannot return till I permit it," he said, and the next second was off at full speed into the woods, with myself close behind him. I had already had some experience of my companion's ability to run swiftly through a dense wood, and I now had the further proof of his power almost to see in the dark. For, once we left the open space about the tents, the trees seemed to absorb all the remaining vestiges of light, and I understood that special sensibility that is said to develop in the blind—the sense of obstacles.

And twice as we ran we heard the sound of that dismal howling drawing nearer and nearer to the answering faint cry from the point of the island whither we were going.

Then, suddenly, the trees fell away, and we emerged, hot and breathless, upon the rocky point where the granite slabs ran bare into the sea. It was like passing into the clearness of open day. And there, sharply defined against sea and sky, stood the figure of a human being. It was Joan.

I at once saw that there was something about her appearance that was singular and unusual, but it was only when we had moved quite close that I recognised what caused it. For while the lips wore a smile that lit the whole face with a happiness I had never seen there before, the eyes themselves were fixed in a steady, sightless stare as though they were lifeless and made of glass.

I made an impulsive forward movement, but Dr. Silence instantly dragged me back.

"No," he cried, "don't wake her!"

"What do you mean?" I replied aloud, struggling in his grasp.

"She's asleep. It's somnambulistic. The shock might injure her permanently."

I turned and peered closely into his face. He was absolutely calm. I began to understand a little more, catching, I suppose, something of his strong thinking.

"Walking in her sleep, you mean?"

He nodded. "She's on her way to meet him. From the very beginning he must have drawn her—irresistibly."

"But the torn tent and the wounded flesh?"

"When she did not sleep deep enough to enter the somnambulistic trance he missed her—he went instinctively and in all innocence to seek her out—with the result, of course, that she woke and was terrified—"

"Then in their heart of hearts they love?" I asked finally.

John Silence smiled his inscrutable smile. "Profoundly," he answered, "and as simply as only primitive souls can love. If only they both come to realise it in their normal waking states his Double will cease these nocturnal excursions. He will be cured, and at rest."

The words had hardly left his lips when there was a sound of rustling branches on our left, and the very next instant the dense brushwood parted where it was darkest and out rushed the swift form of an animal at full gallop. The noise of feet was scarcely audible, but in that utter stillness I heard the heavy panting breath and caught the swish of the low bushes against its sides. It went straight towards Joan—and as it went the girl lifted her head and turned to meet it. And the same instant a canoe that had been creeping silently and unobserved round the inner shore of the lagoon, emerged from the shadows and defined itself upon the water with a figure at the middle thwart. It was Maloney.

It was only afterwards I realised that we were invisible to him where we stood against the dark background of trees; the figures of Joan and the animal he saw plainly, but not Dr. Silence and myself standing just beyond them. He stood up in the canoe and pointed with his right arm. I saw something gleam in his hand.

"Stand aside, Joan girl, or you'll get hit," he shouted, his voice ringing horribly through the deep stillness, and the same instant a pistol-shot cracked out with a burst of flame and smoke, and the figure of the animal, with one tremendous leap into the air, fell back in the shadows and disappeared like a shape of night and fog. Instantly, then, Joan opened her eyes, looked in a dazed fashion about her, and pressing both hands against her heart, fell with a sharp cry into my arms that were just in time to catch her.

And an answering cry sounded across the lagoon—thin, wailing, piteous. It came from Sangree's tent.

"Fool!" cried Dr. Silence, "you've wounded him!" and before we could move or realise quite what it meant, he was in the canoe and half-way across the lagoon.

Some kind of similar abuse came in a torrent from my lips, too—though I cannot remember the actual words—as I cursed the man for his disobedience and tried to make the girl comfortable on the ground. But the clergyman was more practical. He was spreading his coat over her and dashing water on her face.

"It's not Joan I've killed at any rate," I heard him mutter as she turned and opened her eyes and smiled faintly up in his face. "I swear the bullet went straight."

Joan stared at him; she was still dazed and bewildered, and still imagined herself with the companion of her trance. The strange lucidity of the somnambulist still hung over her brain and mind, though outwardly she appeared troubled and confused.

"Where has he gone to? He disappeared so suddenly, crying that he was hurt," she asked, looking at her father as though she did not recognise him. "And if they've done anything to him—they have done it to me too—for he is more to me than—"

Her words grew vaguer and vaguer as she returned slowly to her normal waking state, and now she stopped altogether, as though suddenly aware that she had been surprised into telling secrets. But all the way back, as we carried her carefully through the trees, the girl smiled and murmured Sangree's name and asked if he was injured, until it finally became clear to me that the wild soul of the one had called to the wild soul of the other and in the secret depths of their beings the call had been heard and understood. John Silence was right. In the abyss of her heart, too deep at first for recognition, the girl loved him, and had loved him from the very beginning. Once her normal waking consciousness recognised the fact they would leap together like twin flames, and his affliction would be at an end; his intense desire would be satisfied; he would be cured.

And in Sangree's tent Dr. Silence and I sat up for the remainder of the night—this wonderful and haunted night that had shown us such strange glimpses of a new heaven and a new hell—for the Canadian tossed upon his balsam boughs with high fever in his blood, and upon each cheek a dark and curious contusion showed, throbbing with severe pain although the skin was not broken and there was no outward and visible sign of blood.

"Maloney shot straight, you see," whispered Dr. Silence to me after the clergyman had gone to his tent, and had put Joan to sleep beside her mother, who, by the way, had never once awakened. "The bullet must have passed clean through the face, for both cheeks are stained. He'll wear these marks all his life—smaller, but always there. They're the most curious scars in the world, these scars transferred by repercussion from an injured Double. They'll remain visible until just before his death, and then with the withdrawal of the subtle body they will disappear finally."

His words mingled in my dazed mind with the sighs of the troubled sleeper and the crying of the wind about the tent. Nothing seemed to paralyse my powers of realisation so much as these twin stains of mysterious significance upon the face before me.

It was odd, too, how speedily and easily the Camp resigned itself again to sleep and quietness, as though a stage curtain had suddenly dropped down upon the action and concealed it; and nothing contributed so vividly to the feeling that I had been a spectator of some kind of visionary drama as the dramatic nature of the change in the girl's attitude.

Yet, as a matter of fact, the change had not been so sudden and revolutionary as appeared. Underneath, in those remoter regions of consciousness where the emotions, unknown to their owners, do secretly mature, and owe thence their abrupt revelation to some abrupt psychological climax, there can be no doubt that Joan's love for the Canadian had been growing steadily and irresistibly all the time. It had now rushed to the surface so that she recognised it; that was all.

And it has always seemed to me that the presence of John Silence, so potent, so quietly efficacious, produced an effect, if one may say so, of a psychic forcing-house, and hastened incalculably the bringing together of these two "wild" lovers. In that sudden awakening had occurred the very psychological climax required to reveal the passionate emotion accumulated below. The deeper knowledge had leaped across and transferred itself to her ordinary consciousness, and in that shock the collision of the personalities had shaken them to the depths and shown her the truth beyond all possibility of doubt.

"He's sleeping quietly now," the doctor said, interrupting my reflections. "If you will watch alone for a bit I'll go to Maloney's tent and help him to arrange his thoughts." He smiled in anticipation of that "arrangement." "He'll never quite understand how a wound on the Double can transfer itself to the physical body, but at least I can persuade him that the less he talks and 'explains' to-morrow, the sooner the forces will run their natural course now to peace and quietness."

He went away softly, and with the removal of his presence Sangree, sleeping heavily, turned over and groaned with the pain of his broken head.

And it was in the still hour just before the dawn, when all the islands were hushed, the wind and sea still dreaming, and the stars visible through clearing mists, that a figure crept silently over the ridge and reached the door of the tent where I dozed beside the sufferer, before I was aware of its presence. The flap was cautiously lifted a few inches and in looked—Joan.

That same instant Sangree woke and sat up on his bed of branches. He recognised her before I could say a word, and uttered a low cry. It was pain and joy mingled, and this time all human. And the girl too was no longer walking in her sleep, but fully aware of what she was doing. I was only just able to prevent him springing from his blankets.

"Joan, Joan!" he cried, and in a flash she answered him, "I'm here—I'm with you always now," and had pushed past me into the tent and flung herself upon his breast.

"I knew you would come to me in the end," I heard him whisper.

"It was all too big for me to understand at first," she murmured, "and for a long time I was frightened—"

"But not now!" he cried louder; "you don't feel afraid now of—of anything that's in me—"

"I fear nothing," she cried, "nothing, nothing!"

I led her outside again. She looked steadily into my face with eyes shining and her whole being transformed. In some intuitive way, surviving probably from the somnambulism, she knew or guessed as much as I knew.

"You must talk to-morrow with John Silence," I said gently, leading her towards her own tent. "He understands everything."

I left her at the door, and as I went back softly to take up my place of sentry again with the Canadian, I saw the first streaks of dawn lighting up the far rim of the sea behind the distant islands.

And, as though to emphasise the eternal closeness of comedy to tragedy, two small details rose out of the scene and impressed me so vividly that I remember them to this very day. For in the tent where I had just left Joan, all aquiver with her new happiness, there rose plainly to my ears the grotesque sounds of the Bo'sun's Mate heavily snoring, oblivious of all things in heaven or hell; and from Maloney's tent, so still was the night, where I looked across and saw the lantern's glow, there came to me, through the trees, the monotonous rising and falling of a human voice that was beyond question the sound of a man praying to his God.

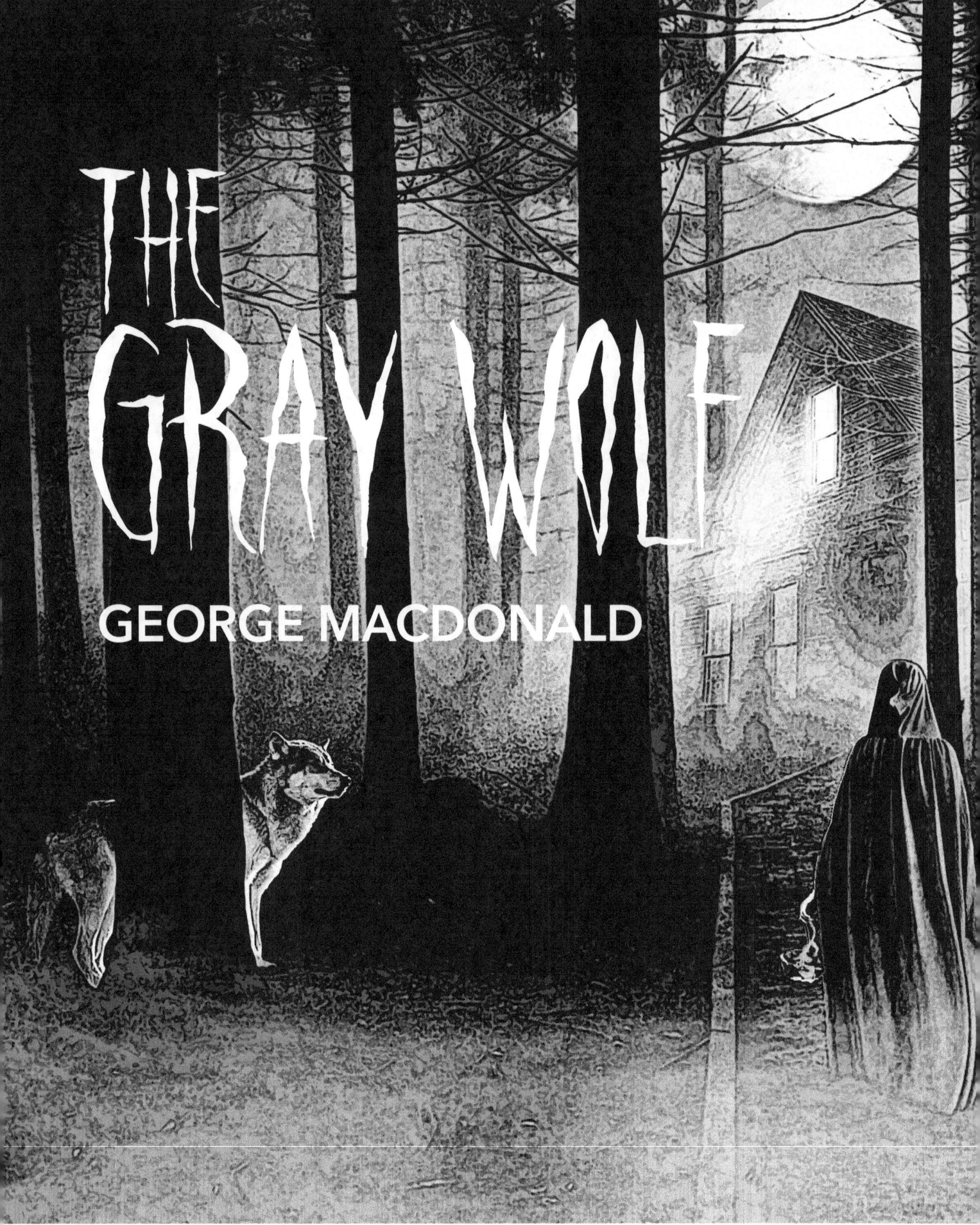

THE GRAY WOLF

GEORGE MACDONALD

One evening-twilight in spring, a young English student, who had wandered northwards as far as the outlying fragments of Scotland called the Orkney and Shetland Islands, found himself on a small island of the latter group, caught in a storm of wind and hail, which had come on suddenly. It was in vain to look about for any shelter; for not only did the storm entirely obscure the landscape, but there was nothing around him save a desert moss.

At length, however, as he walked on for mere walking's sake, he found himself on the verge of a cliff, and saw, over the brow of it, a few feet below him, a ledge of rock, where he might find some shelter from the blast, which blew from behind. Letting himself down by his hands, he alighted upon something that crunched beneath his tread, and found the bones of many small animals scattered about in front of a little cave in the rock, offering the refuge he sought. He went in, and sat upon a stone. The storm increased in violence, and as the darkness grew he became uneasy, for he did not relish the thought of spending the night in the cave. He had parted from his companions on the opposite side of the island, and it added to his uneasiness that they must be full of apprehension about him. At last there came a lull in the storm, and the same instant he heard a footfall, stealthy and light as that of a wild beast, upon the bones at the mouth of the cave. He started up in some fear, though the least thought might have satisfied him that there could be no very dangerous animals upon the island. Before he had time to think, however, the face of a woman appeared in the opening. Eagerly the wanderer spoke. She started at the sound of his voice. He could not see her well, because she was turned towards the darkness of the cave.

"Will you tell me how to find my way across the moor to Shielness?" he asked.

"You cannot find it to-night," she answered, in a sweet tone, and with a smile that bewitched him, revealing the whitest of teeth.

"What am I to do, then?"

"My mother will give you shelter, but that is all she has to offer."

"And that is far more than I expected a minute ago," he replied. "I shall be most grateful."

She turned in silence and left the cave. The youth followed.

She was barefooted, and her pretty brown feet went cat-like over the sharp stones, as she led the way down a rocky path to the shore. Her garments were scanty and torn, and her hair blew tangled in the wind. She seemed about five and twenty, lithe and small. Her long fingers kept clutching and pulling nervously at her skirts as she went. Her face was very gray in complexion, and very worn, but delicately formed, and smooth-skinned. Her thin nostrils were tremulous as eyelids, and her lips, whose curves were faultless, had no colour to give sign of indwelling blood. What her eyes were like he could not see, for she had never lifted the delicate films of her eyelids.

At the foot of the cliff, they came upon a little hut leaning against it, and having for its inner apartment a natural hollow within. Smoke was spreading over the face of the rock, and the grateful odour of food gave hope to the hungry student. His guide opened the door of the cottage; he followed her in, and saw a woman bending over a fire in the middle of the floor. On the fire lay a large fish broiling. The daughter spoke a few words, and the mother turned and welcomed the stranger. She had an old and very wrinkled, but honest face, and looked troubled. She dusted the only chair in the cottage, and placed it for him by the side of the fire, opposite the one window, whence he saw a little patch of yellow sand over which the spent waves spread themselves out listlessly. Under this window there was a bench, upon which the daughter threw herself in an unusual posture, resting her chin upon her hand. A moment after, the youth caught the first glimpse of her blue eyes. They were fixed upon him with a strange look of greed, amounting to craving, but, as if aware that they belied or betrayed her, she dropped them instantly. The moment she veiled them, her face, notwithstanding its colourless complexion, was almost beautiful.

When the fish was ready, the old woman wiped the deal table, steadied it upon the uneven floor, and covered it with a piece of fine table-linen. She then laid the fish on a wooden platter, and invited the guest to help himself. Seeing no other provision, he pulled from his pocket a hunting knife, and divided a portion from the fish, offering it to the mother first.

"Come, my lamb," said the old woman; and the daughter approached the table. But her nostrils and mouth quivered with disgust.

The next moment she turned and hurried from the hut.

"She doesn't like fish," said the old woman, "and I haven't anything else to give her."

"She does not seem in good health," he rejoined.

The woman answered only with a sigh, and they ate their fish with the help of a little rye bread. As they finished their supper, the youth heard the sound as of the pattering of a dog's feet upon the sand close to the door; but ere he had time to look out of the window, the door opened, and the young woman entered. She looked better, perhaps from having just washed her face. She drew a stool to the corner of the fire opposite him. But as she sat down, to his bewilderment, and even horror, the student spied a single drop of blood on her white skin within her torn dress. The woman brought out a jar of whisky, put a rusty old kettle on the fire, and took her place in front of it. As soon as the water boiled, she proceeded to make some toddy in a wooden bowl.

Meantime the youth could not take his eyes off the young woman, so that at length he found himself fascinated, or rather bewitched. She kept her eyes for the most part veiled with the loveliest eyelids fringed with darkest lashes, and he gazed entranced; for the red glow of the little oil-lamp covered all the strangeness of her complexion. But as soon as he met a stolen glance out of those eyes unveiled,

his soul shuddered within him. Lovely face and craving eyes alternated fascination and repulsion.

The mother placed the bowl in his hands. He drank sparingly, and passed it to the girl. She lifted it to her lips, and as she tasted—only tasted it—looked at him. He thought the drink must have been drugged and have affected his brain. Her hair smoothed itself back, and drew her forehead backwards with it; while the lower part of her face projected towards the bowl, revealing, ere she sipped, her dazzling teeth in strange prominence. But the same moment the vision vanished; she returned the vessel to her mother, and rising, hurried out of the cottage.

Then the old woman pointed to a bed of heather in one corner with a murmured apology; and the student, wearied both with the fatigues of the day and the strangeness of the night, threw himself upon it, wrapped in his cloak. The moment he lay down, the storm began afresh, and the wind blew so keenly through the crannies of the hut, that it was only by drawing his cloak over his head that he could protect himself from its currents. Unable to sleep, he lay listening to the uproar which grew in violence, till the spray was dashing against the window. At length the door opened, and the young woman came in, made up the fire, drew the bench before it, and lay down in the same strange posture, with her chin propped on her hand and elbow, and her face turned towards the youth. He moved a little; she dropped her head, and lay on her face, with her arms crossed beneath her forehead. The mother had disappeared.

Drowsiness crept over him. A movement of the bench roused him, and he fancied he saw some four-footed creature as tall as a large dog trot quietly out of the door. He was sure he felt a rush of cold wind. Gazing fixedly through the darkness, he thought he saw the eyes of the damsel encountering his, but a glow from the falling together of the remnants of the fire revealed clearly enough that the bench was vacant. Wondering what could have made her go out in such a storm, he fell fast asleep.

In the middle of the night he felt a pain in his shoulder, came broad awake, and saw the gleaming eyes and grinning teeth of some animal close to his face. Its claws were in his shoulder, and its mouth in the act of seeking his throat. Before it had fixed its fangs, however, he had its throat in one hand, and sought his knife with the other. A terrible struggle followed; but regardless of the tearing claws, he found and opened his knife. He had made one futile stab, and was drawing it for a surer, when, with a spring of the whole body, and one wildly contorted effort, the creature twisted its neck from his hold, and with something betwixt a scream and a howl, darted from him. Again he heard the door open; again the wind blew in upon him, and it continued blowing; a sheet of spray dashed across the floor, and over his face. He sprung from his couch and bounded to the door.

It was a wild night—dark, but for the flash of whiteness from the waves as they broke within a few yards of the cottage; the wind was raving, and the rain pouring down the air. A gruesome sound as of mingled weeping and howling came from somewhere in the dark. He turned again into the hut and closed the door, but could find no way of securing it.

The lamp was nearly out, and he could not be certain whether the form of the young woman was upon the bench or not. Overcoming a strong repugnance, he approached it, and put out his hands—there was nothing there. He sat down and waited for the daylight: he dared not sleep any more.

When the day dawned at length, he went out yet again, and looked around. The morning was dim and gusty and gray. The wind had fallen, but the waves were tossing wildly. He wandered up and down the little strand, longing for more light.

At length he heard a movement in the cottage. By and by the voice of the old woman called to him from the door.

"You're up early, sir. I doubt you didn't sleep well."

"Not very well," he answered. "But where is your daughter?"

"She's not awake yet," said the mother. "I'm afraid I have but a poor breakfast for you. But you'll take a dram and a bit of fish. It's all I've got."

Unwilling to hurt her, though hardly in good appetite, he sat down at the table. While they were eating, the daughter came in, but turned her face away and went to the farther end of the hut. When she came forward after a minute or two, the youth saw that her hair was drenched, and her face whiter than before. She looked ill and faint, and when she raised her eyes, all their fierceness had vanished, and sadness had taken its place. Her neck was now covered with a cotton handkerchief. She was modestly attentive to him, and no longer shunned his gaze. He was gradually yielding to the temptation of braving another night in the hut, and seeing what would follow, when the old woman spoke.

"The weather will be broken all day, sir," she said. "You had better be going, or your friends will leave without you."

Ere he could answer, he saw such a beseeching glance on the face of the girl, that he hesitated, confused. Glancing at the mother, he saw the flash of wrath in her face. She rose and approached her daughter, with her hand lifted to strike her. The young woman stooped her head with a cry. He darted round the table to interpose between them. But the mother had caught hold of her; the handkerchief had fallen from her neck; and the youth saw five blue bruises on her lovely throat—the marks of the four fingers and the thumb of a left hand. With a cry of horror he darted from the house, but as he reached the door he turned. His hostess was lying motionless on the floor, and a huge gray wolf came bounding after him.

There was no weapon at hand; and if there had been, his inborn chivalry would never have allowed him to harm a woman even under the guise of a wolf. Instinctively, he set himself firm, leaning a little forward, with half outstretched arms, and hands curved ready to clutch again at the throat upon which he had left those pitiful marks. But the creature as she sprung eluded his grasp, and just as he expected to feel her fangs, he found a woman weeping on his bosom, with her arms around his neck. The next instant, the gray wolf broke from him, and bounded howling up the cliff. Recovering himself as he best might, the youth followed, for it was the only way to the moor above, across which he must now make his way to find his companions.

All at once he heard the sound of a crunching of bones—not as if a creature was eating them, but as if they were ground by the teeth of rage and disappointment; looking up, he saw close above him the mouth of the little cavern in which he had taken refuge the day before. Summoning all his resolution, he passed it slowly and softly. From within came the sounds of a mingled moaning and growling.

Having reached the top, he ran at full speed for some distance across the moor before venturing to look behind him. When at length he did so, he saw, against the sky, the girl standing on the edge of the cliff, wringing her hands. One solitary wail crossed the space between. She made no attempt to follow him, and he reached the opposite shore in safety.

GABRIEL-ERNEST

SAKI (H.H. MUNRO)

"There is a wild beast in your woods," said the artist Cunningham, as he was being driven to the station. It was the only remark he had made during the drive, but as Van Cheele had talked incessantly his companion's silence had not been noticeable.

"A stray fox or two and some resident weasels. Nothing more formidable," said Van Cheele. The artist said nothing.

"What did you mean about a wild beast?" said Van Cheele later, when they were on the platform.

"Nothing. My imagination. Here is the train," said Cunningham.

That afternoon Van Cheele went for one of his frequent rambles through his woodland property. He had a stuffed bittern in his study, and knew the names of quite a number of wildflowers, so his aunt had possibly some justification in describing him as a great naturalist. At any rate, he was a great walker. It was his custom to take mental notes of everything he saw during his walks, not so much for the purpose of assisting contemporary science as to provide topics for conversation afterward. When the bluebells began to show themselves in flower he made a point of informing everyone of the fact; the season of the year might have warned his hearers of the likelihood of such an occurrence, but at least they felt that he was being absolutely frank with them.

What Van Cheele saw on this particular afternoon was, however, something far removed from his ordinary range of experience. On a shelf of smooth stone overhanging a deep pool in the hollow of an oak coppice a boy of about sixteen lay asprawl, drying his wet brown limbs luxuriously in the sun. His wet hair, parted by a recent dive, lay close to his head, and his light-brown eyes, so light that there was an almost tigerish gleam in them, were turned toward Van Cheele with a certain lazy watchfulness. It was an unexpected apparition, and Van Cheele found himself engaged in the novel process of thinking before he spoke. Where on earth could this wild-looking boy hail from? The miller's wife had lost a child some two months ago, supposed to have been swept away by the millrace, but that had been a mere baby, not a half-grown lad.

"What are you doing there?" he demanded.

"Obviously, sunning myself," replied the boy.

"Where do you live?"

"Here, in these woods."

"You can't live in the woods," said Van Cheele.

"They are very nice woods," said the boy, with a touch of patronage in his voice.

"But where do you sleep at night?"

"I don't sleep at night; that's my busiest time."

Van Cheele began to have an irritated feeling that he was grappling with a problem that was eluding him.

"What do you feed on?" he asked.

"Flesh," said the boy, and he pronounced the word with slow relish, as though he were tasting it.

"Flesh! What flesh?"

"Since it interests you, rabbits, wildfowl, hares, poultry, lambs in their season, children when I can get any; they're usually too well locked in at night, when I do most of my hunting. It's quite two months since I tasted child-flesh."

Ignoring the chaffing nature of the last remark, Van Cheele tried to draw the boy on the subject of possible poaching operations.

"You're talking rather through your hat when you speak of feeding on hares." (Considering the nature of the boy's toilet, the simile was hardly an apt one.) "Our hillside

hares aren't easily caught."

"At night I hunt on four feet," was the somewhat cryptic response.

"I suppose you mean that you hunt with a dog?" hazarded Van Cheele.

The boy rolled slowly over on to his back, and laughed a weird low laugh, that was pleasantly like a chuckle, and disagreeably like a snarl.

"I don't fancy any dog would be very anxious for my company, especially at night."

Van Cheele began to feel that there was something positively uncanny about the strange-eyed, strange-tongued youngster.

"I can't have you staying in these woods," he declared authoritatively.

"I fancy you'd rather have me here than in your house," said the boy.

The prospect of this wild, nude animal in Van Cheele's primly ordered house was certainly an alarming one.

"If you don't go I shall have to make you," said Van Cheele.

The boy turned like a flash, plunged into the pool, and in a moment had flung his wet and glistening body halfway up the bank where Van Cheele was standing. In an otter the movement would not have been remarkable; in a boy Van Cheele found it sufficiently startling. His foot slipped as he made an involuntary backward movement, and he found himself almost prostrate on the slippery weed-grown bank, with those tigerish yellow eyes not very far from his own. Almost instinctively he half-raised his hand to his throat. The boy laughed again, a laugh in which the snarl had nearly driven out the chuckle, and then, with another of his astonishing lightning movements, plunged out of view into a yielding tangle of weed and fern.

"What an extraordinary wild animal!" said Van Cheele as he picked himself up. And then he recalled Cunningham's remark, "There is a wild beast in your woods."

Walking slowly homeward, Van Cheele began to turn over in his mind various local occurrences which might be traceable to the existence of this astonishing young savage.

Something had been thinning the game in the woods lately, poultry had been missing from the farms, hares were growing unaccountably scarcer, and complaints had reached him of lambs being carried off bodily from the hills. Was it possible that this wild boy was really hunting the countryside in company with some clever poacher dog? He had spoken of hunting "four-footed" by night, but then, again, he had hinted strangely at no dog caring to come near him, "especially at night." It was certainly puzzling. And then, as Van Cheele ran his mind over the various depredations that had been committed during the last month or two, he came suddenly to a dead stop, alike in his walk and his speculations. The child missing from the mill two months ago—the accepted theory was that it had tumbled into the millrace and been swept away; but the mother had always declared she had heard a shriek on the hill side of the house, in the opposite direction from the

water. It was unthinkable, of course, but he wished that the boy had not made that uncanny remark about child-flesh eaten two months ago. Such dreadful things should not be said even in fun.

Van Cheele, contrary to his usual wont, did not feel disposed to be communicative about his discovery in the wood. His position as a parish councillor and justice of the peace seemed somehow compromised by the fact that he was harboring a personality of such doubtful repute on his property; there was even a possibility that a heavy bill for damages for raided lambs and poultry might be laid at his door. At dinner that night he was quite unusually silent.

"Where's your voice gone to?" said his aunt. "One would think you had seen a wolf."

Van Cheele, who was not familiar with the old saying, thought the remark rather foolish; if he *had* seen a wolf on his property his tongue would have been extraordinarily busy with the subject.

At breakfast next morning Van Cheele was conscious that his feeling of uneasiness regarding yesterday's episode had not wholly disappeared, and he resolved to go by train to the neighboring cathedral town, hunt up Cunningham, and learn from him what he had really seen that had prompted the remark about a wild beast in the woods. With this resolution taken, his usual cheerfulness partially returned, and he hummed a bright little melody as he sauntered to the morning-room for his customary cigarette. As he entered the room the melody made way abruptly for a pious invocation. Gracefully asprawl on the ottoman, in an attitude of almost exaggerated repose, was the boy of the woods. He was drier than when Van Cheele had last seen him, but no other alteration was noticeable in his toilet.

"How dare you come here?" asked Van Cheele furiously.

"You told me I was not to stay in the woods," said the boy calmly.

"But not to come here. Supposing my aunt should see you!"

And with a view to minimizing that catastrophe Van Cheele hastily obscured as much of his unwelcome guest as possible under the folds of a *Morning Post*. At that moment his aunt entered the room.

"This is a poor boy who has lost his way—and lost his memory. He doesn't know who he is or where he comes from," explained Van Cheele desperately, glancing apprehensively at the waif's face to see whether he was going to add inconvenient candor to his other savage propensities.

Miss Van Cheele was enormously interested.

"Perhaps his underlinen is marked," she suggested.

"He seems to have lost most of that, too," said Van Cheele, making frantic little grabs at the *Morning Post* to keep it in its place.

A naked homeless child appealed to Miss Van Cheele as warmly as a stray kitten or derelict puppy would have done.

"We must do all we can for him," she decided, and in a very short time a messenger, dispatched to the rectory, where a page boy was kept, had returned with a suit of pantry clothes, and the necessary accessories of shirt, shoes, collar, etc. Clothed, clean and groomed, the boy lost none of his uncanniness in Van Cheele's eyes, but his aunt found him sweet.

"We must call him something till we know who he really is," she said. "Gabriel-Ernest, I think; those are nice suitable names."

Van Cheele agreed, but he privately doubted whether they were being grafted on to a nice suitable child. His misgivings were not diminished by the fact that his staid and elderly spaniel had bolted out of the house at the first incoming of the boy, and now obstinately remained shivering and yapping at the farther end of the orchard, while the canary, usually as vocally industrious as Van Cheele himself, had put itself on an allowance of frightened cheeps. More than ever he was resolved to consult Cunningham without loss of time.

As he drove off to the station his aunt was arranging that Gabriel-Ernest should help her to entertain the infant members of her Sunday-school class at tea that afternoon.

Cunningham was not at first disposed to be communicative.

"My mother died of some brain trouble," he explained, "so you will understand why I am averse to dwelling on anything of an impossibly fantastic nature that I may see or think that I have seen."

"But what did you see?" persisted Van Cheele.

"What I thought I saw was something so extraordinary that no really sane man could dignify it with the credit of having actually happened. I was standing, the last evening I was with you, half-hidden in the hedgegrowth by the orchard gate, watching the dying glow of the sunset. Suddenly I became aware of a naked boy, a bather from some neighboring pool, I took him to be, who was standing out on the bare hillside also watching the sunset. His pose was so suggestive of some wild faun of Pagan myth that I instantly wanted to engage him as a model, and in another moment I think I should have hailed him. But just then the sun dipped out of view, and all the orange and pink slid out of the landscape, leaving it cold and gray. And at the same moment an astounding thing happened—the boy vanished too!"

"What! vanished away into nothing?" asked Van Cheele excitedly.

"No; that is the dreadful part of it," answered the artist; "on the open hillside where the boy had been standing a second ago, stood a large wolf, blackish in color, with gleaming fangs and cruel, yellow eyes. You may think—"

But Van Cheele did not stop for anything as futile as thought. Already he was tearing at top speed toward the station. He dismissed the idea of a telegram. "Gabriel-Ernest is a werewolf" was a hopelessly inadequate effort at conveying the situation, and his aunt would think it was a code message to which he had omitted to give her the key. His one hope was that he might reach home before sundown. The cab which he chartered at the other end of the railway journey bore him with what seemed exasperating slowness along the country roads, which were pink and mauve with the flush of the sinking sun. His aunt was putting away some unfinished jams and cake when he arrived.

"Where is Gabriel-Ernest?" he almost screamed.

"He is taking the little Toop child home," said his aunt. "It was getting so late, I thought it wasn't safe to let it go back alone. What a lovely sunset, isn't it?"

But Van Cheele, although not oblivious of the glow in the western sky, did not stay to discuss its beauties. At a speed for which he was scarcely geared he raced along the narrow lane that led to the home of the Toops. On one side ran the swift current of the millstream, on the other rose the stretch of bare hillside. A dwindling rim of red sun showed still on the skyline, and the next turning must bring him in view of the ill-assorted couple he was pursuing. Then the color went suddenly out of things, and a gray light settled itself with a quick shiver over the landscape. Van Cheele heard a shrill wail of fear, and stopped running.

Nothing was ever seen again of the Toop child or Gabriel-Ernest, but the latter's discarded garments were found lying in the road, so it was assumed that the child had fallen into the water, and that the boy had stripped and jumped in, in a vain endeavor to save it. Van Cheele and some workmen who were near by at the time testified to having heard a child scream loudly just near the spot where the clothes were found. Mrs. Toop, who had eleven other children, was decently resigned to her bereavement, but Miss Van Cheele sincerely mourned her lost foundling. It was on her initiative that a memorial brass was put up in the parish church to "Gabriel-Ernest, an unknown boy, who bravely sacrificed his life for another."

Van Cheele gave way to his aunt in most things, but he flatly refused to subscribe to the Gabriel-Ernest memorial.

LEONARD BILSITER was one of those people who
have failed to find this world attractive or interesting, and who have sought compensation in an "unseen world" of their own experience or imagination—or
invention. Children do that sort of thing successfully, but
children are content to convince themselves, and do not
vulgarise their beliefs by trying to convince other people.
Leonard Bilsiter's beliefs were for "the few," that is to say,
anyone who would listen to him.

His dabblings in the unseen might not have carried
him beyond the customary platitudes of the drawing-room

visionary if accident had not reinforced his stock-in- trade
of mystical lore. In company with a friend, who was interested in a Ural mining concern, he had made a trip across
Eastern Europe at a moment when the great Russian railway strike was developing from a threat to a reality; its outbreak caught him on the return journey, somewhere on the
further side of Perm, and it was while waiting for a couple
of days at a wayside station in a state of suspended locomo-
tion that he made the acquaintance of a dealer in harness
and metalware, who profitably whiled away the tedium of
the long halt by initiating his English travelling compan-

THE SHE-WOLF

SAKI (H.H. MUNRO)

ion in a fragmentary system of folk-lore that he had picked up from Trans-Baikal traders and natives. Leonard returned to his home circle garrulous about his Russian strike experiences, but oppressively reticent about certain dark mysteries, which he alluded to under the resounding title of Siberian Magic. The reticence wore off in a week or two under the influence of an entire lack of general curiosity, and Leonard began to make more detailed allusions to the enormous powers which this new esoteric force, to use his own description of it, conferred on the initiated few who knew how to wield it. His aunt, Cecilia Hoops, who loved sensation perhaps rather better than she loved the truth, gave him as clamorous an advertisement as anyone could wish for by retailing an account of how he had turned a vegetable marrow into a wood pigeon before her very eyes. As a manifestation of the possession of supernatural powers, the story was discounted in some quarters by the respect accorded to Mrs. Hoops' powers of imagination.

However divided opinion might be on the question of Leonard's status as a wonderworker or a charlatan, he certainly arrived at Mary Hampton's house-party with a reputation for pre-eminence in one or other of those professions, and he was not disposed to shun such publicity as might fall to his share. Esoteric forces and unusual powers figured largely in whatever conversation he or his aunt had a share in, and his own performances, past and potential, were the subject of mysterious hints and dark avowals.

"I wish you would turn me into a wolf, Mr. Bilsiter," said his hostess at luncheon the day after his arrival.

"My dear Mary," said Colonel Hampton, "I never knew you had a craving in that direction."

"A she-wolf, of course," continued Mrs. Hampton; it would be too confusing to change one's sex as well as one's species at a moment's notice."

"I don't think one should jest on these subjects," said Leonard.

"I'm not jesting, I'm quite serious, I assure you. Only don't do it to-day; we have only eight available bridge players, and it would break up one of our tables. To-morrow we shall be a larger party. To-morrow night, after dinner—"

"In our present imperfect understanding of these hidden forces I think one should approach them with humbleness rather than mockery," observed Leonard, with such severity that the subject was forthwith dropped.

Clovis Sangrail had sat unusually silent during the discussion on the possibilities of Siberian Magic; after lunch he side-tracked Lord Pabham into the comparative seclusion of the billiard-room and delivered himself of a searching question._

"Have you such a thing as a she-wolf in your collection of wild animals? A she-wolf of moderately good temper?"

Lord Pabham considered. "There is Loiusa," he said, "a rather fine specimen of the timber-wolf. I got her two years ago in exchange for some Arctic foxes. Most of my animals get to be fairly tame before they've been with me very long; I think I can say Louisa has an angelic temper, as she-wolves go. Why do you ask?"

"I was wondering whether you would lend her to me for to-morrow night," said Clovis, with the careless solicitude of one who borrows a collar stud or a tennis racquet.

"To-morrow night?"

"Yes, wolves are nocturnal animals, so the late hours won't hurt her," said Clovis, with the air of one who has taken everything into consideration; "one of your men could bring her over from Pabham Park after dusk, and with a little help he ought to be able to smuggle her into the conservatory at the same moment that Mary Hampton makes an unobtrusive exit."

Lord Pabham stared at Clovis for a moment in pardonable bewilderment; then his face broke into a wrinkled network of laughter.

"Oh, that's your game, is it? You are going to do a little Siberian Magic on your own account. And is Mrs. Hampton willing to be a fellow-conspirator?"

"Mary is pledged to see me through with it, if you will guarantee Louisa's temper."

"I'll answer for Louisa," said Lord Pabham.

By the following day the house-party had swollen to larger proportions, and Bilsiter's instinct for self- advertise-ment expanded duly under the stimulant of an increased audience. At dinner that evening he held forth at length on the subject of unseen forces and untested powers, and his flow of impressive eloquence continued unabated while coffee was being served in the drawing- room preparatory to a general migration to the card-room.

His aunt ensured a respectful hearing for his utterances, but her sensation-loving soul hankered after something more dramatic than mere vocal demonstration.

"Won't you do something to CONVINCE them of your powers, Leonard?" she pleaded; "change something into another shape. He can, you know, if he only chooses to," she informed the company.

"Oh, do," said Mavis Pellington earnestly, and her request was echoed by nearly everyone present. Even those who were not open to conviction were perfectly willing to be entertained by an exhibition of amateur conjuring.

Leonard felt that something tangible was expected of him.

"Has anyone present," he asked, "got a three-penny bit or some small object of no particular value -?"

"You're surely not going to make coins disappear, or something primitive of that sort?" said Clovis contemptuously.

"I think it very unkind of you not to carry out my suggestion of turning me into a wolf," said Mary Hampton, as she crossed over to the conservatory to give her macaws their usual tribute from the dessert dishes.

"I have already warned you of the danger of treating these powers in a mocking spirit," said Leonard solemnly.

"I don't believe you can do it," laughed Mary provocatively from the conservatory; "I dare you to do it if you can. I defy you to turn me into a wolf."

As she said this she was lost to view behind a clump of azaleas.

"Mrs. Hampton—" began Leonard with increased solemnity, but he got no further. A breath of chill air seemed to rush across the room, and at the same time the macaws broke forth into ear-splitting screams.

"What on earth is the matter with those confounded birds, Mary?" exclaimed Colonel Hampton; at the same moment an even more piercing scream from Mavis Pellington stampeded the entire company from their seats. In various attitudes of helpless horror or instinctive defence they confronted the evil-looking grey beast that was peering at them from amid a setting of fern and azalea.

Mrs. Hoops was the first to recover from the general chaos of fright and bewilderment.

"Leonard!" she screamed shrilly to her nephew, "turn it back into Mrs. Hampton at once! It may fly at us at any moment. Turn it back!"

"I—I don't know how to," faltered Leonard, who looked more scared and horrified than anyone.

"What!" shouted Colonel Hampton, "you've taken the abominable liberty of turning my wife into a wolf, and now you stand there calmly and say you can't turn her back again!"

To do strict justice to Leonard, calmness was not a distinguishing feature of his attitude at the moment.

"I assure you I didn't turn Mrs. Hampton into a wolf; nothing was farther from my intentions," he protested.

"Then where is she, and how came that animal into the conservatory?" demanded the Colonel.

"Of course we must accept your assurance that you didn't turn Mrs. Hampton into a wolf," said Clovis politely, "but you will agree that appearances are against you."

"Are we to have all these recriminations with that beast standing there ready to tear us to pieces?" wailed Mavis indignantly.

"Lord Pabham, you know a good deal about wild beasts—" suggested Colonel Hampton.

"The wild beasts that I have been accustomed to," said Lord Pabham, "have come with proper credentials from well-known dealers, or have been bred in my own menagerie. I've never before been confronted with an animal that walks unconcernedly out of an azalea bush, leaving a charming and popular hostess unaccounted for. As far as one can judge from OUTWARD characteristics," he continued, "it has the appearance of a well-grown female of the North American timber-wolf, a variety of the common species CANIS LUPUS."

"Oh, never mind its Latin name," screamed Mavis, as the beast came a step or two further into the room; "can't you entice it away with food, and shut it up where it can't do any harm?"

"If it is really Mrs. Hampton, who has just had a very good dinner, I don't suppose food will appeal to it very strongly," said Clovis.

"Leonard," beseeched Mrs. Hoops tearfully, "even if this is none of your doing can't you use your great powers to turn this dreadful beast into something harmless before it bites us all—a rabbit or something?"

"I don't suppose Colonel Hampton would care to have his wife turned into a succession of fancy animals as though we were playing a round game with her," interposed Clovis.

"I absolutely forbid it," thundered the Colonel.

"Most wolves that I've had anything to do with have been inordinately fond of sugar," said Lord Pabham; "if you like I'll try the effect on this one."

He took a piece of sugar from the saucer of his coffee cup and flung it to the expectant Louisa, who snapped it in mid-air. There was a sigh of relief from the company; a wolf that ate sugar when it might at the least have been employed in tearing macaws to pieces had already shed some of its terrors. The sigh deepened to a gasp of thanksgiving when Lord Pabham decoyed the animal out of the room by a pretended largesse of further sugar. There was an instant rush to the vacated conservatory. There was no trace of Mrs. Hampton except the plate containing the macaws' supper.

"The door is locked on the inside!" exclaimed Clovis, who had deftly turned the key as he affected to test it.

Everyone turned towards Bilsiter.

"If you haven't turned my wife into a wolf," said Colonel Hampton, "will you kindly explain where she has disappeared to, since she obviously could not have gone through a locked door? I will not press you for an explanation of how a North American timber-wolf suddenly appeared in the conservatory, but I think I have some right to inquire what has become of Mrs. Hampton."

Bilsiter's reiterated disclaimer was met with a general murmur of impatient disbelief.

"I refuse to stay another hour under this roof," declared Mavis Pellington.

"If our hostess has really vanished out of human form," said Mrs. Hoops, "none of the ladies of the party can very well remain. I absolutely decline to be chaperoned by a wolf!"

"It's a she-wolf," said Clovis soothingly.

The correct etiquette to be observed under the unusual circumstances received no further elucidation. The sudden entry of Mary Hampton deprived the discussion of its immediate interest.

"Some one has mesmerised me," she exclaimed crossly; "I found myself in the game larder, of all places, being fed with sugar by Lord Pabham. I hate being mesmerised, and the doctor has forbidden me to touch sugar."

The situation was explained to her, as far as it permitted of anything that could be called explanation.

"Then you REALLY did turn me into a wolf, Mr. Bilsiter?" she exclaimed excitedly.

But Leonard had burned the boat in which he might now have embarked on a sea of glory. He could only shake his head feebly.

"It was I who took that liberty," said Clovis; "you see, I happen to have lived for a couple of years in North-Eastern Russia, and I have more than a tourist's acquaintance with the magic craft of that region. One does not care to speak about these strange powers, but once in a way, when one hears a lot of nonsense being talked about them, one is tempted to show what Siberian magic can accomplish in the hands of someone who really understands it. I yielded to that temptation. May I have some brandy? the effort has left me rather faint."

If Leonard Bilsiter could at that moment have transformed Clovis into a cockroach and then have stepped on him he would gladly have performed both operations.

THE WEREWOLF

EUGENE FIELD

In the reign of Egbert the Saxon there dwelt in Britain a maiden named Yseult, who was beloved of all, both for her goodness and for her beauty. But, though many a youth came wooing her, she loved Harold only, and to him she plighted her troth.

Among the other youth of whom Yseult was beloved was Alfred, and he was sore angered that Yseult showed favor to Harold, so that one day Alfred said to Harold "Is it right that old Siegfried should come from his grave and have Yseult to wife?" Then added he, "Prithee, good sir, why do you turn so white when I speak your grandsire's name?"

Then Harold asked, "What know you of Siegfried that you taunt me? What memory of him should vex me now?"

"We know and we know," retorted Alfred. "There are some tales told us by our grandmas we have not forgot."

So ever after that Alfred's words and Alfred's bitter smile haunted Harold by day and night.

Harold's grandsire, Siegfried the Teuton, had been a man of cruel violence. The legend said that a curse rested upon him, and that at certain times he was possessed of an evil spirit that wreaked its fury on mankind. But Siegfried had been dead full many years, and there was naught to mind the world of him save the legend and a cunning-wrought

spear which he had from Brunehilde, the witch. This spear was such a weapon that it never lost its brightness, nor had its point been blunted. It hung in Harold's chamber, and it was the marvel among weapons of that time.

Yseult knew that Alfred loved her, but she did not know of the bitter words which Alfred had spoken to Harold. Her love for Harold was perfect in its trust and gentleness. But Alfred had hit the truth the curse of old Siegfried was upon Harold—slumbering a century, it had awakened in the blood of the grandson, and Harold knew the curse that was upon him, and it was this that seemed to stand between him and Yseult. But love is stronger than all else, and Harold loved.

Harold did not tell Yseult of the curse that was upon him, for he feared that she would not love him if she knew. Whensoever he felt the fire of the curse burning in his veins he would say to her "To-morrow I hunt the wild boar in the uttermost forest," or, "Next week I go stag-stalking among the distant northern hills." Even so it was that he ever made good excuse for his absence, and Yseult thought no evil things, for she was trustful, ay, though he went many times away and was long gone, Yseult suspected no wrong. So none beheld Harold when the curse was upon him in its violence.

hopeless, yet knowing not how to combat it

Now, it befell in those times that the country round about was ravaged of a werewolf, a creature that was feared by all men howe'er so valorous. This werewolf was by day a man, but by night a wolf given to ravage and to slaughter, and having a charmed life against which no human agency availed aught. Wheresoever he went he attacked and devoured mankind, spreading terror and desolation round about, and the dream-readers said that the earth would not be freed from the werewolf until some man offered himself a voluntary sacrifice to the monster's rage.

Now, although Harold was known far and wide as a mighty huntsman, he had never set forth to hunt the werewolf, and, strange enow, the werewolf never ravaged the domain while Harold was therein. Whereat Alfred marvelled much, and oftentimes he said: "Our Harold is a wondrous huntsman Who is like unto him in stalking the timid doe and in crippling the fleeing boar? But how passing well doth he time his absence from the haunts of the werewolf. Such valor beseemeth our young Siegfried."

Which being brought to Harold his heart flamed with anger, but he made no answer, lest he betray the truth he feared.

It happened so about that time that Yseult said to Harold, "Wilt thou go with me tomorrow even to the feast in the sacred grove?"

"That can I not do," answered Harold. "I am privily summoned hence to Normandy upon a mission of which I shall some time tell thee. And I pray thee, on thy love for me, go not to the feast in the sacred grove without me."

"What sayst thou?" cried Yseult. "Shall I not go to the feast of Ste. Ælfreda? My father would be sore displeased were I not there with the other maidens. 'T were greatest pity that I should despite his love thus."

"But do not, I beseech thee," Harold implored. "Go not to the feast of Ste Ælfreda in the sacred grove! And thou would thus love me, go not—see, thou my life, on my two knees I ask it!"

"How pale thou art," said Yseult, "and trembling."

"Go not to the sacred grove upon the morrow night," he begged

Yseult marvelled at his acts and at his speech. Then, for the first time, she thought him to be jealous—whereat she secretly rejoiced (being a woman).

"Ah," quoth she, "thou dost doubt my love," but when she saw a look of pain come on his face she added—as if she repented of the words she had spoken—"or dost thou fear the werewolf?"

Then Harold answered, fixing his eyes on hers, "Thou hast said it, it is the werewolf that I fear."

"Why dost thou look at me so strangely, Harold?" cried Yseult. "By the cruel light in thine eyes one might almost take thee to be the werewolf!"

"Come hither, sit beside me," said Harold tremblingly, "and I will tell thee why I fear to have thee go to the feast of Ste. Ælfreda tomorrow evening. Hear what I dreamed last night. I dreamed I was the werewolf—do not shudder,

Alfred alone bethought himself of evil things "'Tis passing strange," quoth he, that ever and anon this gallant lover should quit our company and betake himself whither none knoweth. In sooth't will be well to have an eye on old Siegfried's grandson."

Harold knew that Alfred watched him zealously, and he was tormented by a constant fear that Alfred would discover the curse that was on him; but what gave him greater anguish was the fear that mayhap at some moment when he was in Yseult's presence, the curse would seize upon him and cause him to do great evil unto her, whereby she would be destroyed or her love for him would be undone forever. So Harold lived in terror feeling that his love was dear love, for 't was only a dream.

"A grizzled old man stood at my bedside and strove to pluck my soul from my bosom.

" 'What would'st thou?' I cried.

" 'Thy soul is mine,' he said, 'thou shalt live out my curse. Give me thy soul—hold back thy hands—give me thy soul, I say.'

" 'Thy curse shall not be upon me,' I cried 'What have I done that thy curse should rest upon me? Thou shalt not have my soul.'

" 'For my offence shalt thou suffer, and in my curse thou shalt endure hell—it is so decreed.'

"So spake the old man, and he strove with me and he prevailed against me, and he plucked my soul from my bosom and he said, 'Go, search and kill'—and—and lo, I was a wolf upon the moor.

"The dry grass crackled beneath my tread. The darkness of the night was heavy and it oppressed me. Strange horrors tortured my soul, and it groaned and groaned gaoled in that wolfish body. The wind whispered to me; with its myriad voices it spake to me and said, 'Go, search and kill.' And above these voices sounded the hideous laughter of an old man I fled the moor—whither I knew not, nor knew I what motive lashed me on.

"I came to a river and I plunged in. A burning thirst consumed me, and I lapped the waters of the river—they were waves of flame, and they flashed around me and hissed, and what they said was, 'Go, search and kill,' and I heard the old man's laughter again.

"A forest lay before me with its gloomy thickets and its sombre shadows—with its ravens, its vampires, its serprents, its reptiles, and all its hideous brood of night I darted among its thorns and crouched amid the leaves, the nettles, and the brambles. The owls hooted at me and the thorns pierced my flesh. 'Go, search and kill,' said everything. The hares sprang from my pathway; the other beasts ran bellowing away; every form of life shrieked in my ears—the curse was on me—I was the werewolf.

"On, on I went with the fleetness of the wind, and my soul groaned in its wolfish prison, and the winds and the waters and the trees bade me, 'Go, search and kill, thou accursed brute, go, search and kill.'

"Nowhere was there pity for the wolf; what mercy, thus, should I, the werewolf, show? The curse was on me and it filled me with hunger and a thirst for blood. Skulking on my way within myself I cried, 'Let me have blood, oh, let me have human blood, that this wrath may be appeased, that this curse may be removed.'

"At last I came to the sacred grove. Sombre loomed the poplars, the oaks frowned upon me. Before me stood an old man—'twas he, grizzled and taunting, whose curse I bore. He feared me not. All other living things fled before me, but the old man feared me not. A maiden stood beside him. She did not see me, for she was blind.

" 'Kill, kill,' cried the old man, and he pointed at the girl beside him.

"Hell raged within me—the curse impelled me—I sprang at her throat. I heard the old man's laughter once more, and then—then I awoke, trembling, cold, horrified."

Scarce was this dream told when Alfred strode the way.

"Now, by'r Lady," quoth he, "I bethink me never to have seen a sorrier twain."

Then Yseult told him of Harold's going away and how that Harold had besought her not to venture to the feast of Ste Ælfreda in the sacred grove.

"These fears are childish," cried Alfred boastfully. "And thou sufferest me, sweet lady I will bear thee company to the feast, and a score of my lusty yeoman with their good yew-bows and honest spears, they shall attend me There be no werewolf, I trow, will chance about with us."

Whereat Yseult laughed merrily and Harold said: "'T is well; thou shalt go to the sacred grove, and may my love and Heaven's grace forefend all evil."

Then Harold went to his abode, and he fetched old Siegfried's spear back unto Yseult, and he gave it into her two hands, saying, "Take this spear with thee to the feast tomorrow night. It is old Siegfried's spear, possessing mighty virtue and marvellous."

And Harold took Yseult to his heart and blessed her, and he kissed her upon her brow and upon her lips, saying, "Farewell, oh, my beloved How wilt thou love me when thou know'st my sacrifice. Farewell, farewell, forever, oh, alder-liefest mine."

So Harold went his way and Yseult was lost in wonderment.

On the morrow night came Yseult to the sacred grove wherein the feast was spread, and she bore old Siegfried's spear with her in her girdle. Alfred attended her, and a score of lusty yeomen were with him. In the grove there was great merriment, and with singing and dancing and games withal did the honest folk celebrate the feast of the fair Ste. Ælfreda.

But suddenly a mighty tumult arose, and there were cries of "The werewolf!" "The werewolf!" Terror seized upon all—stout hearts were frozen with fear. Out from the further forest rushed the werewolf, wood wroth, bellowing hoarsely, gnashing his fangs and tossing hither and thither the yellow foam from his snapping jaws. He sought Yseult straight, as if an evil power drew him to the spot where she stood. But Yseult was not afeared; like a marble statue she stood and saw the werewolf's coming. The yeomen, dropping their torches and casting aside their bows, had fled; Alfred alone abided there to do the monster battle.

At the approaching wolf he hurled his heavy lance, but as it struck the werewolf's bristling back the weapon was all to-shivered.

Then the werewolf, fixing his eyes upon Yseult skulked for a moment in the shadow of the yews and thinking then of Harold's words, Yseult plucked old Siegfried's spear from her girdle, raised it on high, and with the strength of despair sent it hurtling through the air.

The werewolf saw the shining weapon, and a cry burst from his gaping throat—a cry of human agony. And Yseult saw in the werewolf's eyes the eyes of some one she had seen and known, but 't was for an instant only, and then the eyes were no longer human, but wolfish in their ferocity.

A supernatural force seemed to speed the spear in its flight. With fearful precision the weapon smote home and buried itself by half its length in the werewolf's shaggy breast just above the heart, and then, with a monstrous sigh—as if he yielded up his life without regret—the werewolf fell dead in the shadow of the yews.

Then, ah, then in very truth there was great joy and loud were the acclaims, while, beautiful in her trembling pallor, Yseult was led unto her home, where the people set about to give great feast to do her homage, for the werewolf was dead, and she it was that had slain him.

But Yseult cried out: "Go, search for Harold—go, bring him to me. Nor eat, nor sleep till he be found."

"Good my lady," quoth Alfred, "how can that be, since he hath betaken himself to Normandy?"

"I care not where he be," she cried. "My heart stands still until I look into his eyes again."

"Surely he hath not gone to Normandy," outspake Hubert. "This very eventide I saw him enter his abode."

They hastened thither—a vast company. His chamber door was barred.

"Harold, Harold, come forth!" they cried, as they beat upon the door, but no answer came to their calls and knockings. Afeared, they battered down the door, and when it fell they saw that Harold lay upon his bed.

"He sleeps," said one. "See, he holds a portrait in his hand—and it is her portrait. How fair he is and how tranquilly he sleeps."

But no, Harold was not asleep. His face was calm and beautiful, as if he dreamed of his beloved, but his raiment was red with the blood that streamed from a wound in his breast—a gaping, ghastly spear wound just above his heart.

THE THING IN THE FOREST

BERNARD CAPES

Into the snow-locked forests of Upper Hungary steal wolves in winter; but there is a footfall worse than theirs to knock upon the heart of the lonely traveller.

One December evening Elspet, the young, newly wedded wife of the woodman Stefan, came hurrying over the lower slopes of the White Mountains from the town where she had been all day marketing. She carried a basket with provisions on her arm; her plump cheeks were like a couple of cold apples; her breath spoke short, but more from nervousness than exhaustion. It was nearing dusk, and she was glad to see the little lonely church in the hollow below, the hub, as it were, of many radiating paths through the trees, one of which was the road to her own warm cottage yet a half-mile away.

She paused a moment at the foot of the slope, undecided about entering the little chill, silent building and making her plea for protection to the great battered stone image of Our Lady of Succour which stood within by the confessional box; but the stillness and the growing darkness decided her, and she went on. A spark of fire glowing through the presbytery window seemed to repel rather than attract her, and she was glad when the convolutions of the path hid it from her sight. Being new to the district, she had seen very little of Father Ruhl as yet, and somehow the penetrating knowledge and burning eyes of the pastor made her feel uncomfortable.

The soft drift, the lane of tall, motionless pines, stretched on in a quiet like death. Somewhere the sun, like a dead fire, had fallen into opalescent embers faintly luminous: they were enough only to touch the shadows with a ghastlier pallor. It was so still that the light crunch in the snow of the girl's own footfalls trod on her heart like a desecration.

Suddenly there was something near her that had not been before. It had come like a shadow, without more sound or warning. It was here—there—behind her. She turned, in mortal panic, and saw a wolf. With a strangled cry and trembling limbs she strove to hurry on her way; and always she knew, though there was no whisper of pursuit, that the gliding shadow followed in her wake. Desperate in her terror, she stopped once more and faced it.

A wolf!—was it a wolf? O who could doubt it! Yet the wild expression in those famished eyes, so lost, so pitiful, so mingled of insatiable hunger and human need! Condemned, for its unspeakable sins, to take this form with sunset, and so howl and snuffle about the doors of men until the blessed day released it. A werewolf—not a wolf.

That terrific realization of the truth smote the girl as with a knife out of darkness: for an instant she came near fainting. And then a low moan broke into her heart and flooded it with pity. So lost, so infinitely hopeless. And so pitiful—yes, in spite of all, so pitiful. It had sinned, beyond any sinning that her innocence knew or her experience could gauge; but she was a woman, very blest, very happy, in her store of comforts and her surety of love. She knew that it was forbidden to succour these damned and nameless outcasts, to help or sympathize with them in any way. But—

There was good store of meat in her basket, and who need ever know or tell? With shaking hands she found and threw a sop to the desolate brute—then, turning, sped upon her way.

But at home her secret sin stood up before her, and, interposing between her husband and herself, threw its shadow upon both their faces. What had she dared—what done? By her own act forfeited her birthright of innocence; by her own act placed herself in the power of the evil to which she had ministered. All that night she lay in shame and horror, and all the next day, until Stefan had come about his dinner and gone again, she moved in a dumb agony. Then, driven unendurably by the memory of his troubled, bewildered face, as twilight threatened she put on her cloak and went down to the little church in the hollow to confess her sin.

'Mother, forgive, and save me,' she whispered, as she passed the statue.

After ringing the bell for the confessor, she had not knelt long at the confessional box in the dim chapel, cold and empty as a waiting vault, when the chancel rail clicked, and the footsteps of Father Ruhl were heard rustling over the stones. He came, he took his seat behind the grating; and, with many sighs and falterings, Elspet avowed her guilt. And as, with bowed head, she ended, a strange sound answered her—it was like a little laugh, and yet not so much like a laugh as a snarl. With a shock as of death she raised her face. It was Father Ruhl who sat there—and yet it was not Father Ruhl. In that time of twilight his face was already changing, narrowing, becoming wolfish—the eyes rounded and the jaw slavered. She gasped, and shrunk back; and at that, barking and snapping at the grating, with a wicked look he dropped—and she heard him coming. Sheer horror lent her wings. With a scream she sprang to her feet and fled. Her cloak caught in something—there was a wrench and crash and, like a flood, oblivion overswept her.

It was the old deaf and near senile sacristan who found them lying there, the woman unhurt but insensible, the priest crushed out of life by the fall of the ancient statue, long tottering to its collapse. She recovered, for her part: for his, no one knows where he lies buried. But there were dark stories of a baying pack that night, and of an empty, bloodstained pavement when they came to seek for the body.

THE WHITE DOG

FEODOR SOLOGUB

Everything was irksome for Alexandra Ivanovna in the workship of this out-of-the-way town. It was the shop in which she had served as apprentice and now for several years as seamstress. Everything irritated Alexandra Ivanovna; she quarreled with everyone and abused the apprentices. Among others to suffer from her tantrums was Tanechka, the youngest of the seamstresses, who had only recently become an apprentice.

In the beginning Tanechka submitted to her abuse in silence. In the end she revolted, and, addressing her assailant, said quite calmly and affably, so that everyone laughed, "Alexandra Ivanovna, you are a dog!"

Alexandra Ivanovna scowled.

"You are a dog yourself!" she exclaimed.

Tanechka was sitting sewing. She paused now and then from her work and said, calmly and deliberately, "You always whine . . . you certainly are a dog . . . You have a dog's snout . . . And a dog's ears . . . And a wagging tail . . . The mistress will soon drive you out of doors, because you are the most detestable of dogs—a poodle." Tanechka was a young, plump, rosy-cheeked girl with a good-natured face which revealed a trace of cunning. She sat there demurely, barefooted, still dressed in her apprentice clothes; her eyes were clear, and her brows were highly arched on her finely curved white forehead, framed by straight dark chestnut hair, which looked black in the distance. Tanechka's voice was clear, even, sweet, insinuating, and if one could have heard its sound only, and not given heed to the words, it would have given the impression that she was paying Alexandra Ivanovna compliments.

The other seamstresses laughed, the apprentices chuckled, they covered their faces with their black aprons and cast side glances at Alexandra Ivanovna, who was livid with rage.

"Wretch!" she exclaimed. "I will pull your ears for you! I won't leave a hair on your head!"

Tanechka replied in a gentle voice: "The paws are a bit short . . . The poodle bites as well as barks . . . It may be necessary to buy a muzzle."

Alexandra Ivanovna made a movement toward Tanechka. But before Tanechka had time to lay aside her work and get up, the mistress of the establishment entered.

"Alexandra Ivanovna," she said sternly, "what do you mean by making such a fuss?"

Alexandra Ivanovna, much agitated, replied, "Irma Petrovna, I wish you would forbid her to call me a dog!"

Tanechka in her turn complained: "She is always snarling at something or other."

But the mistress looked at her sternly and said, "Tanechka, I can see through you. Are you sure you didn't begin it?

You needn't think that because you are a seamstress now you are an important person. If it weren't for your mother's sake—"

Tanechka grew red, but preserved her innocent and affable manner. She addressed her mistress in a subdued voice: "Forgive me, Irma Petrovna, I will not do it again. But it wasn't altogether my fault.

* * *

Alexaridra Ivariovria returned home almost ill with rage. Tanechka had guessed her weakness.

"A dog! Well, then, I am a dog." thought Alexandra Ivanovna, "but it is none of her affair! Have I looked to see whether she is a serpent or a fox? It is easy to find one out, but why make a fuss about it? Is a dog worse than any other animal?"

The clear summer right languished and sighed. A soft breeze from the adjacent fields occasionally blew down the peaceful streets. The moon rose clear and full, that very same moon which rose long ago at another place, over the broad desolate steppe, the home of the wild, of those who ran free and whined in their ancient earthly travail.

And now, as then, glowed eves sick with longing; and her heart, still wild, not forgetting in town the great spaciousness of the steppe, felt oppressed; her throat was troubled with a tormenting desire to howl.

She was about to undress, but what was the use? She could not sleep, anyway. She went into the passage. The planks of the floor bent and creaked under her, and small shavings and sand which covered them tickled her feet not unpleasantly.

She went out on the doorstep. There sat the *babushka* Stepanida, a black figure in her black shawl, gaunt and shriveled. She sat with her head bent, and seemed to be warming herself in the rays of the cold moon.

Alexandra Ivanovna sat down beside her. She kept looking at the old woman sideways. The large curved nose of her companion seemed to her like the beak of an old bird.

"A crow?" Alexandra Ivanovna asked herself.

She smiled, forgetting for the moment her longing and her fears. Shrewd as the eyes of a dog, her own eyes lighted up with the joy of her discovery. In the pale green light of the moon the wrinkles of her faded face became altogether invisible, and she seemed once more young and merry and light-hearted, just as she was ten years ago, when the moon had not vet called upon her to bark and bay of nights before the windows of the dark bathhouse.

She moved closer to the old woman, and said affably, "*Babushka* Stepanida, there is something I have been wanting to ask you."

The old woman turned to her, her dark face furrowed with wrinkles, and asked in a sharp, oldish voice that sounded like a caw, "Well, my dear? Go ahead and ask."

Alexandra Ivanovna gave a repressed laugh; her thin shoulders suddenly trembled from a chill that ran down her spine.

She spoke very quietly: "*Babushka* Stepanida, it seems to me—tell me is it true?—I don't know exactly how to put

it—but you, *babushka*, please don't take offense—it is not from malice that I—"

"Go on, my dear, say it," said the old woman, looking at Alexandra Ivanovna with glowing eyes.

"It seems to me, *babushka*—please, now, don't take offense—as if you, *babushka*, were a crow."

The old woman turned away. She nodded her head, and seemed like one who had recalled something. Her head, with its sharply outlined nose, bowed and nodded, and at last it seemed to Alexandra Ivanovna that the old woman was dozing. Dozing, and mumbling something under her nose—nodding and mumbling old forgotten words, old magic words.

An intense quiet reigned out of doors. It was neither light nor dark, and everything seemed bewitched with the inarticulate mumbling of old, forgotten words. Everything languished and seemed lost in apathy.

Again a longing oppressed her heart. And it was neither a dream nor an illusion. A thousand perfumes, imperceptible by day, became subtly distinguishable, and they recalled something ancient and primitive.

In a barely audible voice the old woman mumbled, "Yes, I am a crow. Only I have no wings. But there are times when I caw, and I caw, and tell of woe. And I am given to forebodings, my dear; each time I have one I simply must caw. People are not particularly anxious to hear me. And when I see a doomed person I have such a strong desire to caw."

The old woman suddenly made a sweeping movement with her arms, and in a shrill voice cried out twice: "Kar-r, Kar-r!"

Alexandra Ivanovna shuddered, and asked, "*Babushka*, at whom are you cawing?"

"At you, my dear," the old woman answered. "I am cawing at you."

It had become too painful to sit with the old woman any longer. Alexandra Ivanovna went to her own room. She sat down before the open window and listened to two voices at the gate.

"It simply won't stop whining!" said a low and harsh voice.

"And uncle, did you see?" asked an agreeable young tenor.

Alexandra Ivanovna recognized in this last the voice of the curly-headed, freckled-faced lad who lived in the same court.

A brief and depressing silence followed. Then she heard a hoarse and harsh voice say suddenly, "Yes, I saw. It's very large—and white. It lies near the bathhouse, and bays at the moon."

The voice gave her an image of the man, of his shovel-shaped beard, his low, furrowed forehead, his small, piggish eyes, and his spread-out fat legs.

"And why does it bay, uncle?" asked the agreeable voice.

And again the hoarse voice did not reply at once.

"Certainly to no good purpose—and where it came from is more than I can say.

"Do you think, uncle, it may be a werewolf?" asked the agreeable voice.

"I should not advise you to investigate," replied the hoarse voice.

She could not quite understand what these words implied, nor did she wish to think of them. She did not feel inclined to listen further. What was the sound and significance of human words to her?

The moon looked straight into her face and persistently called her and tormented her. Her heart was restless with a dark longing, and she could not sit still.

Alexandra Ivanovna quickly undressed herself. Naked, all white, she silently stole through the passage: she then opened the outer door (there was no one on the step or outside) and ran quickly across the court and the vegetable garden, and reached the bathhouse. The sharp contact of her body with the cold air and her feet with the cold ground gave her pleasure. But soon her body was warm.

She lay down in the grass, on her stomach. Then, raising herself on her elbows, she lifted her face toward the pale, brooding moon, and gave a long-drawn-out whine.

"Listen, uncle, it is whining," said the curly-haired lad at the gate.

The agreeable tenor voice trembled perceptibly.

"Whining again, the accurst one!" said the hoarse, harsh voice slowly.

They rose from the bench. The gate latch clicked.

They went silently across the courtyard and the vegetable garden, the two of them. The older man, black-bearded and powerful, walked in front, a gun in his hand. The curly-headed lad followed tremblingly, and looked constantly behind.

Near the bathhouse, in the grass, lay a huge white dog, whining piteously. Its head, black on the crown was raised to the moon, which pursued its way in the cold sky; its hind legs were strangely thrown backward while the front ones, firm and straight, pressed hard against the ground.

In the pale green and unreal light of the moon it seemed enormous. So huge a dog was surely never seen on earth. It was thick and fat. The black spot, which began at the head and stretched in uneven strands down the entire spine seemed like a woman's loosened hair. No tail was visible; presumably it was turned under. The fur on the body was so short that in the distance the dog seemed wholly naked, and its hide shone dimly in the moonlight, so that altogether it resembled the body of a nude woman who lay in the grass and bayed at the moon.

The man with the black beard took aim. The curly-haired lad crossed himself and mumbled something.

The discharge of a rifle sounded in the night air. The dog gave a groan, jumped up on its hind legs, became a naked woman, who, her body covered with blood, started to run, all the while groaning, weeping and raising cries of distress.

The black-bearded one and the curly-haired one threw themselves in the grass, and began to moan in wild terror.

HE OF THE HAIRY FACE

SIR HUGH CLIFFORD

If you put your finger on the map of the Malay Peninsula, an inch or two from its exact centre, you will find a river in Pahang territory which has its rise in the watershed that divides that state from its northern neighbours Kĕlantan and Trĕnggânu. It is called the Tĕmbĕling, and after its junction with the Jèlai, at a point some two hundred miles from the sea, the combined rivers are named the Pahang. The Tĕmbĕling is chiefly remarkable for the number and magnitude of its rapids, for the richness of its gutta-bearing trees, and as being the scene of some of the most notable exploits of the legendary magician Sang Kĕlĕmbai, whose last days on earth are supposed to have been spent in this valley. The inhabitants of the district were, in my time, a ruffianly lot of jungle-dwelling Malays, preyed upon by a ruling family of Wans—a semi-royal set of nobles, who did their best to live up to the traditions of their class. Chiefs and people alike were rather specially interesting because-though of this they had no inkling—they represented the descendants of one of the earliest waves of Malay invaders of the Peninsula—folk who came, not from Sumatra, as did the ancestors of the bulk of the natives of British Malaya, but from the islands of the Archipelago further south. In many localities the offspring of the earlier invaders have resisted conversion to Muhammadanism, and are regarded by the Malays of to-day as part of the aboriginal pagan population of the Peninsula; but the people of the Tĕmbĕling valley have embraced the faith of Islam, and their origin is not suspected by themselves or their neighbours. It is clearly to be traced, however, in certain peculiar customs that have been preserved among them, and by the use of a few local words, not generally understood of the people of the Peninsula, but common enough in northern Borneo and other parts of the Archipelago.

The Tĕmbĕling Valley is bisected by a set of rapids, which render navigation excessively difficult for a distance of some five miles, and above which large boats cannot be taken. Below this obstruction, the natives are chiefly noted for the quaint pottery which they produce from the clay that abounds there, and the rude shapes and the ruder tracery of their vessels have probably suffered no change since the days when the men who dealt with the middle men who trafficked with Solomon's emissaries, sought gold and peafowl and monkeys in the fastnesses of the Malay Peninsula—as everybody knows. Above the rapids the natives, from time immemorial, have planted enough *gambir* to supply the wants of the entire betel-chewing population of Pahang; and as the sale of this commodity brought in a steady in- come, they were for the most part too indolent to plant their own rice. Rice being the staple of all Malays, without which they cannot live, the grain used to be sold to them by downcountry Malays at an exorbitant price, and the profits on the *gambir* crop was thus skilfully diverted into the pouches of wiser men.

A short, distance upstream from the junction of the Tĕmbĕling and the Jelai, and midway between that point and the big rapids, there is a straggling village called Ranggul, the houses of which, built of wattled bamboos and thatched with palm leaves, stand on piles upon the river bank, amid groves of cocoanut and areca-nut palms, fruit trees and clumps of smooth-leaved banana plants. The houses are not set very close together, but a man calling can make himself heard with ease from one to another; and thus the cocoanut palms thrive, for they, the Malays aver, grow not with pleasure beyond the range of the human voice.

The people of Ranggul are no more indolent than other upcountry Malays. They plant a little rice in the swamp behind the village, when the season comes round. They work a little jungle-produce-rubber, rattans, *dâmar-pitch*, and the like—when the pinch of poverty drives them to it. The river is, of course, their principal highway, and they never walk if a boat will take them to their destination. For the rest, they take life very easily. If you chance to visit Ranggul during any of the hot hours of the day, you will find most of its male inhabitants lying about in their dark, cool houses, or seated in their doorways. They occupy themselves with such gentle tasks as whittling a stick or hacking aimlessly at the already deeply scored threshold-block with their heavy wood-knives. Sitting thus, they croak snatches of song, with some old-world refrain to it, breaking off, from time to time, to throw a remark over their shoulders to the women~ folk, who share the dim interiors of the huts with the cats, the babies, and the cooking-pots, or to the little virgin daughter,, carefully secreted on the shelf overhead amid a miscellaneous collection of dusty rubbish, the disused lumber of years. Here the maiden is securely hidden from the sight of the passing neighbour, who stops to gossip with the master of the house, and sits for a space, propped upon the stairladder, lazily masticating a quid of betel nut. Nature has been very lavish to the Malay, and has provided him with a soil that produces a maximum of food in return for a minimum of grudging labour; but, rightly viewed, he has suffered at her hands an eternal defeat. In the tropics, no less than in the arctic regions, Nature has proved too strong a competitor for mankind. In the latter she has forced men to hibernate, paralyzing their energies for more than half the year; in the former, she has rushed in to obliterate the works of human beings with so appalling a rapidity, if for a moment their efforts to withstand her have been relaxed, that here, too, they have abandoned the unequal contest. In the far north and in the tropics alike, it is men drawn from temperate climates, where they have learned to bend Nature in her weaker phases to their will, who have come to renew the struggle with weapons which they have wrested from the enemy in the course of the age-long conflict. But in neither instance can the newcomers look for active assistance from the people of the lands they have invaded. The cool, moist fruit groves of Malaya woo men to the lazy enjoyment of their ease during the parching hours of midday, and the native, who long ago has retired from the fight with Nature, and now is quite content to subsist upon her bounty, has caught the spirit of his surroundings, and is very much what environment and circumstances have combined to make him. Those of us who cry shame upon the peoples of the tropics for their inertia would do well to ponder these things, and should realize that energy is to the natives of the heat-belt at once a disturbing and a disgusting quality. It is disturbing because it runs counter to the order of Nature which these people have accepted. It is disgusting because it is opposed to every tenet of their philosophy.

Some five and fifty years ago, when Che' Wan Ahmad—who subsequently was better known as Sultan Ahmad Maatham Shah K. C. M. G.—was collecting his forces in Dungun, preparatory to making his last and successful descent into the Tĕmbĕling Valley, whence to overrun and conquer Pahang, the night was closing in at Ranggul. A large house stood at that time in a somewhat isolated position, within a thickly planted compound, at one extremity of the village. In this house seven men and two women were at work on the evening meal. The men sat in the centre of the floor on a white mat made of the plaited leaves of the *meng-kûang* palm, with a plate piled with rice before each of them, and a brass tray, supporting numerous small china bowls of curry, placed where all could reach it. They sat cross-legged, with bowed backs, resting their weight upon their left arms, the hands of which lay flat on the floor, with the wrists so turned that the fingers pointed inward. They messed the rice with their right hands, mixing the curry well into it, and expressing the air between grain and grain, ere they carried each large ball of it swiftly to their mouths, and propelled it into them with their thumbs along the surfaces of their hollowed and closely joined fingers. If rice is your staple, it is almost a necessity that you should eat it in this fashion, for when a spoon is used it is aerated, windy stuff of which it is impossible to consume a sufficient quantity. As for the cleanliness of the thing, a Malay once remarked to me that he could be sure that his fingers had not been inside the mouths of other folk, but had no such feeling of certainty with regard to the spoons of Europeans.

The women sat demurely in a half-kneeling position, with their feet tucked away under them, ministering to the wants of the men. They uttered no word, save an occasional exclamation when they drove away a lean cat that crept too near to the food, and the men also held their peace. Malays regard meals as a serious business which is best transacted in silence. From without there came the hum of insects, the chirping of crickets in the fruit trees, and the deep, monotonous note of the bullfrogs in the rice-swamps.

When the men had finished their meal, the women carried the dishes to a corner near the fireplace, and there set to on such of the viands as their lords had not consumed.

If you had looked carefully, however, you would have seen that the cooking-pots, over which the women presided, still held a secret store reserved for their own use, and that the quality of the food in this *cache* was by no means inferior to that of the portion which had been allotted to the men. In a land where women wait upon themselves, labour for others, and have none to attend to their wants or io forestall their wishes, they generally develop a sound working notion of how to look after themselves; and since they have never known a state of society, such as our own, in which women occupy a special and privileged position, it does not occur to them that they are the victims of male oppression.

Each of the men had meanwhile folded a lime-smeared leaf of the sink-vine into a neat, oblong packet, within which was enclosed parings of the betel nut and a fragment or two of prepared *gambir*, taking the ingredients of their quids from the little brass boxes in the clumsy wooden box that lay before them on the mat. Next they had rolled a pinch of Javanese tobacco—potent stuff which grips you by the throat as though you were a personal enemy—in a dried shoot of the *nîpah-palm*, had lighted these improvised cigarettes at the damar-torch which provided the only light, and at last had broken the silence which so long had held them.

The talk flitted lightly over many subjects, all of a concrete character; for talk among natives plays for the most part around facts, rarely around ideas, and the peace of soul induced by repletion is not stimulating to the mind. Che' Sĕman, the owner of the house, and his two sons, Awang and Ngah, discussed the prospects of the crops then growing in the fields behind the village. Their cousin, Abdullah, who chanced to be passing the night in his relatives' house, told of a fall which his wife's step-mother's brother had come by when climbing a cocoanut tree. Mat, his *biras* (for they had married two sisters, which established a definite relationship between them according to Malay ideas), added a few more or less repulsive details to Abdullah's description of the corpse after the accident. These were well received, and attracted the attention of the two remaining men, Pôtek and Kassim, who had been discussing the price of rice and the varying chances of *getah*-hunting; whereupon the talk became general. Pôtek and Kassim had recently come across the mountains from Dungun, in Trĕnggânu, where the claimant to the sultanate of Pahang was at that time collecting the force, which later invaded and conquered the country. They told all that they had seen and heard, multiplying their figures with the daring recklessness common to a people who rarely regard arithmetic as one of the exact sciences; but even this absorbing topic could not hold the attention of their audience for long. Before Pôtek and Kassim had well finished the enumeration of the parts of heavy artillery, the hundreds of elephants and the thousands of the followers, with which they credited the adventurous but slender bands of ragamuffins who followed the fortunes of Che' Wan Ahmad, the master of the house broke into their talk with words on a subject which just then had a more immediate interest than any other for the people of the Tĕmbĕling Valley. Thus the conversation slipped back into the rut in which the talk of the countryside had run, with only casual interruptions, for many weeks.

"He of the Hairy Face[1] is with us once more, Che' Sĕman suddenly announced; and when his words had caused a dead silence to fall upon his hearers, and had even stilled the chatter of the women and children near the fireplace, he continued:

"At the hour when the cicada becomes noisy, I met Imam Sidik of Gemuroh, and bade him stay to eat rice, but he would not, saying that He of the Hairy Face had made his kill at Lâbu yesternight, and that it was expedient for all men to be within their houses before the darkness fell. And so saying, he paddled his boat down stream, using the "dove" stroke,[2] Imam Sidik is a wise man, and his talk is true. He of the Hairy Face spares neither priest nor prince. The girl he killed at Lâbu was a daughter of the *Wans*— *Wan* Esah was her name."

"That makes three-and-twenty whom He of the Hairy Face had slain in one year of maize," said Awang, in a low, fear-stricken voice. "He toucheth neither goats nor kine, and men say he sucketh more blood than he eateth flesh."

"It is that that proves him to be the Thing he is," said Ngah.

"Your words are true," said Che' Seman solemnly. "He of the Hairy Face was in the beginning a man like other men—a *Semang,* a negrit of the woods. Because of his cruelty and his iniquities and the malignity of his magic, his own people drove him forth from among them, and now he lives solitary in the jungles, and by night transforms himself into the shape of Him of the Hairy Face, and feasts upon the flesh of human beings. This is a fact well known and attested."

"It is said that it is only the men of Korinchi who possess this art," interposed Abdullah, in the tone of one who seeks to be reassured.

"They also practise magic of a like kind," rejoined Seman. "But it is certain that He of the Hairy Face was in the beginning a *Semang*—a negrit of the woods; and when he goeth abroad in human guise, he is like all other *Semang* to look upon. I and many others have come upon him, now and again, when we have been in the forests seeking for jungle-produce. He is old and wrinkled and very dirty, covered with skin disease, as with a white garment; and be roameth alone naked and muttering to himself. When he spies men he makes haste to hide himself; and all folk know that it is He who harries us by night in our villages. If we venture forth from our houses during the hours of darkness, to the bathing-raft at the river's edge, to tend our sick, or to visit a friend, Si-Pûdong is ever to be found watching, and thus the tale of his kill waxeth longer and longer."

"But at least men are safe from him while they sit within their houses," said Mat.

"God alone knoweth," answered Che' Seman piously. "Who can say where safety abides when He of the Hairy Face is seeking to glut his appetites? He cometh like a shadow, slays like a prince, and then like a shadow he is gone. And ever the tale of his kills waxeth longer and yet more long. May God send Him very far away from us! *Ya Allah!* It is He, even now! Listen!"

At the word a dead silence, broken only by the hard breathing of the men and women, fell upon all within the house. Then very faintly, and far away upstream, but not so faintly but that all could hear it, as they listened with straining ears and suspended heartbeats, the long-drawn, howling, snarling moan of a hungry tiger rose and fell above the murmur of the insect-world without. The Malays call the roar of the tiger *äum,* and as they pronounce it, the word is vividly onomatopoetic, as those of us who have heard it in lonely jungle places during the silent night watches can bear witness. All who have listened to the tiger in his forest freedom know that he has many voices. He can give a barking cry, which is not unlike that of a deer; he can grunt like a. startled boar, and squeak like the monkeys cowering and chattering at his approach in the branches overhead; he can shake the earth with a vibrating, resonant purr, like the sound of distant thunder in the foothills; he can mew and snarl like an angry wildcat; and he can roar almost like a lion. But it is when he lifts his voice in the long-drawn moan 'that the men and beasts of the jungle chiefly fear him. This cry means that he is hungry, but also that he is so sure of his kill that he cares not if all the world knows that his belly is empty. There is in its note something strangely horrible, for it is as though the cold-blooded, dispassionate cruelty, peculiar to the feline race, has in it become suddenly articulate. These sleek, glossy-skinned, soft-footed, lithe, almost serpentine creatures torture with a grace of movement and gentleness in strength which have in them something infinitely more terror-inspiring than the blundering charge and savage goring of the gaur, or the clumsy tramplings and kneadings with which the elephant destroys its victims.

Again the long-drawn moan broke upon the stillness. The water-buffaloes in the byre heard it, and were panic-stricken. Mad with fear they charged the walls of their pen, bearing all before them, and a moment later could be heard plunging wildly through the brushwood and splashing through the soft mud of the *padi*-fields, the noise of their stampede growing fainter and fainter with distance. The lean curs, suddenly awakened, whimpered miserably and scampered off in every direction, while the sleepy fowls, beneath the flooring of the house, set up a drowsy and discordant screeching. The folk within were too terror-stricken to speak; for extremity of fear, which lends voices to the animal world, renders voluble human beings dumb. And all this while the cry of the tiger broke out again and again, ever louder and louder, as He of the Hairy Face drew nearer and yet more near.

At last it sounded within the very compound in which the house stood, and its sudden proximity caused Mat to start so violently that he overturned with his elbow the pitch-torch at his side, and extinguished the flickering light. The women, their teeth chattering like castanets, crowded up against the men, seeking comfort in physical contact with them. The men gripped their spears, and squatted trembling in the half-light cast by the dying embers of the fire, and by the flecks cast upon floor and wall by the moonbeams struggling through the interstices of the wattling and the thatch of the roof.

"Fear not, Minah," Che' Seman whispered, in a hoarse, strained voice, to his little daughter, who nestled quaking against his breast. "In a space He will be gone. Even He of the Hairy Face will do us no hurt while we sit within the house."

Che' Seman spoke with his judgment supported by the experience of many generations of Malays; but he knew not the nature of the strange animal with which he was now confronted. Once more the moan-like howl set the still air vibrating, but this time its note had changed, and gradually it quickened to the ferocious, snarling roar, which is the charge-song of the tiger, as the beast rushed at the house and flung itself against the bamboo wall with a heavy, jarring thud. A shriek from all the seven distraught wretches within went up on the instant; and then came a scratching, tearing sound, followed by a soft *flop,* as the tiger, failing to effect a landing on the low roof, fell back to earth. The men leaped to their feet, clutching their weapons convulsively, bewildered by fear and by the darkness; and led by Che' Seman, they raised s~bove the wailing of the women, a quavering, half-hearted *sôrak*—the Malayan war-cry, which is designed as much to put courage into those who utter it, as to dismay the enemy whom it defies.

Mat, the man who had upset the torch, alone failed to add his voice to the lamentable outcry of his fellows. Seeking to hide himself from the raging brute without, he crept, unobserved by the others, up into the shelflike loft, in which Mînah had been wont to sit, when strangers were about, during the short days of her virginity. This place consisted of a platform of stout laths suspended from the roof in one corner of the house, and amidst the dusty lumber that filled it, Mat now cowered, sweating with terror. A minute or two of silence and of sickening suspense followed the tiger's first unsuccessful charge. But presently the howl broke forth anew, quickened rapidly to the charge-roar, and again the house shook beneath the impact as the weight of the great animal was hurled at it. This time the leap of Him of the Hairy Face had been judged more surely; and a crash overhead, a shower of leaflets of thatch, and an ominous creaking of the beams apprised the cowering folk within the house that their enemy had secured a foothold on the roof.

The fragmentary, throaty *sôrak*, which Che' Seman had urged his companions to raise, died away into a sobbing silence, disturbed only by the sound of breaths drawn thickly and by the hysterical weeping of the women. Then all were smitten with dumbness, as gazing upward in awful fascination, they saw the thatch torn violently apart by the great claws of the tiger. There were no firearms in the house, but instinctively the men clutched their spears, and held them in readiness to resist the descent of their assailant; and thus for a moment all remained spellbound, with their eyes fastened upon the horror above them. A flood of moonlight, infinitely quiet and peaceful, poured in upon them through the yawning gap in the thatch, and against it the immense, square head of Him of the Hairy Face was darkly outlined, the black bars on the brute's hide, the flaming eyes, and the long cruel teeth being plainly visible, framed in the hole which its claws had made.

The timbers of the roof bent and cracked anew under the unwonted weight, and then, with the agility of a cat, He of the Hairy Face leaped lightly down, and was in among them before they knew. The striped hide was slightly wounded by the upthrust spears, but the shock of the beast's leap bore all who had resisted it to the floor. The tiger never stayed to use its jaws. It sat up, much in the attitude of a kitten playing with a ball of worsted dangled before its eyes, and striking out rapidly and with unerring aim, speedily disposed of all its victims. Che' Seman and his two sons, Awang and Ngah, were the first to fall. Then Iang, Che' Seman's wife, was flung reeling backward against the wall with her skull crushed out of all resemblance to any human member by a single, playful buffet from one of those mighty pads. Kassim, Pôtek, and Abdullah fell before the tiger in quick succession; and Mînah, the little girl who had nestled against her father for protection, lay now beneath his body, sorely wounded, almost demented by terror, but still alive and conscious. Mat, cowering on the shelf overhead, and gazing fascinated at the carnage going on below him, was the only inmate of the house who remained uninjured.

He of the Hairy Face killed quickly and silently while there were yet some alive to resist him. Then, purring gently, he passed from one crumpled form to the other, sucking at the blood of each of his victims, after the manner of a mongoose. At last he reached the body of Che' Seman; and Mînah, seeing him draw near, made a feeble effort to evade him. He pounced upon her like a flash, and then, under the eyes of the horrified Mat, an appalling scene was enacted. The tiger played with and tortured the girl, precisely as we have all seen a cat treat a maimed mouse. Again and again Mînah crawled laboriously away, only to be drawn back by her tormentor when he seemed at last to have exhausted his interest in her. At times she lay still in a paralysis of inertia, only to be goaded into agonized motion once more by a touch of the tiger's claws. Yet, so cunningly did he manipulate his victim, that—as Mat afterward described it—"a time sufficient to enable a pot of rice to be cooked" elapsed ere the girl was finally put out of her misery.

Even then, He of the Hairy Face did not quit the scene of slaughter. Mat, lying prone upon the shelf, watched him through the long hours of that night of terror, playing with the mangled corpses of each of his victims in turn. He leaped from one to the other, apparently trying to cheat himself into the belief that they still lived, inflicting upon them a series of fresh wounds with teeth and claws. The moonlight, pouring through the torn thatch, revealed him frolicking among the dead with all the airy, lighthearted agility and grace of a kitten playing with its own shadow on a sunny lawn; and it was not until the dawn was beginning to break that he tore down the door, leaped easily to the ground, and betook himself to the jungle.

When the sun was up, an armed party of neighbours came to the house to see if aught could be done to aid its occupants. They found the place a shambles, the bodies hardly to be recognized, the floor-laths dripping blood, and Mat lying face-downward on the shelf, with his reason tottering in the balance. The corpses, though they had been horribly mutilated, had not been eaten, the tiger having contented himself with drinking the blood of his victims, and playing his ghastly game with them till daybreak interrupted him.

This is, I believe, the only well-authenticated instance of a tiger attacking men within their closed house in the heart of a Malayan village; and the circumstances are so remarkable in every way, that it is perhaps only natural that the natives of Pahang should attribute the fearlessness of mankind, and the lust of blood displayed by Him of the Hairy Face, to the fact that he was no ordinary wild beast, but a member of the human family who, by means of magic agencies, had assumed a tiger's shape, the better to prey upon his kind.

[1] *Si-Pûdong*—He of the Hairy Face—is one of the names used by jungle-bred Malays to describe a tiger. They will not use the beast's ordinary name, lest the sound of it should reach his ears, and cause him to come to the speaker.

[2] The "dove" stroke is a very rapid stroke made with the paddle lifted high in the air, and driven into the water and drawn back with great force. It is always used far the finish of a canoe-race. The origin of the term is unknown.

THE WERE-TIGER

SIR HUGH CLIFFORD

I

In the more remote parts of the Malay Peninsula five and twenty years ago we lived in the Middle Ages, surrounded by all the appropriate accessories of the dark centuries. Magic and evil spirits, witchcraft and sorcery, spells and love-potions, charms and incantations are, to the mind of the unsophisticated native, as much a matter of everyday life, and almost as commonplace, as is the miracle of the growing rice or the mystery of the reproduction of species. This basic fact must be realized by the European, if the native's view of human existence is to be understood, for it underlies all his conceptions of things as they are. Tales of the marvellous and of the supernatural excite interest and it may be fear in a Malayan audience, but they occasion no surprise. Malays, were they given to such abstract discussions, would probably dispute the accuracy of the term "supernatural" as applied to much that white men would place unhesitatingly in that category. They *know* that strange things have happened in the past and are daily occurring to them and to their fellows. Such experiences are not common to all, just as one man here and there may be struck by lightning while his neighbours go unscathed; but the manifestations of electric force do not appeal to them as less or more unnatural than other inexplicable phenomena which fill human life with awe.

The white man and the white man's justice are placed by this in a position at once anomalous and embarrassing. Unshaken native testimony, we hold, provides evidence which justifies us in sentencing a fellow creature to death or to a long term of imprisonment; yet we hesitate to accept it or to regard it as equally conclusive when it points, no less unerringly, to the proved existence of, say, the Malayan *loup garou*. The Malays of Sâiyong, in the Pêrak Valley, for instance, know how Haji Abdullah, the native of the little state of Korinchi, in Sumatra, was caught stark naked in a tiger-trap, and thereafter purchased his liberty at the price of the buffaloes he had slain while he marauded in the likeness of a beast. The Malays of other parts of the Peninsula know of numerous instances of Korinchi men who have vomited feathers, after feasting upon fowls, when for the nonce they had assumed the likeness of tigers; and of other men of the same race who have left their garments and their trading-packs in thickets, whence presently a tiger has emerged. The Malay, however, does not know that his strange belief finds its exact counterpart in almost every quarter of the globe where man has found himself in close association with beasts of prey, but such knowledge would neither strengthen nor weaken his faith in that which he regards as a proven fact. The white man, on the other hand, may see in the universality of this superstition nothing more than an illustration of the effect of an abiding fear upon the human mind; but that explanation—if explanation it can, indeed, be called—does not carry him much farther along the path of discovery. Meanwhile, he has to shoulder aside as worthless masses of native evidence, which in any other connection he would accept as final.

II

The Slim valley lies across the mountain range which divides Pahang from Pêrak. It used to be peopled by Malays of various races—Râwas and Menangkâbaus from Sumatra, men with high-sounding titles and vain boasts wherewith to carry off their squalid, dirty poverty; Pêrak Malays from the fair Kinta Valley, prospecting for tin or trading skilfully; fugitives from troublous Pahang, long settled in the district; and the sweepings of Java, Sumatra, and the Peninsula.

Into the Slim Valley, some thirty years ago, there came a Korinchi trader named Haji Mi, and his two sons, Abdulrahman and Abas. They came, as is the manner of their people, laden with heavy packs of *sárong*—the native skirt or waistcloth—trudging in single file through the forest and through the villages, hawking their goods among the natives of the place, driving hard bargains and haggling cunningly. But though they came to trade, they stayed long after they had disposed of the contents of their packs, for Haji Ali took a fancy to the place. In those days, of course, land was to be had almost for the asking; wherefore he and his two sons set to work to clear a compound, to build a house, with a grove of young cocoanut trees planted around it, and to cultivate a rice swamp. They were quiet, well-behaved people; they were regular in their attendance at the mosque for the Friday congregational prayers; and as they were wealthy and prosperous, they found favour in the eyes of their poorer neighbours. Accordingly, when Haji Ali let it be known that he desired to find a wife, there was a bustle in the villages among the parents of marriageable daughters, and though he was a man well past middle life, a wide range of choice was offered to him.

The girl he finally selected was named Patîmah, the daughter of poor folk, peasants who lived on their little patch of land in one of the neighbouring villages. She was a comely maiden, plump and round and light of colour, with a merry face to cheer, and willing fingers wherewith to serve a husband. The wedding-portion was paid; a feast proportionate to Haji Ali's wealth was held to celebrate the occasion; and the bride, after a decent interval, was earned off to her husband's house among the newly planted fruit trees and palm groves. This was not the general custom of the land, for among Malays the husband usually shares his father-in-law's home for a long period after his marriage. But Haji All had a fine new house, brave with wattled walls stained cunningly in black and white, and with a luxuriant covering of thatch. Moreover, he had taken the daughter of a poor man to wife, and could dictate his own terms, in most matters, to her and to her parents.

The girl went willingly enough, for she was exchanging poverty for wealth, a miserable hovel for a handsome home, and parents who knew how to get out of her the last ounce of work of which she was capable, for a husband who seemed ever kind, generous, and indulgent. She had also the satisfaction of knowing that she had made an exceedingly good marriage, and was an object of envy to all her contemporaries. None the less, three days later, at the hour when the dawn was breaking, she was found beating upon the door of her father's house, screaming to be taken in, trembling in every limb, with her hair disordered, her garments drenched with dew from the underwood through which she had rushed, and in a state of panic bordering on dementia.

Her story—the first act in the drama of the were-tiger of Slim—ran in this wise:

She had gone home with Haji Ali to the house in which he lived with his two sons, Abdulrahman and Abas, and all had treated her kindly and with courtesy. The first day she had cooked the rice insufficiently, and though the young men had grumbled Haji Ali had said no word of blame, when she had expected a slapping, such as would have fallen to the lot of most wives in similar circumstances.

She had, she declared, no complaint to make of her husband's treatment of her; but she had fled his roof forever, and her parents might "hang her on high, sell her in a far land, scorch her with the sun's rays, immerse her in water, burn her with fire," ere aught should induce her to return to one who hunted by night in the likeness of a were-tiger.

Every evening, after the hour of evening prayer, Haji Mi had left the house on one pretext or another, and had not returned until an hour before the dawn. Twice she had not been aware of his return until she had found him lying on the sleeping-mat by her side; but on the third night she had remained awake until a noise without told her that her husband was at hand. Then she had arisen and had hastened to unbar the door, which she had fastened on the inside after Abdulrahman and Abas had fallen asleep. The moon was behind a cloud and the light she cast was dim, but Patîmah had seen clearly enough the sight which had driven her mad with terror.

On the topmost rung of the ladder, which in this, as in all Malay houses, led from the ground to the threshold of the door, there rested the head of a full-grown tiger. Patimah could see the bold, black stripes that marked his hide, the bristling wires of whisker, the long, cruel teeth, the fierce green light in the beast's eyes. A round pad, with long curved claws partially concealed, lay on the ladder-rung, one on each side of the monster's head; and the lower portion of the body, reaching to the ground, was so foreshortened that, to the girl, it looked like the body of a man. Patîmah stood gazing at the tiger from the distance of only a foot or two, for she was too paralyzed with fear and could neither move nor cry out; and as she looked, a gradual transformation took place in the creature at her feet. Much as one sees a ripple of cool air pass over the surface of molten metal, the tiger's features palpitated and were changed, until the horrified girl saw the face of her husband come up through that of the beast, just as that of a diver comes up from the depths through still waters. In another moment Patîmah understood that it was Haji Au, her husband, who was ascending the ladder of his house, and the spell which had held her motionless was snapped. The first use which she made of her recovered power to move was to leap past him through the doorway, and to plunge into the jungle which edged the compound.

Malays do not love to travel singly through the forest, even when the sun is high, and in ordinary circumstances no woman could by any means be prevailed upon to do such a thing. But Patîmah was distraught with fear; and though she was alone, though the moonlight was dim and the dawn had not yet come, she preferred the terror-haunted depths of the jungle to the home of her were-tiger husband. Thus she forced her way through the brushwood, tearing her clothes, scarifying her flesh with thorns, catching her feet in creepers and trailing vines, drenching herself to the skin with dew, and so running and falling, and rising to run and fall again, she made her way to her father's house, there to tell the tale of her appalling experience.

The story of what had occurred was speedily noised abroad through the villages, and was duly reported to the nearest white man, who heard it with the white man s usual scepticism; while the parents of marriageable daughters, who had been mortified by Haji Ali's choice of a wife, hastened to assure Patîmah's papa and mamma that they had always anticipated something of the sort.

A really remarkable fact, however, was that Haji All made no attempt to regain possession of his wife; and this acquires a special significance owing to the extraordinary tenacity which characterizes all Sumatra Malays in relation to their rights in property. His neighbours drew a natural inference from his inaction, and shunned him so sedulously that thenceforth he and his sons were compelled to live in almost complete isolation.

But the drama of the were-tiger of Slim was to have a final act.

One night a fine young water-buffalo, the property of the Headman, Penghûlu Mat Saleh, was killed by a tiger, and its owner, saying no word to any man, constructed a cunningly arranged spring-gun over the carcase. The trigger-lines were so set that if the tiger returned to finish his meal—which, after the manner of his kind, he had begun by tearing a couple of hurried mouthfuls out of the rump— he must infallibly be wounded or killed by the bolts and slugs with which the gun was charged.

Next night a loud report, breaking in clanging echoes through the stillness an hour or two before the dawn was due, apprised Penghûlu Mat Saleh that some animal had fouled the trigger-lines. The chances were that it was the tiger; and if he were wounded, he would not be a pleasant creature to meet on a dark night. Accordingly, Penghûlu Mat Saleh lay still until morning.

In a Malayan village all are astir very shortly after daybreak. As soon as it is light enough to see to walk, the doors of the houses open one by one, and the people of the village come forth, huddled to the chin in their sǝlîmut, or coverlets. Each man makes his way down to the river to perform his morning ablutions, or stands or squats on the bank of the stream, staring sleepily at nothing in particular, a motionless figure outlined dimly against the broad ruddiness of a Malayan dawn. Presently the women of the village emerge from their houses, in little knots of three or four, with the children astride upon their hips or pattering at their heels. They carry clusters of gourds in their hands, for it is their duty to fill them from the running stream with the water which will be needed during the day. It is not until the sun begins to make its power felt through the mists of morning, when ablutions have been carefully performed and the drowsiness of the waking-hour has departed from heavy eyes, that the people of the village turn their indolent thoughts toward the business of the day.

Penghûlu Mat Saleh arose that morning and went through his usual daily routine before he set to work to collect a party of Malays to aid him in his search for the wounded tiger. He had no difficulty in finding men who were willing to share the excitement of the adventure, for most Malays are endowed with sporting instincts; and he presently started on his quest with a ragged following of nearly a dozen at his heels, armed with spears and *kris* and having among them a couple of muskets. On arrival at the spot where the spring-gun had been set, they found that beyond a doubt the tiger had returned to his kill. The tracks left by the great pads were fresh, and the tearing up of the earth on one side of the dead buffalo, in a spot where the grass was thickly flecked with blood, showed that the shot had taken effect.

Penghûlu Mat Saleh and his people then set down steadily to follow the trail of the wounded tiger. This was an easy matter, for the beast had gone heavily on three legs, the off hind-leg dragging uselessly. In places, too, a clot of blood showed red among the dew-drenched leaves and grasses. None the less, the Penghûlu and his party followed slowly and with caution. They knew that a wounded tiger is an ill beast to tackle at any time, and that even when he has only three legs with which to spring upon his enemies, he can on occasion arrange for a large escort of human beings to accompany him into the land of shadows.

The trail led through the brushwood, in the midst of which the dead buffalo was lying, and thence into a belt of jungle which covered the bank of the river and extended upstream from a point a few hundreds of yards above Penghûlu Mat Saleh's village to Kuâla Chin Lâma, half a dozen miles away. The tiger had turned up-river after entering this patch of forest, and half a mile higher he had come out upon a slender foot-path through the woods.

When Penghûlu Mat Saleh had followed the trail thus far, he halted and looked at his people.

"What say you?" he whispered. "Do you know whither this track leads?"

His companions nodded, but said never a word. They were obviously excited and ill at ease.

"What say you?" continued the Penghûlu. "Do we follow or not follow?"

"It is as you will, O Penghûlu," replied the oldest man of the party, speaking for his fellows. "We follow whithersoever you go."

"It is well," said the Penghûlu. "Come, let us go."

No more was said when this whispered colloquy was ended, and the trackers set down to the trail again silently and with redoubled caution.

The narrow path which the tiger had followed led on in the direction of the river-bank, and ere long the high wattled bamboo fence of a native compound became visible through the trees. Penghûlu Mat Saleh pointed at it, turning to his followers.

"See yonder," he said.

Again the little band moved forward, still tracing the slot of the tiger and the flecks of blood upon the pass. These led them to the gate of the compound, and through it, to the 'ârnan, or open space before the house. Here the spoor vanished at a spot where the rank spear-blades of the *lâlang* grass had been crushed to earth by the weight of some heavy body. To it the trail of the limping tiger led. Away from it there were no footprints, save those of the human beings who come and go through the untidy weeds and grasses which cloak the soil in a Malayan compound.

Penghûlu Mat Saleh and his followers exchanged troubled glances.

"Come, let us ascend into the house," said the former; and forthwith led the way up the stair-ladder of the dwelling where Haji Mi lived with his two sons, and whence a month or two before Patîmah had fled during the night time with a deadly fear in her eyes and an incredible story faltering upon her lips.

The Penghûlu and his people found Abas, one of the Haji's sons, sitting cross-legged in the outer apartment, preparing a quid of betel nut with elaborate care. The visitors squatted on the mats and exchanged with him the customary salutations. Then Penghûlu Mat Saleh said:

"I have come hither that I may see your father. Is he within the house?"

"He is," replied Abas laconically.

"Then, make known to him that I would have speech with him."

"My father is sick," said Abas in a surly tone, and again his visitors exchanged glances.

"What is that patch of blood in the *lâlang* grass before the house?" asked the Penghûlu conversationally, after a slight pause.

"We killed a goat yesternight," Abas answered.

"Have you the skin, O Abas?" enquired the Headman. "I am renewing the faces of my drums and would fain purchase it."

"The skin was mangy and therefore we cast it into the river," said Abas.

The conversation languished while the Penghûlu's followers pushed the clumsy wooden betel-box along the mat covered floor from one to the other, and silently prepared their quids.

"What ails your father?" asked the Penghûlu presently, returning to the charge.

"He is sick," a rough voice said suddenly, speaking from the curtained doorway which led into the inner apartment.

It was the elder of the two sons, Abdulrahman, who spoke. He held a sword in his hand, a kris was stuck in his girdle, and his face wore an ugly look. His words came harshly and gratingly with the foreign accent of the Korin-chi people. He continued to speak, still standing near the doorway.

"My father is sick, O Penghûlu," he said. "Moreover, the noise of your words disturbs him. He dèsires to slumber and be still. Descend out of the house. He cannot see you. Attend to these my words."

Abdulrahman's manner and the words he spoke were at once so rough and so defiant that the Headman saw that he would have to choose between a scuffle, which would certainly mean bloodshed, and an ignominious retreat. He was a mild old man, and he drew a monthly stipend from the Government of Pêrak. He did not wish to place this in jeopardy, and he knew that the white men entertained prejudices against bloodshed and homicide, even if the person slain was a wizard or the son of a wizard. He therefore decided in favour of retreat.

As they were climbing down the stair-ladder, Mat Tahir, one of the Penghûlu's men, plucked him by the sleeve and pointed to a spot beneath the house. Just below the place in the inner apartment where Haji All might be supposed to be lying stretched upon the mat of sickness, the ground was stained a dull red colour for a space of several inches in circumference. The floors of Malayan houses are made of laths of bamboo laid parallel one to another at regular intervals and lashed together with rattan. The interstices thus formed are convenient, as the slovenly Malays are thereby enabled to use the whole of the ground beneath the house as a slop-pail, waste-basket, and rubbish-heap. The red stain, situated where it was, had the appearance of blood—blood, moreover, from some one within the house whose wound had been recently washed and dressed. It might equally, of course, have been the rinsings of a spittoon reddened by the expectorated juice of the betel nut, but its stains are rarely seen in such large patches. Whatever the origin of the stain, the Penghûlu and his people were afforded no opportunity of examining it more closely, for Abdulrahman and Abas, truculent to the last, followed them out of the compound and barred the gate against them.

Then the Penghûlu, taking a couple of his people with him, set off on foot for Tanjong Mâlim in the neighbouring district of Bernam, where lived the white man under whose administrative charge the Slim valley had been placed. He went with many misgivings, for he had had some experience of the easy scepticism of white folk; and when he returned, more or less dissatisfied some days later, he learned that Haji Ali and his sons had disappeared. They had fled down river on a dark night, without a soul being made aware of their intended departure. They had not stayed to reap their crop, which even then was ripening in the fields; to dispose of their house and compound, upon which they had expended. not only labour, but "dollars of the whitest," as the Malay phrase has it; not even to collect their debts, which chanced to be rather numerous. This was the fact which struck the white district officer as by far the most improbable incident of any connected with the strange story of the were-tiger of Slim, and for the moment it seemed to him to admit of only one explanation. Haji Ali and his sons had been the victims of foul play. They had been quietly done to death by the simple villagers of Slim, and a cock-and-bull story had been trumped up to account for their disappearance.

The white man would probably still be holding fast to this theory, were it not that Haji Ali and his sons happened to turn up in quite another part of the Peninsula a few months later. They had nothing out of the way about them to mark them from their fellows, except that Haji Ali limped badly with his right leg.

Running Wolf

ALGERNON BLACKWOOD

The man who enjoys an adventure outside the general experience of the race, and imparts it to others, must not be surprised if he is taken for either a liar or a fool, as Malcolm Hyde, hotel clerk on a holiday, discovered in due course. Nor is 'enjoy' the word to use in describing his emotions; the word he chose was probably 'survive'.

When he first set eyes on Medicine Lake he was struck by its still, sparkling beauty, lying there in the vast Canadian backwoods; next, by its extreme loneliness; and, lastly—a good deal later, this—by its combination of beauty, loneliness, and singular atmosphere, due to the fact that it was the scene of adventure.

'It's fairly stiff with big fish,' said Morton of the Montreal Sporting Club. 'Spend your holidays there up Mattawa way, some fifteen miles west of Stony Creek. You'll have it all yourself except for an old Indian who's got a shack there. Camp on the east side—if you'll take a tip from me.' He then talked for half an hour about the wonderful sport; yet he was not otherwise very communicative, and did not

suffer questions gladly, Hyde noticed. Nor had he stayed there very long himself. If it was such a paradise as Morton, its discoverer and the most experienced rod in the province, claimed, why had he himself spent only three days there?

'Ran short of grub,' was the explanation offered; but to another friend he had mentioned briefly, 'flies' and to a third, so Hyde learned later, he gave the excuse that his half-breed 'took sick', necessitating a quick return to civilisation.

Hyde, however, cared little for the explanations; his interest in these came later. 'Stiff with fish' was the phrase he liked. He took the Canadian Pacific train to Mattawa, laid in his outfit at Stony Creek, and set off thence for the fifteen-mile canoe-trip without a care in the world.

Travelling light, the portages did not trouble him; the water was swift and easy, the rapids negotiable; everything came his way, as the saying is. Occasionally he saw big fish making for the deeper pools, and was sorely tempted to stop; but he resisted. He pushed on between the immense

world of forests that stretched for hundreds of miles, known to deer, bear, moose, and wolf, but strange to any echo of human tread, a deserted and primeval wilderness. The autumn day was calm, the water sang and sparkled, the blue sky hung cloudless over all, ablaze with Light. Toward evening he passed an old beaver-dam, rounded a little point, and had his first sight of Medicine Lake. He lifted his dripping paddle; the canoe shot with silent glide into calm water. He gave an exclamation of delight, for the loveliness caught his breath away.

Though primarily a sportsman, he was not insensible to beauty. The lake formed a crescent, perhaps four miles long, its width between a mile and half a mile. The slanting gold of sunset flooded it. No wind stirred its crystal surface. Here it had lain since the redskins' god first made it; here it would lie until he dried it up again. Towering spruce and hemlock trooped to its very edge, majestic cedars leaned down as if to drink, crimson sumachs shone in fiery patches, and maples gleamed orange and red beyond belief. The air was like wine, with the silence of a dream.

It was here the red men formerly 'made medicine', with all the wild ritual and tribal ceremony of an ancient day. But it was of Morton, rather than of Indians, that Hyde thought. If this lonely, hidden paradise was really stiff with big fish, he owed a lot to Morton for the information. Peace invaded him, but the excitement of the hunter lay below.

He looked about him with quick, practised eye for a camping-place before the sun sank below the forests and the half-lights came. The Indian's shack, lying in full sunshine on the eastern shore, he found at once; but the trees lay too thick about it for comfort, nor did he wish to be so close to its inhabitant. Upon the opposite side, however, an ideal clearing offered. This lay already in shadow, the huge forest darkening it toward evening; but the open space attracted. He paddled over and quickly examined it. The ground was hard and dry, he found, and a little brook ran tinkling down one side of it into the lake. This outfall, too, would be a good fishing spot. Also it was sheltered. A few low willows marked the mouth.

An experienced camper soon makes up his mind. It was

a perfect site, and some charred logs, with traces of former fires, proved that he was not the first to think so. Hyde was delighted. Then, suddenly, disappointment came to tinge his pleasure. His kit was landed, and preparations for putting up the tent were begun, when he recalled a detail that excitement had so far kept in the background of his mind—Morton's advice. But not Morton's only, for the storekeeper at Stony Creek reinforced it. The big fellow with straggling moustache and stooping shoulders, dressed in shirt and trousers, had handed him out a final sentence with the bacon, flour, condensed milk, and sugar. He had repeated Morton's half-forgotten words:

'Put yer tent on the east shore, I should,' he had said at parting.

He remembered Morton, too, apparently. 'A shortish fellow, brown as an Indian and fairly smelling of the woods. Travelling with Jake, the half-breed.' That assuredly was Morton. 'Didn't stay long, now, did he,' he added to himself in a reflective tone.

'Going Windy Lake way, are yer? Or Ten Mile Water maybe?' he had first inquired of Hyde.

'Medicine Lake.'

'Is that so?' the man said, as though he doubted it for some obscure reason. He pulled at his ragged moustache a moment. 'Is that so, now?' he repeated. And the final words followed him down-stream after a considerable pause—the advice about the best shore on which to put his tent.

All this now suddenly flashed back upon Hyde's mind with a tinge of disappointment and annoyance, for when two experienced men agreed, their opinion was nor to be lightly disregarded. He wished he had asked the storekeeper for more details. He looked about him, he reflected, he hesitated, His ideal camping-ground lay certainly on the forbidden shore. What in the world, he wondered, could be the objection to it?

But the light was fading; he must decide quickly one way or the other. After staring at his unpacked dunnage, and the tent, already half erected, he made up his mind with a muttered expression that consigned both Morton and the storekeeper to less pleasant places. 'They must have *some* reason,' he growled to himself; 'fellows like that usually know what they're talking about. I guess I'd better shift over to the other side—for to-night at any rate.'

He glanced across the water before actually reloading. No smoke rose from the Indian's shack. He had seen no sign of a canoe. The man, he decided, was away. Reluctantly, then, he left the good camping-ground and paddled across the lake, and half an hour later his tent was up, firewood collected, and two small trout were already caught for supper. But the bigger fish, he knew, lay waiting for him on the other side by the little out-fall, and he fell asleep at length on his bed of balsam boughs, annoyed and disappointed, yet wondering how a mere sentence could have persuaded him so easily against his own better judgment. He slept like the dead; the sun was well up before he stirred.

But his morning mood was a very different one. The brilliant light, the peace, the intoxicating air, all this was too exhilarating for the mind to harbour foolish fancies, and he marvelled that he could have been so weak the night before. No hesitation lay in him anywhere. He struck camp immediately after breakfast, paddled back across the strip of shining water, and quickly settled in upon the forbidden shore, as he now called it, with a contemptuous grin. And the more he saw of the spot, the better he liked it. There was plenty of wood, running water to drink, an open space about the tent, and there were no flies. The fishing, moreover, was magnificent. Morton's description was fully justified, and 'stiff with big fish' for once was not an exaggeration.

The useless hours of the early afternoon he passed dozing in the sun, or wandering through the underbrush beyond the camp. He found no sign of anything unusual. He bathed in a cool1 deep pool; he revelled in the lonely little paradise. Lonely it certainly was, but the loneliness was part of its charm; the stillness, the peace, the isolation of this beautiful backwoods lake delighted him. The silence was divine. He was entirely satisfied.

After a brew of tea, he strolled toward evening along the shore, looking for the first sign of a rising fish. A faint ripple on the water, with the lengthening shadows, made good conditions. *Plop* followed *plop*, as the big fellows rose, snatched at their food, and vanished into the depths. He hurried back. Ten minute later he had taken his rods and was gliding cautiously in the canoe through the quiet water.

So good was the sport, indeed, and so quickly did the big trout pile up in the bottom of the canoe, that despite the growing lateness, he found it hard to tear himself away. 'One more,' he said, 'and then I really will go.' He landed that 'one more', and was in the act of taking off the hook, when the deep silence of the evening was curiously disturbed. He became abruptly aware that some one watched him. A pair of eyes, it seemed, were fixed upon him from some point in the surrounding shadows.

Thus, at least, he interpreted the odd disturbance in his happy mood; for thus he felt it. The feeling stole over him without the slightest warning. He was not alone. The slippery big trout dropped from his fingers. He sat motionless, and stared about him.

Nothing stirred; the ripple on the lake had died away; there was no wind; the forest lay a single purple mass of shadow; the yellow sky, fast fading, threw reflections that troubled the eye and made distances uncertain. But there was no sound, no movement; he saw no figure anywhere. Yet he knew that some one watched him, and a wave of quite unreasoning terror gripped him. The nose of the canoe was against the bank. In a moment, and instinctively, he shoved it off and paddled into deeper water. The watcher, it came to him also instinctively, was quite close to him upon that bank. But where? And who? Was it the Indian?

Here, in deeper water, and some twenty yards from the shore, he paused and strained both sight and hearing to find some possible clue. He felt half ashamed, now that the first strange feeling passed a little. But the certainty remained. Absurd as it was, he felt positive that some one watched him with concentrated and intent regard. Every fibre in his being told him so; and though he could discover no figure, no new outline on the shore, he could even have sworn in which clump of willow bushes the hidden person crouched and stared. His attention seemed drawn to that particular dump.

The water dripped slowly from his paddle, now lying across the thwarts. There was no other sound. The canvas of his tent gleamed dimly. A star or two were out. He waited. Nothing happened.

Then, as suddenly as it had come, the feeling passed, and he knew that the person who had been watching him intently had gone. It was as if a current had been turned off; the normal world flowed back; the landscape emptied as if some one had left a room. The disagreeable feeling left him at the same time, so that he instantly turned the canoe in to the shore again, landed, and, paddle in hand, went over to examine the clump of willows he had singled out as the place of concealment. There was no one there, of course, nor any trace of recent human occupancy. No leaves, no branches stirred, nor was a single twig displaced; his keen and practised sight detected no sign of tracks upon the ground. Yet, for all that, he felt positive that a little time ago some one had crouched among these very leaves and watched him. He remained absolutely convinced of it. The watcher, whether Indian hunter, stray lumberman, or wandering half-breed, had now withdrawn, a search was useless, and dusk was falling. He returned to his little camp, more disturbed perhaps than he cared to acknowledge. He cooked his supper, hung up his catch on a string, so that no prowling animal could get at it during the night, and prepared to make himself comfortable until bedtime. Unconsciously, he built a bigger fire than usual and found himself peering over·his pipe into the deep shadows beyond the firelight, straining his ears to catch the slightest sound. He remained generally on the alert in a way that was new to him.

A man under such conditions and in such a place need not know discomfort until the sense of loneliness strikes him as too vivid a reality. Loneliness in a backwoods camp brings charm, pleasure, and a happy sense of calm until, and unless, it comes too near. It should remain an ingredient only among other conditions; it should not be directly, vividly noticed. Once it has crept within short range, however, it may easily cross the narrow line between comfort and discomfort, and darkness is an undesirable time for the transition. A curious dread may easily follow—the dread lest the loneliness suddenly be disturbed, and the solitary human feel himself open to attack.

For Hyde, now, this transition had been already accomplished; the too intimate sense of his loneliness had shifted abruptly into the worst condition of no longer being quite alone. It was an awkward moment, and the hotel clerk realised his position exactly. He did not quite like it. He sat there, with his back to the blazing logs, a very visible object in the light, while all about him the darkness of the forest lay like an impenetrable wall. He could not see a yard beyond the small circle of his camp-fire; the silence about him was like the silence of the dead. No leaf rustled, no wave lapped; he himself sat motionless as a log.

Then again he became suddenly aware that the person who watched him had returned, and that same intent and concentrated gaze as before was fixed upon him where he lay. There was no warning; he heard no stealthy tread or snapping of dry twigs, yet the owner of those steady eyes was very close to him, probably not a dozen feet away. This sense of proximity was overwhelming.

It is unquestionable that a shiver ran down his spine. This time, moreover, he felt positive that the man crouched just beyond the firelight, the distance he himself could see being nicely calculated, and straight in front of him. For some minutes he sat without stirring a single muscle, yet with each muscle ready and alert, straining his eyes in vain to pierce the darkness, but only succeeding in dazzling his sight with the reflected light. Then, as he shifted his position slowly, cautiously, to obtain another angle of vision, his heart gave two big thumps against his ribs and the hair seemed to rise on his scalp with the sense of cold that gave him goose-flesh. In the darkness facing him he saw two small and greenish circles that were certainly a pair of eyes, yet not the eyes of Indian hunter, or of any human being. It was a pair of animal eyes that stared so fixedly at him out of the night. And this certainty had an immediate and natural effect upon him.

For, at the menace of those eyes, the fears of millions of long dead hunters since the dawn of time woke in him. Hotel clerk though he was, heredity surged through him in an automatic wave of instinct. His hand groped for a weapon. His fingers fell on the iron head of his small camp axe, and at once he was himself again. Confidence returned; the vague, superstitious dread was gone. This was a bear or wolf that smelt his catch and came to steal it. With beings of that sort he knew instinctively how to deal, yet admitting, by this very instinct, that his original dread had been of quite another kind.

'I'll damned quick find out what it is,' he exclaimed aloud, and snatching a burning brand from the fire, he hurled it with good aim straight at the eyes of the beast before him.

The bit of pitch-pine fell in a shower of sparks that lit the dry grass this side of the animal, flared up a moment, then died quickly down again. But in that instant of bright illumination he saw clearly what his unwelcome visitor was. A big timber wolf sat on its hindquarters, staring steadily at him through the firelight. He saw its legs and shoulders, he saw its hair, he saw also the big hemlock trunks lit up behind it, and the willow scrub on each side. It formed a vivid, clear-cut picture shown in clear detail by the momentary blaze. To his amazement, however, the wolf did not turn and bolt away from the burning log, but withdrew a few yards only, and sat there again on its haunches, staring, staring as before. Heavens, how it stared! He 'shoo-ed' it, but without effect; it did not budge.

He did not waste another good log on it, for his fear was dissipated now; a timber wolf was a timber wolf, and it might sit there as long as it pleased, provided it did not try to steal his catch. No alarm was in him any more. He knew that wolves were harmless in the summer and autumn, and even when 'packed' in the winter they would attack a man only when suffering desperate hunger. So he lay and watched the beast, threw bits of stick in its direction, even talked to it, wondering only that it never moved. 'You can stay there for ever, if you like,' he remarked to it aloud, 'for you cannot get at my fish, and the rest of the grub I shall take into the tent with me!'

The creature blinked its bright green eyes, but made no move. Why, then, if his fear was gone, did he think of certain things as he rolled himself in the Hudson Bay blankets before going sleep? The immobility of the animal was strange, its refusal to turn and bolt was still stranger. Never before had he know, a wild creature that was not afraid of fire. Why did it sit and watch him, as with purpose in its gleaming eyes? How had he felt its presence earlier and instantly? A timber wolf, especially a solitary wolf, was a timid thing, yet this one feared neither man nor fire. Now, as he lay there wrapped in his blankets inside the cosy tent, it sat outside beneath the stars, beside the fading embers, the wind chilly in its fur, the ground cooling beneath its planted paws, watching him, steadily watching him, perhaps until the dawn.

It was unusual, it was strange. Having neither imagination nor tradition, he called upon no store of racial visions. Matter of fact, a hotel clerk on a fishing holiday, he lay there in blankets, merely wondering and puzzled. A timber wolf was a timber wolf and nothing more. Yet this timber wolf—the idea haunted him—was different. In a word, the deeper part his original uneasiness remained. He tossed about, he shivered sometimes in his broken sleep; he did not go out to see, but he woke early and unrefreshed.

Again with the sunshine and the morning wind, however, the incident of the night before was forgotten, almost unreal. His hunting zeal was uppermost. The tea and fish were delicious, his pipe had never tasted so good, the glory of this lonely lake amid primeval forests went to his head a little; he was a hunter before the Lord, and nothing else. He tried the edge of the lake, and in the excitement of playing a big fish, knew suddenly that *it,* the wolf, was there. He paused with the rod, exactly as if struck. He looked about him, he looked in a definite direction. The brilliant sunshine made every smallest detail clear and sharp—boulders of granite, burned stems, crimson sumach, pebbles along the shore in neat, separate detail—without revealing where the watcher hid. Then, his sight wandering farther inshore among the tangled undergrowth, he suddenly picked up the familiar, half-expected outline. The wolf was lying behind a granite boulder, so that only the head, the muzzle, and the eyes were visible. It merged in its background. Had he not known it was a wolf, he could never have separated it from the landscape. The eyes shone in the sunlight.

There it lay. He looked straight at it. Their eyes, in fact, actually met full and square. 'Great Scott!' he exclaimed aloud, 'why, it's like looking at a human being!'

From that moment, unwittingly, he established a singular personal relation with the beast. And what followed confirmed this undesirable impression, for the animal rose instantly and came down in leisurely fashion to the shore, where it stood looking back at him. It stood and stared into his eyes like some great wild dog, so that he was aware of a new and almost incredible sensation—that it courted recognition.

'Well! Well!' he exclaimed again, relieving his feelings by addressing it aloud, 'if this doesn't beat everything I ever saw! What d'you want, anyway?'

He examined it now more carefully. He had never seen a wolf so big before; it was a tremendous beast, a nasty customer to tackle, he reflected, if it ever came to that. It stood there absolutely fearless, and full of confidence. In the clear sunlight he took in every detail of it—a huge, shaggy, lean-flanked timber wolf, its wicked eyes staring straight into his own, almost with a kind of purpose in them. He saw its great jaws, its teeth, and its tongue hung out, dropping saliva a little. And yet the idea of its savagery, its fierceness, was very little in him.

He was amazed and puzzled beyond belief. He wished the Indian would come back. He did not understand this strange behaviour in an animal. Its eyes, the odd expression in them, gave him a queer, unusual, difficult feeling. Had his nerves gone wrong, he almost wondered.

The beast stood on the shore and looked at him. He wished for the first time that he had brought a rifle. With a resounding smack he brought his paddle down flat upon the water, using all his strength, till the echoes rang as from a pistol-shot that was audible from one end of the lake to the other. The wolf never stirred. He shouted, but the beast remained unmoved. He blinked his eyes, speaking as to a dog, a domestic animal, a creature accustomed to human ways. It blinked its eyes in return.

At length, increasing his distance from the shore, he continued fishing, and the excitement of the marvellous sport held his attention—his surface attention, at any rate. At times he almost forgot the attendant beast; yet whenever he looked up, he saw it there. And worse; when he slowly paddled home again, he observed it trotting along the shore as though to keep him company. Crossing a little bay, he spurted, hoping to reach the other point before his undesired and undesirable attendant. Instantly the brute broke into that rapid, tireless lope that, except on ice, can run down anything on four legs in the woods. When he reached the distant point, the wolf was waiting for him. He raised his paddle from the water, pausing a moment for reflection; for his very close attention—there were dusk and night yet to come—he certainly did not relish. His camp was near; he had to land; he felt uncomfortable even in the sunshine of broad day, when, to his keen relief, about half a mile from the tent, he saw the creature suddenly stop and sit down in the open. He waited a moment, then paddled on. It did not follow. There was no attempt to move; it merely sat and watched him. After a few hundred yards, he looked back. It was still sitting where he left it. And the absurd, yet significant, feeling came to him that the beast divined his thought, his anxiety, his dread, and was now showing him, as well as it could, that it entertained no hostile feeling and did not meditate attack.

He turned the canoe toward the shore; he landed; he cooked his supper in the dusk; the animal made no sign. Not far away it certainly lay and watched, but it did not advance. And to Hyde, observant now in a new way, came one sharp, vivid reminder of the strange atmosphere into which his commonplace personality had strayed: he suddenly recalled that his relations with the beast, already established, had progressed distinctly a stage further. This startled him, yet without the accompanying alarm he must certainly have felt twenty-four hours before. He had an understanding with the wolf. He was aware of friendly thoughts toward it. He even went so far as to set out a few big fish on the spot where he had first seen it sitting the previous night. 'If he comes,' he thought, 'he is welcome to them, I've got plenty, anyway.' He thought of it now as 'he'.

Yet the wolf made no appearance until he was in the act of entering his tent a good deal later. It was close on ten o'clock, whereas nine was his hour, and late at that, for turning in. He had, therefore, unconsciously been waiting for him. Then, as he was closing the flap, he saw the eyes close to where he had placed the fish. He waited, hiding himself, and expecting to hear sounds of munching jaws; but all was silence. Only the eyes glowed steadily out of the background of pitch darkness. He closed the flap. He had no slightest fear. In ten minutes he was sound asleep.

He could not have slept very long, for when he woke up he could see the shine of a faint red light through the canvas, and the fire had not died down completely. He rose and cautiously peeped out. The air was very cold, he saw breath. But he also saw the wolf, for it had come in, and was sitting by the dying embers, not two yards away from where he crouched behind the flap. And this time, at these very close quarters, there was something in the attitude of the big wild thing that caught his attention with a vivid thrill of startled surprise and a sudden shock of cold that held him spell-bound. He stared, unable to believe his eyes; for the wolf's attitude conveyed to him something familiar that at first was unable to explain. Its pose reached him in the terms of another thing with which he was entirely at home. What was it? Did his senses betray him? Was he still asleep and dreaming?

Then, suddenly, with a start of uncanny recognition, he knew. Its attitude was that of a dog. Having found the clue, his mind then made an awful leap. For it was, after all, no dog its appearance aped, but something nearer to himself, and more familiar still. Good heavens! It sat there with the pose, the attitude, the gesture in repose of something almost human. And then, with a second shock of biting wonder, it came to him like a revelation. The wolf sat beside that camp-fire as a man might sit.

Before he could weigh his extraordinary discovery, before he could examine it in detail or with care, the animal, sitting in this ghastly fashion, seemed to feel his eyes fixed on it. It slowly turned and looked him in the face, and for the first time Hyde felt a fullblooded superstitious fear flood through his entire being. He seemed transfixed with that nameless terror that is said to attack human beings who suddenly face the dead, finding themselves bereft of speech and movement. This moment of paralysis certainly occurred. Its passing, however, was as singular as its advent. For almost at once he was aware of something beyond and above this mockery of human attitude and pose, something that ran along unaccustomed nerves and reached his feeling, even perhaps his heart. The revulsion was extraordinary, its result still more extraordinary and unexpected. Yet the fact remains. He was aware of another thing that had the effect of stilling his terror as soon as it was born. He was aware of appeal, silent, half expressed, yet vastly pathetic. He saw in the savage eyes beseeching, even a yearning, expression that changed his mood as by magic from dread to natural sympathy. The great grey brute, symbol of cruel ferocity, sat there beside his dying fire and appealed for help.

The gulf betwixt animal and human seemed in that instant bridged. It was, of course, incredible. Hyde, sleep still possibly clinging to his inner being with the shades and half shapes of dream yet about his soul, acknowledged, how he knew not, the amazing fact. He found himself nodding to the brute in half consent, and instantly, without more ado, the lean grey shape rose like a wraith and trotted off swiftly, but with stealthy tread, into the background of the night.

When Hyde woke in the morning his first impression was that he must have dreamed the entire incident. His practical nature asserted itself. There was a bite in the fresh autumn air; the bright sun allowed no half lights anywhere; he felt brisk in mind and body. Reviewing what had happened, he came to the conclusion that it was utterly vain to speculate; no possible explanation of the animal's behaviour occurred to him: he was dealing with something entirely outside his experience. His fear, however, had completely left him. The odd sense of friendliness remained. The beast had a definite purpose, and he himself was included in that purpose. His sympathy held good.

But with the sympathy there was also an intense curiosity. 'If it shows itself again,' he told himself, 'I'll go up close and find out what it wants.' The fish laid out the night before had not been touched.

It must have been a full hour after breakfast when he next saw the brute; it was standing on the edge of the clearing, looking at him in the way now become familiar. Hyde immediately picked up his axe and advanced toward it boldly, keeping his eyes fixed straight upon its own. There was nervousness in him, but kept well under; nothing betrayed it; step by step he drew nearer until some ten yards separated them. The wolf had not stirred a muscle as yet. Its jaws hung open, its eyes observed him intently; it allowed him to approach without a sign of what its mood might be. Then, with these ten yards between them, it turned abruptly and moved slowly off, looking back first over one shoulder and then over the other, exactly as a dog might do, to see if he was following.

A singular journey it was they then made together, animal and man. The trees surrounded them at once, for they left the lake behind them, entering the tangled bush beyond. The beast, Hyde noticed, obviously picked the easiest track for him to follow; for obstacles that meant nothing to the four-legged expert, yet were difficult for a man, were carefully avoided with an almost uncanny skill, while yet the general direction was accurately kept. Occasionally there were windfalls to be surmounted; but though the wolf bounded over these with it was always waiting for the man on the other side after he had laboriously climbed over. Deeper and deeper into the heart of the lonely forest they penetrated in this singular fashion, cutting across the arc of the lake's crescent, it seemed to Hyde; for after two miles or so, he recognised the big rocky bluff that overhung the water at its northern end. This outstanding bluff he had seen from his camp, one side of it falling sheer into the water; it was probably the spot, he imagined, where the Indians held their medicine-making ceremonies, for it stood out in isolated fashion, and its top formed a private plateau not easy of access. And it was here, close to a big spruce at the foot of the bluff upon the forest side, that the wolf stopped suddenly and for the first time since its appearance gave audible expression to its feelings. It sat down on its haunches, lifted its muzzle with open jaws, and gave vent to a subdued and long-drawn howl that was more like the wail of a dog than the fierce barking cry associated with a wolf,

By this time Hyde had lost not only fear, but caution too; nor, oddly enough, did this warning howl, revive a sign of unwelcome emotion in him. In that curious sound he detected the same message that the eyes conveyed—appeal for help. He paused, nevertheless, a little startled, and while the wolf sat waiting for him, he looked about him quickly. There was young timber here; it had once been a small clearing, evidently. Axe and fire had done their work, but there was evidence to an experienced eye that it was Indians and not white men who had once been busy here. Some part of the medicine ritual, doubtless, took place in the little clearing, thought the man, as he advanced again towards his patient leader. The end of their queer journey, he felt, was close at hand.

He had not taken two steps before the animal got up and moved very slowly in the direction of some low bushes that formed a clump just beyond. It entered these, first looking back to make sure that its companion watched. The bushes hid it; a moment later it emerged again. Twice it performed this pantomime, each time, as it reappeared, standing still and staring at the man with as distinct an expression of appeal in the eyes as an animal may compass, probably. Its excitement, meanwhile, certainly increased, and this excitement was, with equal certainty, communi-cated to the man. Hyde made up his mind quickly. Gripping his axe tightly, and ready to use it at the first hint of malice, he moved slowly nearer to the bushes, wondering with something of a tremor what would happen.

If he expected to be startled, his expectation was at once fulfilled; but it was the behaviour of the beast that made him jump. It positively frisked about him like a happy dog. It frisked for joy. Its excitement was intense, yet from its open mouth no sound was audible. With a sudden leap, then, it bounded past him into the clump of bushes, against whose very edge he stood, and began scraping vigorously at the ground. Hyde stood and stared, amazement and interest now banishing all his nervousness, even when the beast, in its violent scraping, actually touched his body with its own. He had, perhaps, the feeling that he was in a dream, one of those fantastic dreams in which things may happen without involving an adequate surprise; for otherwise the manner of scraping and scratching at the ground must have seemed an impossible phenomenon. No wolf, no dog certainly, used its paws in the way those paws were working. Hyde had the odd, distressing sensation that it was hands, not paws, he watched. And yet, somehow, the natural, adequate surprise he should have felt was absent. The strange action seemed not entirely unnatural. In his heart some deep hidden spring of sympathy and pity stirred instead. He was aware of pathos.

The wolf stopped in its task and looked up into his face. Hyde acted without hesitation then. Afterwards he was wholly at a loss to explain his own conduct. It seemed he knew what to do, divined what was asked, expected of him. Between his mind and the dumb desire yearning through the savage animal there was intelligent and intelligible communication. He cut a stake and sharpened it, for the stones would blunt his axe-edge. He entered the clump of bushes to complete the digging his four-legged companion had begun. And while he worked, though he did not forget the close proximity of the wolf, he paid no attention to it; often his back was turned as he stooped over the laborious clearing away of the hard earth; no uneasiness or sense of danger was in him any more. The wolf sat outside the clump and watched the operations. Its concentrated attention, its patience, its intense eagerness, the gentleness and docility of the grey, fierce, and probably hungry brute, its obvious pleasure and satisfaction, too, at having won the human to its mysterious purpose—these were colours in the strange picture that Hyde thought of later when dealing with the human herd in his hotel again. At the moment he was aware chiefly of pathos and affection. The whole business was, of course, not to be believed, but that discovery came later, too, when telling it to others.

The digging continued for fully half an hour before his labour was rewarded by the discovery of a small whitish object. He picked it up and examined it—the finger-bone of a man. Other discoveries then followed quickly and in quantity. The *cache* was laid bare. He collected nearly the complete skeleton. The skull however, he found last, and might not have found at all but for the guidance of his strangely alert companion. It lay some few yards away from the central hole now dug, and the wolf stood nuzzling the ground with its nose before Hyde understood that he was meant to dig exactly in that spot for it. Between the beast's very paws his stake struck hard upon it. He scraped the earth from the bone and examined it carefully. It was perfect, save for the fact that some wild animal had gnawed it, the teeth-marks being still plainly visible. Close beside it lay the rusty iron head of a tomahawk. This and the smallness of the bones confirmed him in his judgment that it was the skeleton not of a white man, but of an Indian.

During the excitement of the discovery of the bones one by one, and finally of the skull, but, more especially, during the period of intense interest while Hyde was examining them, he had paid little if any attention to the wolf. He was aware that it sat and watched him, never moving its keen eyes for a single moment from the actual operations, but sign or movement it made none at all. He knew that it was pleased and satisfied, he knew also that he had now fulfilled its purpose in a great measure. The further intuition that now came to him, derived, he felt positive, from his companion's dumb desire, was perhaps the cream of the entire experience to him. Gathering the bones together in his coat, he carried them, together with the tomahawk, to the foot of the big spruce where the animal had first topped. His leg actually touched the creature's muzzle as he passed. It turned its head to watch, but did not follow, nor did it move a muscle while he prepared the platform of boughs upon which he then laid the poor worn bones of an Indian who had been killed, doubtless, in sudden attack or ambush, and to whose remains had been denied the last grace of proper tribal burial. He wrapped the bones in bark; he laid the tomahawk beside the skull; he lit the circular fire round the pyre, and the blue smoke rose upward into the clear bright sunshine of the Canadian autumn morning till it was lost among the mighty trees far overhead.

In the moment before actually lighting the little fire he had turned to note what his companion did. It sat five yards away, he saw, gazing intently, and one of its front paws was raised a little from the ground. It made no sign of any kind. He finished the work, becoming so absorbed in it that he had eyes for nothing but the tending and guarding of his careful ceremonial fire. It was only when the platform of boughs collapsed, laying their charred burden gently on the fragrant earth among the soft wood ashes, that he turned again, as though to show the wolf what he had done, and seek, perhaps, some look of satisfaction in its curiously expressive eyes. But the place he searched was empty. The wolf had gone.

He did not see it again; it gave no sign of its presence where; he was not watched. He fished as before, wandered through the bush about his camp, sat smoking round his fire after dark, and slept peacefully in his cosy little tent. He was not disturbed. No howl was ever audible in the distant forest, no twig snapped beneath a stealthy tread, he saw no eyes. The wolf that behaved like a man had gone for ever.

It was the day before he left that Hyde, noticing smoke rising from the shack across the lake, paddled over to exchange a word or two with the Indian, who had evidently now returned. The Redskin came down to meet him as he landed, but it was soon plain that he spoke very little English. He emitted the familiar grunts at first; then bit by bit Hyde stirred his limited vocabulary into action. The net result, however, was slight enough though it was certainly direct:

'You camp there?' the man asked, pointing to the other side.

'Yes.'

'Wolf come?'

'Yes.'

'You see wolf?'

'Yes.'

The Indian stared at him fixedly a moment, a keen, wondering look upon his coppery, creased face.

'You 'fraid wolf?' he asked after a moment's pause.

'No,' replied Hyde, truthfully. He knew it was useless to ask questions of his own, though he was eager for information. The other would have told him nothing. It was sheer luck that the man had touched on the subject at all, and Hyde realised that his own best role was merely to answer, but to ask no questions. Then, suddenly, the Indian became comparatively voluble. There was awe in his voice and manner.

'Him no wolf. Him big medicine wolf. Him spirit wolf.'

Whereupon he drank the tea the other had brewed for him, closed his lips tightly, and said no more. His outline was discernible on the shore, rigid and motionless, an hour later, when Hyde's canoe turned the corner of the lake three miles away, and landed to make the portages up the first rapid of his homeward stream.

It was Morton who, after some persuasion, supplied further details of what he called the legend. Some hundred years before, the tribe that lived in the territory beyond the lake began their annual medicine-making ceremonies on the big rocky bluff at the northern end; but no medicine could be made. The spirits, declared the chief medicine man, would not answer. They were offended. An investigation followed. It was discovered that a young brave had recently killed a wolf, a thing strictly forbidden, since the wolf was the totem animal of the tribe. To make matters worse, the name of the guilty man was Running Wolf. The offence being unpardonable, the man was cursed and driven from the tribe:

'Go out. Wander alone among the woods, and if we see you we slay you. Your bones shall be scattered in the forest, and your spirit shall not enter the Happy Hunting Grounds till one of another race shall find and bury them.'

'Which meant,' explained Morton laconically, his only comment on the story, 'probably for ever.'

The Hidden Beast

J.D. BERESFORD

His house is the last in the village. Towards the forest the houses become more and more scattered, reaching out to the wild of the wood as if they yearned to separate themselves from the swarm that clusters about the church and the inn. And his house has taken so long a stride from the others that it is held to the village by no more than the slender thread of a long footpath. Yet the house is set with its face towards us, and has an air of resolutely holding on to the safety of our common life, as if dismayed at its boldness in swimming so far it had turned and desperately grasped the life-line of that footpath.

He lived alone, a strange man, surly and reticent. Some said that he had a sinister look; and on those rare occasions when he joined us at the inn, after sunset, he sat aside and spoke little.

I was surprised when, as we came out of the inn one night, he took my arm and asked mc if I would go home with him. The moon was at the full, and the black shadows of the dispersing crowd that lunged down the street seemed to gesticulate an alarm of weird dismay. The village was momentarily mad with the clatter of footsteps and the noise of laughter, and somewhere down towards the forest a dog was baying.

I wondered if I had not misunderstood him.

As he watched my hesitation his face pleaded with me. "There are times when a man is glad of company," he said.

We spoke little as we passed through the village towards the silences of his lonely house. But when we came to the footpath he stopped and looked back.

"I live between two worlds," he said, "the wild and. . ."—he paused before he rejected the obvious antithesis, and concluded—"the restrained."

"Are we so restrained?" I asked, staring at the huddle of black-and-silver houses clinging to their refuge on the hill.

He murmured something about a "compact," and my thoughts turned to the symbol of the chalk-white church-tower that dominated the honeycomb of the village.

"The compact of public opinion," he said more boldly.

My imagination lagged. I was thinking less of him than of the transfiguration of the familiar scene before me. I did not remember ever to have studied it thus under the reflections of a full moon. An echo of his word, differently accented, drifted through my mind. I saw our life as being in truth compact, little and limited.

He took up his theme again when we had entered the house and were facing each other across the table, in a room that looked out over the forest. The shutters were unfastened, the window open, and I could see how, on the further shore of the waste-lands, the light feebly ebbed and died against the black cliff of the wood.

"We have to choose between freedom and safety," he said. "The individual is too wild and dangerous for the common life. He must make his agreement with the community; submit to become a member of the people's body. But I"—he paused and laughed—"I have taken the liberty of looking out of the back window."

While he spoke I had been aware of a sound that seemed to come from below the floor of the room in which we were sitting. And when he laughed I fancied that I heard the response of a snuffling cry.

He looked at me mockingly across the table.

"It's an echo from the jungle," he said. "Some trick of reflected sound. I can always hear it in this room at night."

I shivered and stood up. "I prefer the safety of our common life," I told him. "It may be that I have a limited mind and am afraid, but I find my happiness in the joys of security and shelter. The wild terrifies me."

"A limited mind?" he commented. "Probably it is rather that you lack a fire in the blood."

I was glad to leave him, and he on his part made no effort to detain me.

It was not long after this visit of mine that the people first began to whisper about him in the village. At the beginning they brought no charge against him, talking only of his strangeness and of his separation from our common interests. But presently I heard a story of some fierce wild animal that he caged and tortured in the prison of his house. One said that he had heard it screaming in the night, and another that he had heard it beating against the door. And some argued that it was a threat to our safety, since the beast might escape and make its way into the village; and some that such brutality, even though it were to a wild animal, could not be tolerated. But I wondered inwardly whether the affair were any business of ours so long as he kept the beast to himself.

I was a member of the Council that year, and so took part in the voting when presently the case was laid before us. But no vote of mine would have helped him if I had dared to overcome my reluctance and speak in his favour. For whatever reservations may have been secretly withheld by the members of the Council, they were unanimous in condemning him.

We went, six of us, in full daylight, to search his house. He received us with a laugh, and told us that we might seek at our leisure. But though we sought high and low, peering and tapping, we found no evidence that any wild thing had ever been concealed there.

And within a month of the day of our search he left the village.

I saw him alone once before he went, and he told me that he had chosen for the wild and freedom, that he could no longer endure to be held to the village even by the thread of the footpath.

But he did not thank me for having allowed the search of his house to be conducted by daylight, although he knew that I at least was sure no echo of the forest could be heard in that little room of his save in the transfigured hours between the dusk and the dawn.

John Barron was frankly puzzled. He could not make it out at all. He had lived in the place all his life—save for the few years spent at Rugby and Oxford—and nothing of the sort had happened to him before. His people had occupied the estate for generations past; and there was neither record nor tradition of anything of the kind. He did not like it at all. It seemed like an intrusion upon the respectability of his family. And John Barron had a very good opinion of his family.

Certainly he was entitled to have a good opinion of it. He came from a good stock: his ancestry was one to be proud of: his coat of arms had quarterings that few could display: and his immediate forbears had kept up the reputation of their ancestors. He himself could boast a career without reproach: the short time he had spent at the bar was marked by considerable success and still more promise—a promise cut short by the death of his father and his recall to Bannerton to take up the duties of squire, magistrate and county magnate.

In the eyes of his friends and of people generally, he was a man to be envied. He had an ample fortune, a delightful house and estate, hosts of friends, and the best of health. What could a man wish for more? The ladies of the neighbourhood said that he lacked only one thing, and that was a wife. But it may be that they were not entirely unprejudiced judges—the unmarried ones, at any rate. But up till the time of our story John Barron had shown no sign

THE VOICE IN THE NIGHT

W. J. WINTLE, F.Z.S.

of marrying. He used to boast that he was neither married, nor engaged, nor courting, nor had he his eye on anyone.

And now this annoyance had come to trouble and puzzle him! What had he done to deserve it? True, he might take the comfort to his soul that it was no immediate concern of his. The affair had not happened to any member of his family or household. Why then should he not mind his own business? But he felt that it was his business. It had happened within the bounds of his manor and almost within sight of his windows. If anything tangible could be connected with it, he was the magistrate whose duty it

would be to investigate the matter. But up till the present there was nothing tangible for him to deal with.

The whole business was a mystery: and John Barron disapproved of mysteries. Mysteries savoured of detectives and the police court. When unravelled they usually proved to be sordid and undesirable; and when not unravelled they brought with them a vague sense of discomfort and of danger. As a lawyer he held that mysteries had no right to exist. That they should continue to exist was a sort of reflection on the profession, as well as upon the public intelligence.

And yet here was the parish of Bannerton in the hands of a mystery of the first water. As a magistrate, John Barron had officially looked into the matter; and, as a lawyer, he had spent some hours in carefully considering it; but entirely without any practical result. The mystery was not merely unsolved: it had even thickened!

This was the history with which he was faced. A fortnight before, the occupants of a cottage on the outskirts of the village—a gardener and his wife-had left their little daughter of three years old in the house while they went on an errand. The child was soundly asleep in its cot; and they locked the door as they went out. They were absent about twenty minutes; and were nearing the house when they heard the screams of a child. The father rushed forward, unlocked the door, and the two parents entered together.

The child's cot was in the living room into which the front door opened. As they went in, the screams ceased and a terrible gasping sound took their place. Then they saw that the cot was hidden by some dark body that seemed to be lying on it. This they hardly saw, though they, were quite clear that it was there, for it seemed to melt away like a mist when they rushed into the room. Certainly it was nothing solid, for it completely disappeared without a sound. It could not have dashed out through the door, for the parents were hardly clear of the door when it vanished.

They had returned only just in time to save the life of the child. At first it was doubtful if they were in time, for the doctor held out little hope. But after a day or two, the child took a turn for the better, and was now out of danger. It had evidently been attacked by some kind of savage animal, which had torn at its throat and had only just failed to sever the arteries of the neck. In the opinion of the doctor and of John Barron himself, the wounds suggested that the assailant had been a very large dog. But it was strange that a dog on such size had not done far worse damage. One might have expected that it would have killed the child with a single bite.

But was it a dog? If so, how did it enter the house? The door in front was locked, as we have seen; that at the back was bolted; and all the windows were shut and fastened. There was no apparent way by which it could possibly have got into the house. And we have already seen that its way of going was equally mysterious.

The most careful examination of the room and of the premises generally failed to yield the smallest clue. Nothing had been disturbed or damaged, and there were no footprints. The only thing at all unusual was the presence of an earthy or mouldy odour which was noticed by the doctor when he entered the room and also by some other persons who were on the scene soon afterwards. John Barron had the same impression when he went to the cottage some hours later, but the odour was then so faint that he could not be at all sure about its existence.

By way of embroidery to the story came two or three items of local gossip of the usual sort. An old woman near by said that she was looking out of her window to see the state of the weather a little earlier in the evening, when she saw a huge black dog run across the lane and go in the direction of the cottage. According to her tale, the dog limped as if lame or very much tired.

Three people said they had been disturbed for two or three nights previous by the howling of a dog in the distance; and a farmer in the parish complained that his sheep had apparently been chased about the field during the night by some wandering dog. He loudly vowed vengeance on dogs in general; but, as none of the sheep had been worried, nobody took much notice. All these tales came to the ears of John Barron; but to a man accustomed to weigh evidence they were negligible.

But he attached much more importance to another piece of evidence, if such it might be called. As the injured child began to get better, and was able to talk, an attempt was made to find out if it could give any information about the attack. As it had been asleep when attacked, it did not see the arrival of its assailant; and the only thing it could tell was, "Nasty, ugly lady bit me!" This seemed absurd; but, when asked about the dog, it persisted in saying, "No dog. Nasty ugly lady!"

The parents were inclined to laugh at what they thought a mere childish fancy; but the trained lawyer was considerably impressed by it. To him there were three facts available. The wounds seemed to have been caused by a large dog: the child said she had been bitten by an ugly lady: and the parents had actually seen the form of the assailant. Unfortunately it had disappeared before they could make out any details; but they said it was about the size of a very large dog, and was dark in colour.

The local gossip was of small importance and was such as might be expected under the circumstances. But, for what it was worth, it all pointed to a dog or dog-like animal. But how could it have entered the closed house; how did it get away; and why did the child persist in her story of an ugly lady? The only theory that would at all fit the case was that supplied by the old Norse legends of the werewolf. But who believes such stories now?

So it was not to be wondered at that John Barron was puzzled. He was rather annoyed too. Bannerton had its average amount of crime; but it was in a small way and could generally be disposed of at the petty sessions. It was not often that a case had to be sent to the assizes, and the newspapers seldom got any sensational copy from the quiet little place. He reflected with some small satisfaction that it was lucky the child had not died; for in that case there must have been an inquest and the inevitable publicity. If his suspicions were well founded, the case would have yielded something far more sensational than generally falls to the lot of the local reporter.

But a day or two later he had more to ponder over. Things had developed—and in a way that he did not like. The farmer had again complained that his sheep had been chased about the field during the night; and this time more damage had been done. Two of the sheep had died; but the strange thing was that they had hardly been bitten at all.

Their wounds were so slight that their death could only be attributed to fright and exhaustion. It was very curious that the dog—if dog it was—had not mauled them worse and made a meal of them. The suggestion that it was some very small dog was negatived by the fact that what wounds there were must have been made by a large animal. It really looked as if the animal had not sufficient strength to finish its evil work.

But John Barron had another item of evidence which he was keeping to himself for the present. During each of the two past nights he had woke up without any apparent reason soon after midnight. And each time he had heard the Cry in the Night. It was a voice borne on the night air which he never expected to hear in England; and least of all in Bannerton. The voice came from the moor that stood above the little hamlet; and it rose and fell on the silence like the cry of a spirit in distress. It began with a low wail of unspeakable sadness; then rose and fell in lamentable ululations; and then died away into sobs and silence.

The voice came at intervals for more than an hour: and the second night it was stronger and seemed nearer than the first. John Barron had no difficulty in recognising that long-drawn cry. He had heard it before when travelling in the wilder parts of Russia. It was the howling of a wolf!

But there are no wolves in England. True, it might have been an escaped animal from some travelling menagerie; but such an animal would have made worse havoc of the sheep. And if this was the assailant of the little child, how did it get in; how did it get away; and why did the child still persist in saying that it was not a dog but a lady who bit her?

The next few days saw the plot thicken. Other people heard the voice in the night, and put it down to a stray dog out on the moor. Another farmer's sheep were worried, and this time one of them was partly eaten. So a chase was arranged, and all the local farmers and many other people banded together to hunt the sheep-killer. For two days the moor was scoured, and the adjacent woods thoroughly beaten, but without coming across any signs of the miscreant.

But John Barron heard a story from one of the farmers that set him thinking. He noticed that this man seemed to avoid a little thicket beside the moor, suggesting that there was a better path at some distance from it; and after some pressing he explained the real reason for this. But he was careful to add that of course he was not himself superstitious, but his wife had queer notions and had begged him to avoid the place.

It seemed that not long before, some wandering gipsies who from time to time camped on the moor, had secretly buried an old woman in the thicket and had never returned to the moor since. Of course there were the inevitable additions to a tale of this sort. The old lady was alleged to have been the queen of the gipsy tribe; and she was also said to have been a witch of the most malignant kind; and these were supposed to have been the reasons for her secret burial in this lonely spot. It did not seem to occur to the farmer that the gipsies thus saved the expense of a regular funeral. Very few people knew the story, and they thought it well to hold their peace. It was not worth while to make enemies of the gipsies, who could so easily have their revenge by robbing hen-roosts or even by driving cattle; to say nothing of the more mysterious doings with which they were credited.

John Barron began to put things together. The whole business had a distinct resemblance to the tales of the were-wolf in the Scandinavian literature of the Middle Ages. Here we had a woman of suspicious reputation buried in a lonely place without Christian rites; and soon afterwards a mysterious wolf roams the district in search of blood—just like the were-wolf. But who believes such stories now, except a few ghost-ridden cranks with shattered nerves and unbalanced minds? The whole thing is absurd.

Still, the mystery had to be cleared up; for John Barron had not the slightest intention of letting it simply slide into the refuse heap of unsolved problems. He kept his own counsel; but he meant to get to the bottom of it. Perhaps if he had realised the horror that lay at the bottom of it, he would have let it alone.

In the meantime the farmers had taken their own steps to deal with the sheep-worrying nuisance. Tempting morsels, judiciously seasoned with poison, were laid about; but with the sole result of causing the untimely death of a valued sheep-dog. Night after night the younger men, armed with guns, sat up and watched; but without success. Nothing happened, the sheep were undisturbed, and it really seemed as if the invader had left the neighbourhood. But John Barron knew that once a dog has taken to worrying sheep, it can never be cured. If the mysterious visitor was a dog, he would most certainly return if still alive and able to travel: if it was not a dog—well, anything might happen. So he continued to watch even after the general hunt for the dog had ceased.

Soon he had his reward. One very dark and stormy night, he again heard the distant voice in the night. It came very faintly rising and falling on the air, for the breeze was strong and the sound had to travel against the wind. Then he left the house, carrying his gun, and took up his post on rising ground that commanded the road that led from the moor.

Presently the cry came nearer, and then nearer still, till it was evident that the wolf had left the moor and was approaching the farms. Several dogs barked; but they were not the barks of challenge and defiance, but rather the timid yelps of fear. Then the howling came from a turn in the road so close at hand that John Barron, who was by no means a timid or nervous man, could hardly resist a shudder.

He silently cocked his gun, crept softly from behind the hedge into the road, and waited. Then a small, shrivelled old woman came into sight, walking with the aid of a stick. She hobbled along with surprising briskness for so old a woman until a turn in the road brought her suddenly face to face with him. And then something happened.

He was not a man addicted to fancies; nor was he at all lacking in powers of description as a rule; but he could never state quite clearly what it was that really happened. Probably it was because he did not quite know. He could only speak of an impression rather than of certain experience. According to him, the old woman gave him one glance of unspeakable malignancy; and then he seemed to become dazed or semi-conscious for a moment. It could have been only a matter of a second or two: but during that short space of time the old woman vanished. John Barron pulled himself together just in time to see a large wolf disappear round the turn of the road.

Naturally enough, he was somewhat confused by his startling experience. But there was no doubt about the presence of the wolf. He only just saw it; but he saw it quite clearly for about a second of time. Whether the wolf accompanied the old woman, or the old woman turned into a wolf, he neither saw nor could know. But each supposition was open to many obvious objections.

John Barron spent some time next day in thinking the thing out; and then it suddenly occurred to him to visit the thicket by the moorside and see the grave of the gipsy. He did not expect that there would be anything to see; but still it might be worth while to take a look at the place.

So he strolled in that direction early in the afternoon.

The thicket occupied a kind of little dell lying under the edge of the moor and was densely filled with small trees and undergrowth. But a scarcely visible path led into it; and, pushing his way through, he found that there was a small open space in the middle. Evidently this was the site of the gipsy grave.

And there he found it: but he found more than he expected. Not only was the grave there, but it lay open! The loose earth was heaped up on either side, and had the appearance of having been scraped out by some animal. And, sure enough, the footprints of a very large dog or wolf were to be seen in several places.

John Barron was simply horrified to find that the grave had been thus desecrated—and apparently in a manner that suggested an even worse horror. But, after a moment of hesitation, he stepped to the edge of the grave and looked in. What he saw was less appalling than he feared. There lay the coffin, exposed to view; but there was no sign that it had been opened or tampered with in any way.

There was evidently only one thing to be done, and that was to cover up the coffin decently and fill in the grave again. He would borrow a spade at the nearest cottage on some pretence and get the job done. He turned away to do this; but as he went through the thicket he could have sworn that he heard a sound like muffled laughter! And he could not get away from the notion that the laughter had some quality closely resembling the howling of a wolf. He called himself a fool for thinking such a thing—but he thought it all the same.

He borrowed the spade and filled the grave, beating the earth down as hard as he could; and again, as he turned away after completing the task, he heard that muffled laugh. But this time it was even less distinct than before, and somehow it sounded underground. He was rather glad to get away.

It may well be imagined that he had plenty to occupy his thoughts for the rest of the day; and even when he sought to sleep he could not. He lay tossing uneasily, thinking all the time of the mysterious grave and the events that certainly seemed now to be connected with it. Then, soon after midnight, he heard the voice in the night again. The wolf howled a long way off at first; then came a long interval of silence; and then the voice sounded so close to the house that Barron started up in alarm and he heard his dog give a cry of fear. Then the silence fell again; and some time later the howling was again heard in the distance.

Next morning he found his favourite dog lying dead beside his kennel; and it was only too evident how he had met his end. His neck was almost severed by one fearful bite; but the strange thing was that there was very little blood to be seen. A closer examination showed that the dog had bled to death; but where was the blood? Natural wolves tear their prey and devour it. They do not suck its blood. What kind of a wolf could this be?

John Barron found the answer next day. He was walking in the direction of the moor late in the afternoon, as it grew towards dusk, when he heard shrieks of terror coming from a little side lane.

He ran to the rescue, and there he saw a little child of the village lying on the ground, with a huge wolf in the act of tearing at its throat.

Fortunately he had his gun with him; and, as the wolf sprang off its victim when he shouted, he fired. The range was a short one, and the beast got the full force of the charge. It bounded into the air and fell in a heap. But it got up again, and went off in a limping gallop in the way that wolves will often do even when mortally wounded. It made for the moor.

John Barron saw that it had received its death wound, and so gave it no further attention for the moment. Some men came running up at his shouts, and with their assistance he took the wounded child to the local doctor. Happily he had been in time to save its life.

Then he reloaded his gun, took a man with him, and followed the track of the wolf. It was not difficult to follow, for blood-stains on the road at frequent intervals showed plainly enough that it was severely wounded. As Barron expected, the track led straight to the thicket and entered it.

The two men followed cautiously; but they found no wolf. In the midst of the thicket lay the grave once more uncovered. And there beside it lay the body of a little old woman, drenched with blood. She was quite dead, and the terrible gunshot wound in her side told its own story. And the two men noticed that her canine teeth projected slightly beyond her lips on each side—like those of a snarling wolf—and they were blood-stained.

LADY INTO FOX

DAVID GARNETT

Wonderful or supernatural events are not so uncommon, rather they are irregular in their incidence. Thus there may be not one marvel to speak of in a century, and then often enough comes a plentiful crop of them; monsters of all sorts swarm suddenly upon the earth, comets blaze in the sky, eclipses frighten nature, meteors fall in rain, while mermaids and sirens beguile, and sea-serpents engulf every passing ship, and terrible cataclysms beset humanity.

But the strange event which I shall here relate came alone, unsupported, without companions into a hostile world, and for that very reason claimed little of the general attention of mankind. For the sudden changing of Mrs. Tebrick into a vixen is an established fact which we may attempt to account for as we will. Certainly it is in the explanation of the fact, and the reconciling of it with our general notions that we shall find most difficulty, and not in accepting for true a story which is so fully proved, and that not by one witness but by a dozen, all respectable, and with no possibility of collusion between them.

But here I will confine myself to an exact narrative of the event and all that followed on it. Yet I would not dissuade any of my readers from attempting an explanation of this seeming miracle because up till now none has been found which is entirely satisfactory. What adds to the difficulty to my mind is that the metamorphosis occurred when Mrs. Tebrick was a full-grown woman, and that it happened suddenly in so short a space of time. The sprouting of a tail, the gradual extension of hair all over the body, the slow change of the whole anatomy by a process of growth, though it would have been monstrous, would not have been so difficult to reconcile to our ordinary conceptions, particularly had it happened in a young child.

But here we have something very different. A grown lady is changed straightway into a fox. There is no explaining that away by any natural philosophy. The materialism of our age will not help us here. It is indeed a *miracle*; something from outside our world altogether; an event which we would willingly accept if we were to meet it invested with the authority of Divine Revelation in the scriptures, but which we are not prepared to encounter almost in our time, happening in Oxfordshire amongst our neighbours.

The only things which go any way towards an explanation of it are but guesswork, and I give them more because I would not conceal anything, than because I think they are of any worth.

Mrs. Tebrick's maiden name was certainly Fox, and it is possible that such a miracle happening before, the family may have gained their name as a *soubriquet* on that account. They were an ancient family, and have had their seat at

Tangley Hall time out of mind. It is also true that there was a half-tame fox once upon a time chained up at Tangley Hall in the inner yard, and I have heard many speculative wiseacres in the public-houses turn that to great account—though they could not but admit that "there was never one there in Miss Silvia's time." At first I was inclined to think that Silvia Fox, having once hunted when she was a child of ten and having been blooded, might furnish more of an explanation. It seems she took great fright or disgust at it, and vomited after it was done. But now I do not see that it has much bearing on the miracle itself, even though we know that after that she always spoke of the "poor foxes" when a hunt was stirring and never rode to hounds till after her marriage when her husband persuaded her to it.

She was married in the year 1879 to Mr. Richard Tebrick, after a short courtship, and went to live after their honeymoon at Rylands, near Stokoe, Oxon. One point indeed I have not been able to ascertain and that is how they first became acquainted. Tangley Hall is over thirty miles from Stokoe, and is extremely remote. Indeed to this day there is no proper road to it, which is all the more remarkable as it is the principal, and indeed the only, manor house for several miles round.

Whether it was from a chance meeting on the roads, or less romantic but more probable, by Mr. Tebrick becoming acquainted with her uncle, a minor canon at Oxford, and thence being invited by him to visit Tangley Hall, it is impossible to say. But however they became acquainted the marriage was a very happy one. The bride was in her twenty-third year. She was small, with remarkably small hands and feet. It is perhaps worth noting that there was nothing at all foxy or vixenish in her appearance. On the contrary, she was a more than ordinarily beautiful and agreeable woman. Her eyes were of a clear hazel but exceptionally brilliant, her hair dark, with a shade of red in it, her skin brownish, with a few dark freckles and little moles. In manner she was reserved almost to shyness, but perfectly self-possessed, and perfectly well-bred.

She had been strictly brought up by a woman of excellent principles and considerable attainments, who died a year or so before the marriage. And owing to the circumstance that her mother had been dead many years, and her father bedridden, and not altogether rational for a little while before his death, they had few visitors but her uncle. He often stopped with them a month or two at a stretch, particularly in winter, as he was fond of shooting snipe, which are plentiful in the valley there. That she did not grow up a country hoyden is to be explained by the strictness of her governess and the influence of her uncle. But perhaps living in so wild a place gave her some disposition to wildness, even in spite of her religious upbringing. Her old nurse said: "Miss Silvia was always a little wild at heart," though if this was true it was never seen by anyone else except her husband.

On one of the first days of the year 1880, in the early afternoon, husband and wife went for a walk in the copse on the little hill above Rylands. They were still at this time like lovers in their behaviour and were always together. While they were walking they heard the hounds and later the huntsman's horn in the distance. Mr. Tebrick had persuaded her to hunt on Boxing Day, but with great difficulty, and she had not enjoyed it (though of hacking she was fond enough).

Hearing the hunt, Mr. Tebrick quickened his pace so as to reach the edge of the copse, where they might get a good view of the hounds if they came that way. His wife hung back, and he, holding her hand, began almost to drag her. Before they gained the edge of the copse she suddenly snatched her hand away from his very violently and cried out, so that he instantly turned his head.

Where his wife had been the moment before was a small fox, of a very bright red. It looked at him very beseechingly, advanced towards him a pace or two, and he saw at once that his wife was looking at him from the animal's eyes. You may well think if he were aghast: and so maybe was his lady at finding herself in that shape, so they did nothing for nearly half-an-hour but stare at each other, he bewildered, she asking him with her eyes as if indeed she spoke to him: "What am I now become? Have pity on me, husband, have pity on me for I am your wife."

So that with his gazing on her and knowing her well, even in such a shape, yet asking himself at every moment: "Can it be she? Am I not dreaming?" and her beseeching and lastly fawning on him and seeming to tell him that it was she indeed, they came at last together and he took her in his arms. She lay very close to him, nestling under his coat and fell to licking his face, but never taking her eyes from his. The husband all this while kept turning the thing in his head and gazing on her, but he could make no sense of what had happened, but only comforted himself with the hope that this was but a momentary change, and that presently she would turn back again into the wife that was one flesh with him.

One fancy that came to him, because he was so much more like a lover than a husband, was that it was his fault, and this because if anything dreadful happened he could never blame her but himself for it.

So they passed a good while, till at last the tears welled up in the poor fox's eyes and she began weeping (but quite in silence), and she trembled too as if she were in a fever. At this he could not contain his own tears, but sat down on the ground and sobbed for a great while, but between his sobs kissing her quite as if she had been a woman, and not caring in his grief that he was kissing a fox on the muzzle.

They sat thus till it was getting near dusk, when he recollected himself, and the next thing was that he must somehow hide her, and then bring her home.

He waited till it was quite dark that he might the better bring her into her own house without being seen, and buttoned her inside his topcoat, nay, even in his passion tearing open his waistcoat and his shirt that she might lie the closer to his heart. For when we are overcome with the greatest sorrow we act not like men or women but like children whose comfort in all their troubles is to press themselves against their mother's breast, or if she be not there to hold each other tight in one another's arms.

When it was dark he brought her in with infinite precautions, yet not without the dogs scenting her after which nothing could moderate their clamour.

Having got her into the house, the next thing he thought of was to hide her from the servants. He carried her to the bedroom in his arms and then went downstairs again.

Mr. Tebrick had three servants living in the house, the cook, the parlour-maid, and an old woman who had been his wife's nurse. Besides these women there was a groom or a gardener (whichever you choose to call him), who was a single man and so lived out, lodging with a labouring family about half a mile away.

Mr. Tebrick going downstairs pitched upon the parlour-maid.

"Janet," says he, "Mrs. Tebrick and I have had some bad news, and Mrs. Tebrick was called away instantly to London and left this afternoon, and I am staying to-night to put our affairs in order. We are shutting up the house, and I must give you and Mrs. Brant a month's wages and ask you to leave to-morrow morning at seven o'clock. We shall probably go away to the Continent, and I do not know when we shall come back. Please tell the others, and now get me my tea and bring it into my study on a tray." Janet said nothing for she was a shy girl, particularly before gentlemen, but when she entered the kitchen Mr. Tebrick heard a sudden burst of conversation with many exclamations from the cook.

When she came back with his tea, Mr. Tebrick said: "I shall not require you upstairs. Pack your own things and tell James to have the waggonette ready for you by seven o'clock to-morrow morning to take you to the station. I am busy now, but I will see you again before you go."

When she had gone Mr. Tebrick took the tray upstairs. For the first moment he thought the room was empty, and his vixen got away, for he could see no sign of her anywhere. But after a moment he saw something stirring in a corner of the room, and then behold! she came forth dragging her dressing-gown, into which she had somehow struggled.

This must surely have been a comical sight, but poor Mr. Tebrick was altogether too distressed then or at any time afterwards to divert himself at such ludicrous scenes. He only called to her softly:

"Silvia—Silvia. What do you do there?" And then in a moment saw for himself what she would be at, and began once more to blame himself heartily—because he had not guessed that his wife would not like to go naked, notwithstanding the shape she was in. Nothing would satisfy him then till he had clothed her suitably, bringing her dresses from the wardrobe for her to choose. But as might have been expected, they were too big for her now, but at last he picked out a little dressing-jacket that she was fond of wearing sometimes in the mornings. It was made of a flowered silk, trimmed with lace, and the sleeves short enough to sit very well on her now. While he tied the ribands his poor lady thanked him with gentle looks and not without some modesty and confusion. He propped her up in an armchair with some cushions, and they took tea together, she very delicately drinking from a saucer and taking bread and butter from his hands. All this showed him, or so he thought, that his wife was still herself; there was so little wildness in her demeanour and so much delicacy and decency, especially in her not wishing to run naked, that he was very much comforted, and began to fancy they could be happy enough if they could escape the world and live always alone.

From this too sanguine dream he was aroused by hearing the gardener speaking to the dogs, trying to quiet them, for ever since he had come in with his vixen they had been whining, barking and growling, and all as he knew because there was a fox within doors and they would kill it.

He started up now, calling to the gardener that he would come down to the dogs himself to quiet them, and bade the man go indoors again and leave it to him. All this he said in a dry, compelling kind of voice which made the fellow do as he was bid, though it was against his will, for he was curious. Mr. Tebrick went downstairs, and taking his gun from the rack loaded it and went out into the yard. Now there were two dogs, one a handsome Irish setter that was his wife's dog (she had brought it with her from Tangley Hall on her marriage); the other was an old fox terrier called Nelly that he had had ten years or more.

When he came out into the yard both dogs saluted him by barking and whining twice as much as they did before, the setter jumping up and down at the end of his chain in a frenzy, and Nelly shivering, wagging her tail, and looking first at her master and then at the house door, where she could smell the fox right enough.

There was a bright moon, so that Mr. Tebrick could see the dogs as clearly as could be. First he shot his wife's setter dead, and then looked about him for Nelly to give her the other barrel, but he could see her nowhere. The bitch was clean gone, till, looking to see how she had broken her chain, he found her lying hid in the back of her kennel. But that trick did not save her, for Mr. Tebrick, after trying to pull her out by her chain and finding it useless—she would not come,—thrust the muzzle of his gun into the kennel, pressed it into her body and so shot her. Afterwards, striking a match, he looked in at her to make certain she was dead. Then, leaving the dogs as they were, chained up, Mr. Tebrick went indoors again and found the gardener, who had not yet gone home, gave him a month's wages in lieu of notice and told him he had a job for him yet—to bury the two dogs and that he should do it that same night.

But by all this going on with so much strangeness and authority on his part, as it seemed to them, the servants were much troubled. Hearing the shots while he was out in the yard his wife's old nurse, or Nanny, ran up to the bedroom though she had no business there, and so opening the door saw the poor fox dressed in my lady's little jacket lying back in the cushions, and in such a reverie of woe that she heard nothing.

Old Nanny, though she was not expecting to find her mistress there, having been told that she was gone that afternoon to London, knew her instantly, and cried out:

"Oh, my poor precious! Oh, poor Miss Silvia! What dreadful change is this?" Then, seeing her mistress start and look at her, she cried out: "But never fear, my darling, it will all come right, your old Nanny knows you, it will all come right in the end."

But though she said this she did not care to look again, and kept her eyes turned away so as not to meet the foxy slit ones of her mistress, for that was too much for her. So she hurried out soon, fearing to be found there by Mr. Tebrick, and who knows, perhaps shot, like the dogs, for knowing the secret.

Mr. Tebrick had all this time gone about paying off his servants and shooting his dogs as if he were in a dream. Now he fortified himself with two or three glasses of strong whisky and went to bed, taking his vixen into his arms, where he slept soundly. Whether she did or not is more than I or anybody else can say.

In the morning when he woke up they had the place to themselves, for on his instructions the servants had all left first thing: Janet and the cook to Oxford, where they would try and find new places, and Nanny going back to the cottage near Tangley, where her son lived, who was the pigman there.

So with that morning there began what was now to be their ordinary life together. He would get up when it was broad day, and first thing light the fire downstairs and cook the breakfast, then brush his wife, sponge her with a damp sponge, then brush her again, in all this using scent very freely to hide somewhat her rank odour. When she was dressed he carried her downstairs and they had their breakfast together, she sitting up to table with him, drinking her saucer of tea, and taking her food from his fingers, or at any rate being fed by him. She was still fond of the same food that she had been used to before her transformation, a lightly boiled egg or slice of ham, a piece of buttered toast or two, with a little quince and apple jam. While I am on the subject of her food, I should say that reading in the encyclopedia he found that foxes on the Continent are inordinately fond of grapes, and that during the autumn season they abandon their ordinary diet for them, and then grow exceedingly fat and lose their offensive odour.

This appetite for grapes is so well confirmed by Aesop, and by passages in the Scriptures, that it is strange Mr. Tebrick should not have known it. After reading this account he wrote to London for a basket of grapes to be posted to him twice a week and was rejoiced to find that the account in the encyclopedia was true in the most important of these particulars. His vixen relished them exceedingly and seemed never to tire of them, so that he increased his order first from one pound to three pounds and afterwards to five. Her odour abated so much by this means that he came not to notice it at all except sometimes in the mornings before her toilet. What helped most to make living with her bearable for him was that she understood him perfectly—yes, every word he said, and though she was dumb she expressed herself very fluently by looks and signs though never by the voice.

Thus he frequently conversed with her, telling her all his thoughts and hiding nothing from her, and this the more readily because he was very quick to catch her meaning and her answers.

"Puss, Puss," he would say to her, for calling her that had been a habit with him always. "Sweet Puss, some men would pity me living alone here with you after what has happened, but I would not change places while you were living with any man for the whole world. Though you are a fox I would rather live with you than any woman. I swear I would, and that too if you were changed to anything." But then, catching her grave look, he would say: "Do you think I jest on these things, my dear? I do not. I swear to you, my darling, that all my life I will be true to you, will be faithful, will respect and reverence you who are my wife. And I will do that not because of any hope that God in His mercy will see fit to restore your shape, but solely because I love you. However you may be changed, my love is not."

Then anyone seeing them would have sworn that they were lovers, so passionately did each look on the other.

Often he would swear to her that the devil might have power to work some miracles, but that he would find it beyond him to change his love for her.

These passionate speeches, however they might have struck his wife in an ordinary way, now seemed to be her chief comfort. She would come to him, put her paw in his hand and look at him with sparkling eyes shining with joy and gratitude, would pant with eagerness, jump at him and lick his face.

Now he had many little things which busied him in the house—getting his meals, setting the room straight, making the bed and so forth. When he was doing this housework it was comical to watch his vixen. Often she was as it were beside herself with vexation and distress to see him in his clumsy way doing what she could have done so much better had she been able. Then, forgetful of the decency and the decorum which she had at first imposed upon herself never to run upon all fours, she followed him everywhere, and if he did one thing wrong she stopped him and showed him the way of it. When he had forgot the hour for his meal she would come and tug his sleeve and tell him as if she spoke: "Husband, are we to have no luncheon today?"

This womanliness in her never failed to delight him, for it showed she was still his wife, buried as it were in the carcase of a beast but with a woman's soul. This encour-

aged him so much that he debated with himself whether he should not read aloud to her, as he often had done formerly. At last, since he could find no reason against it, he went to the shelf and fetched down a volume of the "History of Clarissa Harlowe," which he had begun to read aloud to her a few weeks before. He opened the volume where he had left off, with Lovelace's letter after he had spent the night waiting fruitlessly in the copse.

Good God!
What is now to become of me?
My feet benumbed by midnight wandeings through the heaviest dews that ever fell;
my wig and my linen dripping
with the hoarfrost dissolving on them!
Day but just breaking . . . etc.

While he read he was conscious of holding her attention, then after a few pages the story claimed all his, so that he read on for about half-an-hour without looking at her. When he did so he saw that she was not listening to him, but was watching something with strange eagerness. Such a fixed intent look was on her face that he was alarmed and sought the cause of it. Presently he found that her gaze was fixed on the movements of her pet dove which was in its cage hanging in the window. He spoke to her, but she seemed displeased, so he laid "Clarissa Harlowe" aside. Nor did he ever repeat the experiment of reading to her.

Yet that same evening, as he happened to be looking through his writing table drawer with Puss beside him looking over his elbow, she spied a pack of cards, and then he was forced to pick them out to please her, then draw them from their case. At last, trying first one thing, then another, he found that what she was after was to play piquet with him. They had some difficulty at first in contriving for her to hold her cards and then to play them, but this was at last overcome by his stacking them for her on a sloping board, after which she could flip them out very neatly with her claws as she wanted to play them. When they had overcome this trouble they played three games, and most heartily she seemed to enjoy them. Moreover she won all three of them. After this they often played a quiet game of piquet together, and cribbage too. I should say that in marking the points at cribbage on the board he always moved her pegs for her as well as his own, for she could not handle them or set them in the holes.

The weather, which had been damp and misty, with frequent downpours of rain, improved very much in the following week, and, as often happens in January, there were several days with the sun shining, no wind and light frosts at night, these frosts becoming more intense as the days went on till bye and bye they began to think of snow.

With this spell of fine weather it was but natural that Mr. Tebrick should think of taking his vixen out of doors. This was something he had not yet done, both because of the damp rainy weather up till then and because the mere notion of taking her out filled him with alarm. Indeed he had so many apprehensions beforehand that at one time he resolved totally against it. For his mind was filled not only with the fear that she might escape from him and run away, which he knew was groundless, but with more rational visions, such as wandering curs, traps, gins, spring guns, besides a dread of being seen with her by the neighbourhood. At last however he resolved on it, and all the more as his vixen kept asking him in the gentlest way: "Might she not go out into the garden?" Yet she always listened very submissively when he told her that he was afraid if they were seen together it would excite the curiosity of their neighbours; besides this, he often told her of his fears for her on account of dogs. But one day she answered this by leading him into the hall and pointing boldly to his gun. After this he resolved to take her, though with full precautions. That is he left the house door open so that in case of need she could beat a swift retreat, then he took his gun under his arm, and lastly he had her well wrapped up in a little fur jacket lest she should take cold.

He would have carried her too, but that she delicately disengaged herself from his arms and looked at him very expressively to say that she would go by herself. For already her first horror of being seen to go upon all fours was worn off; reasoning no doubt upon it, that either she must resign herself to go that way or else stay bed-ridden all the rest of her life.

Her joy at going into the garden was inexpressible. First she ran this way, then that, though keeping always close to him, looking very sharply with ears cocked forward first at one thing, then another and then up to catch his eye.

For some time indeed she was almost dancing with delight, running round him, then forward a yard or two, then back to him and gambolling beside him as they went round the garden. But in spite of her joy she was full of fear. At every noise, a cow lowing, a cock crowing, or a ploughman in the distance hulloaing to scare the rooks, she started, her ears pricked to catch the sound, her muzzle wrinkled up and her nose twitched, and she would then press herself against his legs. They walked round the garden and down to the pond where there were ornamental waterfowl, teal, widgeon and mandarin ducks, and seeing these again gave her great pleasure. They had always been her favourites, and now she was so overjoyed to see them that she behaved with very little of her usual self-restraint. First she stared at them, then bouncing up to her husband's knee sought to kindle an equal excitement in his mind. Whilst she rested her paws on his knee she turned her head again and again towards the ducks as though she could not take her eyes off them, and then ran down before him to the water's edge.

But her appearance threw the ducks into the utmost degree of consternation. Those on shore or near the bank swam or flew to the centre of the pond, and there huddled in a bunch; and then, swimming round and round, they began such a quacking that Mr. Tebrick was nearly deafened. As I have before said, nothing in the ludicrous way that arose out of the metamorphosis of his wife (and such incidents were plentiful) ever stood a chance of being smiled at by him. So in this case, too, for realising that the silly ducks thought his wife a fox indeed and were alarmed on that account he found painful that spectacle which to others might have been amusing.

Not so his vixen, who appeared if anything more pleased than ever when she saw in what a commotion she had set them, and began cutting a thousand pretty capers. Though at first he called to her to come back and walk another way, Mr. Tebrick was overborne by her pleasure and sat down, while she frisked around him happier far than he had seen her ever since the change. First she ran up to him in a laughing way, all smiles, and then ran down again to the water's edge and began frisking and frolicking, chasing her own brush, dancing on her hind legs even, and rolling on the ground, then fell to running in circles, but all this without paying any heed to the ducks.

But they, with their necks craned out all pointing one way, swam to and fro in the middle of the pond, never stopping their quack, quack quack, and keeping time too, for they all quacked in chorus. Presently she came further away from the pond, and he, thinking they had had enough of this sort of entertainment, laid hold of her and said to her:

"Come, Silvia, my dear, it is growing cold, and it is time we went indoors. I am sure taking the air has done you a world of good, but we must not linger any more."

She appeared then to agree with him, though she threw half a glance over her shoulder at the ducks, and they both walked soberly enough towards the house.

When they had gone about halfway she suddenly slipped round and was off. He turned quickly and saw the ducks had been following them.

So she drove them before her back into the pond, the ducks running in terror from her with their wings spread, and she not pressing them, for he saw that had she been so minded she could have caught two or three of the nearest. Then, with her brush waving above her, she came gambolling back to him so playfully that he stroked her indulgently, though he was first vexed, and then rather puzzled that his wife should amuse herself with such pranks.

But when they got within doors he picked her up in his arms, kissed her and spoke to her.

"Silvia, what a light-hearted childish creature you are. Your courage under misfortune shall be a lesson to me, but I cannot, I cannot bear to see it."

Here the tears stood suddenly in his eyes, and he lay down upon the ottoman and wept, paying no heed to her until presently he was aroused by her licking his cheek and his ear.

After tea she led him to the drawing room and scratched at the door till he opened it, for this was part of the house which he had shut up, thinking three or four rooms enough for them now, and to save the dusting of it. Then it seemed she would have him play to her on the pianoforte: she led him to it, nay, what is more, she would herself pick out the music he was to play. First it was a fugue of Handel's, then one of Mendelssohn's Songs Without Words, and then "The Diver," and then music from Gilbert and Sullivan; but each piece of music she picked out was gayer than the last one. Thus they sat happily engrossed for perhaps an hour in the candle light until the extreme cold in that unwarmed room stopped his playing and drove them downstairs to the fire. Thus did she admirably comfort her husband when he was dispirited.

Yet next morning when he woke he was distressed when he found that she was not in the bed with him but was lying curled up at the foot of it. During breakfast she hardly listened when he spoke, and then impatiently, but sat staring at the dove.

Mr. Tebrick sat silently looking out of window for some time, then he took out his pocket book; in it there was a photograph of his wife taken soon after their wedding. Now he gazed and gazed upon those familiar features, and now he lifted his head and looked at the animal before him. He laughed then bitterly, the first and last time for that matter that Mr. Tebrick ever laughed at his wife's transformation, for he was not very humorous. But this laugh was sour and painful to him. Then he tore up the photograph into little pieces, and scattered them out of the window, saying to himself: "Memories will not help me here," and turning to the vixen he saw that she was still staring at the caged bird, and as he looked he saw her lick her chops.

He took the bird into the next room, then acting suddenly upon the impulse, he opened the cage door and set it free, saying as he did so:

"Go, poor bird! Fly from this wretched house while you still remember your mistress who fed you from her coral lips. You are not a fit plaything for her now. Farewell, poor bird! Farewell! Unless," he added with a melancholy smile, "you return with good tidings like Noah's dove."

But, poor gentleman, his troubles were not over yet, and indeed one may say that he ran to meet them by his constant supposing that his lady should still be the same to a tittle in her behaviour now that she was changed into a fox.

Without making any unwarrantable suppositions as to her soul or what had now become of it (though we could find a good deal to the purpose on that point in the system of Paracelsus), let us consider only how much the change in her body must needs affect her ordinary conduct. So that before we judge too harshly of this unfortunate lady, we must reflect upon the physical necessities and infirmities and appetites of her new condition, and we must magnify the fortitude of her mind which enabled her to behave with decorum, cleanliness and decency in spite of her new situation.

Thus she might have been expected to befoul her room, yet never could anyone, whether man or beast, have shown more nicety in such matters. But at luncheon Mr. Tebrick helped her to a wing of chicken, and leaving the room for a minute to fetch some water which he had forgot, found her at his return on the table crunching the very bones. He stood silent, dismayed and wounded to the heart at this

sight. For we must observe that this unfortunate husband thought always of his vixen as that gentle and delicate woman she had lately been. So that whenever his vixen's conduct went beyond that which he expected in his wife he was, as it were, cut to the quick, and no kind of agony could be greater to him than to see her thus forget herself. On this account it may indeed be regretted that Mrs. Tebrick had been so exactly well-bred, and in particular that her table manners had always been scrupulous. Had she been in the habit, like a continental princess I have dined with, of taking her leg of chicken by the drumstick and gnawing the flesh, it had been far better for him now. But as her manners had been perfect, so the lapse of them was proportionately painful to him. Thus in this instance he stood as it were in silent agony till she had finished her hideous crunching of the chicken bones and had devoured every scrap. Then he spoke to her gently, taking her on to his knee, stroking her fur and fed her with a few grapes, saying to her:

"Silvia, Silvia, is it so hard for you? Try and remember the past, my darling, and by living with me we will quite forget that you are no longer a woman. Surely this affliction will pass soon, as suddenly as it came, and it will all seem to us like an evil dream."

Yet though she appeared perfectly sensible of his words and gave him sorrowful and penitent looks like her old self, that same afternoon, on taking her out, he had all the difficulty in the world to keep her from going near the ducks.

There came to him then a thought that was very disagreeable to him, namely, that he dare not trust his wife alone with any bird or she would kill it. And this was the more shocking to him to think of since it meant that he durst not trust her as much as a dog even. For we may trust dogs who are familiars, with all the household pets; nay more, we can put them upon trust with anything and know they will not touch it, not even if they be starving. But things were come to such a pass with his vixen that he dared not in his heart trust her at all. Yet she was still in many ways so much more woman than fox that he could talk to her on any subject and she would understand him, better far than the oriental women who are kept in subjection can ever understand their masters unless they converse on the most trifling household topics.

Thus she understood excellently well the importance and duties of religion. She would listen with approval in the evening when he said the Lord's Prayer, and was rigid in her observance of the Sabbath. Indeed, the next day being Sunday he, thinking no harm, proposed their usual game of piquet, but no, she would not play. Mr. Tebrick, not understanding at first what she meant, though he was usually very quick with her, he proposed it to her again, which she again refused, and this time, to show her meaning, made the sign of the cross with her paw. This exceedingly rejoiced and comforted him in his distress. He begged her pardon, and fervently thanked God for having so good a wife, who, in spite of all, knew more of her duty to God than he did. But here I must warn the reader from inferring that she was a papist because she then made the sign of the cross. She made that sign to my thinking only on compulsion because she could not express herself except in that way. For she had been brought up as a true Protestant, and that she still was one is confirmed by her objection to cards, which would have been less than nothing to her had she been a papist. Yet that evening, taking her into the drawing room so that he might play her some sacred music, he found her after some time cowering away from him in the farthest corner of the room, her ears flattened back and an expression of the greatest anguish in her eyes. When he spoke to her she licked his hand, but remained shivering for a long time at his feet and showed the clearest symptoms of terror if he so much as moved towards the piano. On seeing this and recollecting how ill the ears of a dog can bear with our music, and how this dislike might be expected to be even greater in a fox, all of whose senses are more acute from being a wild creature, recollecting this he closed the piano and taking her in his arms, locked up the room and never went into it again. He could not help marvelling though, since it was but two days after she had herself led him there, and even picked out for him to play and sing those pieces which were her favourites.

That night she would not sleep with him, neither in the bed nor on it, so that he was forced to let her curl herself up on the floor. But neither would she sleep there, for several times she woke him by trotting around the room, and once when he had got sound asleep by springing on the bed and then off it, so that he woke with a violent start and cried out, but got no answer either, except hearing her trotting round and round the room. Presently he imagines to himself that she must want something, and so fetches her food and water, but she never so much as looks at it, but still goes on her rounds, every now and then scratching at the door.

Though he spoke to her, calling her by her name, she would pay no heed to him, or else only for the moment. At last he gave her up and said to her plainly: "The fit is on you now Silvia to be a fox, but I shall keep you close and in the morning you will recollect yourself and thank me for having kept you now."

So he lay down again, but not to sleep, only to listen to his wife running about the room and trying to get out of it. Thus he spent what was perhaps the most miserable night of his existence. In the morning she was still restless, and was reluctant to let him wash and brush her, and appeared to dislike being scented but as it were to bear with it for his sake. Ordinarily she had taken the greatest pleasure imaginable in her toilet, so that on this account, added to his sleepless night, Mr. Tebrick was utterly dejected, and it was then that he resolved to put a project into execution that would show him, so he thought, whether he had a wife or only a wild vixen in his house. But yet he was comforted that she bore at all with him, though so restlessly that he did not spare her, calling her a "bad wild fox." And then speaking to her in this manner: "Are you not ashamed, Silvia, to be such a madcap, such a wicked hoyden? You who were particular in dress. I see it was all vanity—now you have not your former advantages you think nothing of decency."

His words had some effect with her too, and with himself, so that by the time he had finished dressing her they were both in the lowest state of spirits imaginable and neither of them far from tears.

Breakfast she took soberly enough, and after that he went about getting his experiment ready, which was this. In the garden he gathered together a nosegay of snowdrops, those being all the flowers he could find, and then going into the village of Stokoe bought a Dutch rabbit (that is a black and white one) from a man there who kept them.

When he got back he took her flowers and at the same time set down the basket with the rabbit in it, with the lid open. Then he called to her: "Silvia, I have brought some flowers for you. Look, the first snowdrops."

At this she ran up very prettily, and never giving as much as one glance at the rabbit which had hopped out of its basket, she began to thank him for the flowers. Indeed she seemed indefatigable in shewing her gratitude, smelt them, stood a little way off looking at them, then thanked him again. Mr. Tebrick (and this was all part of his plan) then took a vase and went to find some water for them, but left the flowers beside her. He stopped away five minutes, timing it by his watch and listening very intently, but never heard the rabbit squeak. Yet when he went in what a horrid shambles was spread before his eyes. Blood on the carpet, blood on the armchairs and antimacassars, even a little blood spurtled on to the wall, and what was worse, Mrs. Tebrick tearing and growling over a piece of the skin and the legs, for she had eaten up all the rest of it. The poor gentleman was so heartbroken over this that he was like to have done himself an injury, and at one moment thought of getting his gun, to have shot himself and his vixen too. Indeed the extremity of his grief was such that it served him a very good turn, for he was so entirely unmanned by it that for some time he could do nothing but weep, and fell into a chair with his head in his hands, and so kept weeping and groaning.

After he had been some little while employed in this dismal way, his vixen, who had by this time bolted down the rabbit skin, head, ears and all, came to him and putting her paws on his knees, thrust her long muzzle into his face and began licking him. But he, looking at her now with different eyes, and seeing her jaws still sprinkled with fresh blood and her claws full of the rabbit's fleck, would have none of it.

But though he beat her off four or five times even to giving her blows and kicks, she still came back to him, crawling on her belly and imploring his forgiveness with wide-open sorrowful eyes. Before he had made this rash experiment of the rabbit and the flowers, he had promised himself that if she failed in it he would have no more feeling or compassion for her than if she were in truth a wild vixen out of the woods. This resolution, though the reasons for it had seemed to him so very plain before, he now found more difficult to carry out than to decide on. At length after cursing her and beating her off for upwards of half-an-hour, he admitted to himself that he still did care for her, and even loved her dearly in spite of all, whatever pretence he affected towards her. When he had acknowledged this he looked up at her and met her eyes fixed upon him, and held out his arms to her and said:

"Oh Silvia, Silvia, would you had never done this! Would I had never tempted you in a fatal hour! Does not this butchery and eating of raw meat and rabbit's fur disgust you? Are you a monster in your soul as well as in your body? Have you forgotten what it is to be a woman?"

Meanwhile, with every word of his, she crawled a step nearer on her belly and at last climbed sorrowfully into his arms. His words then seemed to take effect on her and her eyes filled with tears and she wept most penitently in his arms, and her body shook with her sobs as if her heart were breaking. This sorrow of hers gave him the strangest mixture of pain and joy that he had ever known, for his love for her returning with a rush, he could not bear to witness her pain and yet must take pleasure in it as it fed his hopes of her one day returning to be a woman. So the more anguish of shame his vixen underwent, the greater his hopes rose, till his love and pity for her increasing equally, he was almost wishing her to be nothing more than a mere fox than to suffer so much by being half-human.

At last he looked about him somewhat dazed with so much weeping, then set his vixen down on the ottoman, and began to clean up the room with a heavy heart. He fetched a pail of water and washed out all the stains of blood, gathered up the two antimacassars and fetched clean ones from the other rooms. While he went about this work his vixen sat and watched him very contritely with her nose between her two front paws, and when he had done he brought in some luncheon for himself, though it was already late, but none for her, she having lately so infamously feasted. But water he gave her and a bunch of grapes. Afterwards she led him to the small tortoiseshell cabinet and would have him open it. When he had done so she motioned to the portable stereoscope which lay inside. Mr. Tebrick instantly fell in with her wish and after a few trials adjusted it to her vision. Thus they spent the rest of the afternoon together very happily looking through the collection of views which he had purchased, of Italy, Spain and Scotland. This diversion gave her great apparent pleasure and afforded him considerable comfort. But that night he could not prevail upon her to sleep in bed with him, and finally allowed her to sleep on a mat beside the bed where he could stretch down and touch her. So they passed the night, with his hand upon her head.

The next morning he had more of a struggle than ever to wash and dress her. Indeed at one time nothing but holding her by the scruff prevented her from getting away from him, but at last he achieved his object and she was washed, brushed, scented and dressed, although to be sure this left him better pleased than her, for she regarded her silk jacket with disfavour.

Still at breakfast she was well mannered though a trifle hasty with her food. Then his difficulties with her began for she would go out, but as he had his housework to do, he could not allow it. He brought her picture books to divert her, but she would have none of them but stayed at the door scratching it with her claws industriously till she had worn away the paint.

At first he tried coaxing her and wheedling, gave her cards to play patience and so on, but finding nothing would distract her from going out, his temper began to rise, and he told her plainly that she must wait his pleasure and that he had as much natural obstinacy as she had. But to all that he said she paid no heed whatever but only scratched the harder. Thus he let her continue until luncheon, when she would not sit up, or eat off a plate, but first was for getting on to the table, and when that was prevented, snatched her meat and ate it under the table. To all his rebukes she turned a deaf or sullen ear, and so they each finished their meal eating little, either of them, for till she would sit at table he would give her no more, and his vexation had taken away his own appetite. In the afternoon he took her out for her airing in the garden.

She made no pretence now of enjoying the first snowdrops or the view from the terrace. No—there was only one thing for her now—the ducks, and she was off to them before he could stop her. Luckily they were all swimming when she got there (for a stream running into the pond on the far side it was not frozen there).

When he had got down to the pond, she ran out on to the ice, which would not bear his weight, and though he called her and begged her to come back she would not heed him but stayed frisking about, getting as near the ducks as she dared, but being circumspect in venturing on to the thin ice.

Presently she turned on herself and began tearing off her clothes, and at last by biting got off her little jacket and taking it in her mouth stuffed it into a hole in the ice where he could not get it. Then she ran hither and thither a stark naked vixen, and without giving a glance to her poor husband who stood silently now upon the bank, with despair and terror settled in his mind. She let him stay there most of the afternoon till he was chilled through and through and worn out with watching her. At last he reflected how she had just stripped herself and how in the morning she struggled against being dressed, and he thought perhaps he was too strict with her and if he let her have her own way they could manage to be happy somehow together even if she did eat off the floor. So he called out to her then:

"Silvia, come now, be good, you shan't wear any more clothes if you don't want to, and you needn't sit at table neither, I promise. You shall do as you like in that, but you must give up one thing, and that is you must stay with me and not go out alone, for that is dangerous. If any dog came on you he would kill you."

Directly he had finished speaking she came to him joyously, began fawning on him and prancing round him so that in spite of his vexation with her, and being cold, he could not help stroking her.

"Oh, Silvia, are you not wilful and cunning? I see you glory in being so, but I shall not reproach you but shall stick to my side of the bargain, and you must stick to yours."

He built a big fire when he came back to the house and took a glass or two of spirits also, to warm himself up, for he was chilled to the very bone. Then, after they had dined, to cheer himself he took another glass, and then another, and so on till he was very merry, he thought. Then he would play with his vixen, she encouraging him with her pretty sportiveness. He got up to catch her then and finding himself unsteady on his legs, he went down on to all fours. The long and the short of it is that by drinking he drowned all his sorrow; and then would be a beast too like his wife, though she was one through no fault of her own, and could not help it. To what lengths he went then in that drunken humour I shall not offend my readers by relating, but shall only say that he was so drunk and sottish that he had a very imperfect recollection of what had passed when he woke the next morning. There is no exception to the rule that if a man drink heavily at night the next morning will show the other side to his nature. Thus with Mr. Tebrick, for as he had been beastly, merry and a very dare-devil the night before, so on his awakening was he ashamed, melancholic and a true penitent before his Creator. The first thing he did when he came to himself was to call out to God to forgive him for his sin, then he fell into earnest prayer and continued so for half-an-hour upon his knees. Then he got up and dressed but continued very melancholy for the whole of the morning. Being in this mood you may imagine it hurt him to see his wife running about naked, but he reflected it would be a bad reformation that began with breaking faith. He had made a bargain and he would stick to it, and so he let her be, though sorely against his will.

For the same reason, that is because he would stick to his side of the bargain, he did not require her to sit up at table, but gave her her breakfast on a dish in the corner, where to tell the truth she on her side ate it all up with great daintiness and propriety. Nor she did make any attempt to go out of doors that morning, but lay curled up in an armchair before the fire dozing. After lunch he took her out, and she never so much as offered to go near the ducks, but running before him led him on to take her a longer walk. This he consented to do very much to her joy and delight. He took her through the fields by the most unfrequented ways, being much alarmed lest they should be seen by anyone. But by good luck they walked above four miles across country and saw nobody. All the way his wife kept running on ahead of him, and then back to him to lick his hand and so on, and appeared delighted at taking exercise. And though they startled two or three rabbits and a hare in the course of their walk she never attempted to go after them, only giving them a look and then looking back to him, laughing at him as it were for his warning cry of "Puss! come in, no nonsense now!"

Just when they got home and were going into the porch they came face to face with an old woman. Mr. Tebrick stopped short in consternation and looked about for his vixen, but she had run forward without any shyness to greet her. Then he recognised the intruder, it was his wife's old nurse.

"What are you doing here, Mrs. Cork?" he asked her.

Mrs. Cork answered him in these words:

"Poor thing. Poor Miss Silvia! It is a shame to let her run about like a dog. It is a shame, and your own wife too. But whatever she looks like, you should trust her the same as ever. If you do she'll do her best to be a good wife to you, if you don't I shouldn't wonder if she did turn into a proper fox. I saw her, sir, before I left, and I've had no peace of mind. I couldn't sleep thinking of her. So I've come back to look after her, as I have done all her life, sir," and she stooped down and took Mrs. Tebrick by the paw.

Mr. Tebrick unlocked the door and they went in. When Mrs. Cork saw the house she exclaimed again and again: "The place was a pigstye. They couldn't live like that, a gentleman must have somebody to look after him. She would do it. He could trust her with the secret."

Had the old woman come the day before it is likely enough that Mr. Tebrick would have sent her packing. But the voice of conscience being woken in him by his drunkenness of the night before he was heartily ashamed of his own management of the business, moreover the old woman's words that "it was a shame to let her run about like a dog," moved him exceedingly. Being in this mood the truth is he welcomed her.

But we may conclude that Mrs. Tebrick was as sorry to see her old Nanny as her husband was glad. If we consider that she had been brought up strictly by her when she was a child, and was now again in her power, and that her old nurse could never be satisfied with her now whatever she did, but would always think her wicked to be a fox at all, there seems good reason for her dislike. And it is possible, too, that there may have been another cause as well, and that is jealousy. We know her husband was always trying to bring her back to be a woman, or at any rate to get her to act like one, may she not have been hoping to get him to be like a beast himself or to act like one? May she not have thought it easier to change him thus than ever to change herself back into being a woman? If we think that she had had a success of this kind only the night before, when he got drunk, can we not conclude that this was indeed the case, and then we have another good reason why the poor lady should hate to see her old nurse?

It is certain that whatever hopes Mr. Tebrick had of Mrs. Cork affecting his wife for the better were disappointed. She grew steadily wilder and after a few days so intractable with her that Mr. Tebrick again took her under his complete control.

The first morning Mrs. Cork made her a new jacket, cutting down the sleeves of a blue silk one of Mrs. Tebrick's and trimming it with swan's down, and directly she had altered it, put it on her mistress, and fetching a mirror would have her admire the fit of it. All the time she waited on

Mrs. Tebrick the old woman talked to her as though she were a baby, and treated her as such, never thinking perhaps that she was either the one thing or the other, that is either a lady to whom she owed respect and who had rational powers exceeding her own, or else a wild creature on whom words were wasted. But though at first she submitted passively, Mrs. Tebrick only waited for her Nanny's back to be turned to tear up her pretty piece of handiwork into shreds, and then ran gaily about waving her brush with only a few ribands still hanging from her neck.

So it was time after time (for the old woman was used to having her own way) until Mrs. Cork would, I think, have tried punishing her if she had not been afraid of Mrs. Tebrick's rows of white teeth, which she often showed her, then laughing afterwards, as if to say it was only play.

Not content with tearing off the dresses that were fitted on her, one day Silvia slipped upstairs to her wardrobe and tore down all her old dresses and made havoc with them, not sparing her wedding dress either, but tearing and ripping them all up so that there was hardly a shred or rag left big enough to dress a doll in. On this, Mr. Tebrick, who had let the old woman have most of her management to see what she could make of her, took her back under his own control.

He was sorry enough now that Mrs. Cork had disappointed him in the hopes he had had of her, to have the old woman, as it were, on his hands. True she could be useful enough in many ways to him, by doing the housework, the cooking and mending, but still he was anxious since his secret was in her keeping, and the more now that she had tried her hand with his wife and failed. For he saw that vanity had kept her mouth shut if she had won over her mistress to better ways, and her love for her would have grown by getting her own way with her. But now that she had failed she bore her mistress a grudge for not being won over, or at the best was become indifferent to the business, so that she might very readily blab.

For the moment all Mr. Tebrick could do was to keep her from going into Stokoe to the village, where she would meet all her old cronies and where there were certain to be any number of inquiries about what was going on at Rylands and so on. But as he saw that it was clearly beyond his power, however vigilant he might be, to watch over the old woman and his wife, and to prevent anyone from meeting with either of them, he began to consider what he could best do.

Since he had sent away his servants and the gardener, giving out a story of having received bad news and his wife going away to London where he would join her, their probably going out of England and so on, he knew well enough that there would be a great deal of talk in the neighbourhood.

And as he had now stayed on, contrary to what he had said, there would be further rumour. Indeed, had he known it, there was a story already going round the country that his wife had run away with Major Solmes, and that he was gone mad with grief, that he had shot his dogs and his horses and shut himself up alone in the house and would speak with no one. This story was made up by his neighbours not because they were fanciful or wanted to deceive, but like most tittle-tattle to fill a gap, as few like to confess ignorance, and if people are asked about such or such a man they must have something to say, or they suffer in everybody's opinion, are set down as dull or "out of the swim." In this way I met not long ago with someone who, after talking some little while and not knowing me or who I was, told me that David Garnett was dead, and died of being bitten by a cat after he had tormented it. He had long grown a nuisance to his friends as an exorbitant sponge upon them, and the world was well rid of him.

Hearing this story of myself diverted me at the time, but I fully believe it has served me in good stead since. For it set me on my guard as perhaps nothing else would have done, against accepting for true all floating rumour and village gossip, so that now I am by second nature a true sceptic and scarcely believe anything unless the evidence for it is conclusive. Indeed I could never have got to the bottom of this history if I had believed one tenth part of what I was told, there was so much of it that was either manifestly false and absurd, or else contradictory to the ascertained facts. It is therefore only the bare bones of the story which you will find written here, for I have rejected all the flowery embroideries which would be entertaining reading enough, I daresay, for some, but if there be any doubt of the truth of a thing it is poor sort of entertainment to read about in my opinion.

To get back to our story: Mr. Tebrick having considered how much the appetite of his neighbours would be whetted to find out the mystery by his remaining in that part of the country, determined that the best thing he could do was to remove.

After some time turning the thing over in his mind, he decided that no place would be so good for his purpose as old Nanny's cottage. It was thirty miles away from Stokoe, which in the country means as far as Timbuctoo does to us in London. Then it was near Tangley, and his lady having known it from her childhood would feel at home there, and also it was utterly remote, there being no village near it or manor house other than Tangley Hall, which was now untenanted for the greater part of the year. Nor did it mean imparting his secret to others, for there was only Mrs. Cork's son, a widower, who being out at work all day would be easily outwitted, the more so as he was stone deaf and of a slow and saturnine disposition. To be sure there was little Polly, Mrs. Cork's granddaughter, but either Mr. Tebrick forgot her altogether, or else reckoned her as a mere baby and not to be thought of as a danger.

He talked the thing over with Mrs. Cork, and they decided upon it out of hand. The truth is the old woman was beginning to regret that her love and her curiosity had ever brought her back to Rylands, since so far she had got much work and little credit by it.

When it was settled, Mr. Tebrick disposed of the remaining business he had at Rylands in the afternoon, and that was chiefly putting out his wife's riding horse into the keeping of a farmer near by, for he thought he would drive over with his own horse, and the other spare horse tandem in the dogcart.

The next morning they locked up the house and they departed, having first secured Mrs. Tebrick in a large wicker hamper where she would be tolerably comfortable. This was for safety, for in the agitation of driving she might jump out, and on the other hand, if a dog scented her and she were loose, she might be in danger of her life. Mr. Tebrick drove with the hamper beside him on the front seat, and spoke to her gently very often.

She was overcome by the excitement of the journey and kept poking her nose first through one crevice, then through another, turning and twisting the whole time and peeping out to see what they were passing. It was a bitterly cold day, and when they had gone about fifteen miles they drew up by the roadside to rest the horses and have their own luncheon, for he dared not stop at an inn. He knew that any living creature in a hamper, even if it be only an old fowl, always draws attention; there would be several loafers most likely who would notice that he had a fox with him, and even if he left the hamper in the cart the dogs at the inn would be sure to sniff out her scent. So not to take any chances he drew up at the side of the road and rested there, though it was freezing hard and a north-east wind howling.

He took down his precious hamper, unharnessed his two horses, covered them with rugs and gave them their corn. Then he opened the basket and let his wife out. She was quite beside herself with joy, running hither and thither, bouncing up on him, looking about her and even rolling over on the ground. Mr. Tebrick took this to mean that she was glad at making this journey and rejoiced equally with her. As for Mrs. Cork, she sat motionless on the back seat of the dogcart well wrapped up, eating her sandwiches, but would not speak a word. When they had stayed there half-an-hour Mr. Tebrick harnessed the horses again, though he was so cold he could scarcely buckle the straps, and put his vixen in her basket, but seeing that she wanted to look about her, he let her tear away the osiers with her teeth till she had made a hole big enough for her to put her head out of.

They drove on again and then the snow began to come down and that in earnest, so that he began to be afraid they would never cover the ground. But just after nightfall they got in, and he was content to leave unharnessing the horses and baiting them to Simon, Mrs. Cork's son. His vixen was tired by then, as well as he, and they slept together, he in the bed and she under it, very contentedly.

The next morning he looked about him at the place and found the thing there that he most wanted, and that was a little walled-in garden where his wife could run in freedom and yet be in safety.

After they had had breakfast she was wild to go out into the snow. So they went out together, and he had never seen such a mad creature in all his life as his wife was then.

For she ran to and fro as if she were crazy, biting at the snow and rolling in it, and round and round in circles and rushed back at him fiercely as if she meant to bite him. He joined her in the frolic, and began snowballing her till she was so wild that it was all he could do to quiet her again and bring her indoors for luncheon. Indeed with her gambollings she tracked the whole garden over with her feet; he could see where she had rolled in the snow and where she had danced in it, and looking at those prints of her feet as they went in, made his heart ache, he knew not why.

They passed the first day at old Nanny's cottage happily enough, without their usual bickerings, and this because of the novelty of the snow which had diverted them. In the afternoon he first showed his wife to little Polly, who eyed her very curiously but hung back shyly and seemed a good deal afraid of the fox. But Mr. Tebrick took up a book and let them get acquainted by themselves, and presently looking up saw that they had come together and Polly was stroking his wife, patting her and running her fingers through her fur. Presently she began talking to the fox, and then brought her doll in to show her so that very soon they were very good playmates together. Watching the two gave Mr. Tebrick great delight, and in particular when he noticed that there was something very motherly in his vixen. She was indeed far above the child in intelligence and restrained herself too from any hasty action. But while she seemed to wait on Polly's pleasure yet she managed to give a twist to the game, whatever it was, that never failed to delight the little girl. In short, in a very little while, Polly was so taken with her new playmate that she cried when she was parted from her and wanted her always with her. This disposition of Mrs. Tebrick's made Mrs. Cork more agreeable than she had been lately either to the husband or the wife.

Three days after they had come to the cottage the weather changed, and they woke up one morning to find the snow gone, and the wind in the south, and the sun shining, so that it was like the first beginning of spring.

Mr. Tebrick let his vixen out into the garden after breakfast, stayed with her awhile, and then went indoors to write some letters.

When he got out again he could see no sign of her anywhere, so that he ran about bewildered, calling to her. At last he spied a mound of fresh earth by the wall in one corner of the garden, and running thither found that there was a hole freshly dug seeming to go under the wall. On this he ran out of the garden quickly till he came to the other side of the wall, but there was no hole there, so he concluded that she was not yet got through. So it proved to be, for reaching down into the hole he felt her brush with his hand, and could hear her distinctly working away with her claws. He called to her then, saying: "Silvia, Silvia, why do you do this? Are you trying to escape from me? I am your husband, and if I keep you confined it is to protect you, not to let you run into danger. Show me how I can make you happy and I will do it, but do not try to escape from me. I love you, Silvia; is it because of that that you want to fly from me to go into the world where you will be in danger of your life always? There are dogs everywhere and they all would kill you if it were not for me. Come out, Silvia, come out."

But Silvia would not listen to him, so he waited there silent. Then he spoke to her in a different way, asking her had she forgot the bargain she made with him that she would not go out alone, but now when she had all the liberty of a garden to herself would she wantonly break her word? And he asked her, were they not married? And had she not always found him a good husband to her? But she heeded this neither until presently his temper getting somewhat out of hand he cursed her obstinacy and told her if she would be a damned fox she was welcome to it, for his part he could get his own way. She had not escaped yet. He would dig her out for he still had time, and if she struggled put her in a bag.

These words brought her forth instantly and she looked at him with as much astonishment as if she knew not what could have made him angry. Yes, she even fawned on him, but in a good-natured kind of way, as if she were a very good wife putting up wonderfully with her husband's temper.

These airs of hers made the poor gentleman (so simple was he) repent his outburst and feel most ashamed.

But for all that when she was out of the hole he filled it up with great stones and beat them in with a crowbar so she should find her work at that point harder than before if she was tempted to begin it again.

In the afternoon he let her go again into the garden but sent little Polly with her to keep her company. But presently on looking out he saw his vixen had climbed up into the limbs of an old pear tree and was looking over the wall, and was not so far from it but she might jump over it if she could get a little further.

Mr. Tebrick ran out into the garden as quick as he could, and when his wife saw him it seemed she was startled and made a false spring at the wall, so that she missed reaching it and fell back heavily to the ground and lay there insensible. When Mr. Tebrick got up to her he found her head was twisted under her by her fall and the neck seemed to be broken. The shock was so great to him that for some time he could not do anything, but knelt beside her turning her limp body stupidly in his hands. At length he recognised that she was indeed dead, and beginning to consider what dreadful afflictions God had visited him with, he blasphemed horribly and called on God to strike him dead, or give his wife back to him.

"Is it not enough," he cried, adding a foul blasphemous oath, "that you should rob me of my dear wife, making her a fox, but now you must rob me of that fox too, that has been my only solace and comfort in this affliction?"

Then he burst into tears and began wringing his hands and continued there in such an extremity of grief for half-an-hour that he cared nothing, neither what he was doing, nor what would become of him in the future, but only knew that his life was ended now and he would not live any longer than he could help.

All this while the little girl Polly stood by, first staring, then asking him what had happened, and lastly crying with fear, but he never heeded her nor looked at her but only tore his hair, sometimes shouted at God, or shook his fist at Heaven. So in a fright Polly opened the door and ran out of the garden.

At length worn out, and as it were all numb with his loss, Mr. Tebrick got up and went within doors, leaving his dear fox lying near where she had fallen.

He stayed indoors only two minutes and then came out again with a razor in his hand intending to cut his own throat, for he was out of his senses in this first paroxysm of grief. But his vixen was gone, at which he looked about for a moment bewildered, and then enraged, thinking that somebody must have taken the body.

The door of the garden being open he ran straight through it. Now this door, which had been left ajar by Polly when she ran off, opened into a little courtyard where the fowls were shut in at night; the woodhouse and the privy also stood there. On the far side of it from the garden gate were two large wooden doors big enough when open to let a cart enter, and high enough to keep a man from looking over into the yard.

When Mr. Tebrick got into the yard he found his vixen leaping up at these doors, and wild with terror, but as lively as ever he saw her in his life. He ran up to her but she shrank away from him, and would then have dodged him too, but he caught hold of her. She bared her teeth at him but he paid no heed to that, only picked her straight up into his arms and took her so indoors. Yet all the while he could scarce believe his eyes to see her living, and felt her all over very carefully to find if she had not some bones broken. But no, he could find none. Indeed it was some hours before this poor silly gentleman began to suspect the truth, which was that his vixen had practised a deception upon him, and all the time he was bemoaning his loss in such heartrending terms, she was only shamming death to run away directly she was able. If it had not been that the yard gates were shut, which was a mere chance, she had got her liberty by that trick. And that this was only a trick of hers to sham dead was plain when he had thought it over. Indeed it is an old and time-honoured trick of the fox. It is in Aesop and a hundred other writers have confirmed it since. But so thoroughly had he been deceived by her, that at first he was as much overcome with joy at his wife still being alive, as he had been with grief a little while before, thinking her dead.

He took her in his arms, hugging her to him and thanking God a dozen times for her preservation. But his kissing and fondling her had very little effect now, for she did not answer him by licking or soft looks, but stayed huddled up and sullen, with her hair bristling on her neck and her ears laid back every time he touched her. At first he thought this might be because he had touched some broken bone or tender place where she had been hurt, but at last the truth came to him.

Thus he was again to suffer, and though the pain of knowing her treachery to him was nothing to the grief of losing her, yet it was more insidious and lasting. At first, from a mere nothing, this pain grew gradually until it was a torture to him. If he had been one of your stock ordinary husbands, such a one who by experience has learnt never to enquire too closely into his wife's doings, her comings or goings, and never to ask her, "How she has spent the day?" for fear he should be made the more of a fool, had Mr. Tebrick been such a one he had been luckier, and his pain would have been almost nothing. But you must consider that he had never been deceived once by his wife in the course of their married life. No, she had never told him as much as one white lie, but had always been frank, open and ingenuous as if she and her husband were not husband and wife, or indeed of opposite sexes. Yet we must rate him as very foolish, that living thus with a fox, which beast has the same reputation for deceitfulness, craft and cunning, in all countries, all ages, and amongst all races of mankind, he should expect this fox to be as candid and honest with him in all things as the country girl he had married.

His wife's sullenness and bad temper continued that day, for she cowered away from him and hid under the sofa, nor could he persuade her to come out from there. Even when it was her dinner time she stayed, refusing resolutely to be tempted out with food, and lying so quiet that he heard nothing from her for hours. At night he carried her up to the bedroom, but she was still sullen and refused to eat a morsel, though she drank a little water during the night, when she fancied he was asleep.

The next morning was the same, and by now Mr. Tebrick had been through all the agonies of wounded self-esteem, disillusionment and despair that a man can suffer. But though his emotions rose up in his heart and nearly stifled him he showed no sign of them to her, neither did he abate one jot his tenderness and consideration for his vixen. At breakfast he tempted her with a freshly killed young pullet. It hurt him to make this advance to her, for hitherto he had kept her strictly on cooked meats, but the pain of seeing her refuse it was harder still for him to bear. Added to this was now an anxiety lest she should starve herself to death rather than stay with him any longer.

All that morning he kept her close, but in the afternoon let her loose again in the garden after he had lopped the pear tree so that she could not repeat her performance of climbing.

But seeing how disgustedly she looked while he was by, never offering to run or to play as she was used, but only standing stock still with her tail between her legs, her ears flattened, and the hair bristling on her shoulders, seeing this he left her to herself out of mere humanity.

When he came out after half-an-hour he found that she was gone, but there was a fair sized hole by the wall, and she just buried all but her brush, digging desperately to get under the wall and make her escape.

He ran up to the hole, and put his arm in after her and called to her to come out, but she would not. So at first he

began pulling her out by the shoulder, then his hold slipping, by the hind legs. As soon as he had drawn her forth she whipped round and snapped at his hand and bit it through near the joint of the thumb, but let it go instantly. They stayed there for a minute facing each other, he on his knees and she facing him the picture of unrepentant wickedness and fury. Being thus on his knees, Mr. Tebrick was down on her level very nearly, and her muzzle was thrust almost into his face. Her ears lay flat on her head, her gums were bared in a silent snarl, and all her beautiful teeth threatening him that she would bite him again. Her back too was half-arched, all her hair bristling and her brush held drooping. But it was her eyes that held his, with their slit pupils looking at him with savage desperation and rage.

The blood ran very freely from his hand but he never noticed that or the pain of it either, for all his thoughts were for his wife.

"What is this, Silvia?" he said very quietly, "what is this? Why are you so savage now? If I stand between you and your freedom it is because I love you. Is it such torment to be with me?" But Silvia never stirred a muscle.

"You would not do this if you were not in anguish, poor beast, you want your freedom. I cannot keep you, I cannot hold you to vows made when you were a woman. Why, you have forgotten who I am."

The tears then began running down his cheeks, he sobbed, and said to her:

"Go—I shall not keep you. Poor beast, poor beast, I love you, I love you. Go if you want to. But if you remember me come back. I shall never keep you against your will. Go—go. But kiss me now."

He leant forward then and put his lips to her snarling fangs, but though she kept snarling she did not bite him. Then he got up quickly and went to the door of the garden that opened into a little paddock against a wood.

When he opened it she went through it like an arrow, crossed the paddock like a puff of smoke and in a moment was gone from his sight. Then, suddenly finding himself alone, Mr. Tebrick came as it were to himself and ran after her, calling her by name and shouting to her, and so went plunging into the wood, and through it for about a mile, running almost blindly.

At last when he was worn out he sat down, seeing that she had gone beyond recovery and it was already night. Then, rising, he walked slowly homewards, wearied and spent in spirit. As he went he bound up his hand that was still running with blood. His coat was torn, his hat lost, and his face scratched right across with briars. Now in cold blood he began to reflect on what he had done and to repent bitterly having set his wife free. He had betrayed her so that now, from his act, she must lead the life of a wild fox for ever, and must undergo all the rigours and hardships of the climate, and all the hazards of a hunted creature. When Mr. Tebrick got back to the cottage he found Mrs. Cork was sitting up for him. It was already late.

"What have you done with Mrs. Tebrick, sir? I missed her, and I missed you, and I have not known what to do, expecting something dreadful had happened. I have been sitting up for you half the night. And where is she now, sir?" She accosted him so vigorously that Mr. Tebrick stood silent. At length he said: "I have let her go. She has run away."

"Poor Miss Silvia!" cried the old woman, "Poor creature! You ought to be ashamed, sir! Let her go indeed! Poor lady, is that the way for her husband to talk! It is a disgrace. But I saw it coming from the first."

The old woman was white with fury, she did not mind what she said, but Mr. Tebrick was not listening to her. At last he looked at her and saw that she had just begun to cry, so he went out of the room and up to bed, and lay down as he was, in his clothes, utterly exhausted, and fell into a dog's sleep, starting up every now and then with horror, and then falling back with fatigue. It was late when he woke up, but cold and raw, and he felt cramped in all his limbs. As he lay he heard again the noise which had woken him—the trotting of several horses, and the voices of men riding by the house. Mr. Tebrick jumped up and ran to the window and then looked out, and the first thing that he saw was a gentleman in a pink coat riding at a walk down the lane. At this sight Mr. Tebrick waited no longer, but pulling on his boots in mad haste, ran out instantly, meaning to say that they must not hunt, and how his wife was escaped and they might kill her.

But when he found himself outside the cottage words failed him and fury took possession of him, so that he could only cry out:

"How dare you, you damned blackguard?" And so, with a stick in his hand, he threw himself on the gentleman in the pink coat and seized his horse's rein, and catching the gentleman by the leg was trying to throw him. But really it is impossible to say what Mr. Tebrick intended by his behaviour or what he would have done, for the gentleman finding himself suddenly assaulted in so unexpected a fashion by so strange a touzled and dishevelled figure, clubbed his hunting crop and dealt him a blow on the temple so that he fell insensible.

Another gentleman rode up at this moment and they were civil enough to dismount and carry Mr. Tebrick into the cottage, where they were met by old Nanny who kept wringing her hands and told them Mr. Tebrick's wife had run away and she was a vixen, and that was the cause that Mr. Tebrick had run out and assaulted them.

The two gentlemen could not help laughing at this; and mounting their horses rode on without delay, after telling each other that Mr. Tebrick, whoever he was, was certainly a madman, and the old woman seemed as mad as her master.

This story, however, went the rounds of the gentry in those parts and perfectly confirmed everyone in their previous opinion, namely that Mr. Tebrick was mad and his wife had run away from him. The part about her being a vixen was laughed at by the few that heard it, but was soon left out as immaterial to the story, and incredible in itself, though afterwards it came to be remembered and its significance to be understood. When Mr. Tebrick came to

himself it was past noon, and his head was aching so painfully that he could only call to mind in a confused way what had happened.

However, he sent off Mrs. Cork's son directly on one of his horses to enquire about the hunt.

At the same time he gave orders to old Nanny that she was to put out food and water for her mistress, on the chance that she might yet be in the neighbourhood.

By nightfall Simon was back with the news that the hunt had had a very long run but lost one fox, then, drawing a covert, had chopped an old dog fox, and so ended the day's sport.

This put poor Mr. Tebrick in some hopes again, and he rose at once from his bed, and went out to the wood and began calling his wife, but was overcome with faintness, and lay down and so passed the night in the open, from mere weakness.

In the morning he got back again to the cottage but he had taken a chill, and so had to keep his bed for three or four days after.

All this time he had food put out for her every night, but though rats came to it and ate of it, there were never any prints of a fox.

At last his anxiety began working another way, that is he came to think it possible that his vixen would have gone back to Stokoe, so he had his horses harnessed in the dogcart and brought to the door and then drove over to Rylands, though he was still in a fever, and with a heavy cold upon him. After that he lived always solitary, keeping away from his fellows and only seeing one man, called Askew, who had been brought up a jockey at Wantage, but was grown too big for his profession. He mounted this loafing fellow on one of his horses three days a week and had him follow the hunt and report to him whenever they killed, and if he could view the fox so much the better, and then he made him describe it minutely, so he should know if it were his Silvia. But he dared not trust himself to go himself, lest his passion should master him and he might commit a murder.

Every time there was a hunt in the neighbourhood he set the gates wide open at Rylands and the house doors also, and taking his gun stood sentinel in the hope that his wife would run in if she were pressed by the hounds, and so he could save her. But only once a hunt came near, when two fox-hounds that had lost the main pack strayed on to his land and he shot them instantly and buried them afterwards himself.

It was not long now to the end of the season, as it was the middle of March.

But living as he did at this time, Mr. Tebrick grew more and more to be a true misanthrope. He denied admittance to any that came to visit him, and rarely showed himself to his fellows, but went out chiefly in the early mornings before people were about, in the hope of seeing his beloved fox. Indeed it was only this hope that he would see her again that kept him alive, for he had become so careless of his own comfort in every way that he very seldom ate a proper meal, taking no more than a crust of bread with a morsel of cheese in the whole day, though sometimes he would drink half a bottle of whiskey to drown his sorrow and to get off to sleep, for sleep fled from him, and no sooner did he begin dozing but he awoke with a start thinking he had heard something. He let his beard grow too, and though he had always been very particular in his person before, he now was utterly careless of it, gave up washing himself for a week or two at a stretch, and if there was dirt under his finger nails let it stop there.

All this disorder fed a malignant pleasure in him. For by now he had come to hate his fellow men and was embittered against all human decencies and decorum. For strange to tell he never once in these months regretted his dear wife whom he had so much loved. No, all that he grieved for now was his departed vixen. He was haunted all this time not by the memory of a sweet and gentle woman, but by the recollection of an animal; a beast it is true that could sit at table and play piquet when it would, but for all that nothing really but a wild beast. His one hope now was the recovery of this beast, and of this he dreamed continually. Likewise both waking and sleeping he was visited by visions of her; her mask, her full white-tagged brush, white throat, and the thick fur in her ears all haunted him.

Every one of her foxey ways was now so absolutely precious to him that I believe that if he had known for certain she was dead, and had thoughts of marrying a second time, he would never have been happy with a woman. No, indeed, he would have been more tempted to get himself a tame fox, and would have counted that as good a marriage as he could make.

Yet this all proceeded one may say from a passion, and a true conjugal fidelity, that it would be hard to find matched in this world. And though we may think him a fool, almost a madman, we must, when we look closer, find much to respect in his extraordinary devotion. How different indeed was he from those who, if their wives go mad, shut them in madhouses and give themselves up to concubinage, and nay, what is more, there are many who extenuate such conduct too. But Mr. Tebrick was of a very different temper, and though his wife was now nothing but a hunted beast, cared for no one in the world but her.

But this devouring love ate into him like a consumption, so that by sleepless nights, and not caring for his person, in a few months he was worn to the shadow of himself. His cheeks were sunk in, his eyes hollow but excessively brilliant, and his whole body had lost flesh, so that looking at him the wonder was that he was still alive.

Now that the hunting season was over he had less anxiety for her, yet even so he was not positive that the hounds had not got her. For between the time of his setting her free, and the end of the hunting season (just after Easter), there were but three vixens killed near. Of those three one was a half-blind or wall-eyed, and one was a very grey dull-coloured beast. The third answered more to the description of his wife, but that it had not much black on the legs, whereas in her the blackness of the legs was very plain to be noticed. But yet his fear made him think that perhaps she had got mired in running and the legs being muddy were not remarked on as black. One morning the first week in May, about four o'clock, when he was out waiting in the little copse, he sat down for a while on a tree stump, and when he looked up saw a fox coming towards him over the ploughed field. It was carrying a hare over its shoulder so that it was nearly all hidden from him. At last, when it was not twenty yards from him, it crossed over, going into the copse, when Mr. Tebrick stood up and cried out, "Silvia, Silvia, is it you?"

The fox dropped the hare out of his mouth and stood looking at him, and then our gentleman saw at the first glance that this was not his wife. For whereas Mrs. Tebrick had been of a very bright red, this was a swarthier duller beast altogether, moreover it was a good deal larger and higher at the shoulder and had a great white tag to his brush. But the fox after the first instant did not stand for his portrait you may be sure, but picked up his hare and made off like an arrow.

Then Mr. Tebrick cried out to himself: "Indeed I am crazy now! My affliction has made me lose what little reason I ever had. Here am I taking every fox I see to be my wife! My neighbours call me a madman and now I see that they are right. Look at me now, oh God! How foul a creature I am. I hate my fellows. I am thin and wasted by this consuming passion, my reason is gone and I feed myself on dreams. Recall me to my duty, bring me back to decency, let me not become a beast likewise, but restore me and forgive me, Oh my Lord."

With that he burst into scalding tears and knelt down and prayed, a thing he had not done for many weeks.

When he rose up he walked back feeling giddy and exceedingly weak, but with a contrite heart, and then washed himself thoroughly and changed his clothes, but his weakness increasing he lay down for the rest of the day, but read in the Book of Job and was much comforted.

For several days after this he lived very soberly, for his weakness continued, but every day he read in the bible, and prayed earnestly, so that his resolution was so much strengthened that he determined to overcome his folly, or his passion, if he could, and at any rate to live the rest of his life very religiously. So strong was this desire in him to amend his ways that he considered if he should not go to spread the Gospel abroad, for the Bible Society, and so spend the rest of his days.

Indeed he began a letter to his wife's uncle, the canon, and he was writing this when he was startled by hearing a fox bark.

Yet so great was this new turn he had taken that he did not rush out at once, as he would have done before, but stayed where he was and finished his letter.

Afterwards he said to himself that it was only a wild fox and sent by the devil to mock him, and that madness lay that way if he should listen. But on the other hand he could not deny to himself that it might have been his wife, and that he ought to welcome the prodigal. Thus he was torn between these two thoughts, neither of which did he completely believe. He stayed thus tormented with doubts and fears all night.

The next morning he woke suddenly with a start and on the instant heard a fox bark once more. At that he pulled on his clothes and ran out as fast as he could to the garden gate. The sun was not yet high, the dew thick everywhere, and for a minute or two everything was very silent. He looked about him eagerly but could see no fox, yet there was already joy in his heart.

Then while he looked up and down the road, he saw his vixen step out of the copse about thirty yards away. He called to her at once.

"My dearest wife! Oh, Silvia! You are come back!" and at the sound of his voice he saw her wag her tail, which set his last doubts at rest.

But then though he called her again, she stepped into the copse once more though she looked back at him over her shoulder as she went. At this he ran after her, but softly and not too fast lest he should frighten her away, and then looked about for her again and called to her when he saw her among the trees still keeping her distance from him. He followed her then, and as he approached so she retreated from him, yet always looking back at him several times.

He followed after her through the underwood up the side of the hill, when suddenly she disappeared from his sight, behind some bracken. When he got there he could see her nowhere, but looking about him found a fox's earth, but so well hidden that he might have passed it by a thousand times and would never have found it unless he had made particular search at that spot.

But now, though he went on his hands and knees, he could see nothing of his vixen, so that he waited a little while wondering.

Presently he heard a noise of something moving in the earth, and so waited silently, then saw something which pushed itself into sight. It was a small sooty black beast, like a puppy. There came another behind it, then another and so on till there were five of them. Lastly there came his vixen pushing her litter before her, and while he looked at her silently, a prey to his confused and unhappy emotions, he saw that her eyes were shining with pride and happiness.

She picked up one of her youngsters then, in her mouth, and brought it to him and laid it in front of him, and then looked up at him very excited, or so it seemed.

Mr. Tebrick took the cub in his hands, stroked it and put it against his cheek. It was a little fellow with a smutty face and paws, with staring vacant eyes of a brilliant electric blue and a little tail like a carrot. When he was put down he took a step towards his mother and then sat down very comically.

Mr. Tebrick looked at his wife again and spoke to her, calling her a good creature. Already he was resigned and now, indeed, for the first time he thoroughly understood what had happened to her, and how far apart they were now. But looking first at one cub, then at another, and having them sprawling over his lap, he forgot himself,

only watching the pretty scene, and taking pleasure in it. Now and then he would stroke his vixen and kiss her, liberties which she freely allowed him. He marvelled more than ever now at her beauty; for her gentleness with the cubs and the extreme delight she took in them seemed to him then to make her more lovely than before. Thus lying amongst them at the mouth of the earth he idled away the whole of the morning.

First he would play with one, then with another, rolling them over and tickling them, but they were too young yet to lend themselves to any other more active sport than this. Every now and then he would stroke his vixen, or look at her, and thus the time slipped away quite fast and he was surprised when she gathered her cubs together and pushed them before her into the earth, then coming back to him once or twice very humanly bid him "Good-bye and that she hoped she would see him soon again, now he had found out the way."

So admirably did she express her meaning that it would have been superfluous for her to have spoken had she been able, and Mr. Tebrick, who was used to her, got up at once and went home.

But now that he was alone, all the feelings which he had not troubled himself with when he was with her, but had, as it were, put aside till after his innocent pleasures were over, all these came swarming back to assail him in a hundred tormenting ways.

Firstly he asked himself: Was not his wife unfaithful to him, had she not prostituted herself to a beast? Could he still love her after that? But this did not trouble him so much as it might have done. For now he was convinced inwardly that she could no longer in fairness be judged as a woman, but as a fox only. And as a fox she had done no more than other foxes, indeed in having cubs and tending them with love, she had done well.

Whether in this conclusion Mr. Tebrick was in the right or not, is not for us here to consider. But I would only say to those who would censure him for a too lenient view of the religious side of the matter, that we have not seen the thing as he did, and perhaps if it were displayed before our eyes we might be led to the same conclusions.

This was, however, not a tenth part of the trouble in which Mr. Tebrick found himself. For he asked himself also: "Was he not jealous?" And looking into his heart he found that he was indeed jealous, yes, and angry too, that now he must share his vixen with wild foxes. Then he questioned himself if it were not dishonourable to do so, and whether he should not utterly forget her and follow his original intention of retiring from the world, and see her no more.

Thus he tormented himself for the rest of that day, and by evening he had resolved never to see her again.

But in the middle of the night he woke up with his head very clear, and said to himself in wonder, "Am I not a madman? I torment myself foolishly with fantastic notions. Can a man have his honour sullied by a beast? I am a man, I am immeasurably superior to the animals. Can my dignity allow of my being jealous of a beast? A thousand times no. Were I to lust after a vixen, I were a criminal indeed. I can be happy in seeing my vixen, for I love her, but she does right to be happy according to the laws of her being."

Lastly, he said to himself what was, he felt, the truth of this whole matter:

"When I am with her I am happy. But now I distort what is simple and drive myself crazy with false reasoning upon it."

Yet before he slept again he prayed, but though he had thought first to pray for guidance, in reality he prayed only that on the morrow he would see his vixen again and that God would preserve her, and her cubs too, from all dangers, and would allow him to see them often, so that he might come to love them for her sake as if he were their father, and that if this were a sin he might be forgiven, for he sinned in ignorance. The next day or two he saw vixen and cubs again, though his visits were cut shorter, and these visits gave him such an innocent pleasure that very soon his notions of honour, duty and so on, were entirely forgotten, and his jealousy lulled asleep.

One day he tried taking with him the stereoscope and a pack of cards.

But though his Silvia was affectionate and amiable enough to let him put the stereoscope over her muzzle, yet she would not look through it, but kept turning her head to lick his hand, and it was plain to him that now she had quite forgotten the use of the instrument. It was the same too with the cards. For with them she was pleased enough, but only delighting to bite at them, and flip them about with her paws, and never considering for a moment whether they were diamonds or clubs, or hearts, or spades or whether the card was an ace or not. So it was evident that she had forgotten the nature of cards too.

Thereafter he only brought them things which she could better enjoy, that is sugar, grapes, raisins, and butcher's meat.

By-and-bye, as the summer wore on, the cubs came to know him, and he them, so that he was able to tell them easily apart, and then he christened them. For this purpose he brought a little bowl of water, sprinkled them as if in baptism and told them he was their godfather and gave each of them a name, calling them Sorel, Kasper, Selwyn, Esther, and Angelica.

Sorel was a clumsy little beast of a cheery and indeed puppyish disposition; Kasper was fierce, the largest of the five, even in his play he would always bite, and gave his godfather many a sharp nip as time went on. Esther was of a dark complexion, a true brunette and very sturdy; Angelica the brightest red and the most exactly like her mother; while Selwyn was the smallest cub, of a very prying, inquisitive and cunning temper, but delicate and undersized.

Thus Mr. Tebrick had a whole family now to occupy him, and, indeed, came to love them with very much of a father's love and partiality.

His favourite was Angelica (who reminded him so much of her mother in her pretty ways) because of a gentleness which was lacking in the others, even in their play. After her in his affections came Selwyn, whom he soon saw was the most intelligent of the whole litter. Indeed he was so much more quick-witted than the rest that Mr. Tebrick was led into speculating as to whether he had not inherited something of the human from his dam. Thus very early he learnt to know his name, and would come when he was called, and what was stranger still, he learnt the names of his brothers and sisters before they came to do so themselves.

Besides all this he was something of a young philosopher, for though his brother Kasper tyrannized over him he put up with it all with an unruffled temper. He was not, however, above playing tricks on the others, and one day when Mr. Tebrick was by, he made believe that there was a mouse in a hole some little way off. Very soon he was joined by Sorel, and presently by Kasper and Esther. When he had got them all digging, it was easy for him to slip away, and then he came to his godfather with a sly look, sat down before him, and smiled and then jerked his head over towards the others and smiled again and wrinkled his brows so that Mr. Tebrick knew as well as if he had spoken that the youngster was saying, "Have I not made fools of them all?"

He was the only one that was curious about Mr. Tebrick: he made him take out his watch, put his ear to it, considered it and wrinkled up his brows in perplexity. On the next visit it was the same thing. He must see the watch again, and again think over it. But clever as he was, little Selwyn could never understand it, and if his mother remembered anything about watches it was a subject which she never attempted to explain to her children.

One day Mr. Tebrick left the earth as usual and ran down the slope to the road, when he was surprised to find a carriage waiting before his house and a coachman walking about near his gate. Mr. Tebrick went in and found that his visitor was waiting for him. It was his wife's uncle.

They shook hands, though the Rev. Canon Fox did not recognise him immediately, and Mr. Tebrick led him into the house.

The clergyman looked about him a good deal, at the dirty and disorderly rooms, and when Mr. Tebrick took him into the drawing room it was evident that it had been unused for several months, the dust lay so thickly on all the furniture.

After some conversation on indifferent topics Canon Fox said to him:

"I have called really to ask about my niece."

Mr. Tebrick was silent for some time and then said:

"She is quite happy now."

"Ah—indeed. I have heard she is not living with you any longer."

"No. She is not living with me. She is not far away. I see her every day now."

"Indeed. Where does she live?"

"In the woods with her children. I ought to tell you that she has changed her shape. She is a fox."

The Rev. Canon Fox got up; he was alarmed, and everything Mr. Tebrick said confirmed what he had been led to expect he would find at Rylands. When he was outside, however, he asked Mr. Tebrick:

"You don't have many visitors now, eh?"

"No—I never see anyone if I can avoid it. You are the first person I have spoken to for months."

"Quite right, too, my dear fellow. I quite understand—in the circumstances." Then the cleric shook him by the hand, got into his carriage and drove away.

"At any rate," he said to himself, "there will be no scandal." He was relieved also because Mr. Tebrick had said nothing about going abroad to disseminate the Gospel. Canon Fox had been alarmed by the letter, had not answered it, and thought that it was always better to let things be, and never to refer to anything unpleasant. He did not at all want to recommend Mr. Tebrick to the Bible Society if he were mad. His eccentricities would never be noticed at Stokoe. Besides that, Mr. Tebrick had said he was happy.

He was sorry for Mr. Tebrick too, and he said to himself that the queer girl, his niece, must have married him because he was the first man she had met. He reflected also that he was never likely to see her again and said aloud, when he had driven some little way:

"Not an affectionate disposition," then to his coachman: "No, that's all right. Drive on, Hopkins."

When Mr. Tebrick was alone he rejoiced exceedingly in his solitary life. He understood, or so he fancied, what it was to be happy, and that he had found complete happiness now, living from day to day, careless of the future, surrounded every morning by playful and affectionate little creatures whom he loved tenderly, and sitting beside their mother, whose simple happiness was the source of his own.

"True happiness," he said to himself, "is to be found in bestowing love; there is no such happiness as that of the mother for her babe, unless I have attained it in mine for my vixen and her children."

With these feelings he waited impatiently for the hour on the morrow when he might hasten to them once more.

When, however, he had toiled up the hillside, to the earth, taking infinite precaution not to tread down the bracken, or make a beaten path which might lead others to that secret spot, he found to his surprise that Silvia was not there and that there were no cubs to be seen either. He called to them, but it was in vain, and at last he laid himself on the mossy bank beside the earth and waited.

For a long while, as it seemed to him, he lay very still, with closed eyes, straining his ears to hear every rustle among the leaves, or any sound that might be the cubs stirring in the earth.

At last he must have dropped asleep, for he woke suddenly with all his senses alert, and opening his eyes found a full-grown fox within six feet of him sitting on its haunches like a dog and watching his face with curiosity. Mr. Tebrick saw instantly that it was not Silvia. When he moved the fox got up and shifted his eyes, but still stood

his ground, and Mr. Tebrick recognised him then for the dog-fox he had seen once before carrying a hare. It was the same dark beast with a large white tag to his brush. Now the secret was out and Mr. Tebrick could see his rival before him. Here was the real father of his godchildren, who could be certain of their taking after him, and leading over again his wild and rakish life. Mr. Tebrick stared for a long time at the handsome rogue, who glanced back at him with distrust and watchfulness patent in his face, but not without defiance too, and it seemed to Mr. Tebrick as if there was also a touch of cynical humour in his look, as if he said:

"By Gad! we two have been strangely brought together!"

And to the man, at any rate, it seemed strange that they were thus linked, and he wondered if the love his rival there bare to his vixen and his cubs were the same thing in kind as his own.

"We would both of us give our lives for theirs," he said to himself as he reasoned upon it, "we both of us are happy chiefly in their company. What pride this fellow must feel to have such a wife, and such children taking after him. And has he not reason for his pride? He lives in a world where he is beset with a thousand dangers. For half the year he is hunted, everywhere dogs pursue him, men lay traps for him or menace him. He owes nothing to another."

But he did not speak, knowing that his words would only alarm the fox; then in a few minutes he saw the dog-fox look over his shoulder, and then he trotted off as lightly as a gossamer veil blown in the wind, and, in a minute or two more, back he comes with his vixen and the cubs all around him. Seeing the dog-fox thus surrounded by vixen and cubs was too much for Mr. Tebrick; in spite of all his philosophy a pang of jealousy shot through him. He could see that Silvia had been hunting with her cubs, and also that she had forgotten that he would come that morning, for she started when she saw him, and though she carelessly licked his hand, he could see that her thoughts were not with him.

Very soon she led her cubs into the earth, the dog-fox had vanished and Mr. Tebrick was again alone. He did not wait longer but went home.

Now was his peace of mind all gone, the happiness which he had flattered himself the night before he knew so well how to enjoy, seemed now but a fool's paradise in which he had been living. A hundred times this poor gentleman bit his lip, drew down his torvous brows, and stamped his foot, and cursed himself bitterly, or called his lady bitch. He could not forgive himself neither, that he had not thought of the damned dog-fox before, but all the while had let the cubs frisk round him, each one a proof that a dog-fox had been at work with his vixen. Yes, jealousy was now in the wind, and every circumstance which had been a reason for his felicity the night before was now turned into a monstrous feature of his nightmare. With all this Mr. Tebrick so worked upon himself that for the time being he had lost his reason. Black was white and white black, and he was resolved that on the morrow he would dig the vile brood of foxes out and shoot them, and so free himself at last from this hellish plague.

All that night he was in this mood, and in agony, as if he had broken in the crown of a tooth and bitten on the nerve. But as all things will have an ending so at last Mr. Tebrick, worn out and wearied by this loathed passion of jealousy, fell into an uneasy and tormented sleep.

After an hour or two the procession of confused and jumbled images which first assailed him passed away and subsided into one clear and powerful dream. His wife was with him in her own proper shape, walking as they had been on that fatal day before her transformation. Yet she was changed too, for in her face there were visible tokens of unhappiness, her face swollen with crying, pale and downcast, her hair hanging in disorder, her damp hands wringing a small handkerchief into a ball, her whole body shaken with sobs, and an air of long neglect about her person. Between her sobs she was confessing to him some crime which she had committed, but he did not catch the broken words, nor did he wish to hear them, for he was dulled by his sorrow. So they continued walking together in sadness as it were for ever, he with his arm about her waist, she turning her head to him and often casting her eyes down in distress.

At last they sat down, and he spoke, saying: "I know they are not my children, but I shall not use them barbarously because of that. You are still my wife. I swear to you they shall never be neglected. I will pay for their education."

Then he began turning over the names of schools in his mind. Eton would not do, nor Harrow, nor Winchester, nor Rugby.... But he could not tell why these schools would not do for these children of hers, he only knew that every school he thought of was impossible, but surely one could be found. So turning over the names of schools he sat for a long while holding his dear wife's hand, till at length, still weeping, she got up and went away and then slowly he awoke.

But even when he had opened his eyes and looked about him he was thinking of schools, saying to himself that he must send them to a private academy, or even at the worst engage a tutor. "Why, yes," he said to himself, putting one foot out of bed, "that is what it must be, a tutor, though even then there will be a difficulty at first."

At those words he wondered what difficulty there would be and recollected that they were not ordinary children. No, they were foxes—mere foxes. When poor Mr. Tebrick had remembered this he was, as it were, dazed or stunned by the fact, and for a long time he could understand nothing, but at last burst into a flood of tears compassionating them and himself too. The awfulness of the fact itself, that his dear wife should have foxes instead of children, filled him with an agony of pity, and, at length, when he recollected the cause of their being foxes, that is that his wife was a fox also, his tears broke out anew, and he could bear it no longer but began calling out in his anguish, and beat his head once or twice against the wall, and then cast himself down on his bed again and wept and wept, sometimes tearing the sheets asunder with his teeth.

The whole of that day, for he was not to go to the earth till evening, he went about sorrowfully, torn by true pity for his poor vixen and her children.

At last when the time came he went again up to the earth, which he found deserted, but hearing his voice, out came Esther. But though he called the others by their names there was no answer, and something in the way the cub greeted him made him fancy she was indeed alone. She was truly rejoiced to see him, and scrambled up into his arms, and thence to his shoulder, kissing him, which was unusual in her (though natural enough in her sister Angelica). He sat down a little way from the earth fondling her, and fed her with some fish he had brought for her mother, which she ate so ravenously that he concluded she must have been short of food that day and probably alone for some time.

At last while he was sitting there Esther pricked up her ears, started up, and presently Mr. Tebrick saw his vixen come towards them. She greeted him very affectionately but it was plain had not much time to spare, for she soon started back whence she had come with Esther at her side. When they had gone about a rod the cub hung back and kept stopping and looking back to the earth, and at last turned and ran back home. But her mother was not to be fobbed off so, for she quickly overtook her child and gripping her by the scruff began to drag her along with her.

Mr. Tebrick, seeing then how matters stood, spoke to her, telling her he would carry Esther if she would lead, so after a little while Silvia gave her over, and then they set out on their strange journey.

Silvia went running on a little before while Mr. Tebrick followed after with Esther in his arms whimpering and struggling now to be free, and indeed, once she gave him a nip with her teeth. This was not so strange a thing to him now, and he knew the remedy for it, which is much the same as with others whose tempers run too high, that is a taste of it themselves. Mr. Tebrick shook her and gave her a smart little cuff, after which, though she sulked, she stopped her biting.

They went thus above a mile, circling his house and crossing the highway until they gained a small covert that lay with some waste fields adjacent to it. And by this time it was so dark that it was all Mr. Tebrick could do to pick his way, for it was not always easy for him to follow where his vixen found a big enough road for herself.

But at length they came to another earth, and by the starlight Mr. Tebrick could just make out the other cubs skylarking in the shadows.

Now he was tired, but he was happy and laughed softly for joy, and presently his vixen, coming to him, put her feet upon his shoulders as he sat on the ground, and licked him, and he kissed her back on the muzzle and gathered her in his arms and rolled her in his jacket and then laughed and wept by turns in the excess of his joy.

All his jealousies of the night before were forgotten now. All his desperate sorrow of the morning and the horror of his dream were gone. What if they were foxes? Mr. Tebrick found that he could be happy with them. As the weather was hot he lay out there all the night, first playing hide and seek with them in the dark till, missing his vixen and the cubs proving obstreperous, he lay down and was soon asleep.

He was woken up soon after dawn by one of the cubs tugging at his shoelaces in play. When he sat up he saw two of the cubs standing near him on their hind legs, wrestling with each other, the other two were playing hide and seek round a tree trunk, and now Angelica let go his laces and came romping into his arms to kiss him and say "Good morning" to him, then worrying the points of his waistcoat a little shyly after the warmth of his embrace.

That moment of awakening was very sweet to him. The freshness of the morning, the scent of everything at the day's rebirth, the first beams of the sun upon a tree-top near, and a pigeon rising into the air suddenly, all delighted him. Even the rough scent of the body of the cub in his arms seemed to him delicious.

At that moment all human customs and institutions seemed to him nothing but folly; for said he, "I would exchange all my life as a man for my happiness now, and even now I retain almost all of the ridiculous conceptions of a man. The beasts are happier and I will deserve that happiness as best I can."

After he had looked at the cubs playing merrily, how, with soft stealth, one would creep behind another to bounce out and startle him, a thought came into Mr. Tebrick's head, and that was that these cubs were innocent, they were as stainless snow, they could not sin, for God had created them to be thus and they could break none of His commandments. And he fancied also that men sin because they cannot be as the animals.

Presently he got up full of happiness, and began making his way home when suddenly he came to a full stop and asked himself: "What is going to happen to them?"

This question rooted him stockishly in a cold and deadly fear as if he had seen a snake before him. At last he shook his head and hurried on his path. Aye, indeed, what would become of his vixen and her children?

This thought put him into such a fever of apprehension that he did his best not to think of it any more, but yet it stayed with him all that day and for weeks after, at the back of his mind, so that he was not careless in his happiness as before, but as it were trying continually to escape his own thoughts.

This made him also anxious to pass all the time he could with his dear Silvia, and, therefore, he began going out to them for more of the daytime, and then he would sleep the night in the woods also as he had done that night; and so he passed several weeks, only returning to his house occasionally to get himself a fresh provision of food. But after a week or ten days at the new earth both his vixen and the cubs, too, got a new habit of roaming. For a long while

back, as he knew, his vixen had been lying out alone most of the day, and now the cubs were all for doing the same thing. The earth, in short, had served its purpose and was now distasteful to them, and they would not enter it unless pressed with fear.

This new manner of their lives was an added grief to Mr. Tebrick, for sometimes he missed them for hours together, or for the whole day even, and not knowing where they might be was lonely and anxious. Yet his Silvia was thoughtful for him too and would often send Angelica or another of the cubs to fetch him to their new lair, or come herself if she could spare the time. For now they were all perfectly accustomed to his presence, and had come to look on him as their natural companion, and although he was in many ways irksome to them by scaring rabbits, yet they always rejoiced to see him when they had been parted from him. This friendliness of theirs was, you may be sure, the source of most of Mr. Tebrick's happiness at this time. Indeed he lived now for nothing but his foxes, his love for his vixen had extended itself insensibly to include her cubs, and these were now his daily playmates so that he knew them as well as if they had been his own children. With Selwyn and Angelica indeed he was always happy; and they never so much as when they were with him. He was not stiff in his behaviour either, but had learnt by this time as much from his foxes as they had from him. Indeed never was there a more curious alliance than this or one with stranger effects upon both of the parties.

Mr. Tebrick now could follow after them anywhere and keep up with them too, and could go through a wood as silently as a deer. He learnt to conceal himself if ever a labourer passed by so that he was rarely seen, and never but once in their company. But what was most strange of all, he had got a way of going doubled up, often almost on all fours with his hands touching the ground every now and then, particularly when he went uphill.

He hunted with them too sometimes, chiefly by coming up and scaring rabbits towards where the cubs lay ambushed, so that the bunnies ran straight into their jaws.

He was useful to them in other ways, climbing up and robbing pigeon's nests for the eggs which they relished exceedingly, or by occasionally dispatching a hedgehog for them so they did not get the prickles in their mouths. But while on his part he thus altered his conduct, they on their side were not behindhand, but learnt a dozen human tricks from him that are ordinarily wanting in Reynard's education.

One evening he went to a cottager who had a row of skeps, and bought one of them, just as it was after the man had smothered the bees. This he carried to the foxes that they might taste the honey, for he had seen them dig out wild bees' nests often enough. The skep full was indeed a wonderful feast for them, they bit greedily into the heavy scented comb, their jaws were drowned in the sticky flood of sweetness, and they gorged themselves on it without restraint. When they had crunched up the last morsel they tore the skep in pieces, and for hours afterwards they were happily employed in licking themselves clean.

That night he slept near their lair, but they left him and went hunting. In the morning when he woke he was quite numb with cold, and faint with hunger. A white mist hung over everything and the wood smelt of autumn.

He got up and stretched his cramped limbs, and then walked homewards. The summer was over and Mr. Tebrick noticed this now for the first time and was astonished. He reflected that the cubs were fast growing up, they were foxes at all points, and yet when he thought of the time when they had been sooty and had blue eyes it seemed to him only yesterday. From that he passed to thinking of the future, asking himself as he had done once before what would become of his vixen and her children. Before the winter he must tempt them into the security of his garden, and fortify it against all the dangers that threatened them.

But though he tried to allay his fear with such resolutions he remained uneasy all that day. When he went out to them that afternoon he found only his wife Silvia there and it was plain to him that she too was alarmed, but alas, poor creature, she could tell him nothing, only lick his hands and face, and turn about pricking her ears at every sound.

"Where are your children, Silvia?" he asked her several times, but she was impatient of his questions, but at last sprang into his arms, flattened herself upon his breast and kissed him gently, so that when he departed his heart was lighter because he knew that she still loved him.

That night he slept indoors, but in the morning early he was awoken by the sound of trotting horses, and running to the window saw a farmer riding by very sprucely dressed. Could they be hunting so soon, he wondered, but presently reassured himself that it could not be a hunt already.

He heard no other sound till eleven o'clock in the morning when suddenly there was the clamour of hounds giving tongue and not so far off neither. At this Mr. Tebrick ran out of his house distracted and set open the gates of his garden, but with iron bars and wire at the top so the huntsmen could not follow. There was silence again; it seems the fox must have turned away, for there was no other sound of the hunt. Mr. Tebrick was now like one helpless with fear, he dared not go out, yet could not stay still at home. There was nothing that he could do, yet he would not admit this, so he busied himself in making holes in the hedges, so that Silvia (or her cubs) could enter from whatever side she came. At last he forced himself to go indoors and sit down and drink some tea. While he was there he fancied he heard the hounds again; it was but a faint ghostly echo of their music, yet when he ran out of the house it was already close at hand in the copse above.

Now it was that poor Mr. Tebrick made his great mistake, for hearing the hounds almost outside the gate he ran to meet them, whereas rightly he should have run back to the house. As soon as he reached the gate he saw his wife Silvia coming towards him but very tired with running and just upon her the hounds. The horror of that sight pierced him, for ever afterwards he was haunted by those hounds—their eagerness, their desperate efforts to gain on her, and their blind lust for her came at odd moments to frighten him all his life. Now he should have run back, though it was already late, but instead he cried out to her, and she ran straight through the open gate to him. What followed was all over in a flash, but it was seen by many witnesses.

The side of Mr. Tebrick's garden there is bounded by a wall, about six feet high and curving round, so that the huntsmen could see over this wall inside. One of them indeed put his horse at it very boldly, which was risking his neck, and although he got over safe was too late to be of much assistance.

His vixen had at once sprung into Mr. Tebrick's arms, and before he could turn back the hounds were upon them and had pulled them down. Then at that moment there was a scream of despair heard by all the field that had come up, which they declared afterwards was more like a woman's voice than a man's. But yet there was no clear proof whether it was Mr. Tebrick or his wife who had suddenly regained her voice. When the huntsman who had leapt the wall got to them and had whipped off the hounds Mr. Tebrick had been terribly mauled and was bleeding from twenty wounds. As for his vixen she was dead, though he was still clasping her dead body in his arms.

Mr. Tebrick was carried into the house at once and assistance sent for, but there was no doubt now about his neighbours being in the right when they called him mad. For a long while his life was despaired of, but at last he rallied, and in the end he recovered his reason and lived to be a great age, for that matter he is still alive.

THE FOX WOMAN

ABRAHAM MERRITT

CHAPTER I

The Ancient Steps wound up the side of the mountain through the tall pines, patience trodden deep into them by the feet of twenty centuries. Some soul of silence, ancient and patient as the steps, brooded over them. They were wide, twenty men could have marched abreast upon them; lichens brown and orange traced strange symbols on their grey stones, and emerald mosses cushioned them. At times the steps climbed steep as stairs, and at times they swept leisurely around bastions of the mountain, but always on each side the tall pines stood close, green shoulder to shoulder, vigilant.

At the feet of the pines crouched laurels and dwarfed rhododendrons of a singular regularity of shape and of one height, that of a kneeling man. Their stiff and glossy leaves were like links on coats-of-mail . . . like the jade-lacquered scale-armor of the Green Archers of Kwanyin who guard the goddess when she goes forth in the Spring to awaken the trees. The pines were like watchful sentinels, and oddly like crouching archers were the laurels and the dwarfed rhododendrons, and they said as plainly as though with tongues: Up these steps you may go, and down them—but never try to pass through us!

A woman came round one of the bastions. She walked stubbornly, head down, as one who fights against a strong wind—or as one whose will rides, lashing the reluctant body on. One white shoulder and breast were bare, and on the shoulder was a bruise and blood, four scarlet streaks above the purpled patch as though a long-nailed hand had struck viciously, clawing. And as she walked she wept.

The steps began to lift. The woman raised her head and saw how steeply here they climbed. She stopped, her hands making little fluttering helpless motions.

She turned, listening. She seemed to listen not with ears alone but with every tensed muscle, her entire body one rapt chord of listening through which swept swift arpeggios of terror. The brittle twilight of the Yunnan highlands, like clearest crystal made impalpable, fell upon brown hair shot with gleams of dull copper, upon a face lovely even in its dazed horror. Her grey eyes stared down the steps, and it was as though they, too, were listening rather than seeing. . .

She was heavy with child. . .

She heard voices beyond the bend of the bastion, voices guttural and sing-song, angry and arguing, protesting and urging. She heard the shuffle of many feet, hesitating, halting, but coming inexorably on. Voices and feet of the hung-hutzes, the outlaws who had slaughtered her husband and Kenwood and their bearers a scant hour ago, and who but for Kenwood would now have her. They had found her trail.

She wanted to die; desperately Jean Meredith wanted to die; her faith taught her that then she would rejoin that scholarly, gentle lover-husband of hers whom she had loved so dearly although his years had been twice her own. It would not matter did they kill her quickly, but she knew they would not do that. And she could not endure even the thought of what must befall her through them before death came. Nor had she weapon to kill herself. And there was that other life budding beneath her heart.

But stronger than desire for death, stronger than fear of torment, stronger than the claim of the unborn was something deep within her that cried for vengeance. Not vengeance against the hung-hutzes—they were only a pack of wild beasts doing what was their nature to do. This cry was for vengeance against those who had loosed them, directed them. For this she knew had been done, although how she knew it she could not yet tell. It was not accident, no chance encounter that swift slaughter. She was sure of that.

It was like a pulse, that cry for vengeance; a pulse whose rhythm grew, deadening grief and terror, beating strength back into her. It was like a bitter spring welling up around her soul. When its dark waters had risen far enough they would touch her lips and she would drink of them .. . and then knowledge would come to her . .. she would know

who had planned this evil thing, and why. But she must have time—time to drink of the waters—time to learn and avenge. She must live . . . for vengeance . . .

Vengeance is mine, saith the Lord!

It was as though a voice had whispered the old text in her ear. She struck her breast with clenched hands; she looked with eyes grown hard and tearless up to the tranquil sky; she answered the voice:

"A lie! Like all the lies I have been taught of—You! I am through with—You! Vengeance! Whoever gives me vengeance shall be my God!"

The voices and the feet were nearer. Strange, how slowly, how reluctantly they advanced. It was as though they were afraid. She studied the woods beyond the pines. Impenetrable; or if not, then impossible for her. They would soon find her if she tried to hide there. She must go on—up the steps. At their end might be some hiding place . . . perhaps sanctuary. . . .

Yes, she was sure the hung-hutzes feared the steps. . . they came so slowly, so haltingly . . . arguing, protesting. . .

She had seen another turn at the top of this steep. If she could reach it before they saw her, it might be that they would follow her no further. She turned to climb. . .

A fox stood upon the steps a dozen feet above her, watching her, barring her way. It was a female fox, a vixen. Its coat was all silken russet-red. It had a curiously broad head and slanted green eyes. On its head was a mark, silver white and shaped like the flame of a candle wavering in the wind.

The fox was lithe and graceful, Jean Meredith thought, as a dainty woman. A mad idea came, born of her despair and her denial of that God whom she had been taught from childhood to worship as all-good, all-wise, all-powerful. She thrust her hands out to the fox. She cried to it:

"Sister—you are a woman! Lead me to safety that I may have vengeance—sister!"

Remember, she had just seen her husband die under the knives of the hung-hutzes and she was with child. . . and who can know upon what fantastic paths of unreality a mind so beset may stray.

As though it had understood the fox paced slowly down the steps. And again she thought how like a graceful woman it was. It paused a little beyond reach of her hand, studying her with those slanted green eyes—eyes clear and brilliant as jewels, sea-green, and like no eyes she had ever seen in any animal. There seemed faint mockery in their gaze, a delicate malice, but as they rested upon her bruised shoulder and dropped to her swollen girdle, she could have sworn that there was human comprehension in them, and pity. She whispered:

"Sister—help me!"

There was a sudden outburst of the guttural singsong. They were close now, her pursuers, close to the bend of the steps round which she had come. Soon they must turn it and see her. She stood staring at the fox expectantly . . . hoping she knew not what.

The fox slipped by her, seemed to melt in the crouching bushes. It vanished.

Black despair, the despair of a child who finds itself abandoned to wild beasts by one it has trusted, closed in on Jean Meredith. What she had hoped for, what she had expected of help, was vague, unformulated. A miracle by alien gods, now she had renounced her own? Or had her appeal to the vixen deeper impulse? Atavistic awakenings, anthropomorphic, going back to that immemorial past when men first thought of animals and birds as creatures with souls like theirs, but closer to Nature's spirit; given by that spirit a wisdom greater than human, and more than human powers—servants and messengers of potent deities and little less than gods themselves.

Nor has it been so long ago that St. Francis of Assisi spoke to the beasts and birds as he did to men and women, naming them Brother Wolf and Brother Eagle. And did not St. Conan baptize the seals of the Orkneys as he did the pagan men? The past and all that men have thought in the past is born anew within us all. And sometimes strange doors open within our minds—and out of them or into them strange spirits come or go. And whether real or unreal, who can say?

The fox seemed to understand—had seemed to promise—something. And it had abandoned her, fled away! Sobbing, she turned to climb the steps.

Too late! The hung-hutzes had rounded the bend.

There was a howling chorus. With obscene gestures, yapping threats, they ran toward her. Ahead of the pack was the pock-faced, half-breed Tibetan leader whose knife had been the first to cut her husband down. She watched them come, helpless to move, unable even to close her eyes. The pock-face saw and understood, gave quick command, and the pack slowed to a walk, gloating upon her agony, prolonging it.

They halted! Something like a flicker of russet flame had shot across the steps between her and them. It was the fox. It stood there, quietly regarding them. And hope flashed up through Jean Meredith, melting the cold terror that had frozen her. Power of motion returned. But she did not try to run. She did not want to run. The cry for vengeance was welling up again. She felt that cry reach out to the fox.

As though it had heard her, the fox turned its head and looked at her. She saw its green eyes sparkle, its white teeth bared as though it smiled.

Its eyes withdrawn, the spell upon the hung-hutzes broke. The leader drew pistol, fired upon the fox.

Jean Meredith saw, or thought she saw, the incredible.

Where fox had been, stood now a woman! She was tall, and lithe as a young willow. Jean Meredith could not see her face, but she could see hair of russet-red coifed upon a small and shapely head. A silken gown of russet-red, sleeveless, dropped to the woman's feet. She raised an arm and pointed at the pock-faced leader. Behind him his men were silent, motionless, even as Jean Meredith had been—and it came to her that it was the same ice of terror that held them. Their eyes were fixed upon the woman.

The woman's hand dropped—slowly. And as it dropped,

the pock-faced Tibetan dropped with it. He sank to his knees and then upon his hands. He stared into her face, lips drawn back from his teeth like a snarling dog, and there was foam upon his lips. Then he hurled himself upon his men, like a wolf. He sprang upon them howling; he leaped up at their throats, tearing at them with teeth and talons. They milled, squalling rage and bewildered terror. They tried to beat him off—they could not.

There was a flashing of knives. The pock-face lay writhing on the steps, like a dog dying. Still squalling, never looking behind them, his men poured down the steps and away.

Jean Meredith's hands went up, covering her eyes. She dropped them—a fox, all silken russet-red, stood where the woman had been. It was watching her. She saw its green eyes sparkle, its white teeth bared as though it smiled—it began to walk daintily up the steps toward her.

Weakness swept over her; she bent her head, crumpled to her knees, covered again her eyes with shaking hands. She was aware of an unfamiliar fragrance—disturbing, evocative of strange, fleeting images. She heard low, sweet laughter. She heard a Soft voice whisper:

"Sister!"

She looked up. A woman's face was bending over her. An exquisite face . . . with sea-green, slanted eyes under a broad white brow . . . with hair of russet-red that came to a small peak in the center of that brow . . . a lock of silvery white shaped like the flame of a candle wavering in the wind . . . a nose long but delicate, the nostrils slightly flaring, daintily . . . a mouth small and red as the royal coral, heart-shaped, lips full, archaic.

Over that exquisite face, like a veil, was faint mockery, a delicate malice that had in them little of the human. Her hands were white and long and slender.

They touched Jean Meredith's heart . . . soothing her, strengthening her, drowning fear and sorrow.

She heard again the sweet voice, lilting, faintly amused—with the alien, half-malicious amusement of one who understands human emotion yet has never felt it, but knows how little it matters:

"You shall have your vengeance—Sister!" The white hands touched her eyes . . . she forgot. . . and forgot . . . and now there was nothing to remember . . . not even herself . . .

It seemed to Jean Meredith that she lay cushioned within soft, blind darkness—illimitable, impenetrable. She had no memories; all that she knew was that she was. She thought: I am I. The darkness that cradled her was gentle, kindly. She thought: I am a spirit still unborn in the womb of night. But what was night . . . and what was spirit? She thought: I am content—I do not want to be born again. Again? That meant that she had been born before . . . a word came to her—Jean. She thought: I am Jean . . . but who was Jean?

She heard two voices speaking. One a woman's, soft and sweet with throbbing undertones like plucked harp strings. She had heard that voice before . . . before, when she had been Jean. The man's voice was low, filled with tranquillity, human . . . that was it, the voice held within it a humanness the sweet voice of the woman lacked. She thought: I, Jean, am human . . .

The man said: "Soon she must awaken. The tide of sleep is high on the shore of life. It must not cover it."

The woman answered: "I command that tide. And it has begun to ebb. Soon she will awaken."

He asked: "Will she remember?"

The woman said: "She will remember. But she will not suffer. It will be as though what she remembers had happened to another self of hers. She will pity that self, but it will be to her as though it died when died her husband. As indeed it did. That self bears the sorrow, the pain, the agony. It leaves no legacy of them to her—save memory."

And now it seemed to her that for a time there was a silence . . . although she knew that time could not exist within the blackness that cradled her . . . and what was—time?

The man's voice broke that silence, musingly: "With memory there can be no happiness for her, long as she lives."

The woman laughed, a tingling-sweet mocking chime: "Happiness? I thought you wiser than to cling to that illusion, priest. I give her serenity, which is far better than happiness. Nor did she ask for happiness. She asked for vengeance. And vengeance she shall have."

The man said: "But she does not know who—"

The woman interrupted: "She does know. And I know. And so shall you when you have told her what was wrung from the Tibetan before he died. And if you still do not believe, you will believe when he who is guilty comes here, as come he will—to kill the child."

The man whispered: "To kill the child!"

The woman's voice became cold, losing none of its sweetness but edged with menace: "You must not let him have it, priest. Not then. Later, when the word is given you . . ."

Again the voice grew mocking . . ."I contemplate a journey . . . I would see other lands, who so long have dwelt among these hills . . . and I would not have my plans spoiled by precipitancy. . ." Once more Jean Meredith heard the tingling laughter. "Have no fear, priest. They will help you—my sisters."

He said, steadily: "I have no fear."

The woman's voice became gentle, all mockery fled. She said:

"I know that, you who have had wisdom and courage to open forbidden doors. But I am bound by a threefold cord—a promise, a vow, and a desire. When a certain time comes, I must surrender much—must lie helpless, bound by that cord. It is then that I shall need you, priest, for this man who will come . . ."

The voices faded. Slowly the blackness within which she lay began to lighten. Slowly, slowly, a luminous greyness replaced it. She thought, desperately: I am. going to be born! I don't want to be born! Implacably, the light increased. Now within the greyness was a nimbus of watery emerald. The nimbus became brighter, brighter . . .

She was lying upon a low bed, in a nest of silken cushions. Close to her was an immense and ancient bronze vessel, like a baptismal font. The hands of thousands of years had caressed it, leaving behind them an ever deepening patina like a soft green twilight. A ray of the sun shone upon it, and where the ray rested, the patina gleamed like a tiny green sun. Upon the sides of the great bowl were strange geometric patterns, archaic, the spirals and meanders of the Lei-wen—the thunder patterns. It stood upon three legs, tripodal . . . why, it was the ancient ceremonial vessel, the Tang font which Martin had brought home from Yunnan years ago . . . and she was back home . . . she had dreamed that she had been in China and that Martin . . . that Martin . . .

She sat up abruptly and looked through wide, opened doors into a garden. Broad steps dropped shallowly to an oval pool around whose sides were lithe willows trailing green tendrils in the blue water, wisterias with drooping ropes of blossoms, white and pale azure, and azaleas like flower flames. Rosy lilies lay upon the pool's breast. And at its far end was a small pagoda, fairy-like, built all of tiles of iridescent peacock blue and on each side a stately cypress, as though they were its ministers . . . why, this was their garden, the garden of the blue pagoda which Martin had copied from that place in Yunnan where lived his friend, the wise old priest . . .

But there was something wrong. These mountains were not like those of the ranch. They were conical, their smooth bare slopes of rose-red stone circled with trees . . . they were like huge stone hats with green brims . . .

She turned again and looked about the room. It was a wide room and a deep one, but how deep she could not see, because the sun streaming in from a high window struck the ancient vessel and made a curtain, veiling it beyond. She could see that there were beams across its ceiling, mellow with age, carved with strange symbols. She caught glimpses of ivory and of gleaming lacquer. There was a low altar of what seemed green jade, curiously carved and upon which were ceremonial objects of unfamiliar shape, a huge ewer of bronze whose lid was the head of a fox . . .

A man came toward her, walking out of the shadows beyond the ancient Tang vessel. He was clothed from neck to feet in a silken robe of silvery-blue upon which were embroidered, delicately as though by spiders, Taoist symbols and under them, ghostly in silver threads, a fox's head. He was bald, his face heavy, expressionless, skin smooth and faded yellow as some antique parchment. So far as age went he might have been sixty—or three hundred. But it was his eyes that held Jean Meredith. They were large and black and, liquid, and prodigiously alive. They were young eyes, belying the agelessness of the heavy face; and it was as though the face was but a mask from which the eyes had drawn all life into themselves. They poured into her strength and calmness and reassurance, and from her mind vanished all vagueness, all doubts, all fears. Her mind for the first time since the ambush was clear, crystal clear, her thoughts her own.

She remembered—remembered everything. But it was as though all had happened to another self. She felt pity for that self, but it had left no heritage of sorrow. She was tranquil. The black, youthful eyes poured tranquillity into her.

She said: "I know you. You are Yu Ch'ien, the wise priest my husband loved. This is the Temple of the Foxes."

CHAPTER II

"I am Yu Ch'ien, my daughter." His voice was the man's voice which she had heard when cradled in the darkness.

She tried to rise, then swayed back upon the bed, weakness overcoming her.

He said: "A night and a day, and still another night and half this day you have slept, and now you must eat." He spoke the English words slowly, as one whose tongue had long been stranger to them.

He clapped his hands and a woman slipped by the great vase through the bars of the sunlight. She was ageless as he, with broad shrewd face and tilted sloeblack eyes that were kindly yet very wise. A smock covered her from full breasts to knees, and she was sturdy and strong and brown as though she had been carved from seasoned wood. In her hands was a tray upon which was a bowl of steaming broth and oaten cakes.

The woman sat beside Jean Meredith, lifting her head, resting it against her deep bosom and feeding her like a child, and now Jean saw that herself was naked except for a thin robe of soft blue silk and that upon it was the moonsilver symbol of the fox.

The priest nodded, his eyes smiled upon her. "Fienwi will attend you. Soon you will be stronger. Soon I shall return. Then we shall talk."

He passed out of the wide doors. The woman fed her the last of the broth, the last of the little cakes. She left her, and returned with bowls of bronze in which was water hot and cold; undressed her; ministered to her, bathed her and rubbed her; dressed her in fresh silken robes of blue; strapped sandals to her feet, and smiling, left her. Thrice Jean essayed to speak to her, but the woman only shook her head, answering in a lisping dialect, no sound of which she recognized.

The sun had moved from the great Tang font. She lay back, lazily. Her mind was limpidly clear; upon it was reflected all through which she had passed, yet it was tranquil, untroubled, like a woodland pool that reflects the storm clouds but whose placid surface lies undisturbed. The things that had happened were only images reflected upon her mind. But under that placid surface was something implacable, adamant-hard, something that would have been bitter did it not know that it was to be satisfied.

She thought over what Martin had told her of Yu Ch'ien. A Chinese whose forefathers had been enlightened rulers ten centuries before the Man of Galilee had been raised upon the cross, who had studied Occidental thought both in England and France, and had found little in it to satisfy his thirst for wisdom; who had gone back to the land of his fathers, embraced at last the philosophy of Lao-Tse, and had withdrawn from the world to an ancient fane in Yunnan known as the Temple of the Foxes, a temple reverenced and feared and around which strange legends clustered; there to spend his life in meditation and study.

What was it Martin had called him? Ah, yes, a master of secret and forgotten knowledge, a master of illusion. She knew that of all men, Martin had held Yu Ch'ien in profoundest respect, deepest affection . . . she wondered if the woman she had seen upon the steps had been one of his illusions . . . if the peace she felt came from him . . . if he had made sorrow and pain of soul illusions for her . . . and was she thinking the thoughts he had placed in her mind—or her own . . . she wondered dreamily, not much caring . . .

He came through the doors to her, and again it was as though his eyes were springs of tranquillity from which her soul drank deep. She tried to rise, to greet him; her mind was strong but through all her body was languor. He touched her forehead, and the languor fled. He said:

"All is well with you, my daughter. But now we must talk. We will go into the garden."

He clapped his hands. The brown woman, Fien-wi, came at the summons, and with her two blue-smocked men bearing a chair. The woman lifted her, placed her in the chair. The men carried her out of the wide doors, down the shallow steps to the blue pool. She looked behind her as she went.

The temple was built into the brow of the mountain. It was of brown stone and brown wood. Slender pillars hard bitten by the teeth of the ages held up a curved roof of the peacock blue tiles. From the wide doors through which she had come a double row of sculptured foxes ran, like Thebes' road of the Sphynxes, half way down to the pool. Over the crest of the mountain crept the ancient steps up which she had stumbled. Where the steps joined the temple, stood a tree covered all with white blossoms. It wavered in the wind like the flame of a candle.

Strangely was the temple like the head of a fox, its muzzle between the paws of the rows of sculptured foxes, the crest of the mountain its forehead and the white blossoming tree, like the lock of white upon the forehead of the fox of the steps . . . and the white lock upon the forehead of the woman . . .

They were at the pool. There was a seat cut at the end, facing the blue pagoda. The woman Fien-wi piled the stone with cushions and, as she waited, Jean Meredith saw that there were arms to this seat and that at the end of each was the head of a fox, and that over its back was a tracery of dancing foxes; and she saw, too, that on each side of the seat tiny paths had been cut in stone leading to the water, as though for some small-footed creatures to trot upon and drink.

She was lifted to the stone chair, and sank into the cushions. Except for the seat and the little runways, it was as though she sat beside the pool Martin had built at their California ranch. There, as here, the willows dipped green tendrils into the water; there, as here, drooped ropes of wisteria, pale amethyst and white. And here as there was peace.

Yu Ch'ien spoke: "A stone is thrown into a pool. The ripples spread and break against the shore. At last they cease and the pool is as before. Yet when the stone strikes, as it sinks and while the ripples live, microscopic lives within the pool are changed. But not for long. The stone touches bottom, the pool again becomes calm. It is over, and life for the tiny things is as before."

She said quietly, out of the immense clarity of her mind: "You mean, Yu Ch'ien, that my husband's murder was such a stone."

He went on, as though she had not spoken: "But there is life within life, and over life, and under life—as we know life. And that which happens to the tiny things within the pool may be felt by those beneath and above them. Life is a bubble in which are lesser bubbles which we cannot see, and the bubble we call life is only part of a greater bubble which also we may not see. But sometimes we perceive those bubbles, sometimes glimpse the beauty of the greater, sense the kinship of the lesser . . . and sometimes a lesser life touches ours and then we speak of demons . . . and when the greater ones touch us we name it inspiration from Heaven, an angel speaking through our lips—"

She interrupted, thought crystal clear: "I understand you, Martin's murder was the stone. It would pass with its ripples—but it has disturbed some pool within which it was a lesser pool. Very well, what then?"

He said: "There are places in this world where the veil between it and the other worlds is thin. They can enter. Why it is so, I do not know—but I know it is so. The ancients recognized such places. They named those who dwelt unseen there the genii locorum—literally, the spirits of the places. This mountain, this temple, is such a place. It is why I came to it."

She said: "You mean the fox I saw upon the steps. You mean the woman I thought I saw take the place of that fox, and who drove the Tibetan mad. The fox I asked to help me and to give me revenge, and whom I called sister. The woman I thought I saw who whispered to me that I should have revenge and who called me sister. Very well, what then?"

He answered: "It is true. The murder of your husband was the stone. Better to have let the ripples die. But there was this place . . . there was a moment . . . and now the ripples cannot die until—"

Again she interrupted the true thought—or what she believed the true thought—flashing up through her mind like sun-glints from jewels at a clear pool's bottom. "I had denied my God. Whether he exists or does not, I had stripped myself of my armor against those other lives. I did it where and when such other lives, if they exist, could strike. I accept that. And again, what then?"

He said: "You have a strong soul, my daughter."

She answered, with a touch of irony: "While I was within the blackness, before I awakened, I seemed to hear two persons talking, Yu Ch'ien. One had your voice, and the other the voice of the fox woman who called me sister. She promised me serenity. Well, I have that. And having it, I am as unhuman as was her voice. Tell me, Yu Ch'ien, whom my husband called master of illusions, was that woman upon the steps one of your illusions, and was her voice another? Does my serenity come from her or from you? I am no child, and, I know how easily you could accomplish this, by drugs or by your will while I lay helpless."

He said: "My daughter, if they were illusions—they were not mine. And if they were illusions, then I, like you, am victim to them."

She asked: "You mean you have seen—her?"

He answered: "And her sisters. Many times."

She said shrewdly: "Yet that does not prove her real— she might have passed from your mind to mine."

He did not answer. She asked abruptly: "Shall I live?"

He replied without hesitation. "No."

She considered that for a little, looking at the willow tendrils, the ropes of wisteria. She mused: "I did not ask for happiness, but she gives me serenity. I did not ask for life, so she gives me—vengeance. But I no longer care for vengeance."

He said gravely: "It does not matter. You struck into that other life. You asked, and you were promised. The ripples upon the greater pool cannot cease until that promise is fulfilled."

She considered that, looking at the conical hills. She laughed. "They are like great stone hats with brims of green. What are their faces like, I wonder." He asked: "Who killed your husband?" She answered, still smiling at the hatted hills: "Why, his brother, of course."

He asked: "How do you know that?"

She lifted her arms and twined her hands behind her neck. She said, as impersonally as though she read from a book: "I was little more than twenty when I met Martin, Just out of college. He was fifty. But inside—he was a dreaming boy. Oh, I knew he had lots and lots of money. It didn't matter. I loved him—for the boy inside him. He asked me to marry him. I married him.

"Charles hated me from the beginning. Charles is his brother, fifteen years younger. Charles' wife hated me. You see, there was no other besides Charles until I came. If Martin died—well, all his money would go to Charles. They never thought he would marry. For the last ten years Charles had looked after his business—his mines, his investments. I really don't blame Charles for hating me—but he shouldn't have killed Martin.

"We spent our honeymoon out on Martin's ranch. He has a pool and garden just like this, you know. It's just as beautiful, but the mountains around it have snowy caps instead of the stony, green-rimmed ones. And he had a great bronze vessel like that of yours. He told me that he had copied the garden from Yu Ch'ien's even to the blue pagoda. And that the vessel had a mate in Yu

Ch'ien's Temple of the Foxes. And he told me . . . of you . . .

"Then the thought came to him to return to you and your temple. Martin was a boy—the desire gripped him. I did not care, if it made him happy. So we came,

Charles with us as far as Nanking. Hating me, I knew, every mile of the journey. At Nanking—I told Martin I was going to have a baby. I had known it for months but I hadn't told him because I was afraid he would put off this trip on which he had set his heart. Now I knew I couldn't keep it secret much longer. Martin was so happy! He told Charles, who hated me then more than ever. And Martin made a will. If Martin should die, Charles was to act as trustee for me and the child, carry on the estate as before, with his share of the income increased. All the balance, and there are millions, was left to me and the coming baby. There was also a direct bequest of half a million to Charles.

"Martin read the will to him. I was present. So was Kenwood, Martin's secretary. I saw Charles turn white, but outwardly he was pleasantly acquiescent, concerned only lest something really might happen to his brother. But I guessed what was in his heart.

"Kenwood liked me, and he did not like Charles. He came to me one night in Nanking, a few days before we were to start for Yunnan. He tried to dissuade me from the journey. He was a bit vague about reasons, talked of my condition, hard traveling and so on, but that was ridiculous. At last I asked him point-blank—why? Then he said that Charles was secretly meeting a Chinese captain, by name—Li-kong. I asked what of it, he had a right to pick his friends. Kenwood said Likong was suspected of being in touch with certain outlaws operating in Szechwan and Yunnan, and of receiving and disposing of the best of their booty. Kenwood said: 'If both you and Martin die before the baby is born, Charles will inherit everything. He's next of kin and the only one, for you have nobody.' Kenwood said:

"You're going up into Yunnan. How easy to send word to one of these bands to look out for you. And then brother Charles would have it all. Of course, there's no use saying anything to your husband. He trusts everybody, and Charles most of all. All that would happen would be my dismissal.'

"And of course that was true. But I couldn't believe Charles, for all he hated me so, would do this to Martin. There were two of us, and Kenwood and a nice Scotch woman I found at Nanking, a Miss Mackenzie, who agreed to come along to look after me in event of my needing it. There were twenty of us in all—the others Chinese boys, thoroughly good, thoroughly dependable. We came North slowly, unhurriedly. I said that Martin was a boy inside. No need to tell you again of his affection for you. And he loved China—the old China. He said it lived now only in a few places, and Yunnan was first. And he had it in his mind that our baby should be born—here—"

She sat silent, then laughed. "And so it will be. But not as Martin dreamed . . ." She was silent again. She said, as though faintly puzzled: "It was not—human—to laugh at that!" She went on serenely: "We came on and on slowly.

Sampans on the rivers, and I by litter mostly. Always easily, easily . . . because of the baby. Then two weeks ago Kenwood told me that he had word we were to be attacked at a certain place. He had been years in China, knew how to get information and I knew he had watched and cajoled and threatened and bribed ever since we had entered the hills. He said he, had arranged a counter-attack that would catch the trappers in their own trap. He cursed Charles dreadfully, saying he was behind it. He said that if we could only get to Yu Ch'ien we would be safe. Afterwards he told me that he must have been sold wrong information. The counter-attack had drawn blank. I told him he was letting his imagination run away with him.

"We went on. Then came the ambush. It wasn't a matter of ransom. It was a matter of wiping us out.

"They gave us no chance. So it must have been that we were worth more to them dead than alive. That realization came to me as I stood at the door of my tent and saw Martin cut down, poor Mackenzie fall. Kenwood could have escaped as I did—but he died to give me time to get away . . ."

"Yu Ch'ien, what have you done to me?" asked Jean Meredith, dreamily. "I have seen my husband butchered . . . I have seen a man give up his life for me . . . and still I feel no more emotion than as though they had been reeds under the sickle . . . what have you done to me, Yu Ch'ien?"

He answered: "Daughter—when you are dead, and all those now living are dead—will it matter?"

She answered, shaking her head: "But—I am not dead! Nor are those now living dead. And I should rather be human, Yu Ch'ien. And suffer."

He said: "It may not be, my daughter."

"I wish I could feel," she said. "Good God, but I wish I could feel . . ."

She said: "That is all. Kenwood threw himself in front of me. I ran. I came to wide steps. I climbed them—up and up. I saw a fox—I saw a woman where I had seen the fox—"

He said: "You saw a Tibetan, a half-caste, who threw himself upon those who followed you, howling like a mad dog. You saw that Tibetan cut down by the knives of his men. I came with my men before he died. We brought him here. I searched his dying mind. He told me that they had been hired to wipe out your party by a Shensi leader of hung-hutzes. And that he had been promised not only the loot of your party if all were slain, but a thousand taels besides. And that when he asked who guaranteed this sum, this leader, in his cups, had told him the Captain Li-kong."

She cupped her chin in hand, looked out over the blue pool to the pagoda. She said at last: "So Kenwood was right! And I am right. It was Charles. . ."

She said: "I feel a little, Yu Ch'ien. But what I feel is not pleasant. It is hate, Yu Ch'ien. . ."

She said: "I am only twenty-four. It is rather young to die, Yu Ch'ien, isn't it? But then—what was it your woman's voice said while I was in the darkness? That the self of mine whom I would pity died when Martin did? She was right, Yu Ch'ien—or you were. And I think I will not be sorry to join that other self."

The sun was sinking. An amethyst veil dropped over the conical mountains. Suddenly they seemed to flatten, to become transparent. The whole valley between the peaks grew luminously crystalline. The blue pagoda shone as though made of dark sapphires behind which little suns burned. She sighed: "It is very beautiful, Yu Ch'ien. I am glad to be here—until I die."

There was a patter of feet beside her. A fox came trotting down one of the carven runways. It looked up at her fearlessly with glowing green eyes. Another slipped from the cover of the pool and another and another. They lapped the blue water fearlessly, eyes glinting swift side-glances at her, curiously . . .

The days slipped by her, the weeks—a month. Each day she sat in the seat of the foxes beside the pool, watching the willows trail their tendrils, the lilies like great rosy pearls open and close and die and be reborn on the pool's blue breast; watching the crystalline green dusks ensorcell the conical peaks, and watching the foxes that came when these dusks fell.

They were friendly now, the foxes—knew her, sat beside her, studying her; but never did she see the lithe fox with the lock of white between its slanting green eyes. She grew to know the brown woman Fien-wi and the sturdy servitors. And from the scattered villages pilgrims came to the shrine; they looked at her fearfully, shyly; as she sat on the seat of the foxes, prostrating themselves before her as though she were some spirit to be placated by worship.

And each day was as the day before, and she thought: Without sorrow, without fear, without gladness, without hope there is no difference between the days, and therefore what difference does it make if I die tomorrow or a year hence?

Whatever the anodyne that steeped her soul—whether from vague woman of the steps or from Yu Ch'ien—it had left her with no emotion. Except that she knew she must bear it, she had no feeling even toward her unborn baby. Once, indeed, she had felt a faint curiosity. That this wise priest of the Foxes' Temple had his own means of learning what he desired of the outer world, she was well aware.

She said: "Does Charles know as yet of the ambush—know that I am still alive?"

He answered: "Not yet. The messengers who were sent to Li-kong did not reach him. It will be weeks before he knows."

She said: "And then he will come here. Will the baby be born when he comes, Yu Ch'ien?"

He answered: "Yes."

"And shall I be alive, Yu Ch'ien?"

He did not answer. She laughed.

It was one twilight, in the middle of the Hour of the Dog, that she turned to him, sitting in the garden beside the pool.

"My time has come, Yu Ch'ien. The child stirs."

They carried her into the temple. She lay upon the bed, while the brown woman stooped over her, ministering to her, helping her. The only light in the temple chamber came from five ancient lanterns of milky jade through whose thin sides the candles gleamed, turning them into five small moons. She felt little pain. She thought: I owe that to Yu Ch'ien, I suppose. And the minutes fled by until it was the Hour of the Boar.

She heard a scratching at the temple door. The priest opened it. He spoke softly, one word, a word often on his lips, and she knew it meant "patience." She could see through the opened door into the garden. There were small globular green lights all about, dozens of them, like gnome lanterns.

She said drowsily: "My little foxes wait. Let them enter, Yu Ch'ien."

"Not yet, my daughter."

The Hour of the Boar passed. Midnight passed. There was a great silence in the temple. It seemed to her that all the temple was waiting, that even the unfaltering light of the five small moons on the altar was waiting. She thought: Even the child is waiting . . . and for what?

And suddenly a swift agony shook her and she cried out. The brown woman held tight her hands that tried to beat the air. The priest called, and into the room came four of the sturdy servants of the temple. They carried large vessels in which was water steaming hot and water which did not steam and so, she reasoned idly, must be cold. They kept their backs to her, eyes averted.

The priest touched her eyes, stroked her flanks, and the agony was gone as swiftly as it had come. She watched the servants pour the waters into the ancient

Tang font and slip away, backs still turned to her, faces averted.

She had not seen the door open, but there was a fox in the room. It was ghostly in the dim light of the jade lamps, yet she could see it stepping daintily toward her . . . a vixen, lithe and graceful as a woman . . . with slanted eyes, sea-green, brilliant as jewels . . . the fox of the steps whom she had called sister . . .

And now she was looking up into a woman's face. An exquisite face with sea-green, slanted eyes under a broad white brow, whose hair of russet-red came to a small peak in the center of that brow, and above the peak a lock of silvery white . . . the eyes gazed into hers, and although they caressed her, there was in them a faint mockery, a delicate malice.

The woman was naked. Although Jean Meredith could not wrest her own eyes from the slanting green ones, she could see the curve of delicate shoulders, the rounded breasts, the slender hips. It was as though the woman stood poised upon her own breasts, without weight, upon airy feet. There was a curious tingling coolness in her breasts . . . more pleasant than warmth. . . and it was as though the woman were sinking into her, becoming a part of her. The face came nearer . . . nearer . . . the eyes were now close to hers, and mockery and malice gone from them . . . in them was only gentleness and promise . . . she felt cool lips touch hers . . .

The face was gone. She was sinking, sinking, unre-

sistingly . . . gratefully . . . through a luminous greyness . . .then into a soft blind darkness . . . she was being cradled by it, sinking ever deeper and deeper. She cried out once, as though frightened: Martin! Then she cried again, voice vibrant with joy: Martin!

One of the five moon lamps upon the jade altar darkened. Went out.

The brown woman was prostrate upon her face beside the bed. The priest touched her with his foot. He said: "Prepare. Be swift." She bent over the still body.

There was a movement beside the altar. Four foxes stepped daintily from its shadows toward the Tang front. They were vixens, and they came like graceful women, and the coat of each was silken russet-red, their eyes brilliant, sea-green and slanting, and upon each forehead was a lock of silvery white. They drew near the brown woman, watching her.

The priest walked to the doors and threw them open. Into the temple slipped fox after fox . . . a score, two score . . . the temple filled with them. They ringed the ancient font, squatting, red tongues lolling, eyes upon the bed.

The priest walked to the bed. In his hand was a curiously shaped, slender knife of bronze, double-edged, sharp as a surgeon's knife. The brown woman threw herself again upon the floor. The priest leaned over the bed, began with a surgeon's deftness and delicacy to cut. The four vixens drew close, watching every movement —

Suddenly there wailed through the temple the querulous crying of a new-born child.

The priest walked from the bed toward the font. . . He held the child in his hands, and hands and child were red with blood. The vixens walked beside him. The foxes made way for them, closing their circles as they passed. The four vixens halted, one at each of the font's four sides. They did not sit. They stood with gaze fastened upon the priest.

The priest ringed the font, bending before each of the four vixens, holding out the child until each had touched it with her tongue. He lifted the child by the feet, held it dangling head down, high above his head, turning so that all the other foxes could see it.

He plunged it five times into the water of the font.

As abruptly as the first moon lantern had gone out, so darkened the other four.

There was a rustling, the soft patter of many pads. Then silence.

Yu Ch'ien called. There was the gleam of lanterns borne by the servants. The brown woman raised herself from the floor. He placed the child in her hands. He said: "It is finished—and it is begun. Care for her."

Thus was born the daughter of Jean and Martin Meredith in the ancient Temple of the Foxes. Born in the heart of the Hour of the Fox, so called in those parts of China where the ancient beliefs still live because it is at the opposite pole of the Hour of the Horse, which animal at certain times and at certain places, has a magic against which the magic of the Fox may not prevail.

CHAPTER III

The home of heavenly anticipations honored with its presence Peking, not yet at that time renamed Peiping. It was hidden in the heart of the Old City. The anticipations discussed there were usually the reverse of heavenly—or, if not, then dealing with highly unorthodox realms of beatitude.

But except for its patrons none ever knew what went on within its walls. There was never any leakage of secrets through those walls. Peculiarly ultimate information could be obtained at the Home of Heavenly Anticipations—so long as it did not pertain to its patrons.

It was, in fact, a clearing house for enterprises looked upon with a certain amount of disfavor even by many uncivilized countries: enterprises such as blackmail, larceny on the grand scale, smuggling, escapes, piracies, removal of obstacles by assassination and so on. Its abbots collected rich tithes from each successful operation in return for absolute protection from interruption, eavesdropping and spies, and for the expert and thoroughly trustworthy advices upon any point of any enterprise which needed to be cleared up before action.

Prospective members of the most exclusive of London's clubs were never scanned with such completeness as were applicants for the right to enter the Home of Heavenly Anticipations—and one had to be a rather complete scoundrel to win that right. But to those who sought such benefits as it offered, they were worth all the difficulty in securing them.

Charles Meredith sat in one of its rooms, three weeks to a night from the birth of Jean Meredith's baby. He was not a member, but it was the privilege of accredited patrons to entertain guests to whom secrecy was as desirable as to themselves—or who might prove refractory.

It was a doubtful privilege for these guests, although they were not aware of it, because it was always quite possible that they might never appear again in their usual haunts. In such event it was almost impossible to trace them back to the Home of Heavenly Anticipations. Always, on their way to it, they had been directed to leave their vehicle, coolie-carriage or what not at a certain point and to wait until another picked them up. Beyond that point they were never traced. Or if their bodies were later found, it was always under such circumstances that no one could point a finger at the Home of Heavenly Anticipations, which was as expert on alibis for corpses as for crooks.

Although he knew nothing of this, Charles Meredith was uneasy. For one thing, he had a considerable sum of money in his pocket—a very considerable sum. To be explicit, fifty thousand dollars. For another thing, he had not the slightest idea of where he was.

He had dismissed his hotel coolie at a designated point, had been approached by another who gave the proper word of recognition, had been whisked through street after street, then through a narrow alley, then through a door opening into a winding passage, thence into a plain reception hall where a bowing Chinese had met him and led him to the room. He had seen no one, and he heard no sound. Under the circumstances, he appreciated privacy—but damn it, there was a limit! And where was Li-kong?

He got up and walked about nervously. It gave him some satisfaction to feel the automatic holstered under his left arm-pit. He was tall, rather rangy and his shoulders stooped a little. He had clear eyes whose grey stood out a bit startlingly from his dark face; a good forehead, a somewhat predatory beaked nose; his worst feature, his mouth, which hinted self-indulgence and cruelty. Seemingly an alert, capable American man of affairs, not at all one who would connive at the murder of his own brother.

He turned at the opening of the door. Li-kong came in. Li-kong was a graduate of an American college. His father had cherished hopes of a high diplomatic career, with his American training as part of its foundation. He had repaid it by learning in exhaustive detail the worst of American life. This, grafted to his natural qualifications, had given him high place in the Home of Heavenly Anticipations and among its patrons.

He was in the most formal of English evening dress, looked completely the person his father had hoped he would be instead of what he actually was—without principles, morals, mercy or compunction whatever.

Meredith's nervousness found vent in an irritable, "You've been a hell of a long time getting here, Likong!"

The eyes of the Chinese flickered, but he answered urbanely: "Bad news flies fast. Good news is slow. I am neither early nor late."

Meredith asked suspiciously: "What the hell do you mean by that?"

Li-kong said, eyes watchful: "Your honorable elder brother has ascended the dragon."

Meredith's grey eyes glittered. The cruelty stood out on his mouth, unmasked. Li-kong said before he could speak: "All with him, even his unworthy servants, ascended at the same time. All except—" He paused.

Meredith's body tightened, his head thrust forward. He asked in a thin voice: "Except?"

The eyes of the Chinese never left him. He said:

"When you rebuked me a moment ago for slowness, I answered that I was neither early nor late. I must therefore bear good news and bad—"

The American interrupted: "Damn you, Li-kong, who got away?"

The Chinese answered: "Your brother's wife."

Meredith's face whitened, then blackened with fury. He whispered: "Christ!"

He roared: "So you bungled it!" His hand twitched up to the gun under his arm-pit, then dropped. He asked: "Where is she?"

The Chinese must have seen that betraying movement, but he gave no sign. He answered: "She fled to the Temple of the Foxes—to your brother's old friend, the priest Yu Ch'ien."

The other snarled: "What were your bunglers about, to

let her go? Why didn't they go after her?"

"They did go after her! Of what happened thereafter, you shall hear—when you have paid me my money, my friend."

"Paid you!" Meredith's fury mastered him at this. "With the bitch alive? I'll see you in hell before you get a cent from me."

The Chinese said calmly: "But since then she has also ascended the dragon in the footsteps of her lord. She died in childbirth."

"They both are dead—" Meredith sank into the chair, trembling like one from whom tremendous strain has lifted. "Both dead—"

The Chinese watched him, malicious anticipation in his eyes. "But the child—lived!" he said.

For a long minute the American sat motionless, looking at him. And now he did not lose control. He said coldly: "So you have been playing with me, have you? Well, now listen to me—you get nothing until the child has followed its father and mother. Nothing! And if it is in your mind to blackmail me, remember you can bring no charge against me without sending yourself to the executioner. Think over that, you leering yellow ape!"

The Chinese lighted a cigarette. He said mildly:

"Your brother is dead, according to plan. His wife is dead through that same plan, even though she did not die when the others did. There was nothing in the bargain concerning the child. And I do not think you could reach the child without me." He smiled. "Is it not said, of two brothers, he who thinks himself the invulnerable one—that is the fool?"

Meredith said nothing, eyes bleak on him. Li-kong went on: "Also, I have information to impart, advice to give—necessary to you if you determine to go for the child. As you must—if you want her. And finally—is it not written in the Yih King, the Book of Changes, that a man's mind should have many entrances but only one exit! In this house the saying is reversed. It has only one entrance but many exits—and the door-keeper of each one of them is death."

Again he paused, then said: "Think over that, you welching white brother-killer!"

The American quivered. He sprang up, reaching for his gun. Strong hands grasped his elbows, held him helpless. Li-kong sauntered to him, drew out the automatic, thrust it into his own pocket. The hands released Meredith. He looked behind him. Two Chinese stood there. One held a crimson bow-string, the other a double-edged short-sword.

"Two of the deaths that guard the exits." Li-kong's voice was courtesy itself. "You may have your choice. I recommend the sword—it is swifter."

Ruthless Meredith was, and no coward, but he recognized here a ruthlessness complete as his own. "You win," he said. "I'll pay."

"And now," smiled Li-kong.

Meredith drew out the bundle of notes and passed them to him. The Chinese counted them and nodded. He

spoke to the two executioners and they withdrew. He said very seriously: "My friend, it is well for you I recognize that insults by a younger people have not the same force that they would have if spoken by one of my own race, so much older than yours. In the Yih King it is written that we must not be confused by similitude, that the superior man places not the same value upon the words of a child as he does upon those of a grown man, although the words be identical. It is well also for you that I feel a certain obligation. Not personally, but because an unconsidered factor has caused a seed sown in this house to bring forth a deformed blossom. It is," continued Li-kong, still very seriously, "a reflection upon its honor—"

He smiled at that, and said, "Or rather, its efficiency. I suggest, therefore, that we discuss the matter without heat or further recrimination of any kind."

Meredith said: "I am sorry I said what I did, Likong. It was childish temper. I apologize."

The Chinese bowed, but he did not take the hand the other extended. Nor did he recall his own words.

He said: "The child is at the Temple of the Foxes. In Kansu, it is an extremely sacred shrine. She is in charge of Yu Ch'ien, who is not only wise but powerful, and in addition was your honorable late brother's devoted friend. If Yu Ch'ien suspects, then you will have great difficulty in adding to your brother's and your sisterin-law's happiness in Heaven by restoring to them their daughter. You may assume that Yu Ch'ien does suspect—and knows."

Meredith asked incredulously: "Why should he suspect? How could he know?"

Li-kong tapped his cigarette thoughtfully before he answered: "The priest is very wise. Also, like myself, he has had the advantage of contact with your admirable civilization. The woman was with him for weeks, and so he must know who would benefit by the—ah, expungement of your revered relatives. He might think it highly suspicious that those responsible for the regrettable affair did not pursue the custom of holding the principals for ransom instead of—ah, expunging them on the spot. Naturally, he would ask himself why. Finally, Yu Ch'ien is locally reported to have sources of information not open to other men—I mean living men. The dead," observed Li-kong sardonically, "of course know everything."

Meredith said contemptuously: "What do you mean? Spiritism, divination—that rot?"

Li-kong considered pensively, answered at last: "No—not exactly that. Something closer, rather to the classical idea of communion with elemental intelligences, nature spirits, creatures surviving from an older world than man's—but still of earth. Something like the spirits that answered from the oaks of Dodona, or that spoke to the Sybyl in the grotto of Cumae, or in more modem times appeared in, and instructed Joan of Arc from, the branches of the arbre fee, the fairy tree of Domremy."

Meredith laughed. "Good God! And this—from you!"

Li-kong said imperturbably: "This from me! I am—what I am. I believe in nothing. Yet I tell you that I would not go up those steps to the Temple of the Foxes for all the gold you could give me. Not—now!"

Meredith thought: He is trying to frighten me. The yellow dog is trying to keep me from the temple. Why? He spoke only the last word of the thought: "Why?"

The Chinese answered: "China is old. The ancient beliefs are still strong. There are, for example, the legends of the fox women. The fox women are nature spirits. Intelligences earthy but not human—akin to those in Dodona's oaks, Cumae's grotto, Joan of Arc's fairy tree. Believed in—especially in Kansu. These—let us say spirits—have certain powers far exceeding the human. Bear with me while I tell you of a few of these powers. They can assume two earthly shapes only—that of a fox and that of a beautiful woman. There are fox men, too, but the weight of the legends are upon the women. Since for them time does not exist, they are mistresses of time. To those who come under their power, they can cause a day to seem like a thousand years, or a thousand years like a day. They can open the doors to other worlds—worlds of terror, worlds of delight. If such worlds are illusions, they do not seem so to those for whom they are opened. The fox women can make or mar journeys."

Meredith thought: Come, now we're getting down to it.

The Chinese went quietly on: "They can create other illusions. Phantoms, perhaps—but if so, phantoms whose blows maim or kill. They are capricious, bestowing good fortune or ill regardless of the virtue or the lack of it of the recipient. They are peculiarly favorable to women with child. They can, by invitation, enter a woman, passing through her breasts or beneath her finger nails. They can enter an unborn child, or rather a child about to be born. In such cases, the mother dies—nor is the manner of birth the normal one. They cannot oust the soul of the child, but they can dwell beside it, influencing it. Quaint fancies, my friend, in none of which I have belief. Yet because of them nothing could induce me to climb the steps to the Temple of the foxes."

(Meredith thought: He's trying to frighten me away! What the hell does he think I am—to be frightened by such superstitious drivel? He said, in that thin voice with which he spoke when temper was mastering him:

"What's your game, Li-kong? Another double-cross? You're trying to tell me that if I were you, I wouldn't go to the temple for the brat. Why?"

The Chinese said: "My friend, I have played the game with you. I do not say that if I were you, I would not go. I say that if you were I, you would not. A quite different thing."

The other swung clenched fist down upon the table. "Don't tell me you expect me to take seriously that farrago of nonsense! You don't expect me to give up now because of a yellow—" He checked himself abruptly.

The Chinese completed the sentence politely: "Because of a yellow man's superstition! No, but let me point out a few rather disquieting things. The Temple of the Foxes is believed to be the home of five of these fox women. Five—spirits—who are sisters. Three messengers were sent me with the news of the ambush. The first should have reached me within three weeks after it happened. He has vanished. The second was despatched with other news a week later. He too vanished. But the third, bearing the news of the death of your brother's wife, the birth of the child, came as on the wings of the wind. Why the failure of the first two? Because someone desired to keep you in ignorance until after that birth? Who?

"Again, no word has come from Kansu, except by this messenger, of the attack on your brother's party. This, my friend, places you in a dilemma. You cannot betray your knowledge of his death without subjecting yourself to questioning as to how that knowledge came to you. You cannot, therefore, send for the child. You must yourself go—upon some pretext. I think that whoever sped the third messenger on his way intends that you shall go—yourself. Why?"

Meredith struck the table again. "I'll go!"

"Third," continued Li-kong, "my messenger said that the woman who fled ran up the steps of the Temple of the Foxes. And that when they were almost upon her—a fox stood between her and them. And that fox changed into a woman who changed their leader into a mad dog. At which—they ran. So I think," said Likong meditatively, "would I have run!"

Meredith said nothing, but his hand beat steadily on the table and the grey eyes were furious.

"You are thinking," said the Chinese, "'The yellow dogs! Of course they would run! Filled with rum or opium! Of course!'"

It was precisely what he had been thinking, but Meredith made no answer.

"And finally," said Li-kong, "your brother's wife died when the child was born—"

"Because, I suppose, the fox bitch crawled into her!" jeered Meredith, and leaning back, whined thin, high-pitched laughter.

The Chinese lost for a moment his calm, half arose, then dropped back. He said patiently: "If you go up the steps—ride a horse. Preferably an English horse that has hunted foxes."

He lighted another cigarette. "But that is superstition. Nevertheless, if you go, take two men with you as free from taint—as you are. I know two such men. One is a German, the other French. Bold men and hard men. Travel alone, the three of you, as far as you can. At all times keep as few Chinese with you as possible. When you go to the temple, go up the steps alone. Take no Chinese with you there." He said gravely: "I vouch for these two men. Better still, the Home of Heavenly Anticipations vouches for them. They will want money, of course."

Meredith asked: "How much?"

"I don't know. They're not cheap. Probably five thousand dollars at most."

Meredith thought: Here's what he's been leading up to. It's a trap!

Again it was as though Li-kong had read his thoughts.

He said very deliberately: "Meredith, listen to me! I want nothing more from you nor through you. I have not spoken to these men. They do not know, nor will they know from me, anything of that transaction for which you have just paid. I am through with it. I am through with you! I do not like you. I hope never to see you again. Is that plain American talk?"

Meredith said, as deliberately: "I like it. Go on."

"All that they need know is that you are anxious about your brother. When in due time during your journey you discover that he and his wife are dead, and that there is a child, you will naturally want to bring that child back with you. If you are denied the child, and killing is necessary, they will kill. That is all. I will put you in touch with these two men. And I will see to it that none with whom I have relations embarrass you on your way to Kansu, nor on your way back—if you come back. Except for that obligation of which I have spoken, I would not do even this. I would not lift a finger to help you. After you leave this house, you shall be to me as though you never had been. I want nothing to do with Yu Ch'ien and those who go to the Temple of the Foxes. If we should meet again—never speak to me! Do not show you have known me! Never speak to me, never write to me, do not think of me. I am through with you! Is that clear?"

Meredith nodded, smiling. He thought: I was wrong about him wanting to keep me from the place. The yellow rat is frightened . . . he believes in his own bogies! America and everything else couldn't knock the superstition out of him!

The thought amused him. It gave him a contemptuous tolerance of Li-kong, a pleasant knowledge of superiority. He said, not bothering to keep the contempt from his voice: "Clearer than you know, Li-kong. Where do I meet your friends?"

"They can be at your hotel at one, if it suits you."

"It suits me. Their names?"

"They will tell you. They will bear credentials from me."

Li-kong arose. He stood beside the door, bowing courteously. Meredith passed through. They went along another passage and through a winding alley out into a street. It was not the same street from which he had entered. Nor did he recognize it. A coolie-car waited. Li-kong bowed him into it.

"May our shadows never touch again," said Li-kong ceremoniously. He added, for the first time menacingly: "For your health."

He turned and passed into the alley. The coolie broke into a swift trot, and away.

CHAPTER IV

It was mid-afternoon a month later that he rode out of the green glen and looked up the first steep flight of the ancient steps to the Temple of the Foxes. Riding beside him were von Brenner and Lascelles, the two bold and hard men Li-kong had recommended. They were all of that, but

they were also discreet men. They had accepted without comment his explanation of seeking news of his brother, had been properly sympathetic and had asked him no embarrassing questions. Both could speak the Mandarin as well as several of the dialects. Lascelles knew Kansu, was even familiar with the locality in which was the Temple of the Foxes.

Meredith had thought it wise to make inquiries at various places through which he knew Martin had passed, and here the German and the Frenchman acted as his interpreters. When they reported that at these points his brother's party had been in excellent health, they did so with every outward evidence of belief that such tidings were welcome to him.

Either they were excellent actors or Li-kong had kept faith with him and told them nothing beyond what had been agreed. Confidence in the second possibility however had been somewhat disturbed shortly after entering Kansu. The Frenchman had said he thought, somewhat too casually, that if it was desirable to get to the temple without passing through any village within a day's march, he knew a way. He added that while undoubtedly the temple's priest would know they were coming, he would expect them to follow the usual route. Therefore, he could possibly be taken by surprise.

Meredith smelled a trap. To accept the suggestion was to admit that the temple had been the real object of his journey, the reason he had given a subterfuge, and the anxious inquiries he had made along the line of march a blind. He answered sharply that there was no reason for any surprise visit, that the priest Yu Ch'ien, a venerable scholar, was an old friend of his brother, and that if the party had reached him there was no further cause for anxiety. Why did Lascelles think he desired any secrecy in his search? The Frenchman replied politely that if he had known of such friendship the thought would not have occurred to him, of course.

As a matter of fact, Meredith felt no more fear of Yu Ch'ien than he did of Li-kong's fox woman. Whenever he thought of how the Chinese had tried to impress him with that yellow Mother Goose yarn, he felt a contemptuous amusement that more than compensated him for the humiliation of having been forced to pay the blood money. He had often listened to Martin extol Yu Ch'ien's wisdom and virtues, but that only proved what a complete impractical ass Martin had been . . . gone senile prematurely, in brain at least . . . that was plain enough when he married that golddigger young enough to be his daughter . . . no longer the brother he had known . . . who could tell what he might have done next . . . some senility which would have brought ruin to them all . . . a senile crazy brain in Martin's still sound body, that was all . . . if Martin had been suffering from some agonizing and incurable disease and had asked him to put him out of his misery, he would certainly have done so . . . well, what was the difference between that and what he had done? That the girl and her brat should also have to suffer was too bad . . . but it had been made necessary by Martin's own senility.

Thus he justified himself. At the same time there was no reason why he should take these two men into his confidence.

What he should do with the brat when he had it was not quite clear. It was only two months old—and it was a long journey back to Peking. There must be some woman taking care of it at the temple. He would arrange that she go with them to Peking. If some accident happened, or if the child caught something or other on the way back—that would not be his fault. Her proper place, obviously, was with her father's family. Not in a heathen temple back of nowhere in China. Nobody could blame him for wanting to bring her back . . . even if anything did happen to her.

But on second thought, not so good. He would have to take back proof that this child was theirs. Proof of birth. It would be better to bring her alive to Peking . . . even better, it might be, if it lived until he had taken it back to the States and the whole matter of trusteeship and guardianship had been legally adjusted. There was plenty of time. And he would have his half-million, and the increased percentage from the estate to tide him over the gap between now and until—something happened, and the whole estate would be his. He thought callously: Well, the brat is insured as far as Peking at any rate.

They had passed through a village that morning. The headman had met them, and in answer to the usual questioning, had given a complete account of the massacre, of Jean's escape, of her death later at the temple and of the child's birth. It was so complete, even to the dates, that he felt a stirring of faint suspicion. It was a little as though the story had been drilled into this man. And now and then he would call this one or that among the villagers for corroboration. But Charles had shown the proper shades of grief, and desire to punish the killers. And Brenner and Lascelles had exerted themselves to comfort him in orthodox fashion.

He had said at last: "The first thing to do is get the baby safely back to Peking. I can get capable white nurses there. I'll have to find a woman here to look after it until we reach Peking. I want to get the child to the States and in my wife's care as soon as I can. And I want to start the machinery going to punish my brother's murderers—although I realize that's a forlorn hope."

They had agreed with him that it was most desirable to get the child to his wife in quickest possible time, and that hope of punishing the killers was indeed a forlorn one.

And now he stood looking up the ancient steps at whose end was the child. He said: "You couldn't ride a horse up that, unless it was a circus horse. And these are not."

Lascelles smiled. "It is impossible to ride to the temple. There are steeper flights than this. And there is no trail or other road. We must walk."

Meredith said suspiciously: "You seem to know a lot about this place, Lascelles. Ever been to the temple?"

The Frenchman answered: "No, but I have talked to those who have."

Meredith grinned. "Li-kong told me to take a horse. He said the fox women were afraid of it."

Brenner laughed. "Die Fuchs-Damen! I haf always wanted to see one. Joost as I always wanted to see one of those bowmen of Mons they haf spoken so highly of in the War. Yah! I would like to try a bullet on the bowmen, but I would haf other treatment for the fox women. Yah!"

Lascelles said noncommittally: "It's hard to get some things out of the mind of a Chinese."

Brenner said to Meredith: "There is one question I haf to ask. How far iss it that we go in getting this child? Suppose this priest thinks it better you do not haf it? How far iss it that we go to persuade him, hein?" He added meditatively: "The headman said that there are with the priest three women and four men." He said even more meditatively: "The headsman he was very full of detail. Yah—he knew a lot. I do not like that—quite."

Lascelles nodded, saying nothing, looking at Meredith interrogatively.

Meredith said: "I do not see for what reason or upon what grounds Yu Ch'ien can deny me the child. I am its uncle, its natural guardian. Its father, my brother so designated me in the event of his death. Well, he is dead. If the priest refuses to give it up peaceably I would certainly be justified in using force to secure it. If the priest were hurt—we would not be to blame. If his men attacked us and were hurt—we would be blameless. One way or another—I take the child."

Lascelles said somewhat grimly: "If it comes to fighting, we ride back along that way I told you of. We will go through no village within a day's journey from here. It will not be healthy for us in Kansu—the speed at which we must go will not be healthy for the child."

Meredith said: "I am sure we'll have no trouble with Yu Ch'ien."

They had brought a fourth horse with them, a sturdy beast with wide Chinese saddle such as a woman rides. They tethered the four horses and began to mount the steps. At first they talked, then their voices seemed to be absorbed in the silence, to grow thin. They stopped talking.

The tall pines watched them as they passed—the crouching shrubs watched them. They saw no one, heard nothing—but gradually they became as watchful as the pines and bushes, alert, hands gripping the butts of their pistols as though the touch gave them confidence. They came over the brow of the hill and the sweat was streaming from them as it streams from horses frightened by something they sense but can neither see nor hear.

It was as though they had passed out of some peril-haunted jungle into safety. They still said nothing to each other, but they straightened, drew deep breaths, and their hands fell from their pistols. They looked down upon the peacock-tiled roof of the Temple of the Foxes and upon its blue pool of peace. A man sat beside it on a stone seat. As they watched him, he arose and walked toward the temple. At each side of him went a pair of what seemed russet-red dogs. Suddenly they saw that these were not dogs, but foxes.

They came down over the brow of the hill to the rear of the temple. In its brown stone there was no door, only six high windows that seemed to watch them come. They saw no one. They skirted the temple and reached its front. The man they had seen at the pool stood there, as though awaiting them. The foxes were gone.

The three halted as one, involuntarily. Meredith had expected to see an old, old man—gentle, a little feeble, perhaps. The face he saw was old, no doubt of that—but the eyes were young and prodigiously alive. Large and black and liquid, they held his. He was clothed in a symboled robe of silvery blue on whose breast in silver was a fox's head.

Meredith thought: What if he isn't what I expected! He shook his head impatiently, as though to get rid of some numbness. He stepped forward, hand outstretched. He said: "I am Charles Meredith. You are Yu Ch'ien—my brother's friend—"

The priest said: "I have been expecting you, Charles Meredith. You already know what happened. The village headman mercifully took from me the burden of delivering to you the first blossom of sorrowful knowledge."

Meredith thought: How the devil did he know that?

The village is half a day away. We came swiftly, and no runner could have reached here before us.

The priest had taken his outstretched hand. He did not clasp it palm to palm, but held it across the top, thumb pressed to wrist. Meredith felt a curious tingling coolness dart from wrist to shoulder. The black eyes were looking deep into his, and he felt the same tingling coolness in his brain. His hand was released, the gaze withdrawn. He felt as though something had been withdrawn from his mind with it.

"And your friends—" Yu Ch'ien grasped von Brenner's hand in the same way, black eyes searching the German's. He turned to Lascelles. The French thrust his hands behind him, avoided the eyes. He bowed and said: "For me, it is too great honor, venerable father of wisdom."

For an instant Yu Ch'ien's gaze rested on him thoughtfully. He spoke to Meredith: "Of your brother and your brother's wife there is nothing more to be said. They have passed. You shall see the child."

Meredith answered bluntly: "I came to take her with me, Yu Ch'ien."

The priest said as though he had not heard: "Come into the temple and you shall see her."

He walked through the time-bitten pillars into the room where Jean Meredith had died. They followed him. It was oddly dark within the temple chamber. Meredith supposed that it was the transition from the sunny brightness. It was as though the chamber was filled with silent, watchful brown shadows. There was an altar of green stone on which were five ancient ramps of milky jade. They were circular, and in four of them candles burned, turning them into four small moons. The priest led them toward this altar. Not far from the altar was an immense vessel of bronze, like a baptismal font. Between altar and vessel was an old

Chinese cradle, and nestled in its cushions was a baby. It was a girl child, fast asleep, one little dimpled fist doubled up to its mouth. The priest walked to the opposite side of the cradle.

He said softly: "Your brother's daughter, Charles Meredith. Bend over. I desire to show you something—let your friends look too."

The three bent over the cradle. The priest gently opened the child's swathings. Upon its breast, over its heart, was a small scarlet birth-mark shaped like a candle flame wavering in the wind. Lascelles lifted his hand, finger pointing, but before he could speak, the priest had caught his wrist. He looked into the Frenchman's eyes. He said sternly: "Do not waken her."

The Frenchman stared at him for a moment, then said through stiff lips: "You devil!"

The priest dropped his wrist. He said to Meredith, tranquilly: "I show you the birth-mark so you may know the child when you see her again. It will be long, Charles Meredith, before you do see her again."

A quick rage swept Meredith but before he succumbed to it he found time to wonder at its fury. He whispered: "Cover him, von Brenner! Throttle him, Lascelles!"

He bent down to lift the baby from the cradle. He stiffened, hands clutching at empty air. The baby and cradle were gone. He looked up. The priest was gone.

Where Yu Ch'ien had stood was a row of archers, a dozen of them. The light from the four lanterns shone shadedly upon them. They were in archaic mail, black lacquered helmets on their heads; under their visors yellow slanted eyes gleamed from impassive faces. Their bows were stretched, strings ready to loose, the triangular arrow heads at point like snakes poised to spring. He looked at them stupidly. Where had they come from? At the head of the line was a giant all of seven feet tall, old, with a face as though made of gnarled pear-wood. It was his arrow that pointed to Meredith's heart. The others—

He sprang back—back between von Brenner and Lascelles. They stood, glaring unbelievingly as he had at that line of bowmen. He saw the German lift his pistol, heard him say thickly: "The bowmen of Mons—" heard Lascelles cry: "Drop it, you fool!" Heard the twang of a bow, the hiss of an arrow and saw an arrow pierce the German's wrist and saw the pistol fall to the temple floor.

Lascelles cried: "Don't move, Meredith!" The Frenchman's automatic rang upon the temple floor.

He heard a command—in the voice of Yu Ch'ien. The archers moved forward, not touching the three, but menacing them with their arrows. The three moved back.

Abruptly, beneath the altar, in the light of the four lanterns, he saw the cradle and the child within it, still asleep.

And beside the cradle, Yu Ch'ien.

The priest beckoned him. The line of archers opened as he walked forward. Yu Ch'ien looked at him with unfathomable eyes. He said in the same tranquil tones, utterly without anger or reproach:

"I know the truth. You think I could not prove that

truth? You are right. I could not—in an earthly court. And you fear no other. But listen well—you have good reason to fear me! Some day your brother's child will be sent to you. Until she comes, look after her interests well and try in no manner directly or indirectly to injure her. You will have the money your brother left you. You will have your interest in her estate. You will have at least seven years before she comes. Use those years well, Charles Meredith—it is not impossible that you may build up much merit which will mitigate, even if it cannot cancel, your debt of wickedness. But this I tell you—do not try to regain this child before she is sent to you, nor attempt to molest her. After she comes to you—the matter is in other hands than mine. Do you understand me, Charles Meredith?"

He heard himself say: "I understand you. It shall be as you say."

Yu Ch'ien thrust his hand into his robe, drew out a package. He said: "Here are written the circumstances of your brother's death, his wife's death and the birth of the child. They are attested by me, and by witnesses of mine. I am well known far beyond the limits of this, my temple. My signature will be sufficient to prove the authenticity of the statements. I have given my reasons why I think it useless to attempt to bring the actual murderers of your brother and his party to justice. I have said that their leader was caught and executed. He was! My real reason for acting as I am may not be known by you. Now pick up those useless weapons of yours—useless at least here—take these papers and go!"

Meredith took the documents. He picked up the guns. He turned and walked stiffly through the bowmen to where von Brenner and Lascelles stood close to the temple doors, under the arrows of the bowmen. They mounted the hill and set their feet upon the ancient road.

Silent, like men half-awake, they passed through the lines of the watchful pines and at last into the glen where their horses stood tethered —

There was an oath from the German. He was moving the wrist gingerly. And suddenly all three were like men who had just awakened. Von Brenner cried: "The arrow! I felt it—I saw it! But there iss no arrow and no mark. And my hand iss good as ever."

Lascelles said very quietly: "There was no arrow, von Brenner. There were no bowmen. Nevertheless, let us move from here quickly."

Meredith said: "But I saw the arrow strike. I saw the archers."

"When Yu Ch'ien gripped our wrists he gripped our minds," answered Lascelles. "If we had not believed in the reality of the bowmen—we would not have seen them. The arrow could not have hurt you, von Brenner. But the priest had trapped us. We had to believe in their reality." He untied his horse. He turned to Meredith, foot on stirrup: "Did Yu Ch'ien threaten you?"

Meredith answered with a touch of grim humor:

"Yes—but he gave me seven years for the threats to take effect."

Lascelles said: "Good. Then you and I, von Brenner, get back to Peking. We'll spend the night at that village of the too well informed headman—go back by the open road. But ride fast."

He gave the horse his knee and raced away. The other two followed. The horse with the wide Chinese saddle placidly watched them go.

Two hours after dusk they came to the village. The headman was courteous, provided them with food and shelter, but no longer was communicative. Meredith was quiet. Before they rolled into their blankets he said to Lascelles: "When the priest grasped your hand you were about to say something—something about that birth-mark on the child's breast. What was it?"

Lascelles said: "I was about to say that it was the Symbol of the fox women."

Meredith said: "Don't tell me you believe in that damned nonsense!"

Lascelles answered: "I'm not telling you anything, except that the mark was the symbol of the fox women."

Von Brenner said: "I'fe seen some strange things in this damned China and elsewhere, Pierre. But neffer an arrow that pierced a man's wrist and hung there quivering—and then was gone. But the wrist dead—as mine wass."

Lascelles said: "Listen, Franz. This priest is a great man. What he did to us I have seen sorcerers, so-called, do to others in Tibet and in India. But never with such completeness, such clarity. The archers came from the mind of the priest into our minds—yes, that I know. But I tell you, Franz, that if you had believed that arrow had pierced your heart—your heart would not be alive as your wrist is! I tell you again—he is a great man, that priest."

Meredith said: "But—"

Lascelles said: "For Christ's sake, man, is it impossible for you to learn!" He rolled himself in his blankets. Went to sleep.

Meredith lay awake, thinking, for long. He thought;

Yu Ch'ien doesn't know a damned thing. If he did—why would he promise me the child? He knows he can't prove a thing. He thought: He thinks he can frighten me so that when the child comes of age she'll get what's coming to her.. And he thought: Lascelles is as crazy as Li-kong. Those archers were hidden there all the time. They were real, all right. Or, if it was a matter of hypnotism, I'd like to see myself believe in them in New York! He laughed.

It was a damned good arrangement, he concluded. Probably the priest wouldn't send the brat back to him for ten years. But in the meantime—well, he'd like to see that file of archers in one of the Bronx night clubs! It was a good arrangement—for him. The priest was as senile as Martin . . .

He was well satisfied. He went to sleep.

YEAR'S BEST
HARDCORE
HORROR

COMETPRESS

cometpress.us/years-best-hardcore-horror/

"Not for the faint of heart or weak of stomach, this new best-of annual anthology feature episodes of graphic gore and violence—including torture, dismemberment, self-mutilation, and home abortion—that are designed to push buttons as well as boundaries…strictly for hardcore horror fans."

—PUBLISHERS WEEKLY

VISIT COMET PRESS ON THE WEB:
www.cometpress.us
facebook.com/cometpress
twitter.com/cometpress

MAGAZINE OF EXTREME HORROR AND HARDCORE DARK CRIME

RED ROOM

ISSUE 1 FALL 2017

FICTION

JACK KETCHUM

MEG ELISON

TIM WAGGONER

DAVID JAMES KEATON

LARRY HINKLE

TOM BARLOW

JOSH SCOTT WILSON

NICK MANZOLILLO

FEATURES

AN EXCERPT FROM

A GATHERING OF EVIL

BY GIL VALLE, THE NYPD'S "CANNIBAL COP"
AND INTERVIEWED BY DAVID L. TAMARIN

INTERVIEW WITH MEG ELISON
BY THE RED ROOM EDITORS

PLUS

BOOK REVIEW BY BEN ARZATE: HELL HOUND

MOVIE REVIEW BY PATRICK KING: A DARK SONG

ARTICLE: TO DEPRAVE AND CORRUPT BY DUANE BRADLEY

BARFLY BOB'S HIGHBALLS & LOWBALLS

BRIAN J. MCCARTHY: THE ROGUE REPORT